Contents

Before you Begin...

The Devils of Sun Valley High series is recommended for mature
readers 17+

If you are easily triggered, these books may not be for you as they
do deal with sensitive subject matter.

Please look at reviews for more details regarding specific triggers
though do be aware that in doing so, it may spoil large portions of
the books for you.

WICKED
DEVIL

Wicked Devil

Roman Valdez is the Devil.

He sneers at me.

He hates me.

He wants to hurt me.

Let him try.

He thinks he's untouchable.

The self-appointed Devil of Sun Valley High.

But I've already lost everything and everyone I care about.

It's me he should be afraid of. Not the other way around.

Because I have nothing left to lose, and he can't break what's already broken.

At least, that's what I thought.

"Alejandra, you're going to be late for school." Janessa calls out using my full name. I sigh and choose to ignore her. She won't think anything of it. She's done her job and informed me of the time, as I'm sure my father instructed her to do. *My father*. Thinking of Gerald Ulrich as anything aside from an absolute and total stranger just feels ... *weird*.

I worry my bottom lip and stare at my reflection in the floor-length mirror, bracing myself for what will be my first day at a new school, in a new town, with a new family. Because clearly, my life wasn't hard enough.

Tears prick my eyes but I blink hard to clear them. *Come on, Allie. Hold it together.* I refuse to allow myself to cry. Not today. Not tomorrow. Not again.

If I do, I'm not sure I'll ever stop.

Sucking in a shuddering breath, I take in my appearance. I look okay, I guess. Except the girl staring back at me is nothing like the

Alejandra Ramirez I've been the past seventeen years. She looks preppier. Richer. Honestly, the girl staring back at me looks like a stuck-up bitch.

I look nothing like me. I'm wearing a pair of white skinny jeans that are all but painted onto my body and a soft pink floral top. It has sheer flowing sleeves and exposes a thin strip of my tanned midriff. It's beyond feminine. If my best friend Julio could see me now, he'd probably keel over laughing. This is not my look.

Not that anyone here cares.

Back home, I would have gone to school in ripped jeans, a vintage band tee with an oversized hoodie, and a pair of black K-Swiss sneakers. White if I felt like being fancy that day. It would have been okay to toss my hair into a messy bun and wear my gold hoop earrings with winged eyeliner and little else as far as makeup was concerned. Hell, most days I didn't bother with even the eyeliner. I'd always been a bit of a tomboy. I was still a tomboy.

Though looking at me now, you'd never know it.

But last week when I met my bio-dad, he took one look at me in his polished gray suit and disgust quickly curled his upper lip. Being a tomboy was unacceptable. I needed to look the part, as Janessa—his personal assistant—had reminded me on, so far, three separate occasions in the same number of days. I am Gerald Ulrich's daughter, not some *chola* from the wrong side of town. Gerald is a prominent member of his community. Gerald is a businessman. Gerald has a flashy car and money and probably only carries black credit cards in his wallet.

His daughter needs to hold herself to certain *standards*.

Bring on the eye roll and insert an insane amount of sarcasm here.

Until a week ago, I'd been his estranged and forgotten daughter.

Not anymore.

Not since my mom died.

I rub at the ache in my chest. *Why did you hide all of this from me, Mom? There had to be a reason.*

You'd think given everything I'd been through, the guy would cut me some slack. He'd ... I don't know, try and get to know me.

I huff out a breath and try to squelch the flicker of hurt inside my chest. Mom can't answer my questions. She's dead and I'm here.

Emotion clogs my throat.

Dammit. I refuse to let grief wash over me again. I shouldn't care if I'm not good enough for the guy. I'm here. That means something, right? I mean, he technically fought to get me here.

He could have left me back in Richland. I could have spent the remainder of my senior year as a foster kid. Though, if I'm being entirely honest with myself, I'm not sure I wouldn't have preferred that. At least then I'd be in my hometown. I'd have Julio and Gabe and Felix—my friends—people who actually care about me.

But minors don't get a say in these kinds of things.

If Mom were here, she'd tell me to be strong. To be brave. She should be here. But she isn't, so I need to be brave on my own.

Alrighty then. I can do that.

There's no other alternative.

Janessa had provided my first-day-of-school outfit, along with the rest of my new wardrobe, since mine had been destroyed in the fire. Technically, it isn't really the first day of school. I transferred to Sun Valley High near the end of the first trimester, but it would be *my* first day at this particular school.

Yay.

I hate the outfit. The wardrobe. The makeup and perfumes. But when I hinted that it isn't really my style, she'd scowled as if I'd offended her and then proceeded to remind me that I need to let go of my past.

She hadn't meant to hurt me with her words. At least, I don't think she did. Janessa doesn't strike me as a cruel person. But she thinks my life before the here and now is beneath me. Beneath the Ulrich name. And she's only my bio-dad's assistant.

After she told me how lucky I am to be reunited with my father, I decided it was easier to just go along and not rock the boat. It's my senior year. I'll be eighteen soon and after graduation, I can go back to my old life. I can leave this house. This town. These people.

Then I will grieve.

I leave my long, dark brown hair down, using the flat iron Janessa gave me to straighten it into sleek, glossy strands before applying a hint of makeup.

I need to make a great first impression.

A touch of concealer to hide the bags under my eyes from lack of sleep. A little blush and bronzer to mask my paleness. A touch of mascara and clear lip gloss to make me look a little more alive. Janessa would approve.

It isn't me, and while I hate that, I also know I don't really want to be me right now. I don't want to be the girl who lost her mom. The girl whose boyfriend dumped her the same night. Or the girl who lost her one female friend to that same boyfriend. The jerk had cheated on me. With her. And now, I get to start at a new school and live with a parent I barely know. The cherry on top of the sundae that is my life.

My shoulders slump. I grab my new, pale pink backpack—so not my color—and slide my feet into a pair of Chloe Lauren sneakers. They cost nearly five hundred dollars.

How ridiculous is that? Who spends five hundred dollars on shoes? That's like, rent. Well, maybe not. But it's enough to cover a utility bill and then some.

A sigh escapes me. I know I should be grateful. They're nice. But all the money and high-end stuff makes me a little uncomfortable. I didn't have stuff like this growing up. Mom was a single mom. She worked two jobs to make ends meet and I bought most of my stuff at Ross or Target. You should have seen the look on Janessa's face when I suggested shopping there to replace my things.

I head out of my room, jogging down the stairs and into the kitchen to grab a cup of coffee. Janessa stands by the marble island, a wide smile on her face and no Gerald in sight. She hands me a travel mug. "Here, darling. I made your coffee. We need to get going so you're not late for your first day."

I nod and follow her, quickly scanning the room as I take a sip of the sickly sweet coffee. *Yuck.* I drink my coffee black, not with whatever flavored concoction she's added to the mug. I'm tempted to pour it out and grab a fresh cup. But I don't. That would be *rude.*

Janessa sees my wandering gaze and answers my unspoken question. "Your father is at the office already. His schedule is pretty full and your arrival wasn't"—she pauses—"planned."

I press my lips into a thin line. No, it certainly wasn't. I bet he loved getting *that* particular phone call from social services. I'd stayed with Julio's parents the first week after Mom died while they confirmed my paternity. Dear old Dad had to be sure. I had hoped to stay with my best friend through my senior year; Julio's parents had been on board with the idea. But as soon as the test came back confirming Gerald Ulrich is my father, that option was thrown out the window.

He wanted me. So, there's that, I remind myself. I am wanted. Though, he'd yet to act like it.

Outside, I climb into Janessa's white Porsche Taycan 4S. It sits ridiculously low to the ground and costs more than my old house did. I googled it. The cost of her car. I don't know how much Gerald pays her to be his personal assistant but it must be a lot if she can afford this. I wouldn't be surprised if she's more than his assistant, though, based on the few times I've seen them together. Office romance is more like it. What a cliché.

He's fifty-two and she's barely graduated college. Easily young enough to be my big sister. But who am I to judge?

Up until a week ago, I didn't even know I had a dad. I mean, obviously I knew someone contributed to me being born and all that, but I didn't know he was out there. That he knew about me. I kinda assumed he was dead if I'm being honest with myself. And I'd been okay with that.

Mom never talked about him and I wasn't one of those kids who felt like I was missing a piece of myself without a dad. She'd always been enough.

Tears sting the backs of my eyes and I push my old memories away.

It takes twenty minutes to get to Sun Valley High. Janessa rambles on about nonsense and I tune her out for most of the drive. Pulling into the school parking lot, her Porsche sticks out like a sore thumb and all eyes turn toward us as she parks. I swallow hard and rush to unbuckle. She puts the car in park as though she plans to come in with me. "I'll be fine," I assure her. "I'm a big girl." I grab my bag, purposefully leaving behind the coffee, and rush to open the door.

"But it's your first day. I can walk you in. I'm sure there's paperwork and—"

"It's okay. I got it." I don't miss the gazes of the students passing by. Some are curious but most look annoyed. I don't want that annoyance to morph into disdain. And I don't want to get labeled as a snob.

I'd had to beg Gerald to let me attend Sun Valley High. He wanted me to go to Suncrest Academy. The top private school in the area and the third most prestigious high school in the country. He didn't like the idea of me attending a public school with the *riffraff* of town. His words, not mine. But ever since winning that one, I hadn't fought him on anything else. Not the clothes. Not the living arrangements. Not the rules—only because I know a losing battle when I see one—but he'd conceded and given me this, and Janessa is about to ruin it.

"Are you sure? Your father wouldn't be happy if— "

"I'm good. Promise." I slam the door behind me, not giving her the chance to comment further, and rush across the parking lot to the school's front entrance. A large red devil mascot stares down at me.

Welcome to Sun Valley High, home of the Red Devils.

I pass through the open doors, a sense of foreboding washing over me, but I quash it.

I will be okay.

Mom was strong. I can be strong, too.

I just have to take things one day at a time.

The school was informed of my arrival late last week, so they had everything ready for me. I got my schedule from the school counselor—Mr. Kemp—along with a few forms he said I'd need to take home and bring back with Gerald's signature. I got my locker assignment and combination, though if Sun Valley High is anything like my old school, it would sit empty most of the year. I'll lug my books in my backpack between classes rather than dropping them off in my locker to save on time.

Since Sun Valley High is on a trimester system, I only have four classes. English, Calculus, Spanish 4, and Welding. Calculus will kick my butt. Math was never my strong suit. But the rest should be easy enough to get caught up on.

"Your, umm, Janessa informed me of your ... situation," Mr. Kemp says, a sympathetic frown tugging at his features. "If you need to talk to anyone, my office door is always open."

Always the diligent assistant. Janessa has taken care of everything, including airing my business. *Wonderful.*

"Thanks." I nod, not that I have any plans of taking him up on the offer. But Mr. Kemp seems nice enough. He's younger than most of the faculty I've seen so far. Late twenties, maybe early thirties. He has reddish brown hair and dark blue eyes. He's attractive enough and carries an easy smile. He seems to be one of the *cool* staff members, judging by the number of students shouting out hellos when they walk past his office door. A lot of "Yo, Mr. K." But I don't need a shoulder to cry on and I prefer not to build relationships with guidance counselors. They have the tendency to make things weird. I learned that my freshman year and I don't plan on having a repeat incident.

Besides, he's a stranger. I haven't bothered to confide in my new dad. Why on earth would I confide in *him?*

The warning bell rings signaling that first period is about to start. I stand up to leave, tucking my schedule into the front pocket of my pants. Before I can make it out of his office, a boy saunters in with a swagger and, what I'm sure, is his perpetual smirk. He tilts his head toward Mr. Kemp in greeting before plopping down in the chair I just vacated, not bothering to spare me a glance.

Rude. But, whatever. I'm the new girl. If Sun Valley High is anything like virtually every other high school in America, the students here won't be welcoming. But all of that is a-okay. I don't need to make friends here. I have Julio, Gabe, and Felix to get back to. I don't plan on sticking around long once I graduate.

"Mr. Valdez. To what do I owe the pleasure?" Mr. Kemp says with a stern tone, but I don't miss the slight curve to his mouth. I know right away that this guy, Valdez, is one of those kids who spends a lot of time in the office. There's an air of smug hostility about him, but Mr. Kemp doesn't seem bothered by it. He seems ... amused.

When the boy finally looks my way, he gives me a slow once-over before his upper lip curls in disgust. He mutters, "*Chiflada*," under his breath with a roll of his pretty brown eyes.

"Hey!" I snap. He doesn't know me and I don't care how cute he is, I am not a spoiled brat.

He sneers at me and turns back to Mr. Kemp without bothering to respond to my outburst, a bored look on his face.

"Roman." There was a warning in there, but the boy didn't seem to care.

Mr. Kemp waits.

My cheeks heat and I'm practically vibrating with irritation.

"What? Look at her." Roman shrugs. "Just calling it like I see it."

I bite my bottom lip to keep from snapping at him again before turning to leave. I don't need this.

"Ms. Ulrich," Mr. Kemp calls out.

I freeze. "That's not my name." There's a bite in my tone I hadn't intended but what I said is true. Ulrich isn't my name. Gerald wants me to take his last name. He's some hotshot in town and thinks his name will help open doors for me, but I don't want it. I've been Alejandra Ramirez—Allie for short—for the last seventeen years. I have zero plans of changing that in this life or the next.

Roman's brows lift, sudden interest sparking over our exchange.

"My apologies. *Alejandra*."

"Allie," I correct again.

He grimaces and tilts his head toward the guy. "Allie, this is Roman. He's a senior, like you. And he happens to also have first period English." And I'm supposed to care why? "He'll show you to your first class and help you settle in. Think of him as your guide for the week."

My mouth drops open and I don't miss the look he directs at Roman. This isn't optional for him. I gape at Mr. Kemp before finding my words. "No, thanks. I'm fine." I try and wave him off.

He releases a sigh and leans back in his chair ignoring me completely. His eyes train on Roman who still has that bored expression on his face. "You here because you mouthed off again?"

Roman shrugs. "Maybe."

I roll my eyes. He's totally one of *those* guys. He's probably a jock too. He definitely looks like the athletic type. Broad shoulders, a muscular build. I can see the hint of a tattoo peeking out of the collar of his shirt too. He's a bad boy and he makes sure everyone knows it. Even his teachers.

I did not have time for a guy like him.

Mr. Kemp smiles. "Well then, rather than the usual detention, you'll have the pleasure of showing Allie around and helping her feel welcome. She's new to Sun Valley High and doesn't know anyone. Be a model student for once and help the girl out."

"I'm good," Roman says. "I'll take the detention."

Thank God.

Mr. Kemp folds his arms across his chest and raises a single brow. "You sure about that? This is your third visit to my office this trimester which means you'll get a full week of detention instead of the usual one day. You'll miss a week's worth of practice..." He trails off and levels Roman with a knowing look.

Roman curses. "That's bullshit." He shoots out of his chair. "You can't do that, Mr. K."

"It's out of my hands," he says, his hands lifted in a placating gesture. "You're the one incapable of keeping your mouth shut. Now, I'm not one to offer alternatives but I don't want to earn Coach Samson's wrath any more than you do. So, what'll it be Mr. Valdez? The girl or detention?"

Roman shoots me a withering glare.

"Wait, don't I get a say in this?" I do not need the kind of attention this will surely draw. I have every intention of blending in with the crowd. Being a nobody here at Sun Valley High. I have a feeling that anyone who associates with this Roman guy is not going to go by unnoticed. He's athletic, good-looking, and more arrogant than any other guy I've had the misfortune of crossing paths with, which can only mean one thing. He's popular. I don't do the popular crowd.

"No," both men say at the same time.

Urgh!

This is so unfair. Why am I being punished for this guy's attitude?

After several tense seconds, Roman mutters out a "fine" and storms past me. When I don't immediately move to follow, he glares back at me from the doorway. "You coming or what? I don't have all day, vanilla."

I bite the inside of my cheek but follow him.

Great. Looks like I'm already off to a great start.

THREE

Roman

_____

Kemp did me a favor saving me from detention. Doesn't mean I have to like it. That girl is going to be a pain in my ass, I can already tell. She has fire. She'll buck against being put in line. And for some strange reason, just the idea of going to battle with her brings eager anticipation and a cruel smile to my face.

I almost feel sorry for the girl. *Almost*. It's her first day here and I don't plan on making it easy for her. Like every other student here at Sun Valley High, she'll need to learn her place. At the bottom.

I rule this school. Me and the other Devils—Dominique Price and Emilio Chavez. Which is how I know that despite his words, Kemp couldn't care less if I'm friendly to the girl. It works in my favor because when she decides she's had enough and goes crying to his office, he'll offer her words of comfort and little else. All he cares about—all any of the teachers at this school care about—is whether or not my friends and I will win the next game and what they need to do to keep us happy so we don't throw the next one to get back at them.

I like to think I'm above such petty bullshit. I have a full-ride scholarship lined up to attend Suncrest U and my performance on the field determines whether I'll keep it. Football is all that matters. I'd never jeopardize my future. But I'm not above holding that threat over the Sun Valley faculty. They need me on the field and they need me to win. It's how the school continues to rake in funding for all the shit they want to do.

I made varsity my freshman year and ever since then, we've gone on undefeated. Football might not seem like a big deal to some, but it opens doors, and not just for the players. It's why the Devils get preferential treatment and why, most of the time, teachers turn a blind eye when we mouth off or start a fight.

But Mrs. Jennings is the one and only teacher who doesn't seem to give a fuck about football. I don't know why she hasn't been fired yet. She's the only one to ever try and call me on my shit. I don't see her lasting long if I or Coach Samson have anything to say about it.

Allie's steps are nearly silent as she follows me down the hallway to first period English. She looks so fucking innocent as she hugs a textbook to her chest, looking around the hallway with wide doe eyes, and all I want to do is dirty her perfect image.

Underneath her first-class exterior is a spitfire just waiting to come out—and that's my job.

She's pretty, if you look past the preppy shit she's wearing. Long, dark hair. Brown eyes. Her white jeans hug her ass and highlight her hips. I wish she was walking in front of me instead of behind so I could watch that ass bounce with every step.

She's most definitely Latina but on the fairer side. Kemp called her Ms. Ulrich and there is only one Ulrich in these parts and he's an old white dude. Bet she's half on her mom's side.

I can already feel that familiar spark of interest. I want to play with her. Make her my shiny new toy. I don't usually bother with the chicks here. Most look at me as a status piece, a way to climb the social ladder. Or they see dollar signs because I'm a beast on the field and they think if they hook me early, they'll live the easy life when I finally go pro.

Allie doesn't seem like those girls. No. Those girls will do damn near anything for my attention. If I ask Allie to get on her knees and suck my dick in the janitor's closet, she'll blush and run the opposite direction. Or maybe I'll see some more of that fire of hers and she'll tell me off? No. Allie isn't the easy lay type. I wonder if I can change that...

My pulse quickens, morphing from a slow and steady thrum to a fast and hard clip just thinking about all the things I want to do to her. I don't care who she's related too. My pops would be pissed if he knew I plan on messing around with this girl. Gerald Ulrich is a big deal in this town. It might make some things difficult for my pops if word made it back to him that I'd sullied the man's daughter.

Good thing I don't care.

We reach the door to first period. The bell's already rung, and the door is closed. I make a big show of swinging it open, letting it slam against the wall so all heads turn in our direction. "After you, vanilla." I wave her in with a flourish.

She scowls and then freezes when she realizes we've grabbed the entire classes' attention.

I smirk. "You going to keep everyone waiting?"

Her cheeks turn an impressive shade of pink as she steps forward. I don't get out of her way, forcing her to brush against me as she passes. The room is quiet, all eyes on us.

She tries to slip into the first available seat. It's in the back row and closest to the door but the girl sitting beside it shakes her head. "You don't want to sit there," she says in a loud whisper.

"Why?"

I snort and the girl flicks her gaze toward me. "It's his seat."

Allie turns to look over her shoulder, giving me another frown.

I offer her a bored expression, wondering if she'll fight back on the seat or do the smart thing and move along. I'm almost disappointed when she huffs and walks toward the front of the class. She has to go around the entire room to reach the last remaining open seat clear on the other side, three rows from the front. By the time she sits, the class still dead silent, her cheeks are a brilliant scarlet. Like a rose. Can't wait to see her thorns.

"Alright class," our teacher begins. She makes Allie introduce herself, doing the whole bit of having her stand up. Asking her where she moved from, does she have any siblings? All the boring basic stuff.

I discover she moved from Richland. No siblings. No pets. She lives with her dad. *Interesting.* I never knew Gerald Ulrich had a daughter. I wonder where he's been hiding her all these years?

When she finally completes her interrogation, Mrs. Beck leaves her alone the rest of the period. I have the advantage of being able to watch her without her being able to watch me in return. She takes notes and actually pays attention. She's a goody-goody for sure which will make it all the more fun when I ruin her. This is just what I needed. Senior year was looking boring but now things are about to get interesting. I can hardly wait.

I get lost in my fantasies; my gaze glued to the back of her head as I imagine all the ways I want to hurt her. Fuck her. Ruin her. It's a sport, and one I just so happen to excel at. If she plays her part well, I might soothe some of the hurt I inflict. We'll see.

When the bell rings, I wait for her just outside the door. Her eyes are downcast as she stares at a piece of paper in her hands, not seeing me until she ends up crushing the paper between our bodies. Contact. *That's what I'm talking about.*

"Watch it, vanilla." I snatch the paper from her fingertips, scanning my eyes over her class schedule. I could have just asked what her next class was, but where's the fun in that?

"Hey!" She tries to grab for it but I lift my hand high above her head, tilting my gaze up to scan over the text. There's no way she can take it back unless I want her to. Or unless she decides to climb me like a tree. I would be okay with that.

She's five-two. Maybe five-three. Tiny in comparison to all six feet of me towering over her. Her hands clench into tiny fists at her sides. Her lips press together in a firm line. My dick twitches in the face of her anger but beyond that initial outburst, she stays silent.

Hmmm... I wonder what it would take for her to really get angry. To break out of this little mold of manners and contained ire?

English, Calculus, Spanish 4 ... hmmm. I eye her. Spanish 4 is for native speakers. I was right in my assumptions about her. "Mexican or Puerto Rican?" I ask, giving her another once-over. I'm betting Mexican but I've been wrong once or twice in my life.

"Mexican."

Right again.

I tuck her schedule into my back pocket and move down the hallway.

"Hey, I need that." She rushes to keep pace with me, her shorter legs having to work double time just to keep up. Students eye her with open interest and I decide to make things interesting.

Without missing a step, I toss an arm over her shoulder and pull her close to my body as I lead her through the halls. She stiffens. "Chill. I'm walking you to class. Just helping out the new girl."

Her mouth tightens but she nods, and I decide not to be a complete ass and slow my steps just a little. Not really for her benefit, but because I want to delay this little stroll and make sure as many students see the two of together as possible.

The guys in the hall eye her with a mix of fascination and confusion. The girls though, they're looking at her with open disdain. Perfect.

I spot one of my best friends—Emilio—further up the hallway waiting for me outside our next class. He lifts a single brow in question. The corner of my mouth lifts and I give him a knowing look. He doesn't bother to hide his annoyance. Emilio isn't one for games. He's one of those *you'll get more bees with honey* types, but he won't interfere. It's not his style to go against me.

I stop when we reach Allie's next class and once again I make a show of opening the door for her, only this time I shove her inside. "Yo, Silvia?" I holler.

Silvia Parish whips her head toward me. Her light brown eyes widen in surprise and the beginning of a smile curls her lips — until she spots Allie.

"Take care of my girl." I wink in Allie's direction and close the door.

Let the chips fall where they may. Silvia is going to have a field day with this one. The girl's been trying to get with me for as long as I can remember. She'll make Allie's life hell if she thinks she's a threat to her shot at the prize, and I just put a bright red bullseye on Allie's forehead.

A small group of students have formed behind me but as soon as I turn, they scatter, even though they'd been waiting to get into the class I just walked away from. I smirk. I'll never tire of being the reigning Devil here.

Emilio is waiting for me outside Economics and he doesn't look pleased. "That the new girl everyone's talking about?"

I shrug. "Might be."

His eyes darken.

"Why? You trying to call dibs or some shit?"

He shakes his head. "Do you always have to be a dick?"

Another shrug. "Don't act like you care."

He punches me in the shoulder. "We had a deal, remember? Football. That was what the three of us are supposed to be focusing on. No chicks. No more head games. We had an agreement, *cabrón*."

"My head is in the game. Stop stressing out over nothing. Kemp asked me to help her out this week as a way to avoid detention. I'm only doing what I was told."

Emilio doesn't look convinced but lets it drop with a shake of his head. "You don't ever do what you're told. Not unless you're getting something out of it. If this game of yours fucks up what we have going on the field, I'm coming for your ass and you know Dom will back me up."

Yeah. Yeah. Whatever.

FOUR

Allie

The looks I'm getting aren't friendly. I'm pretty sure that girl—Silvia—wants to murder me. I didn't miss the way she looked at Roman when he called for her. She all but preened under his attention. Until she saw me. She wants him. I can't really blame her. Before dating my ex—Ryker—I might have wanted him, too. The bad-boy type every girl thinks she can tame. But I learned my lesson going down that road once before and my heart's been through enough as it is.

I'm not some masochist, so she doesn't have anything to worry about from me.

He asked her to take care of me—*his girl*. Does he have any idea how much those two little words have royally screwed me? It's easy to tell Silvia is the one, if not the one and only, Queen B here at Sun Valley High. She's polished within an inch of her life and has a resting bitch face strong enough to peel paint. Following her lead, by the end of the day, every girl in this school is going to hate me.

Thankfully I don't have to sit by her and Calculus passes uneventfully with little more than hushed whispers and sneers aimed in my direction, but what can I do?

Nothing. That's what.

Sun Valley High is everything I expected it to be. Your typical public school. But I failed to take into account just how much of a stir I would cause as the new girl. It didn't help that I'd started school halfway through the first trimester. If I'd started on the very first day of school like everyone else, I might have had a chance of going by unnoticed. Maybe. Probably. Unless I'd run into Roman day one then, too.

I tug at the hem of my shirt, fighting off a wave of self-consciousness. No one here is dressed like me. Janessa made me believe they would be, going on and on about what popular things kids here liked, but she was way off base.

Most of the students are wearing ripped jeans, hoodies, and casual shirts. There's a small cluster of kids dressed to the nines—like Silvia—and I have a feeling they're the Sun Valley elite. The preppy jocks and spoiled rich kids. But their version of preppy is Rock Revival jeans and Free People tops.

Still over the top if you ask me but my shoes cost more than most of their outfits and it doesn't go by unnoticed. I get a lot of whispered "stuck up, bitch" comments directed my way, and by lunch I've picked up a new nickname, "Daddy's little princess."

I hate that one even more than when Roman calls me "vanilla."

He's waiting for me outside of class for lunch, taking me by surprise. I don't delude myself into thinking we'll become friends. Guys like him aren't friends with girls. I know the type. All I am is his punishment and it's evident he isn't happy about it, even if he is toying with me. Ryker used to do crap like this, too.

I follow Roman into the cafeteria and we each grab our lunches before heading to a table in the far-right corner. Two other boys are already seated at it. One is a tall black guy wearing charcoal gray sweatpants, a plain white t-shirt, and rocking a pair of Beast Mode sneakers.

Huh, a Marshawn Lynch fan. I can get behind that.

Well, Marshawn Lynch when he went to the Raiders. I was never one for the Seahawks.

He has full lips, and dark brown, wide-set eyes. His hair is braided tight against his head and he has two slashes through his left brow that I'm pretty sure were shaved into twin lines as opposed to being remnants of a scar. It gives him a more severe look and enhances his already good looks.

I take in the other guy beside him. He's shorter than the first but still around six feet tall. He's Hispanic like Roman and me but his eyes lift at the edges a bit more and his cheekbones are a little sharper. Not Mexican, I don't think. Maybe Honduran. He's the thinnest of the three but his arms are still wrapped in corded muscle. He just hasn't filled out as much.

He wears a white tank top, low slung jeans that expose the top two inches of his black boxers, and a silver chain around his neck.

He's gorgeous. All three of them are. And one look around the cafeteria shows me that these three are the cream of the crop. All of the girls stare at them with lust and hunger on their faces.

Can they be any more obvious?

The other Hispanic guy glances at me as I follow behind Roman, a question in his stare, but Roman doesn't seem inclined to answer.

"Por qué está ella aquí?" *Why is she here?* he asks when we finally reach the table.

Roman grunts, not offering a response. Wonderful.

I debate leaving. I can go to the library, have lunch there. Despite Roman dragging me over, the other two guys don't seem inclined to be all that welcoming, but I decide to introduce myself anyway.

"Me llamo, Alejandra. Allie." I decide to say in Spanish. I don't want to be a jerk, but I don't want him thinking he could use Spanish to talk about me without me realizing what he's saying, either.

He smirks and a surprised laugh escapes him. "Ooo, I love it when a girl speaks Spanish to me." I roll my eyes ignoring his attempt at flirting. He waggles his brows and asks. "What's your story, vanilla?"

Him too? I try not to glower. "It's Allie. Not vanilla," I say, working to keep the bite out of my tone. Neither of these guys did anything wrong to me and I don't want to alienate myself further. But I'm really not on board with the nicknames.

"Whatever you say, vanilla." *Urgh. I just might strangle him.* "I'm Emilio." He points to himself. "That silent fucker is Dom." He indicates the black guy beside him. Dom nods but doesn't seem all that interested in introductions. "There a reason you kicking it at our table? No offense, but we don't like to mix with the fairer sex these days."

Oh. *Oh.* "I'm just … I mean … No judgments here." I raise my hands in a placating gesture. "Really. If you're into other guys or each other—"

"We're not gay." Dom deadpans.

My cheeks heat. They're not? "Umm…"

I have no idea what to say.

Dom sighs and shifts to face me. "What Emilio meant to say— " he pauses and smacks him upside the head.

"Hey!"

Dom scowls at Emilio and continues, "…is that it's our senior year. We don't have time for chicks. We're focused on football. Only football. So, if you're trying to get with Ro— "

"I'm not. Oh, my god, I'm really not." My cheeks are flaming by this point but I don't want anyone here getting the wrong idea. "I'm his punishment. That is literally the only reason I'm here right now. Something about him having to show me around this week to avoid detention."

Emilio whistles. "No shit?" He eyes me up and down like I'm a piece of meat before turning to Roman with a wide grin on his face. "How'd you manage to get a hot piece of ass as punishment?" He says it like a joke but there's a certain level of concern in the question.

"It's not a big deal. Just Mrs. Jennings being Mrs. Jennings."

Both guys groan. I ignore what's said next and decide to check my cell.

I pull out my phone. It was buzzing on and off during first and second period but I didn't want to risk looking at it and having it confiscated. I don't know how strict the teachers are here.

I scroll through my text messages. I have three from my ex, Ryker.

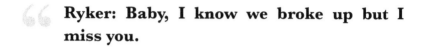 **Ryker: Baby, I know we broke up but I miss you.**

Ryker: Let's make plans soon to meet up.

Ryker: I miss your kiss. The way you taste...

Gross. The last includes a photograph. A dick pic. Wonderful. What an asshole. He broke up with me. The day my mom died. Who does that? And he cheated on me. With my only female friend. And none of these texts are an apology for that. Not that I'd forgive him even if they were. Instead he treats me like some booty call as if I asked for a stupid picture of his pencil dick.

I delete his messages, not bothering to respond and move on to the other two waiting for me.

> **Adriana: I know I messed up. I'm sorry. Talk to me? Please.**

DELETE.

> **Julio: If Adriana messages you, ignore her. She and Ryker are still fucking.**

I SIGH. AT LEAST HE DOESN'T SUGARCOAT IT.

> **Me: Thanks for the heads up.**

HE RESPONDS ALMOST INSTANTLY.

> **Julio: I've always got your back. Miss you *Chica*.**

> **Me: Miss you too J.**

JULIO'S BEEN MY BEST FRIEND SINCE GRADE SCHOOL. EVER since Mimi Johnson stole my ice cream cone in the park and called me stupid. He told her she was fugly and that my stolen ice cream would make her fat. We've been thick as thieves ever since.

J knows me inside and out and I know he's always got my back. Only now he's got it from two hours away. I hate the distance between us, but I just need to make it through this year.

With a smile still on my face, I shove my phone back in my pocket. When I look up, Roman is staring at me. He doesn't say anything so neither do I. The other guys seem to consider me and then Emilio asks, "Hot boyfriend?"

I snort "No. Just some people from my old school." I tell him. There's no reason to lie.

He lifts a brow as if to say, *elaborate*.

When I don't, he says, "You get dick pics from people often?"

Oh, my god. He saw that?

"What? No." I hide my face behind my hands and all three chuckle. "It's not what you think. God. No." I shake my head and they laugh harder.

"Damn, vanilla. No judgment here. You can have all the dick pics you want. Tell you what, I can go in the bathroom right now and take one for you. Give me your digits and we'll make shit happen."

Mortification rolls through me. "It's not..." I shake my head in a definite no before exhaling an exasperated sigh. "My ex is trying to get me back. Sort of." I frown. "I'm pretty sure what he really wants is a booty call but that's not happening. So, no, I don't get dick pics often. He's just a moron and hasn't realized it's over. And no, I don't want pictures of your dick, either. Thanks."

"Holy shit, vanilla. Your life is the prequel to a telenovela. What else you got?"

I snort. "Nothing. My life is not exciting." A little tragic, maybe, but no one else needs to know those parts.

The guys talk football the rest of lunch. All three are on the varsity team which isn't surprising. There's a game on Friday but they don't seem concerned about it. The game two weeks from now has most of their attention. It's Sun Valley High's rival game against the Suncrest Academy Saints. Based on their expressions, it's a really big deal.

I try and track their conversation. Julio and I use to watch football together. Ryker plays for my old school but I never really went to his games. I'd just watch NFL with Julio and sometimes the high school recaps if the game was big enough that the news decided to cover it.

Adriana was always there, though. She was on the cheer squad. Maybe that was one of the reasons he never asked me to come?

As the guys talk, I learn that Dom is the school's quarterback. Roman plays wide receiver. And Emilio is a cornerback. All three seem to live and breathe football. Emilio makes a point of including me in their conversation, which is a little surprising since he didn't seem thrilled that I was here in the first place.

He peppers me with questions but I don't have much to contribute. I understand the game. I know how plays work and I thankfully don't get lost when Dom goes off on a tangent about a blitz the Saints made that worked out for them in last week's game against another school. The guys are intense and it's clear they do their homework on their opponents. I surprise them a few times when it becomes clear I know what they're talking about and I start to find my footing a bit.

These guys aren't that different from my crew back home. Roman is a lot like Julio. The leader of the pack, though more brooding and definitely more of a player. Emilio has a carefree attitude like Felix. He's quick with the jokes and always wears a comfortable smile. And Dom is the strong silent type like Gabe.

I start to feel like maybe today doesn't completely suck but I don't delude myself into thinking that once Roman's little punishment ends that any of these guys will want to still talk to me. Emilio already made it clear they don't mix with the girls of this school. They can't afford any distractions. Aside from that, it's evident we come from different social circles. They're the guys all the girls want and the guys all the other guys want to be. You can see it in the way everyone watches them. And me, I'm the girl who just wants to survive her senior year.

When the bell rings, Roman dumps his tray and presumably heads toward Spanish, not bothering to wait for me. I consider calling out for him but immediately decide against it. He seemed to grow more and more agitated as lunch progressed. I haven't done anything to him so I don't know why he has such a stick up his butt.

No one talks to me as I wander the halls trying to find my Spanish class. Roman still has my schedule and I don't really know where I'm going. I try and ask a few students but all I get are sneers and eye rolls. No words. No help.

Yes, I'm the new girl.

Yes, I sat at lunch with the cute guys who I've now learned are also the school's jocks.

And no. I didn't want to cause any waves in the stupid high school social hierarchy.

I didn't miss the fact that the guys don't sit with the rest of the football players, who are easy enough to spot based on their rowdy behavior and letterman jackets. But if you're the QB like Dom, you're practically high school royalty. So, if the guys always stuck to themselves, me being there isn't going to go over well with the rest of the school.

Which was made abundantly clear once I got a new copy of my schedule from the front office and stepped inside my next class.

The teacher doesn't make me stand and do the whole introductions thing, for which I'm grateful. I hate being the new girl and I hate being put on the spot even more. I already feel out of place and the extra attention and scrutiny makes my skin itch. The girl who sits behind me makes it a point to kick the back of my chair at least four times during class, and then when class ends, she calls me a slut and knocks my notebook off my desk as she walks past.

Wonderful.

Roman sees all of it and his only reaction is to smirk. This guy is some piece of work. One minute he's kind of nice and helps me and then the next he's openly hostile and encouraging this kind of behavior toward me. I start to wonder if maybe he called me "his girl" last period just to make things difficult for me. Like he somehow knew the reaction that would garner.

When she walks past him, he makes a show of throwing his arm around her and walking out of the class beside her.

So dumb.

I ignore it all, though, and head to my last class of the day. Welding.

After a quick trip to the restroom, I make it to class just after the bell rings. I'm greeted by a sea of confused expressions as I stand in the open doorway. There are maybe twenty kids in the class and all of them are boys. Not surprising. The class has already started and I don't want to interrupt, but when the teacher notices everyone's confused faces staring at something behind him, he turns and spots me.

"Are you lost?" he asks me with a frown.

I shake my head. "No. I have Welding fourth period," I tell him, stepping closer to hand him my schedule. "I'm a late transfer," I add sheepishly.

His frown deepens, his nearly white brows furrowing together like two fuzzy caterpillars.

"Were you dropped in here because of space issues?" he asks, seemingly still confused.

"No. I chose Welding as my elective."

That throws him off.

"Are you one of the boy-crazy ones?" There's annoyance in his tone.

I snort. At my old school, a lot of the girls would take weightlifting as their P.E. elective because all the jocks took it. It was a good way to bump elbows with the cool crowd, but I wasn't one of those girls. I actually liked this class.

"No, sir. I enjoy welding."

He raises a single brow. "You've welded before?"

I nod. "My old school offered it so this'll be my third year. I'm decent at MIG and Stick. My TIG welding is," I lift my hand and twist it side to side. "It's just okay."

His eyes widen but he nods his head and returns my schedule. "Alright then. Grab a seat. We're doing a bit of a refresher today, anyway."

I head to the only available chair. When I sit down, a boy leans over his desk toward me. "Hey, you're new here, right?"

I nod, bracing myself for whatever he says next.

"I'm Aaron. What's your name?"

"Allie," I say, surprised by the introduction.

"Cool. Nice to meet you, Allie." He flashes me a brilliant smile. He's cute. *Really cute.* He has shaggy blond hair that hangs down in his face and bright green eyes. Dressed in black Volcom pants and an O'Neill shirt he gives off a skater vibe, but it's cool and it definitely fits him. My assumption is confirmed when I spot the skateboard resting on the floor beside his desk.

I match his smile before turning my attention to our instructor.

Most of what he goes over I already know. He gives us a refresher on safety protocols. I guess they had an injury the day before.

Always wear your face shield. Always wear closed-toe shoes. Wear a long-sleeved nonflammable shirt when welding along with a welding jacket. Wear gloves.

He shows us where the eyewash station is and then goes over the equipment. Most of the kids ignore him but I pay attention just in case there's anything he might do differently from what I learned before.

"First trimester we cover MIG welding," Aaron tells me as we resume our seats. No surprise there since it's the easiest form of welding there is. It's like the hot glue gun of the welding world.

The teacher—Mr. Moyer—explains how the welder works and just as he starts diving into how to prep for your weld, the bell rings, signaling the end of class.

"We'll continue where we left off tomorrow," he says to the class. "Study your syllabus and get a parent signature on your safety waiver," he reminds me as I grab my things to head out.

I nod and pull my phone from my pocket, realizing I have a text.

It's from Janessa.

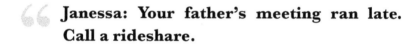 **Janessa: Your father's meeting ran late. Call a rideshare.**

I FROWN BUT THEN DECIDE IT'S PROBABLY GOOD HIS MEETING ran late. I wasn't exactly looking forward to the ride home with Gerald. I search the App Store on my phone for the Uber app and hit download. I haven't needed to Uber before, but it's not rocket science.

Aaron sidles up beside me and peaks over my shoulder at my phone.

"Something wrong?"

"No. Ger—my dad is just running late so I'm gonna catch an Uber."

"I can give you a ride."

"You don't even know me." I give him an incredulous look.

He shrugs and gives me back a boyish grin. "I know. But I'd like to get to know you."

Heat creeps up my face, but before I can respond, Roman is suddenly beside me. "Back off, Henderson." He shoves Aaron back into the lockers.

My mouth drops open and I grab for his arm. "What the heck, Roman?"

He raises a brow and the corners of his mouth lift in a devilish smirk. "Heck? Really?"

I glower at him. As Aaron shoves away from the locker, his face red and angry, I jump between them. With my back to Aaron, I scowl at Roman. "School's out. You don't need to babysit me anymore." Not that he was doing a great job of it to begin with.

Dom and Emilio walk up beside him and both level menacing gazes on the boy behind me.

"What is your deal?" I ask, not understanding where all of their hostility is coming from.

"You know him?" Emilio asks, tipping his chin toward Aaron.

I shrug. "Sort of. Yeah. We have Welding together." I can feel the anger radiating off Roman in front of me. His eyes are narrowed, his hands clenched into white fists at his sides, but he doesn't say anything. He just stares Aaron down behind me like he can kill him with just a look.

"He's bad news, vanilla. Make sure you don't ever get in a car with this one." Emilio says.

"Would you stop calling me that? I have a name." And why does he care if I maybe get a ride with Aaron? Is he some daredevil driver or something?

No one says anything for several seconds. I feel Aaron's hand on my hip a moment later and I turn to face him. "I'll catch you later," he grits out between clenched teeth. I give him a tight smile and a nod.

What else can I do? *So much for the lift.*

The three guys in front of me watch Aaron's retreating form with varying degrees of hostility. When I turn to head the same direction, Roman's hand shoots out, grasping me by my wrist.

"Henderson is bad news."

I pull away. "And I'm just supposed to take your word for it?"

He nods.

"Look. I don't know what your deal is but Aaron is the only person who's bothered being nice to me. I'm not going to stay away from him just because you say so."

"Hey! We've been nice," Emilio calls out.

I shrug. "You two have," I say, signaling to him and Dom. "But he," I point a finger in Roman's direction. "along with the rest of this school, have been complete jerks."

A tick forms on Roman's jaw but I'm not having it. I might look the part of a meek little wallflower but I'm not one.

I storm off toward the school's exit, ignoring him as he calls after me.

FIVE

Allie

The week goes by in a blur. After that first day, Roman stopped playing guide and I was fine with it. Sure, I missed the glimmer of camaraderie we shared at lunch that first day, but I wasn't looking for a replacement crew. Besides, he's a brooding jerk anyway.

I ignore him whenever I see him in first period or in the halls, and the rest of the school—aside from Aaron—thankfully decides to ignore me now that they've realized hanging out with Roman and his crew isn't going to be a repeat event.

Adjusting to life in Sun Valley is a new experience and it feels a lot like being trapped in purgatory. I see Gerald's assistant more than I see him. She's there every morning at half past seven, eager and willing to cart me off to school, though all week I've had to catch a rideshare to get home.

It would be easier if I just took the bus but the look on Janessa's face when I'd made the suggestion made that an immediate no.

The bus is beneath me. Seems fine for everyone else in this town but somehow an Uber is the classier, more refined choice.

Urgh.

I'm making my way out of my last class—eyes glued to my phone as I punch in the address of the school for a ride request—when Aaron calls out to me in the hallway.

"Hey."

I slow my steps and wait for him to catch up.

"Hey." I smile.

He tugs on the straps of his backpack, his skateboard strapped to the back of it, and a boyish smile on his face. "Got any plans this weekend?"

I shrug. "Not really. I'm still the new girl so I'll probably just hang out at home and get caught up on homework."

He nods and sucks on his upper lip. "Well, there's a party this weekend. It's sort of a pre-game tradition. A bunch of us go out in the woods and camp for the weekend before our big rival game against the Saints."

"You're into football?" I ask giving him a speculative look.

"Nah. But I'm into camping and partying so..." He shrugs.

"Oh. Cool," I say, not really sure where he's going with this.

He tilts his head, a question in his eyes, but I'm not sure what response he's looking for. He runs a hand through his hair and shakes his head. "So, uh, would you maybe want to come? With me, I mean? I can pick you up if you're cool with that..." He trails off and looks away, a slight blush on his cheeks.

Oh. *Oh!* "You're inviting me?" I squeak out. As soon as the words leave my lips, I want to smack myself.

The corners of his mouth twitch into the beginning of a smirk. "Yeah. I think it'd be fun. If you came, I mean. I think you would have a lot of fun."

I bite my bottom lip. I want to go. I could really use some fun in my life right now. And Aaron is the only person who talks to me, so I'm banking on him being my one and only friend while I'm stuck here. I don't want to disappoint him by turning him down, but would Gerald even let me go? How would I even go about asking him? I haven't seen him all week. Literally not once. He's always working and his meetings seem to run late every night.

"Um...." I glance around the hallway and I catch sight of Roman, Emilio, and Dom. All three of them are standing by the exit with matching scowls on their faces as they watch our exchange. I still don't know what their deal is with Aaron, but thankfully, this time they keep their distance.

Aaron follows my gaze and sees them, his grin quickly morphing into a grimace. "Are you into those guys?"

I'm a little thrown by his question. "What? No!" I rush to say.

He considers me for a moment like he isn't quite sure whether or not to believe me. "You sure? All the girls at Sun Valley High like the Devils."

"Definitely not this one."

He releases a relieved sigh. "That's good. They're assholes. I wouldn't want to see you hurt."

I don't argue because, well, they are, and the fact he's concerned about me is kinda nice.

I pull out my phone and shoot a text off to Janessa.

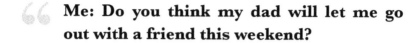 **Me: Do you think my dad will let me go out with a friend this weekend?**

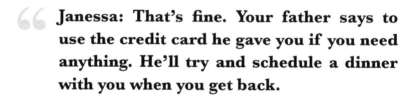 **Janessa: Dates, Times, Location?**

I TURN TO AARON. "MY DAD'S ASSISTANT WANTS TO KNOW for how long and where we'd be going?"

He lifts a brow. "Assistant?"

"Yeah. I know it's weird but I'll get a faster response if I go through her rather than trying to track him down."

He nods like he understands. "Shadle Creek. Today until Sunday morning."

I shoot her the information and watch as the three little dots appear. Then they stop. Then they appear again. *Urgh.* Come on. Answer already.

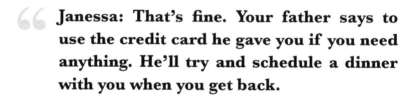 **Janessa: That's fine. Your father says to use the credit card he gave you if you need anything. He'll try and schedule a dinner with you when you get back.**

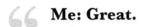 **Me: Great.**

I ROLL MY EYES. I LOVE THE IDEA OF HAVING TO SCHEDULE A dinner with my dad. I shove my phone back into my pocket and turn to meet Aaron's expectant gaze. "I'm in."

His eyes light up. "Really?"

I nod.

"Awesome!"

AARON GIVES ME A RIDE HOME AND FOLLOWS ME INSIDE. He sits on the edge of my bed, watching as I hastily pack a bag with the essentials. Underwear. Toothbrush. Hairbrush. Toothpaste. I'm not sure what all I'll need but it doesn't take long to realize none of the clothes Janessa got for me are going to work. Everything is white or blush and definitely not suitable for camping.

I dig through my dresser drawers and raid my closet looking for something passable. Aaron looks out of place in the space as he leans back against the pink floral bedspread covering the bed.

He's wearing his usual black Volcom pants, though today he's paired them with a Hurley long-sleeved thermal tee and a pair of checkered Vans. His shoulders are well defined, even beneath the fabric of his shirt, and his tee rides up, exposing an inch of smooth, tanned skin dusted with a light trail of blond hair.

I force myself to look away from the curve along his hips that I know leads to an Adonis belt I have no business admiring. How did guys get that? I've seen him eat. He's like a garbage disposal in the lunchroom, but looking at him now, you'd never know it.

"I can't believe you live here," he says, a touch of wonder in his tone.

"Yeah, well, only up until a week ago."

His head tilts in question and I sigh, not really wanting to explain but not really seeing a way around it either. "My mom died." I stuff down my emotions and force the words past my lips. "Dad's the only surviving relative I have, so I was shipped off here. I just moved in the week before last, so none of this," I wave at everything around me. "Is mine or even resembles the life I grew up with."

"No shit?" He shakes his head and his face pulls down into a frown. "Damn. I'm sorry."

I shrug. "It's okay. You didn't know."

Silence stretches between us, and after looking through the final drawer in my dresser, I give up in defeat. "I don't think this is going to work. I don't really have anything appropriate for camping," I say, resignation in my voice. I didn't realize just how badly I wanted to go until it became apparent I might not be able to.

Aaron considers me a moment before coming over to take my hands and pulling me from the floor where I'd been sitting. "It's cool. You can borrow some sweats of mine if you want. My bag is already packed in my trunk. Or we can always run by a store?"

"I don't think I'd fit in anything of yours," I say, eyeing his physique. Aaron is tall and thin, probably just shy of six feet. He's built like Chester Bennington from Linkin Park but with a young Ryan Sheckler hot skater-guy vibe.

"Is there, I don't know, a Target nearby or on the way?" I ask.

He chuckles. "I didn't take you for the Target type but yeah, there is."

My shoulders sag as I lean against the wall, relief sweeping through me. "I don't come from money. All of this, my dad's assistant bought it all for me when I moved in. I'm very much a Target kind of girl."

He grins this goofy lopsided smile. "I think I like you even more with that revelation. Come on. Let's get you some new kicks and go have some fun."

I've never been one for shopping but I absolutely raid Target as soon as we get to the women's section. I'm not the picky type so I grab the basics. Things I can mix and match with little effort. A few solid white shirts and a couple with band logo graphics. Some black ripped skinny jeans. A pair of shorts even though it's past fall and nearing winter. A swimsuit, just in case. And a few pairs of leggings along with a hoodie for good measure.

Aaron is a good sport, helping me carry the piles of clothes as I wander up and down the aisles without a single complaint. When I feel like I have enough, we make our way to the registers.

I feel bad when the cashier rings me up and gives me the total. Four hundred and thirteen dollars. I swallow hard as I hand over Gerald's credit card and guilt sweeps through me, reminding me I need to find a job so I don't have to rely on him. I'll be eighteen soon, and I need to be prepared for that.

It only takes a few minutes after she hands me my receipt to remember my mom just died and Gerald hasn't bothered to be around all week. What kind of father does that?

That helps sweep away any lingering guilt over how much I'm spending today. I'll still need to search for a job, though.

"Woah, Allie. You look good." Aaron says when I step out of the restroom.

As soon as I'd paid, I rushed to change into the ripped black jeans and a white V-neck shirt I'd just purchased. I even bought myself a pair of fake gold hoops. I was an idiot for thinking I wanted to be anyone other than myself. I hate all the expensive white and peach and pink clothes Janessa bought for me. And I really hate the way people judge me when I'm in them.

"Thanks." I tuck a strand of hair behind my ear and smile.

I was comfortable. I was me again.

I'd missed me this week.

With my arms full, Aaron helps me carry my load to his car and we toss everything in the back of his Subaru WRX. As I shopped, he told me about the cabin we'd be staying in. I was relieved when I learned I wouldn't need to worry about getting a tent or a sleeping bag. Camping with Aaron sounds more like staying in a hotel, so clothes and toiletries are all that is required.

I can tell Aaron comes from money. Not like Gerald does. That's an entirely different level. But Aaron's family is better off than just comfortable. It makes me wonder what he'd think if he'd seen my former home. If he'd still want to be my friend if he'd met the old me? The me before my mom died who lived in a one-bedroom, one-bathroom home on the wrong side of town with bars on the windows.

Then I shove that thought away because I realize I'm silently judging him the same way the students at Sun Valley High have been judging me. I'm not like that.

The drive to Shadle Creek takes a little over an hour. Aaron and I listen to The Red Jumpsuit Apparatus, All American Rejects, and Panic! At the Disco, and for the first time in over a week, I feel myself relaxing. The wind blows tendrils of my hair loose and I can't help but smile wide as Aaron navigates us down the winding roads, both of our windows rolled down and the sun shining through.

There's no pressure here. No hate-filled stares. Aaron is surprisingly funny and despite having a horrible singing voice, he has no problem belting out the lyrics to I Write Sins Not Tragedies right along with me.

Before I know it, the asphalt road turns to gravel and we're pulling into a clearing ringed with cabins. Dozens of teenagers—some I recognize from school and others I don't—are milling around, chatting, and drinking beer. Some are pitching tents and another group is getting a bonfire started in the center of the clearing.

As soon as we get out of the car, I close my eyes and breathe in the forest around me.

My shoulders relax, my breathing slows. I exhale and it's like all the tension from earlier this week melts away.

I catch Aaron ginning at me over the top of his car.

"Glad you came?"

I nod and grab my bags, following him as he leads the way to the first cabin on our right. "Yeah. This place is really cool," I say as he unlocks the door and we step inside. He drops his own bag just inside the doorway and I take in the rustic yet clean A-frame cabin. It's simple and screams teenager hangout with the mismatched sofas and already set up red Solo cups on the dining table. A game of beer pong is definitely in our future tonight, not that I'm complaining.

There's a surround sound system set up in every corner and an old school boombox with mini subwoofers built beneath the speakers resting on a cherrywood entertainment center. I spot the CD booklet sitting next to it and can hardly wait to rifle through it. MP3 players and streaming are so overrated. Mixed CDs are where it's all at.

"Thanks. My family owns this one and the cabin right next to us, but I'm letting a few buddies of mine use that one. We'll probably have some crashers here on the sofas later tonight. Usually, we leave our cabins open to whoever decides to stay, but there's a bedroom in the back so we'll have some privacy."

Oh.

We?

Crap.

I bite my lower lip as Aaron gives me the full tour. It's an open floorplan. There's a kitchen to our right. The fridge is already full of beer and not much else. When I ask Aaron about food he laughs and says they grill outside and most of the food is kept in coolers. I shrug and decide not to worry about it. It's not like I've been eating much as it is.

Next, he shows me through the living room area on our left and then down a wide hallway leading toward the back of the cabin.

"This here is the main bathroom. People will come in and out all night to use this one but in here," he opens another door that leads into the lone bedroom. "There's an attached bathroom that will be just ours. Everyone knows to stay out of bedrooms unless you know the cabin owner and have permission, so you won't have to worry about anyone barging in on you."

I nod, eyeing the single bed in the middle of the room. A queen-sized wooden sleigh bed. But there's just the one and I don't know Aaron all that well.

Sensing my apprehension, Aaron reaches out and places a hand on my shoulder. "You okay?" His brows pull down and a small crease appears on his forehead.

I nod. "Yeah. I was just wondering ... ummm ... where should I sleep?"

He clears his throat and shuffles his feet before saying, "I kinda figured you'd crash here, with me. I mean, If that's okay."

I flick a glance toward him and then back to the bed, twisting the teal corded bracelet around my wrist.

"I'm not expecting anything to happen between us," he rushes to add. "I probably didn't think this through but I figured you'd take one side and I'd take the other. Cool?"

I bite my lip. It makes sense. I'm mature enough to share a bed with a cute boy. I can do this. Right? No big deal.

Shoving my apprehension aside, I say, "Yeah. Cool."

He grins.

"Alright, then. Let's go out and grab a beer. I don't know about you, but after the drive, I could use one."

SEVEN

Roman

I pull up to the Shadle Creek campgrounds in Dominique's Escalade. I would have preferred to drive my old-as-shit El Camino but Dom's ride has more space, so here we are. Emilio sits passenger while Dominique is sprawled out in the backseat, snoring louder than a lawnmower. He doesn't usually let me drive. He's got control issues. But he's fucking beat. We all are.

We killed it in tonight's game winning twenty-four to three. It was a slaughter. But because of tonight's game, we're getting out to the campgrounds later that I would have liked. At least we still managed to make decent time.

"Wake up, *cabrón*. We're here."

Dominique groans but pushes himself into a sitting position before rubbing the sleep from his eyes. The three of us stare at the circle of cabins in front of us with varying expressions. Emilio is hyped as fuck and already has his door flung open. His hair is still wet. We all showered after the game in the locker rooms before heading out, so when he whips out of the car, water droplets smack me in the face.

Asshole.

Dom is his usual impassive self but side-eyes me as he grabs his shit from the back. It only takes a second for me to figure out why when all the blood inside me heats and anger spikes in my chest.

Allie is here, and just exited the first cabin with Aaron Henderson. *Fucking Henderson.* Just the sight of that wannabe asshole makes my blood boil. I told her to stay away from him.

I grit my teeth and tighten my hands on the steering wheel.

"Bro, come on," Emilio calls, slamming his door and grabbing his duffel from the back. Dom meets my eyes in the rearview mirror.

"You gonna eye-fuck the girl all weekend?" he asks.

"Fuck you." I flip him off.

He snorts and climbs out of the backseat, grabbing his bag before heading off to follow Emilio to our cabin. I watch them in my peripheral but I don't take my eyes off Allie. She looks good. Real good. She's changed her clothes since I last saw her at school, trading in her white jeans and flowing top for black, ripped jeans and a basic t-shirt. The top dips low in the front exposing a thin line of cleavage and I'm already envisioning her naked breasts.

I scrub a hand over my face. I need to stop checking her out. Emilio's been on my ass all week to focus on the field and yeah, we kicked ass tonight, but I didn't bring my A game and she's the cause of it.

I've stayed away from her all week, avoiding her in the hallways like a fucking coward. It was risky, especially if she decided to whine to Kemp about it, but she stayed quiet like I knew she would. Which makes her all the more intriguing. She didn't rat me out and land me in detention. She didn't beg for attention like other girls would have after being on the receiving end of my cold shoulder.

No. She kept her head down and acted like I didn't even exist. No chance glances my way. No longing looks.

I don't know what it is about her but I can't get her out of my head and it pisses me right the fuck off. I thought if I avoided her it would lessen my attraction to her, but seeing her now makes me realize that was a big fucking failure. If anything, I want her more. I want her as consumed with thoughts of me as I am with her.

It's becoming an obsession.

What am I doing to myself? I pull out a cigarette and light it up. I take one deep pull, holding the smoke in until my eyes burn before I release it. Fuck. I toss the cigarette out the window and then shove the smokes into the glove box before Dom sees. If either he or Emilio realize I still carry a pack on me, they'll both have my ass.

You can't be a star wide receiver and a smoker. The two don't go hand in hand. But damn if I don't want to smoke my way through the entire pack right now.

Dominique's parents own the cabin we're staying in. It's the nicest one out here. Two stories tall, it has four bedrooms and four bathrooms making it more of a vacation home than a cabin. Dom comes from money—enough to rival even Gerald Ulrich—and while the fucker may hate it, it does have its perks. We stay here at least once a month. It's nice to get away from things. Or it would have been if everyone else didn't have the same idea this weekend.

I glare at Henderson and Allie once more before slipping on a pair of mirrored aviators and following my boys. I don't care that it's late. No one is gonna say shit to me about the sunglasses.

The clearing is packed with people illuminated by firelight. Most hang out next to their cars, or in small clusters by the fire. No one speaks to me and everyone gives me and my boys a wide berth as we make our way toward our cabin.

A few guys I recognize from the football team are stupid enough to nod in my direction as if to say *sup?*

I don't reciprocate the gesture. I might talk to some of these assholes on the field when I have to, but I sure as shit am not going to tolerate them off the field. I am not one of them. Never will be and sure as shit don't want to be. They don't take the game seriously. It's all fun and games for them but for us, for me, Dom, and Emilio, football is life. We live, breathe, and sleep football.

All three of us have plans to go pro and we've all earned scholarships at division-one schools. It's a big part of why we don't hang out with the team. We can't afford to get sucked into their bullshit.

Football has to come first.

A group of bikini-clad juniors walk toward me. Emilio slows his steps a few paces ahead while Dom reaches the cabin porch and disappears inside. Beers in hand and wide grins on their faces, the girls sway their hips and offer flirtatious looks and stupid giggles.

I stifle a groan. At school, these chicks usually just give me googly eyes but leave me be unless I approach them, but I can tell they've already had some booze.

One of them is particularly brave. "Hey, Rome. You gonna party with us tonight?" she calls out.

At the mention of my name, I see Allie's head jerk in my direction. *That's right, pretty girl. I'm here.* I don't bother hiding my smirk. "Maybe." I holler back to the girl, wanting to gauge Allie's reaction. She scowls and turns away while the bikini chick giggles. Fucking giggles. I swear these girls get stupider each year, but I eye her rack anyway. Stupid or not, she's got a good one.

Maybe a quick fuck will get Allie out of my head?

"Come find me later," she says and I give her a noncommittal grunt.

I need to get laid, but the idea of fucking her doesn't pique my interest. Allie on the other hand... *Fuck.*

Inside the cabin, Dom flicks on all the lights and we each throw our stuff in our respective rooms. Our cabin is off limits to everyone outside of our group. We've been known to bring a few girls back for the night but our cabin isn't one of the open ones for partiers.

"I see your girl is here," Emilio comments with a shit-eating grin when I make my way back to the porch. I accept the beer he offers me and my eyes track Allie as she follows Henderson over to a group of his skater friends.

My hand clenches around my beer and I clench my jaw. The fucker smiles at her as he leans down to whisper something in her ear.

"I don't have a girl," I say.

That earns me a grunt from Dom. "Then why are you eye-fucking her?" he asks.

I flip him off with my free hand. "You can't see my eyes, asshole. I'm not even looking in her direction."

"Liar," Emilio adds. "Just fuck her and get it out of your system already."

I roll my eyes, not that he can see it. "I'm not interested in fucking her. I— "

"Right. You want to be a dick and toy with her, that it? You need a new pet project to focus on?"

"What the hell is your problem, man?" I flick up my aviators and glare at him.

Emilio laughs but there's an edge to his voice. "Nothing. You do you. Fuck her. Don't fuck her. I don't care. Just make up your mind already so we can enjoy the damn weekend. I'm too tired for your games so whatever you have planned, leave me out of it."

"Count me out, too," Dom adds. He leans back in one of the wooden porch seats, his legs wide and a beer in hand, pretending like he doesn't have a care in the world. "We agreed we'd focus on our futures. You don't have time to be chasing tail. Get laid. Don't get laid." He shrugs. "I don't really care. But you were off today and you know it. She's in your head, so do what you need to do to get her out. If that means playing one of your mind games with her, so be it. But we're not backing you this time around." He tips back his beer.

I grind my teeth together. "Fine." Assholes. We've always messed around with the same girls in the past. It made things fucking convenient, but whatever. I didn't need them to get what I wanted out of Allie.

Emilio downs his beer before reaching for a new one. "I'm going to go find myself a piece of ass. I earned it after tonight's game. I'll catch up with you two later."

He jogs down the steps and heads straight for the bikini girls, throwing his arms around two of them. I won't be surprised if both end up in his bed tonight. Emilio's been known to enjoy his fair share of threesomes and even the occasional foursome.

"I'm surprised his dick hasn't fallen off yet with how many holes he sticks it in," Dom says.

I lift a brow. "Like you're one to talk."

He shrugs. "I'm taking this year easy. Focusing on what's important." I follow his gaze and catch him staring at Kasey Henderson. He tracks her movements like a lion hunting its prey.

"You want Henderson's little sister?"

He shrugs but doesn't take his eyes off her.

"Dude. She's a freshman."

Another shrug.

"Whatever. If you want jailbait, go for it. You've got two months before she's off limits so I suggest you work fast."

He grins. "I'm always up for a challenge."

H e's here. I don't know why I assumed he wouldn't be.
Maybe because of the game? He doesn't seem the
social type apart from the two guys I met earlier this
week. He sticks to Dom and Emilio and they have a bit of a
fearsome threesome going on. No wonder everyone calls them the
Devils. They're always together, and I haven't missed the fact that
everyone else seems to give them a wide berth. They're popular,
sure, but it's almost like they're unwilling participants in the game
that is high school social hierarchy.

Rulers who don't really want to rule.

I haven't made friends at Sun Valley High—at least none aside
from Aaron, but I've heard the whispers in the halls when those
three walk by. Everyone seems to want to get their hands on one of
the Devils. I don't even think the girls have a preference between
the three.

Aaron hands me another beer and I gratefully accept it before
noticing Emilio heading my way with a lopsided grin on his face.

His arms are wrapped around two girls. One a leggy blonde with a bright red bikini top, the other a brunette with a black bikini and a pair of cut-off shorts. Don't these two realize it's cold? It can't be more than fifty degrees outside. Fall is upon us and winter is fast approaching but these two don't seem to have gotten the memo.

"Yo, vanilla. How's it going?" Emilio calls out across the fire. I hate that nickname and I'm almost positive he and Roman use it just to get a rise out of me.

I force a tight smile and lift my beer in greeting. "It's going," I say, hoping he'll turn his attention back to the two girls beside him. They're running their hands all over him and one is actively trying to suck on his neck but she's just a few inches too short to reach and he doesn't seem inclined to accommodate her.

"Tonight, stop by our place." He turns and points with his beer to the monstrosity of a cabin behind him. "Alright?"

"Why does he want you to go to his cabin later?" Aaron whispers beside me. "I thought you weren't into any of the Devils?"

"I'm not. And who knows. I don't get these guys."

Before I can answer Emilio, Aaron decides to do it for me. "She's got plans tonight," he says, throwing an arm around my shoulders. There's a possessiveness to his touch and I'm not sure how to feel about it. I like Aaron. He's nice and he's cute, but I just got out of a relationship. I'm not looking to dive into another one, and Aaron seems the relationship type.

Emilio's eyes narrow and laser in on the contact.

I cringe.

"Maybe later, then?" he says.

I can hear the bite in his tone, but I don't know if it's directed at me or Aaron. "Sur—"

"Nah. Sorry, man. She's busy *all* weekend." He drags out the word "all," and without saying anything else he's sunk a heavy amount of innuendo into that one sentence.

I turn to him with a confused expression, but he doesn't seem to be paying me any attention. His eyes are narrowed and there's a triumphant look on his face as he and Emilio glower at one another. Like he's won something. Like he's won me.

I'm not some prize in these guys' pissing contest. Whatever issue they have with one another, I don't want any part of it.

As unassuming as I can, I shrug out from under Aaron's arm and stand up. "I'm going to explore a bit. I'll catch up with you later." He scowls but nods, and I turn to head in the opposite direction from him and Emilio.

I make it twenty feet when my phone buzzes in my pocket. I'm surprised I even have cell reception out here. I check the screen and release an audible groan when I see who the message is from.

 Ryker: Come on, A. I miss you. Stop icing me out over something stupid.

ANGER BUBBLES UP INSIDE OF ME AND BEFORE I CAN TALK myself out of it, I message him back.

Me: You broke up with me the day my mom died!

THOSE THREE LITTLE DOTS APPEAR AND I STARE AT THEM AS I wait for his response. But instead of another text, my phone rings in my hand.

Ryker.

"Chingada madre!"

Do I really want to talk to deal with him right now? As I stare at the illuminated screen trying to decide, the ringing stops, saving me from having to make a decision. But then it starts right back up again. I must be a glutton for punishment because on the fourth ring, I answer.

"What do you want, Ry?" I ask.

I walk toward the back of Aaron's cabin and step onto the back patio. Thankfully, no one else is out here so I claim a spot on a wooden bench and lean back, waiting for Ryker to respond.

He's quiet for a second and it's as if I can hear the gears turning in his head. Ryker was always good at that. Finding the right words to say to calm me down. Looking back, I can think of at least a dozen instances when he manipulated me into forgiving him for one thing or another. He was never a good boyfriend. I don't know why it took me so long to realize that.

I finish the beer in my hand and since Ryker still hasn't said anything, I dip inside the cabin through the rear entrance in search of something stronger. I'm going to need it for the conversation I'm about to have.

"Baby," he breathes out, longing in his voice. I roll my eyes and spot a stray bottle of tequila. I swipe it and pour a shot into a red cup before adding in some Sprite as a mixer.

"Don't 'baby' me," I tell him, taking a healthy swallow of my new drink. "I can't believe what you did, Ry. I can't..." I choke on my words, unable to force them out as the tequila burns down my esophagus, making me cough. I probably should have taken a smaller sip. I give myself a few seconds, take another drink because, yes, I am a glutton for punishment. "You hurt me." I don't know why I'm saying this. Maybe a part of me wants him to understand just what he did to me. Maybe then he'll finally leave me the heck alone. "You hurt me when I was already hurting."

"Fuck," he mutters. "I know, baby. I know. I'm sorry. Okay? I fucked up. I was drinking and I wasn't thinking straight. *Fuck.*"

I can hear him pacing on the other end as I step back outside and reclaim my spot on the bench.

"What do you want me to say?"

"The truth. For once in your life, Ry. Can you just be honest with me?" I still don't know the full story. I know he cheated on me with Adriana but I don't know any of the details and I don't know why he broke things off between us the way he did. Ryker was an asshole, but until then, he'd never been cruel.

Another curse. "Baby, it's not that simple. Adriana, she came on to me and at first I thought she was you." His words are rushed. "You've got to believe that. I would never—"

"You expect me to believe that?" Is he kidding? Does he really think I'm *that* stupid? I seethe. "Ry, I'm not an idiot."

He groans. "I know. I know. But it's the truth. I was wasted, babe. And I didn't mean to break up with you."

I snort. "Oh really? Then what did you mean when you texted me —the same day my mom died I might add—saying, 'I think we should see other people'. Huh? How is that anything other than breaking up with me?"

There's a loud bang on the other end of the line like maybe he hit something.

"Look, I'm not proud of this, okay. And I didn't know your mom had died when I sent it. Adriana told me you found out about us. That you were going to dump me. I just"—he sighs—"I was stupid and I wanted to break things off with you first before you turned around and ended things with me."

Wow. Just wow.

What an asshole.

He's quiet for a beat and I take another drink from my cup. The alcohol burns and I relish the pain. My throat tightens so I take another drink, eager to chase away the ache forming in my chest because it still hurts and I hate that. I hate that he still has any sort of hold over me.

"I loved you," I tell him, my voice cold.

"Baby, I love you, too. So much."

I shake my head even though he can't see the movement. "No, Ry. Loved. I *loved* you. I don't anymore. Not after what you did."

"Allie, baby. Please. Don't be like this. We can fix this. I know we can."

"Nope." The 'p' makes a popping sound to emphasize my decision. Another drink and my cup is empty. I set it aside and lean back, relishing the slight spinning my head is doing right now. "I might have been able to get past the cheating if you'd been honest with me. I was that invested." He'd been my first kiss. My first love. The guy I lost my virginity to. Maybe that was why I'd put up with so much for so long. Not anymore. I deserved better. I knew that. "But Ry, you dropped me when I needed you the most. There's no coming back from that. Stop texting me. Stop calling. I'm not going to forgive you. Not for that."

A movement to my left draws my attention and I spot Roman leaning against a tree, staring at me. His face is blank, but he's removed his aviators, giving me a glimpse of his dark brown eyes. There's fire in his gaze, and I shiver. When he sees I've spotted him he steps forward and sits beside me.

He puts a hand out, silently asking for my phone. I frown, but what the heck? I hand it to him.

He lifts the phone to his ear and says in a gruff voice, "Listen to her. Stop calling. Stop texting. You two are done. Got it?"

"Who the fuck are you?" I hear Ryker bite out.

"Your replacement." Roman deadpans. He hands me back my phone after he ends the call. It starts ringing almost right away but I silence it and shove it in my back pocket. He offers me his beer and I take it. I tilt the bottle back to my lips, letting the cool liquid slide down my suddenly dry throat.

My vision blurs for a second but I blink fast to clear it and hand the beer back to him. Heat rushes up my neck and I can feel the effects of the alcohol kicking in even more now. Good.

I don't want to be sober. Not tonight.

Neither of us say anything after that. Both content to gaze up at the starless night sky. Roman takes a few pulls from his beer bottle and I watch as his Adam's apple bobs with each swallow.

When the seconds turn to minutes, I feel my cheeks go numb and my head begins to swim. I've always been a lightweight. Drinking and partying was never really my thing. I hadn't expected the liquor to hit me this quickly, though I can't say I regret that it has and I'm already wishing I had more.

Roman nudges me with his shoulder and I meet his gaze. The mask is still in place. His expression unreadable. A tendril of dark brown hair has fallen forward and I reach out, brushing it back.

His hand shoots up to grab my wrist and I gasp, but rather than tightening his hold on me, his thumb rubs small circles along my pulse as he lowers my hand between us. He doesn't release me. He continues to rub lazy circles across my skin and goosebumps break out on my arms. He tugs at the teal bracelet on my wrist drawing my attention.

His eyes meet mine again and this time, I see him. I see the want and the need there. The desire.

I swallow hard and a bout of nerves has my stomach tightening.

"That the ex?" he asks. His voice is smooth and he's still rubbing those darn circles along my skin. I can't think with him touching me.

"Yeah." My voice is more breathless than I'd intended, but all of a sudden, it's like I can't get enough air inside my lungs. Walk away, Allie. You don't need to fall for another asshole.

"He cheated?"

I nod.

"And your mom's dead?"

Another nod.

He seems to ponder my words. "So, who are you living with now? Your pops?"

I nod. "Yeah. Bio-dad."

He tilts his head in question and he shifts so our bodies are closer to one another. One arm curls around my shoulder, the other still on my wrist, but I can feel the heat from his body so close to mine now.

"I, uh... don't really want to talk about it." I stutter my words. Being so close to Roman has me on edge. I'd done so well avoiding him this past week that I'd almost tricked myself into believing he's forgotten about me. Clearly, that was a stupid thought because here he is, in the flesh. A gut feeling has me believing he's planned this meeting. Why else would he have followed me to the back of Aaron's cabin? What other reason did he have for being here?

"Allie?" His voice is flat yet somehow filled with so much suppressed emotion.

I swallow hard and tug my hand free from his hold.

Silence hangs between us again and I push up from my seat. "I'm going to get another drink," I say, needing a reason to escape his presence. There's something about Roman that has me convinced he's dangerous, yet I'm drawn to him all the same.

He doesn't say anything and he doesn't try to follow me. He brushes a hand through his thick, dark hair, his nostrils flaring, but no sound escapes him. I pause by the door, giving myself one last second to drink him in before I escape inside, cursing myself for being stupid. Roman is trouble, and I'm not going to make the same bad decisions again.

NINE

Allie

"Allie!" Aaron shouts as soon as I step into the living room. He must have come inside after I left the bonfire. "Come play with me." He's standing in front of the dining table. Red cups set up to form triangles on either end.

I smile but it's forced. "I was wondering when the beer pong games would begin," I say and head toward him.

The cabin is packed and I have to weave my way through the sea of bodies to get to Aaron. No one bothers to get out of my way but when I finally reach him, he tugs me closer, an arm wrapping around my shoulder as he lifts a beer high in the air. "I've got my partner. Who's brave enough to be our challengers?" Cheers go up and I can smell the beer radiating off him as though it's seeping through his pores.

How many has he had?

I pull away from his hold and shake my head. "I'm not really in the mood to play tonight. But I'll watch."

His bottom lip juts out. "Aw, come on, Allie."

I shake my head. "N— "

The leggy blonde from earlier steps up beside Aaron. "Hey, Henderson. I'll be your partner," she purrs.

He looks at her and I track his gaze as he takes in her barely covered body. His lips press into a tight line but his eyes don't leave her. I can tell he's tempted so I decide to give him a nudge in the right direction.

"Cool. Thanks," I tell her. "I appreciate you taking my place."

She sneers at me. "I'm not doing you any favors. Why are you even here?"

I suck in a breath, taken aback by the open hostility. I open my mouth and then close it. Unsure how to respond. A few other girls beside her start laughing and I stumble back a step.

"Good one, Sarah," a girl remarks.

The blonde, Sarah, beams at her friends and then turns back to me with an obvious look of contempt. "Really, though. No one wants you here. Why don't you slink back to whatever stuffy prep school you were expelled from? I'm sure Daddy Warbucks can help you out."

"Hey. Not cool." Aaron finally comes to my defense.

The girl rolls her eyes. "Come on, Aaron. You know she doesn't belong here." She wraps her arms around his neck and mashes her breasts against his chest. "Send her away already so you and I can have some fun," she whines. The sound grates on my ears. Does she think guys like that?

Aaron's gaze flicks between us with uncertainty.

Seriously? He invited *me*.

Anger ignites in my chest.

Seeing my expression, he pulls her arms away from his neck and takes a step back. "Sorry, Sarah. Allie's my friend. I'm not cool with you talking to her like that."

Her eyes widen and her mouth hangs open for a second before she snaps it closed. "Excuse me?"

He shrugs and runs a hand over the back of his neck. "Look. I know— "

"Screw you! Your loss, Henderson. Don't expect to get a second chance." She brushes past me to leave the room, shoulder checking me along the way. I bite the inside of my cheek to keep from lashing out at her and turn grateful eyes toward Aaron.

"Thanks. You didn't have to do that," I mutter.

He shrugs. "Yeah. I did. I invited you. And Sarah can be a real bitch when she wants to be. She doesn't usually seek me out at parties like this. She's younger but she's with the 'elite' crowd." He makes air quotes for the word elite and sighs. "We don't run in the same circles. But she's my neighbor. We sort of grew up together and sometimes she can be a decent human being." He pauses as though choosing his words carefully. "She's used to being the center of attention. Honestly, I wouldn't be surprised if she only came on to me right now because you showed up."

Oh.

"I'm sorry. That's a crappy thing to do. Are you into her?" I ask, not wanting to cock block him because, yes, he did invite me and I'm grateful he came to my defense, but if he wants to *carpe diem* and all that, I won't stop him. I know how guys can be sometimes.

If he were Felix, he'd have gone with her, had his fun, and then apologized to me later.

But Aaron only shakes his head. "No. Not really. I know the kind of girl she is and that's not what I'm after. I think between the beer and her boobs, I got a little confused."

I can't help but grin. Aaron has a sheepish expression on his face as he says, "So, any chance I can change your mind and convince you to be my partner after all?"

I start to shake my head but then I spot Emilio, Dom, and Roman as they crowd into the space. Emilio's smile is wicked as he looks at me and says, "Come on, vanilla. Let's play. We can make things interesting."

Great. Vanilla again. I scowl, but I'm curious now. "What sort of interesting?"

"If we win," He points to the three of them. "You wear a bikini the rest of the weekend. Day and night. No exceptions."

I snort. Typical. "And if I win?"

He shrugs. "What do you want?"

I consider this. I don't know if they're any good and I don't know if Aaron is either but I do know that I am. As long as Aaron isn't god-awful, there's a decent chance we can win. I've always been one of the guys and beer pong is a party go-to. Julio and I use to make off at parties like thieves. We'd make things interesting with cash on the table, but this is my first party with this crowd, and I don't know what the expectations are here. They don't really seem like the gambling type.

I'm still riding a decent buzz so I decide to focus on that and turn tonight around despite my ex's call and Roman's strange behavior.

"If I win, you three wear bikinis all weekend. Day and night. No exceptions, either."

The crowd cheers on the idea and Emilio's grin widens while Dom and Roman's matching scowls deepen. I don't even bother trying to hold back my laugh.

"Alright. Alright. I can get behind that."

"No," Dom says. "You fuckers have at it. My black ass is not wearing a bikini."

Emilio chuckles. "But Dom, you'd look fine as fuck in one and you know it."

His scowl deepens even more and I clutch my stomach, laughing, as I picture Dominique in a bikini. "Alright. You get a pass," I say when I can catch my breath again. "But only because teams need to be equal. Two on two."

I turn to Aaron and he gives me a reassuring smile. He's in, even though I'm pretty sure if we lose, the guys only care if I'm the one in a bikini. Good thing I bought one today.

Then I turn to Roman and lift a single brow. I'm almost positive he'll bow out like Dominique did but he surprises me when he grabs a ping pong ball and says, "Rack them up."

TEN

Roman

I'm going to murder my best friend for getting me into this. Allie and Henderson are kicking our asses. They're two cups away from handing me my ass and a fucking bikini is not going to be enough to cover it.

Allie's eyes are glassy. The booze is hitting her hard, but with a grin on her face she raises her hand, shoots, and lands the damn thing in my cup.

Fuck.

She jumps up and down, her tits bouncing with the motion, and Henderson high-fives her.

Emilio grabs the cup. Downs it in one swallow and then takes aim.

The fucker misses and I bite back a groan.

Shit.

"I'm going to kill you," I tell him, low enough that only he should hear but I don't miss Dominique's dark chuckles behind us. He's enjoying this shit. He's probably hoping we lose, too.

"Nah, man. You won't," Emilio tells me. "Because I'm helping a brother out by putting you front and center for her. You might hate losing but you want that girl's attention."

"No. I don't," I mutter. "She's no one to me."

Emilio ignores my comment and now it's Henderson's shot. He takes aim for the last cup on our side and at the last second, his eyes flick up to mine and I stare him down. He falters and I let a murderous grin wash over my face. My vision tunnels and all I can see is him. His green eyes darken and I know his surroundings are fading away from him. The crowd around us cheers him on.

"Shoot."

"Shoot."

"Shoot."

I narrow my eyes further. His jaw tightens and he shoots but the fucker isn't looking at the cups. He's still looking at me like he's two seconds away from pissing himself.

He misses.

I grin and blink, breaking the stare off between us and he curses.

That's right, fucker.

It's my turn so I grab the ball and without any fanfare, I shoot it into one of their three remaining cups. Henderson swears again, downs the cup, and hands the ball to Allie.

She smirks at me, completely in her element, and lands the ball in our final cup. Emilio moans beside me but I know it's all for show. He couldn't care less whether we win or lose. It's all a game for him. He lives for this kind of shit even if he tries to claim otherwise.

Slowly, making sure to keep my eyes locked on hers, I lift the cup and down the remaining beer.

"You lose," she says and her satisfaction is clear.

"I did. Guess you better go grab me that bikini of yours," I tell her.

"Mine?"

I nod and suck in my bottom lip with a nod. "Yeah, vanilla. I want yours."

"You can have mine," one of the chicks beside me says.

I lift a brow. "And you are?"

She looks surprised I don't know who she is, but why would I?

"Silvia. Silvia Parish. I have second period with her." She reminds me, angling her head toward Allie. Recognition clicks back to when I told her to watch out for *my girl*. Guess I do know her name after all.

I shrug. "Well, Silvia Parish," I say, "Thanks. But no thanks. I want Allie's. Only hers will do."

Silvia pouts and Allie rolls her eyes. Her annoyance is sexy as hell. "Whatever. *Andale pues.*"

I don't think she realizes she told me to hurry up in Spanish, but I like it. I like that it rolls off her tongue like it's natural. It probably is. And I really fucking like that Henderson has no idea what the fuck she just said. It wasn't anything sexy. There was no hidden meaning there. But he doesn't know that.

I make sure to shoulder check him as I shove past to follow Allie.

"Watch it, Henderson," I say so low only he can hear. "I wouldn't get in my way."

His jaw locks and I wait, making sure he gets my meaning.

It takes longer than I like, but eventually, he nods. *Good.*

I follow Allie through the crowd of people, shoving against bodies when they get too close. This is why we don't open up our cabin. I don't like people in my space.

She leads me back to a bedroom and as soon as I step inside the dimly lit room, I shut the door. I exhale in relief and Allie laughs. "Not one for crowds?" she asks.

"Not one for idiots," I retort.

She smiles and digs through a bag until she retrieves a black two-piece swimsuit. The bottoms are taller, like they'd go past her hips, and the top is a thick band that ties in the back. Hmmm. Interesting. "No slutty string bikini?"

She shakes her head. "Not really my style." She holds her hands out, but before I accept it, I pull off my shirt and let the fabric fall to the floor before unbuckling my jeans.

She sucks in a breath. "What are you doing?"

I can't help my grin at her freaked-out tone. When I look up and see her eyes locked on my abs, heat simmers in my chest and my dick twitches. Her gaze rolls over me with blatant interest and my smile widens. I shove my jeans down, leaving my black boxer briefs on and then step out of the jeans, discarding my socks and shoes along with them.

"Like what you see?" I ask, holding my hands out wide with a cocky smirk on my face. I know I look good. Her expression confirms in.

A delicate hand reaches out as if to touch my tattoos and I wait, eager to feel her hands on me though I can't explain why. *What is it about this girl that draws me to her?*

Hands pressed together in prayer are inked on my right side, a strand of rosary beads between their fingers. My right arm sports a half sleeve filled with an intricate Aztec falcon totem. And on my left collarbone, climbing up my neck and down over the top of my bicep and pectoral, is an Aztec devil mask.

My gaze heats as I watch her eyes drink me in but instead of trailing her fingers over the designs, she hovers over the left side of my rib cage. She has her bottom lip trapped between her teeth and a hint of concern flickers across her face. *Concern for me?* I'm surprised when I spot the emotion.

I look down and realize her eyes are glued to a purplish yellow bruise that's formed across my left side.

I remember the hit I took in the fourth quarter. I'd been running for a touchdown and the guy had come out of nowhere, tackling me in the end zone even though I'd already dropped the ball. Ref threw a flag but it didn't matter. The game was over by then.

Her fingers brush over the damaged skin and she whispers, "Does it hurt?"

I bite back the groan I want to release at her featherlight touch. "Nah. It looks worse than it is."

She steps back and her eyes widen, as though realizing that she'd just been intimately close. A pretty blush spreads across her cheeks. I step closer to her before she can retreat further, and I wrap my hand around her delicate wrist. "You gonna give me the suit?" I ask.

She's maybe five-two to my six-one. A tiny little thing so she's forced to tilt her head back to meet my gaze. All it would take is me dipping my head a few inches to catch her lips with my own, but I don't. Her eyes glaze over as she stares back at me. She licks her lips and I trail the movement.

"Ww...What?"

I quirk a brow. "The suit," I say again, tugging on the material that's clutched in her hands.

"Oh. Oh!" She drops the fabric like it's hot to the touch and steps back, her face even redder than it had been before. Taking the swimsuit, I stretch the top over my chest, the fabric barely able to tie in the back over my broad chest. Then I hold up the bottoms and meet her gaze. "I'm not sure these will fit over my legs, but if you want me to try, I will. Or..." I trail off and wait.

She swallows hard, licking her lips again. "Or what?"

I toss her swim bottoms back to her. "Or I can go like this. My boxer briefs don't cover much more than those would." I point to the swim bottoms. "More leg but less abs." I lift my shoulders in a shrug. "It's your call."

"Oh. Yeah. Sure. That's fine."

ELEVEN

Allie

I don't know why I care that Roman is wearing my swimsuit top. It's just a stupid top. But he's wearing it and it's mine. My stomach flip-flops and I toy with the teal bracelet on my wrist. Following him out of Aaron's room, I try to slow my racing heart. The crowd presses in on us, forcing us to take a few steps back until Roman shoves one of the football players out of his way with a two-handed shove. He's wearing his jersey as are a bunch of other guys, making them easy to spot.

The guy whirls on Roman with a fist raised as if to swing, but suddenly halts before dropping his hand back to his side. "Hey, Rome. My man, uh..." He rubs the back of his neck. "Sorry, man. I didn't realize it was you."

Roman doesn't say anything. He just stares, his eyes narrowed into slits and the guy backs up, hands lifted in surrender. "Yeah. Sorry. Let me get out of your way." He gives Roman a nervous chuckle as he moves.

I expect Roman to shove past him leaving me behind but instead, he turns back, grabs my wrist, and hauls me after him. I squeak and stumble, my body brushing up against a few of the players, but as soon as I come into contact with them, they step back. What is it about him and grabbing me by the wrist? "I'm perfectly capable of walking," I say, but he either doesn't hear me or chooses to ignore me.

We exit the house and find Emilio wearing a neon pink bikini top over his bare chest and string bikini bottoms over his dark blue boxer briefs. I have no idea how he manages to make it look good. But he does.

Emilio has tattoos as well and his chest piece is on full display. A gothic portrait of a woman with her hair flying back and a mix of sparrows and ravens flying around her with strands of her hair lifted in their beaks.

It's surprisingly beautiful. When he catches me staring he rubs his chest and bites his bottom lip. His eyes become hooded and he lifts his brows in a suggestive manner. Roman steps in front of me with a growl and Emilio explodes into a fit of laughter.

I spot Dominique beside him, his shoulders shaking. His lips are pressed together and I can tell he's fighting to contain his own laugh but in the end, he fails.

"Rome, if you could see your face right now."

I move forward to gauge his expression but the mask he usually wears is firmly in place. "Well, uh, I'll let you guys do your thing." I inch around Roman and head back toward the fire, my eyes scanning around for Aaron. When I spot him, there's a girl in his lap kissing at his neck. I can't make out her face but...

My steps falter.

I look again and yep, it's Sarah. The bitchy girl from earlier. Awesome.

Warm breath on my neck catches me off guard and then I hear his voice. "Looks like your boy is busy tonight." His voice is low, his tone suggestive. "Fool. Going for that when he could have had this instead." His fingers brush up my spine and I release an involuntary shiver.

"No one is having *this*," I snap, hating what he's implying. "Besides, we're just friends. He can go after whoever he wants."

Another caress, this one along the back of my hip. "Yeah?"

"Yeah."

Roman's fingers tighten on my hip into an almost bruising grip as he draws me tight against his body. "What if I decided I want you?"

My breath hitches and he's still behind me, trailing his lips up the column of my exposed neck. It's not a kiss. The touch is featherlight but it feels like he's marking me, branding me as his. "I'd tell you to screw off."

"Liar."

I step away from his body, instantly missing his warmth.

"Come with me." He twines his fingers with mine and despite knowing better, I allow him to lead me toward one of the larger cabins.

I stumble after him, but he doesn't pause or slow his steps. He just tugs my hand harder, forcing me to quicken my pace. "Where are you taking me?" I ask, finding my voice.

He smirks over his shoulder. "You scared, vanilla?"

I scoff but continue to follow him, my steps hurried as I try to keep up with his longer strides. "Hardly."

The cabin is empty aside from the two of us and I take everything in. Much like the outside, it looks more like a regular home than a cabin. A large leather sectional takes up most of the room in front of a wood-burning fireplace. And the kitchen and dining area look like they came straight out of a magazine.

Roman watches me as I soak everything in, gauging my reaction though I'm not sure what he's hoping for. Everything inside screams expensive, but it's tasteful and you can tell that each piece in the space was carefully thought out.

Looking at it makes me think of movies in front of the fire huddled up with friends. Julio and Adriana and I would do that sometimes. Sometimes Gabe or Felix would join us. Before she did what she did. Before my mom died.

We'd watch stupid movies and eat popcorn. Julio always poured a bag of Swedish fish in my bowl so I could find sweet surprises. We'd fight over who got to eat the last one and the night almost always ended with Adriana sprawled out on our only sofa, Julio and I on the floor. He'd lean against the sofa with me lying beside him, my head in his lap.

I think of what it would be like being huddled up next to Roman in front of that fire and warmth spreads inside my chest. It wouldn't be like when I watched movies with Julio. There would be no easy carefree affection.

"What are you thinking?" he asks, stepping closer to me.

"Nothing."

"Mentirosa." *Liar*, he says.

Maybe I am, but I know better than to share my true thoughts with him, so I say, "I was just thinking this place is nice. Homey. I know it probably cost a fortune but it doesn't feel cold." *Like my new living arrangements.* But I don't say that out loud. "I like it."

He nods and heads toward the kitchen, leaving me to follow him. He opens the refrigerator and starts pulling out ingredients. Carrots, celery, a package of ground beef. Then he opens up cupboards and pulls out onions, garlic, potatoes, spices, a few cans —corn and tomatoes from the looks of them—followed by a bag of rice.

"What are you doing?"

"I'm cooking."

A laugh escapes me. "I can see that but what are you making, and why?"

"I didn't eat after the game." A shrug, his broad shoulders flexing with the movement, and I fight the urge to trace every contour of his body with my gaze. He should look ridiculous in my swim top. But he doesn't. It's unnerving.

I still haven't decided if he's the enemy or not. He runs hot one minute. Cold the next. I can't get a solid read on him.

"I'm making *albóndigas.*"

My heart seizes in my chest and memories of my mom and me cooking at the stove wash over me. "Yo...you are?" I turn to hide the sudden tears pricking the corners of my eyes, barely catching his nod.

Thankfully, he doesn't look up from what he's doing. He peels the onion and with quick efficiency, dices it into small neat squares. "Here." He hands me a second cutting board and a sharp knife. "Dice these." Then he hands me the celery, potatoes, and carrots.

I take them and do as instructed, ignoring the sudden emotion clogging my throat. "You know albóndigas take at least two hours to make, right?" And even then the flavors aren't completely melded. My mom would make the soup and let it simmer on low on our stove for several hours, making sure everything married nicely together. There's no way the soup will be done in time to eat tonight.

He nods. "I know. I'm cheating."

I look up from my task and spot him pointing to an Instant Pot, of all things, on the back counter. I can't help the laugh that bubbles out of me.

"My mother would be mortified."

He gives me a devilish smile. "Mine, too. And my grandmother would probably disown me, so this is top secret. No sharing trade secrets, vanilla." He winks. "I don't want burgers or hot dogs. I want real food. Food I'd eat at home." Another shrug. "This will cut back on time. Once we get everything in there, we'll have fresh soup that tastes like it's been cooking all day within fifteen minutes."

I smile to myself. "You're not what I expected you to be."

He eyes me up and down and I almost miss the hunger in his eyes before it disappears. "Neither are you."

TWELVE

Roman

She's smiling. A real smile, not one of the forced, fake ones she gives everyone else at school. This one is genuine, and I don't miss the glimmer of tears in her eyes before she banishes them away. The girl has demons. Hell, hers might even be worse than mine.

I've got an overbearing pops whose expectations I never seem to measure up to. She's got a dead mom and a cheating ex. What other damage is she hiding behind that smile?

Maybe that's what draws me to her. I want to hurt her. Bite her delectable lips until they bleed. Caress her body until it bruises. I'm not a gentle lover. I kiss hard and fuck even harder. But I also want to protect her. Something in me wants to hold her. Mark her as mine and shield her from the world even as I strip her bare of all her protections and expose her to me and me alone.

The anticipation of having her builds inside me.

I never should have brought her here.

I put everything in the pot and set the time on the pressure cooker before making quick work of cleaning up the mess we made getting everything together.

"I'll wash that," Allie says, taking the cutting board from my hands as she moves to the sink. She then puts it back in the drawer I'd pulled it out of earlier. With her back to me, I step into her space and place my hands low on her hips. I dip my head down, drawing in her woodsy vanilla scent as my nose drags along her neck.

She sucks in a breath but doesn't move. I draw her back until our bodies are flush with one another before trailing my lips down the column of her neck. She tilts her head to the side, granting me better access and fuck, her skin is so smooth. I nip and bite at the tender flesh. She hisses from the sting of pain but doesn't pull away, surprising me, so I do it again. This time biting hard enough to leave a small bruise behind. I chase away the sting with a kiss and suck on her sensitive skin ensuring that she'll carry my mark after the weekend is over.

One of my hands slides over her hip to trail up her stomach until I'm cupping one of her breasts.

"Roman...?" Her voice is quiet, hesitant.

There's a question there but I can't answer her. I don't have the words for it, because I have no fucking idea what I'm doing, and I sure as hell am not going to admit that.

She cranes her neck to look at me and I see the same want and need inside of me reflected in her gaze. I've never cared what a girl is thinking about or what she might be feeling, but with Allie, I can't help myself from wanting to figure her out. Does she miss her old school? Her old life? What is she planning to do once she graduates?

She's become my obsession and even as I tell myself she's nothing, no one, I dip my head down and capture her lips with mine, desperate to taste her. She gasps and I take full advantage, sweeping my tongue inside her mouth and drinking down her soft moans.

My other hand moves up to cup the back of her neck, angling her head more so I can deepen the kiss while I squeeze her breast, and fuck, does she have nice ones. Full and round. Just enough to fill my hand. I grip the plump flesh, satisfaction flaring within me when she arches her back, pushing her breast further into my grasp before twisting in my arms.

She's so responsive. So fucking hot. Her arms come up to wrap around my neck. Her breasts press against my chest and I'm two seconds away from stripping her out of her clothes and fucking her right here on the kitchen counter when voices outside grow nearer.

She tears her mouth from mine. "Roman." Her breathing is heavy. Her chest heaves up and down and I realize mine is, too. I want this girl, and I have no fucking idea why. I steel myself and mask the need to sink myself inside her, fitting a bored expression on my face as our eyes connect.

"I..." Her brows furrow as she takes in my expression. Confusion flashes over her features.

The voices grow louder and she takes a step back, trying to put distance between us, but I'm not ready to let her go. I grip her hips with bruising force, refusing to let her back away. She's not the one in control here. I am.

The door to the cabin opens and Emilio strides in, Dom hot on his heels.

"I told him you'd be busy," Dominique says in way of greeting. I lift a single brow as if to say the interruption is of little consequence.

Emilio's still got two girls, one under either arm beside him. He's got that junior chick from earlier on his right and Silvia on his left. I can tell he's drunk. His eyes are glazed over and he has a stupid happy smile on his face as he takes in the scene in front of him. "Hey, vanilla. You going to bang my bro, Rome, tonight?" It's all I can do not to punch him in the face. Silvia's eyes shoot to Allie and she visibly stiffens. I step forward, blocking Allie from view and Dominique smacks Emilio upside the head, muttering "stupid fucker," under his breath.

"Hey!" Emilio cries out, rubbing his head as if Dominique actually hurt him. We both know it's all an act. "Not cool, man. What the hell?"

Dominique points down the hallway. "Take your women to your room or send them on their way." He takes a deep inhale before a grin spreads across his face. He's had a few, too, because Dom isn't usually one for smiles. "Roman's cooking tonight."

Emilio perks up like a five-year-old about to get an ice cream cone or some shit and his gaze snaps toward me. "You cooked?"

I nod.

"What'd you make?" He's all but forgotten about the two girls with him. Silvia and the other chick whose name I don't know and have no interest in learning stand just behind him with worried expressions on their faces. Looks like things aren't going as they'd hoped.

"Albóndigas," I tell him.

His smile widens and he turns. "Ladies, it's been real." He ushers them back to the front door despite their protests. Silvia is clearly digging her heels in, not liking that she's being shown the door.

"But, Emilio. I thought we were gonna party," she whines.

"Sorry, uhhh..." He pauses and gives her an apologetic look.

Her mouth drops open and her eyes narrow before she responds with a drawn out, "Silvia."

He snaps his fingers together. "Right. Silvia. Sorry. Something came up. I'll call you later, okay?"

Her cheeks heat and she pushes out her bottom lip. "You haven't even asked for my number yet."

He grins at her. "I'll get it. I have my ways. Don't worry that pretty little head of yours."

Before she can respond, he gives her and her friend one last little push and closes the door behind them. Then he turns back to me. "I just gave up some prime pussy so you better feed me, fucker."

We all laugh. "You've got ten more minutes. Go find something to watch and I'll get tortillas going."

He nods and then moves toward Allie.

I growl.

"Hey, man. I was just gonna show your girl around. Chill."

I glower at him. He doesn't need to show her around anything. Knowing Emilio, the first place he plans to show her is his bedroom. Dominique knows this too, and interrupts before things have a chance to get heated. I might claim disinterest when it comes to Allie but I am anything but disinterested in her and I do not share my toys with others. I want to know everything about her. To own all her secrets and learn all her desires. I need ammunition against this girl. She already has too strong a hold over me.

"Wanna help pick the movie for tonight?" Dom asks her.

Her brows pinch together and she gives us all an assessing look. I can tell what she's thinking. It's written all over her face. We're the grade-A assholes of Sun Valley High. The Devils. So why are we holed up in our cabin when it's barely midnight instead of partying it up outside with everyone else? And what she probably wants to know even more than that is why the hell we're being nice to her when all week we've pretended she doesn't exist.

Dominique answers her first unspoken question. "We're beat from the game today. And that out there," He throws a thumb toward the direction of the front door. "Isn't our scene."

Her lips purse. "You guys don't party?"

"Oh, we party." Emilio chuckles and gives her a suggestive look. "But we do it on our terms and we don't need wannabe assholes around to do it. Besides, today was a game day. That means tonight is a recovery night and Roman is a greedy bastard who doesn't cook for us often. We gotta enjoy it while we can."

"Oh. Okay." She follows Dom towards the sofa and he gives me a quick nod before showing her to our DVD stash. We don't have WiFi out here, so streaming something isn't an option.

As they dig through the movie selection, Emilio heads to his room and comes back in a pair of sweatpants. He's still got his ridiculous bikini on over them but he walks in like he's the hottest shit there ever was. I chuckle under my breath. The guy's got no shame.

Allie hides her smile behind her hand when she spots him. "You don't have to keep that on." She's taken the corner spot on the sectional and has the throw blanket tucked tight around her body. Is she cold? Do I care? I frown, not wanting to examine my feelings where her well-being is concerned.

Emilio looks down at himself, a smug expression on his face as he says, "I mean, I'm all for rocking my birthday suit, but I don't think these two would appreciate it."

"I was talking about the swimsuit," she says. I watch as heat creeps up her cheeks. She has the prettiest blush.

"What? I look damn fine in this thing." He cups his junk over the ridiculously bright fabric. "Pink is my color. Besides, a bet is a bet."

She rolls her eyes and turns to me. "It's just the four of us. You don't have to wear it either. But I'm holding you to wearing it anytime you step outside this cabin this weekend. Fair is fair." Her lip curls into a satisfied smirk giving away that she's a hint competitive. I'll have to file that bit of information away for later use.

"I can get behind that." I untie the black top and toss it on the counter just as the Instant Pot beeps letting me know it's finished. I turn on the *comal*—a cast iron griddle of sorts—and warm up tortillas before portioning out the soup. Normally I'd make them serve themselves but I don't want Dominique eating all of it in one go. Emilio and I are used to home cooking. Dom's not, and every time it's offered the man wolfs it down as though he's been starved.

My mom practically lives in the kitchen and there is always something hot and ready as soon as I or my pops walk in the door. But Dom's parents are rarely home and dinner is almost always some catered solitary affair. It's why Emilio and I try and have him over to our houses for dinner throughout the week. No one should eat alone. Food is meant to be enjoyed with family and those two fuckers are as family as it gets for me.

"Grab your food," I tell the guys as I grab two bowls, handing one to Allie. Then I go back for the tortillas and place a few on a napkin on the empty seat beside her. I sit down and tug some of the blanket from her lap. I don't actually want it, but I want an excuse to be close to her. I haven't had the chance to catalog her features. To memorize her expressions so I know exactly what she's feeling when she's feeling it.

"Hey!" Her eyes narrow and there's visible tension in her shoulders.

"I'm in my underwear. It's cold." I lie because I'm definitely not cold, but I really want under the blanket now.

She rolls her eyes but doesn't object again. *Score one for this Devil.*

Dominique gets the movie going and credits begin rolling as we all dig into the meal.

Allie moans and I fight back a smirk. There's something satisfying about knowing she likes it. That she's enjoying something I made for her. "This is so good. I haven't had albóndigas since—"

She cuts herself off and I turn to look at her. She blinks rapidly then stares down at her bowl like she's fighting back tears. I take in her bottom lip as it wobbles. The red splotches that appear beneath her eyes as if she's already cried her eyes out.

An unfamiliar jolt of something I don't want to realize hits me in the chest. *Fuck.* She hasn't had albóndigas since her mom died. That's what she'd been about to say.

Emilio sees her reaction and meets my gaze with a concerned look of his own. I lift my shoulders just enough as if to say *I have no fucking clue what's set her off,* because I sure as shit am not about to share her secrets with him. They're mine, and mine alone. But in typical Emilio fashion, he saves the night with a wise ass joke.

"Damn, Allie. You can't moan like that over soup. My head's going all sorts of directions after hearing that sexy noise out of you."

She laughs but there's a hiccup in there. "You're such a guy." She throws a tortilla at him before swiping one of mine to replace the one she just lost. I pretend not to notice.

"Don't hate. I can't help I was born with one of these." He grabs himself underneath the bright pink bikini bottoms covering his sweats and then takes a big bite out of the tortilla she hit him with.

She groans again, this time in feigned annoyance. "I don't even know what to do with that statement." This time, her voice isn't as tight, and some of the redness has receded from her face.

"Yo. Pipe down. Movie's starting," Dominique cuts in, and all of our attention goes back to the screen just as Norman Reedus and Sean Patrick Flanery appear on-screen and walk past the priest to kiss Jesus's feet.

Emilio groans, cocking his head to one side before shaking it. "Boondock Saints. Again?"

To which Dom replies, "Don't gripe at me. Allie picked it. Girl's got good taste. Not our fault you don't."

Emilio harrumphs but leaves it be and focuses on the albóndigas as we all turn our attention to the screen.

As soon as Allie finishes her food, I whisk the bowls back to the kitchen. The movie is almost halfway through and it's just now getting to the good stuff.

I reclaim my seat and tug at her blanket once more. She scowls at me and tugs some of it back so I jerk at it again. This time I'm met with a glare. "What are you doing?" she whispers.

"Shhh—" Emilio snaps, engrossed in the show. He might complain about how often we watch this movie when we come out here but he loves it just as much as we do.

Ignoring Allie's question, I lift the blanket and shift closer until our sides are pressed up against one another. I wrap one arm around her shoulders and pull her closer to my chest while adjusting the blanket until it comfortably covers the two of us.

Her body stiffens for just a moment before she relaxes against me and a small thread of satisfaction filters through me. One of her hands presses to my chest right over my heart and I wonder if she can feel it pounding. This girl makes me feel things I'm not entirely sure I want to feel.

My eyes stray to the teal bracelet on her wrist. She's worn it every time I've seen her. Is it sentimental or something? The urge to ask her about it is strong but I hold myself back, unwilling to expose just how much she intrigues me.

Allie definitely isn't like other girls. Those girls want to get with me or my boys because we can do something for them. If they're connected to one of us, their social status goes up. Even if all we do is sleep with them, more guys after that will want them. They want what the Devils have had.

Allie doesn't seem to care about any of that. She doesn't seem to care about status or power.

And knowing that draws me to her even more.

THIRTEEN

Allie

I don't know what is going on between us. It's like something has shifted, the air is charged and the tension thick. Roman's muscular bronze chest is warm beneath my cheek and I find myself absently trailing the devil mask tattoo on his collarbone.

He sighs in contentment and pulls me closer. I'm certain it's a subconscious reaction, because there's nothing sexual about the touch at all. And despite the warning bells in my head, I'm not uncomfortable in his arms. In fact, I'm very comfortable. Like, this is where I belong. Right here in his embrace.

It's not the platonic feeling with him the way it's always been with Julio, however. I have stupid butterflies in my stomach and an ache in my core that has me clenching my thighs together. I don't remember being this drawn to Ryker, as though I want to sink into his skin, share the air he breathes.

Maybe it is sexual.

It's all so confusing. I barely know Roman Valdez, and what I do know paints him as an arrogant jerk. I shouldn't be here with him.

I shouldn't let him hold me like this. But I am and no matter how many times I tell myself I need to leave, I stay.

The movie ends and Dominique quietly slips away to his room. Emilio hesitates like he wants to hang out some more but a single death glare from Roman sends him on his way.

Alrighty then. So much for having a buffer.

I stand up once they leave, feeling awkward and out of place. I have no idea what time it is but the commotion outside has quieted. It's safe to assume most of my classmates have gone to bed or are in the process of doing so.

I fold the blanket we'd been using and place it on the back of the sectional before slipping my feet into my sneakers.

"What are you doing?" Roman asks, his arms folded over his chest and his legs spread wide.

Well, someone sure has a self-assured look on his face. I wish I knew what he was thinking. I feel like I'm about to do the walk of shame when I step outside the cabin door, yet we haven't even done anything. Well, unless that kiss earlier counts.

"I was, uh, just getting ready to head out." I shrug.

Roman clasps my hand and tugs me toward him. "Why?"

I bite my bottom lip. He tugs at my hand again, this time harder, and I stumble forward. He catches me and adjusts my weight so I'm straddling his lap, his face now only inches from mine.

I'm drawn into his dark brown gaze and heat pools between my legs. My core tightens and I feel his cock harden beneath me. I'm tempted to shift and rock against him but I don't. I shouldn't. I can't.

"Why are you planning to leave, vanilla?"

With that one word, it's like a bucket of water is dumped over me. "Why do you keep calling me that? What is your deal?" My voice is heated. I hate that he keeps making digs at me. I thought... I don't know what I thought. But I don't like him making fun of me.

He chuckles and my annoyance spikes. "I call you vanilla because..." he trails off with a grin.

I smack his chest lightly. "Come on."

His smile widens into the devilish smirk I've quickly grown accustomed to seeing on his face. He leans forward to whisper in my ear, "It's my favorite flavor."

His breath heats the shell of my ear and I can't fight the tingles that race up and down my spine. "Your favorite flavor?" I ask, confused.

He nuzzles me and murmurs, "Mmm.... Mexican vanilla. The sweetest taste there is."

Oh. My. God.

He trails kisses along my neck, his hands digging into my hips before he pulls back.

"I..." I swallow hard. "It's late. I'm supposed to stay in Aaron's cabin." At the mention of his name Roman growls, a deep throaty sound that leaves more liquid heat pooling between my thighs.

His eyes lock on mine for the briefest of moments before his lips come crashing down on my mouth, and then I'm drowning in him. His touch. His taste. I can't seem to figure out up from down. All I know is that I want him. No. I need him.

My hips thrust forward and I grind against him. He groans and I want to hear that sound again, so, so bad. I press my core against him harder and swivel my hips. His fingers dig into me hard enough to bruise as he clutches me tight to his chest.

"What are you doing to me?" His voice is husky.

I have no answer for him so I kiss him again. I continue rocking against him, swallowing his groans as he greedily drinks down mine. The reality that one of the other guys can walk in on us at any moment doesn't matter. All I can think of is how good he feels.

One calloused palm rises beneath my shirt and tugs down the cup of my bra. He pinches one hard peak and I cry out. It's as if my nipple and clit are connected and I feel my release move closer, hovering just out of reach.

"Oh, God," I gasp and try to move away. This is too much, too fast but Roman chases after me with his lips and I give in to him, too weak to shove him away. I trail my fingers over his bare chest, reveling in the feel of every dip and valley. He tugs my shirt up and I raise my arms, allowing him to pull it from me.

A quick motion at my back and the clasp on my bra comes free. It slips down my shoulders before Roman tugs it forward, discarding it somewhere to the side.

He drinks me in. His hungry gaze locks on my breasts. "So... fucking... beautiful," he murmurs right before his mouth is on me. His lips wrap around my nipple and his tongue lashes at me as his other hand kneads my tender flesh.

I can't take it. I writhe on top of him, pressing myself closer. Wishing there was nothing between us. I need to feel him inside of me. I need to feel something good. Something that can take all the pain and grief away. I know what I'm doing now and for a moment, guilt slams into me before I shove it aside.

I'm using him. But isn't he using me, too?

With me still in his lap, Roman cups my rear and stands. I wrap my legs around his waist and allow him to carry me down the darkened hallway. I kiss his neck. His shoulder. I can't stop touching him.

When we reach a closed door, he fumbles to open it and then steps inside and carries me to the large bed in the center of the room. He lays me down with surprising care and just stands there, looking down at me with wonder on his face.

The emotion worries me. I need whatever we're doing right now to have boundaries.

"Roman?" I push up to my elbows and he cocks his head to the side, his eyes boring into mine. I lick my lips. "This ... whatever this is ... it's just fun. Okay?"

Anger flashes for a split second and then it's gone as though it'd never been there. An easy smile tugs at the corner of his mouth and he reaches for me, his hand trailing up my side to my face before gripping my jaw as he brushes his thumb along my lower lip. "I want you." There's an edge to his voice. It's all I can do not to reach out for him, draw him closer. His hands move to the button on my jeans. "I want to fuck you. I want you to scream my name. And I want you to come on my cock."

I suck in a shuddering breath.

"But I don't do relationships, vanilla, so don't get this twisted. I'm not a nice guy. Right now, I only want one thing from you and that's access to your pussy." As soon as my jeans are undone he slips a hand inside, sinking two fingers deep inside me.

I hiss.

The rational side of me knows this is a bad idea. He'll hurt me. He'll use me and toss me aside and no matter how many times I tell myself I'll use him too, that this is a fair exchange, I know it isn't. But I refuse to worry about that now.

Roman Valdez is like a drug and I'm desperate to get my fix, all the while praying I don't develop an addiction after just one hit.

He slides out of me before hooking his finger in my jeans and panties and in one smooth motion, he whisks both of them off, and then I'm bare to him.

He groans again, his eyes hooded as he drinks in my naked form.

A hand runs up my thigh before pushing my legs apart, exposing my most intimate flesh to his hungry gaze. Instead of climbing onto the bed like I expect him to, he kneels down at the edge of the mattress, bringing his face eye level with my core.

Instinctively, I try and close my legs but his hands on either side keep me spread and open to him. "I'm going to kiss you," he tells me and then begins trailing hot wet kisses along the inside of my leg. He bites the sensitive skin of my inner thigh, forcing me to stiffen and cry out from the unexpected sting. But then he's laving his tongue over the small wound, kissing the slight pain away, and I relax in his hold again. When he gets close to my core he repeats the movements on my other thigh, taking his time. His teeth scrape against my skin and I'm panting now. A complete puddle as my limbs tighten in eager anticipation.

When his face finally comes back to my center, his eyes darken, drunk with need. He takes a deep breath, inhaling me before his tongue darts out and licks me back to front. My hips buck off the bed and I cry out at the sensations. *Holy... wow.*

After that one lick, Roman buries his face between my thighs. Licking, sucking, biting. Sensations tumble through me, too many to count and the next thing I know my release is thundering toward me. I'm so close. I can feel my release *right* there. And then, like breaking through a damn, it crashes through me. It's like a tsunami I can't escape, the fastest, hardest orgasm I've ever experienced, and I cry out with my release, screaming his name. "Roman."

Then he's on top of me. He's removed his boxer briefs and his hard length is pressed against my lower stomach as he pulls my legs up on either side of him, nestling himself between me. He slides against my wet center and I tilt my hips back, widening my legs to grant him a better angle.

He rears back and curses. "Fuck."

I startle and my eyes go wide. "What?"

He climbs off of me and runs a hand through his dark brown hair.

Humiliation sweeps through me and I jerk into a seated position, wrapping my arms around my chest to cover myself.

"Condom," he bites out. Then he looks at me and his eyes narrow. "What are you doing?"

"I..." A blush warms my cheeks as he stands there in all his naked glory without a care in the world. "I... Ah..." I have no words.

He steps closer and leans down, kissing me hard and deep before biting my bottom lip and giving it a tug. My hands fall away from my breasts and I moan into his mouth.

He pulls back with a devilish smirk, "I'm getting a condom and then I'm fucking that tight little pussy of yours."

I swallow hard. "O-okay," I whisper, hating how unsure I sound. I brush loose strands of hair from my face and then his words slam into me. *Condom.* Oh my god. I almost had sex with him without one. What was I thinking?

He strides out of the room completely naked, only to come back seconds later with a square foil packet in his hands. He tears it open with his teeth, rolls it on his thick, hard length, and then is right back in front of me. He kisses me again and leans forward, pressing me back against the mattress.

"Ready for me?" he asks as he lines his cock up with my center. His eyes are hooded, his expression now serious.

"Yes," I say, because right now the idea of him anywhere but inside of me gives me a panicky feeling. When the head of his erection nudges against my core, he locks his eyes with mine and he holds my gaze.

"I won't be gentle."

I nod in consent and with that one small motion, he's slamming into me in a single hard, smooth trust. Stars explode behind my eyelids and I push my hips up to meet his, gasping at how full I feel. He lets out a string of curses. One hand tightens on my hip, pressing me down into the mattress as the other rests beside my head, bracing his body above mine.

"So fucking good, vanilla."

I whimper his name and kiss the strong column of his neck, nipping playfully.

He slides out of me, slow and smooth before thrusting back inside, this time even harder. Deeper. I grab hold of his biceps, holding onto him like my life depends on it. His groans undo me.

He grips my jaw and slams his mouth down on mine, devouring me like he's starved for my mouth. He kisses my lips, my neck, my shoulder, and then he's thrusting hard and fast, not giving me a chance to catch my breath. His kisses grow more aggressive as he all but punishes my body. His hold on me is so tight I know I'll have bruises in the morning and I don't even care.

I'm on fire. Every cell in my body humming with greedy need and expectation. I can feel another orgasm building inside me and I offer no resistance.

A needy moan climbs up my throat, my body winding tighter and tighter. *Oh my god.* "I'm going to come again," I pant.

Roman pulls out of me and I cry out at the loss of contact but then he's flipping me over onto my stomach, pulling at my hips until my ass is raised high up in the air. Then he slams his cock back inside of me. This angle has him thrusting deeper almost to the point of pain. But it's the best pain.

"Come for me, Allie. Come hard." He tangles one hand in my hair, pulling my head back as far as it will go, my spine arches and my breasts thrust forward. My inner walls clench tight around him and my orgasm shatters around me. Colors explode like fireworks behind my eyelids. He feels that good. So, freaking good.

He begins driving himself harder into me, grinding his teeth with each savage stroke. "Mine," he snarls, biting my shoulder like a wild animal. He fucks me raw and angry, pounding into me without mercy as though he's exorcising his demons. My hands itch to touch him. To roam his muscular body. But I can't in this position. All I can do is barely manage to hold on to my sanity as he fucks me like I've never been fucked before, effectively ruining me for anyone else who might come after him.

I scream his name again as my body locks up for the third time, my inner walls gripping him tight as I shatter, drowning in the waves of yet another release. I collapse face first onto the mattress, the sensations too much for my body to bear. His hands hold my hips back and he stiffens behind me, his body shuddering against mine with his own release before he pulls out, leaving me empty and aching.

His lips find my ear and he says, "My pussy. Got that? For as long as I want it."

I want to deny him. To tell him to fuck off because he doesn't own me, but at the moment, all I can manage is a grunt and I don't even know if it's in agreement or denial.

He tugs me into his arms, nestling me beneath his chin as we both struggle to catch our breath, and when I finally do manage to get my breathing under control, I decide not to address his statement. I can't form the words let alone digest the meaning behind what he just said.

It's possessive in the extreme.

After a few minutes pass, he gets up, leaves the room still gloriously naked, and disposes of the condom. He comes back with a warm washcloth and with surprising care he wipes away the remnants of my release from my thighs before tossing the washcloth in a dark corner of the room.

I consider getting up and leaving. Finding my clothes and heading for Aaron's cabin. I shouldn't stay here. It would send the wrong message. This is just fun. No strings. No emotions.

But when he tugs me toward the head of the bed and helps me slip beneath the covers, I resign myself to the fact that I don't have it in me to fight him.

Neither of us says a word. Roman reels me in until I'm resting splayed across his chest, my ear pressed against his beating heart and the night melts away. My body slips into the first restful sleep I've had since my mom passed away.

FOURTEEN

Roman

I wake up to a loud banging at the front door. What the fuck?

Allie is asleep beside me. Her hair is a tangled mess of brown waves and her expression is relaxed. I watch her for a moment as her chest rises and falls, the sheet barely covering her pert breasts.

Just as I'm about to lean down and suck on her beautiful tits before rolling her over and sliding into her wet heat, the knocking that woke me up in the first place sounds again, though this time louder, closer.

Someone better be dying because Dom and Emilio know not to come knocking this early in the fucking morning.

I groan and throw my legs over the edge of the bed, rubbing my eyes to clear the sleep from them. Finding my boxers, I slip them on and then open my bedroom door with a scowl on my face.

"What?"

Dominique stands on the other side, an amused expression on his face as his eyes wander past me, spotting Allie in my bed. I step to the side, blocking his view of her as I cross my arms over my chest and raise a brow. "*Cabrón*, there better be a good fucking reason you're waking me up right now."

He tilts his head back toward the front of the cabin. "Henderson's looking for her. Figured you'd want to deal with that."

Any good mood I woke up with instantly sours at the sound of his name. "What the fuck does he want?"

Dom shrugs. "What you've got in that bed of yours would be my guess."

I flip him off. "Keep your voice down. You're going to wake her up." He nods and I throw on a pair of sweats and a Sun Valley High hoodie.

Dressed, I head toward the front of the cabin and find Henderson pacing on the front porch. His brows are furrowed and he runs his hands through his shaggy blond hair. Asshole looks like a Bieber wannabe.

When he spots me, his eyes narrow into slits and his fists clench at his sides. He looks me up and down, hate evident in his glare. I wait. As if this fucker can scare me. He'll need to do a hell of a lot better than that.

He takes in my outfit as though searching for evidence of what happened last night. I snort. Is he expecting to find me with the condom still wrapped around my dick?

"Where is she?" he bites out.

"Sleeping," I tell him, enjoying the anger I see bubbling up inside of him. He wants to hit me. I can tell by the tick in his jaw and the way he keeps clenching then unclenching his fists, but Aaron Henderson isn't a complete idiot. He knows he can't take me. He may hit the gym and ride that stupid board of his but I dominate on the field and take hit after hit day in and day out. Doling out some of my own in return both on and off the field.

Henderson wouldn't stand a chance against me and he knows it.

"What did you do to her?"

I roll my eyes, not even bothering to pretend I didn't fuck her brains out. Better for this asshole to learn now that she's mine. Mine to use. Mine to fuck. He lost the game before he even had a chance to play. "Nothing she didn't want." I let my words sink in.

He takes a menacing step forward. "I want to see her," he snarls, inches away from my face.

I lean against the doorway giving him a bored expression. "Why? So you can apologize for fucking the girl who was a bitch to her? You think that will get you inside her tight little pussy?"

He draws back in surprise and flicks his eyes up toward me. "She saw that?"

I fold my arms over my chest. It's not my job to explain shit to him. I don't want him thinking Allie's only here with me because he fucked up. I'm not her second choice. She came eager and willing. It had nothing to do with this asshole.

He looks away, nodding his head and muttering to himself, but I don't bother listening. "What do you want, Henderson? It's early and I haven't had any coffee so get to the point of this little visit and then get off my fucking porch."

He tugs at his blond hair, making it stick out in all directions. "I just wanted to check on her. Make sure she was okay. She didn't come back to the cabin last—"

I cut him off. "If you were that concerned, you would have been looking for her last night. Not this morning after your piece of ass slinked out of your bed."

Guilt flashes across his face confirming what I'd suspected. Henderson got his dick wet and didn't once think about Allie until after he'd gotten what he wanted. "Good thing for you, I took *real good* care of her. Fucked her all night long." I push off the porch and step toward him, using my height to tower over him. "And fuck, Henderson. You don't know what you're missing. She's so tight and when she begs for it"—I grab my crotch in a suggestive manner—"music to my fucking ears."

I have no fucking idea why I'm saying any of this. Why I want—no need—Henderson and every other asshole at our school to know that Allie Ramirez is off limits until I deem otherwise.

We agreed to fun. No strings. No commitments. I'm not the relationship type, so hearing that from her last night should have made me happy. Instead, it made my blood run hot. It filled my ears with a roar and I took my anger out on her hot little body. I was the one in charge. I decided whatever this was or wasn't between us.

I should wake her up and send her on her way as soon as this fucker leaves. It's what I would do with any other girl. But that idea has me gritting my teeth.

If I do that, Henderson will just make another play at her. I'll keep her this weekend to stick it to the asshole. Remind him that I can take any girl I want when I want. Yeah, sounds like a great fucking idea.

I step back inside and slam the door in Henderson's face, not giving him a chance to respond. I can't stand guys like him. He's such a fucking tool.

Back inside, Dom waves toward the fresh pot of coffee. I wave him off. "Later," I say. Because right now there is a naked woman in my bed and I have plans to do wicked, wicked things to her body.

FIFTEEN

Allie

I wake to unfamiliar surroundings. Bright light filters in through the window. I close my eyes against the early morning rays as the scent of chorizo and eggs assails my senses. Mmmm. Stretching my arms above my head, my face still pressed against the mattress, I work out some of the lingering aches in my body.

Who's cooking? Mom? I wonder with a frown, face still buried in my pillow.

That can't be right. What day is it today ... Saturday? She'd be working at ...

Then I remember she wouldn't be working anywhere because she's gone.

I'm immediately hit with a crushing wave of sadness. I choke on a gasp but before my grief can consume me, I feel fingers skim lightly down my back. A roughened jaw scrapes against my skin. Memories of last night and who I shared them with come rushing to the forefront of my mind. And when Roman rolls me over to my back, splaying my legs wide and teasing my body with skilled fingers, I arch toward him, immersing myself in the sensations of his touch as I push away the ache in my chest.

He worships my body and I drown in him. His taste. His touch. Breathing in the scent of sun, coriander, and musk that is uniquely him, it's as if I'll die without him in my lungs.

When emotions threaten to bubble up inside of me, I urge him to go faster. Harder. And he's all too happy to comply. Fucking me to the edge of orgasm again and again without letting me dive off that particular cliff as I cling to him, almost afraid for when I fall.

Each time I get close to the edge, he shuts it down until I'm a writhing ball of desire, unable to think beyond the need coursing inside of me.

He's just as rough with me this morning as he'd been the night before only this time, he doesn't mask his hunger. His bone-deep desire to consume me. It should scare me. But it doesn't. I need this just as much as he does.

My orgasm is right there, so close yet so far away, when Roman slows down his thrusts.

I cry out in frustration, desperate for my release.

"You wanna come, vanilla?"

I nod, unable to form coherent words and I clench around him, chasing what I know waits just around the corner.

"Beg. Beg for it and maybe, just maybe, I'll let you come." His words are harsh, his tone mocking.

I bare my teeth at him, hating that he has this power over me. I shake my head, refusing to voice the words he's asking for. I need to come but not like this. Not at his mercy.

His eyes narrow, a tick forming in his jaw as he slows his thrusts once again.

"Beg, baby girl." He nuzzles my neck, nips my jaw. "Or I'll leave you wanting."

"No."

Something deep inside makes me rebel against his command. To show him he isn't the only one in control here. I know he wants me. This. Whatever it is. Just as much as I do. I can feel his need. He's shaking with it.

With a snarl he slams his mouth to mine, our lips meeting in a furious kiss of tongue and teeth before he bites my bottom lip hard enough to make me gasp. "Don't say I didn't warn you."

I open my mouth to smart off but before I can speak a single word, he flips our position until I'm on top of him, forcing me to ride his cock. For a split second, I'm relieved. I can set the pace I want, and I do. I grind my hips against his pelvis and he thrusts up into me, driving himself deeper until, in three harsh strokes, he's shuddering beneath me. I curse, knowing he came and not being able to do a damn thing to stop it. I grind up and down on his now softening dick and he folds his arms up behind his head to watch the show. But nothing is going to happen because his dick is getting soft and dammit, I still haven't come. Fury thrums through me. I tighten my jaw and dig my fingernails into his chest as I push myself off of him.

He almost manages to hide his flinch. "Should have begged for it," he says.

"You're an ass."

"Never pretended not to be," he calls to my back as I gather my clothes to get dressed. *Un-fucking-believable.*

"Oh, and by the way, Henderson came looking for you this morning." I pause but before I can ask what he said, he continues, "Don't worry though. I told him I took *real good* care of you."

EMILIO OFFERS ME A BREAKFAST BURRITO AS I HEAD OUT THE door but I decline. Not the least bit hungry. I haven't been eating much since Mom died, and after what just happened with Roman, I have absolutely zero appetite. I'm fuming over the fact he took his pleasure and then denied me mine. Who the hell does he think he is? *Stupid devil.*

I go searching for Aaron uncertain of what sort of reception I'll get. I can't believe Roman said that.

Asshole.

I march across the clearing in search of Aaron, pissed at myself for allowing Roman to get under my skin and determined to smooth things over with Aaron in person. I can't afford to screw up one of the few friendships I have in this town.

I find him easy enough. He's sitting on the back of someone's tailgate, drinking a beer, and joking with a group of guys similarly dressed. They all look like they just walked out of a Zumiez so I figure they're boarders like Aaron.

When he spots me walking toward him, he sets down his beer and leans back against the bed of the truck. I can't see his eyes masked behind a pair of blue mirrored Ray Bans but I can tell by the downward curve of his lip that I'm not going to get a warm reception.

"Hey," I say and offer a small wave. *Really Allie? A wave?* Because that wasn't awkward.

"Hey."

I stand there, shifting from one foot to the other. He doesn't say anything else and the other three guys with him are now staring at me like I've grown three heads while wearing a tutu.

"Can we talk?" I ask.

He shrugs. "Sure. Talk."

Okay then. I guess I should have expected that. I lick my lips wishing I could see his eyes, gauge just how mad he is with me right now.

"*Aaron,*" I drag out his name.

He huffs out an exasperated sigh. "Whatever. Fine." Jumping down from the tailgate he walks toward his cabin and stops just in front of the porch to lean against the railing. "What can I do for you?" He waves his beer with an over exaggerated flourish.

"You don't have to be a jerk," I mutter, folding my arms across my chest.

He's silent for a beat and I realize he's not going to say anything. Awesome. Now it's my turn to sigh. "Look, I just wanted to apologize for bailing on you last night. I saw that girl on your lap by the fire and figured you'd want the room to yourself." I shrug and do my best to adopt an apologetic look. "I wasn't trying to ghost you."

Silence.

"If you don't want me here anymore, I'll grab my things and get a ride back to town."

Nothing.

Wonderful.

"Whatever." I turn to head inside his cabin to grab my stuff, praying I can catch an Uber out here in the middle of boom-freaking-nowhere when his hand on my elbow stops me.

I pause, but don't turn back to him.

Gravel crunches beneath his feet as he steps closer, moving around me until we're facing one another. He rubs the back of his neck in an almost nervous gesture, but I must be reading that wrong.

"I'm sorry. I was a dick." The corner of his mouth curls up in an apologetic smile.

Really? "I'm sorry too. I really wasn't trying to be a B and ghost you." It's true. Granted, I also wasn't trying to steer clear so I wasn't a cock-block either. But he doesn't need to know that. He also doesn't need to know I was swept away by good looks and hot tattoos. Wouldn't be the first time I'd made poor decisions while intoxicated. First Ryker. Now Roman. *Urgh.* And if I'm being honest with myself, it probably wasn't my last. And if I was really, really honest, booze had nothing to do with it. "Are we cool?" I ask, shoving away my inner monologue. I could berate myself and my poor decision-making skills later. "Because I like hanging out with you. I don't have many friends here and it'd be nice not to lose that with you."

He exhales sharply. "Yeah. I know I'm overreacting, it's just," he pauses. "I have bad history with the Devils, ya know?"

I quirk a brow in question because no, I don't know. I have no idea what issues lie between them. Only that it appears to be mutual.

"They're all assholes. Especially Roman. I don't want to see you get hurt. Those three can be cruel to girls after they get what they want from them." He gives me a knowing look.

I can't stop the heat I know is spreading across my cheeks, so I look away. Is that what's going to happen? Is Roman going to move on now that he's had his fun? If he does, it's not like I should be surprised.

But I'm not looking for a relationship. I have too much baggage for something like that right now. I wanted fun, and last night I got that. Sure, this morning sucked and Roman is a complete asshole, but it's not the end of the world either.

Aaron reaches out and tucks a strand of hair that escaped my braid behind my ear.

I still can't see his eyes and have no idea what he's thinking, so I go with my gut. "You don't have to worry. We came here to have fun, right? You got laid. I got laid. Neither of us needs to make a big deal of it. Is what's-her-name you hooked up with the love of your life?"

He snorts.

"That's what I thought. Let's not make mountains out of molehills. How about we hang today? Just you and me and whatever friends you have here that you actually like? No Devils allowed."

His smile widens, giving me a glimpse of dimples I hadn't noticed before. "Yeah?"

"Yeah."

SIXTEEN

Roman

She doesn't look at me the rest of the weekend. I should have expected this. Calculated the risk. I know she's not some meek little wallflower, no matter that she sometimes pretends to be. She's punishing me for leaving her hanging and it's fucking working. What was supposed to be a punishment for *her*, a reminder of who the fuck was in charge here, ended up backfiring on me and now I'm watching her like some lovesick dog without his bone.

I keep forgetting she isn't like the rest of the girls here at Sun Valley High. She doesn't give two shits who I am and she's making that abundantly clear. She sticks close to Henderson all day Saturday, leaving me little room to swoop in and take her. Not unless I want to make a big show of it, and yeah, that's not happening. So, I'm left to stew as she laughs with the motherfucker, drinks with him, lets him touch her. It's not romantic. At least I don't think it is for her. But every time that asshole throws an arm around her shoulders, I want to pummel his face in.

Allie Ramirez is mine. Mine to fuck. Mine to hurt. Mine to soothe, should I decide to. I'm itching to touch her and it's doing things to my head I don't like.

"Ro, what's your deal, man?" Dom asks as I brood on the cabin porch sipping on a glass of water, nursing back a bit of a hangover from the night before. I don't drink often. None of us do. Football is too important. But the few beers and the game of beer pong are leaving their mark today. "I figured you'd fuck the girl out of your system and walk away. What gives?"

I grunt. "Maybe I just want a few more fucks before I move along."

Before I finish the sentence, he's already shaking his head. "Nah. I've seen you with girls. This one is different. I get the whole mind-games shit you like to pull with chicks, but even that's different with her. You cooked last night, and don't try and bullshit me into believing that was for me or Emilio. You did that for her. Why?"

Emilio interrupts, stepping outside, still rocking that stupid bright ass bikini over his sweat pants. "I like Allie. Can we keep her?"

Dom and I both jerk our heads toward him. "What?" I ask, surprise coloring my voice.

"I said, can we keep her?"

"She's not a puppy," Dom chides, but his brows furrow like he's wondering the same thing.

"Why?" I ask again.

Emilio rolls his eyes. "Hello, I just said because I like her. Are you even paying attention? What is up with you today, man?"

I turn to Dom but all he does is shrug and raise a brow as if to say, *don't ask me.* Some help he is. I don't get this side of Emilio. Sure, the guy's nice to pretty much everyone, but only at face value. He doesn't actually like people. I don't even think he cares for Dom or I all that much and we're his best fucking friends.

"What happened to you two fuckers saying I needed to focus on the field?"

"I changed my mind. I wanna keep her. If you're not into her anymore now that you've had your fun just say the word. I don't mind sloppy seconds. Based on the sounds I heard coming from your room last night, that girl is well worth the trouble."

I stand and take a menacing step toward my best friend, ready to nail the asshole in the face with my fist when Dom steps between us. "What are you planning here?"

"To wipe that smug look off his face." I point my water bottle right at Emilio and the fucker smiles at me.

Dom shakes his head. "Not with numb nuts over there. What are you planning with Allie?"

My jaw tightens and I glare at him. "I don't have any plans," I bite out, "Why the fuck are you two down my throat about her all of a sudden?"

"She's not like other girls," he says.

"I'm aware. If she was, she'd be over here kissing my boots instead of playing around with Henderson all goddamn day. What do you want from me?"

Emilio shoves himself between the two of us and flicks his gaze back and forth. "He wants you to lay out your intentions, Rome.

We both do." And for once the dude has a serious expression on his face.

I glower. "Why the hell are you two so goddamn interested in who I fuck all of a sudden?"

Dom grunts. "Because Emilio is right. We like her. Neither of us wants you to fuck things up for us."

My mouth drops open. "For *us*?"

Emilio nods and smacks me in the chest light-heartedly. "Yeah, fucker. For us. Like I said, we like her. She fits in with our crew. She doesn't see dollar signs when she looks at any of us like every other chick in this town. We could use a feminine touch up in here. Too much testosterone with you two jackasses all the time if you ask me, and your dick is going to fuck that up so this is us telling you not to do that. Lo entiendes?" *Do you understand?* Was he fucking with me right now? "Say whatever you need to say to her. You fucked something up this morning or she wouldn't be hanging with that ass wipe and you wouldn't be over here brooding."

My jaw clenches. "This isn't how things roll with us." There's a bite in my tone I usually reserve for everyone but the two people beside me. Dominique and Emilio are like my brothers. They're family. But I don't take orders from anyone and I don't have to explain myself to them.

Emilio meets my stare and his eyes narrow, sparking with something I'm not used to seeing in his gaze. "She's the relationship type."

I work my jaw harder. "And this matters to you because..."

"You're not."

"Never tried to claim I was," I remind him. And then I add in for good measure, "She laid her cards out first. She wants fun. No strings. Don't jump down my throat for giving the girl exactly what she asked for."

Both their expressions consider me for a moment, searching for any deception. Then Dom asks, "She really said that?" He doesn't sound convinced.

"Yeah, fucker. She did. So calm down."

"Fine, let's assume we buy that. What'd you do to piss her off?"

My shoulders sag and I grit my teeth.

"Come on, fucker. Spill." Emilio says, all but bouncing beside me. The guy is wired this morning. I need to remember to hide the coffee from him.

"I fucked her."

"And...?"

I huff out a breath. "And I withheld her orgasm when she refused to beg for it."

Dominique whistles and Emilio whoops, then says, "I always knew you were a shady asshole with control issues but fuck, man, that's cold. And let me guess, you still got yours?"

I nod.

Emilio cackles, covering his mouth as he folds over at the waist before he straightens. There are tears of laughter shining in his eyes. "Damn. If you want inside that pussy anytime soon, expect to do some groveling."

Not. Fucking. Happening.

SEVENTEEN

Allie

The hallway is teeming with activity as I walk toward my first class Monday morning. I ignore the looks directed my way as I have been since I transferred here, but something about a few of them make the hairs on the back of my neck stand on edge.

There's more hostility in them now. Not just the usual indifference I'd grown used to last week.

I'm not winning any popularity contests this year, not that I expected to being the new girl, but I have a feeling the camping trip is why I've suddenly earned the extra attention, in particular from the girls of this school. If looks could kill, let me tell you, it's like I just walked onto the set of *Mean Girls* and every girl walking past is another Regina George with their eyes locked on me, marking me as prey.

I shiver and cast a quick glance over my shoulder as I head to my English class. Spotting Silvia and a group of her friends, I step to the side, hugging close to the lockers to avoid her, but of course she sees me, and before I can slip into my first period, she's shoving her way through the crowded halls right toward me.

I cringe. This isn't going to end well.

I'd kind of expected a confrontation up at Shadle Creek and was relieved when one never happened, but it looks like she's been biding her time and now this seems to be her golden opportunity to put the new girl in her place.

Her upper lip curls into a sneer and four more girls close in beside her. I brace myself for whatever verbal lashing she has to offer, knowing it likely has to do with her being kicked out of the Devil's cabin that first night, when the next thing I know, an open palm slaps me across the face. My head snaps to the side, my mouth dropping open as my hand jerks up to clutch my cheek. I barely register the sting and all I'm thinking is, *WHAT. THE. HELL?*

The blow had come out of nowhere. I'm so startled by the violence that I don't react other than to clutch at my face, my eyes wide and my body immobile.

"You're such a stupid whore," she snarls, spittle flying toward me coupled with her vile words. All eyes turn toward us, the silence in the previously boisterous hallway deafening.

Goddammit. I can't hit her back. Her friends have stepped forward, forming a half circle around me. If I hit her, they'll step in and help. I don't have friends here and I don't feel like being jumped, but the urge to fight back has me clenching my hands beside me into tight fists as I take a deep breath, my nostrils flaring.

I step forward determined to force my way past her but she shoves me back into the lockers. My back slams into the cool metal surface and a single manicured finger lifts and points arrogantly in my face.

I grit my teeth together, refusing to rise to the bait. The shove was hard. The slap harder. But she isn't that strong. Neither have done more than surprise me and I refuse to stand here and cower to the school's resident mean girl.

I tilt my chin up, meeting her emerald gaze head on.

Silvia's one of the it girls. In the eyes of the students here, she's at the top. And I'm at the bottom. I don't expect anyone to come to my aid, which is why I'm surprised when the crowd parts and Emilio swaggers toward me, an easy grin on his face—but I don't miss the bright hot fury in his eyes.

He assesses the situation before him, a tick forming along his jaw and between one second and the next, I can tell he's come to some sort of conclusion about what's going on here.

A flash of concern crosses over Silvia's face when she spots him before she tries to mask it with cool indifference. Hands propped on her hips she purses her lips while she continues to stare down her nose at me.

Emilio makes a noise to catch her attention before snapping his fingers like he's just realized something interesting. "You were at the campout this weekend, right?" he asks, moving closer toward us.

When he's only a foot away, he leans next to the lockers beside me, lifts one hand and rubs his bottom lip with his thumb as he gives Silvia a considering look as though he's trying to place her.

She mistakes it for interest and turns her full attention toward him. Her scowl is now a seductive smile, and at this point I'm all but forgotten. "I was." Her words are breathy. She pushes her shoulders back, ensuring her breasts are thrust out toward him before lowering her head so she can look up at him through her lashes.

I roll my eyes, at her come-hither expression. It's so blatantly obvious I can't imagine guys actually fall for this crap.

Emilio pushes off from the locker, his eyes darkening as he closes the distance between them. I guess her little seduction tactics really do work.

"Yeah, I remember you. I almost fucked you." His words are husky, shot full of arrogance.

When he's a scant few inches away, he raises his hand to cup the side of her neck, his thumb resting in the center of her throat. "MmmHmm. We can rectify that anytime you'd like." She leans toward him as he dips his head to whisper just loud enough for our ears to hear.

"Pass. You must either be blind or stupid then, because if you were paying attention, you'd know Allie's with us. She's Devil property and we don't take kindly to people fucking with what's ours."

His thumb presses firmly against her throat and she gasps. The skin around his grip whitens and her eyes are wide, suddenly filled with fear.

Then he releases her and steps back as if nothing happened. An easy smile slips into place and he tosses an arm around my shoulder, drawing me in to his side.

"We gonna have problems, Silvia?"

Her lips tighten, heat now coloring her face and neck.

"She's an outsider," one of the girls beside Silvia spits out.

It's the wrong answer to Emilio's question. His fists clench at his sides and he looks around the hallway, all eyes still glued to the scene in front of us.

"Ice them out," he says to no one in particular, but heads all around us nod.

Silvia sucks in a breath as her four friends all take quick steps back, putting distance between themselves and her. "You can't do that."

He chuckles, but it's a dark, dangerous sound. "I can do whatever the fuck I want. You made a mistake. I suggest you learn from it."

She opens her mouth to respond just as another voice calls out over the sea of students.

"What's going on over here?" A man's voice booms through the hallway. "Break it up. Everyone get to class." The hall empties just as the first bell rings and everyone heads to their first period.

Silvia waits for a beat before she, too, leaves, but not before I see the hate-filled look in her eyes telling me things between us are far from over. If anything, Emilio stepping in only added fuel to the fire. If she didn't hate me before, she certainly does now.

Mr. Alvarez—the school principal—comes into view, eyeing Emilio and me warily. "Mr. Chavez, Ms. Ramirez, get to class." He claps his hands and I jump and move to do as I've been told but Emilio's grip on my wrist stops me from making my escape.

"That shit happens again, you find me. Got it?" His dark brown eyes meet mine.

"Why?" I'm so confused as to why he'd help me in the first place. Is this because I slept with his friend? Emilio comes off like the nice guy, sure. He reminds me a lot of my friend Felix back home.

Which is how I know Emilio never makes a move that isn't calculated and he had no reason to step in just now and help me.

He frowns at me. "That's a dumb-ass question, vanilla. What do you mean, why?"

I shrug my shoulders and rather than answering him, I say, "Fine. I'll find you."

"See that you do." Satisfied, he releases me and we both head off to our first class. I spot Roman waiting for me outside the door leading into English. He doesn't say anything. His dark brown eyes meet mine but I can't get a read on him. I know he saw what just happened but whether he cares or not is a complete mystery to me. I wish I could crack his hard exterior shell. I'm still pissed at him. He was a complete ass Saturday morning and never bothered apologizing for it afterward, not that I'd expected him to. However, I did expect him to talk to me again, but I got nothing. Not even a goodbye on Sunday as everyone drove out heading back into town.

Without a word he turns and heads into class. I sigh. I do not have the energy to deal with both Silvia and Roman today.

By lunch, the entire school is buzzing with news that the Devils have claimed me. And not just one Devil. No, though that would have been more than enough, but Emilio made sure to say *ours* as if he speaks for all of them, making me the property of not one asshole but three. I'm not entirely sure what being *claimed* by them means, but the stares and whispers have definitely increased tenfold. If I thought this morning was bad, the afternoon is even worse.

So much for flying under the radar till graduation.

I grab my lunch as quickly as possible, intending to take it and hide out in the library, but Dominique puts an end to that idea when he lifts my tray from my hands and with his own, carries them both over to the table in the corner forcing me to follow if I want to eat. I almost consider letting him just have my food. It's not like I plan on eating much of it anyway.

I've lost six pounds since mom died. I should eat more but I just can't seem to stomach it. Though I had no problems eating the *albóndigas* Roman made for us.

Dom sets my tray down on the table beside Roman before rounding to the other side and taking a seat next to Emilio. No one says anything about my arrival, they just dive into conversation about an upcoming game like nothing is weird about me sitting with them.

Alrighty then.

I poke at my lunch—a chicken patty with mashed potatoes and gravy on the side. The lunch lady said it was chicken fried steak day but nothing about this looks like chicken fried steak. Still, I make an effort to swallow a bite before using my fork to move things around so it at least looks like I ate something.

I spot Aaron a few tables away, his gaze trained on me. When he realizes I'm looking at him, he flicks on his mirrored shades and turns back to the guys he was talking to.

I deflate and look away only to see Roman's gaze lasered in on me. His mouth is set in a hard line as dark brown eyes search mine. "Something going on between you and Henderson?" he asks.

I roll my eyes. "He's my friend and he doesn't seem all that fond of you three. That answer your question?"

Roman nods and sucks his bottom lip into his mouth before throwing an arm over my shoulder and giving Aaron a fuck-you grin. God. Guys can be such assholes sometimes.

I shrug out from under his hold. "Stop trying to stir up trouble," I tell him, smacking his arm.

He grips my chin and turns my face toward him. I lick my lips and his eyes track the movement, hunger in his gaze. "Allie, haven't you learned I'm nothing but trouble?"

His head dips and he presses his lips to mine. At first, it's a soft press but then his teeth are tugging on my bottom lip, urging me to open for him. I do and his tongue darts in for a quick taste that leaves me reeling in my seat.

He pulls back, cocky arrogance stamped on his face before I catch him looking over my shoulder. I don't need to turn to know he and Aaron are locked in a stare down. My cheeks heat and anger unfurls inside of me.

"When you decide to stop being a jerk, let me know." I stand to leave the table but his hand around the back of my thigh stops me.

"Sit down."

I snort and take a step but his grip only tightens. "Allie—" there's a warning in his voice, one I choose to one hundred percent ignore.

"I'll catch up with you guys later."

I pull away and make my way over to Aaron's table, knowing Roman would never follow me. Guys like him can't be seen chasing after a girl, let alone a no one like me. When I reach Aaron, his glasses are still on so I reach down and push them up over the top of his head.

"Hey." I pause, suddenly unsure of what to say to him. The drive back from Shadle Creek had been fine. I thought we had things sorted but judging by the look on his face, he's still pissed.

He tilts his chin toward Roman and the guys. "You looked cozy."

I fold my arms over my chest. "And you look mad."

He shakes his head. "Nah. Not mad. Disappointed. But why should I be, right?"

"Excuse me?"

He stands and moves closer to me, his mouth so close his lips brush along the shell of my ear. "Every girl in this school wants to spread their legs for Roman Valdez. I just assumed you wouldn't be one of them. My bad. From what I hear, it sounds like you're screwing all three."

EIGHTEEN

Allie

I'm still reeling from Aaron's words when I get home from school. I have nothing but time on my hands so, of course, I stew. I can't believe his nerve. I'm not some whore. I don't sleep around. Roman is literally the second person I've slept with and I sure as hell don't allow myself to get passed around like some hood rat. I am not one of *those* girls.

I pace my room, leaving a worn path in the pale beige carpet, and I finally decide enough is enough. I can't let his opinion consume me. I know who I am. If he wants to be an ass, let him. I don't need him.

Powering up my laptop, I catch up on some homework before touching up my resume and sending it off to at least a dozen local businesses. I need a job. All this downtime is driving me insane. I need to find a way to stay busy. I spot the sneakers I bought at Target and an idea forms in my head.

Stripping out of the white skinny jeans and lavender blouse I wore today, I throw on a pair of leggings, a band shirt, and my new

Target sneakers. I curse when I realize I don't own a sports bra but figure what I'm wearing will do. Throwing my hair up in a messy bun, I tuck my phone into the hidden zipper pouch on the side of my leggings and grab my wireless earbuds and a water bottle.

Janessa sent me a calendar notification earlier letting me know Gerald has requested my presence at dinner this evening. I confirmed that I'd be there, though I'm still not sure where *there* is exactly, since under location it said TBD, but I do know the time. She scheduled dinner for six, so I have a little over an hour before I need to be back in order to have enough time to shower and get ready.

Jogging down the stairs, I tuck in my headphones, blaring some old-school Linkin Park. *Numb* drowns out my thoughts as I head outside and let myself get sucked into the heavy thrum of music. It's still fairly warm, despite it being November, and a thin sheen of sweat coats my body within the first fifteen minutes of my run. My breathing is heavy, my legs already cramping, but I push myself to keep going. I need this. I've never been much of a runner but already I can tell I'll be doing this again.

Fifteen minutes turns to thirty before I stumble to a stop. Bracing my hands on my knees I suck in lungfuls of air. The sun is setting, suburban streetlights illuminate the streets. A car rumbles in the distance, growing closer, but I don't bother looking up until I realize it's slowed to a stop and is now idling beside me.

I stand to my full height, propping my hands on the back of my hips as I try and catch my breath, while at the same time, I'm ready to run hard and fast should I need to. But then I see it's Aaron in his WRX.

Mouth pressed into a tight line, he looks me up and down. "You look like shit."

I flip him off, not even bothering with civility at this point.

He leans over and opens the passenger side door. "Come on. I'll give you a lift home."

"I'm only a few blocks away."

He lifts a single brow as if to say, *so?*

"Fine." I climb in, immediately sinking into the cool leather seats. Cold AC fans my face and I sigh, closing my eyes.

"I didn't realize you were a runner."

"I'm not. Just ... needed to clear my head."

He's quiet so I open my eyes and glance at him through my peripheral. He pulls up to the mansion that is Gerald's elaborate home and I move to open the door. "Thanks for the lift."

Before I can step out, he halts me with a hand on my arm. "Wait."

I stop and turn to face him, leaving the door open.

He scrubs both hands down his face before dragging his gaze back to me. "I hate the Devils."

My anger flares and I suddenly remember what he said to me earlier and why I should still be pissed off with him. "Noted." I get out and step away from the car, slamming the door behind me.

The engine shuts off and Aaron's door opens and closes, but I'm already heading for the front door. "Allie, wait," he calls out, but I don't bother stopping. I'm almost to the door when it swings open and Gerald's stern face greets me, bringing me to a hard stop.

"Alejandra, is that you shouting out here?"

His pale eyes flick from me to the boy I know is standing a few paces behind me. "Sorry." I wilt under his scrutiny. "We didn't mean to disturb you."

"Have some decorum. We have neighbors."

My face falls and I nod. "Sorry," I mutter, hating that this man I barely know has the power to make me feel two inches small. I'm just about to slip in past him when I feel Aaron step in beside me.

"I'm Aaron Henderson, sir. I go to school with Allie. It's nice to meet you." Aaron thrusts out his hand and surprisingly, Gerald takes it, giving it a firm shake and giving Aaron an assessing look.

"You're Allen's boy?" he asks.

Aaron nods. "Yes, sir."

Okay, hold up. What is going on right now?

"I'm happy to see my daughter making respectable friends. I was worried when I agreed to send her to Sun Valley Public instead of Prep, but it was your father who reminded me he'd made a similar decision with you. Thank you for looking after her."

Aaron nods. I shoot him a questioning look but he either doesn't see it or chooses to ignore it.

"Well uh, thanks for the ride." I give Aaron a small wave, cringing at the awkwardness of it when Gerald does the unthinkable and invites him in.

"Allie, why don't you run along and get ready for dinner. Aaron and I will be in my study when you're done."

What?

Aaron's expression brightens at the invitation, and when Gerald steps back, opening the door wider to grant us both entrance, Aaron sweeps right on in as though he's been here a dozen times.

"Uh..."

Aaron meets my gaze giving me a small nod.

Alright then. "I guess I'll go take a shower."

Neither one of them respond. Gerald grips Aaron's shoulder in an almost fatherly embrace as he leads him away from me and toward his study.

I jog up the stairs, stripping my sweat-soaked clothes off as soon as the door to my bedroom is firmly closed behind me. Why would Gerald want to talk with Aaron in his study? Clearly, he knows his parents but ...

I rush through washing my hair and body, taking the fastest shower of my life. Something about leaving Aaron and Gerald alone together is setting off alarm bells in my head. And what was all that about looking after his daughter? Why didn't Aaron mention that our dads knew each other?

I dry off at record speed before pulling my hair into a wet and tangled messy bun. I'm assuming dinner will be here since Gerald invited Aaron to join us. I throw on a knee-length, long-sleeved dress in a soft blue, cinching a belt around the waist and slipping my feet into a pair of strappy sandals.

I don't bother putting on any makeup before heading toward Gerald's office. Murmured words greet my ears as I approach but I can't make them out. I haven't been in Gerald's office before. He's always given the impression that it was off limits and I never wanted to impose. After knocking three times, I reach for the handle and let myself in.

Gerald is sitting at his desk, a cigar in one hand and a glass of amber liquid in the other. He's smiling. I've never seen him smile, but whatever Aaron must have just said clearly amused him.

Aaron is sitting in a leather lounge chair opposite Gerald, a matching glass of liquor in his hand, though his glass looks untouched.

"Umm..."

"Alejandra, come in." Gerald says in a booming baritone. "Aaron was just telling me all about the camping trip the two of you went on together."

I frown, worried Gerald will get the wrong impression and I'll wind up in trouble. He'd given me his permission to go but I'd intentionally left out the fact that I was going away with a boy, assuming he'd think I'd made girlfriends. But he seems pleased anyway, not shocked or upset as I would have expected. Mom would have murdered me. I wasn't even allowed to have Julio over without leaving my bedroom door wide open. "Oh," is all I manage to say before taking a seat in the chair beside Aaron. He gives me a reassuring smile. I'm not sure what to think of that.

Aaron certainly looks comfortable. Like this is an everyday occurrence for him. He's dressed in his usual Volcom black jeans and a charcoal Hurley t-shirt, ever the skater boy and at complete odds with Gerald who's wearing a custom-tailored suit, crisp white dress shirt, and burgundy tie. Yet the two are chatting as though they're old friends. Aaron's even holding himself taller. Like he's not just your average high-school kid.

My head is spinning. I take my seat and fold my hands in my lap. Gerald's eyes zero in on the movement before his scrutinizing gaze takes in my appearance. "I see Janessa's provided you with adequate clothing."

I nod.

"Though it seems a trip to the salon may still be in order."

My head snaps up toward him. "Excuse me?"

He turns to Aaron. "Women often need help making themselves presentable. Don't judge my daughter too harshly. She didn't have the upbringing she should have. But a project can be rewarding. Alejandra here is our diamond in the rough."

My cheeks are flaming. I can't believe he's criticizing me right now. In front of Aaron.

Aaron laughs but I can hear the strain in his voice. "It's one of the things I like about your daughter, sir. She isn't like the girls I've grown up with. She's comfortable in her own skin."

Gerald looks like he's just bitten into a lemon. "Hmm. Yes, well, she could still use some lessons in behaving like a proper young lady. Really, Alejandra. You look like you have a bird's nest on top of your head."

I force my hands to remain in my lap instead of adjusting the bun on my head. I don't care what he thinks. He's not anyone to me. A sperm donor who decided to show up too late in the game. I clench my jaw and tilt my chin up. "I didn't realize I needed to impress my own father when I'm in my own … *home*." I keep my tone even, but this isn't my home. It's a halfway house until I get to wherever it is I'll be going after graduation.

"You need to be presentable at all times, even in your own home. You never know who may be stopping by. Just look at yourself. And you have a guest here, one you were well aware of before you came downstairs." He shakes his head, his upper lip curling in disgust. "If I'd known about you sooner, we could have gotten a handle on this, but at the rate you're going, you're going to end up just like your mother."

He may as well have just slapped me the way he spoke of her, as if being anything like my mother is an insult. It's not. My mother was a proud, hard-working woman. She was compassionate and loving and she always, *always*, made time for me, despite working two jobs. Which is more than I can say for the man sitting in front of me. He missed out on seventeen years of my life, yet I can count the number of times I've seen him on one hand since moving to Sun Valley.

I'm not ashamed of my mother. I aspire to be like her.

I bite the inside of my cheek until the tangy bite of copper hits my taste buds. My anger rises and with it comes a crashing wave of emotion. Blinking rapidly to keep my vision clear, I push myself out of my seat. "You'll have to excuse me. I forgot I have homework I need to catch up on."

Gerald doesn't even acknowledge my departure, too engrossed in whatever subject he's moved onto with Aaron. I storm up to my bedroom, opening my laptop to send off another dozen resumes. I need a job. I won't allow myself to be trapped here any longer than I have to be.

Twenty minutes later there's a knock on my door. But before I can tell whoever it is to go away, it opens and Aaron steps inside. The chagrined look on his face is the only thing that keeps me from snapping at him.

He pads over toward me, claiming the seat beside me on the bed as I roll onto my back and stare at the ceiling. He's quiet for a moment before heaving a long-suffering sigh. "I'm sorry about that," he says.

I keep my eyes pinned on the light fixture above me. A stupidly feminine bedroom chandelier with wrought-iron roses and dangling crystals. "Why? Are you worried I'll end up like my dead mother too? Am I doomed to become a commoner?" I sneer.

He scrubs a hand over his face. "That's not what I meant and you know it."

I flick my gaze toward him. "Do I? You seemed pretty chummy with Gerald there."

He sighs. "My dad works with yours. They golf together. He's been to my house for holidays." A shrug. "I've never been here before we went to Shadle Creek. I didn't put two and two together until he opened the door or I would have said something. I... I don't really know what else to say. Gerald is an ass. He shouldn't have said what he did and"—another sigh—"I should have come to your defense. I'm sorry. That was a dick move."

I push myself into a sitting position. He sounds genuine, but... "Then why didn't you?"

Green eyes search mine, no doubt trying to understand what's going on inside my head. "Because I'm an idiot. Our parents have certain expectations. I guess I just fell into the comfortable role of not wanting to rock the boat."

I nod because, yeah, it sucks, but I get it.

"You hungry?" he suddenly asks just as my stomach rumbles. We both laugh.

"Yeah. You could say that. I was supposed to have dinner with my dad, but I think I'll go back to avoiding him after today."

He pushes to his feet and holds out a hand for me. "Come on, I know the perfect spot. A hole-in-the-wall diner with the best burgers in town."

I hesitate. "Aaron I—"

"Allie," he cuts me off. "I was an ass. I'm sorry. Not just for now but for earlier too. At school. I shouldn't have said what I did. I was being an asshole because I was jealous. It won't happen again. I promise. Give me another shot at being your friend. I won't fuck up this time."

I worry my lower lip, indecision sweeping through me. Then again, it's not like people were knocking down my front door begging to be my friend. "Alright. But can we not talk about my dad? Or the Devils. Or anything that will upset either one of us?"

He chuckles. "Deal."

NINETEEN

Allie

I ride with Aaron to the Sun Valley Diner, a local twenty-four-hour restaurant on the edge of town. The bell above the door jingles, announcing our arrival, and one of the waitresses waves at Aaron with familiar recognition before returning her attention to her customer.

Stepping inside, I'm immediately taken in by the old-fashioned vibe of the place. Black and white checkered floors are paired with red and white vinyl booths, and the bar counter boasts black, Formica countertops.

Aaron heads straight for the counter, claiming one of the red barstools as I climb onto the one beside him. A boy I don't recognize heads toward us and says something to Aaron, but I don't hear what it is as I'm too busy taking everything in. The diner almost reminds me of a Johnny Rockets, though maybe not as polished. I turn in time to see Aaron slap something into the boy's hand in a discreet gesture. I miss whatever it is before the boy shoves his hand into his pocket and makes a hasty retreat after a quick nod in thanks.

"Who was that?" I ask, my curiosity getting the better of me. I'm pretty sure I know what just went down, and I'd be lying if I said I wasn't surprised. I never would have pegged Aaron as the dealer type.

"Just a guy from class." He shrugs, but when I don't say anything else, he continues. "I borrowed twenty bucks from him last week after losing my wallet. It was stupid." He offers me a sheepish grin. "I barely know the guy but he helped me out. I was just paying him back."

Oh. I guess that makes sense. All of a sudden I feel like a complete jerk for assuming the worst of him. What is wrong with me? Obviously he's not some low-life drug dealer. What had I been thinking?

A waitress bounces toward us, her perky ponytail bobbing behind her. "Hey, little Henderson, you off tonight?"

Aaron smiles up at her, his dimples making a sudden appearance. "Yep. I've got the rest of the week to myself."

Her eyes sparkle with mischief. "Lucky. Who's the hot date?"

I cough, thrown off by her assumption. I'm just about to correct her when a group of familiar male voices enters the diner. "Ro, Dom, grab the booth in the back. I'm gonna take a leak." It's Emilio's voice. I see him out of the corner of my eye stalking toward a small hallway to my right. I hunch my shoulders and angle my head away from the walkway, but perky waitress over here decides to draw his attention.

"Hey, handsome. Can I put in a drink order for you?"

Emilio lifts a hand to wave her off, but he catches sight of me and who I'm sitting next to. He comes to an abrupt stop and quirks a brow. "Well, well, well. What do we have here?" He comes closer and a knot forms in the pit of my stomach just as he calls out, "Yo, Rome. Your girl's here."

My cheeks heat and I wish more than anything I could disappear beneath the counter. It's almost comical how quickly I go from relaxed and at ease to epically uncomfortable and Aaron sees it. His jaw tightens, a vein in his neck popping out.

The waitress's eyes narrow in confusion as she flicks her gaze between Aaron and a now standing-and-heading-in-our-direction Roman who, I might add, looks royally pissed. This isn't going to end well.

"I'll leave you three love birds to your squabble," Emilio chuckles and heads to the bathroom.

I grit my teeth. *Bastard.*

Roman crowds in beside Aaron, propping his forearm on the counter as he drinks me in. I don't miss the hunger in his gaze or the fury rising in it. I flick a glance toward Dominique who's settled back in the booth with an amused smirk on his face as if he's settling in to watch the show. Roman clears his throat, drawing my attention back toward him.

"Care to explain?" His lips press into a thin line. I don't know why I'm looking at his lips. Scratch that. I absolutely do know and it's because he kissed me in the lunchroom today. I'm still pissed at him for it, too. Why does he continue being the asshole showing off that he's got the girl when he doesn't even want me?

"She doesn't have to explain anything to you, man." Aaron pushes up from his barstool, but a firm hand on his shoulder shoves him back down into his seat. Roman doesn't even look at him. His eyes stay locked on mine, a tick now forming along his jaw.

"Alejandra..." He draws my name out, the sound low and seductive, sending fire through my veins. He's using his bedroom voice, and God does it do things to me that it shouldn't.

I take a deep breath. *Come on, Allie. Be strong.* I square my shoulders. "I'm having dinner with a friend," I say, proud when my voice comes out even. "Is there a problem with that?"

His eyes darken as he straightens. "Yeah," he says, "there is."

"Umm..." Our waitress opens and closes her mouth. She looks like a goldfish, and I almost laugh.

"We're good, Heather. Thanks." Aaron waves her off, and we all watch as she scurries away to help other customers before Aaron turns to face Roman head on. "Look, man. I get you don't like me or trust me—the feeling is mutual, by the way—but Allie's my friend. I don't care what you two have going on, that's your business, but stop being an asshole for no reason. Why don't you try being a normal guy and, I don't know, call her or ask her out sometime?"

The urge to say "Yeah," in a snarky *told you so* voice is strong, but I hold myself back and wait for Roman's reaction. With exaggerated slowness, he swivels his head to give Aaron his undivided attention. I swallow hard at the look in his eyes. White. Hot. Rage. Had I been standing I would have taken several steps back—and I'm not even the one on the receiving end of that look.

Aaron's Adam's apple bobs up and down, but he manages to meet Roman's glare and hold it. *Impressive.* Whatever issues lie between them, Aaron's no coward.

Hostility radiates off both boys as Roman stares at him, unmoving, never saying a single word. Tension builds in the air. It's suffocating. I rub my palms over the tops of my knees debating whether or not to intervene when Emilio finally pops out of the hallway, oblivious to the tension in the air.

"Hey, fuckers. We still chatting?"

Like a bubble being popped, the pressure releases and I noisily exhale. "Nope." I turn to Emilio, a fake smile plastered across my face. "Roman's just being Roman. You guys should probably get back to Dom, though. He's looking lonely over there."

Emilio looks over my shoulder and his grin widens. "Yeah, he doesn't look so lonely." I turn and spot our waitress—Heather— leaning toward him, her breasts intimately close to his face. Dom licks his lips.

I sigh. And then my stomach does the unthinkable and growls like a rumbling bear. How *em-barr-essing*. "Come on, vanilla. We need to put some meat on those bones." Emilio tugs me from my seat angling me toward the booth Dom is still sitting in but I dig in my heels.

He stops and scowls over his shoulder at me. "What?"

I tilt my head toward Aaron and Emilio snorts. "You're going to pick Henderson over us?" he asks as if the very idea of doing exactly that is unfathomable.

"Uh, yeah. I came here with him. I'm not going to just bail because you three showed up."

He frowns like he never thought of it like that and I have to smother a laugh. The Devils really are used to always getting whatever they want. I tug my hand free from his grip and reclaim my seat, but rather than heading to the booth as I'd expected, Emilio grabs the stool beside me and Roman takes the empty seat beside Aaron, who looks anything but thrilled to be seated beside him. As soon as he reaches for a menu, Dom rises and heads toward us, taking the last empty seat next to Roman.

Aaron's jaw ticks and he clenches his hands into fists on the counter. I rest a hand on his knee and mouth one word—*Sorry*. Roman sees the touch and his eyes narrow so I quickly snatch it away.

"We can head out," I mutter. "Grab something on the way back to—"

"Nah. Don't be like that." Emilio moves to squeeze between Aaron and me, throwing his arms around both our shoulders and pulling us toward him in a weird side-hug embrace. "Stay. You want us to get along, right?" he says to me. "Be friendly and shit?"

I nod.

"Alright then. We're doing our part. Henderson,"—he meets Aaron's frustrated green gaze—"you don't mind, do you? It'll be just like old times."

Aaron shoves out of his seat, forcing Emilio to stumble back a few steps. "I'm not fucking doing this." His chest rises and falls with each heavy breath and he bares his teeth. Roman and Dom also stand, folding their arms over their chests.

I jump to my feet, eyes wide. "Hey, it's fine. We can—"

"No. It's not fucking fine."

I flinch at Aaron's tone.

"Don't talk to her like that." Roman comes to my defense, taking a menacing step forward. All of this is escalating way too fast.

"Hey. *Hey!*" I draw everyone's attention back to me. "What am I missing here?"

"Nothing," Aaron is quick to snap back.

Emilio laughs. "Keeping secrets, Henderson? Then again, that is your M.O., isn't it?"

"Fuck off. I'm not dealing with your shit." Aaron storms past him, making a beeline for the door before he catches himself and turns back to me. "Come on, Allie." I step forward to follow, but a hand on my elbow stops me.

"Not happening. You wanna storm out that's on you. But she's not going anywhere with you like this."

Before I can argue—because, yeah, Aaron is angry but it's not like he'd hurt me—he's cursing out a, "Whatever." And leaving me behind.

Un-freaking-believable. I consider chasing after him. He's my ride after all, but a firm shake of Roman's head has me deciding against it. Was it too much to ask to have a normal day for once? No mean girls or asshole fathers or stupid boys to ruin it?

My stomach rumbles again. "Come on, vanilla." Roman steers me toward a nearby booth. "Let's feed you. I'll take you home after."

TWENTY

Roman

A flare of something eerily close to jealousy burns hot in my chest at the thought of Allie on a date with Aaron *fucking* Henderson. No. Scratch that. I'm not jealous. I'm pissed. Who the hell does Henderson think he is?

I told him to stay away from her. Emilio made it public knowledge that she belonged to the Devils. He saw us together at Shadle Creek. He *knows* she's mine. And he's still sniffing around.

It's like the guy has a death wish. After what happened that summer before junior year—when the asshole nearly got all four of us killed—you better believe I'm not taking his shit anymore. I can't believe I was ever friends with that asshole.

I pull Allie closer to me, conscious of my mounting anger. My arm wraps around her narrow waist as I lead her to our usual spot. Lust stirs and my dick twitches as I take in her slim legs and narrow waist, breathe in the strawberry scent of her shampoo. She isn't wearing a lick of makeup, exposing a faint sprinkling of freckles on the top of her nose. God, she's so fucking beautiful.

And she was here with him. The get-up she's in is all for *him*.

I grind my teeth together as we take our seats. Heather returns, takes our drink orders, and slaps a few menus down on the tabletop before retreating to the counter. She isn't trying to flirt with Dom anymore and that's fine by me. Every chick in this place is team Henderson. His aunt owns the place, so I'm not surprised.

For a while there we stopped coming around, but the Sun Valley Diner has the best burgers, and after sweating my ass off on the field, I decided I'd earned a little reward. It's a good thing we came into enemy territory, too, or who knows what Aaron would have tried to pull with Allie. I don't trust the fucker. He might seem squeaky clean now, but I'm not buying it. He's just good at hiding his demons.

She's quiet as the guys jump right into talking about the upcoming game. It's the biggest one of the season and we're all hyped for it. The Saints are the only school with a shot of ruining our record. So far we're undefeated, and once we beat them, it'll be smooth sailing all the way to state. Scouts will also be there, and while we all have a scholarship lined up, it's never a bad idea to have a back-up.

My parents are even showing up for the game, which was one hell of a surprise when my mom told me. Neither of my parents support my decision to go pro. Hell, neither supports my decision to go to college. My pops wants me to go straight into the police academy following graduation. *Not fucking happening.* He might enjoy being a boy in blue, but I have zero plans to follow in his footsteps. Mom does the whole *I just want to see you happy* bit, but really, she wants me to do whatever will make my pops happy to make her own life easier. If she really cared about my happiness, she wouldn't nod and smile and tell me how my father knows best every night at the dinner table. He does not fucking know best. Not where my life is concerned.

They humored me during my freshman and sophomore years. Even came to a few of my games. But when that pending scholarship offer came through end of junior year from Suncrest U and they realized just how serious I am about playing football, everything changed. *Football isn't a career. It's a game. I'm almost eighteen now. I need to be a man. Show some responsibility.* Blah, blah, fucking blah.

Pops is married to his badge. All the man ever does is work. And I get it. It's how he provides for his family. But as the Sun Valley Police Chief, he's got time for little else beyond work. Certainly not time to see his only son play ball. But he's coming to Friday's game—the first one he'll be at all year— and I know once he sees me on the field, sees how good I am, he'll finally drop the subject of me going to the academy. Friday's game is more than just a chance to secure scholarships. It's a chance to prove to my pops that this is what I was born to do.

Allie's quiet as the guys talk until Emilio asks what we've all been secretly wondering. "So, you and Henderson a thing now?"

She stiffens beside me and swings her head toward him, frowning. She better not say what I think she's about to because no, no fucking way is she going to date that douchebag. She's way too good for a tool like him.

I brace myself for the admission, not that it'll matter, because Allie Ramirez is mine. She can like Henderson all she wants, I'll wedge myself right in the middle if I have to.

But instead of confirming their relationship, she says, "We're just friends." I raise a brow and she sighs, shaking her head. "Why is that so hard to believe?"

Our waitress drops off our orders before making a hasty retreat.

Emilio pops a fry into his mouth before saying with a grin, "Because Aaron wants to bone you." He chews, swallows, then eats another. "Can't say I blame him. You're hot as hell, Allie." She blushes. "But I know who you belong to. Henderson does, too, and he's still making his plays." He taps his temple with his index finger. "Not smart on his part but Henderson never was the sharpest crayon in the box."

"I don't belong to anyone."

I snort, leaning back in the booth and spreading my legs to get comfortable. "Yeah, you do." She frowns, looking from Emilio to me. "Time to get with the program, vanilla. Admit you're mine. It's not nice messing with a guy's emotions like that. Letting Henderson believe he has a chance."

"I'm *not*," she snaps.

"Yeah, you are. Admit it."

She scoffs before hissing, "You do not own me. I do not 'belong' to you. I am my own person with my own autonomy."

"Keep telling yourself that, but look where I am and look where you are. This is a thing between us and I for one do not fucking share."

She sets her jaw, turning away from me. Gripping her chin, I force her to meet my gaze, fully aware of Dominique and Emilio's interested stares. "You. Are. Mine. Got it?"

She jerks away. If it weren't for the fact that she's trapped beside me in the booth, I'm sure she'd have already stormed off. "Screw you."

"Already have. And I'm happy to make a repeat go at it, too."

She makes a sound of disgust in the back of her throat, but it's all for show.

"Don't pretend you're anything but flattered. You don't want Henderson. You don't want anyone else. Just admit it already. You want me. I want you. Stop being a child and we can all move on."

Swallowing hard, she swings her glare back to me. Her eyes narrow and her expression is considering before she bites out, "Fine."

Woah. "Fine?"

A shrug. "Yeah, fine. I want you. You're hot and the first time around the sex was good." Her nose crinkles. "Not so much the second time but we all have our off days."

"Burn." Dominique gives a rare chuckle.

"Right to the *cojones*," Emilio adds.

"That wasn't very nice," I bite out.

"Neither is being left without an orgasm. And just so you know, I'm all about second chances in life, but don't expect a third." Her smile is slow as it morphs into a warning. There's that fire I knew was buried inside her.

A slow grin stretches across my face. "Alright. I'll try and remember that."

"Be sure that you do."

I demolish my food. Coach has us running two-a-day practices to prepare for the game and within minutes Dom, Emilio, and I have all cleared our plates, but I notice Allie has barely touched hers.

Maybe half a chicken strip and a few fries. She catches me staring and looks away.

"I thought you were hungry?"

She shrugs. "Yeah. It's not really sitting right with me."

I haven't known Allie long but she looks thinner than she did when she first arrived at Sun Valley High, but I brush it off. If the food isn't settling with her then it isn't settling. I'm not her mom. She can take care of herself.

"So, Allie, you coming to watch us play this weekend?"

She perks up in her seat and when Heather returns to clear our plates, Allie passes her unfinished food to her with little concern. I frown but don't comment. The girl needs to eat, but maybe she'll grab a bite when she gets home?

"I wasn't really planning on it..." she begins.

"You have to come. If you're one of us then you gotta represent. No excuses. Game's Friday night at seven. Plan on being there."

She worries her bottom lips then freezes when my thumb pulls down on her abused lip, my eyes meeting hers. "Come to the game."

"Is that an order?" she quips.

I run my tongue along my teeth. "If it is?"

She shrugs, tearing her napkin into small little squares. "I might have other plans."

I growl and pull her against me. I don't know why it's suddenly important that she be there but it is. "You don't have any other plans. You're coming to the game. End of discussion." She doesn't say anything else, but I catch the small smile playing on her lips and triumph floods through me. She'll be at the game.

TWENTY-ONE

Allie

I slip into English class with seconds to spare when an unfamiliar face pauses beside my desk. "Um... you're Alejandra, right?" a girl asks.

"Allie," I correct her while nodding and she slides into the seat beside me.

"I'm Kasey."

I frown. Why is she talking to me? "Uh, okay."

The bell rings and the last of the students claim their seats, but there's no sign of Mrs. Beck anywhere, and as soon as the rest of the class realizes she's MIA, they all begin talking, visiting their friends' desks, and tossing crumpled paper balls around in a game of catch.

My gaze wanders over the heads in the room and I meet Roman's stare. I swear it burns right through me. Heat flashes through my chest with each passing second and my heart rate picks up before

Kasey draws my attention back with a small wave of her hand. "So, yeah. Hi."

I raise both brows. "Hi."

"I know we haven't talked before. I kept meaning to introduce myself but you seemed a little standoffish and"—her eyes dart around the classroom—"well, anyway. I was just wondering if you had a thing for Aaron Henderson?"

I scowl at her. Was she for real right now? "Why? Do *you* have a thing for Aaron Henderson?" I don't need to turn to know that Roman's stare is still boring into me but I decide to ignore it, giving Kasey my full attention.

She chokes on a laugh, her blond curls bouncing around her heart-shaped face as she claps her hand over her mouth. "What? No! He's my brother."

"Your brother?"

She laughs. "Yeah, sorry. I probably should have led with that. I kind of assumed you knew."

I'm shaking my head. "No. I didn't. He never mentioned he had a little sister."

She sighs. "Yeah, we're not very close. Four years between us and all. But he's a good big brother. Maybe a little absent but what can I expect? You know?" No. I didn't know. I didn't have any brothers or sisters.

"So that makes you a..."

"Freshman. Yep."

I raise a brow. "And you're in this class because...?

"Oh. I have a non-schedule first period. I usually hang out in the library since I ride to school with Aaron but Mrs. Beck asked me to T.A. for her today so here I am."

Oh. Okay.

"Anyway, so...umm... do you?"

I tilt my head to the side before her earlier question comes back to me. "Oh. No." I shake my head. "We're just friends."

Her smile drops and she purses her lips together. "Oh."

Why does she care?

I reach out and touch her forearm offering what I hope is a reassuring gesture. "It's not like that with us. On either side. You don't need to worry about me stringing him along or anything. He knows I'm only looking for friendship."

She nods but doesn't look wholly convinced. "Is it because of..." She flicks her gaze toward Roman just as the classroom door opens and I'm saved from having to answer.

"Good morning, class. Sorry for the delay. Please open your books to..."

Class goes by as usual. Kasey helps Mrs. Beck pass out this week's assignment. A ten-page persuasive essay on a controversial current event. Should be easy enough. And then, before I know it, the bell rings, signaling the end of the period and everyone rushes from their seats to head to the door.

I take my time shoving my books in my bag when a familiar sense of awareness has goosebumps breaking out along my skin. I look up and spy Roman waiting for me near the door with a devilish smirk on his face as he looks me over from head to toe with open want.

When I get close to him he takes my hand and drags me out the door before shoving me into the first empty classroom we come across.

"Hey! What—"

His lips land on mine and a small whimper escapes me. One hand settles on my hip, the other coming up beneath my hair, dragging me closer. I tense, but when he groans against my lips I melt into him. The bell rings but neither of us come up for air.

"What are you doing to me?" I arch against him as his lips trail down my neck, teeth nipping at my collarbone.

"Whatever I want." His fingertips slide inside my jeans and he pulls back to meet my gaze. His tongue peeks out to lick his lips, as his fingers get dangerously close to my needy center.

"Roman." My eyes dart up to look at him through my lashes. And then he's there. Right there. His fingers dip inside me before making a hasty retreat as he swirls my clit with my own juices.

"Just making up for before." There's a wicked smile to his voice.

I cling to him, the muscles in his biceps flexing as he works me over with skilled fingers. "We're supposed to be in class," I rasp.

"Are you asking me to stop?"

I moan and my body tightens, chasing away my release. God, no. I don't want him to stop. But when I don't respond, he must take my silence as agreement and withdraws his hand from my jeans. A strangled sound of protest leaves my lips and he chuckles before kissing me into silence as his hands work quickly to unbutton my pants and shove them down over my thighs, leaving me exposed.

My head falls back against the classroom wall and when he shoves two fingers deep inside me, curling them to find just the right spot, I shudder in his grip. He kisses my jaw before trailing his lips down my neck, his free hand coming up to play with my breasts. He pushes down the stretchy material of my top, giving him better access to pinch my right nipple.

I gasp, my knees going weak.

He circles my clit, his movements quickening. I cry out when out of nowhere, my release slams into me. He covers my mouth with his hand, muffling my cries as his fingers milk every last drop of my orgasm from me.

"I need to fuck you," he says, pulling me forward and bending me over the nearest desk, my bare ass in the air and on full display. I shiver, a whimper leaving me as I hear the telltale sound of his belt being unbuckled. His jeans sliding over his hips.

"Condom?" I rasp and he curses behind me.

"I'll pull out."

I'm about to object but then he presses against me and I arch back to meet him as he slides his dick inside my pussy in a single fluid thrust.

We groan in unison as he flexes his hips, holding me in place. "God you feel incredible," he says. His hands tighten on my hips with bruising force as he pulls back and then thrusts inside me once again. "So fucking wet."

I'm panting, barely able to catch my breath as he pounds into me. Each thrust harder than the one before until the desk is sliding beneath me with the force of his movements, screeching across the floor. I cling to the edge and he grinds his hips against my ass.

I cry out his name, losing myself to the feel of him inside of me, completely forgetting that we're at school and that anyone can walk in on us. His hips slam frantically into me and I know he's chasing his own release when suddenly he jerks back and then his hot cum is coating my ass, dripping down over the backs of my thighs.

He slides his dick over the trail of cum he coated me in before smacking me lightly on the rear. I groan and peer over my shoulder. Roman's smirk greets me as he considers my still bare ass. "You should probably clean that up," he suggests. I narrow my eyes as he laughs. "I might be persuaded into helping you out under a few conditions." He tucks himself back into his jeans before folding his arms over his chest, leaving the top button unbuttoned, but saying nothing.

"Do you ever want to do this again?" I ask.

He grins. "Every day of the week."

"Then get me something to wipe your cum off my ass or I won't let you near me with so much as a ten-foot pole."

"You say that now, but—"

Voices can be heard in the hallway. *Crap.* Everyone is supposed to be in class. "Now, Roman."

Thankfully, he does as I ask and finds a roll of paper towels in a closet and helps to clean me up before tossing them in the trash. I shimmy back into my jeans and am adjusting my top just as the door bursts open and Silvia Parish's startled brown eyes meet my own.

She takes in the scene, her eyes narrowing on our rumpled clothes and my unruly hair. When Roman steps closer to me, they narrow farther and I can't help the grin that spreads across my face.

"Did you need something?" he asks, not a care in the world that she knows exactly what we were just doing. "You're interrupting."

"We all heard you fucking in Calc," she sneers at me. "You sound like a dying rhino."

Feeling extra bold with Roman beside me, I roll my eyes and flip her off. I don't have time for her mean girl antics today. "Whatever." Not my strongest comeback, but it's better than wilting under her glare.

She whirls and leaves as quickly as she came. Roman leans down, smacking my ass and giving me a meaningful look. "If that's what a dying rhino sounds like, I better be hearing it again. *Soon.*"

I shiver in response to the blatant desire in his gaze before Roman walks out of the room. I decide to stop by the bathroom and just skip Calc entirely. A look at one of the clocks in the hallways shows me that there's only ten minutes left until the bell rings for lunch, so I decide to loiter for a bit and save myself some embarrassment.

I wash my hands and splash water on my face before running my fingers through my hair in an effort to smooth it out. The door opens behind me and I don't pay it any attention until a body slams me forward and my stomach collides with the porcelain sink. I stumble and am shoved harshly to the ground. My hair covers my face as a foot slams into my chest. *Shit. Ow.* I suck in a pain-filled gasp and another kick comes at me from behind, slamming into my back with the force of a sledgehammer.

I curse and roll, narrowly avoiding the third kick when a fist slams into my cheek. My head snaps back and my vision blurs. Someone grips my hair, jerking my face up as my eyes meet Silvia's.

"Bitch." I spit blood in her face and she reels back. Then I kick out, connecting with her shin and she stumbles back into her two asshole friends who decided to join her. I scramble to my feet and rush out the bathroom door just as the bell rings and the hallway crowds with people.

I suck in a breath and clench my hands into tight fists to keep them from shaking.

Careful to keep my head down, I lose myself in the sea of bodies, hugging my ribs as I fight through a wave of pain. *Fuck.* I think I'm going to vomit. I stumble toward a classroom door and lunge for the first receptacle I see to throw up my breakfast in.

Acid burns my throat and tears fill the corners of my eyes making it hard to see. The next thing I know, a boy crouches beside me, a comforting hand smoothing down my back, but I flinch at the contact. "What the hell, Allie? Are you okay?" Aaron says.

I hold a hand out to keep him at bay as I dry heave over the trashcan, my stomach intent on puking some more, despite it now being empty.

When the heaving stops, I sink to the floor still clutching my aching stomach and lean my head back against the wall. Aaron crouches down in front of me. His eyes are wide and filled with worry.

The door opens and Dominique steps inside, his eyes immediately zeroing in on me. "What's going on here?" His nostrils flare and he rushes toward me. "What the fuck did you do?" He turns a hot glare toward Aaron who stands and takes several steps away.

"I didn't do anything. She stumbled in here and I followed her to see if she needed help."

He reaches for me, but I shake my head and slowly come to my feet. I use the counter as support to steady myself as my head spins and everything blurs for a few seconds. Nausea rolls through me again.

The door opens again and Emilio steps inside. "Yo, Dom. What's taking you so—fuck!"

I lift my head and take in his wide-eyed stare. "Someone better start talking before Roman gets here." The door opens again and Roman walks in. Emilio whistles. "Too late."

Roman spots me and his eyes flare. "What the fuck happened to you?"

"Nothing." I shrug, but the movement causes me to wince.

"Nothing?" Roman stalks closer, his hand reaching out, tilting my jaw toward the light. His thumb grazes my lip and I hiss. He releases me. "This doesn't look like nothing."

The other three boys crowd me until Dominique shoves Aaron back. He curses but stays put as all three Devils level me with varying shades of anger. "Spill, Alejandra," Emilio says, and woah, we must be serious because Emilio never uses my name. It's always Allie or vanilla.

I swallow and look down at my sneakers. "It's nothing. I was walking out of the bathroom as someone else was walking in. The door slammed into my face." Three sets of disapproving eyes meet my gaze.

"You're lying," Dominique says. And yeah, maybe I am. But I don't need any of them making things worse by creating a scene.

Silvia is the petty mean girl type and she's mad she isn't getting her way. I can handle her. I wasn't expecting an attack like this but looking back, after the hallway incident, I should have seen it coming. I won't make that mistake again.

I shake my head at Dom's accusation but then stop when the room spins. "No, I'm not. You guys are making a big deal out of nothing. I got smacked in the face with a door and I'm on my period. Can we drop it now?"

"That the story you're sticking with?" Roman asks, unconvinced.

"Yep."

He glares. "For the record, you're not on your fucking period and I don't like liars."

I shrug. "Whatever. Look, I just had the pleasure of throwing up my breakfast and would love to wash my mouth out. Can we move this show along?" I shove past them and head for the door, grateful when no one rushes to immediately follow.

TWENTY-TWO

Roman

"She was jumped," Emilio says as soon as Allie leaves the room.

A snort from behind has all three of our heads turning. Aaron shakes his head, his jaw clenched and his hands fisted at his sides. "Yeah, she was. Wonder who's fucking fault that is?"

"What the hell is that supposed to mean?" I advance on him, but he doesn't cower, which only serves to piss me the fuck off.

"You know exactly what I mean, Roman. Or did you forget we used to be friends? I know how that head of yours works. You don't think I know you wanted her targeted when she first showed up here? That you didn't plant your little seeds in the school to make her life difficult?" He briefly looks up to the ceiling and laughs, but the sound is harsh and mocking. "Every fucking girl in this school is going to go after her now. And you"—he digs his finger into my chest—"you're the one who put the target on her back." He shakes his head. "I might have my demons, but at least I'm not a selfish prick like you." He storms out of the classroom, leaving me reeling with his last statement.

"Fuck," I yell as soon as Aaron is gone from the room.

Two sets of grim stares meet my own. "We didn't really consider how chicks would respond when you claimed her," Dominique tries to reassure me, but we all know what Aaron said is true. I did this. Me. No one else. I knew what would happen and I did it anyway. I might not have known the girls would stoop to jumping her, but I should have suspected this after what went down with her and Silvia before. Stupid. I am so fucking stupid.

"I need to fix this." Neither one disputes my statement. The question now is, how?

Emilio rubs the back of his neck. "I didn't make things better when I told the school to ice out Silvia. This could be retaliation for that. She can't do anything to us, but..."

I shake my head. "I appreciate what you're doing, but, no. This is on me." I fucked up and I'll own it. "Besides, we don't even know if Silvia was involved. We need more information."

Emilio snorts. "One of us is going to need to be with her at all times," Emilio says.

"How the fuck are we supposed to manage that?" I ask, anger burning a hole in my gut. She was hurt. Someone put their fucking hands on my girl and hurt her.

"Yeah. It doesn't look like Allie will be forthcoming with that," Dom remarks.

"We start by finding her and then make sure whoever did this doesn't decide to have another go at it," Emilio says and I nod.

I don't give a shit if Allie wants to sweep this mess under the rug. I want to know who did this and I'm going to make *damn sure* it doesn't happen again. Everyone at this school needs to know they can't hurt my girl and get away with it.

We head out to find Allie but she's elusive. She isn't in the lunchroom and she's not in her next class either. After searching for twenty minutes straight, I find out from the front office that she signed herself out for the day. I release a harsh sigh of relief. At least with her home, I don't have to worry about someone else coming after her.

I fill the guys in when we meet up later after school and we come up with a plan to shadow her during the next school day. I've got her covered before school and during first. I'll walk her to second and Dom will follow her after second to third. Emilio's next to her fourth period class so he'll have eyes on her until she makes it to class and then I'll catch her as soon as she's done for the day.

We shouldn't have to worry about anything happening to her during classes. No one is *that* stupid. And fourth period she's got Welding with Aaron. I don't like the idea of relying on that fucker, but whatever his motives, he seems to care for her, and thankfully there aren't any catty bitches in that class for her to have to deal with.

It's a solid plan and I should be cool with it, but I can't get the idea of her abused body out of my head. Every time I close my eyes I see her face. The bruises. The split lip. It's like a dagger to the stomach, and thinking of what she must have felt makes the blade twist inside me.

Practice that afternoon is grueling. I push all my anger and frustration into completing each pass and running hard until my heart feels like it's going to burst out of my chest, but it doesn't matter. I'm responsible for a pass-interception that I should have completed and then I fumble a fucking catch. Coach is screaming at me to get my head out of my ass and I'm trying but, *fuck*. I'm so out of it.

"We cannot afford for you to play like this come Friday," Coach shouts.

I grit my teeth to keep from lashing out. I know he's right but —*Fuck*. I tear my helmet from my head and throw it on the field.

"Roman!" Coach shouts, but I ignore him, stalking to the locker room to strip out of my gear and shower before the rest of the team finishes.

"Valdez, get your ass back on the field," he tries again.

Dominique heads toward Coach to smooth over my little outburst, but I don't stick around long enough to see if it works.

I need to see Allie, and recognizing that makes me feel all sorts of ways that I don't want to think about. It's three days till the big game. I should be focused on plays. Football is all that matters.

I know she's home. I know she's safe. I need to let this insatiable need to see her go but, dammit, I fucking can't. I'll be useless on the field until I know without a shadow of a doubt that she's okay.

FORTY MINUTES LATER I'M PULLING UP TO HER HOUSE—IF you can even call it that. I used my dad's Sun Valley residents service app that he doesn't know I have installed on my phone to look up Gerald Ulrich's address. Having a father who's the chief of police comes with a few perks, but what I pull up to is not a home. It's a fucking mansion.

The place has got to be five thousand square feet or more. It's got twin pillars flanking the front door and massive floor-to-ceiling windows on all sides of the house. The lawn is perfectly kept and rose bushes ring the grass. This place rivals even Dominique's, and that's saying something, because that fucker has more money than any person can spend in a lifetime.

For a minute I idle in front of the place, staring at the front door as though I can *will* her to step out of it. I press down the gas, letting the roar of the engine fill the street, and a flutter of movement at one of the second-story windows pulls my gaze.

Allie peaks through pale pink curtains and I wave, still willing her to come outside. The curtains close and I wait. She knows I'm here. She'll come.

A few short minutes later she's closing the front door behind her. Wearing white jeans and an oversized hoodie, she stops beside my car and frowns. "What are you doing here?" She tucks her hair behind her ear, exposing the purple bruise on her lower jaw.

But all I see is red.

"Get in."

She shakes her head. "What do you want, Roman? Shouldn't you be at practice or something?"

I try and tamp down my irritation at her refusal. "Nah. Ended thirty minutes ago. Come on." She's still not moving. "Get in the car, Alejandra." Something about saying her full name gets a reaction out of her, and with a muttered curse, she's opening the passenger side door and sliding inside. "Put on your seatbelt."

She does.

Thank fuck for small favors.

We ride in silence for the first ten minutes before I take her to a different side of town where the houses are smaller, some with bars on their windows and heavy iron screen doors covering their wooden counterparts.

"Where are we going?" she finally asks just as I pull onto a familiar street.

"My place." I'm not entirely sure why I'm taking her home with me. We come from two different worlds. But I want her beside me. I need to know that she's okay.

I pull into the driveway of a three-bedroom, ranch-style home and put the car in park. "Come on."

Allie gets out hesitantly, checking her surroundings with an inquisitive stare. "This is where you live?"

I nod, searching for any sort of reaction that my life isn't good enough, but I see none from her. I release a breath. There's no judgment in her gaze as she takes in the stucco exterior of my home or the fact that the garage door is wide fucking open and my garage looks like a second living room packed full of mismatched sofas with a pool table in the middle.

A car door slams one house over and a voice shouts, "Yo, what's for dinner?" as Emilio jogs toward us.

"What's—"

"We're neighbors," I tell her as he nears.

"Please tell me your mom's going to feed me. Coach is killing me with these two-a-days and I need some fucking calories in me before my stomach decides to eat itself."

"Come on, *cabrón*. Let's see what she's got."

Allie follows behind but I don't miss the curiosity on her face as I lead her through the garage and straight into the kitchen. As soon as we're inside, we're enveloped in the heady smell of my mother's cooking.

"*Mamá,*" I shout into the house, knowing she can't be far. I check the stove, lifting the lid off a large stockpot, finding fresh warm tamales steaming inside.

"Hijo, no toques," *Don't touch that,* she admonishes just as she turns a corner. I'm about to ask her what's wrong, because my mom only ever makes tamales for two occasions. A holiday like Thanksgiving or Christmas, or because my pops is upset about something—usually where I'm concerned—and she's trying to smooth things over the only way she knows how. With food. But before I can ask, she spots Allie and her eyes widen in surprise.

"You brought home a girl?" Her accent is thick but her English is clear as she takes Allie in from head to toe and a wide smile spreads across her face. Fuck. I don't think I thought this all the way through.

"Mija, let me see you." My mother pulls Allie toward her, not bothering to introduce herself or offer any sort of hello before spinning her around and taking her in.

Allie accepts this like it's completely normal, a hesitant smile on her face as she circles back around to face my mother. My mom is a small woman, a few inches shy of five feet making Allie, who's tiny compared to me, look tall for once.

"You're beautiful," my mother tells her, leaning in to give Allie a kiss on the cheek.

Allie returns the gesture. "Thank you. I'm Alejandra." Her voice is small but her smile is genuine.

"And how long have you been dating my son?" she asks, and I groan while Emilio chuckles.

"*Mamá!*"

"What? A mother should know these things."

I shake my head. "No, she shouldn't. Don't scare away the first girl I've introduced you to."

"Sorry, Mrs. Valdez, Allie here is mine." Emilio tosses his arm around Allie's shoulders.

My mother's frown is immediate, forcing me to bite off a laugh. "Tell him you won't feed him unless he gives her back."

Her eyes, lined with age, spark with mischief and she smiles.

Emilio groans. "Not cool, bro. Not. Cool."

I tug Allie from his arms. She comes willingly and I tuck her beside me, leading her to the table. I'm just as hungry as Emilio. He wasn't kidding when he said our two-a-day practices have been killer.

When Allie's back is to my mother, my mom's concerned eyes meet mine and she makes a small gesture, brushing her thumb under her own jaw. I tilt my head, letting her know with that small gesture that I know why the bruise is there and that she has nothing to worry about.

She trusts me, so with a satisfied nod, Mom returns to the stove, dishing up three plates of food while we take our seats. Within a few short minutes, rice, beans, and tamales are in front of me and I don't hesitate to dive in. Emilio eats like he's been starved, which earns him a beaming smile and a second helping. Mom won't eat until Pops comes home from work, so after making sure we're all settled, she retreats to her room.

I wish I knew what was up, but our family is private and she would be embarrassed if I brought up family matters in front of guests, so I'll wait to talk to her when Allie's gone.

The first few minutes we focus on our food. Allie's bites are small, her chewing almost methodical as if she's savoring the flavors. I've noticed she doesn't eat a lot at school but she's eating now, so it doesn't look like there's reason to be concerned.

"You're such a lucky asshole," Emilio says, now on his third tamale and I smirk.

"Consider yourself lucky I put up with you or you'd miss out on all of this."

Allie laughs. "It is really good."

"Better than my albóndigas?" I ask and she blushes.

"I don't know. That's a hard one. I'm not sure I could choose."

"Roman's ma's tamales. Hands down. She only makes them like twice a year. I would kill for these."

I ignore him, leaning toward Allie and capturing her lips with my own in a quick kiss. When I pull back her eyes are wide and uncertain as her fingers come up to touch her mouth.

"What was that for?"

I shrug. "Because I wanted to."

Emilio, having missed the exchange, talks on about how amazing my mom's food is and how I'm a greedy bastard who doesn't share often enough. Some of it is a joke but there's a thread of painful honesty there too. Emilio's mom bailed when he was seven, leaving behind her husband and four children. He has two older brothers and a little sister. And let's just say his dad isn't the domestic type.

But Emilio's always been welcome here and my mom loves feeding the fucker. As we eat, Allie relaxes, her smiles coming more easily as Emilio and I bitch and moan about practices. Every now and then she sends me questioning looks. I know she's waiting for me to ask her what happened back at school, but I want her comfortable first. I'm also waiting for Dominique to show up. I have a feeling I'm going to need all the help I can get to pry the names I need from Allie's mouth.

When we finish eating I draw Allie back outside to the garage and pull her down beside me as Emilio takes a seat on the opposite couch, his expression now serious. The sun is setting and a cool breeze floats through the open space.

My knee bounces and I'm itching for a smoke but refrain from pulling one out. I haven't taken a hit since Shadle Creek weekend and it's better not to blow my little streak.

As soon as Dom's black Escalade pulls into the driveway, Emilio shifts over to make room for him. Dom steps out in black slacks and a black button-up shirt with the sleeves rolled up. He heads toward us and Emilio whistles at him.

Dom doesn't react aside from flipping him off. Seeing Dom dressed up isn't all that unusual. His family is the sort to dress for dinner and use fine china, so I appreciate that he came here straight afterward and didn't take the unnecessary time to change.

He sits back on the sofa and gives me a look that says, *now what?*

Allie catches it and turns to look at me. "What's going on?" Her tone is wary.

I run my fingers through my hair and sigh. "We need to know who jumped you today."

She starts to stand but I pull her back down beside me. "No more running. Someone hurt you and we want to know who."

"Why do you care?" she hisses.

Is she kidding me right now? "I care because you're my—"

"I'm not *your* anything."

Clenching my jaw, I cup her face and force her to meet my gaze. "We've gone over this. You're mine. My girl. Got it?" She swallows hard but doesn't respond. "Anyone who fucks with you is asking to be fucked with by me."

"Us," Dom corrects and she whips her head around toward him.

"Why?"

I open my mouth to speak but she cuts me off. "And yeah, I get it. You're a possessive asshole. I'm yours until you decide I'm not. I know. But we've gone over this, too"—she indicates the space between us, a small frown on her face—"and we both agreed this is for fun. We're passing the time. You don't need to go all alpha protector on me. I can take care of myself."

Silence.

No one says a thing as I glare into her dark brown eyes, pretending it doesn't bother me one bit to hear her say that whatever we have between us doesn't fucking matter. Like she said, we're just passing the time. I'm not catching feelings for some girl I barely know and clearly she's not catching any for me. Good.

I release my grip on her jaw before I add to her bruises and give an exaggerated eye roll. "Stop reading into this, vanilla. If I can't protect what's mine then how can I expect anyone to take me seriously. I have a reputation to uphold."

Emilio opens his mouth to say something but I send him a murderous look, shutting him up.

Allie's brows furrow as she considers my words with a sigh. "I can handle this on my own."

"Right. Because you've done such a great job already."

"Will you just drop it?"

All three of us shake our heads.

"We're going to find out one way or another. Why are you so adamant to face this alone?" Dominique presses.

"Because I can. It's mean-girl shit. You're blowing it out of proportion. Just because three girls decided—"

"Three?" Emilio questions and Allie's eyes widen, realizing her mistake. "Names, Alejandra?" he presses.

"I don't even know all their names," she mutters, folding her arms over her chest like a petulant child not getting her way.

"Maybe not, but you know at least one, am I right?"

She glares at me and I smirk.

"Maybe."

I turn to Emilio and Dom. "Can you guys give us a minute?" They nod and head back inside. Once they're gone I turn Allie toward me, pulling her close until her chest is pressed against my side. I rub my thumb over her jawline before dragging it against her bottom lip. "Who did this?"

Her eyes plead with me to drop it, so I go for a different tactic and crash my lips against hers. She immediately kisses me back as I tug her onto my lap, her legs now straddling my waist. She rocks against me and I'm instantly hard inside my jeans. I devour her mouth, drinking down her soft moans. When I finally break the kiss, I rest my forehead against hers, our chests heaving, her small hands clinging to the fabric of my shirt. "Who?" I try again, capturing her mouth once more and then pulling away. "Tell me, Allie."

She groans, chasing after my lips but I deny her, instead trailing kisses up the column of her neck. "Allie?" I scrape my teeth against her skin and she shivers in my arms. "Come on, baby. One name. Tell me who did this and I'll help you forget all about it."

"Silvia," she says.

I smile triumphantly before gripping her ass. I stand, wrapping her legs around my waist as I head over to the door, slapping a hand down on the garage door opener to give us some small measure of privacy. Dom and Emilio will know what we're doing once they hear the sound of the door closing and they'll make sure we're not interrupted.

TWENTY-THREE

Allie

He's getting under my skin. It's been a few days since the bathroom incident and one of the Devils is always at my side. I know they're doing it to protect me, but it's getting annoying. I can't even go to the bathroom without having one of them try and tag along. The first time I went to go pee I had to forcefully shove Emilio out of the bathroom and that was only after he'd stormed in and kicked everyone else out making sure it was clear.

It's a good thing I wasn't worried about my reputation here at this school before, because a guy forcefully clearing a bathroom usually only ever meant one thing.

Even Aaron has been extra attentive and sticks around until he spots one of the Devils, and then it's like a handoff. I don't know if they somehow hashed out my babysitting details or if this is some unspoken guy thing, but I'm ready for it to be over. The one positive in all this is that I've somehow managed to make a female friend. Roman likes me sticking around at their practices until he can take me home himself and since it's not like I have anything better to do, I agreed.

Somehow, Kasey Henderson wound up keeping me company the first day and we sort of just hit it off. I've managed to convince her to stick around two other times and realized it's nice having a girlfriend. It makes me miss Adriana even more, but that's not a friendship with any chance of recovery.

The big game is today and it's all the guys are talking about. "You're still coming to support, right?" Emilio asks, tossing a french fry at me.

I nod and take my seat beside Roman at the lunch table. He pulls me close and I lean my head on his shoulder, feeling more tired than usual. I poke at my food, not making any real effort to eat before pushing my tray toward Dominique who's already finished his. "Here, you need fuel for the big game."

He grins and picks up my burger, eating the whole thing in four bites. I don't bother hiding my laugh. Dom is practically a garbage disposal when it comes to food. They all are.

I know I should probably try and eat some of my lunch but the very idea of it makes bile rise in my throat. I've lost more weight and my clothes are starting to hang loose on my body. Between the lack of appetite and the running I've taken up, I'm getting leaner. I still have curves but I've lost some of the softness around my stomach and thighs, not that I'm complaining.

"Why aren't you eating?" Roman asks, surprising me.

Saving me from having to respond, Kasey picks that moment to plop down beside me, setting her tray down on the table with a loud smack. "Urgh, can you believe her," she practically snarls.

I lift my head, giving her a questioning look.

She rolls her eyes. "Sarah. She's all over Aaron and it's disgusting. I can't stand her."

I look across the cafeteria and spot Sarah standing behind Aaron who's sitting at a table. Her arms are wrapped around his neck, her breasts pressed against his back. "I take it you're not her biggest fan?"

Her lip curls in disgust. "Definitely not. She's a bitch and she's only all over Aaron because she thinks it'll make him jealous." She points a finger toward Emilio before shoving a fry in her mouth, still glaring in her brother's direction.

"Me?" Emilio's balks, eyes wide and a horrified expression on his face. "I don't want none of that."

I lift my water bottle to take a sip just as Kasey snorts. "You slept with her last weekend. She's my neighbor. I totally saw your walk of shame the next morning." I choke on the water and Roman slaps my back a few times before the coughing subsides.

"You slept with that piranha?" I ask.

Emilio glares at Kasey, stabbing a finger at her in return. "Not cool, baby Henderson."

"Gross. Don't call me that."

"Hold on. You slept with Sarah Draven?" I ask again.

Emilio sighs and Roman fights a grin. "What baby Henderson left out is, there was a party. I was drunk. That basket of crazy over there took advantage of me."

I snort. "*Riiiight.*"

"Hey, at least I learn from my mistakes. You're still sleeping with this asshole."

Roman shoots him a glare and Kasey snickers. I give Roman a quick kiss on the cheek and his glower instantly softens. "I happen to like this asshole," I tell him and everyone else at the table makes gagging sounds.

I roll my eyes and steal a fry off Kasey's tray only to throw it at Emilio who somehow manages to catch it in his mouth.

"So, the game...?" Emilio says, trying to shift the focus off himself. "Who are you going with, because you can't show up alone."

I roll my eyes but notice Roman scowling. I guess he hadn't considered that. "I'll be fine. Nothing has happened since the whole bathroom incident and nothing is going to happen. You three went all psycho on Silvia and she's been avoiding me ever since." Every head turns to look where she's currently seated, alone and in a far corner picking at her lunch with a look of complete misery on her face.

All three give me smug smiles. As soon as Roman learned Silvia was behind the attack he went all caveman and pulled in every guy on the football team to make sure that her status as an outcast stuck. She's a social pariah now. I almost feel bad. Her own friends have abandoned her and the school pretends she doesn't exist. People will walk into her without batting an eyelash. I noticed in second period even our teacher ignores her. I have no idea how the Devils managed that but they did.

"No way." Roman shakes his head. "You can't show up alone. All three of us will be on the field. We won't be able to protect you."

"I don't need protection—"

"I can go with you," Kasey says. All eyes swing toward her.

"Are you sure?" I ask. "You hate football." I know because she's whined on at least four separate occasions about how boring it is and how stupid it is that the school treats the players like gods. Kasey isn't fond of athletes in general, which has made her little addition to our group pretty interesting, to say the least.

"Yeah, I'm sure. I like hanging out with you. Besides"—the corner of her mouth lifts into a smirk as she turns her attention toward Dominique—"then I can watch him throw an interception and give him shit for it."

Dom glowers and our entire table erupts into a fit of laughter.

"Not fucking likely," he deadpans.

I don't know what's going on with those two. Likely nothing because Dom will be eighteen in a few short months and Kasey's only a freshman, but she seems intent on getting under his skin any chance she gets, despite the fact that he usually ignores her.

The bell rings signaling the end of lunch and we make our way out of the cafeteria. Roman stops me just outside my third-period class and plants a lingering kiss on my lips that leaves me breathless.

"Don't be late tonight," he tells me, nipping my lower lip.

"Are you suddenly worried I won't show up?" I ask, fingering my bracelet.

He smirks. "Nah, I know you'll be there, but it never hurts to have some reassurances."

I tug my bracelet off and take his hand in mine, trying it around his wrist. "Consider yourself reassured. This is important to me. You can give it back to me after the game."

He kisses me deep and slow, leaving me breathless before walking backward toward his own class. "Later, baby."

TWENTY-FOUR

Roman

F riday night came too fucking fast. I'm sitting in the locker room and can barely hear what coach is saying as he gives his little pep talk before we rush out onto the field. I tighten my laces, my gaze meeting Dom's. We nod, both ready to lay it all out on the field. Tonight's a big night. If we win, it'll be smooth sailing from here on out. Coach drones on and on about how proud he is of each of us. How we've played an incredible season. And then he yells at us not to fuck it up.

Emilio elbows me in the ribs, a grin on his face as he sucks on a *palerindas*—a tamarind-flavored sucker—his game day ritual. Personally, I can't stand the things, but Emilio's an addict and always has a few in his bag.

I bounce my leg, waiting for coach to hurry up so we can get out on the field. Tonight the Devils play the Saints and I'm determined put those fuckers through hell.

The stadium lights light up the field and hundreds of people in the bleachers as I jog beside my team. I scan the crowd, not seeing

Allie yet, but I know she'll be here. Seats are packed, everyone on the home side decked out in red and black with devil horns on their heads.

I make sure Allie's bracelet is tucked beneath my glove before following the other guys to the center of the field. Dom is our captain and quarterback and all eyes are on him as we huddle up and run through the details of our first play.

I'm hyped as fuck and bouncing on the balls of my feet, ready to leave the Saint's defense in a cloud of dust. One last scan of the bleachers shows that Allie still isn't here, but I shake off the irritation as soon as I spot my pops in the stands. I puff out my chest and when Dom calls the play and snaps back, I'm off. I sprint wide to the left, before spinning to catch the ball I know is aimed right for me. My hands connect with the laces and I clutch the damn thing like my life depends on it before taking off straight for the goal posts.

I'm tackled twenty yards from the end zone but I'm still grinning because we picked up way more ground on the first play than we should have. Looks like the Saints are going to have an off day.

It's the end of the second quarter and we're ahead by seven. The stadium is packed, making it harder to find my girl, but as I take my seat on the bench, Dominique points out Henderson's little sister. "Baby Henderson's here. That means Allie is, too."

I nod, scanning the surrounding crowd for her dark brown hair. The spot beside Kasey is vacant. Maybe Allie went to the restroom? The idea alone is enough to have me clenching my hands into tight fists. "Yeah, but do you see her?"

He looks and shakes his head. "No."

"Me, either. Which means she's off somewhere at this packed fucking game alone right now."

"Maybe she just went to grab a soda?"

"I don't care if she needed to take a shit. She knows the deal. She's not supposed to go anywhere at this school alone."

He nods, a scowl on his face letting me know he doesn't like this any more than I do, but there isn't anything either of us can do about it from the field. Coach calls us back to the locker room for our half-time pep talk and I have no choice but to follow the rest of the guys.

When we return for the beginning of the third, the seat beside Kasey is still fucking empty. Worry worms through me, followed quickly by anger when I catch my pops getting up from the stands, his phone to his ear because of course he can't leave work at the office.

I'm tracking his movements as he leaves through the gate entrance and miss Dom's words as he calls out the play before the snap. Fuck. I take off, hoping I'm heading in the right direction. When Dom throws, I realize I'm way the fuck off and have to kick it into gear to reach his intended mark. My fingers glance across the ball but I fumble the catch. Thankfully, one of my teammates is close by to recover it. I kick at the field, unearthing a chunk of grass as I curse and head back to the start-up line.

The rest of the game goes similarly, but I'm not the only one affected now. It's like everything went to shit the second half. Dom throws an interception and we miss two field goals that we should have had in the bag. Emilio lets two running backs slip past him, allowing the Saints to score. We're still in the lead but we're down to the wire and if we don't score, there's a good chance the Saints will on their next play and we'll lose. There isn't enough time on the clock. I have to score.

I know the play. I've done this maneuver a million times before, so I focus on my breathing, narrowing my field of vision as I zero in on where I need to be and how to get there as quickly as possible. My pops never returned after stepping out and I still haven't caught sight of my girl. Focusing all of my anger and frustration into our last play I sprint up the field, adrenaline rushing through my veins. My hands find the ball and then I'm running up the field, racing along the boundary line.

Two players are hot on my heels and I have no one from my own team anywhere close to help. One of the assholes—number eleven —is gaining on me, but with the ball tucked under my right arm I shove out with my left, shoving him away and then TOUCHDOWN!

My team rushes me. Helmets knock into mine and fists knock me in the shoulder. There's less than two minutes on the clock and the other team has no time-outs left. I cheer with my team. We won. We'll run out the clock, but my job here is done.

I'm riding a high and smiling like an idiot until I look back up at the stands.

Kasey's nowhere to be found now, and neither is Allie.

My smile tightens. And I turn back to the guys, accepting their good-natured high-fives and shouts of congratulations, all the while thinking in my head, *where the fuck is she?*

TWENTY-FIVE

Allie

I'm running late getting to the game. Kasey was going to meet me at my place and we'd drive over together but something came up with her aunt, so she sent a text letting me know she'd have to meet me at the school.

I call an Uber and get the oldest grandma in the history of Uber drivers who happens to drive five miles an hour below the speed limit the entire way, but I get there just as the first quarter ends and make my way over to the bleachers where Kasey said she'd be.

"Hey. Sorry I'm late." I claim the empty seat beside her.

"Damn, Allie. Looking good," she says, taking in my painted stomach. I blush. It hadn't been planned, but I knew that some of the girls painted their boyfriend's or favorite player's number on their midriff, so I painted Roman's—a number four—and a small red devil on my abdomen.

"Thanks. Think he'll like it?"

Her brows wiggle. "I think he'll *love* it." She smirks, then winks. "Also, don't hate me, but I might have to leave early."

Oh. I look around, instantly realizing I don't have anyone else to hang out with here if she leaves, but I promised the guys I'd be here so I can't very well bail.

"My aunt is running short-staffed at the diner," she tells me. "I don't usually work there but she's in a bind. That's why I was late. I filled in after school for one of the girls who was a no-show. I can stay for most of the game, but I'll need to leave before the end of the fourth so I can get there before the football crowd shows up."

"Oh. That's totally fine." It's great, actually. I won't be alone the whole game. Just for part of the fourth. No big deal.

I look out on the field and instantly find Roman—number four. My heart quickens and I watch him run up the field, scoring for the Sun Valley Devils. The entire stadium cheers, including me. I jump up and down like a moron screaming his name in the hopes he'll see me.

"Oh, and here. I brought us these to make the game more interesting." Kasey opens her purse to show me the stash of mini booze bottles tucked away inside.

"You snuck alcohol into a school game?"

She grins. "How else was I supposed to get through this game?" Pulling two out, she hands one to me. A mini Malibu rum. I roll my eyes but accept it. "To Dominique throwing an interception."

"I can't toast to that."

She shrugs. "I can. You can toast to Roman scoring the winning touchdown."

I laugh but concede. "Okay. I'll toast to that." Cracking the cap, I take a drink, downing half of the rum in one swallow before tucking the bottle into my pocket. "That's kind of awful," I tell her.

"I know, but it was all I could find on short notice. Aaron keeps a stash of these in the bottom drawer of his dresser."

My phone buzzes in my pocket. I look down and recognize Julio's number flashing across the screen and smile.

"Hello?"

"Hey—" His words are hard to hear through the thundering noise of the crowd.

"Give me a second to get somewhere quiet," I shout into the phone. "I'll be back. I need to take this," I tell Kasey. She waves me off, her attention focused on her own phone as her fingers fly over the keyboard. Standing, I make my way through the stands, slipping through the bleachers and heading for the parking lot gate.

The half-time show is starting up and everyone is on their feet dancing to whatever song the cheer squad has going on.

"Excuse me. Sorry." I brush past a group of parents and finally make it outside the gate. It's still loud out here but the noise level is no longer deafening.

"Sorry about that. How are you?" I ask as I stride further across the darkened lot toward the corner of the school. The lights barely illuminate the space but it's still hard to hear Julio over the crowd so I resign myself to a phone call in the dark.

"I'm good. Now, tell me about this guy you mentioned you're seeing."

I laugh, hearing the protective tone in his voice. "Chill with the big brother vibes. Nothing serious is going on."

He snorts. "Allie, you don't date. Ryker was the exception and we saw how that went."

I groan. "Please don't remind me." If I could forget ever being with Ryker, that'd be the day.

"I'm serious, though. Is he good to you?"

A smile spreads over my face as I think about Roman. He's still an asshole to everyone else in this school but in the small pockets of time we happen to get alone, he's different. Still cocky and possessive but also kind, thoughtful, and surprisingly funny. Just thinking about this past week we've had together is enough to make butterflies dance in my stomach.

"Yeah, Julio. He is. I don't know what it is about him but..." I trail off and narrow my eyes in the dark as I spot two men ten yards away from me. They're not doing anything, just standing there watching me, but still ... goosebumps spread across my skin.

"You still there?" Julio asks.

"Ye...Yeah. I'm here. Sorry, umm, what was I saying?" I turn away from the men and head back across the parking lot, finally realizing I'd pulled myself away from the safety of the crowd. Everything looks different now. Darker, more sinister. My heart races in my chest and I can barely make out Julio's words as panic bubbles inside me.

I scan the lot and see Silvia across the parking lot, but there's no way I'm going to her for safety. I'm not that stupid. I don't see anyone else close by, though. I chance a look behind my shoulder and just as I turn, my phone is snatched from my fingertips. The call is ended and my phone is tossed carelessly to the ground. "Hey!"

The man who took it grabs me by the throat and slams me against the brick wall of the school. My head slams against the hard surface and my vision blurs, a strangled cry pouring from my lips.

"This her?" Another voice asks.

A grunt. "Yeah. It's her."

The man holding my throat whirls me around, one arm bands beneath my chest, pinning my arms to my sides while the other one grips my throat. He shoves me forward. "Come on, we'll take her over here."

I try to scream but all I can muster is a wheezing sound. I spot Silvia across the lot again. Her face is trained away from me and I'm silently begging her to look my way. To see what's happening right now. But she never turns, her gaze caught on something or someone else.

I try to cry out again, shouting her name but nothing comes out. My head is pounding and I squirm against his hold but he has me in a vice-like grip. My vision clears and I can see that he's leading me further from the parking lot into a more remote area where the lights don't reach. My stomach drops.

I fight harder, kicking out with my legs, and when that doesn't work I drop my weight, but he still doesn't release me.

"Girl's got some fight in her," the second man says. I twist to see him but all I can make out is a dark shadow.

The man holding me grunts and his grip on my throat tightens to the point that I know it'll leave a bruise. Spots form in my field of vision and I claw at his fingers, desperate for air. "Just means this'll be more fun." His hot breath heats the side of my neck and I recoil. What does he mean, more fun? What are they planning to do to me?

Tears track down my cheeks, but I'm not resigned to my fate. Not yet. I try kicking again and this time I manage to hit his knee.

The man holding me curses and the hand around my throat loosens enough that I can finally suck in a deep breath.

I make it count and scream with everything in me. "Help! Somebody help me!"

The fist comes out of nowhere. A crack along my cheek that leaves me reeling.

"Dumb bitch." He releases me and I crash to the ground, my hands meeting cool grass. I choke on a sob and reach up with a shaking hand to cradle my cheek.

The men don't give me any time to recover. I'm shoved face first down in the cool, wet grass, my injured cheek pressed hard against the ground. I cry out again but it's cut off when his hand comes up to cover my mouth. "You're going to be nice and quiet if you want to leave here alive," he spits at me. The threat in his voice settles deep in my bones, freezing me in place.

"Please—"

"That's it. Beg for it."

I try to shake my head but I can't move. His weight has me pinned in place. "Please." I hiccup. "Don't do this."

He releases my throat and leans back. His legs straddle my own and his other hand shoves beneath me to release the button of my jeans. *This can't be happening.* I struggle against his hold, squirming and kicking, but he's just so much bigger than me. My struggles make little difference. Deciding I have no other choice, I scream again. "Help. Som—"

Crack!

He grabs the back of my head and slams my face into the ground. *Hard.* Pain lances through me and sheer terror rips my insides apart.

"I won't tell you again. Shut the fuck up," he growls just before tugging my jeans and underwear down, exposing my bare rear to the cold night air.

Panic tightens my throat, but I manage to say, "Why are you doing this?" in a choked-out sob. My head is throbbing and black is quickly filling my field of vision, but I fight to stay awake and aware. I can't black out. I refuse to pass out and be at their mercy.

The other man is chuckling beside us. "This is a message for dear old dad." Ice freezes in my veins. "We want to make sure he knows that when he fucks with what's ours, we'll fuck with what's his."

What? I struggle to comprehend what he's telling me, but as soon as I feel the other man press himself against my naked rear, my mind blanks.

No. No. No.

One hand pins me down, the other is beside my face as he braces himself against me. I hear the sound of a foil wrapper being torn open followed by more chuckles.

Tears prick the corners of my eyes and I struggle to breathe over the mounting pain in my chest. This isn't happening. *This isn't happening.* I repeat the words over and over again in my head but it doesn't make them true.

A sharp intrusion makes my stomach lurch. I gasp and without realizing what I'm even saying, I beg him to stop. To let me go. I promise him anything and everything I can think of if he will just let me go. He doesn't. Fighting doesn't do anything but make him rougher. He grips me tighter, his hand bruising as he grabs my hips and forces his way inside of me. The other man presses his boot to the side of my face, holding me down.

My breaths are heavy. He moves behind me, grunting like an animal and vomit threatens to rise in my throat.

Everything hurts. My vision continues to swim as I force the bile down. I lock my gaze on his hand and force my mind to think of something, anything else.

The full moon manages to illuminate his tanned skin. The calluses on the side of his thumb. He has short fingernails with a thin line of dirt beneath each of them. I focus on the scars that cover the top of his hand. On the age lines. I force myself to count every hair follicle.

Time passes. I keep counting. I keep tracing the lines on his hand, blocking out the sounds he's making. And then he stops. I sob in relief as his weight leaves me until he says, "Don't fucking move."

I don't. I keep myself planted on the ground, my breathing shallow and my cheek still mashed against the lawn of the school. I need to move. To run and escape but my limbs are locked and frozen in place. I'm drowning in the realization that I was just—

Then the second man steps closer.

No. The word echoes in my mind before a raw animalistic sound pours out of me. He straddles my hips like the man before him did and I'm already shaking my head as another sob lodges itself in my throat, but just as he reaches for me, a voice speaks out in the distance.

A man.

His voice comes closer. I can't tell what he's saying but his words get louder as he nears. "Help," I try to call out, but my words are little more than a whisper. My throat aching and scraped raw from crying.

"Shut up." The man behind me says with a growl. "Do you think he's spotted us?" He directs his questions to the other guy. I shift my head, still unable to see either of their faces. Both men are dark shadows in the night. A heavy presence I'm desperate to escape. I can't go through this again. I don't care if they kill me. I can't—

"*Help!*" This time my words are louder.

The two men curse and the one behind me shoves up from me, using my back to press himself forward. I groan from the weight of him, my spine protesting his movements. "We need to get gone," he says.

"Hey! Stop!" The newcomer shouts and the two men curse. Footsteps pound across the pavement toward me. I can't tell how far away he is but a trickle of hope spills into me. I move to push myself up when one of the men grabs my hair and jerks my head up, my scalp stinging and fresh tears forming in the corners of my eyes.

I cry out.

"Be sure to relay our message. If Ulrich fucks with one of our deals again, we'll be more than happy to make another visit," the man says before dropping me harshly back to the ground.

They run in the opposite direction just as a new man runs up alongside me. "*Dammit.*" He curses and reaches for me but I recoil from his touch. "I'm not going to hurt you. I work for the Sun Valley P.D. Everything is going to be okay." He tears off his jacket and throws it over my exposed skin before flipping open his cell phone. "I need an ambulance at Sun Valley High. Sexual assault. Yes."

I wrap his coat around myself as I struggle to lift my pants back into place. My fingers are numb and my hands shake, making it nearly impossible. When I finally pull them up I gingerly roll to my back. Dark night sky greets me.

I swallow hard and the man comes into my field of vision. His phone is still held up to his ear. He's saying something but I can't hear him. Darkness crowds my vision and this time, I welcome it.

TWENTY-SIX

Allie

Janessa storms into my hospital room with a no-nonsense air to her and for some strange reason, my shoulders relax.

She looks to the nurse who's still completing my admittance paperwork and asks, "Can we have a moment? Alone."

The nurse sends a sympathetic look my way and bobs her head before saying to me, "I'll give you and your mom a few minutes and then I'll come back and we'll get started. Okay, Allie?"

I nod, not bothering to correct her as dread courses through me. She means we'll get started with the rape kit and God, I don't even want to think about everything that involves.

I stare down at my hands, noting the bruises on my knuckles. The bloody tears on my fingernails. I suck in a shuddering breath and start counting each bruise on my hands and arms. One. Two. Three. Four....

When we're alone, Janessa pulls a chair closer to me.

Five. Six...

Taking a seat, she reaches out for my hands but I stiffen and jerk away.

She nods to herself and takes a deep breath. I keep my eyes trained on my hands. I know what she's going to say.

"Your father couldn't—"

"I know," I whisper, not needing her to finish her sentence. Gerald is in an important meeting. He can't get away. I've heard it all before. I shouldn't have expected anything different.

So why is my stomach twisted up in tight ugly knots?

I swipe a tear away from my face.

I'm his kid. You're supposed to care about your kids, right? When your daughter is attacked you're supposed to be there. Mom would have been here. She would have held my hand and smoothed my hair back. She would have told me to cry. That it was going to be okay. And she would have held me.

But none of this is going to be okay. *I* wasn't going to be okay.

Another tear escapes and I furiously swipe that one away, too. Mom isn't here so I can't cry. No one will hold me. No one will promise me that I'll make it through this. I can't break down because no one will be there to help me pick up the pieces.

Janessa releases a breath. It's a resigned sound. "I'm sorry this happened to you, Allie. So terribly sorry."

I sit there. What am I supposed to say to that? Am I supposed to comfort her because she feels bad for me? Am I supposed to say I'm sorry it happened, too? Should I tell her how angry I am with myself for being there in the first place? That I'd known better. That I shouldn't have—

She interrupts my train of thought with a question. "Do you know who did this to you?"

I shake my head as bitter acid coats my tongue. Isn't that the kicker. That bastard did this to me and I don't even know who he is. He didn't know me. We'd never met before but he still did this.

"Did you see his face?"

"No," I choke out with a hard shake of my head. I ignore the spinning sensation that hits me with the movement and bite back the bile in my throat. The nurses think I have a concussion. He gave me a concussion when he slammed my head against the brick wall of the school. And that's the least of it all.

"Do you remember anything that might identify him in a lineup?"

I hang my head again. All I remember is his voice. His words. The feel of his body against mine. The pain of him inside of me. And his hand. I remember his hand. I stared at it while he ... no. I don't want to relive it. I don't want to remember.

I shove the memories as far down as they'll go and tuck them away with the emotions I refuse to let free right now.

I shake my head.

"Have they done a rape kit, yet?"

I swallow hard and whisper out another, "No."

She nods to herself. "Do you know if he used a condom?"

My brows pinch together. Why does she want to know that? My mind goes back to that moment. To him pushing me down and ripping my pants off of me. I was turned away from him. He shoved my face down on the ground. Pressed my cheek in the dirt. But I remember the sound of a foil packet. I heard the distinct sound of him tear something open behind me before forcing himself—

My breaths come out as shallow pants and suddenly Janessa is right in my face.

"Allie. Allie." She snaps her fingers in front of me.

I can't breathe. I claw at my own throat, desperate for air.

Janessa grabs the back of my neck and forces my head between my legs.

I cry out at the sudden movement but don't fight her. I can't. I still can't breathe.

"Breathe, honey. Just breathe." Her grip tightens on my neck and inside I'm screaming for her to let go. Not to touch me. But I can't get the words out. Seconds tick by. Then minutes.

When my breathing finally slows down she lets go and steps back.

"It was just a panic attack," she says as I lift my head back up.

My vision blurs for a moment but then she comes back into focus.

"Take another breath."

I do as she tells me and when I no longer feel like my lungs are going to collapse in on me, I mutter out the answer to her last question.

"I... I think he did. I think he used one."

"Good. That's good."

She pulls out her phone and her fingers frantically type across her keyboard before she puts it back in her purse.

Then she leans down and lifts a small bag from the ground that I hadn't noticed when she first walked in. "Here. I brought you some clothes. Let's get you dressed and I'll take you home."

I nod, accepting the bag but then I stop. "What about the...?" I make a small wave with my hands unable to say the words aloud. Tears prick the corners of my eyes again as I brace myself for what I know will be another form of violation and shame blooms in my chest.

I can't do it. I just can't.

They're going to look at me and touch me. I've seen the movies. There will be pictures. Doctors will see me without my clothes. I'll be exposed. I can't I just. I can't.

Janessa takes a step closer and saves me from my panic. "We don't need to worry about that today."

I give her a tear-filled, half-hearted smile. "We don't?"

She shakes her head. "No, sweetheart. We don't."

Relief sweeps through me before reality sets in. "But...if we don't, how will they find him? How will..." I trail off. Because they have to find him, right? He can't get away with this. He'll do it again. What if he finds me again? He said he would come back if...

She places a tentative hand on my arm and I stiffen and jerk away from her.

There's an apology in her gaze as she asks, "Allie, were you drinking this evening?"

I swallow past the lump in my throat and answer honestly with a nod. "But I wasn't drunk. I didn't even have one whole drink." I remember that Kasey snuck mini liquor bottles into the game. She'd given me one. I only took a sip. Drank maybe half of it before I got the call from Julio. "I—"

"I know, honey. I know. But you *were* drinking and you're a minor. You don't know who did this and since you think he used a condom, there won't be any semen to use to find him, if he is even in the system."

I stare at her. Stunned. Is she... no. *No.*

"You're a young girl. You're beautiful and smart and you have your whole life ahead of you. But this, this could ruin you. This could ruin your father."

My father. That's what this was really about.

"If Ulrich interferes in our deals again, I'll be happy to make another visit..."

Cold dread consumes me. He's going to stay out there. He's going to get away with this. Because of Gerald. Because of my dad.

No. No. *No.* That's not right. He'll find me. If Gerald messes up again. I don't even know what he did. Why the man came after me. But I do know deep down in the marrow of my bones that he'll do it again and I have no way of knowing. No way of protecting myself because I don't even know what he looks like.

I shake my head. No. *No!* I can't breathe.

Janessa cups my cheeks as tears fall freely down my face now. "Allie. If we do a rape kit this goes on record. There's no taking it back. You'll be questioned. You'll be blamed. It's not right. This wasn't your fault. None of it was your fault. You need to believe that." Her eyes glass over and I want to shove away from her because how dare she look at me like that. I was the one raped. I was the one who had something taken away from them. Me. Not her. She has no right to act like this hurts her. It only hurts me.

"I know you're dealing with a lot. I know this is a lot to take in, but I need you to see how this looks on paper. You were drinking while underage. You were dressed provocatively." I think back to what I'd been wearing. The ripped jeans and crop top hadn't seemed provocative at the time. It was our big rival game. Everyone dressed up. My stomach had been painted with a red devil and a number 4. It was Roman's number. So many other students had done something similar. But ... was she right? It was a lot of skin, wasn't it? My entire midriff had been showing.

Oh God.

"Honey, even if they find this guy, if they press charges, his lawyer is going to drag you through the mud. They'll tarnish your name. Your reputation. And this trauma will consume your life for six months or more. You'll have to tell a courtroom full of people what happened. Every single detail over and over. The defending attorney will twist your words and turn the blame on you. They'll make you relive what happened in the hopes that you slip up. That you make a mistake in your story."

She thumbs my tears away and I bite back a scream as I digest her words because she's right. I know she's right. But it feels wrong. He shouldn't be free. He shouldn't get away with this.

"They won't find enough evidence to find who did this. If he didn't use a condom, if they had his...his fluids, it still might not be enough evidence to convict. I don't want that for you."

I shudder and turn away from her. I choke back my sobs and straighten my spine, letting everything she says sink in and settle deep in my bones. *Come on, Allie. Be strong. Don't fold now. You've been through too much. You cannot fold now.*

"He did this because of my dad," I tell her, because I have to tell someone. Her eyes widen in shock but I don't give her a chance to respond. "When he..." I pause before forcing the word out. "After he *raped* me, he told me why. He said Dad fucked up some deal of his." Another deep shudder as I repeat the message he gave me. She gasps in response.

Then I push the next words out of my mouth uncaring of how broken and bitter I sound. I'm allowed to feel bitter.

"But you're still right. It doesn't matter because he was smart and I didn't see him. I was raped because of my own father—because of my father's *business*—and it doesn't even matter."

Silence.

I reach for the bag again and move toward the attached bathroom to get dressed. When I brush past her I barely make out her words but they're there, hanging in the air between us. "I'm so sorry, Allie."

Yeah. I was too. But sorry wasn't going to change a damn thing.

I catch my reflection in the mirror before jerking away as I strip down, trying to bottle up all my emotions. The urge to shower is strong. I want any traces of him scrubbed off my skin. When I first got here the nurse told me I had to wait. How important it was that I not shower or even wash my hands until they have a chance to gather their *evidence*. But that doesn't matter anymore. I turn on the sink, waiting until steam rises from the faucet. I pump a large amount of hand soap into my hands and begin washing. I get lost in the motions, making sure I scrub my hands up to my forearms until my skin is coated in a white foaming lather. The water is scalding when I shove my hands beneath it but I don't care. I force myself to rinse the soap off leaving my hands and forearms beneath the spray until they're pink and angry. I've endured worse.

If I could shower in the sink I would but that will have to wait until I get to Gerald's.

When I come back into the room, Janessa and one of the nurses are facing off against one another. They turn to me and I stop.

"Allie. I was trying to explain to your—" the nurse begins.

"She is a minor and the decision has been made. We're leaving."

I bow my head. I don't have it in me to argue with anyone. Let them figure it out.

I slip my feet into my shoes and hear the distinct buzz of a cell phone as Janessa uses her *take no prisoners* tone with the nurse.

I don't bother listening to their conversation. I know how this will go and I'm already resigned to my fate.

I locate my phone on the bedside table, grateful it was recovered at the scene, and unlocked the screen.

Four missed messages.

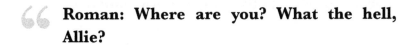 **Roman: Where are you? What the hell, Allie?**

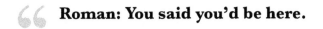 **Roman: You said you'd be here.**

> **Roman: After everything that's happened will you at least let me know if you're okay?**

> **Roman: Tracked down Kasey. She said you bailed for some phone call. Where are you?**

I GLANCE AT THE TIME. IT'S JUST AFTER TEN. THE GAME would have ended almost an hour ago. He would have come out of the locker rooms, expecting to find me waiting for him, but I wasn't there. How long had he waited for me?

My fingers shake over the keyboard. What do I say? I can't tell him where I am. What happened. I can't tell anyone. But I don't want to lie to him, either.

Another text flashes across my screen.

> **Emilio: Way to fucking support our boy.**

THEN ANOTHER

Roman: You know what, whatever. You do you.

A FRESH WAVE OF TEARS CASCADES DOWN MY CHEEKS. I CAN'T stop them. I swipe them away but they just keep coming.

Janessa calls my name and I turn to her, shoving my phone into the pocket of the pants she brought for me, then I follow her to the door. On my way out, the nurse hands me a small pill and a glass of water. I don't ask what it's for. I know.

I place the pill in my mouth and take a drink, swallowing it down before handing the cup back to the nurse who nods like I've done something good, but she's still not happy.

Janessa watches the exchange with a tight-lipped frown but she doesn't say anything.

A pair of police officers and a man that must be their boss meet us halfway down the hallway. I don't recognize the officers but the man with them, he's the one who found me. I remember that. He's wearing a uniform like the others. It's similar to the boys in blue but there are more pins on it. More stars on the shoulders. He has an air of authority the other two don't have.

I want to thank him. He helped me. But I can't make the words form. All I can do is stare at his hands. They're rough and tan and—

I take several steps back.

Janessa turns her head to look at me but all I can see are his hands.

They're not the same, Allie. They're not the same.

I know that. My mind knows that. But my heart is racing out of my chest because they're not the same but they're similar and I can't stop looking at them. He takes a step in my direction and my muscles lock up.

My head snaps back to look him in the face and he freezes.

"Miss?" His hands are lifted as if in surrender and I can see the worry in his gaze. He takes another careful step closer and my chest heaves. He's approaching me like I'm some rabid animal. I need ... I need ...

Janessa takes two steps to her left and suddenly she's blocking him from my view. She says something but I don't hear it. I can't hear anything over the roaring in my ears.

His hands aren't the same. I tell myself again and again like a mantra that will somehow make this all better. I try to think of something else. Anything else. But then my mind latches onto Roman and how mad he must be with me right now. How disappointed all of them are. I promised I'd be there. They'd wanted me to be there. And then I wasn't.

Janessa tugs on my sleeve and I glance up, she guides me around the officers and I don't miss their pity as she ushers me outside the hospital doors. I don't want their pity.

When we're outside I slowly start locking myself down. I will my mind to go numb. To block out everything I'm feeling. To forget everything that happened. I just want to forget it all.

TWENTY-SEVEN

Allie

I wake with a start. My chest heaves and my eyes pop open. Daylight filters in through my bedroom curtains, letting me know it's morning. Or maybe afternoon. It doesn't matter.

I stare up at the ceiling, willing myself to go back to sleep. I don't want to be awake. It hurts too much.

There's a knock at my door.

I ignore it.

Another knock.

I roll to my side just as the door opens. "Allie," Janessa calls.

I squeeze my eyes shut hoping she'll think I'm asleep and leave me alone.

She doesn't.

I hear her steps fall across the carpet as she comes closer. My bed dips under her weight as she sits on the corner. I stiffen when she reaches out and touches my leg. "Allie, you need to eat something. Why don't you come downstairs? Your father ordered breakfast. It'll be good for you to get out of bed."

I say nothing.

She tries another tactic. "Some friends of yours from school have stopped by."

They have? A part of me wants to know who. Wants to know if it was Roman. If he's still angry with me? He hasn't messaged me since that night and I miss him but ... every time a man has come close to me I've panicked. Gerald tried speaking to me once. I freaked out. I curled into a ball like a child and sobbed. I still don't know why. It just happened and I couldn't stop it.

He hired a doctor to come look at me. That didn't go well either. For the past three days the only person that I've allowed in my room has been Janessa. I don't like it when she's close, and I really don't like it when she touches me, but at least her presence doesn't send me into a mindless panic. It's enough.

So, while I might want to see Roman, I don't want him to see me like this. I don't want to risk losing myself again. With him. But curiosity burns through me so I open my eyes and ask, "Who?"

She shifts her weight. "A few boys. Two Latinos and a black guy. They said they were your friends?"

I nod.

"What did you tell them?"

"That you weren't seeing visitors right now."

I swallow. "Anything else?"

She's quiet for a moment and I hold my breath. "I didn't tell them what happened but ... one of the boys got angry when I refused to let him in. He started shouting. I might have yelled at him. Told him you didn't want to see anyone. Even him." She grips my leg in apology. "He didn't seem happy. I'm sorry, sweetheart. I just didn't know how else to make him leave."

I blink back the moisture in my eyes. "It's okay."

She sighs and stands to leave. "Will you at least think about coming down to eat?"

I nod, knowing I won't. I haven't left my bed since that night to do anything more than use the bathroom or shower. Something I've been doing at least three times a day. Sometimes more. I can't seem to get the feel of his hands off of me. The smell of his skin.

Janessa starts to say something else but I can't listen to her anymore. I'm losing myself to my memories. I want her to go away. I need to go back to sleep. It's the only place I feel safe anymore. Childishly I cover my ears. "Please," I whisper. "Go away."

TIME PASSES FROM ONE DAY TO THE NEXT, EVEN WHEN IT feels impossible. Even when it seems like I'm losing myself with each passing hour. Each passing minute. I don't understand how the sun manages to rise each day when I can barely open my eyes to greet it.

I lose count of how many days go by.

Some days Janessa comes to try and get me to come downstairs. Some days she doesn't. I manage to drink the bottled water she brings me. On occasion the tea. But I rarely touch the food. The few times I've tried have resulted in me bent over my toilet heaving whatever I consumed right back out. My body doesn't feel like it's mine anymore. I know this isn't normal. I know I need help. But I can't find the energy or want to ask for it. I'm numb and I'm afraid to be anything else but numb.

Roman doesn't message me. Neither does Emilio. Dominique reached out once asking me if something happened. If I was okay. But I didn't respond. What could I say?

I wake to the sound of heated voices in the hallway outside my bedroom door. Rubbing the sleep from my eyes I try and muster interest in what they're saying. I stare at the closed door, pulling my covers tighter around myself as if that's enough to keep me warm. But it's not. All I feel is a bone-aching chill. It never leaves.

"She needs more time."

"She doesn't need time. There's nothing wrong with her and she's done nothing but sleep. It's been nearly a week—"

"What else would you have her do? The girl is traumatized."

"She needs to get over it."

I don't hear what they say next. I look at the clock on my bedside table. It's just after seven in the morning.

I take a deep breath.

I'm okay.

I will get through this.

You're strong, Allie. You're strong like Mom.

I take another deep, shuddering breath and force back a fresh wave of tears. *Why am I crying?*

"You're strong like Mom," I whisper to myself. I wipe my tears away and make myself get out of bed. I'm numb. I can be numb and move. I can be numb and do things. Go places. Right? Maybe.

Mom died. My boyfriend cheated. My boyfriend dumped me. My best girlfriend turned her back on me. I lost my home. I had to go to a new school in a new town. My dad never has time for me. I was ra...

I force myself to finish the thought.

I was *raped.*

I'd been through so much in such a short amount of time. But it was done. Over. Finished. All of it had already happened. I'd push forward. *One day at a time, Allie. You can do this.*

Numb. So fucking numb.

Janessa's voice rises again. There's mention of a therapist.

I don't know what Gerald says in response but I can tell by Janessa's tone that she doesn't agree.

That's okay.

I'm okay.

Or at least, I will be. Time heals all wounds, right? That's what all the inspirational quotes and memes on social media say.

The day I arrived in Sun Valley I told myself all I needed to do was survive this year, graduate, and then I could go home.

That is still the plan. I can go home. Things will be better once I'm back in Richland. There won't be a school full of people who hate me. There won't be bad men lurking around corners, hurting me to get to my dad. I will be safe. I just have to survive here a little bit longer.

Letting that resolve settle inside of me, I shower. The hot water scalds my skin, but it's still not enough to warm the bone-deep chill. I scrub at my arms and legs, wishing I could clean myself, but I've already learned it doesn't matter how many times I wash my body, I still feel dirty. I can't get the smell or feel of him off me.

I spend thirty minutes in the shower before giving up and drying off. I put on a pair of jeans and a long-sleeved purple top, careful to cover every inch of skin I can reasonably manage and add a silk scarf to cover the bruising on my neck for good measure.

Leaving my hair down, I blow it dry and add a heavy layer of concealer along my jaw, my right cheek, and beneath my bottom lip. It's not enough, so I add a layer of foundation on top and then another layer of concealer on top of that. It covers the bruises but I can't do much to conceal the swelling. With some lip liner and gloss, it should be less noticeable. I hope.

Even with a full face of makeup, my skin is still a little discolored but if I keep my head down like I usually do I should be fine. No one will give me a second glance.

There's a knock on my door and before I can answer, it swings open.

Janessa walks in to find me sitting on the floor in front of the full-length mirror in my room.

"You're ready?" she asks, sounding surprised.

"Yeah." I stand and reach for my backpack. My eyes lock on my hands and I freeze, staring at them as though for the first time. My knuckles are bruised. My nail beds torn and cracked with dried blood.

Makeup can't cover that. I frown. I'll have to keep my hands in my pockets if I want to avoid any questions. Dread wells up inside of me. I can't handle any questions.

I grab a zip-up hoodie from my closet. One of the pieces I picked up with Aaron during our Target run.

Janessa frowns when she sees the black garment and then steps over to my closet. She flicks through the clothes hanging there and pulls out a soft white sweater with pale pink sleeves.

Turning, she hands it to me, gently taking the hoodie and placing it back inside my closet. "This goes with what you're wearing," she tells me.

I want to scream.

But I don't.

Screaming doesn't do anything. It doesn't help. I know that, so I nod and slip my arms into the sweater, feeling another piece of myself die inside. Why does the sweater matter so much?

When we step outside to head to school, an unfamiliar car sits in the driveway.

Dominique stands there, leaning against the hood of his black Escalade, arms folded over his chest.

I freeze.

"Allie," he calls out and tilts his head back to his car. "I'm giving you a lift. Come on."

My heart rate picks up and my eyes turn to Janessa, pleading with her to say something. Anything.

I can't go with him. My breathing becomes erratic. *I can't.*

Understanding washes over her face. She gives me a barely perceptible nod and turns to him. "I'm sorry, young man, but you need to leave."

Dom smirks. "I'll get right on that. As soon as Allie gets in the car." He flashes her a dazzling smile. "I'm a friend from school. I've given her rides before. She's plenty safe with me, ma'am."

Janessa flicks a look to me as if to ask, *what now?*

But how the heck should I know. I have no idea what to do in this situation. I wasn't prepared to face him. I had an entire pep talk ready to give myself on the drive to school today. Before I saw him. Before I saw anyone. My hands are clammy and a cold sweat drips down my spine.

My heart hammers in my chest. Faster. Harder. My breaths quicken and I know a panic attack lingers right there on the edge. I can't let him see me like this. My temples pound, a headache now coming on strong, beating inside me like a battering ram.

"Allie?" she whispers.

I can't. I can't.

I know Dom is safe. He's my friend. He's safe. I know that. But the idea of being in a car with him right now is sending my mind into a spiral. I can't.

I turn and rush back inside the house, ignoring both of them as they call out for me.

I can't.

I'm not ready.

I just can't.

TWENTY-EIGHT

Allie

More time passes. I don't know what I was thinking trying to go to school. I was an idiot.

It's been three days since. Maybe four. I don't know for certain and I try not to care. There's a knock at the door and I sigh, but when I roll over to tell Janessa to go away, my breath freezes in my lungs.

Julio steps inside, Janessa right behind him. "Allie," she hedges.

I swallow hard and push up into a sitting position, clutching my blankets tight to my chest. "What are you doing here?" I whisper, my eyes zeroed in on Julio as he stands just inside my room.

His dark brown eyes soften and he takes a step toward me. I lock up with that one small movement. He stops and turns to Janessa, a question in his gaze.

"She has a hard time with men right now."

He nods. Taking a step back, he leans against the wall before sliding down to the floor and folding his hands in his lap. "Hey," he tries again.

I shift in my bed, putting a few more inches between us. "Hi."

Janessa hovers in the doorway. "Do you want me to stay?" she asks.

I take a deep breath. Exhale. Then take another one and shake my head. "I... no. I'm okay."

She nods but doesn't look convinced.

"I'll stay right here for however long she needs," he tells her. "I won't push."

"I'll be right downstairs if you need me," she tells me and then pulls the door shut behind her.

Julio and I stare at one another for several seconds before he finally breaks the silence. "Are you okay?"

That one question has my eyes brimming with tears. I look away and swipe at my cheeks.

"Fuck, Allie." Julio hangs his head, his chest rising and falling with heavy breaths. "I..." He looks at me, his eyes stark and raw with pain. "I don't know what to say. How to fix this."

I choke on a laugh. "She told you?"

He nods. "I tried calling you a few times but your phone kept going to voicemail. Then this chick calls me out of nowhere asking if I'd be willing to come here for a few days. See if I can help." He shrugs. "Allie, when she told me what happened to you. What you went through..."

My eyes sting and shame blossoms in my chest. Pressing my lips into a tight line I look down at the covers clenched between my fingertips. He must think I'm so weak. So dirty.

"Hey."

I don't look up.

"Hey!"

I shake my head. I don't want to see the pity or disgust I know must be in his gaze. If Julio looks at me differently... I can't handle this anymore.

"Allie. Babe. I love you. You are my best friend. Let me be here for you."

A tear slips down my cheek and I furiously swipe it away. "You shouldn't be here," I tell him.

"Alejandra. Por favor. Déjame ayudarte." *Please. Let me help you.*

I want help. I do. But—

"How?" I choke on the word. "How can you help me? Julio, I feel like I'm dying inside and I wish I was dying on the outside, too. I don't want to be here. I don't want to feel this. Anything. *I can't.* I can't do this anymore. I just—"

He pushes from the ground, but stays by the door. A sob mixed with a whimper passes through my lips. He freezes. Hands clenched into fists at his sides, his eyes plead with me but I don't know what he wants.

A tick forms along his jaw and he scrubs a hand over his face leaving behind a weary expression. "I want to hold you. Can we... do you think we can try?"

I have no freaking idea. Closing my eyes, I slow my breathing while my mind races, rationalizing his request. The only person who's touched me is Janessa. But Julio is my friend. I trust him. I know him. I ...

"Can I see your hands," I ask.

He frowns, confused but raises them palms out to face me. I shake my head. "Turn them around."

He does without question. I take in the backs of his hands already knowing what I'll find. Both hands are inked, one sporting a large skull with red roses on either side. The other is tattooed with a strand of rosary beads and a cross resting between his thumb and index finger.

I focus on the ink, tracing the lines of the designs with my gaze. I force myself to recognize the differences between his hands and those of my attacker. Beyond the ink I take in the gold band he wears on his right middle finger. His clean, short nail beds.

My breathing slows and my shoulders relax. Julio is patient with me, letting my eyes drink their fill. Several minutes pass before I feel confident enough to let him step closer.

With exaggerated slowness, he walks to the edge of my bed. When he reaches it, he inclines his head, asking if it's okay to sit. I nod.

Beside me now, we both wait. When I don't have a panic attack, he shifts closer, leaning beside me against the headboard.

I swipe at my eyes and hold myself perfectly still as he slowly and carefully places one arm around my shoulders. Neither of us moves. My deep, deliberate breaths are loud in the quiet room, but he doesn't seem to mind. We sit there and as the minutes pass, I slowly shift until I'm turned toward him, my ear pressed against his chest over the sound of his beating heart. His grip around me tightens and I manage to breathe through it.

One hand comes up to mindlessly stroke my hair. "I'm so fucking sorry, Allie," he says.

I nod against his chest. "Me, too," I whisper, almost afraid to break the silence in the room. "But I'm really happy you're here."

"And I'm not going anywhere. I'll stay as long as you need me."

I SPEND THE MORNING WITH JULIO AND FOR THE FIRST TIME since the attack, I feel like I can breathe again. He tells me he's staying all week. Longer, if I need it. He already got it cleared with his parents and teachers and he's staying in the guest room in the pool house. There are plenty of empty rooms in the main house for him to stay in, but he seems content to stay in the pool house, so I don't question it. It's probably Gerald being Gerald. I'm surprised he allowed Julio to visit in the first place, so I'm not about to say anything that might jeopardize that.

I'm happy Julio's here. I missed him. I hadn't realized how much until he arrived.

Julio fills me in on the particulars of his stay. He'll be going to school with me. I don't know how but Janessa got him cleared as a visiting student. I guess the plan is for him to attend all my classes with me for the first week so I won't have to face it alone.

I still don't know if going back to school is a good idea. But when I broached the subject of getting my GED, Janessa shot it down and said it wasn't even worth trying to bring up to my father. Anything less than a diploma meant I couldn't get accepted into an Ivy League school—not that I'd personally applied to any—but Janessa seems to be under the impression that I'll be attending one. The idea of college right now seems so out there that it's not worth thinking about. I'd always planned on doing two years of community college first. It's all I can reasonably afford but I don't tell her that. Right now, I just want to focus on today. Maybe tomorrow. Anything past that is too much.

The following morning when my alarm goes off, I force myself to get out of bed. The heaviness in my chest I've had since the attack is lighter. It's still there, but today, it feels bearable.

I've had enough time to wallow in my own misery. More time than I ever gave myself after Mom died. It'll have to be enough. I need to graduate. Missing so much school is going to make that hard enough as it is, and I refuse to let the men who did this to me take anything else.

After spending all day yesterday with Julio, I've convinced myself I'll be okay.

We didn't talk about the assault. He knows what happened and I don't have any desire to relive the memories just so he can hear the story from my own mouth. Thankfully, he never pushes me. Not that I expected him too. Julio is the strong silent type. He's the mountain that refuses to move no matter how hard the wind blows. Growing up, he was my rock. The big brother I never had. He gets me. He gets what I need.

And being held, knowing that I was safe in his arms, that the world couldn't hurt me as long as he was there, gave me the reprieve I needed to pull myself together.

We spent most of the day watching Netflix and eating junk food. Well, he did at least.

I still haven't been eating, but I did pick at some of the popcorn for his benefit.

I know Julio noticed. But he didn't say anything and I'm grateful for it. My ribs stand out in sharp relief beneath my chest. I can count each one while in the shower. It's not healthy but I don't know how to make myself want to eat. Sometimes even the scent of food gets to me and sends me running for the bathroom.

When I go downstairs in the morning, I expect to find Janessa waiting to take us to school, but instead, she hands me a set of keys and gives me a small smile.

"Your father pulled this from the garage for you at my suggestion." She tilts her head to the set of keys. "This way, if you need to leave, to get away, you can."

I stare at the keys in my hand. Tears form in the corners of my eyes and I swipe them away. I keep crying. I'm always crying. I hate it, but I never thought I'd be so relieved to have access to a car. Before all of this, I would have refused it. I didn't want Gerald's money. I didn't need it and I like earning my own way in life. It's why I'd been applying for jobs in the first place. But I couldn't afford a car on my own right now. Not even a beater. And this, this would give me an escape.

"Thank you."

Her smile widens just a bit. "If you ever want to talk…"

Julio comes in the back door. "Hey." He lifts a hand in greeting and walks toward me.

My stomach tightens as he approaches but I do what I did yesterday every time my body reacted to his proximity. I look at his hands and the anxiety subsides. Then to Janessa I say, "Thanks. But I'm good."

She nods. Hands me a to-go cup of coffee and Julio and I both head outside.

I find a silver Audi RS 5 in the driveway. I push a button on the key fob, somewhat surprised when the Audi chirps back. He's letting me drive an RS? Why can't he be like normal dads and just get me a Jetta? Preferably a used one.

"Damn," Julio draws out. "This is sick."

I roll my eyes. "Yeah, yeah. You can drool over the interior. Come on or we're going to be late."

TWENTY-NINE

Roman

Emilio sidles up beside me. "She's back," he mutters under his breath. My jaw tightens and all our heads turn to see her step out of a silver car a few rows down from us.

"Is that a..." Emilio starts.

"Brand new Audi RS 5? Yeah. It is," Dom answers and a quick look his way shows he's not all that happy to see her, either.

Guess she's still living the good life or maybe now she's just happier to embrace it. She's dressed in that rich preppy shit she wore the first week of school.

I guess we're back to that again, too.

I shrug my shoulders and catch Emilio and Dom's gazes. "Doesn't matter what she's driving. She's here. I want some fucking answers." That chick that works for her dad blew us off when we showed up, but I'm not buying the whole Allie-doesn't-want-to-see-me crap. Something else has to be going on. I tried waiting around for Allie to leave the house, hoping to catch her and corner her into talking to me, but she never fucking left her house. Not once. Not that I ever saw, at least. And I was there, every fucking day for eight days straight. I went full-fledge stalker and don't even care.

I push off from the hood of my ride, intent on speaking with her, but then I catch sight of a guy getting out of the passenger seat of the same vehicle.

"What the fuck?" Emilio says beside me. He scratches the back of his head. "This is new."

"Yeah," I bite out. "It is."

I watch as he moves around the car until he's right beside her. He reaches a hand out to her. It's tentative, like he's unsure if she'll accept his touch and for a second my heart races in my chest. She's going to brush him off. I know she is. If this were a thing, if he was competition, he wouldn't look so hesitant to touch her. I grin. The fucker has no idea what he's trying to get in between.

Allie's mine. She has a lot to answer for and I'm pissed as hell with her, but she's still mine.

I take another step toward them and my boys follow suit. But then she smiles up at the guy and accepts his hand. She threads her fingers with his and the two of them turn their backs on us and head to the school's front entrance.

I stop in my tracks, my eyes glued to their hands. Their fucking entwined fingers like this is middle school or some shit.

What. The. Fuck.

Dominique puts a hand on my shoulder and squeezes. "You alright, bro?"

"I'm fine."

Emilio swears beside me. "Who the fuck is that dude?"

I grind my teeth.

"We still need answers," Dom says beside me. "You guys didn't see her last week. Something happened."

"I don't fucking care. Ice her out." Anger bubbles up inside me. "I don't have time for petty bitches and their games. That's not how we roll." Both of them nod their agreement, but Emilio looks hesitant.

"There's gotta be an explanation," he hedges. I glare at him and he puts his arms up, palms out in surrender. "Whatever you say, man. We'll ice her out."

I nod. She ghosted us. Ghosted me. And for what? This guy? I don't know him. Don't even recognize his face. Not once have I ever seen him near her before. But she blew me off for *that* guy. She made me look like a fool. And now, hand in hand, she's making sure the entire school knows she's dropped me.

She didn't even have the decency to call. My pops showed up to the game. He never comes to my games. He never has the time. But he came to our rival game against the Saints and I had it all planned out. He was going to meet my girl. I told my fucking parents about her. My mom knew Allie was supposed to be there and she no-showed. Fucking no-showed. No call. No text. Nothing.

A tick forms in my jaw and I glare at her retreating form. As if she can sense my attention her head swivels to look over her shoulder and her eyes lock on mine. Pools of chocolate brown meet my stare head-on and she flinches.

I hope she sees just how pissed off I am. How done I am with her.

The guy beside her slows his steps. I watch as she untangles her hand from his and he frowns at her. She says something to him. She's shaking her head and glancing over at me again. He says something back and they argue for a moment before a decision is made.

She turns around and heads in my direction—the new guy hot on her heels. She chews on her bottom lip, worry lines deepening with every step she takes. Good. She should be worried. If she's expecting a warm welcome, she won't find it.

The guy has a blank expression. I can't get a read on him but he stays close to Allie. Almost like he wants to protect her. His hands are tatted and he has two diamond studs in his ears. He's dressed in dark denim jeans and a black hoodie with the words Richland printed on the back. Then it clicks. This dude is from her hometown. Is he the ex? The ex that doesn't look like he's an ex anymore?

They're almost to us when Dom asks, "What's the plan?"

I shake my head. I don't know. She's coming over to us but she's with him. They clearly have some sort of relationship with each other and I have no fucking clue what's going on. Was I some side piece of hers? She said in the beginning, she didn't want anything serious. We didn't use labels. I never called her my girlfriend, but fuck, she was my girl. She'd been *my girl*.

None of it matters now. "Stick to the plan. Ice her out. I'm done."

They nod and we each grab our bags, heading straight toward them. Allie's steps falter and her skin pales, highlighting the sharp angles of her cheekbones. Has she lost more weight?

When we're right in front of them she says, "Ro?" My name on her lips is whisper-soft and it does something to me, twisting my insides around, but I don't respond. I don't react. Instead, I push right between her and her new guy and head straight to the doors. My steps never slow.

She gasps before saying a little bit louder, "Roman?"

I keep going. Then the asshole with her calls out, "Bro, what's your problem?"

I whirl on him. Dropping my backpack on the pavement, I close the distance between us and get right in his face. He holds his ground and fury flashes in his eyes.

Allie sucks in a breath and takes several steps back. She's as white as a sheet but I can't find it in me to fucking care.

"I don't know who the fuck you think you are, but this is my school. My town. Don't talk to me again. Ever. We clear."

He doesn't answer, meanwhile Allie's all but hyperventilating beside us as she watches the exchange.

Slowly, so fucking slow, I turn my head to glare at her. "The same goes for you. Don't speak to me. We're not friends. We're not anything. I don't fraternize with whores." She jerks back as if I've slapped her and the next thing I know a fist smashes into my face and I stumble back a few steps. Dom and Emilio rush up beside me and I shake my head, blinking hard to clear my vision as it meets the angry glare of the guy she came with.

His nostrils flare and his hands clench into tight fists at his sides as though he's barely keeping himself from hitting me again.

I spit and my blood smacks the pavement. "You're gonna regret that."

"Don't call her that again. Are we clear?" His tone is hard, his eyes murderous.

I can't help it. I laugh. "Whatever you say, *cabrón*. Just know she was underneath me two weeks ago. Who knows how many guys she's had since?"

"You worthless *sonovabitch*. Do you have any idea what she's—"

"Julio, don't!" she cries out and we both turn to see her tear-filled gaze. "Please. Don't."

Guilt tears into me at the sight of those tears before I push it away. No way am I going to feel sorry for her. She's got *Julio* now. That's this fucker's name. So not the ex.

His eyes soften as they drink her in and he moves toward her. He cups the back of her neck and draws her face toward his chest. She goes willingly, wrapping her arms round his waist and fuck, it's like a punch to the gut. Seeing that, seeing her in his arms hurts more than that fucker's punch to my face ever could.

I don't say anything. I have no fucking words. I turn around and head back to the entrance, refusing to look back.

"Watch your back," Dom warns him before moving in step beside me.

"What the hell was that?" Emilio mutters when we're out of hearing distance from the happy couple.

I don't answer him.

When Silvia Parish walks past me, rather than ignoring her like I usually would, I call her over. Her eyes are hesitant, but they brighten when I give her a smile. She slows her steps, waiting for me.

"Hey, Ro," she purrs.

I see the confusion in my boys' gazes but I ignore them. "Ready to be out of the dog house?" I ask her.

She pouts. "That was really mean of you."

"Yeah. Well, maybe later I'll make it up to you. What do you say?"

Lust darkens her eyes and she nods her head in agreement. "Mmmmm. I'd love to." She settles in beside me. "Are you and the little do-gooder over?"

I shake my head, then look down at her and give her a devilish grin. "Nothing to be over," I tell her. "Shit never even started."

THIRTY

Allie

I f Julio wasn't with me, I wouldn't have survived today. He follows me to all my classes. A few girls give him interested looks but he ignores them, his full attention on me.

Roman is a no-show first period. A part of me wonders if he's off screwing Silvia in the locker rooms or something. I know he's mad but he didn't need to say what he did.

I want to talk to him, to explain why I didn't call or text. I know if he knew my reasons, if he knew everything that happened, he'd understand. At least, I hope he would. But I can't convince myself to expose myself like that to him. His words cut deep. He wanted to hurt me and he did. What if he doesn't understand? What if telling him what happened only confirms what I am in his eyes? A whore.

Julio tries to comfort me throughout the day. Every time I catch sight of Roman, Dominique, or Emilio, he distracts me with a question or a dumb joke. Sometimes it works. But most of the time, it doesn't.

"Hey," he tilts my chin up, forcing me to meet his gaze. "You don't need them. Seven more months and you're coming home with me."

I nod. I'll be eighteen in four months. Graduate in seven. It feels like forever and a day away but in reality, it's not that far. Falling out like this with the Devils hurts, but maybe it was for the best.

We eat lunch in the library without incident. Well, Julio does at least. I manage two bites of pizza before throwing my tray away, unable to stomach the food any better than I have been at Gerald's.

Spanish goes by without a hitch. When I get to Welding, Julio draws a little more attention than he had in my previous classes, but this time, since it's a class full of guys, Julio doesn't ignore them.

"This the new beau?" Aaron asks, a smile on his face. It's a forced smile but it's a smile nonetheless. I stiffen as he nears but Julio positions himself between us, easing some of the tension before he answers Aaron for me.

"Nah, man. Allie's like my little sister. I'm a friend from back home." He reaches out a hand and Aaron shakes it. His smile morphs to one that's more genuine as he gives Julio a once-over.

"Sister, huh? You two could have fooled me. All the hand holding, the looks..." He trails off and I know there's a question in there, but he doesn't come out and ask it.

Julio and I have been affectionate since he arrived. I'm not entirely sure why. Back home, we never really held hands, but we've cuddled watching movies together and neither of us have ever shied away from physical contact. But it's always been platonic. Saying I'm like a sister is one hundred percent accurate. I don't have any biological siblings but if I did, I imagine my relationship with them would be like what I have with Julio. Easy. Comfortable. And with zero romantic feelings for the other person.

"I've known J since grade school." I shrug. "I don't think either of us realized how people might take things."

Julio snorts beside me. "We also don't care."

Aaron seems to mull that over. "So... how's Roman handling this? I saw him earlier with—" He cuts himself off and looks away. Rubbing his hand over the back of his neck he offers me an apologetic look. "Sorry. I know it's none of my business but I think you deserve to know." He pauses. "Roman was all over Silvia Parish at lunch today."

A rock falls to the pit of my stomach. "It didn't take him long to move on."

Aaron's face twists into a grimace. "Did something happen? All the Devils have been acting weird. I know you and he were—"

"No. Nothing happened. Things ran their course. That's all."

Julio's vibrating with anger beside me. I know he wants to say something. He's made it clear what he thinks about Roman, but thankfully he keeps quiet about it all.

"Well, for what it's worth, I hope you're doing okay. Roman is an asshole. You deserve better."

Julio whistles and the teacher's head jerks in our direction with a glare. In a quieter tone he says, "You can say that again. That guy is a grade-A asshole."

Aaron high fives him and I stifle a groan as the two dive into a heated conversation about just how much of a dick Roman is. *Great.*

Just as class ends Aaron's phone chimes with a message. He pulls out his cell and scowls. "Shit."

"Something wrong?" I ask.

He ruffles his sandy blond hair before shoving his phone in his back pocket and grabbing his skateboard. "One of our dishwashers at the diner just bailed. No notice either. Tonight is going to suck."

"You work at a diner?" Julio asks.

He nods. "Yeah. My aunt owns it—the Sun Valley Station. Best burgers in town. I work there after school sometimes to help her out." He shrugs. "I don't really need the money but it gets me out of the house."

An idea forms and before I can talk myself out of it I say, "I can help. I mean, if you think she'd want to fill the position. I'm looking for a job."

His brows furrow. "You are?"

I bob my head enthusiastically.

"Allie, you sure this is a good idea?" Julio whispers beside me. I give him an affirming nod. This is a great idea. Exactly what I need.

"Yeah. I've put in a few applications around town, but I haven't gotten any callbacks."

"I've seen your place and your new ride. You're not hurting for cash. Why would you want to scrub dishes at a diner?"

"Because I don't want to have to rely on my bio-dad for everything. I barely know the guy. You know what he's like. Would you want anything from him?"

He shakes his head with a grimace, probably remembering Gerald's words when he'd last been over.

"If you helped me get this job you'd be doing me a huge favor."

His lips twist as he considers it. "You'd be able to work tonight?"

I nod.

"Alright. I'll talk to her. I can't make any promises but plan on working the closing shift. It's four to eleven."

"Thank you. You have no idea how much I appreciate it." The bell rings signaling the end of class and we all get up, gathering our things.

Aaron smiles and steps forward. His arms open as if to hug me and instantly I stiffen. Julio intercepts the touch, reaching out to shake Aaron's hand while pulling him into a bro hug. Aaron's eyes widen in confusion over Julio's shoulder.

"Thanks for helping my girl out, man. I'm glad she'll have a friend around after I head back home."

"Uh, yeah. Of course."

Julio steps away and then tugs me toward the door.

"See you tonight," I tell him, rushing to leave.

THIRTY-ONE

Roman

I sit on the hood of my El Camino, my legs wide and Silvia standing between them. Her manicured hands rest on the top of my pants and she's leaning into me, trying hard to be seductive.

I ignore her. She thinks I'm lingering because I want to be in her fucking presence when in reality, that is the last thing I want. Keeping her close today is already biting me in the ass. She's a stage-five clinger with a serious complex but Allie's Audi is four cars down and I want her to see Silvia between my thighs.

I want her to see just how over her I am, so I wait.

"Yo. We going to practice?" Emilio asks, tossing his bag into my backseat. Dom's already in the locker room. He's our QB and he can't afford to show up late. Coach would rip him a new one.

"Yeah, we're going."

He gives me a sideways glance until he spots Allie and the new fucker walking beside her. Realization dawns on Emilio's face and he does me a solid. Walking toward the gym doors he shouts, "Come on, fucker. You can bone Silvia later."

Allie's head jerks toward his voice. Then she follows his gaze and sees what I wanted her to see. Hurt flashes in her eyes. What the hell does she have to be hurt about? I might not admit it to anyone else, but she's the one who dropped me. She showed up with some random, held his fucking hand, and now wants to act like this is all on me.

Not happening.

I grip Silvia's hips and draw her closer. Nuzzling her neck, I keep my eyes locked on Allie's as I let my other hand wander until I'm grasping Silvia's tight ass.

She moans in my embrace and presses herself closer to me. "Roman, you feel so good."

I bite back my scathing response, hating the feel of her body pressed against mine when it should be Allie instead.

I scrape my teeth along the column of her neck. She visibly shudders. So fucking dramatic but it works to my benefit.

Allie stands there, ten feet away from her car, watching us. It's like she's frozen in place and I take full fucking advantage. When Silvia's hand dips down to stroke my dick over my jeans, I shift, making sure Allie has a nice view.

Her cheeks heat, a pretty pink blush staining her cheeks but whether in anger or embarrassment I have no fucking clue.

Julio calls her name. When she doesn't respond, he tugs on her hand and draws her to her car. Her eyes stay locked with mine the entire way until she finally steps inside and the tinted windows block her from my view.

As soon as her car leaves the lot, I push Silvia away and head toward the gym.

"Hey—" she squeaks.

"I got practice." I'm already halfway across the parking lot.

"Oh. Okay. Call me later!"

I throw a wave over my shoulder. I won't call her, and yet she'll still be waiting for me tomorrow when I get to school. So damn predictable.

THIRTY-TWO

Allie

I got the job.

Just as Julio and I are walking in the door, I get a text from Aaron.

> **Aaron: My aunt said you can work tonight as a trial run. If it works out, the job is yours. Closing shift 3x a week.**

> **Me: THANK YOU SOOOOOO MUCH!**

"You look happy," Julio says as we drop our bags beside the kitchen island. I grab two glasses from the cupboard and fill both with water before handing one to him. "Thanks."

"I am happy. Aaron said I got the job. Finally, something good. Ya know?"

He nods but his brows are pinched together as he looks down at his glass. "I don't want to rain on your parade, but are you sure this is a good idea?"

I stiffen. "Why wouldn't it be?"

He runs a hand through his dark brown hair and lifts his gaze. "Allie, you've been through a lot."

"I know that," I snap, not liking the direction this conversation is going. Not two minutes ago I was elated. Now, he's popping my balloon and for no reason.

"How are you going to handle being around everyone? The customers? The other staff? What if Aaron goes to give you a friendly goodbye hug again?"

I chew on my fingernail. "I'll figure it out," I tell him, determined to make this work. "I'm fine. I didn't have any major breakdowns at school today. This will be good for me."

He doesn't look convinced, but he lets the subject drop. I check the time and notice I have forty minutes to get ready and be at the diner. "I need to get ready. Do you want to drop me off and you can keep the car in case you want to do anything?"

He shakes his head. "No. I have some independent study homework I need to catch up on. You okay to drive yourself?"

I nod. "I'll be fine."

He still doesn't look convinced, but says nothing as I jog upstairs to change.

THE SUN VALLEY STATION IS PACKED FOR A WEEKNIGHT. Nearly every booth is filled and only two barstools remain empty at the front counter. I recognize a few students from school but, thankfully, I don't spot the Devils. I don't think I could deal with seeing Roman right now.

Aaron waves me over as soon as I walk in the door. "Hey, follow me." He catches the attention of one of the servers and calls out an, "I'll be right back."

She nods and Aaron leads me through a set of swinging doors and down a private hallway to an office. He knocks twice on the door before opening it.

"Aunt Emma, this is Allie." A middle-aged woman with ash-blond hair looks up from her desk. Her features are severe. Sharp nose, high cheekbones, and thin lips. A pair of reading glasses sit perched atop her head.

"You go to school with my nephew?" She leans back in her seat, setting aside the papers she'd been looking at to give me her full attention.

"Yes, ma'am."

"Ah, manners on this one," she says to Aaron before turning back to me. "Do you have any work history?"

"I was a barista back in my hometown for a summer." It's not much but it's something and it did teach me to work at a fast pace.

"Did Aaron fill you in on the particulars? This is a dishwashing job. It's not glamorous. You won't be waitressing and you won't be earning tips. From time to time you might buss tables if the girls up front need the help but for the most part, you'll be in the back. You good with that?" She gives me a scrutinizing once-over.

I hadn't known what to wear so I put on a pair of black skinny jeans and a long-sleeved black t-shirt and paired it with white sneakers. I assumed black would be safest.

"Sounds good," I tell her.

"Okay, then. Aaron will get you an apron and show you to the back. If you keep up today, the job is yours. It's minimum wage but you'll get a dollar raise once you last six months. Schedule changes each week but you'll be guaranteed three shifts."

I nod. "Thank you."

Aaron leads the way back through the hallway and into the kitchens. I'm greeted by two cooks, but both are elbow deep in work so they only offer me a wave and a smile. I stiffen when I realize it'll be just the three of us back here, but my shoulders relax when Aaron leads me further into where the washing station is.

It sits away from the cooks in a small corner. "Servers and busboys will stack dishes here." He points to a low counter already piled high with dirty plates and glasses. "And then when you're done with them, you put them here. Silverware and glasses all get put inside the automatic runner so they're sanitized but you'll wash plates and bowls by hand."

"Sounds easy enough." I give him a smile. "I think I got it."

"Okay, and if you get stuck or need help, I'll be up front." He places a hand on my shoulder and I instantly lock up. Panic rushes into me and Aaron doesn't miss my reaction. His hand immediately lifts and he takes two steps back.

"What just happened?"

I open my mouth to answer but nothing comes out.

"Allie, you're really pale."

I wrap my arms around myself and look away. Julio was right. This was a horrible idea. What had I been thinking?

I worry my lower lip struggling to give Aaron an explanation for my behavior when he says, "Something happened to you while you were gone?"

I meet his concerned gaze knowing my own is glassy-eyed with unshed tears and nod.

"Fuck." He rubs the back of his neck. "That's why your friend stepped in when I went to hug you today?"

Another nod.

"Okay. Okay." He paces in front of me as he takes this all in and I brace myself for whatever he has to say next. "I don't need to know what happened. It's none of my business. If you decide you want to tell me at some point, you can, okay? I'm here, for whatever you need." My heart melts at his confession. I knew Aaron was a good guy. "But..." A shake of his head as he expels a harsh breath. "You don't want to be touched. Is that it?"

I nod. "Yeah. Pretty much."

"Is that why your friend is here in town? To help you out with whatever you're dealing with?"

"Yeah."

"I'll help, too. Whatever you need. I know he can't be with you twenty-four seven. When you're here, I've got your back. Okay?"

A tear slips down my cheek and I swipe it away. "You're a really great guy, Aaron. Thank you."

THIRTY-THREE

Roman

She's not eating. I don't know why I care but the girl never eats. Not at school anyway. Her cheekbones are sharper. Her clothes fit looser. Something is up and I have no fucking clue what.

I know my boys notice. They give her the same concerned glances I do when they think I'm not looking.

The urge to force her to tell me what's wrong is strong, but she's still with that fucker, Julio. And worse, she's hanging out more with Henderson. One of them is always with her. She's never alone. Not in her classes. Not at lunch. Hell, even when I spot her going to take a piss, one of these assholes is always right outside the door.

I'm tempted to find a way to distract them so I can pull her away but I talk myself out of it. I shouldn't care that she's losing weight. What difference is it to me? She wasn't eating a ton before. This is just more of the same. Maybe she's still upset over her mom.

That's probably all it is. I can't say I blame her, but it is not my problem. Not anymore.

Just then, Silvia struts toward me. I groan. The girl is clingy as shit. "Yo, Rome," Emilio calls. "The wife is coming."

I flip him off and ignore the annoyance Silvia's presence brings. Sarah is right beside her, making stupid eyes at Emilio. He tilts his chin at her in greeting and the girl swoons. Pathetic.

Kasey Henderson walks by just then and sneers with a dramatic eye roll. "Getting desperate, boys," she calls out before heading to the table Allie's sitting at. I ignore her comment and throw my arm over Silvia's shoulder and as expected, she presses herself into me, her breasts and the inch-thick padding in her bra mashing up against my chest.

"Are we going to get to spend some time together this weekend, Ro?" she asks, fluttering her lashes in what I'm sure she thinks is a seductive manner, but really she ends up looking like she's got something stuck in her eyes.

I shrug my shoulders. "Dunno. I got plans with the boys. We'll see."

Her bottom lip juts out and I know she's not happy. Chick's been trying to screw me all week. I've kissed her but that is as far as things have gone and only ever in public. If I'm going to lower my standards to a girl like her, there's gotta be a reason for it, and ensuring it gets back to Allie is reason number one. Silvia wants more. She wants to fuck. But the idea of screwing her makes my dick limper than a soft noodle.

I can barely manage to shove my tongue down her throat as it is.

A few weeks ago, I'd have fucked her in a heartbeat. Silvia's got a tight ass, curves, and a decent rack. Her teeth are straight, and she's got long, sleek hair I'd normally enjoy wrapping around my fist. But now, all I see when I look at her is a pathetic girl who can't seem to understand just how uninterested I am in her.

She's a means to an end. A way to pass the time. The season's over and I don't have football practice anymore to use as a distraction, so instead I try and come up with creative ways to screw over the girl who decided to stomp on my fucking heart.

When Allie's gaze turns my way, I lean into Silvia's touch and capture her lips with mine. She moans dramatically into the kiss and I force myself to close my eyes, pretending it's Allie I'm kissing. Allie whose mouth I'm tasting.

Silvia moans again, not bothered in the least that we're in a crowded cafeteria and she sounds like a porn star. I wish she would shut the hell up. When she moans for the third time I pull away. Her pupils are dilated and her smile wide as she struggles to catch her breath. I flick my gaze back to Allie's table but it's empty now. She's gone.

THIRTY-FOUR

Allie

———————

The week passes and before I know it, it's Saturday night. I work the closing shift again at Sun Valley Station, only this time, Aaron has the night off so he can go watch the girls' basketball game. The season just started and Kasey plays on the JV team, though not by choice. She hates sports but I guess her parents are forcing her into some extracurriculars. Aaron's going so he can make fun of his sister later.

I was originally given the night off too, and Aaron invited me to come, but I couldn't stomach the idea of attending another school event.

The diner is slow the first few hours I'm here, but I know once the game is over that'll change. Everyone will either go out and party or come here for food since other restaurants in the area will be closed, so I take advantage of the reprieve and make sure all the dishes are clean and stacked so that when the rush hits, I'm ready.

Julio had to head back home this morning. I was bummed to see him go but he can only take so much time off from school. He offered to stay longer but I didn't want to take advantage of him. I appreciate the week he gave me, though. I've only had one panic attack since Monday and true to his word, when Julio wasn't around, Aaron did his best to step in and help make me comfortable.

The volume in the front of the diner increases and I chance a look at the clock, noting that it's just after nine. Less than two hours until closing and we're just now getting busy.

I keep myself occupied, scrubbing dishes down while I listen to some older *My Chemical Romance* songs. I'm bouncing to *Black Parade* a little over an hour later when Emma pops her head in the back and says, "I have to leave early and handle some stuff. Julie will be the one closing up with you tonight."

I nod. Julie's one of the waitresses who works here full-time. She's in college and from what I've gathered, also a family friend so she's trusted with a key and closing out the register.

Tonight's cooks, Rodrick and Ben, let me know they're heading out when they fulfill the last order of the night and I wave goodbye to them. They've mostly kept to themselves since I started working here and a part of me wonders if Aaron said anything to them about me. I wash the last of the dishes just as the double doors swing open and Julie bounces into the room.

"Are you almost done?" she asks.

I nod. "Yeah, just a few more."

She eyes my stack of dishes with a frown. It's not that big and should take ten minutes tops to get through. "I'm supposed to meet some friends at a party and I'm already running late. Are you okay if I head out? The doors are already locked and the till is zeroed out. All you have to do is make sure the door is closed all the way when you leave."

"Yeah. That's fine."

She squeals. "Thank you so much. You're a doll. I'll see you next week."

And then she's gone.

I finish up the dishes, no longer in a hurry, and then collect my bag and hoodie. I shut off the lights and I'm just about to open the door when I spot a man standing across the street. All the lights are out inside the diner so I'm confident he can't see me, but it's like he's staring right at me anyway, even though I can't make out his eyes.

Goosebumps break out all over my skin.

The streetlight casts him in shadow, hiding his face but illuminating enough of his body that I can make out his dark washed jeans and flannel shirt. He's big. Built like a man and not one of the boys I go to school with.

Fear freezes me before I stumble back a few steps away from the door. The man never moves. I glance toward the parking lot, spotting my Audi right where I left it. In the furthest spot on the lot because I hadn't wanted to be parked close to anyone.

The ten yards or so between it and me feels like a mile.

Can I make it to my car before him? If I run I probably can. Maybe. What reason does he have for standing out there, lurking?

"Come on, Allie. Pull yourself together," I mutter to myself. Just because I was attacked once before doesn't mean it will happen again. But my attacker's words echo in my mind as if he's standing over me again. *I'd be happy to make another visit,* he'd said. What if this is him, or his friend? What if Gerald messed up again?

Gerald and I never talked about what caused the attack in the first place. He just said he'd take care of it and then he never brought it up again. I should have brought it up again. I should have made sure something like that could never happen to me another time.

Oh God. I'd been so stupid.

I slump into one of the booths toward the back, away from the windows, and pull my phone out with shaking fingers. I dial Julio's number before I realize he can't help me and hang up. Okay. Plan B. I'll try Aaron.

I call him and wait. The line rings once, twice, six times.

Voicemail.

Dang it.

I try again.

Voicemail again.

I wipe my clammy hands on my knees and stare at the screen of my phone. I don't know who else to call. Feeling desperate I try Janessa. She doesn't pick up. Against my better judgment, I try Gerald next.

"You've reached the voicemail box of..."

I hang up.

My heart skips a beat. The man is still out there. What is he waiting for? A knot of dread expands in my chest. It crawls through me and my entire body begins to shake. I squeeze my eyes shut. I need to get it together. I can't think if I panic.

My breaths are ragged as if I've just run a marathon. My chest heaves up and down. I press my forehead down on the cool surface of the table and force myself to slow down my breathing. I can't have a panic attack. Not here. Not now.

Think, Allie. Just think.

The idea to call Roman leaves me as quickly as it came. I swallow hard and chew on my bottom lip until I'm certain I've bitten through the tender flesh and the tang of copper fills my mouth.

I try Dominique.

He answers on the second ring. "Allie?"

"Oh, thank God." I choke out the words on a sob.

"What's going on?"

His voice is hard, and a sense of urgency has me rushing to say, "I just got off work and there's a man outside. I think he's waiting for me. I let Julie leave early and I'm alone and my car is far away and—"

"Breathe, Allie. Take a breath. Slow down."

I try to do as he instructs but I can't seem to slow down.

"Where are you at?"

"The Sun Valley Station."

"Okay. I'm on my way. I'll give you a lift. We can get your car tomorrow morning."

I nod even though he can't see me. "Thank you."

"Just hang tight. Go in the back. I'll be there in ten."

THIRTY-FIVE

Allie

I'm huddled on the floor in the kitchen hiding behind one of the cook stations. My knees are pressed to my chest and I have my arms wrapped around them as though through sheer will, holding myself tight will keep me from falling apart.

My phone chimes and I lift it to glance at the illuminated screen.

> **Dom: I'm here.**

"Thank God."

I squeeze my eyes shut once before forcing them open. Dominique is here. I'm safe. He's a big strong football player and whoever the man is outside won't want to mess with him. He's probably gone by now anyway. I'm okay. Everything is okay.

Me: Be right out.

I PUSH MYSELF UP FROM THE GROUND, MY LEGS STILL shaking as I shove my phone in my back pocket and try and catch my bearings.

I take several deep breaths and press my hand over my chest. My heart is racing but there isn't anything I can do about it. I force myself to move toward the front of the diner. My steps are slow and I keep checking my surroundings to make sure I'm still alone. I know the man couldn't have gotten inside. The doors are all locked. But I still feel the urge to double and triple check.

I spot Dominique's Escalade parked right out front and a small sigh of relief escapes me. I'm almost to the door when a police cruiser pulls up behind it. I stop. Did he call the cops? I look around and don't spot the man outside any longer. Inwardly, I groan. I'm going to have to explain the false alarm to an officer. He's going to think I'm an idiot for getting all worked up over nothing.

Dominique is sitting in the front seat of his car seemingly not paying attention. His eyes are on his phone, the screen casting light on his face in the darkened vehicle.

I watch as the officer gets out of his car. He draws his gun from his holder and moves around the vehicle until he's facing Dom's driver-side window.

What the—

The officer starts shouting. Dominique raises his hand in the air and then steps out of his car. I move to the corner of the diner to get a better look and notice another police cruiser pull up. This one follows suit and two men exit that car, both with weapons drawn.

Dominique is shaking his head vigorously, hands still lifted in the air.

He turns around to face me and I see stark fear in his eyes. *No. No. No.*

I pull my phone out of my back pocket and rush outside just as Dom lowers himself to his knees, his hands coming to rest behind his head. I look up and down the street but aside from Dominique and the police, the street is empty.

"Ma'am, I need you to step back inside the restaurant."

What? No. I shake my head. "What's going on, officer?" I ask, my feet rooted in place.

Dom is on his knees, but the police have three guns drawn and trained on my friend. My phone is still clutched in my hand so as discreetly as possible I dial Roman's number. His dad is the chief of police. I remember him telling me that. Instinctively, I know I have to call him. I know he can help.

I don't bother waiting to see if he answers, I put the phone on speaker and turn all my attention to the officer closest to Dominique.

"Ma'am. Get back inside the diner." His voice is hard, his eyes narrowed as he looks me over.

"I...I can't. It's locked now. Why are you pointing your gun at him? He didn't do anything wrong." As I'm talking I hear the call connect and Roman swears on the other line quietly enough that only I can hear him.

"This man is suspected of auto theft." The officer tells me. "We got a tip and he fits the description."

I frown at that. No way would Dom steal a car. His family is loaded. He has no reason to.

"Officer, I know him. Dominique Price is not a thief. He's here to give me a ride home. I called him at the end of my shift here at the Sun Valley Station." I say all of this, hoping Roman will hear and call his dad. Maybe he can show up and help defuse the situation, or make a call so these guys back off.

Dominique isn't saying anything but his normally dark complexion has taken on an ashen quality. His eyes are wide and he's not looking at me. I'm not even sure he's aware of what's going on anymore.

I take a step toward Dom when another officer shouts, "Ma'am we need you to stay away from the suspect."

Suspect? Dom isn't a suspect. He's a kid. He's seventeen. He's just a kid like me.

"But I ... I know him." My voice wobbles. "Why are your guns drawn? He's not dangerous. He's not..."

"Ma'am. Please step back. It's for your own safety."

"Put your guns away and I will. He isn't doing anything to justify this type of force."

At my words, Dominique flinches and all three officers start shouting.

"Get back."

"Get on the ground."

"Keep your hands in the air."

They're not talking to me. They're shouting at Dominique, but he barely moved.

Dom's eyes flick to mine.

"I'm not leaving you," I mouth.

His lower lip trembles. My eyes prick with tears. Dom, strong, quiet Dom is on the verge of tears. This cannot be happening.

Then one of the officers gets angry when Dominique doesn't move to comply but he's already on his knees. What more do they want? "Get on the ground. Get on the fucking ground," he shouts, stepping forward. "I said, get on the fucking ground." His hands shake and I can see hatred burning in his gaze.

No. *No!*

I drop my phone, purse, and sweater so there's no way any of them can think I'm hiding anything. Then I move closer.

"Ma'am!"

"Miss!"

I keep my arms raised as I walk toward Dominique, my steps measured. I don't look at the officers. I don't look at the guns. I keep my gaze locked on Dom and watch as he tracks my movements with his eyes but he doesn't move. He's still as a statue.

When I'm right beside him I finally look up and meet the gaze of the closest officer. Then I step in front of Dom, protecting him with my body.

My voice shakes as I say, "His name is Dominique Price. He's seventeen years old. He goes to Sun Valley High." My heart is pounding in my chest. I can barely hear myself, but I push more words past my lips, determined to make them understand. "He's here to pick me up from work. He was giving me a ride."

The officer closest to me, an older white man with dark brown hair shot through with streaks of silver, eyes me warily.

"He's driving a brand-new Escalade. We have reason to believe the vehicle is stolen."

"It's not!" I shout the words. I don't know why I'm not scared anymore. But I'm not, all I'm feeling is anger. Cold and visceral. They have no right to do this. To make Dom feel a certain way when he didn't do anything wrong.

"Miss. I understand you know this man but—"

"He's a *kid*. A seventeen-year-old kid. The car is his. His family has money. Why are you doing this?" I can hear the hysteria in my voice but can do nothing to quash it.

"We have reason to believe—"

"How? Why? Because he's black?"

His eyes narrow. "This has nothing to do with race. We received a call—"

I cut him off. "Do you know the chief of police?" I ask him. "Do any of you know Police Chief Valdez?" I shout.

One of the men nods so I push on. "His son, Roman, goes to Sun Valley High. He's best friends with Dominique Price. This is Dominique Price. Chief Valdez has known Dominique forever. Please, just put the guns down and call the chief. He'll clear this up. He'll tell you—"

Another cruiser pulls in. Two more officers exit and add two more guns raised in our direction.

I can't catch my breath. Panic rises in my gut.

My voice is frantic now. "Call the chief. I'm not letting you shoot my friend. This is not happening." The last part I say to myself.

It takes every shred of courage in me to turn my back on them but I do. I turn around and the crouch down behind Dominique. I take in his broad back and raised hands. I look at his hands. Always hands. *This is Dom.* I tell myself. *He's my friend. I can do this. I have to do this.* Wrapping my arms around his waist I use my body as a human shield. Panic floods through me at the contact but I close my eyes and shove it away. It's just Dominique. Dominique is safe. He would never hurt me. I'm touching him. He's not touching me. I'm okay. I'm okay. I'm okay.

To him I say, "Don't move. I've got you. I won't let them shoot you for being black. I've got you."

He trembles beneath me. Seconds stretch into minutes, but I don't move. Neither of us do. I can hear the officers in the background arguing amongst themselves, but I block out their voices.

My legs begin to shake but I hold on tighter, refusing to move away and abandon my friend. Then a familiar voice calls out from the crowd. "Allie?"

I turn my head but still don't release Dom.

"Roman?" My word is a whisper and I feel Dominique's shoulders slump in relief.

Roman shoves through the cluster of officers, a severe-looking older man right behind him. A man I recognize. *Oh shit!* The man who found me that night. That's Roman's father? I can see the resemblance now.

"Drop your weapons and stand down. Now," he orders the men.

A breath whooshes out of me as one by one the officers holster their weapons.

"Everyone but the first officer on the scene, get the hell out of here. Beat it."

No one argues, and once I can see that they're clearing out and there aren't any more guns trained our way, I loosen my hold on Dominique and stand. My heart pounds in my chest now for an entirely different reason.

Police Chief Valdez meets my gaze. There's concern there but it's fleeting. Then he turns and starts in on the officer forced to stay behind.

Roman is there, yanking me into his arms. "What the hell were you thinking? Fuck. Were you trying to give me a heart attack? Seeing you like that just shaved ten years off my life."

I freeze in his arms and close my eyes. Silent tears track down my face. I... I can't... I can't breathe.

He releases me and turns toward Dom, completely unaware of the meltdown taking place inside of me.

"What the hell happened?" Roman asks.

No answer. I swallow several times trying to force the lump in my throat down.

"Dom?"

He's not getting up. Roman sends me a worried look and I force my feet to move. I step around him until I'm standing in front of him and I bend down to catch his gaze. "Dom?"

His jaw is locked. His eyes glassy and far away. I send a worried gaze toward Roman but he shrugs, unsure of what to do. I bite my bottom lip. Words aren't getting through to him.

I take a deep shuddering breath and swipe the tears from my face with the backs of my hands before turning my attention to his. They're still held above his head.

I shove past my fear and with shaking fingers, reach out and cup Dom's cheeks in my palms. "Dominique?" His gaze flickers to mine. "It's okay. You're okay. They're gone. It's okay."

His hands slowly lower but his arms are trembling. He sucks in a shuddering breath. "I need..."

I know and I force myself to give it to him. I wrap my arms around his neck and hug him close. His strong arms wrap around me in an almost painful embrace. I bear it and when my limbs lock up and my breath becomes erratic, I just squeeze him tighter.

"It's okay. I've got you."

THIRTY-SIX

Roman

Allie took off ten minutes ago. I tried to convince her to let me give her a ride but as soon as Dom released her, she took off straight for her Audi with barely a backward glance.

I was tempted to go after her. I don't know what the hell came over me but seeing her like that, in the line of fire, I've never been so fucking scared in my life. My girl was in danger. *My girl.*

Fuck all the bullshit with her and Julio. Fuck the fact that she ghosted me. She's mine. She ran off tonight but as soon as I get Dom settled, she and I are going to have words.

It's just the three of us now. Dom, me, and my pops. We're sitting in Dominique's Escalade but I'm in the driver's seat. No way am I letting him drive himself home tonight. Dom gave my dad a recount of what happened, and one thing for sure is heads are going to roll Monday morning when my dad gets to his office. He assures Dominique that all of the officers will face consequences. I'm almost positive the first asshole on scene will lose his badge.

You can't be a racist prick on my dad's force. He has zero tolerance for that shit.

"You boys going to be alright tonight?" my dad asks.

"Yeah. I'll drive Dom home and crash at his place. What were you doing here, anyway?" I ask him.

Color is coming back to his face. He seems a little more like himself. "Allie called me. She was freaked out. I guess there was some dude outside and she didn't feel comfortable leaving the diner by herself."

A stab of pain hits me in the gut when I realize she was afraid and she called him. Not me. But before I say anything, my pops curses.

I flick my gaze toward him, and he asks, "Are you two close with her?"

We both shake our heads. "Used to be. We don't talk anymore," I tell him.

He frowns but I have no idea why. What does he care whether or not I talk to Allie?

"What's that mean exactly?" he asks.

I shrug, not wanting to get into it with him. Allie and I were on the outs but after tonight, I plan to rectify that. "Nothing. It's whatever."

His frown deepens and his eyes flicker with disappointment. "That girl's been through hell," he says.

Anger rises up inside me. "How would you know?"

He scrubs a hand over his face, and I know he's going to give me some non-answer. Hell, no. Not this time. If he knows something about my girl, I should know it, too. "Pops, how do you know Allie?"

His mouth tightens. He's quiet for a minute so I press again. "If something's going on, I should know. You have to tell me."

"The night of your game. The one your mother and I came to watch you play in..." he hesitates.

"Yeah? What about it?" I remember that he'd stepped out to make a phone call and then left shortly after. Mom said a case came up or some shit.

"She was assaulted in the parking lot."

Wait. What?

My chest seizes and my mouth drops open. "What do you mean, assaulted?" Was that why she wasn't at my game? She'd been hurt? *Fuck.* She'd been hurt and I'd been a complete asshole. No wonder she didn't message me back.

His face hardens. "I don't want you spreading rumors about this girl, feel me?"

Dread settles deep in my stomach. "What kind of assault are we talking about here?" There's only one that would warrant his tone, and I need him to confirm it.

"We believe she was raped."

I suck in a breath. And then I fucking explode. "What? Are you fucking kidding me right now?" I jump out of the driver's seat and start pacing in front of the car, unable to remain still.

My dad and Dom both get out after me.

"Fuck." Then his words settle over me and I whirl on him. "What do you mean you think?" Either someone is raped or they aren't. There isn't really a gray area here.

"She wouldn't consent to the rape kit. She told the nurses she was raped upon arrival and it was clear she'd been when I found her. She was—" He shakes his head. "It doesn't matter. But she told the nurses about the assault when we got there. I rode in the ambulance with her. She had all the signs of a rape victim. Torn clothes. Bruises. All of it. But before the nurses could start the kit, some woman in a suit stormed in and tore out of there with her like she was on a mission. When me and another officer tried to confront her, she shut us down. The girl's a minor. We couldn't question her without parental consent and they weren't giving it."

I pull at my hair and resume my pacing. "And she was okay with that?" Goddammit. This is so much worse than I thought. Raped? Fuck. I iced her out and she'd been raped.

She'd been in trouble today and she'd called Dom. Not me. I fucked up. She's been hurt and I royally fucked up.

My dad lifts his shoulders and releases a weary exhale. "I don't know. She was in shock. She shut down. I can't say I blame her." He shakes his head. "Whoever hurt her made sure to leave their mark. I can't fault her for calling you when she saw a man outside." He directs that statement to Dom, and I notice his eyes are no longer distant. Instead, they're alight with remembered fury.

"The guy who hurt her?"

Pops shakes his head. "Still out there."

Fuck.

THIRTY-SEVEN

Allie

I

t's Saturday morning. Against my initial hesitations, I decide to go on a run to clear my head. I couldn't sleep last night. I kept replaying what happened at the diner again and again, visualizing all the ways that things could have gone. It was bad enough, what happened. But it could have been a thousand times worse. Deep down, I know that, and it's left me shaken.

I can only imagine how Dominique must feel. Speaking of... I spot a familiar black Escalade as I round the corner of my street, my sneakered feet smacking against the pavement.

I wipe the sweat from my forehead, but I don't slow down. Not until the car gets close enough for me to spot Dominique through the windshield. I let out a small breath of relief. I was pretty sure it was him, but it helps having the confirmation.

The Escalade pulls up beside me and slows, keeping pace with my jog as one of the windows rolls down and Roman hangs an arm out of the passenger side window. My heart stutters in my chest, despite everything that's happened. I spot Emilio in the backseat. Looks like the gang is all here.

"Allie," Roman calls my name. His voice is hard and I instantly bristle at his tone. "Get in the car."

"Pass," I tell him, picking up my pace. I swallow hard, forcing myself not to focus on the sound of his voice. Longing sweeps through me, but I push it aside and keep my eyes trained ahead of me.

"Allie." There's a warning in his voice. He's angry. Does he blame me for what happened last night? *Probably.*

"Go away, Roman."

The Escalade jerks to a stop and Roman jumps from the car. I squeal when he rushes me and between one second and the next, he has me hoisted over his shoulder and unceremoniously throws me into the backseat beside Emilio before slamming the door and getting back in the front seat.

"Bro, what the fuck?" Emilio snaps. "What happened to playing this cool?"

"Buckle up." Roman barks, ignoring him.

I rush to right myself and then press against the door as far away from Emilio as I can get as Dom pulls the car back onto the road. My breaths are loud and heavy in the quiet space and I can feel all their eyes on me.

"Let me out." Adrenaline floods through me and I close my eyes. *It's just the guys.* I'm fine. They're not going to hurt me. Even if Roman is angry with me, he wouldn't hurt me. Not like that.

It doesn't matter. Telling myself I'm safe doesn't stop the panic coursing through my veins. I'm hyperventilating now.

"Allie, it's okay. We just want to talk." Emilio unbuckles and slides closer to me and I lose it in a haze of blind terror.

"Let me out. Let me out!" I scream and my fingers claw at the door. Finding the handle, I jerk it open. Dominique slams on the brakes just as I throw myself from the car. I slam against the pavement, asphalt scraping against my skin and three sets of doors open and slam shut. Curses fly but I'm already scrambling to my feet, uncaring of the scrapes or bruises I know I have. Blood drips down my forearm and all three guys step toward me.

"Stop! Don't come any closer." I hold a hand out toward them, urging them to stay away. My other hand clutches my head as I struggle to get air into my lungs. My head is pounding, an incessant beat growing louder and louder as each second passes.

"Allie, we won't come any closer. Breathe. We won't hurt you. You know that." Dom's voice cuts through some of my panic. I step back on the pavement until my feet meet grass and then I collapse. Pressing my head between my knees I rock back and forth, sucking in air.

"I'm okay. I'm okay. I'm okay." If I say it enough, it'll be true.

"What do you need?" Dominique again.

I shake my head.

"Allie?" Emilio's voice is higher than usual. I look up and all three are standing maybe fifteen feet away with a mix of worried and confused expressions.

I swallow hard. "Hands." My voice shakes. "I need to see your hands."

Three scowls greet me but without hesitation, Dominique holds his hands out and takes two steps forward. "Okay. Here are my hands."

I take in his darker skin. The contrasting pink of his palms. I force myself to recognize how different his hands are from the men who hurt me. He takes another step. Then another. My breathing slows and I shudder.

Dominique crouches down in front of me, hands still lifted. I reach out and take one of his hands in my own. I turn his palm over. Safe. Dom is safe. Emilio steps closer, his hands lifted as well.

The sun-kissed color of his skin has my chest rising and falling faster and faster. I close my eyes. "I'm sorry. I—" I shake my head. Dom waves him back and without me having to ask, he steps further away from me.

"What is it about hands?" Dominique asks.

I shake my head. I don't want to talk about it. I know I'm freaking out and I know they want answers but I can't—

"We know you were assaulted." His voice is gentle, but his words are like a slap.

What? All the blood drains from my face.

"Baby—"

I jerk my head toward Roman. His voice is filled with pain as his wide, haunted eyes meet mine. His hands are clenched into white-knuckled fists at his sides. He steps closer and I flinch.

Cursing, he rounds to the opposite side of the car. "Dammit."

"You're not helping. Get your shit together," Dominique tells him. He turns back to me. "Can you explain what it is about hands. We just want to help. We didn't know. Not until last night..."

Last night, after Roman's dad showed up. He must have told them. Shame washes over me in cascading waves that leave me drowning in self-loathing and disgust. They know. All three of them know. Tears fill my field of vision and I press the heels of my palms against my eyes, fighting to keep them from falling.

"Allie—"

"Your hands are different," I choke out. I gasp for breath and force more words past my lips. "The man who hurt me... I only saw his hands. I... Your hands are different. I know you won't hurt me. I'm not saying Roman would. I know it doesn't make sense but...." I give him a pleading look, begging with him to understand.

Dom's eyes tighten and he runs a hand over his tightly braided hair. "Your mind gets it but your body doesn't." He shakes his head. "It's okay. I get it."

My shoulders slump in relief. "Your hands are different. He wasn't black. It's easy for me to convince myself you're safe."

He nods. "And with Roman and Emilio?"

I shrug. "I think he was maybe Latino, too. I don't know, but his hands, they were tan. Darker than mine. Like..."

"Like theirs."

I nod, unable to look at either of them. God, what they must be thinking right now.

"The guy who's been with you all week—?" Dominique doesn't finish but I know what he's asking.

"Like a brother. I've known him since grade school. And he has tattoos." I trace the back of my hand. "They cover the tops of his hands. A skull and roses... rosary beads..." I say all of this hoping he understands. I know I'm not making complete sense but I don't have another way to put into words why hands matter.

He nods again. "Okay. Okay. Let me think." He stands and goes back toward his car. He says something to Roman and Emilio and Roman explodes, throwing his hands up in the air and cursing. He pulls at his hair, but when he looks at me, all of his anger evaporates. In its place is stark need and devastation.

My chest tightens. He's not hiding any of his emotions from me. Not this time. He lets me see all of it. Every painful piece of what he's feeling. And it leaves me reeling. I don't know how to interpret his anguish. Is he upset because of what happened? Because I'm such a mess?

He doesn't come any closer. Just stares at me with unmasked emotion, and it's suddenly too much. Seeing him hurts too much.

I swallow hard and push back up to my feet. My eyes stray to his clenched fists and I notice that he's still wearing my bracelet. The one I gave him before the game. I try not to read into it but does that mean—

"Allie, baby." His voice is raw. "I never—" His voice cracks and he looks away. "I fucked up. I thought some things and they weren't true and I wasn't there when you needed me." He turns back to me and I can see the despair in his eyes. "I messed up. But I'm here now. I want to be there for you. You have to let me be there."

I shake my head. I can't deal with all of this right now. Wrapping my arms around myself, I take a step away, retreating back the way I'd come. "I... I can't do this. I'm sorry."

"Allie!"

I pause, hating how weak I feel right now. How broken and shattered I am inside.

"I won't hurt you. I would *never* hurt you." He takes a tentative step forward and I jerk away. He stops and offers me a sad smile. "I would never hurt you. You've gotta know that."

"Wouldn't you?" My own voice cracks as the words spill out on their own. I'm not sure if I'm asking or challenging him, but he did hurt me. He's been hurting me.

Roman's face falls. He rubs the back of his neck and averts his gaze. "I'm so fucking sorry. I didn't know. If I'd known I never would have... Allie, I never meant..."

"But you never asked." Tears fall freely down my cheeks. I don't even bother to wipe them away. I want him to see them. I want him to see every ugly broken thing about me and know he had a part in it. I want him to hurt the same way he made me hurt. Because just like Ryker, he left me. Right when I needed him the most. "I tried to talk to you. That first day I came back to school. As soon as I saw you, I walked straight up to you and do you remember what you said? What you called me?"

Anguish fills his gaze, but I can't find it in me to hold back.

"You called me a whore." I shake my head, more silent tears falling down my face, enough so that Roman is a blurry shadow in front of me, his features no longer recognizable. "I can't do this. Just... leave me alone. I think I've been through enough."

I turn and jog home. Thankfully, no one follows.

THIRTY-EIGHT

Roman

She won't meet my gaze. I try and talk to her at school, but she gives me the cold shoulder, and hell knows I deserve it. I try and catch her eyes in first period but not once does she look my direction. To make matters worse, Silvia is waiting for me outside the class and the look on Allie's face when Silvia makes an attempt to kiss me sends a spear of self-loathing straight to my gut.

I push Silvia away but the damage is already done and before I can call out to her to wait up, Allie is gone, swallowed up by the crowded sea of people in the hallway.

"Silvia," I bite out.

"Yeah, babe?" she purrs, stroking a hand over my chest. I pull her hand away, my lip curling in disgust. "I've had my fill. I'm moving on. I suggest you do, too."

Her eyes widen before narrowing into slits. "Let me guess, you're going back to daddy's little princess?"

I take a menacing step toward her. "Say one more thing about Allie Ramirez and I'll make sure you regret it. You've already had a taste of what it's like to be on my bad side. Want to be there again?"

She swallows hard and shakes her head.

"Good. Now make yourself scarce. I've moved on."

I don't bother waiting for an answer and head out to find Emilio. He's smoother when it comes to girls. Maybe he'll have an idea of how I can get Allie back.

I catch Allie talking to Dominique in the halls as they head to lunch, but as soon as I approach, she takes off and sits at Henderson's table. I try to ignore how gutted I feel at her dismissal, but it's hard. Dom pats me on the shoulder. "She just needs time, man."

I nod, knowing he's right but it doesn't mean I have to like it. I messed up royally when I pushed her away. I won't make that mistake again. Won't give up on her or what we have. I've never felt about a girl the way that I do about Allie. It's why even when I was pissed as hell at her, when I thought she'd moved on with Julio, leaving me in the dust, I still couldn't get her out of my head. She lives there. Takes up space and refuses to move the fuck out.

At lunch, I sit with my face in my hands, going over all the ways I can win her back. When the lunch bell rings, I track her with my gaze, watching like some love-sick puppy as she leaves the cafeteria, Kasey and Henderson close on her heels.

I shove away from the table and storm after them.

"What do you think you're doing?" Dom shouts somewhere behind me.

I shake my head. I have no fucking idea but I have to do something. Allie slips into her third-period class and I walk past it, my eyes trained on Henderson, and just before he reaches the door to his own class, I jerk him back by the fabric of his shirt.

"Hey, man—" Startled green eyes meet my own when he sees who grabbed him. "What the hell, Roman?" He jerks away, adjusting the collar of his shirt.

"You've been hanging out with Allie a lot lately." I meant it as a question, but it comes out as an accusation and Aaron's jaw tightens.

"Why do you care? You've been a complete asshole to her ever since she came back. Do the girl a favor and leave her alone. She's been through enough and she doesn't need your shit."

I slam my fist into the locker beside him. "I didn't know!" A few people in the hall turn to look at us and I snarl at them. "Move the fuck along." Heated faces turn and rush to their classes, effectively clearing the hall of everyone but the two of us. "I didn't know what happened to her. Not until just recently."

"And that's supposed to somehow make this all better? Fuck you, Roman."

"Henderson—" It's a warning.

He shakes his head. "No. You fucked up. I don't know why you're even talking to me. I'm not going to help you fix your mistakes. I don't owe you any—"

"Yeah, you do."

His eyes narrow.

"You owe me and you fucking know it. You want me to stop hating you? You want the Devils to stop hating you for what you put us through the summer before junior year?"

His mouth presses into a sharp line and he gives me a single sharp nod.

"Then help me talk to her. She doesn't feel comfortable with me." He snorts and the urge to punch him in his smug face is strong, but I ignore it. "I care about her. I want to be there for her. Help me talk to her and I'll forget what happened. We'll wipe the slate clean."

He considers this. It's no secret I hate him. I've hated him since junior year. He used to be my friend. We were like brothers. All four of us. But then he had to go and fuck it all up. He'd just gotten his license. He was the only one of us old enough to drive and we were all heading to Shadle Creek to camp for a week over summer.

But the fucker did drugs. None of us knew. He hid his addiction because he knew what we'd say about it, and on the way up to Shadle Creek, high as a fucking kite on coke, he hit a truck head-on. We were in a WRX. His first one, not the one he drives now. The force of the impact sent Emilio shooting out the window and broke Dominique's arm in two places. He had to have surgery to repair the break and spent all summer in a cast. It could have ended his chances of playing football and we all could have died. Emilio surprisingly came out the least scathed. Scrapes and bruises. A concussion, but nothing life threatening. And me, I had the pleasure of a ruptured spleen, and after surgery that shit took four long weeks to recover from.

To make matters worse, as I was freaking the fuck out trying to help Dom out of the car and find Emilio because we had no fucking idea where he'd been thrown, Henderson was ranting about how much trouble he was in. How screwed he was. We all could have died and all he'd cared about was whether or not he'd be going to jail.

He should have. Maybe it would have straightened him out. But for whatever reason, I convinced my pops to go easy on him. There was history there. Years of friendship I couldn't turn my back on, even though not once did he visit Dom or me in the hospital.

He got a slap on the wrist. Community service and his parents had to pay a fine to the city. But after that, I cut ties, and to this day, the asshole still hasn't apologized.

I never thought I'd forgive him, but to get Allie back, I'll do damn near anything.

"You'd do that? Forget what happened?" He swallows, his Adam's apple bobbing. "Forget what I did, and all I have to do is get Allie to talk to you."

I nod.

"I can't make any promises."

"I don't need promises or assurances. I just need a chance. One fucking chance to make this right."

"Okay."

I exhale a breath. "Okay."

THIRTY-NINE

Allie

Roman calls me now. All of the Devils do. Emilio sends me a joke each morning. Or a funny meme he found online. He wants to make me smile. And while I appreciate the gesture, it's a lot to take in. The sudden shift in their behaviors.

One second they hate me. Now it's like they're smothering me in distant affection.

Dominique is the only one I talk to at school. He sometimes walks me to class when Aaron isn't around. He makes sure no one gets too close. I didn't ask him to play guard dog, and when I told him as much, he just gave me this serious stare and carried on like I hadn't said anything. I've learned not to push. If he wants to make himself late to class each day, that's his prerogative.

Roman messages me each morning. A variation of **good morning, beautiful**, and calls me every night. I don't respond to the texts and never answer the calls. He doesn't leave any voicemails which is probably for the best. Hearing his voice at school is bad enough. If he left me messages, I know myself well enough to know I'd replay them again and again, obsessing over the sound of his voice. Trying to peel back any hidden meaning. It's already what I do with his texts. Sometimes he adds an emoji and it's enough to leave me guessing, hoping. For what, I'm not really sure.

But without fail at nine o'clock each evening my phone lights up and his name flashes across the screen. A part of me has come to look forward to that phone call. When eight fifty nears, I start counting down the minutes, hoping he'll call, and that alone scares me. Because sooner or later, he's going to give up. He'll stop calling. He'll stop texting. And he'll move on. I want him to move on.

I can't afford to need anyone else in my life. I've lost too much, and I don't think my heart can take any more. It doesn't matter that I miss him or that his presence sets my heart racing.

What happens when he's no longer there?

I'm already dreading when the calls stop.

It's been a week since he found out what happened to me. A week of pretending I don't want him. Of trying to convince myself that I'm better off without him. But I'm slipping.

I catch myself staring at him when he's not looking. And I hang onto every word Dom says whenever he mentions Roman. How he's doing. Where he's at. What they're eating for lunch. It's borderline obsessive and I know it, but I'm desperate to know every little detail.

Aaron has mentioned him a few times, too, which was surprising at first. He's always made it clear how he feels about Roman. I know they have history, and while I'm curious, I also know it's none of my business. But even he's tried to convince me to talk to Roman. To at least hear him out. He thinks it'd be cathartic for me. And maybe it would be. But....

"Hey, Allie?" A hesitant voice calls out and I turn away from my locker to find Emilio standing a few feet away. He mashes his lips together, his eyes on the ground near my feet. "You doing okay?"

"Hey. Umm, yeah. How are you?" I glance around the hallway, class will be starting soon.

He shrugs and looks up, giving me a small smile. "I'm good. I, uh..." he trails off and looks away. "I wanted to try something. If you're okay with it?"

I nod and brace myself.

"I know you said hands were a thing for you. So, I, ah..." He raises his hands so the tops of them face me. He's painted his nails an inky black and has a gold band on his left thumb and another on his right-hand middle finger. "I was hoping this might make a difference for you." He shrugs again with an almost sheepish expression on his face, and I can't help but smile as I take in what he's done, focusing on his nail beds and the jewelry. I take a tentative step forward. When my heartbeat stays steady, I take another. Emotions clog my throat and I take another step.

Emilio bites his upper lip, his eyes anxious as he waits for me to close the last bit of distance between us. When I do, I reach out and take one of his hands in mine, turning it over to trace the lines of his palms. I give him a tentative smile. "You going to wear nail polish all the time now? It might mess with your player status both on and off the field."

He smirks. "I think the black makes me look cool. I'm going for that whole emo-rocker look with some Latino flare."

"Ah, is that where the gold comes in?"

He smiles and hesitantly reaches for my elbow tugging me close. When I don't object, his arms wrap around me and I breathe in the smell of him. Spice and mint. His embrace tightens for a split second and I stiffen but he's quick to release me, taking a single step back. "I missed you, vanilla."

"I missed you, too."

He winks. "So, uh, you maybe wanna—" His eyes flick to someone over my shoulder, and I turn to find Roman standing just outside the door leading to our first-period class.

"He misses you, too," Emilio says behind me.

I shake my head. "I can't fix that E. Rome and I," I brush my hair out of my face and give him a tight-lipped smile. "We were just each other's way to pass some time. We both said as much from the beginning. A happy ever after was never in the cards. It's time to move on."

"Do you really believe that?" he asks.

I shrug. "Yes. I don't know. Maybe. It doesn't matter now."

He shakes his head. "I've known Roman almost my entire life. I'm closer with him than I am my own brothers. He's not the best at showing how he feels, but he cares about you, Allie. A lot. I don't want to push you. You've been through enough but just ... don't write him off yet, okay?"

I bit my bottom lip and look away. "I don't think I can afford to care about him any more than I already do. It hurts—"

"I know, sweetheart. I know. But I think Rome can make you happy. You deserve to be happy."

FORTY

Roman

I watch Allie with Emilio and jealousy hits me like an oncoming train.

She takes his hands and rather than retreating, she steps closer to him. Reaches out and touches him.

Dominique slaps a hand on my shoulder and my gaze jerks toward him. "You need to fix this."

"I'm trying."

"Try harder."

I tug away from him. "She's letting everyone else in *but* me." Even I hear the bitterness in my voice. The second I see Emilio pull her into a hug, I see red. I want to punch the fucker in the face, to hell if he's one of my best friends.

"I know this hurts, man—"

"Hurts?!" I turn to him, eyes wide, and a sneer on my lips. "You think this hurts? Fuck you. I wish all it did was hurt. This shit right here"—I wave in their direction—" it fucking guts me. My girl won't talk to me. Won't look at me. She was fucking r—"

Dominique grabs me and shoves me inside an empty classroom. "Keep your goddamn voice down," he whisper-shouts.

I'm shaking my head, hands already forming fists. I need to hit something. Or someone. I need to funnel all of whatever it is that I'm feeling into *something* or I'm going to lose my goddamn mind.

Dom gets in my face and it takes everything in me not to draw back and hit my best friend.

"This sucks. You're pissed off because you know you fucked up. You had a good thing going and she got hurt." I open my mouth but he cuts me off. "But you're still not getting it Rome. *She* got hurt. Her. Not you. You don't get to be pissed off at her or anyone else because you're a jealous asshole used to getting his way. She deserves better than that."

"Get off me." I shove him back. He takes a few more steps away, his jaw clenched and his eyes narrowed.

"This isn't about you. Not what you want or what you think you need. If you want to get her back then stop being a selfish prick and realize this is about her. What she wants and what she needs. That's all that should matter right now."

I work my jaw. The asshole is right and I hate it. My eyes fall to the floor and I force myself to take a deep breath before dropping down, my ass hitting the cool linoleum with my back against the wall. My eyes hit his once more. "What do I do?"

He rubs the back of his neck, a weary expression on his face. "I don't know, man."

"She won't talk to me," I say, my words hollow and empty.

Dom sighs. "You're making this about you again. It's not just that she won't talk to you. She can't. You saw what happened before. She freaked out and damn near had a panic attack."

Fuck.

It's the hands thing.

Something clicks. An idea forming in my head and suddenly, I know what I have to do now.

I push to my feet and head for the door.

"Where are you going?"

"Out."

"What do you mean, out? We have class."

I shake my head. "I'm skipping. I have something I need to do. Just —" I pause. "Watch out for my girl."

I head straight to the parking lot, ignoring Mrs. Jennings when she pokes her head out of her classroom and asks me where I'm going. Season's over. She can give me all the detentions she wants.

I spot Henderson in the parking lot getting out of his Subaru WRX and make a split-second decision to call out to him. "Yo, Henderson."

His head jerks toward me and he scowls.

"Come on, we're cutting."

"What?"

I stalk toward his car and open the passenger side door. "Get in the car, Henderson. I need a ride. Let's go."

Surprisingly, he does as I ask. I give him directions to The Missing Piece and have him park in the first available space we can find. There's no hesitation as I walk inside. I don't even need to think about what to get. I already know. He follows behind, uncertainty written across his face.

The woman at the desk takes one look at the two of us and her smile brightens. She's wearing a low-cut tank top in the middle of winter, exposing her arms, both covered in ink. "Do you have time for walk-ins?" I ask, ignoring the flirtatious smile she gives me.

"I'll check for you," she turns to her computer before her gaze returns to mine. "And what about him, sugar? You both here for some work?"

Henderson shakes his head in a definitive no.

"Just me," I tell her.

"Alright then. Henry has some time. What are you after?"

I give her a quick rundown of what I'm looking for.

She purses her lips. "Are you sure you want that on your hands?"

I nod and she goes and gets this Henry guy who comes to the front, and I explain again to him what I want. He looks at me the way some tattoo artists do when they think you're making a mistake, but he's not going to say anything because he's happy to take my money.

We sit down together and he works on the sketch for both pieces. Laying the stencil on my hands we go over placement and then we're set. He doesn't bother asking me for ID. I've learned that once you have some ink, no one really cares much about adding more.

"Last chance, man. You sure?"

I nod. I explained to Henry what the tattoos meant, it's not every day a guy walks in asking for what I'm after, and the explanation only cements his belief that this is stupid. But that's okay. This girl is it for me. She's not just my beginning, she's my end. I've been fucking around and going through the girls in this town one right after the other until she showed up. That had worked for me these last few years. I never wanted more than one night with any of them. But with Allie, I don't want just one night. I need more. I need her every day. For all of the days that are to come.

She's the first person I think about when I wake up and the last one on my mind when I go to sleep. She's not just some random. She never was. She's the real deal. I know we're young. I know we said we were having fun. I shouldn't be worried about my tomorrow or my forever, but that's what I want with her.

She needs to know she's it for me. I'll make the sacrifices. I'll step up and put in the work. Because she fucking deserves it. I just hope this shows her exactly what she means to me because if this doesn't do that, I have no fucking idea what else I can do to win her back.

It takes four hours for Henry to finish. When he does, he walks me through the usual list of how to care for the ink. What lotions to use. And gives me the reminder that hand tats are notorious for fading faster than anywhere else on the body. I pay him and give him my thanks after he covers the tops of both my hands in a thin bandage.

There's still around an hour left of school and another twenty minutes or so after that until she gets home. I need to talk to her where she'll feel safe. I don't want to do it at the school. We don't need the audience and I know the parking lot holds bad memories for her, so I decide to head to her place. I don't want to spring this on her or make her uncomfortable, but I don't see an alternative.

"I can't believe you just did that," Henderson says.

I shrug like it's no big deal because it isn't. I'd do a hell of a lot more for that girl than just get a little ink.

He gives me a sideways look as I tell him to head toward Allie's place. "You really care about her?" he asks, sounding surprised.

I grunt because I don't have to justify my feelings for her to him.

He parks across the street from the mansion where she lives, and I recline my seat and settle in to wait. A glance at the clock shows me we have some time before she gets home. Henderson turns off the car and the silence between us stretches, becoming awkward.

"We ever gonna talk about—'

I cut him off. "No. There's nothing to talk about."

He sighs. "I fucked up."

"That's the understatement of the century."

He turns toward me in his seat, nostrils flaring. "You've fucked up too, Rome. Don't pretend like you're some saint."

"Never said I was," I tell him. "But I'm learning from my mistakes. Trying to fix them. Can you say the same?"

His face tightens and he looks away, staring out the windshield. "I was in a bad place back then."

I nod. I'm aware. I might not have been at the time. He was good at covering his tracks, keeping his nose clean, but I found out later what he'd been going through. "We made a deal," I remind him. "You help me, we wipe the slate clean. But, Henderson." I wait until he meets my gaze again, wanting him to see just how serious I am. "I won't make this deal again. Whatever shit you still need to clean up, be sure that you do."

He nods, not denying that he's still in some shit he shouldn't be.

Knowing I shouldn't I ask, "You still doing?"

He shakes his head.

"Dealing?"

A pause and then a single sharp nod.

"Keep that shit away from her. Got it? She likes you. She doesn't have many people here and she's been through too much. Don't let whatever you're into rub off on her life."

"I won't. I would never—"

I snort. "Because it didn't fuck up our lives either, right?" That quiets him and he exhales a harsh breath.

"I'm getting my shit in order. I just ... need time."

"It's been a year and a half."

"I know." His jaw tightens. "But I have my reasons, and I'm working on it."

I nod, letting the subject drop. We wait in silence for a few more minutes before Allie's Audi comes into view.

"So, what's your plan here?"

I turn to him and shrug. "I don't have a plan. I'm winging it. If she's okay to talk to me, make yourself scarce. I'll find a ride back later. If she struggles, stick around and try not to listen as I pour my heart out on the fucking pavement."

He frowns, rubbing the back of his neck. "Uh, okay. I guess I can go with that."

FORTY-ONE

Allie

I've been thinking about what Emilio said all day. I want to believe him. Believe that Roman misses me. It's just so hard to do that when it was so easy for him to push me away.

I pull into my driveway and get out, my mind distracted, when I hear a voice behind me say, "Allie?"

I squeal, whirling to see who's behind me and find Roman and Aaron standing a few yards away.

I press my hand to my chest, willing my racing heart to slow. "Don't scare me like that!"

Roman lifts both hands, "I didn't mean to scare you. I just want to talk."

I frown and flick a glance toward Aaron who's standing a few steps behind Roman. He gives me a sheepish look and shrugs. "I'm just here for moral support."

My scowl deepens. "For me or for him?" I thought they hated each other.

Roman answers. "He's here for you. We're patching up some of our shit. Henderson can be an okay dude when he wants to be. But I asked him to come with me because I wanted him to be here for you."

He did? "Why?"

Roman takes a tentative step forward. "Because I want to talk and I know you trust him. That you're comfortable with him around."

"I'm fine with Dominique too, and he's your friend. Why not ask him?"

He shakes his head. "Because I didn't want to gang up on you. Dominique's my friend. He's yours too, but I didn't want you to think he'd be on my side over yours or that you wouldn't have anyone in your corner. Henderson and I have our history, but when it comes to you and me, he's always going to pick you first. He's in your corner. He's your friend. I want you to feel safe talking to me."

Oh. That's ... thoughtful of him.

He runs his hands over his face and I catch sight of the twin bandages over the top of both his hands.

"What happened to your hands?" I ask, worry clenching my stomach. Is he hurt? Did something happen?

Roman lifts his gaze, his dark brown eyes meeting mine. "That's actually what I came here to show you."

Aaron looks nervous behind him, shifting from one foot to the other.

"Ummm...okay." I wait for him to elaborate but he doesn't. His lips are pressed into a tight line, his eyes downcast. He peels back the bandages and underneath I see that he's sporting new ink. I gasp. "You tattooed your hands?"

He nods but doesn't say anything as he removes the second bandage, shoving both in his back pocket. I swallow hard as I take in the new pieces he's added, fighting the urge to get a closer look. They're beautiful. On his left, he has an anchor surrounded in a sea of crashing waves that covers the entire top of his hand. The detail looks amazing and before I can talk myself out of it, I step toward him, curious about the design.

"Do you want to see them?" he asks, holding perfectly still, almost like he's afraid to breathe. I realize how close I've gotten to him and my own heart races, but I fight through the wave of apprehension and nod.

He holds his hand out and with shaking fingers I trace the design on his left hand before jerking away and putting a foot of distance between us. Hurt flashes in his eyes before he masks it.

I inhale a lungful of air. *It's just Roman.* I remind myself. I force my gaze back to his hands, allowing myself time to take in the dark ink and see the stark differences between his hands and those of my attacker. Seconds pass and when my heart settles I move closer to him once again.

"Why an anchor?" I'm whispering and have no idea why.

"Because when you're adrift, when you can't find your way to shore, I want to be the one who steadies you."

My heart seizes in my chest. "You got this for me?" I ask, dumbfounded.

His smile is hopeful.

"I don't understand," I say. "This is permanent, Roman. You didn't have—"

He cuts me off. "I did, Allie. I need you to see how important you are to me. How much you matter and how incredibly sorry I am. I just... I want a second chance. To do everything the right way. To treat you like you deserve to be treated."

A tear rolls down my cheek and I hastily wipe it away. Forcing down the sudden knot in my throat I ask, "And what is this one? Is it an orchid... or maybe a daffodil?" I examine his right hand. This one is smaller though still covers most of his hand.

Roman shakes his head. "No. Not an orchid or a daffodil."

"What is it then?"

"It's a vanilla planifolia." At my confused expression he adds, "Mexican vanilla."

I gasp, dropping his hands. I look away as emotion threatens to bubble up out of me. It's as if he's shoved his hand in my chest and squeezed my heart until it beats only for him. The walls I've built to protect myself begin to crumble.

I catch sight of Aaron. He's retreated toward his car and is sitting on the hood, giving us some semblance of privacy. His eyes meet mine and he gives me a barely perceptible nod as if to say, *yeah, that just happened.* I turn back to meet Roman's raw gaze.

"Why?" I force myself to ask. None of this makes sense. "Why are you trying so hard to fix something that never really started?"

"Because you're worth it. You're worth all of it. All the fighting, the pain, the feelings. You make me fucking *feel*, Allie." He slaps a hand on his chest right over his heart. "Right here. You made my ice-cold heart beat, and it only wants to beat for one person. You.

Only you. I don't just want you. I fucking *need* you." He steps forward and presses his forehead against mine, cupping my face in his strong inked hands and I close my eyes, breathing him in. Fighting through the fear of being close to a boy I'm not sure I can trust. "Alejandra Ramirez, I need you in my life."

Instinctively, I know Roman would never hurt me. Not physically. But the fear of giving this boy my heart has the air in my lungs freezing.

"Roman, I can't lose a—"

"You won't," he says with conviction. "You fucking won't. I can promise you that. I don't know how to do this whole relationship thing. I'm learning as I go here. But I won't ever turn my back on you like that again. Never, Allie. Just give me this chance. One more chance. I won't mess it up."

"I'm broken," I tell him because it's true. I'm broken, my pieces jagged and sharp. I don't know if I'm even capable or even willing to be intimate with him after everything I've been through, and he doesn't need that. He doesn't need my baggage. For what, a few months of bliss? We're graduating in a few short months. And then what?

"Let me pick up all your broken pieces and put you back together. Let me be your anchor when you're lost and the world keeps spinning around you."

I pull back, and my heart aches seeing the sheer vulnerability on his face. His hands fall from my cheeks to wrap around me and I'm almost surprised when I don't stiffen. "And when we graduate?"

He presses his face into my hair. "We figure it out. I'm not letting you go, vanilla. I need you too much."

My heart does a free-fall and I pray that this time, he doesn't let it splatter on the ground near his feet. My trust is a bruised and battered thing. But I think I love the boy standing in front of me. And I think he loves me, too. Neither one of us knows how to say it. Words don't feel like they'll ever be enough.

But Roman said he needs me, so I take a leap of faith and let my truth pass over my lips, whisper soft. "Maybe we need each other."

FORTY-TWO

Allie: Four months later

"*Happy birthday to you. Happy birthday to you. Happy birthday to Allie. Happy birthday to you.*"

My smile is beaming as I lean forward and blow out the candles on the cake Mrs. Valdez made for me. It's my eighteenth birthday, and while I don't feel any different than I did yesterday, I know that after today, everything is going to change.

It's been four months since Roman and I decided to give a real relationship between us a try. We've had our ups and downs, and I'm still learning to cope with some of the traumas I've experienced, but I've made a lot of progress.

I don't freak out anymore when he comes up behind me and wraps his arms around my waist like he's doing now, leaning in to kiss my neck. "Did you make a wish?" he asks, his breath is hot against my skin, his voice pitched low and seductive.

A slow smile spreads over my face and I shake my head, turning to look at him. "Nope,"

His brows furrow in confusion, and I bite my lower lip to keep from laughing. "I already have everything I could ask for." And it's the truth. All my friends are here. I have the most amazing boyfriend who consistently puts me and my needs first. And I've gotten the help I should have when I was first assaulted. Roman's mom—Maria—made sure of that.

I'm happy and I'm healing. I couldn't ask for anything more.

His face cracks into a wide grin as he turns me to face him, then dips down and presses his lips against mine in a tender kiss. His kisses always start this way. Hesitant and soft. But one nip of his bottom lip has him deepening the kiss and I gasp, opening my mouth to drink him in, silently asking for more.

Voices groan behind us before wandering off.

"Get a room," Emilio calls out and I pull away, fighting hard not to blush.

"Fuck off," Roman says, though there's no heat in his voice.

Emilio rolls his eyes then pries me out of Roman's embrace. "You'll have Allie all to yourself soon enough. Today you have to share."

I squeal as he lifts me into the air, throwing me over his shoulder and racing into the backyard with me, Roman hot on our heels. It's strange to think that a few short months ago I was adrift. Lost to my pain and consumed by my grief. I didn't think I'd find happiness again. Not like this. But I'm not numb anymore. I feel my emotions like a kaleidoscope of sensation and I relish each and every day.

The entire crew moves outside. Roman's parents—Maria and Melchor—Dominique, Aaron, Kasey. Even Julio, Gabe, and Felix made the drive up from Richland to celebrate with me.

Emilio sets me on my feet before gripping my hand and dragging me to the center of the yard. Music is playing on the outdoor speaker system and he draws me into dancing with him as Rombai's *Me Voy* plays. Kasey joins us before long and the three of us sing off key. Despite most of Kasey's words being made up and not actual lyrics, we laugh, dancing without a care in the world because that's how I've chosen to move on.

So much happened that I didn't have control over, and the threat of what tomorrow brings is always there. But my therapist reminds me during our weekly sessions that I need to focus on today and live my life without fear. I've lost so much. More than most people in my short eighteen years. But I don't want to live a life full of fear and what ifs. Which brings us to today. I'm eighteen, and I'm getting the keys to my first apartment this afternoon. Roman is moving in with me, which Maria and Melchor aren't thrilled about since both of us are still in high school, but Maria at least seems to understand.

Living with Gerald isn't an option for me if I want to escape my past. He's a toxic piece of my life with an ever-present threat hanging over my head that we still need to deal with, and to move forward, I need to separate my life from his.

Janessa set up a meeting with him just this morning and I explained that I was moving out. I thanked him for taking me in after my mother's death and told him I'd made other arrangements now that I was a legal adult. He didn't look happy about it, but Janessa managed to smooth things over and help with some of the awkwardness.

He's letting me keep the car, a birthday gift of sorts. He also gave me access to a trust fund that I have no intention of using on anything beyond schooling, but I'm glad it's there. It helps with some of the stress that moving out brings.

Roman smiles at me across the lawn, a beer in his hand as he stands with Aaron on his right and Dom on his left. Kasey stands surrounded by my boys from back home, soaking up all their attention and I fight a grin when I see Dominique's murderous glare aimed their way.

Something makes me think there's something going on between the two of them, but neither has mentioned anything and I haven't asked. I'm just happy. Content, for once, and looking forward to what comes next for us.

It only takes a few lingering looks before Roman sets his drink down and joins me on the lawn, his hips swaying in sync with mine as his arms wrap around me. "You're so beautiful," he tells me.

I can't help the smile that blooms over my face. "You're pretty good-looking yourself," I remark, giving him an obvious once-over and letting heat build in my gaze.

His eyes gain a wicked glint. "I'm so fucking lucky." He presses his lips to mine again before whispering against my mouth, "And I love you so fucking much."

God, this boy. "I love you, too," I say, flinging my arms around his neck and hugging him tight. No matter what our future holds, I know he'll be by my side, and I can't wait for what our next chapter might bring.

"Have you guys seen the new girl?" Aaron asks, taking a seat beside me. He's wearing his signature black Volcom jeans, a long sleeve Fox t-shirt, and checkered Vans.

Roman, Dominique, and Emilio wear matching scowls as they turn toward him. The guys still aren't one hundred percent on board with letting Aaron back into their lives, but they're thawing to the idea a bit. At least, I hope they are. That they haven't barked at him to get lost is already an improvement.

"I thought I was the new girl?" I ask, shoving a french fry in my mouth. As soon as I swallow, Roman hands me another. I roll my eyes but accept the food and toss it in my mouth before meeting his gaze with an exasperated smile.

I might have developed a bit of an eating problem earlier in the school year. Really, it was more of a lack of eating problem. As in, I never really ate, and it definitely showed. But I'm better now.

I still see my therapist every other week and I've been working through some of the trauma I've experienced, finding better coping mechanisms.

Since then, Roman's made it his mission to make sure I eat at least three meals a day. Every chance he gets, he shovels food at me. It would bother the heck out of me if it wasn't for the fact I know he does it because he cares, so I begrudgingly tolerate it.

Aaron shakes his head. "You are. But now we have a *newer,* new girl. The whole school has been buzzing about her all morning. I'm surprised you haven't heard about her."

I scan the cafeteria, looking for any unfamiliar faces, but don't see anyone who stands out.

"That's because Allie's the only new girl who matters," Roman says, earning a smile and a kiss on the cheek.

"Is she hot?" Emilio asks, just as Kasey claims the seat across from him. Dominique scowls at her and, catching his gaze, she sticks out her tongue like a petulant child. I snicker.

"Yeah, man. She is." Aaron says. "Dark brown hair. Blue eyes. She's fucking tiny too. Barely over five feet."

Me and Kasey both roll our eyes. *Boys.* But Emilio's eyes brighten with interest.

"No," Kasey says forcefully and all heads turn to look at her. Her eyes bore holes into Emilio's skull as she waves a french fry in his direction.

"This'll be good," Roman whispers into my ear, his warm breath caressing my neck. I fight a shiver and lean toward him, smiling to myself when he pulls me closer and trails kisses along my bare shoulder, completely ignoring the conversation around us.

"No?" Emilio's brows pull together.

"Yeah. No. Leave this new chick alone. Everyone knows you're fucking Sarah. Though none of us know the hell *why*. Bibiana is nice. She doesn't need attention from any of the devils. Least of all you."

Roman snorts as Emilio's eyes spark with mischief, his upper lip curling into a smirk. "Bibiana, huh? I like it."

Dominique places a fist over his mouth, hiding his own smile as we all lean in, ready to watch the fireworks explode as Kasey and Emilio verbally spar with one another.

"What's the matter, baby Henderson? You jealous?"

She laughs. "Of you? Hardly."

"That's right." He snaps his fingers. "I almost forgot. I'm the wrong flavor, right?"

Kasey glares. "What the hell are you going on about?"

Emilio's smile turns smug. He leans over the table as if he's about to share a secret with her. "We all know you're a fan of dark chocolate." He winks and tilts his head toward Dominique.

Kasey bares her teeth, but she can't hide the crimson staining her cheeks. Dominique coughs. Then chokes. He reaches for his Gatorade to clear his throat.

Kasey glowers at him. "Don't get excited all of a sudden," she snaps. "Emilio's right. I like black guys. But I sure as hell don't like you."

She shoves to her feet and stomps away in a fit of anger.

I sigh and scrub a hand over my face. "Did you really have to do that?" I ask.

Emilio shrugs. "It's fun riling up baby Henderson. I gotta take advantage of every opportunity."

"You're a dick." Aaron says, but there isn't any heat in his voice. Instead, he's watching Dom as Dominique, in turn, watches Kasey's retreating form.

I kick him under the table and his head whips to face me. I angle my head to Aaron and Dom meets his stare. "What?"

"Stay the hell away from my sister."

He snorts. "Don't worry. Jailbait isn't my type."

Satisfied, Aaron stands from the table just as the bell rings, calling an end to lunch. "I'll catch up with you later," he tells me.

I wave goodbye as the rest of us gather our things and head to our next classes. Roman holds my hand in the halls and together we ignore everyone's interested stares. I don't think the Sun Valley High student body will ever get used to seeing Roman in a relationship, but at least they've stopped sneering at me.

Emilio and Dominique turn down a hallway on our left as Roman and I continue forward. Spotting a classroom that brings back heat inducing memories, I tug Roman towards it and shove him inside, closing the door behind me.

I make a point of locking the door before looking at my very hot and very confused boyfriend. "We're going to be late," he says.

I walk towards him and place my hands on his chest. Licking my lips, I lean in close, "I don't want to go to class. I want to stay here.

With you." I pull back, gauging his expression. He frowns, still confused, and I fight back an eye roll. Why is he being so dense?

Taking a deep breath, I reach down and cup his dick over his jeans. He jumps back a few steps and my hand falls between us.

"Allie?" His voice is rough.

"I want you," I please, closing the distance between us again.

Roman sucks on his bottom lip, concern flashing in his dark brown eyes. "You're not ready."

Determination sweeps through me. I'm not a fragile flower. I won't break. Not again. He's treated me with kid gloves since the assault, but I'm ready to move on with my life. To be with him again. I want him. All of him. So freaking bad.

"Do you remember the last time we were alone in this room?" I ask.

His eyes sweep the empty classroom. Recognition brightens his gaze before he gives me a questioning look. "I don't think this is a good—"

Throwing caution to the wind, I tear my shirt over my head, exposing the lacy black bra underneath. His eyes zero in on my chest and his mouth drops open.

Reaching behind me, I unclasp my bra and let it fall to the floor.

He groans.

A smile teases the corners of my mouth as I spot the blatant want on his face. He still hasn't moved, but he will. Roman wants me just as bad as I want him. He just needs a little more encouragement, and I plan to give him exactly that.

I palm one of my breasts, my free hand reaching for his and guiding it over the other. He squeezes my flesh, his eyes darkening, before tugging at one taut nipple.

I gasp, electricity zipping through me and arrowing straight to my core.

Roman's other hand grabs my hip and he tugs me flush against his body. "I don't want to hurt you," he says just before dipping his head and claiming my mouth with a soft, gentle kiss. I moan into the kiss, pouring all of my need and desire into his hot mouth. Encouraging him to go deeper. To devour me the way I want him to.

Roman keeps his kiss gentle. His lips controlled. I hate it. I want him to let go. To just give in to the lust coursing through us both.

My fingers fumble with the zipper of his jeans and when I finally get them undone, I slide my hand beneath his boxers, wrapping my fingers around the smooth skin of his shaft. I pull his cock out of the front of his underwear and give him a careful squeeze.

His hips involuntarily thrust forward in my grasp. He mutters out a harsh, *"Fuck."* and his chin dips down, his gaze locked on my hand pumping his cock.

I smirk and raise one brow.

Dark eyes meet mine. "Allie—"

"Stop talking." I pump his dick up and down, using my free hand to cup his balls. His eyes flash with heat and my heart pounds in my chest. Tension lines his face and I know he's straining to hold himself in place, but I'm determined to make him move.

Dropping to my knees, I take his cock and wrap my lips around the engorged head, swallowing his shaft until the tip presses against the back of my throat.

He grunts. His head rolls back on his shoulders, eyes on the ceiling as he swears in Spanish. "*Maldita sea.* You're going to kill me." He groans, a wicked and starved sound that makes liquid heat pool between my thighs.

I bob my head, working him over, but after a few short minutes, he jerks me to my feet and slams his mouth on mine. He devours me with his kiss and it's all I can do to remain standing.

His tongue tangles with mine. Teeth crashing,

This, right here. This is what I needed. I give myself to him, imagining what it will feel like with him inside of me.

His hands knead my breasts and I writhe against him. Desperate for more.

I grab one of his hands and drag it to my aching center beneath the hem of my skirt. He curses when his fingers meet smooth, bare flesh, having come to school without panties in the hopes of this very thing happening.

"You make me insane," he growls into my mouth, pressing me back against one of the desks.

It's been months since the assault. Months of therapy. Months of adjusting to a new life and a new normal. Of living with the man I love and being unable to show him just how much I want him. He's been patient this entire time. But I'm ready for more. I need him. All of him. So if I make him insane, he makes me absolutely crazy.

We've fooled around. Touched one another and shared moments of intimacy, but he's never let it go all the way and I'm desperate to feel him inside of me, stretching me, claiming me. It's a visceral need I can't shake.

"I want you."

At first, I was grateful he didn't pressure me. Now, being with him is all I ever think about. It's been long enough that we've denied ourselves this.

Practiced fingers delve between my legs, circling my clit. I tense and warmth floods through my veins.

"Are you sure?" He asks. His eyes are hooded, stark need staring back at me.

I swallow hard and mash my breast against his firm chest. "Yes," I hiss.

He teases my entrance before two fingers slip inside me. My head falls back. He pumps his fingers in and out of me as his thumb continues to circle my clit.

Pressing me back, my butt rests on the edge of the desk and he withdraws his fingers to position my legs on either side of it, exposing my center to his hungry stare. With one hand, he grips my thigh, kneading my flesh before slipping his fingers back inside of me.

God, he feels so good. He adds a third finger and my breath hitches.

"Play with your tits, Allie." He demands.

I do as I'm told, massaging my breasts and tugging at my aching nipples. He groans, his fingers working in and out of. Pleasure assaults me as my climax moves closer, but I don't want to come on his fingers. I want to come with him buried inside of me.

Reaching down, I grip his shaft. "Fuck me," I beg. "I need you. Now."

He hesitates for a moment before shaking his head. His fingers withdraw from my needy center and I'm on the verge of angry tears when he surprises me and drops down between my legs. Gripping my thighs, he drags his tongue along my slit.

I moan.

He devours me as though starved, feasting on my lips, my core, my aching clit.

Within seconds, I'm a whimpering puddle, desperate for release. "Roman!"

"Come for me, baby." he murmurs against me, dipping a finger back inside.

I moan at the intrusion, tilting my hips up as I fight to get even closer. He sucks on my clit again and I cry out, stars exploding behind my eyelids. My orgasm crashes over me and he growls between my legs, lapping at my release.

When the trembling in my legs stops, he draws back and disappointment flares inside me, but it doesn't last long.

The next thing I know, he's lining his cock up with my needy pussy, swiping the head through my slick entrance. "Are you sure?" he asks.

"God, yes." I press my feet against the back of his calves, pushing him forward as he slips inside me. He freezes, no more than an inch of him inside me. His breathing is ragged, his gaze hungry, but I catch the worry there too.

Reaching up, I cup the side of his face, forcing him to meet my gaze. "I want you inside of me." I tell him, "I need you to fuck me, Roman. Now. I won't break."

My words have the intended effect and he finally lets himself off his leash. Thrusting forward, he buries himself inside me with a grunt, quickly drawing back and slamming into me again.

One big strong hand wraps around the back of my neck, the other holds my hip, and I lean back, bracing myself on the desk and he fucks me.

His balls slap against my ass with each one of his thrusts, and he drives me toward another frenzy. A mixture of whimpers and moans comes from my throat to add to the wet slurping sounds that fill the room.

He dips his head, lips seeking mine and giving me a taste of myself. I moan into his mouth, surprised by how turned on I am, tasting myself in his kiss.

I arch my hips and he growls, finding a new angle and hitting a spot deep inside me that has my toes curling.

I bite my bottom lip, fighting back the sounds threatening to escape.

"Come on my cock, Allie," he murmurs. "I'm not going to make it much longer."

Reaching between us, he circles my still sensitive clit and within seconds I cry out, my orgasm shattering me. Roman thrusts into me, his movements erratic as my pussy convulses around him.

A harsh groan falls from his lips right before he pulls out and liquid heat splashes over my exposed stomach.

We're both breathing hard in the now still room and Roman looks down at me with so much love and devotion in his eyes it makes my chest physically hurt.

"You're so fucking perfect," he says, leaning down to kiss me. "And all mine."

"Mmmmm." I hum in agreement.

"I love you," he tells me, pressing his forehead against mine.

"I love you, too." My eyes stray to his hands, spotting the vanilla planifolia and anchor tattoos on the back of his hands. God, I love this man. More and more with each passing day.

Pulling back, he looks down at the mess we've made and crudely drags his cum from my stomach over each of my breasts.

I suck in a breath. "What are you doing?"

He grins before circling my nipple. "Marking what's mine." He trails his cum to my other nipple, giving it the same attention. I clench my thighs together, noticing his still half hard erection.

I lick my lips.

Roman catches the direction of my gaze and smirks. "Already wanting more?"

I nod, not bothering to hide my blatant desire despite the thorough fucking he just gave me.

He chuckles. Tucking himself back into his boxers, he zips up his pants before grabbing a roll of paper towels from the classroom counter.

He helps me clean his cum from my stomach, but when I move to wipe over my breasts, he stops me. He shakes his head before stealing a kiss, his teeth playfully tugging at my bottom lip.

"I want you wearing my cum," he says.

I swallow hard, and a shiver of desire works up my spine.

"You're wicked," I tell him, but I don't hate the idea.

He smirks. "You have no idea."

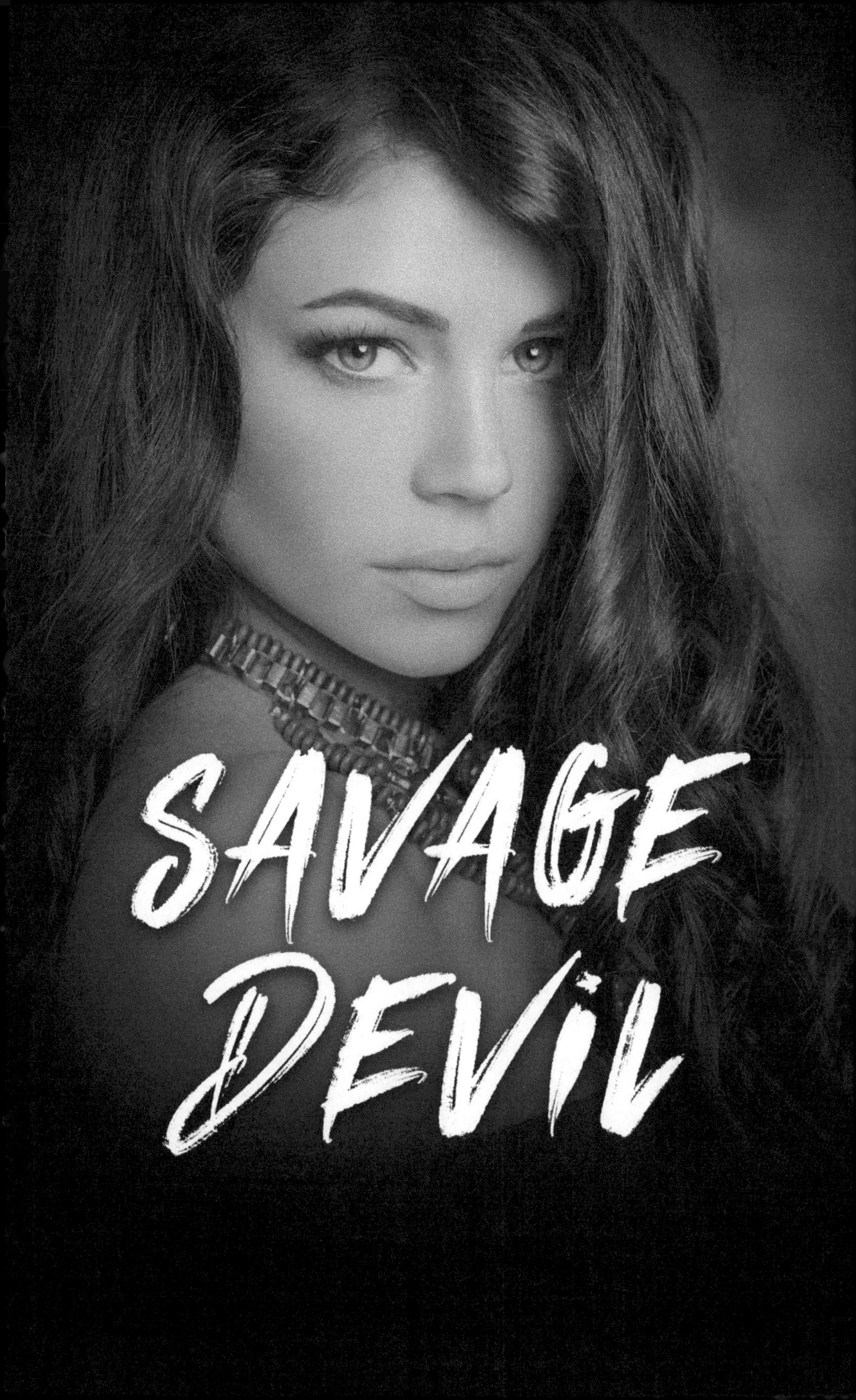
SAVAGE
DEVIL

Savage Devil

One night.
No names.
No numbers.
That is the deal we make.
After tonight, I'll never see him again, and I want to leave town
with zero regrets.

But, a year and a half later, I'm back with a secret I'm terrified to
tell.

Turns out the guy from that one reckless night is football royalty.
One of Sun Valley's infamous Devils.

I didn't tell him I was moving that night.
And, he isn't someone who handles rejection well.

Something I realize when I bump into him at my new school. Sun
Valley High. Home of the Devils.

And he decides to give me a lesson in why you never cross a Devil.

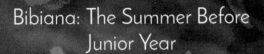

Bibiana: The Summer Before
Junior Year

"**C**ome on, Bibi!" Monique whines before adding a coat of clear gloss over her full lips. "We're going to be late for the party. The one you insisted we go to tonight," she reminds me now as she toys with her hair. The dark brown box braids hang just past her shoulders. She glowers at me through the reflection in the mirror.

"I have nothing to wear!" Yes, now I'm whining, but sifting through my closet for something sexy—or, at the very least, something that doesn't scream "I go to a stuck-up private school"—is next to impossible. And being a Suncrest Saint—even if past tense—isn't something you advertise when mingling with the Sun Valley Devils. With any luck, we won't run into any of the true Devils tonight. That would cause all sorts of problems, especially since Monique's brother happens to be one of them.

He was in a car accident last week and is home recovering, so we should be in the clear. At least, I hope.

"Obviously." Monique reaches into her overnight bag. "That's why I brought you this." She pulls out a sleek, black, bodycon dress and tosses it my way.

I catch it and hold up the barely there dress, an immediate scowl on my face. "No way. I can't wear that," I tell her with a firm shake of my head.

Hand on her hip, she turns to me. "And why the hell not?"

"Because half the dress is missing, that's why," I hiss, careful to keep my voice down as I give the dress another once-over. Mom and her boyfriend—Miguel—are already in bed, and I don't want to wake either of them. Going out tonight isn't exactly approved. But you know the saying, "better to ask forgiveness than permission." Better yet, if Mom doesn't find out, then there's nothing to forgive in the first place.

In my hands, the dress looks no bigger than a t-shirt. A child-sized t-shirt. Yeah, no way am I wearing this.

Monique huffs out a breath. "At least try it on. What happened to you wanting to step out of your comfort zone today, huh? Weren't you the one who said you wanted to do something daring? Live on the edge?" Her brows lift in an expectant expression. "It's your last night in Sun Valley, Bibi."

Urgh, please don't remind me. "That doesn't mean I want to go out looking like a dime-store hooker," I tell her with a huff as a wave of sorrow crashes into me. Tonight is my last night in Sun Valley. Tomorrow, I'm moving. New town. New school. New life. In Richland, of all places. It sucks.

She rolls her eyes before turning away to finish her makeup in the full-length mirror that hangs from the back of my bedroom door.

"Do I look like a dime-store hooker to you?" she asks over her shoulder.

"Obviously not," I snort. Monique is a goddess. Five-foot-eleven with rich brown skin, chestnut-colored eyes, and long braids pulled back into a half pony. She looks like Brandy Norwood from her Moesha days and I would kill to look half as good as she does. Her skin is flawless, and unlike me, she's managed to acquire curves in all the right places. I, on the other hand, am reed thin and straight as a bean pole. Mom swears I'll fill out eventually, but I doubt it. Not with my luck. At least I have boobs. Not much, but they're there.

"Glad we both agree. I'm wearing the exact same dress just in green. Try it on. You'll like it."

I roll my eyes but do as she says. It's not like I have a lot of options here. Most of my things are already packed. And even if they weren't, I still probably wouldn't have anything to wear. "Sexy" isn't really in my wardrobe vocabulary.

"Where did you get this from anyway?" I ask. "And how the heck did you manage to hide it from your mom?"

"Online. And I ordered it when she had a stupid floral shipment arrive for one of her charity things. There were so many delivery people in and out that day, she never noticed my lonely little Fashion Nova box."

"Sneaky," I tell her with a wink.

Monique and I have been best friends since middle school, which is how I know her parents would never approve of her wearing a dress like this. It's all about appearances for the Price family. They even took issue with our school-issued uniform skirts and had hers custom ordered three inches longer than standard. Though the hemline isn't the only thing about the dress they'd object to. They'd also balk at her wearing anything that wasn't designer and didn't cost a fortune. Can't wear the same clothes as the common folk.

Slipping the dress over my head, I smooth down the fabric and eye myself in the mirror.

"Damn, girl." Monique whistles. "You look stunning!"

I grimace. "This is...a lot." Though I can't pull my eyes away from my reflection. Monique is seven inches taller than me, so while her dress comes down just far enough to cover her butt, mine falls to mid-thigh. It's strapless and hugs my body like a second skin, giving the illusion of curves I know I don't have. But...wow.

Monique comes up behind me and pulls the clip from the back of my head, making my long, curly black hair fall around my face.

"This is perfect," she tells me. "It's sexy and screams for the love of God, please take my virginity."

I smack her arm but don't bother fighting my laugh. "I'm not trying to announce I want my virginity taken."

She tosses my hair clip on the bed and hands me a tube of bright red lipstick. "Doesn't change the fact that that is exactly what you're after. Come on, Bibi. This was your idea. Let's be rebels for once. We need this. A last hoorah before you abandon me."

I chew my bottom lip but accept the lipstick and move closer to the mirror to put it on. Squaring my shoulders, I remind myself that I'm leaving Sun Valley with zero regrets. I've spent the last sixteen years of my life being the good girl. The girl who never stepped out of line. Never caused a fuss. Never broke the rules.

I need to breathe. Even if it's only for one night.

At first, I was always on my best behavior because Mom was pregnant. She was older, the pregnancy unplanned, and it wasn't without complications. She needed help and support and I wanted to be there for her.

Then it was because my baby brother was sick. My parents had their hands full dealing with Afonso's condition. I didn't need to add to their plate by being reckless, and I didn't want to take attention away from Afonso. He was my baby brother. He was everything.

Then, right before his third birthday, he died. It gutted our family. Mom needed to grieve. No way would she have been able to handle me acting out on top of everything else. So, I continued to be the good girl. The rule follower. I can count on one hand the number of times my parents have ever needed to scold me.

Less than a year after Afonso passed, Dad left.

My family has been hit in the face with life again and again. There is never a good time to...I don't know...be a kid. To make mistakes. To act impulsively. Guilt worms its way through my chest reminding me now still isn't a good time. But then, when will it ever be? I'm sixteen years old. I want to be young and dumb. Not forever, but for a night. Just this one time. I want to make mistakes I can look back on. I want to know that I was wild and free. That I spread my wings and lived.

Afonso's been gone for three years now. Dad's been gone for two. It's been a whirlwind for Mom and I, but things have gotten better. Mom has a boyfriend. He's kinda weird but she smiles a lot more than she has in years, and I think she really loves him. He makes her happy. And I want her to be happy.

She's been through so much.

It's why I'm not complaining about the move. Well, not out loud at least. And why I stuffed back my tears and smiled ear to ear when she told me the good news. She deserves to be happy. I just...I want that for me, too.

"Okay. Let's go before I lose my nerve."

Monique's smile widens. "Eeeeee! This is going to be so much fun!"

I don't know if I share her enthusiasm, but I'm committed to this course nonetheless. For one night, I'm not going to be Bibiana Sousa—the good girl. I'm going to be the rebel. The wild child. A girl that goes with the flow, lets her hair down, and for once in her life, makes some freaking mistakes.

No one bats an eye as Monique and I stroll up to tonight's party house. I have no idea whose it is, but I also don't care. Suncrest Academy kids don't throw ragers like this, and by crashing a Sun Valley High party, we're less likely to run into anyone we know and have word get back to either of our parents.

"Come on, let's grab a drink." Monique hauls me through the front door and leads me in the obvious direction of the kitchen where a keg has been set up. Grabbing a red cup, she hands it to one of the guys manning the keg and he fills it for her, giving her an interested once-over.

"You here with anyone?" he asks, handing her the beer and tilting his head toward me in silent question. I shake my head, and wave off the offered alcohol, grabbing a water bottle from the open coolers instead. I know plenty of students who have zero issue with underage drinking but...I don't know...coming to the party to hook up with a guy seems risqué enough for me for one night. Drinking when I've just barely turned sixteen feels like I would be pushing it.

"Nope. Just my girl," Monique says, giving him a come-hither look as she takes a sip of her beer. The guys at Suncrest Academy don't give Monique a second glance. I'm pretty sure it's because they're intimidated by her. She's tall, a complete beast on the basketball court, and she has a spitfire personality. But it could also be because they're idiots. Actually, if I had to put money on it, it'd be because they're all idiots.

He tugs her close and she squeaks, though secretly I know she's thrilled by the attention. Like me, Monique is kept in a sheltered little box, rarely let out to play. We might say tonight is my night, but it's equally for her. We both need this escape from the constricting lives we lead, and Monique deserves to feel like the goddess she is.

"I'm gonna go mingle," I tell her, giving her the out she needs to have fun and not worry about me. She makes a face, about to argue, and I shake my head. "Have fun. You can't stick by my side all night, anyway. Remember?"

She rolls her eyes but smiles. "Fine. But find me if you need me, okay? And don't go home with anyone."

"Yes, Mom!" I snicker and turn around, following the sound of music coming from the back of the house.

I cut through the kitchen and dining room until I get to a set of double doors that leads to the back patio. A DJ booth has been set up. People are drinking and dancing, having a good time. I crack open my water bottle, taking a sip as I soak in the cool evening air, letting my gaze wander over the crowd. Everyone is clustered in these little groups as though natural cliques have formed and I kinda hate it. It's so high school.

I continue to scan the clusters when a guy on my far right grabs my attention. He's cute. My age with light blond hair and broad shoulders. He's laughing at something his friend says when our gazes connect. He stares for a second before lifting his cup as if to say hello. I smile. He smiles back. And then he goes back to talking. But every few seconds his eyes come back to me.

I linger where I stand for a moment, debating whether or not to head in his direction. It's obvious he's no longer listening to whatever his friends are saying. And he's not being shy about staring either. His perusal of my body lets me know he's interested but—

No.

Come on, Bibi. You can do this.

I take a deep breath. Be a rebel, I tell myself. I'm not going to just stand here like an idiot hoping he'll approach me. I'm going to be bold. I can do this.

I take a step forward when a voice behind me stops me in my tracks. "I wouldn't waste my time on Carson Bailey if I were you."

I whirl around, a scowl on my face as my eyes land on a boy hovering close behind me. "He has a small dick," he says, a savage grin on his face.

"Who said I was interested in his dick?" I ask, quirking a brow. And okay, yeah, maybe I am, but I don't have to admit it to this guy. Whoever the hell he is.

He snorts. "With a body like yours in a dress like that, you're looking for something, and it's not cookies at a bake sale. My money is on dick."

I roll my eyes. Jerk. "Maybe I just wanted to feel pretty."

He licks his lips, his eyes roving over my body in obvious appreciation. "Nah. You already know you're pretty. You want something else." His dark gaze is challenging as he boldly steps forward, our chests almost touching. A wave of heat floods through me at his proximity, and I take a second to drink him in. He's not just cute like the other guy. He's hot. He has dark brown hair and equally dark eyes that lift the smallest amount at the corners. He's Hispanic. Not Mexican, though. His jaw line is sharp. His brows angular. Not Brazilian like me either.

Honduran, maybe Guatemalan if I had to guess. Latin American for sure, there's a little too much indigenous in his features to be Spaniard but I don't bother asking to confirm.

Dressed in low-slung jeans and a form-fitting black shirt, it does nothing to hide his muscular body. He's most likely an athlete. No surprise there. He definitely has the confident swagger of one.

I force my feet to stay rooted as he towers over my tiny frame. He's much taller than me, maybe six feet. I have to tilt my head back to meet his stare, and a part of me itches to reach up on tiptoe and close the distance between our mouths, the blond boy all but forgotten thanks to his arrival.

My chest rises and falls with each of my breaths. My heart suddenly eager to beat out of my chest. I've never reacted to a boy like this. It's...intoxicating.

The corners of his lips quirk as if he knows exactly what I'm thinking and more surprising, he acts, closing the space between our lips, his mouth pressing firmly against mine. I gasp and he takes full advantage, his tongue exploring my mouth as the taste of sweet oranges and chili explodes across my tastebuds. I moan into his mouth, unable to stop my reaction to him. Man, can he kiss.

One of his hands grips my hip, the other tangles in my curly hair as he pulls me closer, our bodies pressed tight against one another and everything else around me disappears.

Hoots and hollers to get a room cut through the fog of desire and I pull back, breaking the kiss. He releases me with obvious reluctance, his hand still firmly on my hip and a stunned expression on his face.

I'm breathing heavy, my heart racing. That was...I don't know what the hell that was, but I've never been kissed like that. Never felt the need to clench my thighs together and curl my toes. Was it the same for him? I swallow hard and chew on my bottom lip. His gaze locks on my mouth and he licks his lips, my eyes tracking the movement. My hand reaches up almost as if it has a mind of its own, and my fingers curl into the fabric of his shirt needing to ground myself.

"You still want pretty boy over there?" he asks, tilting his head toward...what was his name?

I shake my head. Hell, no. I want him. This guy right here. If I'm going to lose my virginity to anyone, it should be him. Someone who makes me feel lightheaded after just one kiss.

"Good."

Without another word he reaches for my hand and tugs on me to follow as he weaves his way through the crowd, heading toward what I think is a pool house. "Where are we going?" I ask, my voice coming out a little breathless, my lips still tingling from our kiss.

"Somewhere quiet," he says over his shoulder and I notice he's clutching his side and there's a stiffness to his gate.

Is he okay?

I'm suddenly nervous. We're going somewhere quiet which is good. Right? It's what I want only I don't even know this guy. Then again, that is kind of the point of tonight. Only... God. Come on, Bibiana. Stop being such a worrier.

Reaching the pool house, he opens the door and we both slip inside. The room is dark, some outside light filtering in through the sheer curtains. He drags me toward a sofa and sits, a soft hiss escaping his lips before he tugs me down beside him.

"Are you alright?"

The room is silent except for our breathing. I sit stiffly beside him, my fingers still laced with his as my eyes adjust to the darkness. His thumb rubs lazy circles across the back of my hand, then he shifts to face me.

"Just a sports injury. No big deal."

I purse my lips. It's summer. Sports have ended for the year. I guess it's possible some practice over the summer months. I think football does maybe, but...

"Hey." He pulls me closer. "Come here."

He tugs me onto his lap, my thighs straddling his waist. His length presses against my core and I'm barely able to restrain myself from grinding against him.

He trails a finger along the side of my face, down my neck and settles it along the hollow of my throat. There's something strangely intimate about the caress. "What's your name?"

I hesitate.

"You holding back on me, mariposa?" I was right. Definitely Hispanic. His smile is both savage and sinful. There's this energy to him that draws me in, but it also terrifies me. This is supposed to be a one-night thing. Good memories and a fun time, but nothing more. No attachments. But there's something about him that tells me he's someone I'd find myself easily attached to. It's a good thing I'm only in Sun Valley for one more night. Wouldn't want to become one of what I'm sure are his many admirers.

"Hardly, just, why not keep this interesting?" I suggest as casually as possible.

He raises a brow, shadows cast across his face from the moonlight filtering through the room. "You don't wanna exchange names?" If anything, his grin widens.

I shake my head.

"What about phone numbers?" he asks, cocking his head to the side.

Another shake.

He chuckles. "Damn, mariposa. And here I thought I was the player."

If he only knew just how inexperienced I was. Stepping into the role I've set out for myself, I rock my hips against him and he hisses, his eyes glazing over with lust. "You're playing a dangerous game, mariposa."

"Why do you keep calling me a moth?" I ask, a breathy quality to my voice.

He leans forward, nipping at the column of my throat. "Not a moth. A butterfly," he murmurs. His hands find my hips and he presses me down against him, his hips thrusting upward to grind against my center. Electricity crackles between us. He tilts my chin, drawing my lips to his and fusing them together. Stars explode behind my closed lids and every rational thought in my mind floats away.

The more he kisses me, the drunker I am on his taste, and the more I want to throw caution to the wind. This feels good. Right. I don't even know him, but somehow, my body does. It craves him, silently begging for me.

His fingers dig into me, his erection hot between my legs. I weave my fingers through the short strands of his hair, pressing my chest against his, but it isn't enough. His kiss is drugging, pulling me deep into an abyss I have zero desire to escape. When his hands slip beneath the hem of my dress, tugging it over my ass and then my head, bearing me to his dark and hungry gaze, I offer no resistance.

His eyes grow hooded as he lasers in on my chest, a hand coming up to thumb over one taught nipple. I shiver and he grins. The satisfied smile of a boy who knows the effect he has on a girl. He leans forward, capturing my breast in his hot mouth, his teeth grazing my nipple as I rock against him. My body aching and desperate for more friction.

Between kisses, I tug off his shirt. Unbutton his jeans. It takes next to no time for the two of us to find ourselves naked, clawing at one another's skin and he wastes zero time in retrieving a condom from his discarded jeans pocket and rolling it on before pulling me down on top of him and lining himself up with my core.

A part of me wonders if I should say something. Let him know I'm a virgin. I've heard the stories. I know there is usually pain the first time. But I can't convince myself to ruin this moment. I want this. Unequivocally and desperately. I want this.

His cock nudges my entrance and I stiffen, bracing myself for what's to come. His hard, thick length pushes inside of me with slow and measured thrusts. I gasp at the sensations as he stretches me to my limits, to the point where pleasure merges with the sharp bite of pain.

"Fuck, you're tight," he hisses between clenched teeth.

My fingers dig into his shoulders as I seat myself on him. And when I feel that edge of resistance, that last layer of innocence I'm determined to stamp out, I don't let myself think about it. I suck in a breath, steel myself, and press my hips down until he's fully inside of me, pushing past the pain and focusing only on the pleasure.

He groans and slams his mouth against my own, consuming my cries and filling me up until I don't know where I end and where he begins. "Your name, mi pequeña mariposa?" he prompts when I pull back to catch my breath. My little butterfly.

I ignore the question, chasing his mouth instead and shifting my weight on his shaft. A breath hisses between his teeth, but he holds me steady. "You're a virgin."

It isn't a question, so I don't bother responding. Instead, I do the only thing I can—no, the only thing I need—and move.

I rise above him until only the tip of his shaft remains inside me before sinking back down with deliberate slowness.

He drops his head back on the sofa, his Adam's apple bobbing in his throat. "Fuck, what are you doing to me?" His voice is guttural, coated in desire and laced with hunger.

I repeat the movement twice more before he lifts me in his arms, standing to his full height, my legs wrapping around his waist. He walks us to a table, laying me back, our bodies never losing their connection.

"You're playing with fire," he cautions as he pulls out of me before flexing his hips and driving himself back in. Harder. Deeper. I writhe beneath him, uncertain if I'm desperate to get closer or trying to pull away.

My body is burning, my center slick with need as he thrusts into me again and again. Pressure builds inside of me making me needy and desperate for more. For all that he'll give. "Maybe I want to get burned."

He lifts one of my legs, drawing it up and over his shoulder as I hold the other tight, curled over his hip. His cock sinks deeper inside of me as he leans down, his mouth trailing wet kisses across my breasts, up my throat, and to my lips. He hits a deeper angle in this position. Every thrust and every pivot of his hips elicits new sensations.

The pressure inside of me continues to build until I'm spinning, unable to tell up from down. My visions blurs, stars explode behind my eyelids and my body jerks, jolts of pleasure spear through me without warning. He swallows down my cries until they become little more than whimpers and mewls, leaving me breathless and my body boneless.

My chest heaves. My body is slick with sweat and he's still rock-hard inside of me. There's something primal in the way he's looking at me right now. His hungry stare drinking in my sweat-slicked skin and thoroughly fucked gaze.

"You shouldn't have given me your innocence," he says, a fierce glint in his eyes. "I'm going to ruin you for any man who comes after me."

I bite my lower lip. Thank God I'm leaving tomorrow. This boy could easily become an addiction. This moment, these feelings, it's more than I imagined. More than I ever anticipated. And a hell of a lot more than I'm ready for. But to hell with it.

"Do your worst." I tell him.

His eyes flash. "Burn for me, mariposa. Burn."

FORTY-THREE

Bibiana

I'm anxious. More anxious than I should be. I try on half a dozen shirts, hating all of them before I settle on a basic, long-sleeved, black t-shirt and an oversized hoodie, resigned to the fact that today just isn't my day. None of my clothes look right on a body that doesn't feel like it's mine anymore. It's been nine months. And while I've managed to drop most of the weight, I'm still...different.

My breasts are larger. My hips wider. I'm soft in places that were once firm and I just...I exhale a loud breath. I've changed. And not just on the outside. Clothes can only hide so much. There are times like now when I feel like an imposter trapped inside my own body.

Luis chooses that moment to wake, and I silently curse myself for my little outburst. Rushing over to his crib that's positioned beside my bed, I lean down to pick him up, rocking him in my arms while making soft cooing sounds. A quick glance at the clock shows me I need to leave in fifteen minutes. If I'm late for my first day of school, so be it. Luis is more important, and I cherish these moments when it's only the two of us so much.

He's nine months old now, and my days of nursing my sweet little boy are numbered, especially with going back to school. I planned on getting my GED when we returned to Sun Valley, knowing Suncrest Academy would never take me back, but the public high school decided they'd accept my online alternative school credits. Surprisingly, I'm not as far behind as I thought, so I'll have the pleasure of attending Sun Valley High. Yay. Can you sense my sarcasm?

If I survive the last six months of senior year, I get to graduate. Mom thinks it'll be good for me. To find a sense of normalcy and be a teenager again. As if it's that easy. The thought of leaving Luis, even just for classes, is a hard pill to swallow. In such a short amount of time, this little boy has become my entire universe.

I sigh and hug him close as he nurses. These moments are special. I know that. And despite having his face memorized, I still get lost staring into his eyes and have to stifle a smile at how unlike me my own son looks. His eyes are a dark rich brown unlike my cerulean blue. His hair a softer shade of chestnut than my raven black. He even has his father's full lips and straight brows that make him look like he's scowling more often than not.

But he's precious, and he's mine.

A pang of regret hits me in the chest when I think of how he might never know his father, who might never have him to show him how to throw a football or work on a car. I want those things for my son. I want him to grow up with two parents who love him. He deserves the full package. But...I don't know who his father is. Not by name. And a physical description doesn't get you very far.

When I found out I was pregnant, I had no way of finding the boy

I gave a piece of myself to. No way of letting him know he was about to become a dad. All I know about him is that he lived in Sun Valley. And when I told Mom as much after those two little pink lines appeared, she decided it was for the best to just forget all about him.

A thrum of nervous energy courses through me at the possibility of seeing him again. Every time I leave the house, I scan the faces of the people around me, hoping for a glimpse of the boy who inadvertently changed my life forever.

He said he'd ruin me for any man who came after him. He wasn't lying. Even after all this time, I still think back to that night. To the way he made me feel. Maybe I've built it up in my mind. I don't know. But what I do know is that he left a mark. I realized that even before I found out I was pregnant.

Luis finishes nursing and I make quick work of burping him and changing his diaper before picking out his outfit for the day—a pair of soft black cotton pants and a red onesie—and head to the kitchen where I know my mother is waiting for me.

She sees me as soon as I step into the room, and her smile brightens when she catches sight of Luis in my arms. "Oh, he's awake." She holds her arms out. "Come to Grandma, amorzinho," she coos. My little love. I can't help my smile. She used to call me that when I was a little girl.

Luis pulls away from her at first. He can be clingy when he first wakes up, but after a few more softly spoken words and some bribery in the form of a banana, he relents.

Handing him to her, I grab a pão de queijo—a baked cheese roll, just as a honk outside alerts me that my ride is here.

"There's breastmilk in the freezer and I have my phone on me. If he gets too fussy. I can always—"

"Go, Bibiana. We'll be fine," my mom tells me. I hesitate for a moment before the sound of the horn again jerks me into motion. I give Luis a kiss on the cheek, grab my breakfast, and head for the door. "Call me if—"

"Yes. I know, *minha filha*. I raised you, and you turned out fine. Stop worrying. Go. Have fun."

Fun isn't the word I would use to describe high school, but I keep my feelings to myself and hurry outside.

Jaejun Yu—Jae for short—is standing in my driveway beside a sleek, cherry red Acura TLX. He grins when he looks up from his phone and realizes I'm there before he rushes around to the passenger side to open my door.

"Thanks." I offer him a tight smile and slide into the passenger seat, tucking my backpack between my legs on the floor as he jogs around the car to get back in. I hate when he does that. I know he's being chivalrous or whatever, but it still feels weird. Like it means something more than it should.

"You all set?" he asks, a smile on his too-handsome face. He leans forward and tucks a strand of my curly black hair behind my ear, lingering a second longer than he should before settling back in his seat. "You look beautiful, Bibi."

I fight my grimace and mutter out a thank you as I buckle my seat belt.

Don't get me wrong, Jae is great. He's kind and handsome and he's always there to lend a helping hand like right now, taking me to school when he doesn't even go to Sun Valley High. He isn't even in high school. He graduated two years ago, so why he insists on driving me and wasting his time when I know he has classes at Suncrest U that he'll be late for baffles me.

I sound ungrateful. I should probably work on that. It's just that Jae tries really hard. All the time. We met at one of my mom's boyfriend's—Miguel's—work events and we sort of hit it off. But in the let's be best friend's way, not the I want to date you way. I thought we were on the same page, but the more and more we're around one another, I get the feeling that we're not.

I have no idea why he's even remotely interested in me. He's interning with Miguel's security firm while he finishes his degree, and he has his entire life laid out in front of him. Everything meticulously planned to ensure success.

He even has his own townhouse at twenty. He bought it when he was eighteen as an investment property shortly after graduation. Even as a teenager he had a plan. He's smart. Responsible. Has a good head on his shoulders and probably has health insurance.

Meanwhile, I'm an eighteen-year-old single mom with zero plans for my future beyond making it to graduation. I want to do something with my life, sure. But I'm still very much in survival mode here. I don't have the mental capacity to focus on anything or anyone beyond school and Luis and, let's be honest, he could do so much better than me.

Mom likes to nudge me in his direction every chance she gets, but...I sigh. I'm not ready for that.

Jae's an exotic kind of good-looking. Half Korean and half Italian, he has hazel eyes and dark brown hair worn long on top in a bun and shaved on the sides. He turns more than a few heads when he enters a room, and there is zero question as to why. His cheekbones are high and sharp, his jawline angular, and there's just something striking about him that makes it hard to look away.

But I don't have time for a relationship. And even if I did, I'm not sure I want one. No matter how much my mother pushes or how much I try to convince myself that I should give him a chance, I'm not ready to jump back on that particular horse. With my luck, the next person I sleep with will get me pregnant too. I snort. Okay, probably not thanks to the wonderful IUD I got after Luis was born, but still. Accidents happen and while I wouldn't trade Luis for anything in the world, my days of being reckless are over. No more unplanned pregnancies for me, thank you very much.

I haven't been with anyone since Luis's father. Pathetic, I know. I get one night of incredibly reckless sex only to become a spinster afterward. It's unfair. I grit my teeth and silently curse him. Thinking back on that night all this time later, my skin still prickles with heat, my body still desperate and longing for him. It's naive of me to think one day our paths will cross again. I know that. But it doesn't stop me from looking. The little girl inside of me still believes in fairy tales regardless of how stupid it sounds. I think a teeny, tiny piece of me will always wonder what would happen if I saw him again? If he knew about Luis?

It's not like I owe him my fidelity or anything but ... I don't know. A part of me feels like the idea of pursuing something with anyone else would be a betrayal.

It's been eighteen months since Monique and I crashed a Sun Valley Party, and unless he was a lot older than he looked and already graduated, there is a chance he still goes to Sun Valley High.

If he does, I'm going to find him. And if he doesn't, maybe I'll finally be able to put that night behind me.

FORTY-FOUR

Bibiana

_____

High school is the same hell I remember it being, only somehow worse. At the academy, people at least smiled my way before they ignored me. It was like church where everyone is nice to your face for the sake of appearances. They keep their pettiness and bullshit for moments behind your back where you can't hear them.

Which is all fine. There, I had a solid friend group already in place. I knew who to trust. Who was a real friend, and who was fake and should be avoided. As a scholarship kid, I wasn't Miss Popular by any means, but I had Monique and that added a layer of protection. No one fucked with the Price family. If their money didn't intimidate you, Dominique Price, the town's football legend, star quarterback and self-proclaimed Devil would. It only took one time during freshman year for the entire school to realize that Dominique would always defend his sister's honor whether he attended Suncrest Academy or not. And he did one hell of a job using his fists to accomplish that.

Here, there is no mock politeness and there is zero common courtesy in these hallways. I'm the new girl and everyone has already decided to hate me on sight. I'm greeted with looks of disgust or ignored entirely.

It's infuriating and not the reception I'd been hoping for, but there isn't anything I can do about it. The best I can hope for is to skate through and not cause any waves while drawing minimal attention to myself. The school's administration know I'm a breastfeeding mom. They've made some accommodations for me, and my teachers have been made aware that I'll sometimes arrive a few minutes late if I need to pump before class. Thankfully, the school is letting me duck into the nurse's office when I need to, so I don't have to resort to using the girl's bathroom.

I'd rather keep my single-mom status a secret if I can help it.

I'm not ashamed to be a mom. Luis is the best thing that ever happened to me. But I don't want to broadcast it to everyone in the school either. Teenagers are assholes. I would know. And I refuse to give anyone here ammunition against me.

I make it through my first two classes without incident and spend the second half of lunch—after pumping—alone in the library, which is surprisingly pleasant. There's something about being surrounded by worn books that I take a special sort of comfort in. I'm skimming through a fantasy novel when voices a few book stacks away draw my attention. Setting the book back on the shelf, I edge closer, curious to see who's there. The library had been empty when I arrived. I wonder if maybe there are others like me who don't blend in with the crowd hiding out in here.

"Why are you doing this to me?" a girl's voice whines.

I peek my head around the shelves, spotting a blond with her arms folded across her chest. Her hair is a tangled mess of curls thrown into what I'm assuming is supposed to be a bun, but instead is a riot of crazy that she somehow manages to pull off. She's wearing red basketball shorts, white sneakers, a black Sun Valley High Red Devils t-shirt, and an annoyed expression directed at whoever it is she's talking to.

"Kasey, I'm just trying to be supportive," another girl says, though I can't quite make her out from my position.

"Liar. If you come to my game, the Devils will come and you know it."

A snort. "And that's a bad thing because..."

"Because they're assholes." A pause. "Okay, fine. Roman isn't as much of an asshole, but Emilio and Dominique totally are." Devils and Dominique can only mean one thing. The Sun Valley High mascot is a Devil but no one talks about just anyone like that.

"I don't see what the big deal is. Aaron goes to your games."

"He's my brother and he does actually want to support me. The Devils want to go hoping I mess up so they can make fun of me for it later." I pause at the mention of the Devils and consider what I know about Monique's older brother. Yeah, I could see him doing that. He can be a real asshole when he wants to be.

Despite going to Suncrest Academy, I know all about the Devils. Hell, even without for Monique I would know about them. They're legend in these parts. A group of four best friends. Three football gods and one skateboarding king. The Suncrest Academy Saints have always hated the Devils because when they showed up freshman year, the Saints began losing. Every single football game against the Devils from that year on has ended in defeat. As far as I know, the score is still the same.

"Oh, so for the same reason you go to their football games?"

Yep. Definitely those Devils.

"That's not the—"

Having stepped too close to one of the shelves, I accidentally knock over a few books. They make a loud clatter and the voices cut off from what they'd been saying. I silently curse as I rush to pick them up, kicking myself for not paying closer attention to what I was doing.

Footsteps grow closer just as I place the last book back on the shelf. I turn to head in the opposite direction as a voice calls out, "Hey!"

Shoot.

I spin around, hands raised and a grimace on my face. "I'm sorry. I didn't mean to eavesdrop. I just, uh..." I've got nothing. No valid reasons or excuses come out of my mouth as I stand there like an idiot faced with two girls I don't know. God, I hope they're not the catty type. I'm not prepared for an in-your-face confrontation on my first day back.

The blond I spotted initially looks annoyed but the other girl—a petite brunette with distinctly Hispanic features—eyes me curiously without any anger or annoyance in her gaze.

"You're new here, right? I don't think we've met before," she says, offering me a kind smile that takes me by surprise.

"Yeah, sort of." I tuck my hands into my back pockets. "I lived in Sun Valley growing up, but I went to Suncrest Academy before." I wince. Probably should have left that part out. There's no love lost between the two schools. "I moved and did an online school thing for a while. Now I'm back. And here I am." I cringe. "Sorry. I'm rambling. I do that when I meet new people. Just ignore me." Why can I not stop talking? Oh my god, Bibi, get it together.

She laughs off my awkwardness. "You didn't want to go back to the academy when you moved back?" she asks conversationally, and my shoulders relax.

"It wasn't really my choice, not that I'm upset or anything. Sun Valley High is great. Err, well, I hope it'll be great. I guess I can't really judge it after one day, but so far it seems fine." I shrug. "Suncrest Academy doesn't accept subpar credits in their program." I make air quotes when I mention subpar credits and the brunette chuckles. "If I want to graduate on time, I had to come here."

"Well, welcome." Her smile widens. "I'm Alejandra, but everyone just calls me Allie. I transferred in last semester."

I perk up at the mention that she's a transfer student too. "Really? Where from?"

She nods. "Yeah, really. I moved from Richland. This is Kasey." She indicates the girl beside her who offers me a halfhearted wave.

"Oh, I lived in Richland this past year in a half. Before moving back, I mean. It's nice." I am definitely ruining this first impression here. "So uh, are you both seniors?" Please let me have classes with one of these girls. I could seriously use someone who doesn't look at me like I'm ruining their day.

"I am," Allie says. "Kasey here is a freshy."

"Do not call me that. It's as bad as baby Henderson."

Allie laughs. "Ignore her. She's in a mood."

Kasey rolls her eyes. "I'm not in a mood." She folds her arms across her chest, and I fight back my laugh. She's pouting like Luis. Bottom lip jutted out and brows furrowed into a scowl.

"Sure," Allie drawls.

"Urgh. Whatever. Do your friendly chat thing with the new girl. I'm off to ruin Sarah's day." She turns on her heel and heads straight for the exit.

"And how exactly do you plan to do that?" Allie calls after her.

Kasey turns, walking backwards. "I caught Emilio making out with some random in the hallways after first period this morning. Sarah is going to lose it when she finds out." Her eyes glitter with mischief.

"Please tell me he's not still sleeping with that piranha?" Allie groans.

Kasey grins. "He's a Devil with lots and lots of sins. You let him fool you with that smile of his, Allie. You should work on that. Emilio is a player through and through. He'll sleep with anyone who has a rack and a nice pair of legs. Sarah knows it too."

"Then why are you about to start drama?"

She chuckles. "I just want to give her a little reminder that just because she's screwing a Devil, doesn't mean she's special."

Allie mutters out a curse before turning back to me. "Sorry about that. Sarah and Kasey have some history. She sorta screwed over Kasey's brother."

I shrug, not really sure what she has to apologize for. "Don't worry about it," I tell her, though I'm adding Kasey to my be cautious of list because she sounded way too excited to go and mess with whoever this Sarah girl is. "I'm not really following, anyway. Is this Emilio guy a friend or boyfriend or something?" I hope he's not her boyfriend. She seems nice and it would be really screwed up if he was hooking up with a bunch of other girls on the side while seeing her.

Allie laughs. "Just a friend. I don't think Emilio has a single boyfriend bone in his body. Monogamy and him don't mix. But that's probably a story for another day."

"I've got time," I say and I do. The bell won't ring for another ten minutes, and I like her. She's friendly and has this open and welcoming personality. I don't want to get ahead of myself, but she is totally friend material. Monique would love her.

She waves me toward one of the tables. "Come on, I should probably give you the lowdown on the Devils, anyway. If you don't get it from me, you'll get it from someone else and it's probably better you get it from me."

We take our seats and I pull out a small package of *Presuntinho*—Piraque crackers. Allie tosses her bag on the floor and I wave the package toward her. "Want one?" I ask.

She purses her lips before shrugging. "Why not." I hand over a cracker and she takes a bite. She chews slowly, her brows furrow before she swallows. "That's....interesting," she says, but takes another bite.

I nibble on my own and grin. "I take if you're new to ham-flavored crackers?"

"Yeah. You could say that. They're sort of weird but also kind of—"

"Addicting," I finish for her, leaning across the table to hand her another.

She nods and takes it. "They are. Anyway, what was I saying?"

"The Devils," I prompt, because any information about the guys who rule this school is sure to be useful.

"Right. So anyway, the school is run by the Devils. Three guys all the girls want and all the guys want to be."

"I thought there were four?" I ask, thinking back to the gossip I'd heard when I lived here before.

She scowls and thinks for a moment. "Oh! You're probably thinking of Aaron. Hmm..." Tapping her finger against her chin she thinks for a moment. "I guess he was a Devil. Before I arrived at least." A shrug. "He's not really one now. The guys kind of had a falling out. But they're working it out"—she doesn't bother hiding a mischievous grin that makes me think she plays some part in their working it out—"but no one really considers Aaron a Devil. He's too nice for all that."

"That's...good?" I say, not really sure how to respond to that. "Are the Devils all assholes or something?"

She chuckles. "I'm sorry. They're not all bad. The Devils, I mean. Roman, Dominique, and Emilio are great guys. They just take some getting used to. They're not really trusting, which can make them come off as standoffish. But once you get to know them, they're the sweetest guys. Aaron, too. And his outer shell, thankfully, isn't as hard to crack. You'd like him."

I raise a single brow and she laughs. "I'm not trying to play matchmaker or anything. Promise."

That's a relief. "So, if they're standoffish and you're a new girl too, how do you know them so well?"

Her cheeks turn a soft shade of pink. "I'm dating one."

"Not the one screwing the piranha, right? That's what you called her?"

Allie laughs, a deep chuckle that has the librarian shushing us from across the room. We both hunch down lower in our seats, effectively chastised. Allie's next words come out softer. "No. Not that one. I'm dating Roman Valdez. The one Kasey was talking about is Emilio Chavez and the piranha is Sarah Draven. She's a junior and a complete bitch. New girl to new girl, I would avoid her."

"Noted. Thanks for the heads up."

She nods.

"Do you speak Portuguese," I ask.

Brows furrowed, she shakes her head. "No, I'm Mexican, so Spanish."

I frown. "So, why call her a piranha, then?"

She shrugs. "She's like the fish. She hunts down men, has a pack of vicious girls with her at all times, and her mouth cuts like a blade when she opens it."

Ah. That does make sense. "Good description."

"Does it mean something else in Portuguese?" she asks, and I nod.

"Yeah. Slut."

Her lips smash together, and I can tell she's fighting to remain quiet as her shoulders shake with silent laughter. "I think I like your version better," she whisper-shouts when she finally gets control of herself.

Me too, I think to myself, though out loud I ask, "Anyone else I should steer clear of?"

Her features tighten and she nods. "Yeah. Silvia Parrish. She's a senior like us so you might have classes with her. She and some friends jumped me in the bathroom earlier this year. I wouldn't mess with her. I think the guys have effectively put her in the doghouse but still...I'd be careful."

"Oh, my god. You were jumped?"

"Shhhh.... Not so loud."

I cringe. "Sorry. But seriously? Why were you jumped?" That sort of thing would never fly at the academy. There are rules and consequences. No one there can afford to be suspended let alone expelled which is what would happen if you got into a physical altercation with another student.

She huffs out a breath. "It's another long story. But the Cliff Notes version is that she wanted my boyfriend. It's not really worth going into but seriously, steer clear. You can't trust her."

I swallow hard. What sort of school did I walk into this morning? Brawls in bathrooms is not something I signed up for.

"Don't worry, though. She won't try anything with you. At least I don't think she will. She hates me because I have the guy she wants, but unless you start dating a Devil, I think you're in the clear."

Relief washes through me. "No worries there. Not really one for dating guys right now."

"Girls?" she asks, and I choke on my cracker, coughing hard as I smack myself in the chest.

"What? No."

She raises both arms. "Hey, no judgment here. If you're into girls—"

I shake my head. "I'm not. I just...I don't date. I have a lot going on in my life, and boys are a complication I don't need."

She smirks. "I've heard that one before. But if you change your mind, let me know. It might be fun to play matchmaker, you know?"

Ha. I highly doubt that.

FORTY-FIVE

Emilio

"Emilio. Hurry up. I'm not going to be late because of your ass," Aaron calls, heading toward our last class of the day.

"Bro, I'm cutting. If you're late, that shit is on you." As soon as the words leave my mouth, Roman and Dom—who'd been walking beside him—stop and turn toward me, scowls stamped across their faces.

"Why? Something up at home?" Roman asks, concern immediately coloring his voice.

I sigh, wishing I could take my words back. I'd lie, but these two fuckers are like brothers. Hell, I'm closer with them than I am with Roberto and Antonio, my actual blood brothers. Aaron, on the other hand, he's a work in progress. Definitely still a fucker. Dammit. I don't want to lie to their suddenly concerned faces.

"Shit is what it always is, but that's not why I'm cutting. I'm gonna kick it with Sarah. Smooth some shit over if you know what I mean?"

Aaron snorts. "Seriously? You're skipping for a piece of ass?"

My eyes narrow. "I wouldn't have to if your little sister minded her own damn business."

His brows furrow and he glances from me to the other guys, an unspoken question on his face. Aw, man. He really has no idea. He'll figure it out eventually.

Dom chooses to fill him in. "Kasey told Sarah he was getting some on the side." It isn't a lie. But she didn't have to throw me under the bus like that. Baby Henderson should be team Emilio. Or at least stay out of my fucking business. But no, Baby Henderson always has to stir the fucking pot.

Not that it should matter. Sarah knows what we're doing isn't exclusive, but I guess having it thrown in her face hurt her feelings, or some shit and now I have to deal with it.

Aaron's frown deepens. "Why would she do that?" The poor bastard actually sounds confused. His little sister has the wool pulled over his eyes, but she doesn't have the rest of us fooled. Baby Henderson is a hellion, and since she joined our crew—not that we had much of a say in it—she's made it her mission to stir the pot any way she can.

Usually, she reserves her antics for Dominique's benefit—those two are like gunpowder and a lit match when they're in the same room—but lately she's enjoyed fucking with me, too.

I don't like it.

"Because she's demon spawn," I mutter, turning to head for the exit. I need to make my escape before Allie catches sight of me or she'll drag my ass back to class come hell or high water. That girl is the mother hen I absolutely adore but do not fucking need right now. "I'll catch you boys later."

"Rubber up," Roman shouts after me. "You don't need to create any devil spawn anytime soon." Yeah, a definite "no" to that. The spawn, not the rubber. I always remember to wrap my shit.

I give him a two-fingered salute just as Allie turns the corner, some random right beside her.

"Peace, *carbón*." My eyes linger on the unknown girl for a moment. There's something familiar about her. She's wearing snug fit jeans and a giant ass black hoodie. It hides most of her body, but for some damn reason I'm intrigued.

I pause, knowing I shouldn't. It's only going to get me in trouble, but she isn't someone I've seen Allie with before. Allie only ever kicks it with the Devils or Kasey, no one else at Sun Valley High can be trusted. Not after what went down earlier this year. Girls are catty fucking bitches and seeing some random next to her has me both curious and on alert. "Where do you think you're going?" Allie calls, noticing that my feet are still pulling me toward the exit and not in the direction of our class.

The girl beside her lifts her head and our eyes meet, recognition flaring through me. No fucking way. Her bright blue eyes widen and I know right away she recognizes me too. Isn't that a fucking plot twist for today?

I give her another once over, remembering her in a whole new light. Small waist. Flat stomach. Perfectly round tits. The way her hair felt wrapped around my fist. Her pussy convulsing on my cock.

I bite back a groan. Well, fuck me. I need to get laid. Pronto. My eyes narrow on the blast from my past before I shove my thoughts away and turn back toward Allie. No way am I giving this chick even a second of my time. Not after she fucking ghosted me like I was nothing. I refuse to let this girl think she has any sort of hold over me.

"Sorry, vanilla. I gotta run." I edge back closer toward the exit, the new girl still in my peripheral. Look away, dammit. Look away. Her eyes are wide as saucers and glued to me. Her mouth forming a small O. I shouldn't like the attention, her obvious surprise, but I do, and the distraction allows Allie to creep right up on me.

"Oh, no, you don't." She grabs my arm, looping hers through mine and turns me away from the doors I'd almost made it too. "You can't miss fourth. It's the one class we all have together and, my new friend has it too. Come say hi and don't be a jerk. I like her." The last is muttered under her breath.

She tugs me forward, but I keep my feet planted, looking down to meet her determined brown-eyed gaze. "I'll make it up to you. But, I really do need to go. I got someone waiting on me." I make sure to say it loud enough for the other girl to hear.

Allie scowls and turns back to her friend who's still staring, eyes wide and mouth parted. I'm not sure if I should be flattered or insulted that she's yet to tear her gaze off me. Is she remembering our night together in vivid detail like I am? Or maybe she's realizing who the fuck I am and what I can do to her if she steps out of line here. I can make her life her hell if I want to.

We fucked like rabbits that night. I buried myself inside her warm cunt three fucking times. Took her goddamn innocence. You'd think that would matter to a chick, but she acted like it was nothing. Gave as good as she got. No hesitation. No insecurities. Even on the last round when we ran out of condoms, she didn't bat an eye when I suggested I could pull out—something I never fucking do.

I don't know what I expected, but it wasn't passing out beside her with the chick wrapped in my arms only to wake up with her gone and the space on the couch cold beside me.

I swear for a whole week I wondered if I'd dreamt the entire thing up. I never saw her again, and no one knew who the hell she was when I described her. And now, she's here. Wide-eyed and hot as shit, even in that oversized hoodie she's trying to hide in.

I pull out of Allie's grip, giving Roman a nod. I don't have time for this. Thankfully, he understands my meaning and before Allie can move for me again, he wraps his arms around her and pulls her into an embrace. She melts in his arms. God, they're disgustingly cute together. And I speed walk out the door, hearing her muttered curse behind me, but she doesn't run after me again.

Thank god for small favors. I love Allie to death, don't get me wrong. But since she and Roman made things official, she's decided Dom and I are her latest pet projects, and I for one have no desire to be reformed from my savage ways, nor do I have any plans to deal with the new problem staring at my retreating back right now. I can feel her eyes boring into me, but I refuse to give her the satisfaction of knowing just how much her being here is fucking with me.

It won't be long before she learns who I am and what it means to be a Devil.

I run a hand through my hair. Fuck. Who knows what will happen then. Will she turn into every other chick in this school determined to land me? And no, I'm not being arrogant. Every girl at Sun Valley High wants to date a Devil. Some for status, others for what they perceive to be an easy life if they can lock us down early.

Roman, Dominique, and I are football legends around these parts. Each of us with full ride scholarships to Suncrest U and a good chance at going pro in the future. It's why we get so much attention and why I make it a point of never dating exclusively. Women can't be trusted. They always have an ulterior motive.

Will she throw herself at me like the others? Regret leaving me in the pool house like she did? Ghosting me like the sex wasn't fucking magical and shit? I know we said no names. We sure as shit didn't exchange numbers. But I still expected to see the girl at some point.

I suck on my teeth. I know it was just as good for her as it was for me. No way is she unaffected after seeing me today. Hmm... I can work with that. Show her the mistake she made. What she passed up on. And then remind her why she'll never fucking have me.

Outside, Sarah is sitting on the hood of her Jetta. I head straight toward her, a shit-eating grin stamped on my face as a plan begins to form in my mind. The previous appeal of getting my dick wet isn't the same, my mind now full of other more intriguing possibilities. But I'm also not going to let this chick get in my head. I'll fuck my way through the entire school if I have to before I let that happen.

"Ready to blow this place?" I ask Sarah once I'm close. I'm committed to the course of action and I'm always one to follow through. Sure, seeing her with Allie may have thrown me for a loop. I won't deny I've thought about her a time or two this past year and a half. You would too if you'd had awesome sex with a hot chick only to never see her again. But here she is in the flesh.

Hmmm...maybe if shit doesn't blow over with Sarah, I can work out a different arrangement. I mean, she'd been down for a casual fuck before.

No. That's what she wants. Wanted. I'm not giving it to her again. Letting her fucking use me. Nah. Her disappearing act deserves a little punishment. She needs to see what it's like to be left behind. Tossed aside like you don't fucking matter.

A plan starts forming in my mind.

If she and Allie are friends, Allie will have my balls for breaking the girl's heart. I consider this. Fuck it. It'll be worth it. She never should have ghosted me. I told her I'd ruin her for anyone else, and if I didn't accomplish that the first time around, I'll make it my mission here and now.

"I'm ready for you to do some groveling," Sarah retorts, arms folded across her chest, shoving her breasts up higher in her already too-tight green top. "I can't believe you made out with some random this morning."

My grin widens. "Baby, I don't grovel." I lift the hem of my shirt, exposing my cut abs that look amazing thank you very fucking much. "Women beg to be with this, not the other way around. Besides," I drop the hem of my shirt. "I didn't kiss Gwen. She kissed me. What was I supposed to do?"

She pouts. She thinks it's cute. It's not. But I let it slide, knowing she'll come around. Sarah knows the deal between us. She doesn't get to own me. I'm not hers, and this thing between us isn't exclusive. I don't do relationships. Never have. And I have no desire to in the near future. Maybe when I'm thirty. But hell, who knows, I might decide to be a badass bachelor forever.

"Urgh, do not say her name in my presence," she snaps.

Irritation flashes through me but I shove it aside and lower my voice to a growl. "You know you want to beg for me, baby girl."

Her eyes darken and I can see desire burning in her honey-colored gaze. She licks her lips but manages to hold herself in place. Funny. She thinks she's going to make me work for it.

Sarah wants something I refuse to give her. Commitment. And while I'm here, smoothing shit over with her, it's not because I actually give two fucks about losing her. This little arrangement between us is one of convenience. Shit gets too real at home sometimes and she's a hot little body to pass the time in. Nothing more. Nothing less. Well, maybe a little less, but I try not to be a complete asshole about it, which is why I'm here. I should get brownie points or something for that shit.

It's easier for me to cut fourth and give her a rare moment of my undivided attention than to find another piece to bury myself in. A new chick might get clingy. I don't have time for that. I've got a scholarship and football on my horizon. I'm not looking to chain myself to anyone. Then again...my mind flashes to the brief blast from my past before I focus back on the chick in front of me. Stop fucking thinking about her.

"What if I don't want to?" Sarah's lip juts out further and I lean toward her, nipping at it. She moans and arches toward me.

"Then I guess this—like all good things—will come to an end."

She wraps her arms around my neck, pressing her breasts against my chest. "I don't want it to end." Her voice is low and breathy. "But I hate that I have to share you."

I fight the urge to roll my eyes and decide to respond to the first part of her statement, ignoring the second. This is to fucking easy.

"Then you know what to do?"

The corners of her mouth curl into a seductive smile. "My place?"

I nod and accept her keys when she hands them to me. Like I said, too fucking easy.

FORTY-SIX

Bibiana

"Urgh. What is going on with him?" Allie says, but I'm barely paying attention to her because oh my god, that was him.

"Emilio." I whisper his name to myself, liking the way it sounds. Emilio Chavez is what she said his name was. Oh my God. Luis's dad is here. He's really here and he has a name. Well, obviously. He has a name. Everyone has a name.

A million thoughts are running through my mind. I can't seem to focus on any single one of them.

What do I do? Should I go after him? No. That would make me look like a crazy person. He recognized me though, right? At least, it looked like he did. Not that he stuck around. I'm not sure what I expected. It's been eighteen months and it was just a casual hook up. I mean, yes, it was memorable for me. I lost my virginity that night. That's kind a big deal. And even if I hadn't gotten pregnant, I wouldn't be able to forget being with him. We had sex three times. I didn't even know a guy could do that. I thought it was a one and done sort of thing, but Emilio certainly proved me wrong. And I didn't realize a girl could orgasm as many times as I did. I expected pain. Discomfort. Embarrassment. What I did not expect was...that. It sounds so dumb, but it was a dream. Magical.

As stupid as it sounds, slipping out early that morning to get home before Mom and Miguel woke up was physically painful.

He'd been asleep when I left, and I didn't bother to wake him. At the time, I told myself it was because I wanted to avoid an awkward goodbye. But if I'm honest with myself, I think I didn't wake him because I knew it would hurt even more to leave. He made me feel things I didn't realize I could feel, and that scared me.

But judging by his expression when he saw me, I'm just one in a long line of hookups for him. My shoulders slump and my stomach drops. Why does that realization hurt so much? I don't even know him. I knew what the deal was. And hell, I've been dealing with the consequences of that night ever since. Seeing him in the flesh shouldn't suddenly bring about these feelings of loneliness.

Allie's chatting with three boys in the hallway when suddenly she's snapping her fingers in my face, drawing my attention. "Earth to Bibiana. Where'd you go?"

I shake my head. "Sorry. What'd you say?"

Allie rolls her eyes but smiles before turning to the boy closest to her.

"Bibiana, this is my boyfriend, Roman." He inclines his head toward me, his way of saying hello. "This one is Aaron," she indicates the blond boy with the skateboard, "and this ray of sunshine is Dominique." I know she's kidding, because Dominique is definitely not a ray of sunshine. He's wearing the most brooding expression of the bunch, his eyes still trained on the door Emilio just exited out of. Allie elbows him in the stomach and he pretends to wince, rubbing his stomach, but I don't miss her smirk. She knows she didn't really hurt him.

"Ignore him. I swear he knows his manners. He just rarely shows them."

Roman tilts his head back and laughs, a deep chuckle that has Allie's smirk morphing into a wide smile. God, they're cute together. My heart gives a pathetic lurch. I want what they have. It looks so easy. They're so content. What if...no. I can't get ahead of myself here. It was just sex, Bibi. Stop trying to remember it as anything else. And besides, once you tell him about Luis, he still might want nothing to do with you.

Determination straightens my spine when I think of that. He doesn't have to like me. He doesn't owe me any sort of relationship or commitment just because we have a kid together. But he does owe Luis his attention and affections. I just hope he's the kind of guy who will step up once he realizes what we created together.

"You look..." Dom's voice pulls me from my thoughts. His head tilts to the side as he scrutinizes my face. "Familiar," he finishes. "How do I know you?"

Allie's eyes brighten. "You two know each other?" She bounces on her feet.

"Not really." I say with a shrug. I'm not sure if I should be answering her or him, so I go with the less intimidating option of the two. "I'm best friends with Monique. His sister. We used to go to school together."

"Oh! I haven't met her yet. Is she as stoic and broody as her brother?" She turns to him. "And why doesn't she go here?"

Dom grunts and I laugh. "She's Dominique's complete opposite," I tell her. "And she's a senior at Suncrest Academy. Dominique's parents only let him go here because of the football program."

Allie's eyes widen and she whirls on Dominique. "You have a twin!?" She squeals. "Why haven't I met her yet?"

All three guys shake their heads. "She's not my twin. She's my little sister and I haven't introduced you yet because look how well that worked out for us when you hooked up with baby Henderson. I do not need to add fuel to that fire."

Aaron and Roman both nod in agreement.

"If she's not your twin, then how—"

I answer for him. "Monique is smart. Like insanely smart. She skipped eighth grade. That's why they're both seniors. She could probably graduate early if she wanted to."

"Okay, this is great. You know Monique and I'm friends with Kasey. The four of us have to get together this weekend. It'll be so much fun. Girl's night!"

The guys groan in unison just as the bell rings, signaling that we're officially late to class. I should probably be a little concerned about that, but I'm too excited over the prospect of making new friends and finding my son's father to think about anything else.

"Come on. We'll sort out all the details after school. We better hurry or Mr. Chu is going to bite our heads off." I follow her to class, a small ball of warmth unfurling in my chest.

As the teacher drones on about this week's assignment, I slip my cell phone out from my pocket and fire off a text to my mom. It's only been a few hours, but I'm not used to being away from my little boy this long.

 **Me: How is he?**

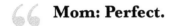 **Mom: Perfect.**

SHE INCLUDES A PICTURE OF LUIS SLEEPING IN HER ARMS and I smile, running a finger across the screen before opening a new text conversation and pulling up Monique's number. There is no way this can wait.

Me: He's here.

THREE DOTS APPEAR ALMOST INSTANTLY BECAUSE OF COURSE she isn't paying attention in class. Like she even needs to.

Monique: Oh my God! Did you tell him?

I ROLL MY EYES. IS SHE SERIOUS? YOU DON'T JUST SEE A GUY for the first time in close to two years and drop a baby in his lap day one.

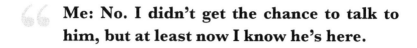

Me: No. I didn't get the chance to talk to him, but at least now I know he's here.

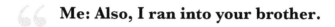

Me: Also, I ran into your brother.

I LEAVE OUT THE PART ABOUT HER BROTHER BEING FRIENDS with Luis's dad. Knowing Monique, she wouldn't be able to stop herself from grilling Dominique about him and I don't want word of Luis getting to Emilio from anyone but me.

Monique: Was he an asshole?

I SNORT. HEADS TURN MY WAY AND I BITE MY LIP, SINKING down lower in my seat.

Me: No. He's friends with this girl, Allie. She introduced us. I think you'd like her.

Monique: Don't get any ideas about replacing me B.

I roll my eyes and smile.

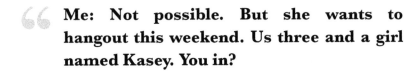 **Me: Not possible. But she wants to hangout this weekend. Us three and a girl named Kasey. You in?**

I hope she says yes. Now that I know Allie and Kasey are friends with Emilio, I have every intention of feeling them out and getting every detail I can about him. He one hundred percent has every right to know he has a son, but that little boy is my everything, and I owe it to him to make sure that whoever I bring into his life isn't going to walk right back out of it either.

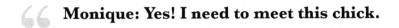 **Monique: Yes! I need to meet this chick.**

Me: Allie?

Monique: No. Kasey. Dom gripes about her ALL THE TIME. Anyone who can rile my brother up like that is someone I need to know.

Me: LOL. Okay. I'll tell Allie you're in. TTYL.

I SHOVE MY PHONE BACK IN MY POCKET JUST AS THE TEACHER walks by my desk, placing a sheet of paper on the surface. "Pop quiz. Let's see what you know and how behind you all are. I like to see what I'm working with. Fair warning, Christmas break is over, and I don't tolerate slackers in my classroom," he says, and the collective room groans.

The rest of class goes by in silence as we all work on the math quiz. I finish before the bell rings and take a few extra minutes to go over my work until I'm satisfied with all of my answers. I need to finish strong this year. I might not know what I plan to do after graduation, but I want college to be an option. Monique is going to Suncrest U. And I don't know...maybe I can work out a way to go there too. It wouldn't be full time. Not with Luis. But it would be something and I'm okay with college taking a little bit longer. I'll do whatever I need to do in order to make sure Luis gets the life he deserves.

I wonder briefly what Emilio's plans are after high school. How his plans might affect my own. But before I get too stuck in my own head, I force myself to take a breath and relax. There's no point in worrying about any of that yet.

For now, I need to figure how to tell him about Luis, which sounds a hell of a lot easier than I know it will be. After that, I can worry about the rest.

FORTY-SEVEN

Emilio

This is one of the absolute worst fucks I've had in my life. I don't know what the deal is. Sarah is into it, but my dick certainly isn't. Her moans are loud and dramatic. And the excessive back scratching is starting to hurt. It's like she's auditioning for a B-rated porn flick.

"Yes. Yes. Oh. My. God. More. Emilio, Yes!" Her moan is obnoxiously loud.

I grit my teeth as she tightens her grip around my hips with her legs and I plow into her, trying to find a rhythm that will do something—anything—for me, but it's no fucking use. Her pussy convulses on my cock, her eyes all but rolling into the back of her head as she finds her release again.

Fuck.

How is she enjoying this? I made her come in the car before she dragged me up here, and she's clearly getting her rocks off a second time, but I'm not even close. I can't get into it. I should be focused on the naked girl beneath me, but instead, my mind wanders to her. To her full lips. Her striking blue eyes. The way she looked lying beside me before I fell asleep.

This was a mistake.

We've been screwing for close to twenty minutes. Sweat drips down my back and my release is literally nowhere in sight. I thrust into her harder. Deeper. I am not going to let her get in my fucking head.

Goddammit. What is wrong with me?

Fuck it. I've had enough. I groan loud and scrunch my eyes closed, faking that I've dropped my load, before I pull out and sag against Sarah's naked body. Thank fuck for condoms. Between that and my hand I should be able to hide my still evident hard on. How fucking embarrassing.

I roll to my side, grab my boxers off the floor and head to the attached bathroom, my hand over my dick as if I'm trying to keep the condom from slipping off. Sarah's breaths are heavy behind me as I close the door and sag against the wall.

I stare at my still erect cock and clench my jaw. "You and me are going to have words," I mutter. Bracing my hands on the countertop, I take a moment to catch my breath and will my cock to stand down. Does it? No. Why? Because my dick is a fucking dick. "Not cool, dude. See if you get action again anytime soon." He won't come in Sarah's cunt, and he's determined to leave me with a case of blue balls.

Fuck me right now. I lean back and fist myself, working my length up and down in an effort to find my own release. I can hear Sarah moving around in her room, but I block out the sounds as I think of the one chick I shouldn't be thinking of. Get it together, man. You're letting her fuck with your head. I tighten my grip, envisioning her tight little pussy. The soft mewls of pleasure she made. The way she clung to me like she couldn't bear to let go. That was seriously a good fucking night.

Out of nowhere, my orgasm slams into me. Fuck. I empty myself into my hand, my chest heaving as I meet my own startled reflection. That was unexpected. I'll have to try that fantasy more often.

Irritation thrums through me. She left. She walked away without a word and now I can't even get off without thinking of her. This is some seriously messed up shit.

Washing my hands, I take care of business, slip on my boxers and go back out to Sarah's room in search of my jeans. Ah. There they are. I start dressing, eager to get the hell out of here, when—still naked—Sarah makes a beeline for me. Her small perky tits bounce with her steps and she gives me a wanton look. What is she up to now?

She runs her manicured nails over my chest and leans up on tiptoe to kiss my neck. "That was fun," she says, her voice husky.

I force myself to remain still and face her. I do the polite thing and plant a kiss on her lips, giving her a sly grin. "Always fun," I tell her. "But I gotta run. I'm supposed to meet Roman after school and"—I check the time on my phone—"school's already out. I'll catch you later," I say, not really meaning it. Coming here was supposed to smooth shit over between us so we could go back to our casual arrangement. An arrangement I'm no longer interested in maintaining.

Her face falls and I hesitate. Tilting her chin up I brush my thumb along her jaw.

"Why the long face, beautiful?" She brightens at the endearment but forces a petulant look on her face. One I can see right through.

"I thought we could, I don't know, hang out?" Her cheeks turn pink and I stifle a groan, forcing the easy and carefree smile to remain on my face. I need to end this. If the shitty fuck wasn't an indication, this whole wanting to hang out bit certainly is.

"Sarah," I draw her name out and tsk.

Her eyes water, and despite feeling like a piece of shit, I force myself to say the next words that come out of my mouth. "We're not a thing. We're friends with benefits—without the friend part."

She sniffles. "And if that's not enough for me?"

I look up the ceiling. We just went over this. "Then I'm out. I don't do complicated pussy." I grab the last of my clothes and head for the door.

"Stop."

I don't.

"Emilio Chavez, if you walk out that door you are never getting with me again," she threatens, as if that is enough to make me reconsider.

"Later, Sarah." This was a mistake. I should have stayed in class.

"Emilio, please."

I sigh, but keep walking, pulling out my phone to text Aaron.

"I drove you. You can't just leave."

Clearly, she doesn't know me if she thinks a thing as simple as a ride will slow me down.

66 **Me: I'm going to your place.**

66 **Aaron: Why?**

I ROLL MY EYES. COME ON, MAN. GET WITH THE PROGRAM.

66 **Me: Shit with Sarah. I need a lift to Roman's.**

66 **Aaron: Fine. I'll drop everything I'm doing and be right over.**

I GRIN. FUCKER THINKS HE'S FUNNY.

66 **Me: Sounds good, friend.**

I SHOVE MY PHONE IN MY BACK POCKET AND CUT ACROSS THE lawn, grateful for once that he lives next door. If I wait on the porch for Aaron to show up, Sarah will just follow me and do the whole begging then yelling then begging again thing, so I make my way to the back gate and take a seat on one of the patio chairs.

Aaron's place is nice. He lives in one of those cookie-cutter gated communities where all the houses look the same and they have to deal with HOAs that tell you exactly how long your grass is allowed to be. His parents do well enough if memory serves. He went to private school for a while before he started kicking it with us. Then he convinced his parents to let him go to Sun Valley High so he could be with his friends.

That blew up in his face. Well, sort of. I guess it's working out now, what with Allie around. Henderson and Roman made some sort of deal I don't have all the details on. All I know is that he helped Roman win Allie back and Roman decided to drop the beef between them. Personally, I'm not that forgiving. He fucked up and we all got hurt because of it.

We might tolerate him these days, but I sure as shit don't trust him.

My phone dings and I glance down at the screen.

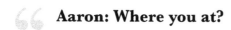 **Aaron: Where you at?**

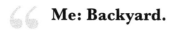 **Me: Backyard.**

A FEW SECONDS LATER THE BACK DOOR OPENS, AND AARON walks outside. He's wearing his usual emo shit. Black pants. Black shirt. Black beanie pulled low over his blond hair. He looks like

Justin Bieber had a baby with Machine Gun Kelley. No wonder the dude is still single. "You could use a little more color in your life," I tell him.

He frowns. "Are you on something?"

"Nope. That's your MO. Not mine," I say with a grin.

His scowl darkens.

"Really, man. You wanna go there right now?"

I shrug. Why not? I'm already having a shitty day. But Aaron decides to flip shit around. Smooth fucker.

"What happened to smoothing shit over with Sarah?" he asks, taking a seat in one of the chairs beside me.

"Decided the pussy wasn't worth the effort. She's getting too attached."

He snorts. "You've been staying the night at her place almost every night for the last month. What did you expect?"

"You've been tracking me?" I ask, remembering he's hooked up with her, too. "Jealous it was me in her bed instead of you?"

He snorts. "Hardly. I try not to repeat my mistakes. And no, fucker, I'm not tracking you. But you're not hard in the mornings when you do the walk of shame to your car early enough to get your sister to school."

I shrug, not meeting his eyes. I don't like that he knows how often I've been here. Aaron's not an idiot, and he demonstrates that even more with his next question.

"What's really going on, Emilio? Why don't you wanna be home?"

I jerk my gaze to his. "What the fuck is that supposed to mean?" It comes out angrier than I intended, but fuck, he's got no right prying into my business.

"It means, I'm not stupid. I know you have issues with your dad. Why haven't you said anything to Roman or Dominique?" Because Roman's got Allie now. I'm not about to crash in on their happy little life. And Dom... I shake my head. Dom's got his own problems. Neither one of them needs to worry about mine.

"It's not a big deal." I push to my feet.

"Stop fronting. What's going on?"

"Drop it," I snarl.

Aaron lifts both hands. "Fine, be an asshole. I was only trying to help."

"Right, well, the only help I need is a lift to Roman's. You going to help with that or not?"

He scowls, but nods. "Come on. But just so you know, screwing random girls isn't going to solve your problems. And getting involved with chicks like Sarah Draven is going to come back and bite you in the ass. I would know."

FORTY-EIGHT

Bibiana

My palms are sweaty. My knees weak. I don't know what to say to him. How to break the news or even start a conversation with the guy, so I do the smart thing and avoid him. Okay, it's also the cowardly thing to do, but it's not like I have a lot of options here. I only manage to make it two days before I'm faced with speaking to Emilio though, and like all the times before, as soon as I see him, it's like everything around me stops.

"Hey, beautiful," he says, taking me completely by surprise as he sits down at the lunch table. It takes me a second to realize he's not talking to me. His words are directed toward Allie, who is seated beside him, but hearing his voice has goosebumps breaking out across my skin. "Who's the new new chick?" he asks, his tone suggestive, but he's still not looking my way and it bothers me. It's not like we're strangers. He can say hello. Just as easily ask me for my name instead of asking Allie when I'm literally sitting right in front of him.

Roman smacks him upside the back of his head as he claims his seat on Allie's other side, but there's a smile on his lips that says he's not actually pissed. "Lay off Allie's new friend," he comments, not making eye contact, but this time I don't take it personally. Given all that I've learned about the Devils of Sun Valley High and how uncommon it is for anyone new to be welcomed into their inner circle, Roman's quiet acceptance of me is enough.

"This is Bibiana," Allie says. "Play nice."

"Bibiana. Hmm..." Emilio says my name as though testing its flavor. The corners of his mouth curl on either side, his expression almost savage as he finally deigns to look at me.

His chocolate brown eyes lock on mine and I freeze like a deer caught in headlights, unable to tear my gaze away as he rakes his bottom lip through his teeth, electricity crackling between us. Was it always like this? I think back to the night we met. The chemistry between us. I swallow hard because yeah, it felt just like this. An imaginary cord stretched taut between us.

Dominique drops his tray beside me, claiming the seat to my left while Kasey claims the seat to my right, pulling my attention away from Emilio and effectively shattering the moment.

Emilio turns to Dominique, ignoring me now as the two dive into a conversation about the upcoming game. Listening in, I learn the Devils made it to the playoffs. No surprise there. They finished their season undefeated, so making it all the way and going to state is their next objective.

Roman joins the conversation, leaving Allie, Kasey, Aaron, and I to talk amongst ourselves. I try to push Emilio from my mind, but every few minutes I can feel his eyes boring into me. His gaze like a physical caress, only when I turn to look at him, he jerks his attention away.

"Hello, Earth to Bibi," Allie calls, and I force my gaze away from him.

"What'd you say? Sorry, I got a little lost in my head."

She smiles. "Right. I was saying, what do you want to do this weekend? We're dragging Aaron along, too." My eyes flick to his as I consider her question.

"Uh..." Crap. Now isn't the time to tell them I have a son, but I can't very well go out on weekends with him either. I'm a mom, and yes, my mom watches him while I'm at school, but I don't like the idea of dumping Luis on her just so I can hang out with friends. I'm his mom. I'm the one who should be taking care of him. He's my responsibility.

I don't want to lose more time with him either, especially when I'm already not seeing him during the day most of the week. It's made him clingier then usual, and he's only going to be my baby a little while longer. Soon, he'll be a toddler. Then a little boy. The thought alone makes my chest ache. He's growing up too fast.

"Why don't we do something at my place?" I suggest. "Movies, junk food. Something casual?" I'll come up with a way to let them know about Luis between then and now. Hopefully it's not a deal breaker for our friendship. Monique loves Luis and Allie seems nice. With any luck, she'll love him too.

Allie's eyes brighten at my suggestion. "Yes! I love that idea. You guys in?" She looks between Kasey and Aaron.

"I'm in. What do you think, little sis?" Aaron asks, ruffling his sister's hair.

"Urgh, don't do that," she whines, smacking his hand away as if she's annoyed, but I don't miss her affectionate smile. "Yes. I'm in. I could use a low-drama night and some junk food."

"Perfect. I'll text you guys the address. Let's plan on, I don't know, seven-ish?"

Everyone nods just as the lunch bell rings and we all rise to drop our trays in the waste bin as we head to our next class. I lose track of the others in the crowd, not really worried since I'll see them again—save for Kasey—fourth period, when a hand wraps around my arm and pushes me into an open classroom door. I stumble forward before whirling around, hands fisted at my sides and ready, only to find Emilio behind me.

He closes the door, pressing the lock and leaning against it as he folds his arms over his chest and gives me a once-over before quirking a brow. "Pretending we don't know each other?" he asks, a sinful expression on his face. The bell rings again and I grit my teeth together. I'm already behind. I shouldn't miss any of my classes without a damn good reason, but Emilio doesn't look like he's going to just let me brush past him. He looks like someone who has something they need to get off their chest, though I can't imagine what it is—I'm supposed to be the one with something to share.

I swallow hard and take a few steps back, managing to put some much-needed distance between us. My heart is racing in my chest, my palms suddenly sweaty. "I'm not pretending," I tell him. "I just didn't know if I should mention—"

"That we fucked." The gravely quality of his voice grates along my senses. "That I buried my dick inside of you three times before you vanished. Poof. Like a ghost."

My brows furrow and I take another involuntary step back. He sounds angry, almost. But that can't be right. He has nothing to be angry about. At least, not yet.

Emilio pushes off the door and stalks toward me, that's the only way I can describe it. His eyes are bright, practically glowing, as he closes the distance between us, a predatory glint in his eyes.

"You running from me, mariposa?"

I swallow hard and manage to shake my head, that nickname eliciting a strange sort of emotion in my chest. Emilio leans into me, his breath fanning across my neck. My hands fly up on their own to clutch at the fabric of his shirt. I don't know if I plan to draw him in or push him away, but the steady thrum of his heartbeat beneath my palms grounds me.

"Good. Because if you run," he trails his nose down the side of my neck and nips at my shoulder with his teeth. "I'll have to give chase."

I shudder, my entire body responding to him, but I force myself to take a deep breath. This...isn't what I expected.

"I remember the way you taste," he whispers, tugging the neckline of my zip-up hoodie to the side and trailing kisses across my skin. "The way your pussy squeezed my cock when I buried myself inside you."

His vulgar words make my thighs tighten, even as a shiver of apprehension races down my spine. He draws back, a savage curl to his lips. "Do you remember?"

My stomach tangles in knots. Of course I remember. I remember every single moment of that night in vivid detail. Every kiss. Every touch. But I don't tell him any of that. I'm stuck standing here, words frozen in my mouth as he looks at me like he wants to devour me, but there's a cruel edge to his smile. One I don't know how to interpret. The boy I met eighteen months ago was wild. He had a devil-may-care attitude. And sure, I don't really know him, but first impressions do mean something. Emilio acted like he didn't have a care in the world. He was the kind of guy always looking to have a good time. Searching for his next thrill.

This Emilio is different.

He doesn't give me the chance to dwell on that. Instead, his lips press against mine, and suddenly I'm drowning in the taste of him. Sweet oranges and chili, just how I remembered him tasting. Each caress of his tongue awakens something dormant inside me. I lose myself to the sensations when his arms band around me as he lifts me from my feet, my legs wrapping around his waist of their own accord.

He carries me over to a desk and sets me down on the smooth surface. One of my hands curls around the edge for support while the others holds onto Emilio, afraid to let go. My heart races behind my rib cage. There are a million reasons why I need to stop this, the most prevalent one being that I still haven't told him about Luis. But I can't think. Can't get enough air to form the words I know need to be spoken.

His kiss is frantic. His grip possessive as he tilts my head, deepening our kiss and pressing his body closer into mine. Then I feel it. The hard length of him pressed firmly against my core. It reminds me that I haven't been with anyone else. Not since that night. Not ever. He was my first. And so far, my only.

The next thing I know, his fingers are unbuttoning my jeans and working their way into my panties. I tear my mouth from his and suck in a lungful of air. "What are you doing?" I gasp as his mouth latches on to the side of his neck, nipping and sucking at my skin in a way I know is sure to leave a mark.

His fingertips graze over my center, and I shudder in his arms. He chuckles, the sound smug and self-assured. "So fucking responsive. What does it look like I'm doing, Bibiana?" The way he says my name makes my toes curls and short-circuits my brain. He manages to slide my jeans down my hips before I realize what's even happening. He unzips the front of my sweatshirt, but when his fingers curl beneath the hem of my shirt, reality sneaks back in, reminding me that I am not the same girl he slept with eighteen months ago. I've changed. My body has definitely changed. And I'm not ready for anyone, let alone the boy who haunts my dreams, to see it.

I stop his hand from tugging up my shirt but have zero clue as to where to redirect it when he makes that decision for me and squeezes my breast over the material of my top. I wince. It doesn't hurt but...gah...if I leak milk right now, I will be so mortified.

I need to put a stop to this entire thing. This, whatever it is, cannot happen right now but—oh my God. His finger rubs over my center, the thin material of my panties hardly a barrier as he presses a finger inside me.

I moan into his mouth. This is a stupid, horrible, insane thing to do right now, but I can't seem to make myself tell him to stop. And I have to accept the fact it's because I don't want him to.

FORTY-NINE

Emilio

She lets out a sweet whimper when I cup her breast in my hand and squeeze it. They're larger than I remember. More than a handful, but fuck me if they're not perfect. Her eyes darken with need, if not a little apprehension. She's nervous. That should bother me, but it doesn't. Seeing her open desire feeds the beast inside me, so I give both of us what we want, slipping one finger inside her dripping cunt. Fuck me. My girl is ready, needy.

Wait. What? She is not my girl. Where did that thought even come from? Gritting my teeth, my cock strains against my zipper, desperate to thrust into her heat, but that's not on the menu today. This isn't about getting my dick wet. It's about proving a point.

A moan leaves her as I sink a second finger into her pussy. Fuck, she's so goddamn tight. I nip at her lips, small mewls of pleasure escaping as I work my fingers in and out, finger fucking her until she's writhing on the desk. Gasping my name.

"You like that, baby girl?" I ask, taking pleasure in watching her squirm. She doesn't answer, but she doesn't need to. Her heavy breaths, the rapid rise and fall of her chest is answer enough.

She wets her lips and the sight of her tongue peeking out does things to my head. Makes me want to devour her. Body, mind, and soul.

I tower over her, our mouths centimeters away from one another. I suck in the air she breathes, my free hand tangling in her thick, black hair before I crush my lips against hers in a punishing kiss. Her legs clench, her back arching as her breasts press against my chest. She's close.

I add in a third finger, stretching the walls of her pussy, making her take all that I can give. Next time, it'll be my cock buried inside her tight little body instead of my fingers.

The thought has me clenching my jaw, nostrils flaring. There isn't going to be a next time, I remind myself.

"Oh, God." She stiffens against me, her jeans dangling from one leg while the other wraps around my hip.

"Come for me, Bibiana," I grind out against her ear, savoring the way her name tastes on my tongue. My thumb finds her clit, circling the bundle of nerves and like glass, she shatters.

Her body goes taught. Her moan muffled by my lips as her orgasm tears through her.

I swallow her cries and suck on her bottom lip until her body relaxes, her shoulders slumping and her pleasure-drunk gaze finding mine.

I withdraw my fingers, adjusting the raging hard on in my jeans before bringing my hand to my lips and sucking her orgasm clean from my fingertips.

Her eyes widen in surprise. A blush heating her cheeks. I don't bother hiding my savage smile before gripping her jaw and forcing her to taste herself on my tongue. When she's breathless once more, I release her and turn to leave.

"W...where are you going?"

I don't answer. I don't turn around. I force myself to take step after step away from her so she knows exactly what it's like to have someone mark you, only to walk away and for you to be forgotten.

I SKIP THIRD PERIOD BUT MAKE SURE I'M IN FOURTH. ALLIE will have my ass if I skip our calculus class again. It's the one class Dom, Aaron, Rome, Allie, and I all have together, and I swear she treats it like it's a family meal. I head to the back of the class where Dom and Aaron are already seated and nod at both of them as I take my seat. Bibiana has fourth with us too, and it looks like this girl doesn't give one fuck about making a scene, because as soon as my ass hits the chair, she storms into class, cheeks tinged pink and eyes ablaze as she heads straight toward me, righteous anger etched into every line of her body. "What the hell was that?" she bites out, slamming her small hand against the top of my desk.

I might not have thought this through completely, but damn if she's not beautiful like this. I'll have to piss her off again sometime. Possibilities race through my mind and a slow smile curls the corners of my mouth. I look her up and down, silently cursing myself for not getting a glimpse when I had the chance of the tanned skin she hides beneath her oversized sweaters. "I don't know what you're talking about." I spread my legs and lean back in my seat, folding my arms across my chest. She stands there. Indignation written all over her face. "Did you need something?" I ask. "Class is about to start."

Her eyes brighter, a lick of fire rising to the surface as her gaze narrows on me. "I don't know what you're trying to do here, but you can't just..." she waves her arm in the air. "You can't do what you did and then walk away like that."

I cock my head to the side. "Why? You had zero problem fucking me and walking away. I thought this was our thing." The students around us snicker but neither of us look their way, too focused on glowering at one another instead.

Bibiana bares her teeth, leaning forward and pressing her face close to mine. I'm tempted to kiss her again. Capture her lips with mine and see how she reacts, but I manage to hold myself back. Barely. The pull between is strong. I don't fucking like it. She's not only under my skin. It's like she's burrowing her way into my goddamn soul. What is it about this girl?

I catalogue her features, taking in her bright blue eyes, her kiss-bitten lips, and her sexy-as-hell scowl, all the while ignoring Dominique's interested stare. The asshole's probably already envisioning my downfall at the hands of the tiny thing in front of me. He's a cruel bastard like that. Seriously though, he and baby Henderson deserve one another. And me, do I deserve her? I'm not sure if I've been given a gift or a curse with Bibiana's arrival.

"What is your problem? We had a one-night stand. Why are you acting like an asshole whose feelings are hurt when you knew the arrangement upfront?"

I scoff. "Baby girl, my feelings are far from hurt. You just seemed a little tense earlier. I figured I'd help you out."

She isn't buying it, but I don't fucking care. The entire room is looking our way. She doesn't know it yet, but her little outburst isn't going to do her any favors here. My jaw tightens. I don't know how to feel about that.

Roman and Allie walk in and like any other day they head straight for me and Dom claiming the seats nearest to us. "Is everything okay?" Allie asks.

I shrug. "Not sure. You should ask your new friend here."

Allie's shoulders drop and she gives me an exasperated look. "What did you do?"

Bibiana smirks. Cute. She's only known Allie a handful of days. Vanilla would never take her side over mine, but I let her think she's won. For the next thirty seconds, at least before I turn to Allie and look her right in the eye. I'll probably go to hell for this. Then again, I'm already a Devil. Hell's been a forgone conclusion for me. "I gave her an orgasm." I say loud enough that the entire class can hear. "Not sure what the problem is. She enjoyed it, but now she's complaining. Sorry, baby girl. I had to get to class. I know you have needs so if you behave, I'll consider helping you out again later." Her cheeks flush and fire licks her gaze.

"Screw you," she curses and turns, looking for a seat, but she isn't left with many options. She can either sit her pretty ass down where she's at, putting her beside Allie and directly in front of me, or she can go sit front and center at the head of the class.

Her nostrils flare and I watch as she considers what to do, her fingers curling into a tight fist at her side.

She does what I expect and claims the seat in front of me, her back ramrod straight and shoulders stiff. I lean across my desk, my mouth hovering behind her ear as I whisper, "That's right. Be a good girl and next time I'll get you off with my mouth instead of my fingers."

I watch in fascination as goosebumps break out across her skin.

"There isn't going to be a next time," she grinds out.

I laugh and lean back in my chair. I thought that too, but I've suddenly changed my mind. No longer content leaving her after just one round. An eye for an eye isn't enough. I don't want to get even. I need to be ahead. To win whatever twisted game it is we're playing.

This girl has me under her spell, and I refuse to be the only one who suffers for it. She deserves to be punished. I need that. Need to know I'm the one in control. I don't want to hurt her. Not physically.

I want to strip her down of her defenses and make her beg. I want to tease and taunt her until she can't take it anymore. And when she's finally had enough, I want to push her a little bit more. Show her just how much she can take. I don't know why I feel this way. But it's an insatiable need, and fuck it, I may hate myself for this later, but it doesn't change the fact that I'm drawn to this girl. And instead of doing the smart thing and keeping the fuck away, I'm going to bury myself in her until neither of us knows up from down. And I'm going to have a hell of a time doing it.

FIFTY

Bibiana

"Relax," Monique tells me.

I'm pacing in the living room and despite Luis being asleep in my arms, nervous energy makes it hard to stand still.

"It's not a big deal."

Easy for her to say. She isn't the one about to tell everyone she has a kid. A kid who happens to also belong to their friend, but I'll save that story for another day. Maybe. Hopefully. Urgh. I don't know. I tried all week to find the courage to tell Emilio about Luis but there was never a good time and then after the whole classroom incident, I don't know. I need to tell him but a part of me also doesn't want to.

He did what he did and then went about his business like it never even happened. And every time I turned around he was either hitting on a girl or making out with one in the hallways at school. It ... sucked.

I haven't been touched in a year and a half. Not that he knows that, but still. He doesn't get to do that. Make my body light up like the world is on fire, only to walk away and pretend like what happened between us isn't a big deal. Like it meant nothing. Because dammit it did. To me at least. Just the thought of him makes my blood boil. Where does he get off? He is such an asshole.

I don't understand him and trying to figure out what is going on in that head of his gives me a migraine. He watches me. Always out of the corners of his eyes like I won't notice but I do. He tracks my movements and more times than not it's like he's waiting for me to show up before he leans into another girl. Like he wants a reaction out of me but I refuse to give it to him. I'm not an idiot and I refuse to be pulled into this twisted game of his.

Ignoring me, the girls, it's all intentional. He wants me to react, though how, I'm still not sure. I have no claim on him. I can't be jealous. Well, I can be, because I clearly I am, but I have zero reason to be. He's not mine. I'm not even sure if I want him to be.

I don't know if the fact that he's doing this all on purpose is a relief or just pisses me off more. But at least I know I'm not the only one affected. Every time another guy that isn't one of the Devil's talks to me, Emilio's jaw tightens. It's a subtle reaction but it's there.

It's petty and immature of me but, I've taken to messing with him at lunch. Intentionally eating my food in a provocative manner. His eyes burn. His jaw clenches. But despite his suggestion two days ago, that next time he'll make me come with his mouth, he hasn't said a single word to me. I've been on the receiving end of heated stares and lingering looks, but that's it. No words. No smiles or openings for conversation. No way to casually say, "did I mention we have a son together?"

I hate it, and I love it, and I have no freaking idea what to do about it. Finding a way to tell Emilio about Luis was complicated enough to begin with. Now it's a cluster fuck of epic proportions.

The doorbell rings, startling me from my thoughts, and I rush to answer it, Luis propped on my hip, his head on my shoulder. I'm equal parts terrified and excited for Allie and Kasey to meet him. I haven't introduced him to anyone outside of family except for Monique, and she's my best friend so that doesn't count.

"Relax, B," Monique says as she joins me. "They're gonna love him."

I gave Allie a heads-up that I wanted to introduce her to someone important to me but I didn't give her any details and I'm pretty sure this isn't who she had in mind.

I open the door and find both girls waiting with Aaron right behind them. Shit. I'd completely forgotten he was coming too. I swallow hard and all three sets of eyes zero in on the little boy I'm holding.

"Hey, come on in," I say, ushering them inside.

Dressed in a knee-length hoodie dress and black K-swiss sneakers, Allie is beaming when she steps inside. "Is he yours?" she asks with open curiosity. I nod. "Oh, my God. He's adorable." She touches one tiny hand, her eyes shining with wonder as she gazes at my precious bundle. "How old is he?"

I swallow hard. "Nine months."

Her smile widens. "You did good, momma." She moves to the side, making way for the others, and I lead everyone through the kitchen and into the living room. "Told you," Monique whispers. I nudge her with my elbow playfully, grateful that things are off to a good start.

"My mom will be here in a little bit and she's going to hang out with him. He usually goes to bed around eight, but he didn't get a nap today, so he zonked out early," I say for everyone else.

Kasey moves closer and gives Luis a quick once over. She's dressed in ripped jeans and a flannel shirt over a black tank top. Her hair thrown in her usual messy bun style. "He's cute," she says in way of greeting. "Doesn't look anything like you."

"Kasey!" Aaron groans.

"What? It's not a bad thing. He'd still be cute if he looked like her too." She rolls her eyes and then turns her attention to Monique, a mischievous glint in her eyes. "I'm Kasey, by the way. You must be Dominique's sister?"

"In the flesh. I'm Monique, and I must say, I'm kind of obsessed with you. You have to tell me what it is that you do to my brother that gets him so worked up damn near every day. I need some pointers." Allie and I laugh, but Aaron has a pinched expression on his face I can't quit read, though he doesn't comment. I don't know Kasey or Dominique very well, but even an idiot can see there's something going on there. Whenever they're in the same room together it's like everyone else has to brace themselves for the oncoming explosion. I can't tell if it's hatred that fuels their responses or if they're secretly into each other. Either way, Dominique and Kasey in the same space for more than a few minutes is a recipe for disaster.

The girls head to the sofa just as my mom walks into the room, setting her purse and keys on a nearby hook.

"Sorry, I'm late. I had a few errands to run." She tells me, pulling Luis from my arms. She rubs his back and makes small shushing sounds when he squirms, and in no time he's back to being fast asleep. "We'll be upstairs, but you kids have fun." She waves to my new friends, exhaustion tugging on her features. She'd normally stop and chat for a few minutes, but I know she's been working late. Helping Miguel with some of his work at his office after she gets off from a full day of work herself.

"Thank you," I mouth and watch as she heads upstairs.

"Where's the baby going?" Allie whines, a mock pout on her lips. "I wanted to hold him."

"Why, with the way you and Roman fuck like rabbits every chance you get you'll probably have one of your own soon enough," Kasey remarks.

Allie smacks her arm, but there's a smile on her face that tells me she doesn't hate the idea.

"Sorry. Come over earlier next time and you can hold him. Promise." I tell her, secretly thrilled that not only do they seem completely fine with the fact I have a child, but genuinely interested in him too.

"Urgh, fine. But if he wakes up, I call dibs on baby snuggles. He's so freaking cute."

My heart warms and I hesitantly ask the one question that's been on my mind since we made plans to get together. "So ... you don't care that I have a kid?" I didn't make many friends in Richland. I wasn't there very long. But what friends I did make when we first moved didn't last long after having Luis. They always wanted me to leave him with my mom. They though it was inconvenient for him to be around even if all we were doing was homework or going to the mall. It was disheartening to say the least. And it's not like he caused problems. He was a newborn at the time. All he did was eat, sleep, and poop.

"Why would we?" Kasey asks. "He's cute. He's yours. I don't see what the big deal is."

"You seriously have no idea how relieved I am to hear that. I was so nervous to tell you guys."

Monique gives me an I told you so look just as Aaron steps forward and places a hand on my lower back. "He's a cute kid. And no one who matters is going to treat you any different for having him."

"Aww," Allie coos. "See. This is why we like having you around."

He snorts. "And here I thought it was for my good looks."

"Gross." Kasey retorts.

Aaron rolls his eyes. "Whatever, baby sis." He turns back to me with a shrug. "Having a baby isn't anything to be ashamed of, and friends don't turn their backs on one another for things they can't control." His jaw clenches at the last bit, his expression stony before he wipes it away and drops his hand, moving to sit beside Allie.

I give him a grateful smile. "Thanks, you guys. All of you. Really."

"Don't let that cute baby smile fool you, though," Monique says. "He can be a little devil when he wants to be." My heart shutters in my chest at her choice of words, but thankfully no one seems to notice. Or at least I don't think anyone does. But then Kasey asks, "So what is going on with you and Emilio?" And I freeze like a deer caught in headlights.

My eyes flick to Monique's, who's sporting a confused expression because I'm a terrible friend and still haven't told her who exactly Luis's father is or that I hooked up with him in a classroom after lunch.

"Yeah. Did you guys really have a thing before? I didn't realize you knew each other." Allie adds.

"Really well, too," Aaron interjects. "Pretty sure Emilio wasn't lying about that orgasm he gave you based on your face when he announced it to the entire class."

My cheeks heat and once again my gaze finds Monique's. Her eyes widen, sudden understanding dawning, and I implore her with my eyes not to say anything.

"Orgasm? You and—" she barely stops herself from blurting out you and Luis's father, but thankfully manages to catch her herself. "You and Emilio Chavez fucked?" she says instead, knowing exactly who he is with him being one of Dominique's best friends. "When? I'm your best friend. How did I not know about this? And eww... Emilio is one of Dominique's best friends. He's like an older brother to me." She visible shivers.

I bury my head in my hands. "Can we please not make this a thing, and we didn't have sex. There was no ..." I shake my head. "Just no. Let's pretend nothing ever happened. Okay? Okay. Glad we cleared that up."

Allie snorts. "You may not have boned but he gave you an O during school hours." She shrugs her shoulders. "I can't judge. Roman's caught me off guard a time or two too." A sly smile curls her lips. "But Emilio doesn't usually hook up on campus, and he's staying tight-lipped about the whole thing, which is unusual for him. It's driving me insane. So hard no. We are definitely not dropping it. I want all the details!"

Kasey snorts. "You mean because he usually brags about his conquests from the rooftops after spending the night at their place?"

My stomach drops, and Allie throws a sofa pillow at her. "He does not. He just..." She huffs and shakes her head. "Emilio is a great guy. A little bit of a man whore but a great guy."

Now it's Aaron who snorts though he raises both hands in surrender when Allie glares his way. "I wasn't disagreeing with the great guy part," he rushes to say. "Only the part about being a little bit of a man whore."

"Ignore him. The guys had a falling out and he's still a little salty. Emilio isn't that bad."

The face Kasey makes says she disagrees. "Right! He's so great that he fooled around with Bibiana and has been all over every senior and junior girl since."

I swallow hard, hating that she's right.

"Please tell me you're smart enough not to get involved with him as anything more than whatever it is you two are now? If you wanna fool around with him, have at it. Do the dirty. Just ... don't get attached," she warns.

"It's really not a thing. I made a stupid mistake. One I don't plan on repeating. Let's...talk about something else. Anything else."

"No way," Allie says. "There was mention that you guys hooked up before you moved. Is that true? Come on, please. Emilio is being so tight-lipped about it and getting anything out of Roman on the subject is like pulling teeth. I need the juicy details. I promise after you tell me everything, I won't bug you again."

"Way to sweeten the deal," Monique chimes in. "But I'm with Allie. Give us all the details." So not helping.

At the mention of our hookup, Aaron gives me a considering look. One that has me fidgeting in my seat.

"There isn't much to tell. We hooked up one time."

"Before you moved, right?"

"Yeah. I've lived in Sun Valley my whole life, so," I shrug. "We were bound to run into each other, but it was no big deal. Really. One hookup. That was it."

"Was it good?" Kasey asks. "I've always wondered why chicks throw themselves at him. I'm assuming he's at least decent in the sack. Is that why you fell for his act and fooled around at school with him?"

"Really?" Aaron admonishes his sister.

"What? It's a valid question."

I scrub my hands over my face. "It was fine. Good. But like I said, it was a one-time thing."

"So, the classroom was—"

"A mistake. And not sex. He just..." I look away and swallow.

"Aw, you like him!" Allie sing-songs and now it's me throwing a pillow at her.

"I'm getting food." I jump to my feet and rush off to grab some coxinha I made earlier. They're these little deep-fried balls of heaven filled with shredded chicken that my mom used to make for my dad. She doesn't make them anymore, but I still do from time to time, and hopefully with food in their mouths they'll drop the Emilio stuff, and we can get on with our night.

"Oh, what are these?" Kasey asks, popping one into her mouth when I return. She closes her eyes and moans. "Oh my god," she says around a mouthful because really, coxinha aren't small enough to be eaten in just one bite. "Soooo good."

I laugh as I grab one of my own. "Thanks. I figured since I dropped the baby bomb on you, I'd feed you. You know, in case having a kid was a deal breaker or something, I would bribe you with my culinary ways."

"You can drop as many bombs as you'd like," she says, eating another. "As long as you make these, I swear I will never care or hold anything against you."

"Deal."

We watch Five Feet Apart, which has all of us girls teary-eyed by the end and then take pity on Aaron and put on Enola Holmes. It's still probably not his cup of tea, but he doesn't complain, which I give him props for. I'm sure hanging out with four girls, one of which being your little sister, is probably not the highlight of his week, but he takes it all in stride and he seems pretty close with Allie so what do I know? Maybe this is how he likes to spend his Friday nights.

"I'm going to make some popcorn," I say hopping up from my seat and heading to the kitchen when it gets to the part when her brothers show up. I've watched this movie at least a dozen times and know the script almost by heart.

"I'll help you," Aaron says, getting up to follow.

"She totally needs help," Kasey mocks, and he throws a pillow at her, not bothering to respond.

"Did you want a drink or anything?" I ask once we're in the kitchen. I toss a bag of popcorn in the microwave and then grab two glasses from the cupboard, filling them both with water and handing one to Aaron as we wait for the popcorn to pop.

"Thanks." He accepts the glass and then leans against the kitchen island, a serious look on his face. "So, uh, I wanted to ask you something."

"Okay. What's up?"

He rubs the back of his neck in a nervous gesture. Is he gearing up to ask me out or something? No. That can't be right. Aaron hasn't shown even a hint of interest in me as anything more than a friend, and even that is still up for debate. Right now, he's tolerating me because of Allie, just like the rest of the Devils. So, I have no idea why he's acting so nervous all of a sudden.

"You said Luis is nine months old, right?"

I nod, not really sure where he's going with this.

"And you hooked up with Emilio two summers ago?"

My body goes on high alert. Shit. Shit. Shit.

I nod again. What else am I supposed to do?

"Kasey's right. He doesn't really look anything like you."

I frown. "Uh, okay."

"But he looks a hell of a lot like Emilio especially if you've seen his baby pictures like I have."

My mouth drops open. The microwave dings and I turn to retrieve the bag. "I don't know what you're—"

He doesn't give me the chance to finish. "I've known Emilio almost my entire life. I've seen the pictures of him that decorate his walls. The timeline adds up. You moved eighteen months ago. You hooked up with Emilio before you left. Tell me I'm wrong."

My back is still to him as I squeeze my eyes closed. This isn't how anyone was supposed to find out. What if he tells Emilio? What if—

"You need to tell him. He'd want to know. He'll want to be a part of that little boy's life."

I fist my shaking hands and force myself to turn around and face him, exposing myself in a way I haven't had to do before. "And what if he doesn't?" I ask, voicing my biggest fear. The thing that keeps me up at night when my mind refuses to go quiet. "What if he doesn't want the responsibility of a child? Aaron—" I force myself to slow down and take a deep breath. "We had a one-night stand. It was never supposed to lead to anything more. He didn't sign up for this." I wave my hands around me.

"Neither did you," his words are softly spoken, not a hint of anger or judgement in them. "Bibiana, I can't imagine being a single mom in high school is easy."

I shake my head because no, it isn't.

"You didn't sign up for this either, but would you change it? Would you give him up?"

I vehemently shake my head. "Never. I love him. Luis is everything to me."

Aaron nods as though he understands, but his next words stab into my chest like a knife. "Don't you think Emilio deserves to love him too?"

Tears prick the corners of my eyes and I hastily wipe them away. "I was going to tell him. I am going to tell him." I suck in a breath. "There just is never a good time and whenever I try and get him alone or have an actual conversation with him—"

"He defaults into putting the moves on you?" Aaron says with a sad smile. I don't bother correcting him because no, Emilio isn't interested in me anymore. It's every other girl with a set of tits that he's chasing after. "I can see how that might be a problem but..." he hesitates then exhales a loud sigh, "you need to tell him. Soon. The longer you wait, the worse it'll be. You've already waited a year in a half."

Not on purpose. "I didn't know who he was." He must think I'm such a horrible person right now. "We didn't exchange information. Not even names. I had no way of letting him know I was pregnant after the fact," I rush to explain. I don't want him thinking I kept Emilio from his son intentionally. That was never the objective here.

"But you knew the first day you came to Sun Valley High?" he hedges.

I nod. "Yeah. I recognized him right away."

He considers me, tapping his forefinger against his chin. "It's been a week. I'll give you one more to find a way to tell him. It would be better if it came from you. But if you can't do it, I have to tell him. He deserves to know."

I swallow hard and open my mouth to ask for more time, but the front door opens and in walks Miguel, pulling both of our attentions his way.

"Hey, Bibi. Your mom upstairs?" Miguel asks as soon as he sees me. "Oh. I didn't realize you had a friend here." He scowls as he takes Aaron in. "Is Jae here too?" he adds, and there's an edge in his voice. I stop myself from rolling my eyes, because of course he would see Aaron and assume he's Jae's competition. It doesn't matter that I've told Jae and Miguel, and my mom for that matter, that I am not interested in dating anyone.

I just want to focus on graduating. Is that too much to ask?

"Who's Jae?" Aaron asks, taking Miguel's bait. Urgh.

"He's Bibi's—"

"Friend." I cut him off. "We're friends and no, he's not here. I haven't seen him since this morning." And only because he still insists on driving me to school every day. "And yes, Mom's upstairs with Luis. She went to bed early. She looked beat."

Miguel nods and grabs a beer from the fridge. "Yeah, she's been helping me with some of the accounting at work," he says as he cracks open the bottle and downs half its contents in one pull. Voices can be heard from the living room, and Miguel cocks his head, pointing his beer toward the hallway. "Who else is here?"

"A few friends. We're just hanging out. Watching movies."

"Sleepover?" he asks, a glint in his eyes that puts me on edge. He's been weird lately. I mean, he's always been a little weird but weirder than usual. Miguel's never been anything but nice to me. Sometimes overly nice and I usually just brush it aside. But right now, Miguel has a distinct creeper factor that is making me uncomfortable.

Just then all three girls come into the room. "Hey, what's taking so long?" Monique asks with a bounce to her step.

"Yeah, I was starting to wonder if you were making out with my brother," Kasey jokes, flicking her gaze between us before settling on Miguel. "But I can see that's not the case. Did you make the popcorn?"

"Here, let me help you out with that." Miguel says, taking the bag of popcorn from the counter and pouring it into a bowl. "What are you girls going to be up to tonight? Hopefully not getting into trouble," he says it with a smirk, and again the creep-o-meter jumps up.

No one answers him. Monique and Kasey are both giving him polite but wary smiles, meanwhile Allie's gone pale as a ghost.

"Are you okay?" I ask her but she doesn't look at me. Her eyes are trained on Miguel, her chest rising and falling at a rapid clip.

He turns his attention to her and recognition sparks. "Well, fuck me."

FIFTY-ONE

Emilio

"Whatm's going on in that head of yours?" Dominique asks in the locker room. We just wrapped up practice and I'm sore as fuck. I drop my football helmet and pads beside my locker as I peel my sweat-soaked shirt over my head, rubbing my stomach in the process. I'm fucking starving.

"Nothing, man. I'm good."

"Liar," Roman says as he comes in the room and drops his gear beside mine.

"What's going on with you and Allie's new friend?" he asks. "Because whatever is eating at you, it has to do with her."

I shake my head. "I don't know what you're talking about. Nothing's eating at me. I'm good."

"Right." Dominique cuffs me on the shoulder. "So good you can't stop staring at the girl every time she walks into a room."

"Drop it," I snarl under my breath. "She's unimportant."

Dom snorts. "And you pissing all over the place to keep people away from her like she belongs to you totally supports that statement."

I clench my jaw and glower. "I'm not pissing on anything."

"*Mentiroso*," Roman says. *Liar.*

I ignore them and head for the showers, but of course the fuckers follow me. "Bro, you've claimed her. The whole fucking school knows it too. You beat the shit out of Carson Bailey during practice because he said she had a nice rack. Which she does, by the way," Dominique adds and my hands fist at my sides.

"See, that right there. That's my point." He indicates my tight fists and I force myself to relax, opening and closing them to bring back circulation. "I'm one of your best friends and you want to swing at me too. What the fuck, man?"

"Carson had it coming and you're being a dick." I stick my head under the running water and try and block out the voices of my friends as they do the same. Fucking Carson Bailey. He wanted her that night and the idiot made it known he was still interested. Sucks to be him though, because he's not getting anywhere near Bibiana if I have any say about it. And trust me, I have a say.

"E—" Roman snaps.

I wipe the water from my eyes and grab the soap, lathering it in my hands to take off today's layer of grime. "We hooked up. What's the big fucking deal?"

"You still hooking up with Sarah?" he asks and isn't that a loaded question. I tighten my jaw and rinse off the last of the suds before reaching for my towel and wrapping it around my waist.

"No." I offer the single-word answer, knowing the fucker is going to read more into it than he should. I'm not hooking up with anyone else and it's a fucking travesty because I should be. Sarah, Kathleen, Kaitlyn, I have a whole host of girls willing but none of them are her.

Neither Dom nor Roman say anything as we all dry off, getting dressed before heading for the exit. "What's the plan tonight?" I ask as we make our way to the school parking lot. It's Friday night and coach has us running two a day during playoffs since he's a sadistic bastard. I'm ready for the weekend and need the time to recharge and get my head on straight.

Antonio is home this weekend. Shocker. My older brother usually makes an effort to be anywhere but home, yet decided he'd watch over our little sister, Sofia, giving me a much-needed break. Sofia is old enough to be home alone but Raul—I refuse to call that waste of space "Dad"—has been hanging around more than usual, and none of us trust him where she's concerned.

I get that the man who contributed half of your DNA being home is probably normal for most families, but not for us. Not since Mom left. He spends most of his nights at the bar. Most of his days in some seedy motel with his flavor of the week. It's better this way. Safer for Sofia. For all of us. But he never stays gone for long. Not as long as he should, at least. He comes by the house on a near-weekly basis and when he does, he's usually drunk and angry. Never a good combination.

Lately, we've lucked out and Sofia's been at a friend's or kicking it at Roman's with his mom when Raul's stopped in. But I have a feeling our luck will run out eventually, which is why one of us is with Sofia at all times. And if we can't be, either because of practice for me or work for Antonio, then we make sure to coordinate a sleepover with a friend or she spends time with

Maria. Roman's mom is the mom we never had and thank God she loves my sister as if she were her own.

Roberto should be here helping make sure she's safe, but he enlisted the day he turned eighteen. It was fucked up when he left, but I can't say I blame him.

"Dunno. Allie is kicking it at Bibiana's with the babies and Henderson."

"The babies?" I ask.

He smirks. "Yeah. Dom and Henderson's baby sisters. The babies."

Dominique scrubs a hand over his face. "Them meeting one another is going to come back and bite me in the ass."

"You're not wrong, man." I grip his shoulder and grin. "And I cannot wait to see your downfall."

He shrugs me off as we reach Roman's El Camino and Dom's Escalade. I rarely drive myself. Why bother when both of these two are control freaks and insist on driving. Nine times out of ten we're going to the same place. We don't need three rides to get there. "My place?" Roman asks and Dominique nods. I open the passenger door to Roman's ride when a cell phone rings. I check my pocket, but it isn't mine that's ringing. Dominique pulls his out and stares down at the screen, a scowl on his face. "What the hell is Kasey calling me for?" he bites out, letting it go to voicemail. As soon as he shoves it back in his pocket, it starts ringing again.

"Looks like things are about to bite you in the ass sooner than you thought."

He flips me the bird but answers the phone with a curt, "What?"

There's shouting on the other line and I freeze, straining to pick up what she's saying.

"Address?" Dom bites out. "Lock yourselves in a fucking bathroom if you have to, got it?"

He's shaking his head. "Dammit. Why can't you lis— Fuck. Put Aaron on the phone."

More shouting.

She must have given Aaron the phone because now Dom is listening, eyes dark as he runs his hands over his tightly braided hair, his fingers flexing as though he wish he could tear it out. "We're on our way." Dominique ends the calls and turns to Roman with rage in his eyes. "Follow me and call your pops on the way. I'll text Emilio the address so you can pass it along to him."

"What's going on?"

His jaw ticks. "Allie thinks she found her rapist, and Aaron is beating the shit out of him as we speak. We need to go."

That's all it takes to get Roman moving. We peel out of the school parking lot, taking the corner so fucking fast I have to grab the oh-shit handle, but I don't tell Roman to slow down. His girl is in trouble and there isn't a mountain on this planet he wouldn't try to move for her. He dials his dad's number, snapping out the situation, and I pass on the address Dominique texted me.

It's a fifteen-minute drive, but we make it in close to five, and before the car is even off Roman is jumping from the front seat and barreling straight for the front door, Dominique and I close behind. We're family. And none of us fight alone.

FIFTY-TWO

Bibiana

Something is seriously wrong here and it has everything to do with Miguel. "Uhh... we're going to get back to our movie." I grab Allie's arm and half drag her toward the hallway, hoping everyone else will follow. Once we're alone I'll ask her what is going on. Her skin is so pale it's virtually translucent. I'm afraid she might pass out.

All of a sudden Allie digs in her heels and pulls her arm away from me, her spine straightening. "It's you," she says, but her voice is so quiet Miguel doesn't hear her. He's already gone back to his beer, and a part of me wonders if it isn't the first one he's had this evening. "It was you," she repeats, this time louder and he snaps his head toward her.

"I'm not sure I know what you're talking about," he tells her, but even I know it's a lie. He's not bothering to hide his smile or the heated look in his gaze as he eyes her up and down like a piece of meat. What is wrong with him? He has to know she's only seventeen.

"What's going on?" I ask, but Monique looks just as confused as I do.

"Allie?" Aaron questions, stepping closer to her and wrapping one arm protectively around her waist. "What's wrong?"

Tears are silently spilling down her face as she points at Miguel, her attention still wholly focused on him. "It was you. You were one of the men who..." She chokes on her words. "It was you." Aaron stiffens beside her and almost in slow motion turns to face Miguel. He tucks Allie behind his back and faces off with my mother's boyfriend, a furious expression washing over his face. "Kasey, call Roman."

"Wha—"

"Now. Tell him to call his dad and get here. Now, Kasey," he snaps.

Kasey pulls out her phone and starts calling, but it goes to voice mail so she tries again. And again.

"You sick sonovabitch," Aaron growls, taking a step forward.

Miguel doesn't even try to deny whatever it is they're accusing him of. He holds one arm out and waves his beer in the other. "Hey, man, you'd tap it too if you had a chance." My stomach rolls at his words. Is he...with Allie? No. No way. No freaking way.

Aaron launches himself at Miguel, and the two crash to the ground.

"Oh, my God," Monique gasps beside me.

I take a step forward but have no clue what to do. Do I intervene? Aaron is on top of Miguel, fists flying as he lands a right hook to his jaw before Miguel lands one of his own and manages to throw

Aaron off him. I push the rest of the girls back as both men climb to their feet. Aaron's chest is heaving but he doesn't look to be in rough shape. Meanwhile, blood is running from Miguel's nose and the corner of his mouth. Yet he's smiling, eyes bloodshot and a manic expression on his face. He spits blood onto the floor and waves at Aaron as if to say come on. Aaron lunges forward again. The two begin rolling across the ground and it's all I can do to track their movements. One second Miguel is on top and the next, Aaron is. Limbs are flying everywhere, fists crashing into whatever body part they can find. A plant is knocked over spreading dirt across the tiles and it mixes with their blood, leaving smears of murk in horrific streaks or brown and red.

Aaron seems to have the advantage despite Miguel being the bigger of the two. He's younger and in better shape, and he makes good use of what advantage that affords him. The two manage to separate, but only for a few seconds before the front door crashes open and all eyes turn toward it. Allie visibly relaxes beside me when she catches sight of Roman—Dominque and Emilio right behind him.

A jolt of fear spears through me. Emilio is here. He can't be here. Not right now. Not like this.

Roman assesses the scene in a matter of seconds before he throws himself forward into the fight, fists flying as he tackles Miguel back to the ground.

Miguel has zero time to react before Roman is pummeling his face into the tile floor, a murderous look in his eyes.

A gasp on the stairs has me looking up to find my mom standing at the top of the staircase, Luis clutched in her arms as she watches the scene below. "What are you doing? Get off of him!" she shouts, and I rush to intercept her as she runs down the steps and heads right for Roman and Miguel. I pull Luis from her arms, my focus completely on my son's safety, just as Emilio steps up to my mother and says in a low voice, "He has this beating coming to him for what he did to our friend."

My mom tries to shove past him but Emilio sidesteps her, blocking her path. She pushes against his shoulders, but he refuses to move. "You can't do this. You have no right—"

"He raped a seventeen-year-old girl," Dominique adds, his expression stony. He hasn't moved since coming in, and despite his words being for my mother, his gaze is glued to the fight in front of us, almost like he's waiting for something.

"Miguel would never do that. Whatever you think you know is a lie. He—"

"Admitted it Mom," I say in a whisper, imploring her with my eyes. My vision blurs but I refuse to let a single tear fall.

She jerks back as if I struck her. "Watch your words, minha filha." My daughter. "You don't know the truth of it. Miguel would never do what they're accusing him of. I'm calling the police."

"They're already on their way," Dominique says, and as soon as the words leave his lips, we all hear the sirens in the distance.

"Time's running out," Emilio says, his words directed at Roman, but he doesn't hear him. Roman is straddling Miguel who's barely moving, his arms no longer able to defend against Roman's fists. "Roman!" Still no response.

His jaw clenches before he meets Aaron's gaze across the room. Silent communication passes through them before they both step forward and rip Roman off Miguel's body. Roman doesn't give up without a fight, and it takes both boys holding him back to keep him from throwing himself back at Miguel who's barely moving on the floor as it is. Roman looks crazed, his eyes ablaze and his lips pulled back in a snarl. "I'll fucking kill you," he shouts. "You're a dead man."

Allie rushes to Roman's side, her arms wrapping around his waist. His nostrils flare but he manages to pull himself together enough to wrap his hands around her and hold her tight against his chest.

My mother rushes to Miguel's side, pulling his head into her lap as she sobs over him, and I just stand there, holding my baby boy, my world falling apart all around me.

Two officers come through the door and one immediately begins barking orders.

"Roman, get Allie and get out of here. I'll get statements from both of you later." Roman nods and leads Allie through the open doorway and outside. The sound of a car starting and pulling out of the driveway can be heard from outside, letting us know they're gone. The officer takes one look at Miguel, who's still on the ground but has managed to push himself up into a sitting position, and says, "You're under arrest for the assault and rape of Allie Ramirez. Anything you say can and..."

I don't bother listening after that. I stumble backward until my back hits the wall and let my body slide down until my butt hits the floor, Luis clutched safely in my arms. Monique is beside me in an instant, but then so is Dominique. "Go wait in the car," he says.

She shakes her head. "I'm not leav—"

"Now, Monique. Don't make me call Mom."

Monique clenches her jaw and turns an apologetic look my way.

"It's fine. I'll talk to you tomorrow," I tell her. No way can she get mixed up in whatever all this is. Her family would never let her see the light of day if they found out what happened. They'd never let her hang out with me again if they knew what my mom's boyfriend was accused of doing. Dominique has the right to get her out of here before any more cops show up or the two who are already here decide to take statements from everyone and get names on the record.

"Call me later and let me know you're okay," she says, and I nod.

Dominique walks her out, but seconds later he's back and heading straight for Kasey. They argue but I can't make out what's said and the next thing I know he's throwing her over his shoulder and storming out of the room as she screeches at him to put her down. Aaron watches the entire thing with a resigned expression before following Dominique out the door, presumably to take his sister home.

The officers pull Miguel to his feet and begin to usher him out the door, my mom right behind them. "Mom—" I call after her and she turns to face me. "Where are you going?"

"I'm sorry, minha filha. But I love him." Tears fall down her cheeks, her expression torn.

My brows furrow. What is she saying right now? "Mom?"

She doesn't say anything else. She just shakes her head and follows the officers out. I'm still standing there, staring at the empty doorway she walked through when Emilio appears beside me. "You okay?"

I jump at his words, managing to startle and wake Luis in the process. How he managed to sleep through all the noise is beyond me, and I wish he would have stayed asleep a little longer because now Emilio is looking at him with open curiosity. "He yours?"

I swallow hard, but nod and push back to my feet.

He flicks his eyes between me and Luis. He opens his mouth. Closes it. Opens it again. I can the see the moment he puts two and two together. His mouth tightens, brows drawn, eyes glued to the boy in my arms.

"Come on," Dominique calls, ducking back inside. "Aaron's in his car with the girls. He'll drop them off and then head to Roman and Allie's so we can all figure our shit out. After Rome's dad drops Miguel off at the station he'll be heading there too. We need to get our stories straight."

Emilio doesn't move.

"E, come on." Dominique grabs his arm but Emilio jerks free and shoves him away. His chest is rising and falling at a rapid pace, his nostrils flaring.

"You have a son?" Pain slashes across his face and a muscle ticks in his jaw as he visibly fights to keep it together. When I don't answer, he takes a step back, and shouts, "I have a son?" It's as if the entire house shakes with the force of his voice.

I don't know what to do or what to say so I just stand there frozen in place. Dominique looks between us, seeing the baby boy in my arms, and his expression tightens. "Emilio, now isn't the—"

"Nah. No way, man. No fucking way." He shakes his head. "Do I even need to ask?" he says to me, and Luis starts to cry. I bounce him on my hip and make soothing noises in the face of Emilio's anger. He's fuming. If it were possible for steam to be coming out of his ears, it would be. His face is red and the veins on his neck stick out in sharp relief. All I can do in the face of his anger is swallow hard and hold Luis to me a little tighter.

Emilio catches the movement and his eyes narrow. "Are you fucking kidding me?" he barks. "You think I'd hurt him? My own kid?" His eyes narrow into slits, "Because that's what he is, right? Mine."

I hesitate.

"Answer me!" he roars.

Dominique steps forward and places a hand on Emilio's shoulder. "Hey, why don't we—"

"Fuck that. Tell me the truth. Is. He. Mine?" I nod, and Emilio shrugs Dominique off again, his movements sharp as he begins to pace. "She kept my kid from me. My son." He slaps a hand over his chest. "My son." His jaw clenches. "What the fuck, Bibiana? What did I ever do to you to warrant that? Huh? Am I not good enough?" His voice rises with each word until he's practically shouting at me, and all I can do is stand there knowing I deserve his anger. His rage.

Luis's crying increases at Emilio's harsh tone, and a silent tear slips past my defenses to trek down my cheek. This isn't how I wanted this to go. None of this is what I wanted.

"Emilio—" Dominique tries again. He flicks his gaze toward me. "Maybe you should—"

"No." He shakes his head, anger etched into every line of his body. "Give me my son." Emilio holds his arms out but I take an involuntary step back.

His eyes blaze. "Let me hold my son, Bibiana," he spits out my name with so much venom, I visibly shudder but manage to stand my ground and shake my head.

"You're angry."

"You would be too," he snaps.

I rock Luis in my arms, running my hand over the back of his head in a soothing gesture as I struggle to remain calm. "I know. I'm not saying you shouldn't be. But you're angry and right now, you're scary." Really fucking scary. I don't think Emilio would hurt me or Luis, but seeing him like this, it's unnerving to say the least. "I'm sorry. But I'm not handing him to you. Not like this."

I sway my body side to side and Luis's cries finally stop. He sniffles a few times before his head rests against my shoulder. Exhaustion finally taking hold. When his eyes close, I release a small sigh of relief and turn back to the angry boy before me. Emilio's entire body is taught like a bow string. I can tell he wants to argue but instead he gives me a stiff nod. He heads to the sofa and sits down, bowing his head and running his hands through his dark brown hair. His shoulders slump in defeat, and so many emotions run through me. Sorrow. Pain. Regret. I chance a look in Dominique's direction, but instead of finding anger or disgust like I expect, I find resignation. I'm not sure that is any better.

"This wasn't how I wanted you to find out," I say the words in little more than a whisper.

"I'm sure you had your reasons for not telling him." Dominique chimes in, not bothering to lower his voice, ensuring Emilio hears his words. "I can't imagine being a single mom is easy. You've had to make some tough decisions. Sometimes they're good ones. Other times maybe they're not."

I nod, worrying my lower lip. This obviously wasn't one of my better ones.

"But, I can see you love that little boy." He tilts his chin toward his friend. "Do right by him and give Emilio a chance to love him too."

It's all I've ever wanted to do. I didn't mean to keep Luis a secret. I wanted to tell him. It just never seemed like the right time. I'm so angry with myself for letting this happen. For letting it come out like this.

Dominique tosses his keys beside Emilio and heads to the door. "I'll catch a ride with Aaron. Call me if you need anything. We'll fill you in later when you have time." Emilio doesn't respond, not that Dominique waits for him to.

When the door closes behind him, I stand there for a few moments, almost afraid to move, before I muster up the courage to say, "I'm going to lay him down in his crib. If ..." I take a deep breath. "If you're still here when I come back and you want to talk, we can do that."

He doesn't answer, so I head upstairs and gently lay Luis down in his crib before slipping into the bathroom. My cheeks are red and blotchy, my eyeliner smudged beneath my eyes and the small wing at the corners long since rubbed away. I wash away the emotions of today and go back downstairs, almost surprised to find Emilio in the exact same spot I left him in.

A part of me was sure he would have left. I'm not sure if I should be relieved that he chose to stay.

When he hears me enter the room, he lifts his head and I freeze. Grief stands out in sharp relief across his face, and it twists me up inside to see him like this.

I sink down on the bottom step of the staircase, wrapping my arms around my knees. I don't know what to say, or if I should even say anything at all. So, I wait. Seconds tick by, turning into minutes as we stare at one another. I hope he can see how sorry I am. That my eyes can convey what my words have failed to give him.

When a full five minutes passes, he shakes his head and stands up, but he doesn't go anywhere. He just...stands there. The anger has drained out from his body, leaving behind a boy who looks lost and alone. Broken. And I'm responsible for that.

"I'm sorry I didn't tell you about him sooner," I say, my words whispered.

"Were you ever going to tell me?" he asks. "If I hadn't found out today, would you have ever said anything?" His words are equally quiet as though he's afraid of the answer.

I push to my feet and move closer to him. "I wanted to tell you the first day I saw you. I had every intention of letting you know right away but..." I bite my lip and Emilio tilts his head back staring at the ceiling. His Adams apple bobs as he swallows.

"But then you heard about my reputation." I exhales a harsh breath. "And then I finger-fucked you in a classroom. Fuck."

He reaches out and jerks me to him, wrapping his arms around my shoulders in a fierce embrace. "I'm so fucking mad at you for keeping him from me," he says into my hair and I tentatively wrap my arms around his waist. I have no idea why he's holding me like this, but I don't really care. I need this. Need the contact. I need to feel like things will be okay. That he isn't going to hate me forever.

"You should have told me. I don't give a fuck about everything else. You should have told me right away."

"It's only been—" He cuts me off, his body trembling beneath my hold.

"A week, Bibiana. It's been a week that you've been here. That's a week I can't get back. A week of not knowing I had a son and of him not knowing me."

"I'm sorry," I say, because he's right. If roles were reversed, I'd feel the same way.

"I want to hate you," he whispers almost too quiet for me to hear, but I do and my heart plummets to the soles of my feet. "And when my head stops spinning, I just might. I don't know if I'll ever be able to get over the fact that you kept him from me. I missed so fucking much." He releases me and takes two steps back.

I feel cold at the loss of contact and wrap my arms around myself.

"I—" I don't know what to say to that.

"I want to get to know him," he says, voice firm. "I want visitation and I want it in writing."

His last statement takes me by surprise, and I swallow hard as a trickle of fear worms its way through me before reason has me locking the emotion away. This is what I wanted. I want my son to have his father. I want him to feel wanted and Emilio demanding visitation is him showing that he wants to be in Luis's life. I take a deep breath and force out my next words.

"I'd like that too."

His eyes widen before he nods his head. "Okay. Good." He shoves his hands into his pockets. "When can I have him?"

I frown. "Um..."

"Can I pick him up tomorrow?"

"You want to pick him up?" I ask, licking my lips. "And take him where?"

"I don't know. The park. Maybe Roman's." He shrugs.

It's the middle of winter. What does he think they're going to do at the park? Luis isn't even walking on his own yet. "Have you ever looked after a baby?" I ask as gently as possible because I really don't want to fight with him about this. "Luis is only nine months old. He ...umm..." I can see that Emilio is about to argue so I rush out my next words. "What if you came here instead? You could take a few days to get to know him. Make sure he's comfortable with you and it'll give you a chance to learn umm ... how to look after an infant?" That sounds a lot more patronizing that I mean it to be.

He considers it and the silence stretches between us. "Fine."

I release a breath I hadn't realized I was holding. "Okay. Good."

We stare at each other for a beat. "His name is Luis?" he asks. His eyes keep flicking toward the staircase, and I know he wants to see him again.

"Yeah. Luis Afonso Sousa."

A muscle ticks in his jaw.

When he doesn't snap or yell at me, I move closer and tentatively reach out, tugging on his sleeve. "Come on," I say and lead him up the staircase to my room.

Outside the door, he hesitates for only a minute before following me inside. The lights are out, but there is a small night-light and sound machine beside Luis's crib that illuminates his sleeping form. Careful not to wake him, I wave toward my bed, indicating that Emilio have a seat. His eyes are glued to our son and a small smile curls the corners of his mouth as he takes a seat, leaning forward for a better view.

"He's perfect," he whispers, and I can't help but match his smile.

"He has your eyes and your mouth," I tell him, claiming the space beside him.

"He does?"

I nod.

We sit in silence, watching our little boy sleep, and despite today being a complete disaster of epic proportions, a small part of me is hopeful. Emilio wants to be in Luis's life, and that alone is more than I could have hoped for.

FIFTY-THREE

Emilio

I stay at Bibiana's until just past midnight watching my boy sleep, the steady rise and fall of his tiny body doing something to soothe the raging devil inside of me. I have a kid. A son. One she kept secret from me for all this time. Fuck. I scrub my hands over my face and look down at her. She drifted off to sleep close to an hour ago, her tiny body curled up beside me on top of her comforter. Exhaustion lines her face and a part of me is sorry for that, but the bigger part of me, the all-consuming asshole deep inside is furious with her. I'm having to try real hard not to explode.

What the actual fuck?

I shove to my feet and lean over the crib railing, giving Luis one last look. "I'll be back later, little man." I tell him, tracing a finger along his cheek. He's so small. Fragile. Looking at him brings home the fact that my entire world is about to flip upside down right now.

I head for the door, leaving Bibiana undisturbed on her bed. She said I could see him tomorrow. Well, technically today. But I need a few hours of sleep and a shower before I'll be in any sort of shape to meet my little boy.

I jog down the stairs, grabbing Dominique's keys along the way and head straight for my place. My mind is roiling and my stomach is twisted into knots. I want to call Roman, but I know he's got his hands full with Allie's shit right now, and she needs him more than I do. And isn't that a fucking plot twist. Bibiana's what? Stepdad, or whatever he is to her, is one of the sons of bitches who raped Allie.

My blood boils as an entirely different sort of anger thrums through my veins. I need to do something. Hit something or someone. I slam my palm against the steering wheel and scream out my frustrations. What the hell am I going to do?

Bibiana seems onboard with me being in his life, but that could be the adrenaline of the night's events talking. A lot has happened. What if she wakes up in the morning and changes her mind? What if she decides I'm not good enough? Or fuck, worse, what if she takes off again? She might. She's done it before and with her mom taking that asshole's side. What if—

Shit. I still don't have the girl's fucking number.

I'm about to turn around and go back when my phone pings with the sound of an incoming text message.

 Allie: Are you okay?

I PULL OVER TO THE SIDE OF THE ROAD AND STARE DOWN AT the illuminated screen.

Me: I should be asking you that. You good, vanilla?

I TAKE A DEEP BREATH THROUGH MY NOSE AND EXHALE loudly through my mouth as I wait for her response. I can't even imagine what she's going through right now, and the fact that she's still worried about me... I hang my head. She's too much. Too good. This is why we all liked her when she transferred in. She's not like other women. She isn't selfish. She's there when you need her. The girl is the strongest person I know.

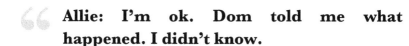

Allie: I'm ok. Dom told me what happened. I didn't know.

EVEN IF SHE DID, I COULD NEVER BE MAD AT HER. ALLIE IS...I don't know. She's my friend. But she's more. Like a sister but not. I don't know how to describe it. What I do know is that she never gives up. She puts everyone else's needs before her own. But this time, she needs to put herself first. She doesn't need my shit. I love her for it. But I'm gonna figure this out. I don't want her worrying about me when she has her own mess to handle.

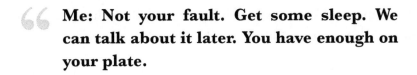

> **Me: Not your fault. Get some sleep. We can talk about it later. You have enough on your plate.**

> **Allie: It's going to be okay. Love you, E.**

> **Me: You too, vanilla.**

I PULL BACK ON THE ROAD AND GO STRAIGHT HOME, PAUSING in the driveway at the sight of Raul's beat up Civic. Shit. I do not have time for this right now. I climb out of the car and head for the door, only then spotting that it's standing slightly ajar. Fuck me.

I take a deep breath and push it open. A broken bottle sits discarded in the entryway. I listen, but don't hear anything. No voices. No footsteps. I creep through the house, careful to keep my steps quiet. Where the hell is my Antonio? Where's Sofia?

One of my questions is answered when I find my brother passed out on the living room floor, dried blood beneath his nose and mouth. Fuck. I drop down to my knees and check for a pulse. It's steady. He's just knocked out. I shake his shoulders and he stirs with a start.

"What the—"

"Where's Sofia?" My heart races as I scan the room for our little sister.

He groans and I know his head has got to be killing him. I help him into a sitting position. "The bastard took me by surprise."

I clench my jaw because that's what he always does. You never know when or if he's going to swing. There's no way to read Raul. One second, he's fine and the next he's in a manic rage trying to kill his own fucking children.

"Sofia," I prompt when my brother doesn't say anything else.

"Shit." He pushes to his feet. "What time is it?"

"Maybe twelve-thirty. Where is she, Antonio?"

His shoulders relax and he heads for the hallway that leads to our rooms. There's more broken glass here and a few drops of blood splattered across the floor. I'm assuming those belong to Raul because they all lead toward his room at the very end of the hallway.

Antonio raises his finger to his lips in the universal sign to be quiet as he slowly opens the door that leads to my bedroom. We step inside and he goes straight for my closet. Sofia is asleep inside, her tiny body curled into the fetal position. We both stare down at her, relief sweeping through me once I can see for myself that she's okay.

I lean down to lift her out, careful not to wake her as I lay her on my bed and tuck the blankets around her. When she's settled, I follow Antonio back into the hall, locking the door behind me. It only locks from the inside, so she can let herself out when she wakes up. I won't be able to get back in until then, at least not without waking her. But it's better this way. I need to talk to my brother and find out what the hell happened, and I can't do that and worry about the bastard down the hall getting to my baby sister.

"What the hell happened?" I asked, my voice pitched low as soon as we're a safe distance away.

He rolls his neck and scrubs a palm down his face, wincing in pain when he brushes over his bruised cheek. "What always happens. He showed up maybe an hour ago." Antonio shakes his head. "I heard his car roll up and hid Sofia before he stepped through the front door. Made her promise not to come out and to keep quiet."

I nod my head. That's what we usually do when Raul comes around. She's looking more and more like our mom as she gets older, and the sight of her alone has been enough to set him off the few times he's dropped by recently.

"You okay?"

Antonio nods. "Yeah. I'm good. I don't remember much after the second punch, but I didn't fight back so he must have gotten bored."

"You should go to the—"

"I said I'm good," he snaps. Antonio hangs his head, palms clenched into fists at his sides. "I fucking hate this." He moves further down the hall to the kitchen and pulls out a bag of frozen corn before taking a seat at the table. He holds it against his face and mutters out a few choice words.

I grab two beers from the fridge, open both, and hand one to him across the table before taking a seat. "What's the plan?" I ask, hoping he's come up with something. Raul is getting worse, and we all have shit going on. We do our best to protect Sofia, but one of these days he's bound to come up on her alone, and none of us knows what will happen when that day comes.

"I don't know, man." He's fighting exhaustion. Shit. We both are. Too much has happened today. Too many things to process. To try and figure out.

"What are you doing home so late? I figured you'd have been here earlier, or later if you crashed at Romans."

I debate telling him about Luis, but before I can make up my mind, my brother proves just how well he knows me with his next words. "What happened?"

"It can wait."

Antonio shakes his head. "No. Don't do that. I know you've got your boys, but you got me too. Come on, Emilio. What happened?"

I grind my teeth down as frustration radiates through every cell in my body. I want to tell him. I want his support, but Antonio doesn't do well when his plate is full. He's like Roberto. He bails rather than dealing with it. He might be doing better than our oldest brother—when shit got too real, he enlisted in the military and never looked back. Antonio, at least, stuck around after his eighteenth birthday—but he still takes off sometimes for a week or more at a time.

"E?"

"Don't you dare bail, you got me?"

His eyes widen, but he nods. "I won't bail."

"I'm serious, Antonio. I can't deal with Raul and my own shit right now. Not by myself."

He nods his head, his face twisted into a solemn expression. "I won't leave."

"Okay." I hesitate and have to swallow past the lump in my throat. "I have a kid."

His eyes widen to the size of saucers. "You knocked a girl up?"

"Yeah," I rub the back of my neck. "A year and a half ago. I just found out tonight."

He curses and drops his head into his hands. "Shit. Are you sure it's yours?"

I nod. "I'm sure. The timing lines up and he looks just like me. Damn near identical to my baby pictures at that age.

"You should get a paternity test," he suggests.

"I don't need it. He's mine. I haze zero doubts. You'll feel the same when you meet him."

He doesn't like my answer, but thankfully doesn't argue either. "We need to call Roberto."

"What?" I shove away from the table. "Why the hell would we call him? He left!" I hiss, but Antonio just shakes his head.

"Can you think of a better option? Raul is a problem. A big one. And now you have a kid. What are you going to do if you have him here and Raul shows up? Huh? Have you even thought that far?"

My blood turns to ice as I digest his words because no, I hadn't thought that far. I'm still dealing with the fact that I'm a dad. That Luis is mine. I hadn't even considered just how vulnerable he is. How dangerous having him with me could be for him. Shit. If Bibiana found out what I was dealing with, no way would she let me be in his life. Fuck. Fuck. Fuck.

"He doesn't have leave coming up. There's nothing he can do—"

"He'll get leave."

"But—"

"Let me handle it, okay? Shit. Boy or Girl?"

Huh. It takes me a second to understand his questions. "Oh. Boy."

"What's his name?"

"Luis," I tell him.

Antonio nods to himself for a second before a wide grin splits his face. "So, I'm an uncle."

I muffle my laugh with my fist. "Yeah, fucker. You're an uncle."

Silence stretches between us, both of us thinking of all the things that have gone wrong and all the possible things that can still happen. It's times like this when I can't breathe. When the pressure builds too much, and I need to find a release. I'm tempted to call some random. It'd be easier if I called Sarah, worked out some of my frustration while Antonio was here but that's not a tree I want to be barking up right now. Fucking her holds zero appeal for me. I don't know what is wrong with me but obviously something is. Maybe it's just her. Our last fuck was awful. But... whatever. I can't leave Antonio and Sofia to deal with Raul on their own whenever he wakes up anyway.

My family might be fucked up, but we do what we can for as long as we can. Let's hope we all have enough fight left in us to deal with whatever comes next.

FIFTY-FOUR

Bibiana

I wake to Luis's garbled baby jabbers and roll over to find the space beside me empty. A glance at the beside clock. It shows that it's just past nine. Emilio must have left sometime after I fell asleep. I pick up my Luis almost as though I'm on autopilot and go through our usual morning routine.

Nurse. Fresh diaper. New clothes. When he's all set, I put him down on the floor with some of his toys and get myself ready, taking a five-minute shower with the door open to try and wash away some of the strain of last night.

Clean and feeling more awake, I straighten up the small mess Luis made before we head downstairs. I pass my mom's room on the way, her door open and the bed empty. I wonder if she ever came home last night. I need to talk to her but I'm not sure what to say.

The entryway and kitchen are a disaster. A lamp is laying on its side, shards of glass scattered in the general area. There are blood smears across the floor. Chairs toppled over and dirt from a potted plan strewn about.

I sigh, already knowing I can't leave it like this. I deposit Luis on the floor in the living room with a few of his favorite toys and turn on some cartoons. "Mommy will be right back."

I grab a garbage bag and the broom, cleaning up all of the dirt and glass and throwing away anything not salvageable. Luis wanders into the kitchen a few times, so the clean-up process takes a little longer having to go back and forth and pause long enough to play with him for a few minutes before he's distracted enough for me to slip away and finish my task.

The blood has stained the off-white tiles leaving them tinged with pink, but I've been scrubbing at them for close to half an hour so it's as good as it's going to get. I'm just about to go dump out the blood-tinged water when there's a knock at the door.

I dry my hands on my pants and head over to it to answer, surprised when I find Jae standing on my doorstep. "Hey," I say opening the door wider for him to come in.

His hair is disheveled. Instead of being neatly pulled back into his usual bun, it hangs over one side of his head, and a sprinkling of scruff covers his jawline. "Hey. Sorry. I would have come sooner, but I didn't want to wake you."

"Is everything okay?"

Luis chooses that moment to crawl into the kitchen. His eyes light up when he sees Jae and he stretches his little arms up in the air. His way of demanding to be picked up. Jae complies, bouncing Luis in his arms for a second. "Hey, little man," he coos, and I don't bother fighting my smile. Jae has always been great with Luis. It's why I always felt like a jerk for never giving the guy a chance.

"So, what brings you by?"

He turns to face me, and his expression grows stony. "I was at the precinct all night. I know Miguel was arrested."

"Oh. That." I'm not sure what else to say. He works for Miguel. They were kind of friends despite the age difference between them. I know Jae looked up to him almost like a mentor. "Did you see my mom?"

He shakes his head. "No. She was at the hospital with Miguel. She called me for help but then I found out what he was being charged with ..." He hangs his head. "Did he... "

"No. It wasn't me. He didn't." I shake my head. "Not me."

He exhales a relieved breath. "Your mom seems to think—"

"He did it. He all but admitted it in front of me. He isn't innocent."

He jaw clenches. "I kinda figured."

"You did?" I ask, surprised. He and Miguel always seemed close, almost like he looked up to him.

"Yeah. Miguel is in some shady shit. The way he talks sometimes when it's just the guys," a shrug. "I brush it off as just talk but now ..."

I place a hand on his arm. "Not your fault. You couldn't have known. None of us knew he was capable of something like this."

"I know. But, I'm... I'm sorry, Bibi. I told your mom I couldn't help. Wouldn't. If he's guilty, I'm not going to use the firm's connections to get him off. They'll have to figure things out on their own."

"Good." Miguel can rot for all I care.

"It's just…" he hesitates. "It looks like your mom is going to stand by him on this one. He's in the hospital. He'll be taken to the precinct once his injuries allow it but…" he trails off.

Moisture pools in the corners of my eyes and I blink it away. I shouldn't be surprised. She'd said as much yesterday.

"So…" I trail off, unsure what it is that I'm asking exactly.

Jae holds one arm out while his other supports Luis's weight. I step into his embrace, relishing the security and comfort of just being held. "I'm here for you. I'm worried about you," he says, conviction in his voice.

I slowly pull away and stare up into his eyes, a fierce determination on his face. "We're not your problem," I tell him, and his jaw tightens.

"You're my friend. That's reason enough to give a damn about your well-being."

Fair enough. "I'm not sure there's really anything you can—"

"Move in with me," he says, his words taking me back.

"What?"

He hands Luis back to me and shoves his hands into his pocket, squaring his shoulders. "Move in with me."

I can't be hearing him right.

"Miguel has an entire team of lawyers working for him. Even if he doesn't get off, he will get out on bail. They're already drawing up the paperwork for his release. You're not safe here. Neither is Luis. I think you should move in with me."

Before he finishes, I'm shaking my head. "I—I can't move in with you." I say, though what choice do I have if what he says is true? If Miguel gets out, this is his house. His home. I can't stay here if he's here. And Mom... I don't even know what she's going to do. We haven't talked since she ran out to follow him. I need to call her. Figure out what she's planning. Convince her that he isn't someone worth defending.

"Bibi—"

I raise a hand to stop him. "I'll think about it," I tell him, and I will. "But he's not here yet. He's still in the hospital and it's the weekend. At best, he'll get out Monday." With any luck it'll be later than that. "Let's just hold off a bit and see what happens."

He doesn't look happen but nods. "Okay. But if you need anything,"

"I know. And thank you. You have no idea how much I appreciate that." I've made friends at school but they're new. Fragile. It's not like I can call Allie or Kasey and ask to move in with them and while Monique would want to help, no way would her family approve. I'm grateful I have Jae at least.

He looks around the room, spotting the garbage bag and bucket of bloody water. "I know he was arrested and is accused of raping a student at Sun Valley High. Wanna fill me in on the rest?"

For whatever reason, I completely unload all of last night's events on Jae. From the second everyone arrived to Emilio finding out he's Luis's father. It's takes twenty minutes to give him all the details and when I finally finish, he's wide-eyed with a stunned expression on his face.

"Shit. That's a lot to process."

"No kidding."

"Do you know what you're going to do next? What he—"

A knock at the door halts his next words. "Let me get it," he says, moving to answer the door. Emilio is on the other side, freshly showered, his hair still wet. His eyes are narrowed at Jae, but they soften when he spots Luis in my arms behind him.

"Hey, can I come in?" He barely acknowledges Jae's existence.

I nod and have to tug on the back of Jae's shirt when he doesn't step aside to let Emilio in.

"Yeah. Follow me. We can go in the living room."

I lead him through the house where Luis's cartoons are still playing. Jae takes a seat on the sofa, a wary look on his face as he sizes Emilio up. I'm not sure what he's looking for, but whatever it is, he doesn't find it because his expression only seems to darken as the seconds go by.

"This is my friend, Jae. Jae, this is Emilio. Luis's—"

"Bio-dad. Got it," he bites out.

I scowl at him, not sure where his hostility is coming from, but also not having the energy to deal with it right now. "Do you think we can get together later?" I ask. "Emilio and I..." I pause. What do we need to do exactly? Talk, I suppose. I'm sure he wants to meet Luis. Play with him maybe.

"I can stay if you'd like," Jae suggests, but I don't miss the narrowing of Emilio's eyes. "It might be good to—"

"That's okay." I cut him off. "This is probably something I should do alone."

His jaw tightens, but he nods and climbs to his feet. "Okay." He kisses the top of my head before doing the same to Luis. "Catch you later, little man. And Bibi," I wait. "Think about what I said. Okay?"

"I'll consider it," I tell him, watching as he leaves. I wait for the sound of the front door closing behind him before I turn and face Emilio.

"Something I should know about?" he asks.

I shake my head. A part of me knows he would have a problem with me living with Jae and it's not something I want to argue about right now. Not when we should be focusing on Luis. "No. It's nothing."

I take a seat on the floor, Luis in my lap and hand him a few blocks to play with. "He takes a few minutes to warm up to strangers," I tell him, immediately regretting my choice of word. "But if you give him some time to adjust, he'll make his way over to you on his own and hand you blocks or cars to play with him with."

Shoulders stiff, Emilio nods and lowers himself to the ground across from me. He shrugs out of his coat, laying it on the sofa behind him. His shirt stretches across his broad shoulders, the fabric hugging his muscular form. I wet my lips and wring my hands in my lap.

Luis captures his entire attention, his gaze never straying from our boy. I watch emotions play over Emilio's face. Curiosity, wonder, joy. He's enamored with him already and a fist squeezes my heart inside my chest seeing the open affection he already has for him.

We both watch our son toddle around the room, one second crawling and the next walking as he collects his toys into one pile before throwing them as far as he can—which isn't that far—across the room one by one, laughing as they hit the hardwood floor.

"He's kind of a terror, isn't he? Emilio asks, affection clear in his voice.

I smile. "Yeah. He likes the sound the blocks make when they hit the floor. It's his favorite pastime these days." One block lands particularly close to Emilio, and Luis crawls toward him to retrieve it. Emilio freezes when Luis sits up on his knees, brown eyes curious, as he holds the block out in his hand for Emilio to take.

"That for me?" he asks. His face is the softest I've ever seen it as he looks down at our son, carefully taking the toy from his tiny fingers. "Thanks." Luis stares at him a moment longer before crawling right into Emilio's lap and turning himself to the side to get comfortable. He reaches for the block in Emilio's hand and he gives it to him, both arms winding around Luis's small body and a wonder-struck expression on his face.

Luis doesn't allow Emilio to hold him long before squirming in his arms to get back on the ground to play and Emilio reluctantly releases him.

"So..." I begin, because there are a lot of things we should probably talk about. "We should talk about, um, what it is you want." God, even to my own ears that sounded lame.

His dark brown gaze finds mine and anger flashes for a split second before he nods once, rubbing the back of his neck. "Yeah. Well, I figured it's pretty obvious." He looks to Luis and his jaw clenches. "I want to be in his life. I want to be his dad."

Okay. That sounds good and all, but...

"And I want regular visitation."

I swallow hard and force my breathing to slow despite the rapid beating of my heart. What he's asking for isn't unreasonable.

"And I want it in writing, Bibiana. I want to be added to his birth certificate. I want our visitation schedule in writing and signed or notarized or whatever it needs to be for it to be official. I need to know you're not going to disappear again and take him from me."

My breath hitches and a trickle of apprehension slips beneath my skin. "I never meant—"

"It doesn't matter. You did. I'm not risking that again, so those are my terms. I'll pay child support or whatever. We'll figure it out and I'll do my part, but I want everything in writing so there is zero question that he is mine and I have rights."

I lick my lips. "And if I don't want to put everything in writing?" I ask because there is a needle of fear that tells me if I give him what he's asking for, it will make it all the easier for him to one day take Luis away from me. I'm not saying he would, just...it's a possibility. I don't know Emilio. Not really. What if we get into an argument? What if he wants to take Luis out of town or to visit a distant relative and then never comes back. I know they're what ifs, but that little boy is my entire world. The thought of losing him—

"Then we'll get the courts involved. I don't want to do that, Bibiana. I don't want things to get any uglier than they already are but..." He trails off and shakes his head, turning his focus to Luis. "I won't risk losing him."

The mention of that word—court—makes my mouth run dry. He could take me to court, make demands, ask for even more than he's asking for now and there is a good chance he would get it. I know people assume that the judge always favors the mother, but will that still hold true if they learn I kept his son from him? That he missed out on the first nine months of his life because of me? No. I don't think it would. If he takes me to court, I could lose everything.

I drop my head and close my eyes, pulling in a lungful of air. "Okay," I whisper, my heart aching in my chest and I raise my gaze up to his. "We'll put it in writing."

He nods once.

"But—"

He frowns.

"The rest we do my way. I'm his mom. He doesn't know you yet, and you're a seventeen-year-old guy with no clue how to look after a baby. I'm not going to just send him off with you after one introduction."

His jaw clenches, his nostrils flaring. "I won't let you keep him from me, Bibiana."

"I don't want to. I just..." I exhale a loud breath. "He's only nine months old. He's still breastfeeding."

His eyes drop to my chest, and a dark look passes over his face before he blinks it away.

"I think you should come here for visits, at least to start," I say and when it looks like he's about to argue I rush to add, "Let him get to know you. Let...let me get to know you so I don't freak out when you walk out the door with the most important person in my universe. Please."

The muscle in his jaw ticks. "Fine," he manages to bite out, and I release the breath I'd been holding.

"Thank you."

FIFTY-FIVE

Emilio

This moment is surreal, seeing my kid play with his toys and bring them to me like he knows me. As if we've been doing this his whole life.

My kid.

Fuck. I still can't wrap my head around the fact I'm a dad.

Luis stumbles across the floor, his tiny legs unsteady, and with each step he takes, I tense, waiting for the moment when he loses his balance and I need to catch him. Somehow, he manages to stay on his feet, his arms held out and a drooly grin on his face.

We watch him play for half an hour when all of a sudden he gets angry with one of his cars, yelling at the thing like it somehow offended him before crawling to Bibiana and shoving his little hand down the front of her shirt.

"Sorry." Her cheeks turn pink. "I think he's hungry." She gets up from the floor, about to leave the room and I realize I don't want her to. It would be one more thing I don't get to be involved in.

"Feed him here." It comes out like an order. She scowls and is about to argue when I add, "Please."

She nods once, and her cheeks turn an even brighter shade of pink.

I try not to stare as she lifts him up and positions herself on the sofa, my boy in her arms. She grabs a blanket from the back of the sofa and attempts to cover herself up as she pulls her shirt up just enough for Luis to reach her breast, but he isn't having it. If anything, her attempts at modesty make it worse because instead of burying his face in her boobs—something that, I won't lie, sounds appealing because she's got great tits—he's fighting with her, yelling and flailing his tiny hands in the air to get the covering off.

I'm sure she'd like a few minutes of privacy, but I can't bring myself to give them to her.

Bibiana huffs, finally giving up, and lets the blanket drop to the side, her full breast exposed save for the back of Luis's head blocking my view of her nipple.

She visibly swallows and won't meet my gaze. It's fucking adorable. Not that the thought should be running through my head. I've cooled off some since last night but I still can't shake the feeling that she did this on purpose. That she didn't think I was good enough for our son. I hate that.

"You good?" I ask. Not that I should care, but seeing her feed our son, take care of him, it awakens something primal inside of me. Fire burns in my throat as she turns her head and meets my stare head on, and want flickers in the recesses of my mind. What the hell is wrong with me?

"Yeah. Just ... didn't want to make you uncomfortable." She shrugs.

A smile curls my lips. "You can pop those out anytime you'd like. Trust me, I'm far from uncomfortable."

Her cheeks go from pink to scarlet. I like it. Like making her uncomfortable. Uncertain.

What she's doing isn't sexual. Far from it, in fact. But ... I exhale a harsh breath. Without letting myself think about what I'm doing, I get up from the floor and move to sit beside her. She gazes up at me, a furrow between her brows, but I've already turned my attention to Luis. His little fists are balled up against her breast, his eyes closed and a relaxed expression on his face.

Emotion threatens to overwhelm me and I almost don't recognize the sound of my voice as I utter my next words. "Marry me," I say, surprising myself, but I don't try and take back the words. Actually, now that they're out in the open, it makes sense. Getting married, I mean. It would resolve all our problems. We wouldn't need to work out custody or visitation. There wouldn't be any worries or unknowns. We'd be a family, for Luis.

Her head snaps up. "What? Are you serious?"

"Deadly."

"No."

I grit my teeth and try not to be offended by her response, even as my chest squeezes all the air from my lungs. "Why not?" It comes out angrier than I intended and her eyes narrow. I was right, a voice in the back of my mind tells me. I'm not good enough.

"Because I don't know you. And you don't know me. We can't go off and get married just because we have a child together."

"Yes, we can," I bite out. It would make things easier, too. We'd be a family. That's what Luis deserves. Why wouldn't she want that? "Luis deserves both parents—"

"And he'll have them. But I'm not going to marry someone I don't even know—who doesn't even like me—just because we have a child together."

My jaw tightens. I like parts of her just fine. Her ass. Her tits. Her tight pussy. There are plenty of things I like about Bibiana, but I don't bother voicing them aloud, already aware that isn't what she means.

I glower at her as though my stare alone can change her mind, but she doesn't cower. If anything, her chin lifts higher in the air.

Okay, so no marriage. For now. We'll shelf that conversation for another day because I sure as shit am not giving up on it. My son deserves everything I never had and more. "Fine."

She releases a breath.

"We'll date first." I can be reasonable. Compromising is important in a relationship. See, very reasonable.

Her blue eyes widen and she shakes her head in a definitive no.

I try not to let my annoyance show. But, why is she being so difficult? I know she's attracted to me. We have chemistry off the charts. This is a win-win situation.

"Let me guess, you have reasons for not wanting to date me too? We've already fucked. Is dating really such a big leap here?"

Her lips press together and she turns her attention back to Luis who's fallen asleep in her arms, his mouth open and her glistening nipple on full display. She covers herself up, careful not to disturb

Luis before she rises to her feet. My dick twitches in my jeans and I glower down at my crotch. Now is not the fucking time.

"I'm going to lay him down in his crib. I'll be right back."

I suck on my teeth as I watch her all but run from the room without answering my questions.

She returns a few minutes later and I decide I'm not going to give her the easy out she clearly wants. "Date me," I say again, ignoring my semi. I swear my dick gets excited just by her walking into a room.

She claims a seat on the sofa across from me instead of sitting beside me like before. "No."

A muscle ticks in my jaw.

"Emilio—" Her voice is soft and I can feel the careful let down she's about to deliver and I don't fucking want it. "I don't know you."

"Then get to know me." That's what dating is for, right? I've never done the whole exclusive thing before but I know how it works. You date before you decide to marry. I'm not missing a step here. At least I don't think I am.

"Aren't you seeing someone? Sarah or Kaitlyn or," she rolls her eyes on a forced laugh, "I don't know, half the senior class? All the girls at least."

Is that what this is about? My reputation? I sleep around, sure. But that doesn't mean I have to. I haven't been with anyone since she came back. I sure as shit don't belong to anyone else. I've never been exclusive with a girl. Bibiana would be the first. The only.

"No," I deadpan. "I'm not seeing anyone. I'd like to see you. The mother of my goddamn child." Why is this such a difficult concept for her to wrap her mind around? I know our cultures are different but we're both Hispanic or Latino or whatever the fuck you want to call it. I'm Honduran. She's Brazilian. Our upbringings couldn't have been so different that she wouldn't at least see the appeal in raising our son together. I'm trying to do the right thing here. Why is she making that so difficult?

"I don't know you," she repeats. Again.

"You know me well enough to let me finger-fuck you in a classroom."

Her eyes narrow to slits.

I run my hands through my hair and try to tamp down my frustration. "Will you get to know me, then? I think our son deserves at least that much from us."

"For Luis?"

Fuck, yes. Fine. "For Luis," I agree.

She nods. "Okay. I'll get to know you."

That's still not an agreement to date.

God dammit.

WE SPEND THE NEXT THREE DAYS GETTING TO KNOW ONE another. All day Saturday and Sunday, and then I show up right after football practice Monday evening. We agreed my next visit would be on Wednesday but Bibiana wasn't at school today and she didn't answer any of my texts. There's an irrational fear inside me that says she's bolted with my boy, but when I show up unannounced on her front porch, she lets me in without question and for the first time, Luis reaches for me.

There are dark circles under her eyes and her hair is haphazardly thrown up into a bun thing on top of her head. "You look," I pause choosing my words carefully, "tired. Everything alright?"

She sighs. "Yeah. Luis is teething so we didn't get much sleep last night."

Oh. "Is that why you weren't at school today?" It makes sense. I pluck Luis from her arms and follow her inside.

Despite her oversized shirt, I can tell her spine is stiff as she hastily picks up Luis's toys from the ground. "Umm... no. My mom usually watches Luis while I'm in school but she's dealing with Miguel stuff today so..." she trails off and then hastily adds, "I have it sorted with my teachers. It's not a big deal."

My brows furrow. Something in her voice contradicts her words, but I decide to leave it alone, knowing it isn't my place. "Cool. Is it alright if I hang for a bit with Luis?"

She nods. "Yeah that would be great actually. Do you care if I take a shower and catch up on some homework? You can have some one-on-one time with him?"

My smile widens and I turn to Luis. "What do you think, little man. Wanna kick it with Dad?"

He gurgles and waves a fist in the air which I take to mean hell yeah, so I turn back to Bibiana with a grin. "Sounds good. Shower away." I try not to think about her naked and wet in said shower but my mind wants to go places it shouldn't. It's been nice these past few days, which is better than I could have expected.

At first it was terrifying. There is so much I don't know and when Luis is tired or hungry, it's not like he can tell me. I don't know his cues, but I learned real fast that my boy has a temper. If I take too long trying to figure out what he wants, my man loses it. Who knew something so tiny could be so explosive? And the diaper changes, my god. Nothing this cute should smell that bad.

The uncertainty has mostly faded now. I still don't know everything there is to know, but I'm learning, and Bibiana's been good about filling me in if she thinks he's trying to tell me something. She doesn't have to make this easy on me. She isn't required to help me figure out how to be a dad. But she has been. Helpful, I mean. And while it's the least she can do after keeping him from me, I guess, I don't know, I appreciate it. Hell, I'm grateful, really. Not that I'll tell her that.

We haven't talked about the whole dating thing again but I think I'm winning her over. It's slow moving, but I can be patient.

She heads upstairs and I move with Luis to the living room, finding the basket of blocks and cars she keeps close by for him. We play on the floor for a bit before grabbing a snack from the kitchen, one of those food pouch things he seems to like.

When he finishes with that he yawns and I know he's ready for a nap, but I haven't quite figured out his routine for that yet. From what I've seen so far, he usually just falls asleep after nursing and well, I don't have tits for my little man to get what he needs. But, I don't want to call Bibiana for that either.

"How's everything going?" she asks, poking her head into the room, as if me thinking of her somehow conjured her here. Her wet hair hangs in loose curls around her make-up-less face. I'm stunned for a moment at the sight of her. She's fucking beautiful.

Wearing an army green tank top that hugs her chest and waist like a second skin, she shows off every inch of her delectable curves. Fuck me. I haven't seen her in anything form fitting since the night we met. She looks good enough to eat. My mouth waters and I wonder what she tastes like.

"We're good," I say, hoping my voice doesn't betray me.

"Do you need me to—"

I shake my head. "Nah. I got it." I give her a wink. "Go. You have homework, right?"

Her eyes are conflicted but she nods and leaves the room with a muttered, "Call me if you need me." But, I'll figure it out. He ate. He played. I check his diaper and we're good on that front too.

I rock Luis in my arms, adjusting his position a few times until we find one that's comfortable for him. He fusses a little but I manage to keep him quiet for the most part. I don't want Bibiana thinking I can't handle this. I want to take him to meet my sister which means she needs to trust me enough to let me take Luis on my own. We agreed we'd do this her way, and I don't want to push, but my baby sister was bouncing off the walls as soon as I told her she's an aunt. I know Antonio wants to meet him too. Hell, Allie was even me asking today at school when I'd be bringing him over despite all the shit she's dealing with right now.

And none of that can happen if the mother of my child barely trusts me alone with him when she's right there in the next room.

"We've got this, don't we, little man?" I whisper and rub circles on his back until his head rests against my shoulder. Holding him in my arms reminds me of how fragile he is. How easy it would be for him to get hurt, and I have to fight back the urge to squeeze him tighter to me. Miguel is Bibiana's mom's boyfriend and he hurt Allie. He beat her and then the fucker raped her. I haven't brought it up with her yet because I don't want to start an argument but I'm nervous about what will happen if the bastard is released. I don't want him anywhere near my kid.

Roman's dad can't make a case for the rape. There isn't sufficient evidence and Allie didn't report it when it happened, but he's doing his damnedest to keep the asshole locked up for something else. They're digging into all of his financials and looking for any skeletons he might be hiding in his closet. Allie was attacked because of something her father did. Some business deal gone wrong that Miguel was involved in.

If the people you work with are shady enough to rape your daughter because you pissed them off, chances are that shit isn't above board, and with any luck, Chief Valdez will find something to pin the fucker with. Then I won't have to bring the subject up with Bibiana at all.

Luis falls asleep and I take a chance, slowly dropping onto the sofa and centering him on my chest. When he doesn't stir, I sigh in relief and look down at the mop of dark brown hair on his head, pressing my lips to his temple.

I prop my feet on the coffee table and settle back in my seat, letting my eyes close as I listen to the steady inhale and exhale of his breaths.

I'm completely content to sit here until he wakes up. There isn't anywhere else I'd rather be.

FIFTY-SIX

Bibiana

The shower is heaven. I haven't been able to take one that wasn't rushed in longer than I can remember. I almost feel guilty for taking my time and going through the motions of shaving my legs and deep conditioning my hair, something it desperately needed.

When Emilio showed up on my porch, I realized I like having him here. In a way, it helps. Sure, I've always had my mom but she never really stepped in for the parenting parts. If Luis was hungry, I fed him. If he needed a nap, I was the one to put him down. If he was having a rough day and insisted he be held twenty-four-seven, I was the one who held him. Mom helps me out if I can't be there because of school, but if I'm home, the responsibility of caring for Luis falls directly on my shoulders. As it should. I'm not complaining.

But with Emilio around, there's someone to help carry that load, even if all he does is play with him on the floor while I shower or make a something to eat. I never noticed how much easier it is to accomplish simple tasks without carrying a baby around with me while I did them.

I towel my hair dry and after checking in to make sure Emilio is doing okay with Luis, I turn on my laptop and check to see if any of my teachers emailed me back. I let them all know last night after I got off the phone with Mom that I wouldn't be there. I came up with an excuse that Luis was sick and thankfully it doesn't seem like any of them are disgruntled about it. They're probably all married with kids of their own and while Luis isn't actually sick, I couldn't very well say, "My mom's boyfriend is in custody and she's refusing to leave his side so I don't have childcare." Well, I guess I could. But I don't really want to air out all of our dirty laundry if I don't have to.

Miguel's in the hospital after the beating he took. He's still under arrest. Handcuffed to his hospital bed according to Mom. But since he's not actually in prison where she can't see him, she's adamant that he needs her and that she has to stay with him while he recovers. I'm not sure what she's hoping for. He raped a teenage girl. Someone who happens to be the same age as her daughter. That she's even speaking to the man is beyond me, but I can't very well tell her all that over the phone.

This might be one of those things she needs to work out for herself, and with any luck, once Miguel is carted off to jail, she will. I don't think the reality of the situation has hit her yet. She's still trying to process everything and still clinging to the hope that this is all some horrible misunderstanding.

It isn't. I've spoken to Allie on the phone a few times since Friday night and she's confident he's the one who attacked her. And after seeing his reaction to her with my own eyes, I believe her.

I download the assignments my teachers sent and get to work on playing catch up. Mom said she'd come home at least long enough for me to go to school tomorrow so with any luck I won't fall too far behind only, I don't know what will come next and I hate being unable to plan.

I spend the next hour catching up on my reading and assignments. There's an exam in my economics class on Friday and I want to make sure I do well. With that finished, I head back downstairs and freeze at the sight of Luis fast asleep on Emilio's chest.

Wow. I'd like to blame what I'm feeling right now on my hormones, but I have a feeling the sight of this arrogant playboy asleep with our son in his arms is something I'll never get used to.

He must not have been too deeply asleep because the next second Emilio is cracking one eyelid open and smiling my way.

"Hey, momma." His voice is rough with sleep. Why do those words make my toes curl? Visions of Rio from Good Girls comes to mind and I have to force myself to walk further into the room instead of standing there dumbstruck. Does Emilio have to be so hot? This would be so much easier if, I don't know, he was average and said all the wrong things instead of unraveling me with his words and voice alone.

"How was your nap?"

His smile grows impossibly wider. "Fan-fucking-tastic. Isn't that right, little man," he whispers, and kisses the top of Luis's head. I swear my ovaries are on overload right now.

"How long has he been out?"

He cranes his neck toward the wall clock, his Adam's apple bobbing before saying, "Maybe twenty minutes."

"His evening nap is usually an hour or two. Do you want me to go put him down in his crib so you can move?"

He shakes his head and beams at me. "Nah. We're good."

The sight of his smile tugs at my heartstrings. Emilio is more than I expected. "You're pretty good at this dad stuff, huh?"

"Learning from the master," he tells me and pats the space beside him.

I take the seat, leaning in to brush a lock of hair from Luis's forehead.

"We made a great kid," he whispers, and if it weren't for the fact I'm sitting down right now, I would melt into a puddle of goo right here on the floor. "You did good, momma."

A lump forms in my throat. "Thanks."

Almost reverently, he rubs Luis back with one arm, his other thrown across the back of the sofa, and his fingers absently stroking my bare shoulder. I'm not sure if he even realizes he's touching me, but I don't bother to point it out.

"Can I come back tomorrow?" Emilio asks, his voice hesitant. "I know we said Wednesday and I know I wasn't supposed to be here today but ... I've missed so much already, and I swear the kid changes every day. I don't want to miss out on even a second of his life that I don't have to."

"I—" A trickle of worry worms its way into me before I push it aside. This is great. Emilio wanting more time with Luis is a good thing. I need to get over the irrational fear that him spending more time with Luis somehow means I'll have less. This isn't a competition, and right now, more time is not only good for Emilio, but it's good for Luis and that's what is more important. "That would be great."

"Really?" His arm drops down from the back of the sofa and he squeezes me to him in a side embrace.

"Yeah. Really."

He kisses my temple, taking me by surprise. "Thank you."

I laugh off his words and his touch with a roll of my eyes. "Don't thank me yet. One of these days Luis is going to clock you in the face with a car and we'll see then how you really feel."

"I'm looking forward to it."

I ignore the fact that his arm is still around me, that I'm still pressed against his side, and decide to just be. I rest my head on his shoulder and place the other on our son, content to share this moment with the man I created this tiny human being with.

FIFTY-SEVEN

Emilio

"How goes fatherhood?" Dominique asks when I take my seat beside him in fourth.

"Amazing," I tell him and pull out my phone to show him the pictures I snapped of Luis earlier in the week. It's Thursday and I've been at Bibiana's every day as soon as football practice let out. Antonio is keeping to his word. He's been watching Sofia, getting her to and from school and making sure she isn't alone while I focus on Luis.

Raul hasn't been back since last week, and I'm hoping our luck holds out a little bit longer.

"There's a lot of Bibiana in this reel," he tells me, quirking a brow.

"She's his mom and she's there. Don't read too much into it." I haven't told any of them that I asked her to marry me. And I sure as shit am not going to mention that she turned me down.

"Don't read too much into what?" Allie asks as she takes her seat, Roman following suit beside her.

"The fact that most of the pictures Emilio has of Luis on his phone are also shots of Bibiana."

"Oooo, let me see," Allie says and without bothering to wait for me to hand it to her, she snatches my phone and begins scrolling. "Oh, my god, he is so freaking cute." She shows Roman a few of the pictures and he gives me his nod of approval. Asshole. Though despite myself I have to try and not puff up at his response. Roman is the head of our little trio, err, foursome. Is that what we are now that Allie is around?

Hold up. Do Kasey and Aaron count? And if they count, what about Bibiana? She's the mother of my child so she better fucking be included, right?

I rub the back of my neck. I'm not even going to try and figure all of that out right now, but whatever we are size-wise, Roman is our fearless, asshole-ish leader, so yeah, him being happy for me gives me those warm and fuzzy feelings I won't admit to out loud. I'm a dad. A teenage dad, which I'm sure comes with the same stigma as being a teen mom, but none of my friends have batted an eye at that. No one is giving me shit. I'm grateful. Roman and Dominique, they're my family. Just as much as Roberto, Antonio, and Sofia are. I want them to be a part of Luis's life, and that they're so clearly interested in my boy is a relief.

"My mom wants you to bring him by. She said she's only going to wait so long to meet her first grandchild before she comes and hunts you down," Roman adds gruffly.

I grin at that. "Aww, you bitter I gave Mama Valdez a baby first?"

He snorts. "No. I'm hoping since you gave her a baby she'll back off with her questions about when Allie and I are getting married and when will we pop out some grand-babies for her."

"Good luck with that."

Allie laughs. "We have time. Right now it's just, when are you going to get married and stop living in sin?"

Roman snorts. "Don't delude yourself. That woman wants babies. I vote we pimp out Emilio's."

I roll my eyes but I'm cut off from responding when our teacher starts his lesson. I don't pay attention for most of it. All of this feels like refresher coming off winter break and my grades are better than most, so I let my mind wander to my future now that Luis is in it.

I have a full ride to Suncrest U after graduation just like Roman and Dom do, but unlike them, football isn't all I've been considering.

For Roman, it's always been football. His pops wants him going to the academy. Having a police chief for a dad puts on some added pressure, but Roman has never once even considered it. He wants to go pro.

Dominique wants to go pro too, and with an arm like his, the fucker is good enough if you ask me, but he also comes from money. He could go to any college in the country and his parents would pave the way for him. Hell, they'd probably prefer he go somewhere else. Suncrest U is a state college, but it's a division one school with the top-ranking football team in the nation which is why we're all going there.

But Dom's parents are loaded and they've got plans for him to take over the family empire at some point. Only time will tell if he makes it playing ball before they drag his ass off the field.

I play cornerback for the Sun Valley Devils. And I'm good. Really good. But, I got offers for educational scholarships too. It helps when you get a 1340 on the SATs and carry a 3.9 GPA, not that I advertise that shit. I could rock the 4.0 if I wanted to, but I cut one too many classes and let's be honest, no one likes an overachiever.

Football has always been the plan for me. Getting a degree in engineering is just a backup plan. But with Luis, where does being a dad fit into things? Next year, I'll have classes, training, my free time will be thin. If I took an educational scholarship instead, gave up on playing ball, I'd have more time in the day.

A rock forms in the pit of my stomach. No. I'll figure something out. I don't need to do the college scene. That was never the plan anyway. Fuck the parties and the booze. I'm going to college with one goal in mind, so I'll have plenty of time if I keep my eye on the prize. Luis, football, school. That's it. I can plan my schedule so it's tight. Back-to-back classes with a break between them and practice so I can see my boy.

I don't need to get a killer GPA in college. I just need to pass well enough to keep my scholarship. No one cares about your grades as long as you walk away with your degree. And fuck, if I get drafted, then my grades really won't mean shit.

I can make this work.

I have to.

The bell rings, snapping me out of my thoughts. I look up to see Allie's gaze locked on mine. "Everything okay?" she asks.

"Yeah, Vanilla. Everything is good."

Roman scowls but I roll my eyes. He isn't the only one allowed to call her that. He pulls out his phone and reads an incoming text. "Practice is cancelled," he tells us.

"Friday funday, fuckers."

"For you, maybe," Allie complains. "I have a shift at the diner."

"You two coming over?" Roman asks Dominique and I as we all make our way out of the classroom. "I'm dropping Allie off at work and then I'll be at my place. We can go over plays. Watch a few recordings."

I shake my head. "Can't. I'm heading to Bibiana's."

"Has she mentioned when she'll be back?" Allie asks, and I hear the worry in her voice.

I suck on my teeth. "No, actually. It hasn't come up. But she said she has it handled with her teachers." I shrug.

Allie doesn't look happy about my response. "I'm worried about her. She can't afford to miss this much school. She was already struggling to meet graduation requirements."

My brows pull together. "What are you talking about?" She hasn't mentioned any of this to me.

Allie sighs. "It's not really my pla—"

"Come on, Vanilla. Help a man out. Please."

Her eyes soften. "Fine." She runs a hand through her hair as we all navigate our way through the parking lot to our cars and I force myself to slow down my steps so she doesn't have to increase her pace to keep up. She's almost as small as Bibiana but not quit. "Her mom isn't coming home until her loser boyfriend is either released or in jail, so she has no childcare."

I stop. "What?"

"That should be any day now. Roman's dad has enough to bring charges and his injuries are mostly healed since Aaron and Roman beat the crap out of him." Roman smirks at that and not gonna lie, Aaron's part in all this definitely makes it harder to keep hating on him.

Speak of the devil. "Hey," Aaron calls out and we all turn to find him a few car lengths away with Kasey beside him. "I'm heading to the diner, want a lift?" His words are meant for Allie but it's Roman who answers him.

"No. I can take her."

Aaron comes closer as Kasey rolls her eyes and climbs inside his Subaru WXR. "Don't be a dick, Roman. I'm working with her. I can take her to work and you can pick her up before shift ends."

"Sounds like a plan," Allie says, not letting Roman argue as she gives him a kiss on the cheek and turns to leave.

"Hold up. What all am I missing about Bibiana?"

She pauses beside Aaron. "Her mom isn't watching Luis for her until things with her boyfriend are sorted." Her lip curls in disgust. "I don't know what is wrong with her. She's acting like her boyfriend isn't a rapist asshole when he is. When he could do to Bibi what he did to me." She shudders. "It's not my problem but I feel bad for Bibi and what she's going through. It's hard knowing that your mom is standing by someone like that."

My jaw tightens. Shit. I didn't know.

"Roman's dad said they'll bring charges against him today. Once they do, he can request bail so they're going to time it with the weekend and hold him as long as possible. Bibiana should be back next week if everything works out. With that creep in jail her mom should be around but," she shakes her head, "I don't know. She can't afford to miss much more school. Even if she manages to keep up on assignments, there are attendance requirements she won't meet. We talked yesterday. I don't know the specifics but I know she's barely treading water."

"Fuck." I run my hands through my hair. "She didn't tell me that. She said she had it figured out."

The look on Aaron's face says it all. I'm an idiot.

"I didn't think—"

"About what it was like to be a single mom, raising a kid on your own when you still have school and shit to worry about?" Aaron finishes for me. Allie smacks him in the chest, but he's not wrong.

"No. I didn't." Dammit. "I gotta go. I'll catch you guys later." I need to talk to Bibiana. Figure this out because she needs to graduate. Luis is my kid, too. She doesn't have to do this on her own anymore. What happened to being a team? Co-parenting? That means I do my part, but I can't if she doesn't keep me in the fucking loop.

FIFTY-EIGHT

Emilio

She opens the door like she has every other day this week, only this time, Luis is nowhere in sight. "Hey," she says, stepping aside to let me in. "You're here early."

"Yeah. Practice was cancelled today," I tell her.

She nods and I debate how to go about this. Bibiana is proud. She won't want me inserting myself into her life. Not on her account. I've noticed this week she's fine when I offer to do something for Luis, but anytime I try to help her, she brushes me aside.

"That's probably nice," she says. "Gives you a chance to rest up before next week's game." I'm surprised she knows our schedule. She hasn't been to any of our games, not that I've made a point of inviting her or anything. I'm not sure she'd want to go even if I did. We're not together, and watching me play feels like a girlfriend thing to do.

"Yeah. I'm always down for a break." Coach has been running us hard. We made it through playoffs and earned our regional championship titles. You would think that'd grant us a reprieve, but, if anything, it's only made things more grueling. Coach isn't going to let up until we take state next week, and then we can all breathe a little easier.

Sun Valley High has won state the last three years in a row. If we win this year, it will be our fourth. I think Coach is worried it'll also be his last with all three of us Devils graduating this year. He's been pushing the underclassmen on the team to step up, asking us to spend more one-on-one time with them than typical so that he has something decent to work with next year. We don't. Well, Roman and I don't, at least. Mingling with the new recruits isn't exactly something we do, but Dom is the school's quarterback so he's been handling business, giving the rest of the team pointers and getting their asses in line.

"Where's my little man?"

She brushes a few stray pieces of hair out of her face. "He actually just went down for a nap. I'm sorry."

I shrug. "No worries. Mind if I hang out until he wakes up?"

"Umm... sure. I guess. I mean, yeah. That's fine." She's nervous but she has no reason to be. Bibiana leads me through the house and into the kitchen, pausing behind one of the barstools at the kitchen island where it looks like she's been doing her schoolwork.

"Keeping up?" I ask, nodding to her open textbooks.

She sighs. "Yeah. I've got it handled."

I step closer to her and tilt her chin toward me. "It's okay to ask for help sometimes," I tell her.

She tugs her chin away. "It's not your job to help me. I've got it covered. Besides, Mom should be back next week."

I clench my jaw. "You said that before and it's been a week already. Can you afford to keep missing school?"

Her expression tightens. "I'm not your problem, Emilio."

I swear this girl is going to be the death of me.

FIFTY-NINE

Bibiana

"I'm not your problem," I tell him.

"What if I want you to be?" he asks. Brown eyes search my own, trying to understand what's going through my head. But if I'm honest, I have no idea. This week has been ... different. Not bad different, though I'm not sure if it's good different either. It's just, different. I feel like I'm playing some elaborate game where we each have a role and a character we're expected to be and I'm terrified to get my part wrong.

I'm already coming to rely on him and it's only been a week. He plays with Luis in the evenings while I get caught up. He helps with bedtime and he makes being a single mom so much easier than it ever was before.

I'm getting attached when I shouldn't be. I don't want to mess everything up. Emilio's only concern should be Luis. I'm not his responsibility. We need rules. Boundaries.

But ... his words from earlier this week come to me.

Date me.

Would that be such a bad thing?

Emilio's eyes darken when I still don't answer, and his thumb drags along my jawline. "Mariposa?"

He hasn't called me that since...

"Why did you call me that?" I ask and yeah, I'm avoiding his question. I'm woman enough to admit it. Doesn't mean I'm going to feel bad about it.

The corners of his mouth quirk up. "Because the night we met, you decided to spread your wings and fly. You transformed from the shy prep-school girl into a sexy-as-sin vixen. *Mi mariposa.*" My butterfly.

My breath hitches. "A moth," I correct for no real reason. I know mariposa translates to butterfly in Spanish, but I need to dispel this moment.

Emilio dips his head toward me, his warm breath skating across my cheek.

"Fine. You can be the most beautiful moth if you'd prefer."

I swallow hard. How does he manage to make that sexy?

"Do you remember that night? How good we were together?"

I gasp when he leans even closer, his stubble scraping along my skin. Heat rushes between my legs and my thighs clench as memories assail me. That night was so much more than I'd expected.

A strong arm wraps around my waist and pulls me flush against his chest, and his free hand cups my jaw, right before his lips press against mine. My heart pounds in my chest as his mouth teases my own. Sucking in a breath, I pull back before the kiss can go much further.

"Emilio—?"

His eyes are hooded and glazed with desire. "Don't. Don't overthink this. I want you. And I'm pretty sure you want me too."

I exhale in a rush as Emilio's hands find their way to the back of my head, tangling in my hair. He tugs me toward him again, his lips an open invitation I'm not strong enough to deny. I didn't realize how badly I craved him. How much deeper my need for him has grown these past few days.

I sag against him, allowing the kiss to deepen, and the next thing I know, he's lifting me onto the kitchen counter and wedging himself between my thighs, the height just enough to line our bodies up perfectly. He devours me as though starved, his kisses deep and hungry. His tongue slips past my defenses, the taste of sweet oranges and chili an addictive flavor I can't seem to get enough of.

For a second, I consider pushing him away, but then he groans into my mouth, his hard length pressing against my center, and any thoughts of putting an end to this escape me.

"Emilio," I breathe. "God, you feel so good." Oh my god, did I just say that out loud?

"Fuck," he moans. "I can't get enough of you." His fingers slip under the hem of my sweatshirt and the next thing I know he has it tugged up and over my head. I gasp as cool air hits my overheated skin and my arms instantly wrap around my middle to cover myself.

He pulls back, a furrow between his brows as I tear my gaze away from him, hunching my shoulders in a vain attempt to hide my body. This was a mistake.

"Hey."

I turn, my eyes scanning the room for my sweater, but he's thrown it on the floor behind him and out of reach.

"Bibiana?"

"I need my sweater," I tell him, hoping he'll grab it and give it back to me. He doesn't. Instead, he takes two steps back, folds his arms across his chest and stares at me. My nursing bra isn't sexy. It's simple. A black full coverage bra that hooks in the back and has snaps above each cup for easy access should Luis get hungry. It's not what I would have chosen if I knew anyone else was going to see it, but it's not the worst bra I could be wearing either. At least this one has shape and isn't one of those uni-boob sports bra types that I happen to have buried in my drawers.

What I'm more worried about is that I didn't have a shirt on underneath my sweater, so not only is my bra on full display, but so is the rest of my body and it isn't pretty. It isn't...what he's used to. The body he's seen before.

My cheeks heat in the worst possible way and I blink back my complete and utter humiliation, refusing to cry over something like this. Stupid hormones. Come on, Bibi. Pull yourself together.

"What happened just now?"

"Nothing, I just want my sweater back. Can you hand it to me? Please." I hold my hand out but he doesn't move.

My vision blurs. Dammit. I shouldn't care. It's not like I want to impress him. What he thinks of my body shouldn't matter. But it does. I don't let people see me like this. I cover up. I wear baggier clothes. I hide the changes having a baby has made to my body. I don't want his scrutiny. His disgust.

"Hey—" His voice softens. "Talk to me. What just happened? We were good and then it's like a switch went off as soon as I..." His brows pull together. "You want your sweater?" he asks, as if that isn't exactly what I've been asking for this entire time.

"Yes. Now, please."

He picks it up from the ground but doesn't hand it to me. I huff out an exasperated breath. "Emilio. Give it to me." I'm still covering my stomach or I'd reach for it myself.

"Why?"

"Because I want it back." I snap. I shouldn't have to explain this to him.

His eyes roam over my body.

I clench my teeth, bracing myself for the look of revulsion I'm sure will come once he realizes what I'm hiding.

He steps closer and I all but lunge for my sweater, but he shifts to the side, keeping it just out of reach. "I want to see you."

The first tear falls. "No. And we shouldn't be—"

He doesn't give me the chance to finish. His lips crash into mine and my mouth opens on a moan. His tongue flicks out, sending tendrils of desire straight to my core. His hands loosen the hold I have on myself as he guides my arms around his neck, pressing our bodies impossibly close so my stomach is flush against his.

He abandons my lips to trail kisses along my neck, sucking and nipping at my skin gently. Shockwaves ripple through me when his hand cups my center, his palm pressing firmly against my clit through the fabric of my jeans.

"You're so goddamn beautiful," he tells me. I wish I could believe him but—

His tongue drags back up my jaw and to my mouth before he pulls back just enough to look me in the eye. "You are beautiful. This body is perfection. Do you understand me?"

I swallow past the lump in my throat. "But—"

He shakes his head. "No buts. You're perfect. Don't ever hide from me." He kisses me again. "I want to see all of you. Every inch so I can worship your body the way I've been dreaming about."

His words undo me and I force myself to relax. If he's repulsed by my body, I'll find out soon enough.

My stomach is soft. My stretch marks visible. That won't ever go away. And if it's going to be a deal breaker, I may as well find out now before putting my heart on the line.

His palm slides down my side, over my hip and to the button on my jeans. He pops them open as I pull at the material of his shirt, tugging it off and exposing his broad chest and muscular abs. My eyes catch on the tattoo that spreads across his chest. A gothic woman's portrait, her hair flying all around her as ravens tug on the strands.

I trace the intricate ink. It wasn't there when we first met. It's amazing. "Is this new?" I ask and there's a note of wonder in my voice. It looks so lifelike, the woman almost familiar.

"Got it on my eighteenth birthday earlier this year," he tells me.

"She's—"

"You."

I jerk my hand away from the tattoo. "What?"

He smirks. "I knew what I wanted, and I needed a description for the girl, so when I got the ink, I described you."

My eyes widen. "Why would you do that?"

A shrug. "Because you were the most beautiful girl I'd ever seen—you still are," he adds with a savage smile. "Being with you that night was a memory I didn't want to forget. Even if you ghosted me after the fact."

My chest squeezes. "Emilio, I—"

He places a finger against my lips to stop me. "We have history. We have a kid. I want to see where this goes. Where we can go. Don't you?"

God, yes. But ... so many things could go wrong. What if this blows up in our faces?

He mistakes my hesitation as acceptance and kisses me, and I'm too far gone to stop him. His fingers hook into the waistband of my pants, and I decide to hell with it. I'm going to be the girl I was when we first met. Reckless and free. I'll spread my wings and soar with Emilio right beside me.

Our breathing is heavy as he drags my jeans and underwear down over my hips and I lift myself up a few inches for him to get them past my butt and down my legs. I hiss when my bare ass hits the counter and he chuckles. "Cold, baby?"

I bite his bottom lip.

He grunts. "Why don't you let me warm you up." His fingertips leave a fiery trail of heat across my skin as he inches closer to my center. I squirm on the counter, one of my legs hooked over his hip. I tug at his jeans, wanting him just as naked and exposed as I am. I haven't been with anyone else. There isn't a lot of time to explore your sexuality when you're pregnant, and there is even less when you have a newborn. I'm desperate to feel his skin against my own.

Unbuckling his belt, I push his jeans and boxers to the floor and his impressive cock springs forward. I swallow hard. I remember him being big, but...did it grow?

"Everything okay?" he asks just as he sinks one finger inside my wet heat.

My back arches toward him and I whimper, needing more.

"Fuck, you're tight." He thrusts in and out of me before inserting another finger and I cry out, tightening my legs around him. He cups my nape and devours my mouth as skilled fingers bring me close to the edge of orgasm. My fingers bite into his biceps, the muscles flexing beneath my touch.

"I have dreamed about fucking you ever since you left. Replayed your moans in my mind every night since you came back."

"I didn't leave, I—"

"You left," he growls. "I'm not letting you go again." He adds a third finger and uses his thumb to stroke my clit and I explode, my body tightening around him as shock waves wrack my system.

I'm shaking as he withdraws his fingers, and the satisfied smile on his face is absolutely savage. He grabs a condom from his jeans pocket and rolls it on his hard length before lining himself up with my center and meeting my gaze. His eyes are hard but his voice is tender when he asks, "You ready for me, baby?"

My chest rises and falls as I struggle to catch my breath. "Mmm hmm." I'm beyond words at this point.

He circles his cock around my opening, teasing every sensitive nerve ending I have before plunging himself inside me in a single hard thrust. I gasp his name as he pulls out only to dive back in, harder than before.

I buck my hips up and he increases his pace. Triumph is stamped across his face as he buries himself inside me, his thrusts coming faster and more urgent. My body responds, arching toward him and leaving me breathless. It feels so good. I can't help but watch him as he towers over me. His muscles bunch. His jaw gets tighter. Sharper. He's beautiful like this—consumed with need.

He drags the cup of the bra I'm wearing down, exposing one breast as he fucks me, and before I can tell him to stop, he's squeezed my breast in his palm before pinching my nipple and drawing a moan from my throat. Sensations surge through me and moisture coats my breast but he doesn't seem to care. He spreads my milk across my chest before exposing my other breast and giving it a similar treatment. Kneading and squeezing the tender flesh.

"Fuck," he swears before leaning forward and raking his teeth against my sensitive nipple. A second orgasm slams into me and I can tell his is close behind. He slams into me, his entire body trembling. His control starts to slip. His movements grow erratic as he thrusts deep into me three more times before his dick is pulsing inside of me. He hisses out a sharp, "Fuck," when he finds his own release and slumps against me, his sweat-slick skin hot against my own.

I wrap my arms around his shoulders, clinging to him as the gravity of what we did settles over me. Milk leaks from my breasts onto his chest and I pull away, looking for something to clean myself up with before he stops me.

"There you go hiding from me again," he whispers. One finger trails down my stomach and I realize he's tracing a particularly dark and thick stretch mark.

I push his hand away. "I'm leaking," I confess, completely mortified.

His mouth smiles against my own as his hand cups my breast and his thumb flicks over my still sensitive and leaking nipple. "Is that supposed to bother me?"

I bite my bottom lip. I mean...shouldn't it?

"Because it doesn't. Like I said, everything about you is perfect."

Luis's cry shatters the moment and as though we're both on fire, we lunge away from one another and for our clothes then rush up the stairs. I manage to grab Emilio's shirt and throw it over my head just as I reach the door and throw it wide.

Luis stands in his crib, eyes red and angry, but he hiccups to a stop when he sees me.

"Hey, benzinho," I coo. My baby. "Come here." Emilio is right behind me. He's managed to slip on his jeans and stands barefoot, his naked chest pressed against my back.

"Hey, little man."

Luis turns toward Emilio and a smile spreads across his face. He gurgles and babbles and whatever he was upset about is history now that he sees his dad. "You wanna come see me?" Emilio asks, putting his hands out, and Luis reaches for him.

"Why don't you get cleaned up and little man and I will wait for you in the living room?" He presses a kiss to my temple and bounces Luis in his arms. "Don't worry, momma. I've got this."

SIXTY

Bibiana

T he weekend passes and I somehow manage not to throw myself at Emilio every time he comes over, despite the heavy tension between us. My mind is a jumbled mess. I don't know what the two of us sleeping together means, and it's driving me insane.

We haven't talked about what this is. I'm not even sure what I want it to mean.

We've kissed. Touched. But we haven't had sex again. My body wants him. Craves him. But my mind tells me I need to slow down. There is too much on the line to rush into whatever this is turning into. I want to believe we can be one big happy family. What girl doesn't want her Cinderella story? But it all seems too good to be true.

Emilio doesn't do commitment. I've heard enough stories. Rumors. The thought that he'll tire of playing family is a feeling I can't shake.

On top of that, I've given up on my mom being available for Luis. I need to take matters into my own hands. This, at least, is something I feel confident in working out.

I walk into my first period class with Luis on my hip. The bell will ring in just a few minutes, so I'll need to make this quick. The rape charges against Miguel were dropped, and he's since been charged with securities fraud and money laundering in addition to extortion. I have no idea what all they found, but the combined charges can lead up to a combined twenty years behind bars and over five hundred thousand dollars in penalties and fines.

He's in jail now, but his bail hearing is set for Wednesday afternoon, and Mom is frantically trying to figure out a way to pull the money together for his release. We don't have it. Miguel doesn't have it stashed away somewhere that I know of either. Which is a relief.

It's insane how ignorant she's behaving. But the fact that the rape charges were dropped just confirms in her mind that he didn't do it. He has her convinced the rest is false. Misunderstandings or mistakes made by his associates. She is completely blind to the fact that he's a criminal and a rapist.

Don't get me wrong, I'd love for Miguel to be innocent. My mom loves him. Truly and completely loves him, but she didn't see the look on his face when confronted with Allie in the kitchen. She didn't hear his admission of guilt. And that's what that was. An admission. He knows what he did, and the fact that he won't be charged for his crime is wrong.

I've never had a great relationship with Miguel, but I never had issues with him either. He was just always ... there. It creeps me way the heck out to know that all this time, I've been living with a rapist. Would he have done to me what he did to Allie if given enough time and opportunity? What if he tried to hurt Luis? He's just a baby, unable to tell me if anyone tries to hurt him.

I shiver just thinking about. It keeps me up at night. Knowing he was there. I'm glad I never left Luis alone with him. Never trusted him enough to watch my boy.

Heading toward Mr. Albert's desk, I consider what I'm going to say just as his head lifts from a stack of assignments he's been grading, judging by the red pen in his hand.

"Ms. Sousa." He gives Luis a curious once-over. "Can I help you with something?"

I shift Luis's weight to my other side and nod. "Yeah. Sorry. I won't be in class today. Actually, I probably won't make it all week. Again." I exhale a sigh. "I was hoping you'd let me make up this week's assignments somehow, and any quizzes we might have coming up since I missed Friday's exam?"

His lips purse and he looks a little closer at the baby boy in my arms. "He yours?"

I nod and offer him a small smile. "Yeah, he's mine."

He nods to himself. "Okay. When you first enrolled we were informed you had a child. I didn't realize he was so young. We'll make it work."

"Thank you so much. I really appreciate it. You have no idea. I promise to stay on top of things. I can even drop my assignments off daily after school gets out. Whatever you—"

"Ms. Sousa, I believe you misunderstand me."

My stomach drops. What? I thought...

"I didn't mean I would send you home with independent study assignments. I meant you could continue coming to class and bring your son with you."

"To class?" No way am I hearing him right. What high school teacher is okay with a nine-month-old in their classroom?

"Yes. And before you leave I'll have you write down the names of your other teachers and get things sorted out with them. If they don't want you in the classroom you can use the teacher's lounge to do your assignments away from other students, or perhaps the library if you'd be more comfortable there."

Emotion clogs my throat and my vision blurs. "Why?" The single word passes my lips in a whisper, and I suck in a shaking breath as I struggle to maintain my composure. "Why are you jumping to help me like this?" Because that's exactly what he's doing. He doesn't have to go out of his way for me. Emailing me assignments and letting me retake tests is already going above and beyond but this ... letting me complete my senior year as a student. This is so much more.

Mr. Albert stands from his chair and moves around his desk. He reaches a tentative hand out and Luis latches onto his finger waving his arm and jabbering away with a drooly grin on his face.

"Ms. Sousa, you are one of the brightest students I have ever had the pleasure of teaching. You are diligent. Studious. You think outside of the box and your creativity in thought knows no bounds. You can make something of yourself should you decide to. Having a child does not mean you have to sacrifice your opportunities. If anything, it means you must get a little ... creative in how you achieve your goals."

I sniff and blink away my tears. "I really appreciate this. You have no idea. But, I'm not so sure the school will let me—"

"You let me take care of that, okay?"

I nod just as the bell rings, signaling that first period is about to start.

"Do you need to miss today or do you have your materials and everything you need for your son with you?"

"I just have to run to my locker. But I have all my things." It's part of why I decided to come in person originally. To pick up some of my books I'd left behind the last time I was at school.

"Good. Do that and hurry back. We're covering the devastating effects of European diseases on native populations. Wouldn't want you to miss any of it."

I smile and rush to grab my books, ignoring the startled looks of my peers as I hurry through the hallway and to my locker. I shove Luis's diaper bag inside, grabbing his favorite toy and a bottle out and shoving that into my backpack before grabbing my history textbook and heading back to class.

I'm almost there when I spot Dominique hovering outside the door to the classroom beside mine. "Everything okay?" The bell rings just as the hallway empties. "I thought I saw you and this little guy but wanted to be sure." He runs a hand over his tightly braided hair.

"Yeah, Mr. Albert is working it out so I can still attend classes with Luis."

He nods his head like this all makes perfect sense to him. "What do you have second?"

"English."

"I have a non-schedule. I can take him and chill in the library if you're cool with that?"

My brows pull together and I worry my bottom lip. "You want to babysit for me?" I ask, making sure I'm hearing him right, because Dominique doesn't seem the type to want to hang out with a baby.

He shrugs. "Why not? He's Emilio's which makes him mine. Don't be surprised when Roman asks you for some time with him too. This little man has a lot of people who love him."

I fight back a wave of unexpected emotion. "Oh. I mean, yeah. That'd be cool."

He nods and steps backward toward his class. "Alright. I'll meet you out here after class." And then he slips inside, leaving me to do the same.

Class is uneventful. I get a few interested looks when I first walk in, but eventually people ignore that I'm sitting there, bouncing Luis on my knee as I take notes. Toward the end Luis gets a little fussy, but before I can even try and soothe him, Mr. Albert comes and plucks him from my arms and goes back to teaching the class while swaying my boy in his arms. I'm not sure I've ever felt this grateful in my entire life.

As promised, Dominique is waiting for me outside the door when class lets out.

"Do you have everything I'll need?" he asks, and I fall into step beside him.

"We'll grab his diaper bag from my locker and then you'll be set."

Emilio is waiting beside my locker, a wide grin on his face as soon as he sees us. I texted him earlier that I'd be here, but he didn't respond, so I'm assuming he got my message.

"Hey, momma." He tugs me close and kisses me, uncaring of who sees. When he pulls away I'm a little breathless and Luis is jabbering away, vying for his daddy's attention.

"There's my boy," Emilio says, lifting him from my arms and carefully tossing him up in the air before catching him and hugging him close to his chest. There are a few interested looks directed our way, and I do my best to ignore them. I don't know how Emilio feels about everyone knowing he's a dad. We never discussed if we were going to keep his involvement secret or—

"Ah! You brought him," Allie's voice calls out, and all heads turn her way. "Bibi, your and Emilio's little boy is the freaking cutest." And that answers that question. By the end of the day everyone will know Luis is ours, and a part of me is surprisingly happy about that, though I don't miss the intense glares from some of the girls who pass us.

"What can I say, I make cute kids," Emilio jokes. "Where are we heading, momma?" he asks, and I can't help but smile up at him.

"To class. Dominique was nice enough to offer to babysit during his non-schedule."

Emilio lifts a single brow. "Uncle Dom, already making moves to become the favorite?"

Dominique takes the diaper bag off my shoulder and pulls Luis from Emilio's arms just as Roman stalks up behind Allie and wraps his arms around her waist.

"I won't have to try very hard. Between me and this fucker, I've got favorite uncle in the bag."

Emilio snorts. "Tell that to Antonio. He'll fight you for the title."

Everyone laughs. "Who's Antonio?" I ask, not recognizing the name.

"My older brother," he tells me. "I have two. A baby sister as well. You'll meet them soon." He tugs me into his side and leads me toward my second period class. "Little man has a whole host of people who are going to compete for his attention."

The thought makes warmth spread through my chest. This is what I wanted. Family. People who will love Luis as much as I do.

"Are you sure you'll be okay with him?" I ask Dominique one last time.

He nods and grins down at my little boy. "Yeah, I've got it. We'll see you guys at lunch."

SIXTY-ONE

Bibiana

Second period is nerve-wracking knowing Dominique has Luis. It isn't that I don't trust him. I know he wouldn't hurt Luis. But he's also a teenage boy. What if Luis gets hungry or tired? What if he throws a fit and Dominique doesn't know how to calm him down? Will he come get me? Get Emilio? This wasn't my best idea. I appreciate the help but I should have said no.

I twist my hands in my lap, watching each second tick past on the clock above the door. "So, is it true?" a voice whispers behind me.

I turn around in my seat.

"Is what true?" I ask the girl, who so far has never bothered to talk to me before. She usually just sits in the back of class and files her nails or texts on her phone.

"Is it true you and Emilio Chavez are together? That your kid is his kid?" Her brows are raised high in open curiosity. News certainly travels fast, though I'm not sure what I expected. Emilio is a Devil. I doubt he could sneeze without someone knowing about it.

"Yeah." I shrug. "We have a son together." I whisper the words over my shoulder and turn back toward the front of the class. I might not be paying attention, but I don't want to get in trouble either. Mrs. Jennings isn't known for being tolerant of disruptions in her classroom.

"No wonder you're always in baggy clothes."

I scowl and turn back around. "Excuse me?"

She smirks and flicks her platinum blond hair over her shoulder. "I mean, the kid probably destroyed you, right? I get it. I'd want to hide that too." The corners of her mouth dip in a mock display of sympathy before she adds, "My sister had a baby two years ago. Absolutely wrecked her. The stretch marks, the loose skin." She shivers. "I am never having children. No, thank you."

I grit my teeth together to keep from snapping at her. My body isn't wrecked. It's different, sure. But it's not...urgh.

No, Bibi. Do not go down that road. Don't let her get to you. She isn't worth your time.

I turn back around again. This class cannot end soon enough. I'm grateful to be here, but I have enough on my plate. I don't need pettiness added to it.

"So, you and Emilio?" she whisper-shouts behind me, and Mrs. Jennings jerks her head in our direction, her ever-present frown on her face.

"Ms. Crisp?"

"Yes?" the girl chirps.

"Is there a reason you're talking instead of paying attention in class?"

I don't need to see the look on her face to know she doesn't care one lick about the reprimand. "Nope."

Mrs. Jennings' scowl deepens. "Refrain yourself then, please. Or you can stay behind after class to catch up on everything you're intentionally missing."

Our teacher returns to the board and I slink down in my seat, but Kaitlyn Crisp, the girl sitting behind me, still doesn't shut up.

"Are you going to answer or not?" she hisses in my ear. My nostrils flair and my lips press into a thin line.

"Shut up," I tell her. "You're going to get me in trouble."

"I'll take that as a no, then," she says with satisfaction.

I ignore it. I don't want to confirm or deny anything when I, myself, don't know what the situation is. Emilio asked me to marry him. God. What was he thinking? And then to suggest we date, as if the proposal is no big deal. It's a huge freaking deal. How can he be so flippant about marriage? But now, I don't know what this is.

Are we dating? Are we simply friends with benefits? I have no clue. Do I need to say yes? To the dating part, I mean. Or is it assumed that we're a thing because he technically asked me, even if I didn't say yes at first.

This is all such a mess.

He kissed me in the hallway though. He isn't treating me like a dirty little secret. Then again, he's never kept any of his relationships secret, if you can even call them that.

We're in this weird going-with-the-flow stage and I'm not sure how to feel about that.

The bell rings and I rush to shove my books in my bag and haul ass toward the cafeteria. We need to talk. I don't like the uncertainty of what is happening, and I'm cognizant enough to know that by not talking I'm setting myself up for heartache. I'm already developing feelings for Emilio, and I don't want to get hurt.

I run into Dominique halfway there and am relieved to see a smiling Luis in his arms.

"How was he?" I ask, reaching for my boy.

He grunts, but there is affection in his voice. "A terror."

"What did he do?"

The corners of his mouth curl into a smile. "Crawled down almost every row in the library and yanked every book he could reach onto the floor." He pats Luis on the head. "Our librarian might not be his biggest fan but we cleaned up the mess and it kept him entertained."

"Did he eat anything?" I ask, hoping he drank the bottle I pumped for him earlier. I don't remember if I gave Dominique specific instructions on that.

He nods. "Downed the entire thing and I changed his diaper. You're welcome."

"Thank you!" I tell him and I mean it. We fall into step beside one another, heading toward the cafeteria, when Emilio comes into view, a pretty blond standing close beside him. I give her a closer look and realize it's Kaitlyn, the girl who sits behind me in second period.

My steps falter. They're right beside the cafeteria doors so I'll have to pass them if I want to go inside. I hesitate, assuming he'll dismiss her after a moment, only he doesn't. He laughs at something she says, and she twirls a piece of her hair, a come-hither expression on her face.

Dominque see's what I'm looking at and his brows pull forward. "I thought he was—" He shakes his head. "Whatever. Come on."

My heart plummets to the bottom of my stomach. Is she... are they... no. I'm getting ahead of myself. For all I know, she's just asking for his notes or something from class. It's harmless flirting. Right?

I force myself to move forward and follow Dominque when I see her press her hand against his chest and lean up on tip toe to plant a chaste kiss on his cheek. He shakes his head and says something to her I can't hear before turning around and going through the open double doors, leaving her behind, but still not noticing me.

I swallow hard.

It's nothing, I tell myself.

When I get to the table, everyone is already there. Roman, Allie, Aaron, Kasey, and Dominique.

"Hey, momma," Emilio says, a wide smile on his face as he shifts to the side and makes more room for me. I accept the seat and he plucks Luis from my arms, handing him a french fry off his tray. "How was your time with Uncle Dom?" Emilio asks him, to which Luis gurgles and grins. "That good?" He turns to Roman. "Looks like you've got your work cut out for you," he tells him.

Roman rolls his eyes, but it's Aaron who surprises us when he holds his arms out and Luis immediately reaches for him. "Hey, what's this?" Emilio says in mock offense. Luis grips Aaron's cheeks and gives him an open-mouthed kiss as he all but tries to eat his nose.

"Who were you saying was his favorite?" Aaron asks and all three of us girls laugh at the boys stunned expressions.

"He was over for girls' night," I remind everyone and then wince. "Sorry."

"Don't be," Allie says, nudging my foot with her own under the table. "Girls' night was good. Besides, I needed the closure, you know?"

I nod, still unconvinced, but I don't want to dig into the topic either.

My phone buzzes in my pocket and I pull it out to see a text flash across the screen.

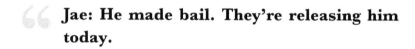 **Jae: He made bail. They're releasing him today.**

I GASP. WHAT? IT'S TOO SOON.

"What is it?" Emilio asks. I turn wide eyes toward him, not wanting to say anything, but everyone's eyes are on me, waiting.

I lick my lips and chance a furtive glance at Allie. "Miguel made bail."

She visibly swallows and nods. Roman tucks her into his side, his jaw tight and his hand fisted on the table.

"I'll call my dad. We'll figure out—"

I block out the rest of his words as my fingers fly over the keyboard.

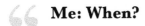 **Me: When?**

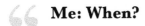 **Jae: This afternoon. Bibi...**

I wait.

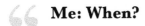 **Jae: Let me come get you. Help you pack. You can't stay there.**

Emilio nudges my shoulder and tilts his chin to my phone. "What's going on, momma?"

I hesitate for only a second before forcing a smile. "Nothing. Just Jae filling me in on what's going on."

"Jae?" Emilio scrapes his teeth over his bottom lip. A muscle ticks in his jaw but whatever is bugging him, he decides to keep to himself.

 Me: Give me until the end of the day to think about it?

> **Jae: Can I at least go to your house and grab some of your things? In case he's there when you get out of school.**

> **Me: Yeah. That would be great. Thank you.**

I SHOVE MY PHONE BACK IN MY POCKET AND TRY TO ENJOY the rest of lunch, but the mood at the table has drastically shifted. This isn't just bad news for me. It's upsetting for all of us, and I'm not sure how any of us are going to handle what happens next.

SIXTY-TWO

Emilio

The rumor mill is running rampant. I can see it eating at Bibiana. She's not used to all of the attention. Personally, fuck what people here think. Let them look and whisper. I'm proud to be a dad. I know she is too — of being a mom. The way she is with Luis, there's just something about it that makes my heart beat faster, my chest squeeze tighter.

I don't want to mess this up.

Everyone is acting like this is some big thing. It's not. Luis is mine. End of discussion. I don't need to explain myself. They all want to know why they never heard of him before. Why we kept him a secret for so long. But that isn't my problem.

It's not my job to keep these fuckers informed, and I sure as shit am not going to throw my girl under the bus and tell everyone I didn't know about him.

My girl. I like the sound of that.

I might be new to this relationship shit, but I know that's not the way to get off on the right foot.

People here should know by now the Devils don't explain themselves. A few words in the halls shut most of the guys down, and the team knows better than to question any of us. But the girls — fuck, they're the worst.

My phone is on silent and I swear it vibrates in my back pocket every other minute. I read the first three this morning before deciding to ignore it the rest of the day. I don't have time for that shit. I thought if I ignored them, they'd eventually stop, but the ones who are bold like Kaitlyn Crisp have taken it upon themselves to just ask me about it in person.

She thought she was subtle, asking how things are going. If I like being a dad. Telling me how cute my boy is and then hinting that being a single dad must be so hard. Puh-leez. She's angling to find out if Bibiana and I are a thing. Single dad. I roll my eyes.

I need to take a page out of Dom's playbook and be the broody, unapproachable asshole so I don't have to deal with people and their bullshit. The bell rings and we all dump our trays in the trash. Aaron reluctantly passes Luis back to Bibiana and I walk her to her next class.

"See? This all worked out," I tell her, placing my hand on the small of her back. She offers me a hesitate smile, shifting Luis's weight to her other side.

"For now. What happens when Luis is sick or has a meltdown?"

I press my lips to her temple. "We deal with it. If he's sick, I'll stay home with him. We'll watch cartoons and chill in my room. And if he has a meltdown," I shrug. "Kids do that. We'll cross that bridge when we get there."

She doesn't look convinced, but she nods. "Okay."

"Do you want me to take him for third?"

She shakes her head. "No. I can manage."

I tuck a strand of hair behind her ear and face her once we reach her classroom door. "I know you can manage, but we're a team, remember? Luis is my responsibility too. Fifty-fifty. If you need a break, tell me."

She nods. "I will."

I scrutinize her looking for the lie, but she seems genuine, so I leave it at that. "I'll see you in fourth." I run my hand over the top of Luis's head. "See you soon, little man."

SIXTY-THREE

Bibiana

"Need a lift?" Emilio asks when the final bell rings and we all head outside, the school day officially over. It was stressful at first, but by the end of the day having Luis with me felt ... normal. I can totally do this. Especially with everyone else helping out.

Dominique has volunteered to take Luis every day during second since he has a non-schedule. I found out today that Aaron TA's third and he's offered to take him then. We're all together during fourth so there are plenty of hands on deck should I need them. This is completely do-able, and there is this giddiness inside of me at the knowledge that not only is everyone willing to help, they want to. They want that one-on-one time with Luis. I know people say it takes a village, but I never realized the true meaning of those words until now.

I catch sight of Jae's Acura TLX as soon as we get outside. He offered to pick me up today, but I didn't realize just how much he'd stand out. He's parked front and center, leaning against the hood with his arms braced behind him. Several girls stop and give him appreciative looks, a few are brave enough to introduce themselves, but he barely glances their way, his eyes focused on me and a genuine smile on his face.

"What is he doing here?" Emilio asks, dark shadows crossing over his face.

"He's my ride," I offer with a shrug. For whatever reason, these two decided to immediately dislike one another. Too bad they're going to need to work past all that, especially if I move in with Jae which is sounding more and more likely. Okay, it's pretty much a done deal. I've thought about his offer all day today and to be honest, it's not like I have any other option. I don't know what this is between Emilio and I, but I do know it's too new for us to shack up together. I texted Monique during class when my teachers were distracted to get an outside opinion and she seems to agree. If I want things to work with Emilio, we need to move slow.

Besides, Jae is my friend. He's always been there for me and I appreciate him being there for me now. If he wasn't, I'm not sure what I would to. I'd probably have to drop out. I'd need a job to support myself and Luis, and I'd still be in a bind when it came to childcare.

Emilio's arm wraps around my waist, his hold possessive and his voice filled with irritation when he says, "Why? Allie or Aaron can take you home on their way to work. Your place is on the way to the Sun Valley Station. Hell, I'll let coach know right now I'll be a few minutes late to practice and I can take you. It's not a big deal." His fingers clench on my hip and I wince.

If it's not a big deal, why is he trying to turn it into one? "Jae is my friend. He offered. I accepted. He's literally been driving me to school all quarter already, so this isn't new. Don't make a big deal out of nothing," I plead.

If anything, his face only darkens. "I don't know him," he bites out.

"And he doesn't know you. Why don't you two make nice and be friends?" It sure as hell would make my life easier.

He snorts. "Not happening."

I rub my temples and remind myself that now isn't the time to get in a fight. Especially over something as stupid as who drives me home. I can already tell that moving in with Jae is going to be a problem. One Emilio is just going to have to deal with.

"I'm going to go home. Go to practice before you're late."

Emilio's nostrils flare, and the next thing I know he jerks me up against him. Luis is still in my arms, but that doesn't stop him as his mouth presses down on my own. One of his hands tangles in my hair, holding me in place while the other cradles our boy so neither of us drops him. The kiss is angry. His teeth bite at my lower lip until I open for him and then he devours my mouth like I'm his last meal.

It ends almost as quickly as it began, and I'm left standing on shaking legs when he steps away.

"Just a ride?" he questions, as though I'm somehow the untrustworthy one. I force my irritation down and give him nod.

"Yeah, man. I'm just giving her a ride," Jae says, having moved closer. His words are innocent enough, but there's the hint of suggestion in his tone and Emilio doesn't miss it. "You all set?" Jae asks, ignoring the tension that's building between them. He places his hand on my shoulder and Emilio's eyes laser in on the touch, his hands now fisted at his sides in a white-knuckled grip. Dominique and Roman both take steps forward, flanking their best friend in an aggressive show of support.

You have got to be kidding me. They can't possibly think it's okay to act like this.

"Really? You guys are going to go all machismo now? Don't you dare even think about starting something. Jae is my friend. What are you thinking?" Roman and Dominique say nothing. Stupid Devils.

Allie tugs Roman's arm and he reluctantly allows her to pull him away, but not before shooting a warning look at Jae that screams, *I can and will hurt you.* I roll my eyes before giving Aaron a pleading look and tilting my head in Dominique's direction just as Kasey joins our group. He gives me a shake of his head. So much for being one of the girls. All right then. No help from him. I try Kasey next and I can tell she's considering it. Her eyes flick between Dominique and Emilio, her lips pursed together. I catch a spark of mischief in her gaze, but also hesitation.

"Please," I mouth.

Jae plucks Luis from my arms and habit has me letting him. Immediately, I know it's a mistake. It's only confirmed when I hear Emilio bites out, "I don't want him around my kid," as he takes a step closer. I shift to intercept him.

"Excuse me?" Where is this possessive asshole crap coming from?

"One of us will get you to and from school. You don't need him to do that, and I don't want him around Luis. I don't know him and I sure as shit don't trust him with my son."

I rub my temples with my fingers, a headache already blooming. Jae says nothing for which I'm grateful. His eyes narrow into slits but he does the right thing and keeps his mouth shut, letting me deal with Emilio's sudden hostility. Luis grabs for his cheeks, smooshing his face and attempting to blow raspberries against his skin. It'd adorable, but only serves to piss off Emilio more.

"Can you buckle him in his car seat?" I ask Jae and he nods, turning to put Luis in the car. Before Emilio can argue I grab his hand and tug him closer to the building away from the growing crowd that is all too interested in what one of the school's Devils is getting himself into. Sometimes I really hate high school.

"You don't get to dictate who I spend my time with," I remind him as soon as we're a safe distance away. "And you do not get to dictate who I have in Luis's life."

"I'm his dad—"

"And I'm his mom. Jae giving me a ride and being in Luis's life doesn't change that any more than Dominique or Roman being in his life."

The muscles of his jaw flex. "You know he has a thing for you."

I don't answer because yeah, I do. And admitting that right now isn't going to do me any favors.

"Jae has been there for me. As a friend," I rush to add when Emilio opens his mouth. "I'm not going to all of a sudden cut him out of our lives because you say so."

Emilio's stare burns through me as he takes a step forward until we're little more than an inch away from one another. His hand comes up to wrap around the column of my throat, his hold possessive. He runs his thumb over my jaw and slowly over my bottom lip. I stay still the entire time, waiting to see what this beautiful boy will do when his anger rides him like this.

"You and Luis are mine."

I quirk a brow.

Fire licks his gaze as his teeth scrape over his bottom lip. "Say it."

"Say what?"

His grip tightens just enough to be a warning. "You're mine."

"What happened to getting to know one another?" I ask. "Taking things slow."

He backs me up against the wall and presses his body against mine. I can feel his cock dig into my stomach, already hard. "You said you wanted to take things slow. I never agreed." He captures my lips in a drugging kiss. How does he undo me like this? His hand moves from my throat down to my chest where he squeezes one breast before trailing down my body to rest his hold on my hips.

"People are watching," I gasp, tearing my mouth from his.

"You think I care?"

I push at his chest because while he might not, I certainly do. His mouth trails kisses down my neck and he presses his pelvis against me, letting me feel every glorious inch of him. My pussy clenches and I force myself to keep from melting into his touch.

"Emilio—"

"Bibiana—" There's a warning in Emilio's voice and he bites at the juncture between my neck and shoulder. I hiss and before I can do more than that, he steps back. I rub at the slight sting and turn an accusing glare his way.

"Was that really necessary?" I ask.

He shrugs. "Just marking what's mine."

"You don't own me," I remind him.

"Keep telling yourself whatever you need to hear."

I shake my head and brush past him, Jae already seated in the driver seat of his car.

I check on Luis to make sure he's properly buckled and that his chest clip is resting where it's supposed to before climbing in the passenger seat. I meet Emilio's stare through the windshield, his face still tight and eyes glaring.

Jae squeezes my knee in reassurance. "Everything good?"

I nod. "Yeah. Let's go."

He puts the Acura in drive and Emilio steps out behind the car, watching us leave. I sigh. I have a feeling he isn't going to take the news of me moving in with Jae very well. Which is why I'm not going to tell him. At least, not anytime soon if I can help it. Now, I just need to figure out a way to keep him from finding out. Easier said than done.

SIXTY-FOUR

Emilio

I'm supposed to be defending my receiver, but I'm taking every chance I get to slam into my teammates during scrimmages. Fuck the plays. I'm going on the offensive. There's a fucking monster simmering beneath the surface of my skin and I need a release. Bashing helmets isn't going to cut it.

What was that guy even doing here? Jae. Pfft. And why the hell would she call him? Today is her first day back. I told her I'd be there. That I'd help. Pull my weight. I thought we went over all of this at her place. I told her she was my responsibility too. I want to take care of her and Luis, but she doesn't even give me the chance.

Dominique throws the ball long, aiming for Roman who is rushing toward the end zone, his cleats flying across the field as the ball spirals right for him. We're playing blue, the other half of our team wearing red. I see one of the guys in red coming my way and I bend my knees, angling my shoulder to take him right in the gut. My smile is savage when our bodies connect, and I hear the air rush out of him as he takes the full brunt of my aggression. My feet slide back across the wet grass, but I manage to stay upward as he stumbles back, crashing flat on his back.

"Fuck!" he shouts, his chest rising and falling as his fists hit the ground beside him. He doesn't get up and I hear Coach's whistle putting an end to the play. I walk over to my teammate, seeing his number and knowing right away it's Carson-fucking-Bailey. "Did you have to lay me out like that?" he growls, trying and failing to push himself up with his hands. He slumps back, his helmet bouncing on the ground and I shrug.

"Yeah. I did."

Coach comes up beside me and slaps my shoulder, but I barely feel it. "Hold onto that fire for this weekend's game. We need it," he tells me as he reaches down to pull Carson up. "But lay off your teammates." He pauses. "At least my starters."

I chuckle. "Sure thing, Coach."

Carson tears off his helmet and flips me off as soon as Coach turns away. "Fuck you, Chavez. I thought we were cool?"

I take my helmet off and brush past him, making sure to shoulder check him along the way. "Not sure what gave you that idea."

He curses. "I didn't even talk to her, man."

I don't bother turning around. He doesn't deserve my anger, but it fucking sucks for him because he's going to get it. "Line up!" Dominique shouts and everyone hustles back into line.

"I'll be in on the next play," I tell him and nod toward one of the juniors on the bench. "You're up."

He startles to attention and then runs for the field, Dominique already shouting for him to hurry his ass up. I stalk toward the locker room and drop my helmet on the bench. I need to get my head on straight, but I can't get the image of her sitting with him out of my head, my kid in the back seat. They looked like the perfect fucking family. Is that why she said no to marrying me? Fuck. To dating me. Because she's already got her eyes set on someone else?

I drag my hand over my face and kick the locker. I need answers. Spinning in the combination to my lock I tear my locker open and dig through my bag for my cell phone, but before I even have a chance to unlock the screen, a call comes in.

Antonio's name flashes across the screen and my stomach drops to my feet. Shit. My fingers fumble as I rush to answer, bringing the phone to my ear, my heart lodged in my throat. Is our little sister okay? Did Raul do something?

"What's up?" I ask as sooner as the call goes through.

"Where are you?" His voice is tight, and my panic increases tenfold.

"School. Football practice," I tell him.

"Can you get away? Somewhere quiet where you can be alone?"

My brows furrow. He doesn't sound upset, just... tense.

"Already am. I'm in the locker room. I needed a breather. What's going on?"

"Sit down."

"Bro— " I cover my apprehension with a laugh. "Get to the point. Who died?" I joke, because if anything had happened to Sofia, he would have told me by now.

"Raul."

What? I stumble back onto the bench and clench the phone to my hear, hunching over as I stare at the ground. There's a ringing in my ears. Antonio is still talking but I can't make out his words. I catch pieces of what he's saying but none of it is making any sense. "Missing. Found at ... drunk. Choked on his own..."

I shake my head to clear it. "He's dead. You're not fucking with me right now?"

There's a beat of silence. "Dad is dead."

I haven't heard him call Raul "Dad" since Mom left, and for some godforsaken reason, hearing it makes my insides twist into knots. It hurts. A physical pain I can't describe, and all because a fucker who needed to die finally did.

"Don't call him that. We haven't had a dad in years. If Raul died, as far as I'm concerned, good riddance."

"Fine. We'll skip over the tears and heartfelt trip down memory lane. But we have a problem?"

I snort. "No. We just got a solution to our problem. A big fucking one at that." There's movement on the other line already, like he's stepping into another room.

"We have Sofia," he reminds me.

"What about her? She's safe now. We don't need to worry about that fucker hurting her anymore." I rub at my chest, trying to alleviate some of the ache. Maybe I took a hit on the field and didn't realize the pain at the time. I can't think of another reason for feeling this way all of a sudden.

"No. Now we have to worry about social services taking her."

Hold on a minute. "You can't be serious." She's our sister. Our blood. We're family. You don't take family away. Social services didn't give a shit about us when Raul was leaving bruises behind. Why the hell would they get involved now?

"I've already gotten a phone call. When the police were called after a maid at the hotel found his body, they ran his records. They know he has kids, and they know Sofia is a minor."

"She has us. It's not like she's alone. You and I are both over eighteen. We've got this."

He exhales a harsh breath. "You're an eighteen-year-old high school senior," he reminds me, and I can hear the thread of panic in his voice. He's serious. Sofia can be taken from us all because our deadbeat father kicked the bucket. Will this man never stop ruining our lives? He even has to do it from the goddamn grave?

"You're not. You have a job. You can be her legal guardian." I still don't understand what the problem is.

"I have a record, E."

All the blood drains from my face. "That was three years ago. They can't—"

"They can. It was assault with—"

"You were defending yourself!" I roar, slamming my fist against the locker. "You were defending us." Antonio did what he had to do to keep us safe, but our asshole of a father pressed charges even though he was the one who swung first.

"I know. Doesn't matter though. That's not how they see it."

"Fuck." I start to pace. "What are we going to do? How do we fix this?" There has to be a way. Letting social services take Sofia is not an option, I'll run with her if I have to. I know Antonio will too. My mind strays to Bibiana and Luis. Shit. I can't take my sister and run. I have my own kid to think about too. Goddammit. What a mess.

Would Bibiana leave with us? I could convince her if I had to, right?

"Roberto is on his way. I called him before calling you. He put in for leave when I told him about Luis. It was approved."

"But for how long? We can't count on him to—"

"We'll figure it out, okay? We have to."

I grind my teeth together and nod, not that he can see it. I don't have a lot of faith in our eldest brother, but if he can stick around long enough for us to figure this shit out, that'll be enough. Then he can crawl back to whatever desert they have him stationed at and go back to pretending his family doesn't exist.

"So, what do we do in the meantime?"

"You get your ass home. We need to show the case worker that we're a stable, loving, family. That we can provide the type of environment Sofia needs to thrive in. They'll be here tomorrow to interview us. I need—"

"I'll be there."

He lets out a relieved breath. "Thank you."

I snort. "You don't have to thank me. She's my baby sister too."

"I know." He sighs. "But you've got your own kid now and—"

"And nothing. I'll let Bibiana know I'll be busy for a little while. She's bringing Luis to school now, so I'll still get to see him every day. We'll figure it out."

"You still need to bring him home sometime. I want to meet my nephew."

"I know I will—"

"Only maybe after we get all of this figured out."

Sounds good to me. I don't want my kid anywhere near where social services is sniffing.

The sound of voices approaching lets me know the guys must have finished up with practice. "I gotta go, but I'll be home in half an hour. An hour max. Okay?"

"Okay. See you soon."

I hang up and shove my phone back into my bag before peeling off my pads. I need a quick shower before the rest of the team uses all the hot water, and then I need to haul ass home. I consider calling Bibiana to let her know what happened, but I never told her about Raul in the first place. Better to leave well enough alone. I'll just tell her I can't come by this week because of practice. She'll understand. She knows we have the state championship this weekend, so it won't be a big deal.

Right?

SIXTY-FIVE

Bibiana

When Jae said he'd grab some of my things from my mom's, I didn't realize he'd meant all of my things. My room wasn't very large to begin with back home, so I didn't have a ton of stuff, but all of my clothes are hanging in the guest room closet and six large boxes lay against one wall filled with Luis's clothes and toys. He even packed my books and knickknacks.

There is a playpen set up beside the bed, and it looks like my makeup and toothbrush are sitting on the nightstand. I can't believe he thought to grab them from my bathroom.

"Did you leave anything behind?" I ask jokingly, though also somewhat serious, because this makes the move feel permanent and that can't be what he has in mind. Right? I mean, no. Of course, this is temporary. A few weeks. Maybe a couple of months at most.

He rubs the back of his neck, his expression sheepish. "I mean, I didn't bring the bed. Or the crib. But we can go back for it if you'd like."

"No. This is fine. Great actually." The play pen is new. I definitely didn't have that before, though Luis is fine to sleep beside me if need be. Half the time he winds up in my bed anyway.

I set Luis down and place a hand on Jae's forearm. "You didn't need to go through all this trouble. I'll figure something out soon. I promise." Maybe I'll get lucky and can wait out Miguel's trial, though from the sounds of it, that could take months, and I don't have months.

"Don't." He sighs. "I mean, you don't need to, and it wasn't any trouble. Living by yourself is overrated. I have this whole place to myself. It could use some life in it, don't you think?"

"Are you sure? Because if you're not—"

"I want you here. You and Luis." His eyes implore me to stay, and without an alternative, I relent.

"Okay. Thank you. I promise we won't get in your way."

He chuckles. "I want you two in my way. That's the entire point of moving you in here so get comfortable. Leave Luis's toys all over the house and help yourself to whatever you need."

I can't help my smile. "You know you're a pretty great guy, right?"

The corner of his mouth lifts into a smile. "Yeah?"

"Yeah. You're going to make some girl insanely happy one day."

His smile dips and he licks his lips, a nervous gesture. "That isn't you though, is it?"

I open my mouth. Close it. Swallow and take a deep breath. "I think Emilio and I are..." I trail off. I'm not sure what we are, but it's something, and I don't want Jae getting the wrong idea. Because even if Emilio weren't in the picture, I just don't feel those sparks with him. It isn't in the cards for Jae and I.

He forces a laugh. "No worries. I get it." He swoops Luis into his arms and rubs his nose against his, giving him an Eskimo kiss. "I hope he knows how lucky he is. And I hope you know if he screws up, I'm available." He winks.

I can't help the laugh that bubbles out of my chest. "Stop. You are not going to be anyone's second choice."

He steps closer and places a chaste kiss along my temple. "I'd be your second choice in a heartbeat if you'd have me."

My breath hitches.

"But I won't push. I value our friendship too much and I want you comfortable while you're here. Why don't you unpack while Luis and I grab a snack?"

"I really do appreciate—"

He shakes his head. "Enough with all that. You and me, we're good. I don't mind being friend-zoned as long as that friendship weathers any storms that might come up. Okay? I know you and Luis's dad are together."

I scowl.

"Or maybe not together?" he corrects.

"I have no clue, to be honest."

"Yeah, guys are stupid at his age." He shrugs. "But you're something, or you're working out what you are to each other at least, and I respect that. Just don't let him shove me out of your life, okay? I remember being eighteen and an idiot too."

"You're not that much older," I remind him.

He smirks. "Old enough to grow out of my idiot phase."

I roll my eyes.

"He's going to be jealous. Possessive too. Can't say I blame him but"—he hesitates, and I can see that this is really important to him —"hang on to the people you want in your life."

"I will. Promise."

"I'll hold you to that."

I spend the next hour unpacking and making sure I have everything I need. I try calling Mom, but she doesn't answer so I shoot her a text hoping she'll see it eventually and respond.

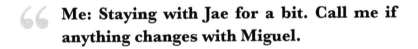

Me: Staying with Jae for a bit. Call me if anything changes with Miguel.

I'm not used to radio silence from her. We've always been close. Especially after Dad died. She talked to me. Told me things most mothers probably wouldn't tell their daughters, but it was okay. I liked the shift in our relationship. I liked knowing she needed me but now—I need her.

I try to push back the emotion bubbling up inside of me. An empty crater opens in my chest and I rub at the ache, hating the hollow feeling inside of me.

"You're not some little kid anymore," I remind myself. I close my eyes and take a deep breath. Everyone has to leave the nest at some time. Now just happens to be mine.

I set my phone on the bedside table before picking it back up. I debate calling Emilio next.

Every day this week he's come over to the house after football practice. But he's clearly upset with me today. It's stupid and beyond immature. I get the feeling he won't stop by today but if he does, I should be the one to tell him. It'll only make him angrier if he shows up at my house and my mom is the one to tell him I moved in with Jae. I don't know how he'll take it. But I imagine it'll be worse than if I tell him myself.

Indecision swirls through me. I don't want to tell him. I want to just pretend like this isn't a thing. Because it shouldn't be. Where I live should play no part in our relationship, whatever it may be. And that kiss. I press my fingers to my lips, remembering his touch. His taste. He's always sweet with a hint of spice, much like the *palerindas*—a tamarind-flavored sucker—I see him eating sometimes.

But I know this is going to be a thing between us. It'll cause a rift and Mom being the one to tell him will only make it so much worse. She knows Emilio is Luis's father. We had that fun, awkward conversation and it went about as well as can be expected.

She thinks he's too young. That I should be careful. That I shouldn't give even an inch when it comes to Luis because he'll take a mile. It's like she expects him to try and take Luis from me or something.

It doesn't help that she's always been a fan of the idea of Jae and I getting together. Luis being around puts a damper on her plans and knowing Emilio was there when Miguel was arrested, doesn't give him any points in her book. I don't need this to boil over into a bigger deal than it needs to be. I love my mom but, she's not thinking clear right now.

Resigned with the knowledge that I do actually have to tell him, I pull up Emilio's number and hit dial, listening as it rings. Once. Twice. Five times. I hit his voicemail. Relief sweeps through me as his voice says, "This is Emilio. You know what to do." The line beeps and I hang up. Voicemail isn't the best way to tell him I've moved out, right? I'll try again later. Probably. But at least I can say I did try.

I check the time. Practice should be out already but be could be running late, or maybe he decided to take a shower or something. Should I send him a text? Maybe just to ask him to call me when he has a moment. Before I can decide, my phone vibrates in my hand and I jump.

Emilio's name flashes across the screen and my fingers fumble to open the incoming message, nerves already slamming into me.

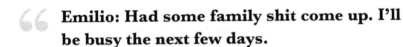

Emilio: Had some family shit come up. I'll be busy the next few days.

OH. MY SHOULDERS SLUMP. HE'LL BE BUSY? WHAT IS THAT supposed to mean? Like, is he too busy for Luis and me? I chew on my bottom lip. Is he really that mad at me that he'd make up some story about family drama?

I shake my head. No. I'll give him the benefit of the doubt. Besides, I wanted to put off telling him I moved out anyway. This at least buys me some time. I sit on the edge of the bed and stare down at my phone.

This is good. Helpful, even.

I exhale a harsh breath. So why does it feel like my stomach is trying to escape through my feet right now?

If he wants to avoid me, there isn't anything I can do about it. It just royally sucks to know that he does.

 Me: Okay. See you at school.

I HIT THE SEND BUTTON, REFUSING TO LET ON HOW MUCH this bothers me. Doubt creeps in and I wonder if this is going to be a recurring thing? Get mad at Bibi and suddenly become unavailable?

Three little dots appear on the screen and I wait for him to respond, but after a few seconds, the dots that signal he's typing fade and no new messages arrive. I sigh. Whatever. Boys are dumb anyway.

SIXTY-SIX

Emilio

It's been three days since I found out Raul died, and life has been an absolute shitstorm. I didn't even make it to practice the last two days, and I barely see Luis. I mean, I see him at school since Bibiana brings him but getting my kid for all of thirty minutes during lunch and then sharing him during fourth period isn't enough. This isn't going to work for me.

I remind myself that it's temporary. As soon as we figure shit out and make sure Sofia doesn't go into the system, I can spend more time with Luis. With my girl. Bibiana has been acting strange. Reserved even. It's like she's folding herself back into a shell and I'm not sure what to think about it. I want to let her know what's going on, but what if she freaks out? I won't risk her keeping Luis from me. I'd like to think we're past that. That she'd never keep him from me, but I can't shake the feeling that she might. I mean, what mother wouldn't be worried with social services sniffing around, right?

"Thank you, boys. I believe that's everything I need for now." The social worker—a Miss Patricia Morgen—says, getting to her feet.

WICKED SAVAGE CRUEL

She holds a legal pad in one hand, the first few pages littered in notes. About what, who the fuck knows. She's been here twice now in three days, and I won't be surprised if I see her again.

It's clear she has decided she doesn't like our situation. She keeps making statements about how important it is to for a young girl to grow up with a mother. And yeah, I'm sure it is. But we don't have one around, and it's more important for Sofia to stay with her family than to be carted off to live with a bunch of strangers. Mother or not, she needs us too.

The possibility of that happening is getting to my baby sister and it shows. Not in a good way either. She's pale and acting skittish. She inches back every time this Morgen lady asks her a question, as if she is trying to sink into the furniture, and she flicks her eyes toward me and Antonio before she answers. It makes her look guilty as hell. If I were Patricia Morgen, I would be concerned too. But she doesn't know us. Dropping in on people and putting the fear of God in them in your first meeting isn't a great way to make someone comfortable.

Antonio jumps to his feet to walk her out and I stay on the couch, pulling Sofia into a hug. God knows she needs it. Her tiny body shudders against mine and I tuck her head beneath my chin. "She's going to take me away, isn't she?" she whispers, tears lodged in her throat.

"Nope. This is all just protocol, baby sis. No one is taking you anywhere." My voice is firm, but inside I'm reeling. They could take her from us and there isn't a damn thing we could do about it.

A few hours pass and the mood in the house is decidedly grim. Sofia's retreated to her room to read her *Meet Josefina* book—they really need to come up with a Honduran girl for that shit—and Antonio are I are sitting in the garage. He's drinking a Modelo while we both stare out across the street, lost in our separate trains of thought.

A car I don't recognize rolls up and I lean forward in my seat. The passenger door opens, and a man steps out. Dressed in combat greens, my brother turns to face us, a military duffle slung over one shoulder. The driver takes off as Roberto stands there, waiting to see his reception.

Antonio is the first to stand up. He meets our brother halfway across the drive and the two embrace. Roberto has filled out since I last saw him. He's both taller and broader, damn near engulfing Antonio in his arms.

They separate and walk together to the garage, Roberto stopping a few paces in front of me, a quirk in his brow. "Long time, *hermanito*." Little brother.

I nod and push to my feet. "Four years," I remind him. Four years with damn near zero contact, I might add. But I don't bother saying that out loud. He already knows how long he's been away.

Roberto ducks his head and releases a harsh breath. "I'm back now."

Obviously. He's standing in front of me. But the question is, for how long?

He flicks his gaze to the side, his jaw stiff before returning his hard hazel stare back to mine.

"Cut him some slack," Antonio asks.

Before I can respond Roberto adds, "I'm out now."

"What's that supposed to mean?" I ask.

He's standing stiff, shoulders squared, and feet almost perfectly spaced. "It means I was eligible to re-enlist when Antonio called. He told me about your kid." A smile splits his face, one of the few genuine smiles I've ever seen on my brother's face. "I decided not to. Even before I knew about Raul." He hesitates, his voice dropping low. "I know I left you. Left like mom. I don't blame you for being pissed off with me. I should have called. Or written." He huffs out a breath. "Look. I'm sorry. But—I'm here now. I want to be here. For Sofia. For you. I want to put our family back together the way it should be."

I work my jaw and give him a stiff nod. "Okay."

"Okay?" he questions, as if he doesn't believe me. I hold my hand out and he clasps it.

"Yeah, man. Okay." I gave up my grudge years ago. He did what he needed to, and I can't say I wouldn't have made the same decision in his place. Okay. Lie. I know I wouldn't have, but still. This, I can let go. For family. For blood.

SIXTY-SEVEN

Bibiana

"We're going to a party this weekend," Kasey says as soon as I sit down for lunch.

"Uh, you do know I have a kid, right?"

She nods, blond hair bobbing around her face. "Yup. I already took care of it." I look at Allie and she shrugs.

"And how exactly did you take care of my child?" I ask just as Emilio and the rest of the boys join us.

"What's this about our child?" Emilio asks, plucking Luis from my arms. He gives me a quick kiss on the cheek and then turns his attention to our son, making faces and blowing raspberries on his neck.

"I got you a sitter," Kasey adds, and I frown. I'm not going to leave Luis with just anyone. "Relax, it's Monique."

Oh. My shoulders relax. "I didn't know you two talked."

Dominique grunts and a wicked smile spreads across Kasey's face. "All the time," she says with a pointed look toward Dominique. "I'm learning so much. That girl is a wealth of information."

I snort, but quickly smother my laugh. I can only imagine what these two are getting up to. "Okay. I'll bite, since I trust Monique, why are we going to a party this weekend?"

At the mention of party, four scowls greet me. Emilio, Aaron, Dominique, and Roman.

Kasey ignores all of them. "The guys have the state championship game this weekend."

"Exactly," Roman says. "So why the fuck would any of us go to a party?"

"You're not invited," she tells him with a flick of her hair.

"If the guys have a game, why wouldn't we go to that?"

Emilio shifts beside me. "You wanna see me play?"

I shrug. "Why not?"

His back straightens and the corners of his mouth curl into a smile. "You guys should come to the game."

Kasey just shakes her head. "We don't do school games, remember?" She gives a pointed look in Allie's direction and everyone at the table is suddenly nodding.

"What am I missing?"

Kasey hesitates, so it's Allie who answers. "When I was... uh... assaulted," she swallows hard, "it was at a football game. They're still kinda a sore spot for me."

Oh. "I'm so—"

She shakes her head. "Don't be. But I'm with Kasey. Let's get out. Go to a party. I haven't been to one since we all got together at Shadle Creek. I could use a fun night with everything going on right now."

Roman places his arm around her and she leans into him. I've been such a crappy friend. I've barely checked in to see how she's holding up with all of the Miguel stuff going on right now. That last I heard from Jae, since he's been keeping tabs on everything for me, is that Miguel was offered a plea deal to give up the other man who assaulted Allie with him.

It's looking like the recent charges are going to stick, and Jae said Miguel is considering it. They offered him a lesser sentence. Ten to fifteen years with a shot at parole for good behavior, so he could be out in as little as seven if he turns on his buddy. We'll see what happens.

"Are you holding up okay?"

She shrugs. "As good as can be expected. I just want it all to be over, ya know? I want to finally put all of this behind me and move on with my life."

I reach across the table and squeeze her hand. "So, girls' night out?"

She nods. "Girls' night out."

I smile wide. I haven't been to a party since... well, since I got pregnant with Luis.

"I don't like the idea of you three going out alone," Emilio says, setting Luis on the table where he promptly twists in an attempt to crawl across the surface.

"Give me," Allie says reaching for him. "I need the baby snuggles."

"We're not going to be alone. We'll be with each other." I shrug.

"Bad idea," Dominique adds. Roman and Emilio both nod in agreement. "Shit could happen. Someone could spike your drink. You guys could get hurt."

Kasey snorts. "It's at Sarah's. I live literally right next door. We don't have to worry about rides or designated drivers and none of us are heavy drinkers. Stop being spoilsports. We'll call Aaron if we get in a bind."

Aaron shakes his head. "I've got plans. You three are on your own."

Kasey whirls on him. "Plans? What plans?"

"Personal ones that my nosey baby sister doesn't need to know about."

Her eyes narrow but surprising us all, she drops it. "Whatever. It doesn't matter. We don't need—"

"No," Roman deadpans like his word is law and all three of us girls raise a brow.

"No?" Allie says, a tilt of her head and a gleam in her eyes. Oh, this is going to be good.

"Vanilla, you know this is a bad idea."

"What I know is that I'm having a much-needed girls' night. And I know you have a football game. State championships in fact, that I also know you can't miss. That's what I know."

Kasey and I both snicker.

Roman opens his mouth to argue and then thinks better of it before he curses under his breath and then steals Luis from her. "I thought you both hated Sarah."

"We do," Kasey chimes in. "But that doesn't mean I'll turn down free booze and a night out."

His lips mash together and Allie smirks in triumph as Roman starts making baby noises and faces at Luis. It's weird how fast his mood shifts.

"Can I keep him next period?" she asks. "I want some nephew time." I love that she considers him family already. That they all do.

"Sure. But don't you have class?"

She nods, holding a finger out to Luis, who tries to bite it. He's teething and everything appears edible, or at least chewable these days.

"Just gym so we'll roll a ball around or something. No one will care."

"Why not?"

The bell rings and we all push up from our seats. "See you in fourth," she calls, claiming my diaper bag as she and Roman head toward the exit.

I'm about to follow when Emilio reaches out and captures my arm. "A party?" he asks, his voice low. "Is that a good idea?"

"Why wouldn't it be?"

He tugs me into falling into step beside him and we spill into the crowded hallway. "Because the last time you went to a party you—"

"Had a one-night stand? Got pregnant?" I grin. "Worried it'll happen again?"

He drags me into an empty classroom and closes the door behind us before spinning around and pressing me up against the wall. My breath hitches as he trails his nose along my jaw line and takes a deep breath. "It better not happen again, unless I'm the one who puts another baby in this oven." He presses a hand against my stomach. My eyes meet his hooded gaze in question.

"Already planning on knocking me up, again?" I joke, but he doesn't smile.

"What if I was?"

My brows furrow. "You're kidding right?"

Silence.

"Emilio…"

"I wasn't there the first time. I missed all of that. Maybe I want to see what it's like." He shrugs like it's no big deal, but there's an emotion in his eyes I don't recognize.

"We're not even—"

"Yeah. We are." He presses himself against me, his lips hovering a hairsbreadth over mine. "We're a thing. You can tell yourself whatever you need to but this, you and me, it's not nothing. This is a thing. And it's exclusive."

I shiver in response. "Emilio Chavez is capable of monogamy? Who could have known?" I only half joke, because despite his words, I have my doubts. Especially with the way he's been acting these past few days.

"You know now," he says, kissing me, his lips ghosting across my own in a way that has me chasing to follow. "And you're the only one who matters." He cups the side of my face and tilts toward me until his lips are pressed against mine. This time, the kiss lingers for a moment and my cheeks heat when I feel the hard press of him against me.

The bell rings, jerking me out of the moment and we break away from one another, but just barely. "We should get to class," I mumble, but make no move to leave.

"We should," he agrees, but Emilio doesn't move either.

My chest rises and falls as my heart pounds in my chest. There's a savage glint in his eyes and a wicked curl to his lips. "Or..."

"Or?" My voice is breathless.

"We could stay."

I swallow hard and lick my lips. His eyes track the movement and the next thing I know he's lifted me into his arms. My legs wrap around his waist and he grinds into me, his hard length pressed tight against my center. "I need to be inside you," he murmurs against my mouth.

"We..." I gasp. "Can't do that... here." I can't catch my breath. His kisses are drugging, stealing the air inside my lungs. He nips at my chin, my jawline, my neck.

"I'll come over after practice. Things are settling down with my brother in town."

I arch against him as his words make their way through a haze of desire. Come over? Today? Brother? Shit.

I pull away and drop my feet back to the ground. Emilio scowls and reluctantly sets me down. "Your brother is in town?" I wrack my brain for any earlier mention of him. I know he has two. And a little sister. I haven't met them yet, but I assumed they all lived here.

"Yeah. My oldest just got out of the army. He's back for good now that..." he trails off.

"Now that what?"

He takes a deep breath and steels himself. "My dad died."

"Oh, my god." My hand flies up to cover my mouth before I rush to hug him. "I'm so sorry," I murmur against his chest.

Emilio pulls away and looks down at me, a strange look on his face. "He was an alcoholic who liked to hit his kids. Don't be sorry he's gone. I'm not."

Oh. I had no idea. "Are you..."

He rubs the back of his neck. "I'm good. Really. I don't want to talk about him though. What I want is," he kisses me again, "to fuck you, preferably in a bed but I'll settle for a desk."

I groan against his mouth. "We are not having sex at school. Someone could come in."

"Fine. Your place tonight."

When I don't answer, Emilio leans back, holding me at arm's length. "Unless you don't want me to come?"

I shake my head. "It's not that..." How do I explain?

"Then what is it?" There's a bite in his tone.

I take a deep breath and decide to rip off the band aid. "I moved out." There, I said it.

"When?"

"Earlier this week. Miguel made bail so…" I shrug.

He steps back and folds his arms over his chest. "And you weren't going to tell me?"

"It's not that I wasn't. I mean, I knew I had to tell you eventually, just…"

He taps his foot.

"I moved in with Jae?" It comes out like a question even though it isn't. As expected, his face reddens and steam practically comes out of his ears.

"Jae? The guy who would fuck you in a heartbeat, Jae?"

"We're just friends."

He shakes his head and backs away from me. "Are you fucking kidding me right now?"

I rush toward him. "Keep it down. It's not a big deal. I needed a place to crash and he offered. Nothing is happening. I swear."

He tugs at the strands of his hair, but instead of yelling at me some more he surprises me and backs me into one of the desks. "Nothing is happening between you two?" he bites out.

I shake my head. "Nothing."

"But I can't come over and fuck my girl at his place. Is that what you're telling me?"

When he says it like that it sounds bad, but still, "It would be weird. Don't you think?"

He quirks a brow and one hand comes up to grip my chin. "You're mine, Bibiana Sousa. Only mine."

I press my lips together to hold in my retort.

"Say the words. You. Are. Mine."

I hesitate and he bites my bottom lip. Hard. Ow. Fuck.

His hand grips my ass and tugs me tight against him. "I'm going to fuck you until I own every part of your mind, body, and soul," he growls.

My pussy clenches in anticipation.

"I won't be gentle," he warns. "You kept something from me. I thought we agreed, no secrets?" There's a savage glint in his eyes, but he waits, almost like he's silently asking for my permission. I swallow hard but manage a nod. "Okay," I tell him, knowing that despite the anger riding him, he needs to hear that I'm alright with this.

He wants to... punish me. I think. For not telling him about Jae. Probably still for the other day when he picked me up from school. I should balk at this, but I don't. I've accepted that Emilio isn't like other boys, and I'll happily take my punishment if it means I can have him.

At his core, Emilio is a good guy. He doesn't want to hurt me. He just needs...

"Turn around," he commands, his voice thick with lust.

I hesitate for only a second before doing as he instructs. I turn around and press my hands down on the desk in front of me, my chest heaving and my heart racing. Emilio presses his cock against me as he drags the waistband of my leggings down. Cool air brushes over my skin, the thin scrap of satin that covers my rear hardly enough to keep the chill away. "What if someone—"

"No one is going to come in. The door is locked. You'll just need to stay... quiet." There's a smirk in his voice.

His fingers trail along my inner thighs, digging into my flesh before sliding up to hook into my panties. Practiced fingers tug them down, but they're left to tangle with my leggings at my feet. My fingers tighten on the edge of the desk. This is really happening. I'm going to let him screw me in a classroom.

My pussy pulses with need and he steps back. I turn to look at him over my shoulder. His eyes burn with want. "So pretty," he coos darkly, but he isn't looking at my face. His eyes are locked on my bare flesh as he licks his lips like the savage devil he is, intent on devouring me. He lowers himself between my thighs, pressing his face against my ass. His hands roam up and down the inside of my legs, forcing them wider for him.

Anticipation hums through me as he parts the folds of my pussy with his thumbs and he licks me front to back like I'm his favorite treat. I cry out at the explosive sensations, but he's just getting started.

"Stay quiet," he warns. My eyes close, but I force them back open and bite my lip to keep my moans locked up inside. He presses a wet, hot kiss to my core and his tongue goes to work as he circles my clit and works me into a frenzy before plunging inside me with his tongue. My back arches and I push back, chasing his sinful mouth.

"So fucking sweet," he says. "Come for me Bibi. I want you to unravel."

"Oh God," I gasp, a little embarrassed at how breathless I sound. How exposed I am.

"Hold still, baby. I've only just begun."

I cry out when he adds his fingers, plunging one deep inside me before adding in a second. I clench around him, my body so starved for contact that I can feel my release hovering close. "Emilio," I gasp as the pressure builds. He thrusts into me with his fingers, curling them inside me as his mouth works my clit and my orgasm tears through me. I buck against his mouth, my body writhing as wave after wave of sensation rockets through me.

He continues sucking on my clit, prolonging my orgasm until my legs feel like jelly my body sated and my limbs boneless. But he isn't finished. He rises to his feet behind me like an avenging angel.

Devil would be more accurate.

I hear him loosen his belt and undo his zipper. I turn back to watch him, kicking off my leggings and panties with my other foot so they're not in my way. His impressive cock juts out and he meets my stare, grinning like the devil himself as he rolls a condom on his impressive dick. "You taste like sin, Bibiana Sousa." He steps back to me and covers my body with his as he cups my jaw, forcing me to twist right before he slams his mouth against mine. I taste myself on him and something about that turns me on. "It's a good thing I'm a Devil." Before I can respond, he releases me and tugs my hips back against his cock.

"Now, I'm going to fuck you like one."

He thrusts inside of me, stretching me as I'm forced to accommodate his size.

"Fuck," Emilio grunts, digging his fingers into my hips in a way I know will leave marks. "You're so fucking tight." He spreads my ass cheeks, exposing me in a completely different way as he pounds into me harder, faster. Taking zero time to let me adjust to his size.

I clutch the desk like my life depends on his, his thrusts so forceful that with nearly each one, we slide forward, forcing him to follow to hold the connection. "You like that, don't you?" He growls and my body coils tight, chasing my release.

I press my face to the desk, hoping it will muffle my moans, but I know it isn't enough. There's a knock at the door and I gasp, but Emilio doesn't stop. If anything, his thrusts become harder, more frantic. Again and again until the knock at the door is all but forgotten. My orgasm tears through me and stars explode behind my vision. But Emilio doesn't relent. He shifts his hips, finding a new angle and milking my orgasm for all that it's worth. His thrusts quicken with mounting urgency and I moan his name.

His grip tightens, his hands on my hips hurting as he pumps into me with wild abandon. His cock nudges my cervix and I see stars. Oh. My. God. He's so deep inside me I can feel him in my throat. And another orgasm threatens to wash over me. "I can't—" I gasp. Unable to get the words out.

It's too much. Too deep. Too everything. But I don't want him to stop.

Just when I think he's about to come, he surprises me and pulls out, spinning me around and pressing me down until my face is level with his shaft. He tears the condom off, weaves his fingers through my hair and thrusts his cock between my parted lips.

I groan around him as he thrusts into my mouth, his cock nudging the back of my throat and inducing my gag reflex, but he doesn't stop. He fucks my mouth mercilessly, sweat glistening on his brow as his eyes bore into mine. "That's it, baby. Suck my cock," he grunts the words, his entire body tense. "Good girl."

God. Why does hearing him say that turn me on? If anything, I should be offended right now, but I'm not. I like this. Hell, I love it.

My pussy clenches just as his cock pulses in my mouth and it's the only warning I get before his hot salty cum coats my tongue and shoots down my throat.

I take all of it, every drop he has to offer and swallow it down greedily. Pulling out, he yanks me up to him and slams his mouth down on mine again, the taste of both our pleasure a heady combination.

"You are mine," he growls the words against my mouth. My heart thumps loud behind my rib cage as I fight to recalibrate my brain and slow down my breathing. "Say the words, Bibiana. I need to hear them. You. Are. Mine."

We stare at one another in the silence, electricity crackling in the air between us. His savage grin is firmly back in place and I wish I knew what to say to him. But clearly, I was supposed to say something because when the silence continues to stretch, he reaches out and grips my jaw. "Mine," he enunciates the word. "Do we have an understanding?"

"Are you mine?" I bite out with a flare of irritation. Now that I've had a few seconds to recover, my brain is kicking back into gear, reminding me again of all of my doubts. The girls I see who flock to him. The flirting. But he does the unexpected and instead of telling me no, he nods his head in agreement. "I'm yours as much as you are mine. Which is to say completely and unequivocally. If you let another man touch you, Bibi, make sure you hate him because he won't be walking once I'm through with him."

My mind instantly snags on Jae and I know this is no idle threat. He grips the back of my head, slams his mouth on mine again and then releases me, all in the span of a few short seconds.

"Don't forget that," he warns before tucking himself back into his jeans. "I have zero intention of sharing you or my son with another man." He reaches for my leggings and panties, picking them up off the floor and handing them to me. Some of the tension has left him as he trails a hand down my neck, my shoulder, and then drags his fingers along my arm.

The knock at the door again startles me and I jump, but Emilio only laughs. He waits a few seconds as I rush to put my clothes back on and he takes care of throwing away his condom. I finger comb my hair and when he opens the door it's to reveal Allie with Luis fast asleep in her arms.

"Skipping school again?" She tsks and my cheeks heat, but Emilio only shrugs.

"From what I hear, you and Roman have made some good use out of an empty classroom a time or two."

Her eyes widen before she masks her horror with a groan. "Of course, you would know about that."

Emilio carefully reaches for Luis, tucking him into his arms and rocking him so as not to wake him.

"Everything okay?" I ask, peering down at my boy in Emilio's arms.

She nods. "Yeah. We ran out of his bottle and he was getting fussy, so I came to find you. Only you were," she smirks, "busy. So I walked around the halls with him until he fell asleep."

"Thank you."

She smiles and the bell rings, doors thrown open and students spill into the hall.

"That would be our cue," she says, tugging me beside her. "Best to slip out now before everyone else knows what you two were up to."

SIXTY-EIGHT

Emilio

I'm pissed as fuck that she moved in with Jae and didn't tell me. That my kid is living with the guy. He's already comfortable with him, but now, living there...

I lean back in my seat in fourth period, Luis fast asleep on my chest. I don't like the idea of another guy being around him. I don't want it confusing him. What if he wants Jae more than me? He's my kid, but he's still getting to know me. How is that supposed to happen now?

I try to push my worries away. There isn't anything I can do about. I understand why she moved out. Hell, I'm glad she did. I just— fuck, I wish it wasn't there.

Class moves at a snail's pace and I'm so done with all this shit. I'm ready to graduate. Move on with my life. We have five months left before we can blow this taco stand, and I'm counting down the weeks. Only shit is different and it's getting more and more complicated as time goes by.

I shift Luis in my arms, slumping lower in my chair to make him more comfortable. I hate not seeing him every day. I hate that I'm not a part of his day-to-day life. We agreed to a visitation agreement, had it submitted to the courthouse and all that shit, but it isn't enough. Bibiana isn't keeping him from me, but I want more time. I want every day.

Living with Jae needs to be a temporary situation, which means I need to figure my shit out so we can get a place. I know she wants to take things slow, but slow with that girl just isn't in my vocabulary. Roman and Allie moved in together, so I don't see why we can't. We were all going to stay in the dorms together when we went off to college, but that plan has changed with Roman and Allie being together, so it was going to be just Dominique and me. With Bibiana though— we could do what Roman and Allie are doing. Get our own apartment. Somewhere not too far away.

I consider what I'd need to do to make that work. Income is going to be our biggest obstacle. Allie has a job. And she got a trust fund from her bio dad the day she turned eighteen, so rent has never been an issue. I don't have that. I'll need to get a job to support my family, but where will I find the time between classes and football? I can work nights maybe, but juggling a job, school and practice and game days will make spending time with them that much more difficult.

Shit. No matter how I look at this, it's a fucking mess. My scholarship covers room and board in the dorms, but they're not co-ed and no way will the university let me waltz my girl and kid in. I suck on my teeth. I need to come up with something. I don't have any other choice.

GAME DAY RITUALS ARE A MUST. WE ALL HAVE OUR THINGS and I stick to mine like a religion, only today I'm off and I know exactly why. Bibiana. Coach goes on about what we're here to do but I tune most of it out. Since the Devils are the reigning state champs, the game is taking place on our field. This should be a big deal. I promised myself this year would be all about football. But all I can think about is the fact that Bibiana is going out to a party. With Kasey, of all people, which means those girls are going to get into trouble. Even with Allie around no way are they going to be on good behavior. And the last time Bibiana went to a party—that dress...

Dominque slams the locker door beside me jerking me from my thoughts. "Get your head in the game, man."

I suck on my palerindas and flip my friend off before turning to Rome.

"How are you dealing with this?" I ask him.

He doesn't bother pretending like he doesn't know exactly what I'm talking about. "I know my girl isn't interested in anyone else's dick. Not much to worry about." He shrugs. "Besides, I'd be more worried if she were here."

I nod because yeah, Allie and football games don't mix. "Any news?" I ask. I've been out of the loop and haven't wanted to bring the matter up with Bibiana.

He nods. "Fucker's days are numbered. He made bail but he is also accepting the deal. He has until next Friday to surrender himself."

"How long?" The longer the better, as far as I'm concerned.

Roman pushes to his feet, keeping his voice down so Coach doesn't lose focus. He's on the whole this-game-can-change-your-lives, so-don't-fuck-up roll. It's his shit way of motivating us and scaring the underclassmen.

"He'll do six years minimum even if he gets parole." His jaw clenches.

"You're obviously not happy about that."

"Would you be?"

I shake my head. "Hell, no. I wouldn't be happy until the fucker was six feet in the ground if he did that to my girl."

"Agreed. But he gave up the other guy. He's looking at three years, so at least Allie will get some time to... fuck. I don't know. Breathe."

"Three? That's it?"

Roman nods. "Crimes of sexual assault come with the least severe punishment. It's a bullshit system if you ask me, but my pops says it's the best we're gonna get unless Allie wants to go to trial."

"Fuck that," Dominique barks and Coach turns to look at us. We draw back further into the locker room.

"I know. I'm not putting her through that."

"I thought the rape charges couldn't stick. How is this guy getting three years—"

"Because he confessed. They won't stick to Miguel because we have no proof, but when they dragged in the other guy, some William Chaiton or some shit, they told him Miguel flipped on him and he told them everything." He exhales a harsh breath. "He told them every goddamn twisted detail and we can't use any of it to nail Miguel because the deal's already been signed.

I push my sucker to my cheek. "Fuck, man. That's rough."

None of us say anything after that. The situation is a dumpster fire. Our system is broken and the fact that two asshole rapists are getting off so easy makes me sick to my stomach. I'm glad they got Miguel for something, even if it wasn't for the rape, but it's still bullshit.

Coach blows his whistle, and we all grab our gear, heading for the doors. Dominique slaps my shoulder, his voice grim as he says, "Focus on getting through the game, kicking their asses, and then we'll go collect what's ours from the party."

I lift a brow in silent question. Ours. Really? We making confessions now?

Dom's jaw locks tight and he gives me a stiff nod, refusing to say anything else as we spill onto the field. Well, isn't that interesting.

SIXTY-NINE

Bibiana

Allie picked me up and we dropped Luis off at Monique's before going to Kasey's to get ready.

I eye the dress Kasey has picked out for me, having flashbacks to the night I first met Emilio. "No." I shake my head and throw the dress back at her.

"Why not?"

Allie plops down on the bed and settles in for the show, already dressed and ready in a red body con dress with long sleeves and a short hemline.

"Because my body is not like your body and I am not going to put every dimple and bulge on display."

Kasey rolls her eyes. "You're right. Your body isn't like mine," she says and my shoulders slump. Ouch. I mean, it's true but still. "It's better. Because you have curves I would kill for but am still a few years away from developing. And you have a rack most girls would die for. So, put on the damn dress."

My brows pull together. "Uh, thanks. But still no."

"Come on, Bibi. Just try it on," Allie pleads.

"I'm serious when I say it's going to look awful. And it's backless. I can't go braless. I will literally leak everywhere."

Kasey's face scrunches up. "Okay. You might have me there." She returns to her closet and flips through the hangers before pulling out a black lace dress with skin colored lining. "Try this one." She tosses me the dress and Allie steps up beside me, fingering the lace.

"This is hella pretty," she says, and I can't help but agree.

"Okay. Give me a minute."

I use Kasey's attached bathroom to slip into the dress. The zipper is on the side, making it easy to get into on my own. I rub my hands down the front, smoothing out any wrinkles as I look at myself in the mirror.

"Woah."

The door opens behind me and Kasey and Allie both step inside.

"Damn," Allie says.

"Told you." The corner of Kasey's mouth lifts into a smirk. "Curves in all the right places."

"Too bad Emilio can't see you like this."

Kasey whips out her phone, her fingers flying over the keyboard. "Oh, he will," she says, right before snapping a picture and sending it to him.

I groan. "I'm pretty sure knowing that this," I wave at myself, "is how I'm going out tonight isn't going to make him happy."

She grins. "I know. Which is exactly why I'm sending it. The guys were already planning on coming over after the game so this will give Emilio a little added encouragement to hurry his ass up."

Allie and I both laugh. "God. The guys aren't wrong. You really do like to stir the pot."

She smirks. "Duh. Hi, I'm Kasey. Have we met?"

THERE ARE TOO MANY PEOPLE HERE. IT'S LOUD AND THE strobe light in the corner of the room is giving me a headache. I might have thought I missed out on the whole party scene since having Luis, but now that I'm here, I'm beginning to think I wasn't really missing out on much of anything.

I check my phone for the hundredth time, knowing Luis is fine. Monique has been sending me updates. It's just that this is his first overnight and it's making me anxious. I've had to run back to Kasey's to pump and dump once already which makes me feel horrible as I pour my liquid gold down the drain. Normally I'd save it, but we're drinking. Or at least Kasey and I am. She suckered me into taking a shot with her before we left, and after being reminded of whose house we're going to, I figured it was necessary. Now that we're here, I know I was right.

Kasey walks through the house like she owns it, making a beeline for the bar covered with booze. "What do you like?" she asks me, and I consider this. I don't drink. I've had the shot at her house—which was disgusting by the way—and I've had a mimosa. Beyond that, my knowledge of alcohol is nil.

"I'm not much of a drinker," I tell her with a shrug.

She rolls her eyes. "Well, you are tonight. I want to have some fun!" she shouts over the music. I glance toward Allie who gives me an expectant look.

"No one is going to make you drink if you don't want to, but how many opportunities do you get to let loose a little?"

I purse my lips. "Okay. One drink." Kasey jumps up and down before turning to the teenage boy manning the bar. He's familiar. From our school, but not someone I've talked to before. She tells him what she wants, and he makes quick work of lining up three red cups and filling them with various liquors before pushing all three toward her. She takes them and hands one to each of us before retrieving her own.

"What is it?" I ask, looking down at the vibrant blue concoction.

"Blue Hawaiian. You'll love it."

I take a tentative sip. Oh. Yum. "That's really good." I take another drink and decide maybe this whole alcohol thing isn't so bad after all. Shots though, I don't need to try those again.

We follow the sound of music to a makeshift dance floor in the middle of the living room and, cups in hand, start dancing to some early two-thousands reggaetón. My hips sway to the beat and I relax a bit.

"So, what's going on with you and Emilio? Are you guys official now?" Kasey asks and Allie smacks her arm.

I take another drink and consider her words. "I mean, I'm not sure. He does this whole caveman thing saying I'm his, but I don't think we have labels or anything. He's never called me his girlfriend or anything like that."

"Do you want to be?" Allie asks, waving a boy off who tries to dance with her.

I shrug and drink a little more. "I don't want to rush into anything. I don't want to mess things up. You know?"

She nods. "Yeah. You have Luis to think about."

Exactly.

"You do realize you're past the whole girlfriend bit, right?" Kasey says. I stare at her and she huffs out a breath. "You have a kid. You can't really date like normal teenagers, so you've basically skipped that part, but you're not *not* a thing. And you're definitely past the whole, this is my boyfriend-girlfriend bit."

"You think so?" I ask, genuinely curious because if I can't figure out what we are exactly, maybe Kasey can shed some light on things for me.

"Absolutely."

The three of us are quick to finish off our drinks and after a second trip to the bar for another blue drink, I'm feeling great. The lights aren't giving me a headache anymore and my body tingles, my cheeks slightly numb.

"You're buzzed," Kasey says, dragging Allie and I back to the dance floor, and I don't deny it. I've never been intoxicated before, but I definitely understand the appeal now. This is pretty fantastic.

SEVENTY

Emilio

—————

"She's trying to get a rise out of you," Dominique says as I stare down at my phone, my jaw tight.

"She's succeeding," I tell him with a shake of my head. Why does Kasey always have to pull this shit? And fuck, why does Bibiana have to look so damn good? I love that dress on her, but I'd love it even more if no one else but me saw her in it. And I'd really like it if it were on the floor and she were naked beside me right now.

I save the picture to my albums because ima need that later, and then I shove my shit in my locker. "Let's roll out," I tell him and he's quick to nod.

"I'm ready." Dominique shoves his gear in the locker and pulls on a clean shirt.

"Shower?" Roman questions with a quirk of his brow.

I send Kasey a text. It's been maybe an hour since she sent the first picture, but knowing Kasey, she'll have her phone on her and respond right away.

 Me: Send Roman Allie.

SHE REPLIES ALMOST INSTANTLY WITH A WINKING EMOJI.

Seconds later Roman's phone buzzes and he looks down at the screen. A switch flips and he goes from tired and worn out from our game—which we won, by the way—to tense and ready to throw the fuck down. "What the hell were they thinking?" he bites out and I smirk. He's not too keen on that shower now is he?

"Really? You thought they were what, going to go out to a party in sweats? *Estúpido.*" Stupid. I shake my head. "Don't act surprised. But hey, if you wanna take the time to shower..." I trail off as his nostrils flare. "I mean, we could wait. Right, Dom?"

"Fuck that. Let's go get our girls," Rome bites out.

Like I thought.

We roll out in Dominique's Escalade. Roman rides shotgun while I sprawl out in the back seat. Kasey gives me a fucking play by play of their evening with a series of photos, now that she knows she's got our attention, and it's easy to see Bibiana is having a good time. Her smile is bright when Kasey catches her unaware as she dances beside Allie, red Solo cup in hand. Shit. She's drinking. Does she do that? Hell if I know. What if she can't handle her liquor? What if some asshole tries to take advantage of her?

"Should we call Aaron to get his sister?" I ask with feigned innocence, curious to see what Dominique thinks about the idea.

He grunts but doesn't say anything. That's cool, the fucker doesn't have to. I don't miss his hands tightening on the steering wheel, and I swear if it weren't for the fact he's black, he'd have a white-knuckled grip. He isn't fooling anyone. I don't know why he's pretending he doesn't want to fuck Baby Henderson. He's already admitted it before so there's no reason to act disinterested now. Hell, if anything, he should hurry his ass up before he turns eighteen because then shit can get complicated.

Just to piss him off, I dial Aaron's number, putting him on speakerphone so Dominique and Roman can hear.

"What?" he says as soon as the call connects.

"Nice to talk to you too," I deadpan. *Cabrón*. Like he isn't happy to talk to me. We all know I'm the lovable one out of the bunch.

He huffs out a breath. "Kinda busy," he says, and I hear movement in the background.

"Who is it?" a feminine voice asks.

Ooh. Damn. Someone really is busy.

"No one. Go back to the bedroom," he murmurs.

"Yo. Henderson's getting some action, boys."

"OH! Ow. Ow!" Dominique and Roman howl from the front and for a second, it's like old times, before the rift between us all developed. Where we mess with each other and give Aaron shit just for the hell of it. There was a time when I considered him as much family as I do the two fuckers sitting in front of me. I rub at my chest and remind myself we're not cool like that anymore but maybe... maybe Roman has the right of it. Maybe it is time to let that shit go.

Aaron groans, but there's a laugh mixed in there as well. "What do you fuckers want?" I can hear the smile in his voice and don't bother fighting my smirk.

"We're about to go crash a party, but I can see you're indisposed so don't you worry. We'll make sure Kasey's taken real good care of," I joke.

"Stay the fuck away from my sister with your dick, Chavez."

"Woah, woah. I got a girl. It's not me you gotta worry about."

He barks out a laugh. "I better not have to worry about any of you assholes."

I meet Dominique's gaze in the rearview mirror and it clicks. He's not going for Kasey because of Aaron. Interesting. "Alright. Alright. You go get yours. I'm about to go get mine. Talk later, *cabrón*."

I hang up the call just as we pull up to Sarah's place. The lawn is packed with bodies, the streets lined with cars.

"Fuck, this is going to be a nightmare," I groan. How the hell are we going to find the girls in this mess?

Stepping inside, we're immediately overwhelmed by the crush of bodies, loud thumping music, and the strong smell of marijuana. "I'll check the living room and hallway. Go check the kitchen and we'll meet at the bottom of the stairs in ten," Roman grunts over the noise.

"I've got the back," Dominique adds, and we all part ways to see who can find our prey first.

I nod, eager to get this over with. Guys and girls are grinding against one another. Another couple is damn near fucking against a wall for everyone to see, the guy's hands down the girl's pants, and it takes zero imagination to know what he's doing.

I scan the heads around me, looking for Bibiana's raven black hair when I hear my name.

"Emilio!" Sarah squeals, launching herself at me. I stumble back a step before I steady myself and peel her arms from around my neck. Her smile falters at my expression. "Did you come to see me?" she asks, a thread of hope in her voice.

I sigh and shake my head. "You know I'm with Bibiana."

She harrumphs. "Then why are you here?" Sarah flicks her hair over her shoulder before folding her arms across her chest, a move I know she does to draw attention to her chest. Too bad for her I'm not even tempted to take a peek. My girl's got the only tits I'm interested in.

"I'm looking for Bibiana, Kasey, and Allie. Have you seen them?"

Her brows furrows. "Maybe." She hesitates.

"Sarah—" She doesn't miss the warning in my voice. I'm not here to play games.

"Urgh, fine. I think I saw them earlier getting a drink. Come on." She turns around, leaving me no choice but to follow as we make our way through to the crowded kitchen. "Do you want something?" she asks, reaching for a red cup and letting the dude manning the keg fill it for her.

"No," I bite out. "I'm not here to party. I'm grabbing the girls and then leaving."

Her lips press into a tight line. "It's only one drink," she says, holding the cup out to me. A guy crashes into her back and she stumbles forward, her drink spilling down my front. Sonova— My nostrils flare as I stare down at my now beer-soaked shirt.

"I am so sorry," she rushes to say. Sarah sets her now empty cup down and hands me a wad of paper towels. I blot at the mess but it's not going to make a lick of difference. The whole fucking cup caught me.

"Great. I'm going to smell like the beer the rest of the night." Maybe I can convince Bibiana to take a shower with me. I know Monique is keeping Luis for the night and she was going to stay the night at Allie's but maybe we can change that.

Sarah's eyes brighten. "I think I have one of your shirts." She looks away with a shrug. "I mean, if you want it back that is."

My brows pull together and I cock my head to the side, not sure if I believe her or if this is some game she's playing. I don't remember leaving clothes here, but I mean, I guess I could have left a beater or hoodie or something like that.

She rolls her eyes. "Don't act so suspicious. I'm pretty sure you left one here from one of the nights you stayed over. It's upstairs." She heads for the staircase and yet again, I'm forced to follow. But honestly, what choice do I have? While the prospect of convincing Bibiana to take a shower with me is promising, I don't want to wear Sarah's drink for the next thirty minutes or however long it takes for me to find her and then get home.

We make our way upstairs and I stand in the middle of her room as she rummages through her drawers. "Take off your shirt and you can throw it in there if you want." She points toward a laundry basket in the corner. "I'll wash it and bring it to school on Monday."

I hesitate and she huffs out a breath. "Emilio, you're being stupid. I get it. You're seeing someone."

Fine. I peel the shirt off, tossing it in the hamper before moving past her and stepping through the open doorway of her bathroom. I wet a rag and run it over my chest and abs to get off some of the lingering beer off before walking back out into her room.

"Shirt?" I ask.

She holds up a black shirt I vaguely recognize and saunters my way, a little extra swing in her step. And here we go. She places the shirt in my hand, but a second after I accept it, she tosses her arms around my neck and stares up at me, longing in her gaze. Fuck. Her eyes have that glazed look too that says she's probably had one too many drinks herself and is about to do something stupid.

"Sarah—" I warn.

"Come on, Emilio. Weren't we good together?" Her voice is breathy, more of her wannabe porn-star shit and I am not in the mood. "Why don't we have one last round together? For old time's sake," she purrs. "I'll make it good for you."

"I'm seeing someone," I remind her, grinding my teeth together. I hold myself back from shoving her off me which is exactly what I want to do, and instead grip her arms with near bruising force to keep her from climbing my body like I'm a goddamn tree. The feel of her hands on my chest makes me shiver, and not in a good way. I hate the press of her body against mine. It's just... wrong.

Despite my hold on her, she still leans up on tiptoe and presses her lips to my neck, her teeth grazing the column of my throat. "I don't mind sharing anymore," she whispers. "I miss you."

I've had enough. Fuck the shirt. Fuck this shit. I don't want her or anyone else that isn't my girl touching me.

"Sarah—" I growl, but the creak of the door stops me from finishing the sentence as my eyes meet twin pools of anguished blue. "Hey ma—"

She doesn't wait for me to finish. She bolts from the hallway, her slender legs taking her quickly from sight as I shove past Sarah and chase after her. "Bibiana, wait!" I shout after her, but she doesn't stop. Fuck.

I lose sight of her raven-colored hair in the sea of people when we make it to the main part of the house. Shit. Where is she?

I scan the crowd, calling out her name. Several heads turn in my direction—none of whom are her—but I don't give a fuck what people think. I need to find my girl. What she thinks happened didn't and I don't want her worried for even a second longer than she needs to be. Allie is the one who drove so she can't go far on her own. That's the one thing I've got going for me right now.

I pull out my phone, firing off a quick text message and praying she takes the time to read it.

 Me: It's not what it looked like. Let me explain.

I STARE AT THE SCREEN FOR SEVERAL SECONDS, WILLING HER to respond.

She doesn't. Shirt still in my hand I throw it on over my head and scan the room again, spotting baby Henderson surrounded by a circle of seniors. Motherfucker. What is she thinking? I make a beeline for her and move to drag her away from her admirers. One of them steps forward to object—some asswipe I recognize from the school's basketball team—but it only takes a second for him to realize who the fuck I am, and he immediately backs off. "Sorry, man. I didn't realize Kasey was Devil property."

"She's not." Kasey tries to wriggle away but I tighten my grip. "But she is my friend's baby sister and she's fourteen. Which makes her too fucking young for you to get your dick wet with." He drops his head, a chastised look on his face. Good. These fuckers need to stop trying to rob fucking cradles.

"Emilio, knock it off," she snaps.

I ignore her, shoving her toward the front door with my hand on the center of her back. "I do not have time for your shit, Kasey. I need you to help me find Bibiana."

She stops struggling and whirls around to face me. "What did you do?" she asks, hands on her hips.

"Nothing." I bite out. "Sarah threw herself at me, but nothing happened. Bibiana doesn't know what she saw."

Her eyes narrow. "I swear to god if you—"

"I didn't do shit," I yell at her, but she doesn't look convinced, and goddamnit if she doesn't believe me how the hell am I going to convince Bibiana?

"Yo," I turn and find Dominique and Roman a few feet away. Allie beside them.

"Either of you seen Bibiana?" All three shake their heads as they move closer. Dominique shifts to Kasey's side, taking a protective stance beside her as his expression screams to every guy within range to back the fuck off.

"No. She was looking for the bathroom before Roman found me. It's been kinda long for that though," Allie says, and I rub the back of my neck.

"Would she have gone to your place?" I ask Kasey. Desperation bleeds into my voice. Where is she?

She shakes her head. "I don't think so."

"Fuck."

"Hey," Allie says, stepping closer. "What's going on? What happened?"

I run my hands through my hair. "Nothing, but Bibiana thinks something did. I just need to find her."

She reaches out and places a hand on my arm. "Take a breath. We will. Let me call her."

I nod, my gaze still scanning the room in case I catch sight of her. Allie dials her number, but then pulls the phone away from her ear to frown down at the screen. "What—"

"One sec. She sent me a text."

I move to peer over her shoulder as she reads it aloud.

Bibi: Catching a ride home. Sorry. I'll explain later.

I RUSH OUT THE FRONT DOOR. WHO THE HELL WOULD SHE get a ride with? Everyone who's fucking trustworthy is right here with me. I don't want some random asshole trying to take advantage of her. If she's leaving though, then she has to be outside somewhere. I ask a few of the kids I recognize if they've seen her when I spot her curly hair in the dark cutting her way through the crowd. Relief floods through me. I take a step forward, and then notice that she's veered straight for the bright red car sitting in Kasey's driveway. One I know doesn't belong to either Henderson.

I squint. "You have got to be kidding me," I curse, heading toward them when the driver comes into view. He is someone I immediately recognize and someone I do not want anywhere near Bibiana right now. Not when she's pissed. Probably hurt over what she thinks she saw. Fucking Jae. Can't this guy just disappear or something?

"Bibiana!" I shout her name and she spins, her face red and splotchy in the moonlight, wet trails running down her cheeks as she stumbles a bit before regaining her footing. My chest tightens. Shit. I did this. "Mariposa, please. Talk to me." The endearment rolls off my tongue, but as soon as she hears it, she flinches as though struck.

I'm almost to her but she manages to swing open the car door, climbing inside and shutting it quickly behind her. I slam my palm against the glass and lift the door handle, but it's locked. "Momma, open the door." She won't look at me. I can tell from their mouths moving that she and the fucker inside are arguing about something, but I can't hear their words. I can feel her slipping through my fingers. If she leaves right now without talking to me, without hearing me out, I know deep down in my gut that we're done. I don't know how I know that, but it's a visceral feeling I can't shake.

I need her to open the door. Now.

SEVENTY-ONE

Bibiana

A text message flashes across my screen.

> **Allie: Stay. I'll take you home if you don't want to see Emilio but you should hear him out. I don't think he did what you think he did.**

My fingers fly over the illuminated screen as tears track down my face. Of course she would take his side.

> **Me: I know what I saw.**

HE HAD HIS SHIRT OFF, HIS HANDS HOLDING HER TO HIM AS she sucked on his neck like a goddamn vampire. So, no. I do not want to hear him out. I don't want to ever talk to him again. Urgh! I press the backs of my hands to my eyes.

Nothing can excuse what he did. What he was about to do. God, I am so stupid. I thought I meant more to him. I thought that the flirting and whatever at school was unintentional. Like maybe he didn't realize what it looked like. I tried to brush it off, but this, I can't ignore this, and god does that hurt. I thought—I thought maybe he wanted to build a life with me. That we could be a family—him, me and Luis. But I was wrong and now I feel sick. Nausea twists and turns in my gut as I buckle my seat belt.

"Can we leave?" I ask Jae, ignoring the look of concern on his face.

Emilio never cared about me. I was convenient. Easy. A heavy weight presses down on my chest as I realize just how insignificant I am to him. Was this all just a ploy to hurt me? Was any of these past few weeks real?

I shake my head, the alcohol making my head spin.

"Bibi—"

I groan and press my head against my seat. "I'm crying. I'm drunk. And my boyfriend or baby daddy or whatever the hell he is supposed to be was with another girl so for the love of God, can we please leave!" My voice is shrill in the car and I don't even care. I can't—my chest heaves and I begin to hyperventilate.

"Are you okay?"

No. I am not okay. I'm pretty sure that's obvious right now, but I don't say that.

"Open the door," Emilio shouts, knocking on the window, startling me as he tries to pry the door open with brute force. Good luck with that. "Mariposa, please. Talk to me."

My upper lip curls at that single word. I am not his butterfly. I am not his anything. I turn to face him and suck in a shaking breath. "Leave me alone!" I scream loud enough for him to hear me.

His hand is still holding the door handle as if he can stop the car from leaving. His nostrils flare and he gives one firm shake of his head. "We need to talk. You can't just run away from—"

"Fuck you, Emilio!" I flip him off. I don't care that it's childish. He deserves it. "Leave me the hell alone." Angry tears spill down my cheeks and I hate myself for them. Hate that I can't lock up my emotions right now. "Why can't I stop freaking crying," I complain out loud, and Jae squeezes my knee.

"It's okay," he says.

Emilio shouts, "Dammit, Bibiana. Nothing happened!"

I want to believe him. Believe he would never throw what we have away, but I know what I saw, and I refuse to let him make a fool out of me. How long has this been going on? Did he ever stop seeing her? Has he been fooling around with her behind my back this entire time?

"Drive Jae."

"Are you sure? If you need to talk to him—"

"Just drive!"

His face is tight with worry, but he nods and puts the car in reverse, backing out of Kasey's driveway.

"Bibi, please—" Emilio's voice cracks.

I can't look at him. Not when it feels like my entire world is crashing down around me. They say when you lose the one you love, your heart breaks. But it isn't only my heart that hurts. My chest aches, my breaths are ragged and shallow. I didn't realize just how much I cared about him before, but the weight of my feelings slam into me like a Mac truck and I feel like I'm going to have a panic attack if I have to look at him even a second longer.

Is this what he wanted? To hurt me? To see me fall apart? To know he owned my heart and then throw it away?

Emilio chases us out of the driveway, panic written all over his face. "Don't do this! It's a misunderstanding. A fucking misunderstanding," he shouts. But I'm done listening.

Jae peels down the street, finally putting some much-needed distance between us. I see Emilio come to a stop in the rearview mirror, arms at his sides and a hopeless expression on his face as he stands in the middle of the street. I stare at him as his figure gets smaller and smaller. The hole in my chest growing wider and wider.

We turn a corner, and as soon as he's out of sight, the tears come faster. Angry, hurt, confused sobs wrack my body, making my chest heave and my shoulders shake.

I bury my face in my hands, a keening sound escaping my lips. Jae pulls over on the side of the road and I hear him unbuckle both our seatbelts before shoving his seat back as far as it will go and dragging me into his lap. His arms wrap around me and he holds me tight in a fierce embrace. "It's going to be okay," he tells me, but I have no reason to believe him. No part of what happened tonight feels like it will ever be okay.

"You've been drinking, B. Things might look different in the morning," he tells me.

I don't bother responding. He wasn't there. He doesn't know anything.

I don't know how long we sit there on the side of the road, but eventually my sobs subside, leaving behind a gaping pit in my chest. "I'm sorry," I tell him when I can form words again. "I didn't mean to drag you into this. I just—"

"Don't apologize. I'm here. For whatever you need. I'll always be here, okay?"

I nod against his chest, taking a few precious seconds to pull myself together before I lift my head from his chest and climb over the center console, taking my seat again. I wipe the tears from my face and suck in a shuddering breath. Get it together, I tell myself and decide here and now that I will be fine. I've been through a lot. I'm strong. I'm independent. And I can do this on my own. I've already proven that. I don't need Emilio to be whole. Brick by brick I will put myself back together. I won't become my mother. I won't settle for a man who doesn't really love me.

SEVENTY-TWO

Emilio

_____

She won't take my calls. I know she moved in with Jae, but I don't know where the fuck that even is. She picked Luis up this morning. Dominique called to let me know she showed up at his place, but I wasn't able to make it there fast enough to intercept her and Monique refused to tell him what time she was coming for me to plan ahead. Fuck. I should have just showed up at seven this morning and waited. That would have been the smart thing to do. The creeper-stalker thing too, but I could live with that.

The girls are locking down hard. Even Allie is vague-booking shit. Telling me to give Bibiana space. That she just needs time to think.

No, the fuck she doesn't because all she's doing is thinking about shit that never fucking happened. Giving her time and space right now is not going to help me in the least. It's only going to make shit worse.

"Take a breath," Allie says, handing me a cup of something warm. Cocoa by the looks of the mug. I accept the drink and take a sip, immediately recognizing the spiced flavor of Abuela's hot chocolate, but I barely taste it. Everything feels bland to my senses, my world a colorless haze of gray.

I take another drink, hoping the warmth will seep into my bones and calm me down, but it does nothing for me. My leg won't stop bouncing. My mind is racing a mile a minute trying to come up with a way to win my girl back. If I could just talk to her...

"Emilio?"

I look up from my cup.

"Whatever you're thinking, stop. It's not that bad." Allie says, dropping down into Roman's lap and leaning against him. We're all sitting in their living room—Dominique, Roman, Allie and I, as I try to come up with a plan, but so far, I've got nothing.

I scrape my bottom lip through my teeth and shake my head. "You don't know that. You didn't see the look on her face when she left—"

"She thinks you cheated. That this probably isn't the first time," Allies admits as if I don't know that already, but hearing it aloud pisses me right the fuck off.

"I didn't cheat!" I snap at her, shoving to my feet. "I never cheated. Not once."

Roman glowers at me. "Calm the fuck down and don't yell at her," he bites out.

Dominique's hand on my shoulder stops me from stepping closer and instead I sit back down, my shoulders slumping in defeat. "I didn't fucking cheat. I told you guys what happened. I wouldn't—"

"We know," Allie says. "And we believe you. Just... give her some time. Right now, she's hurt and—"

"She doesn't need to be. If she would just talk to me. Let me explain. I could fix this."

Allie nods her head, a solemn look in her dark brown eyes. "I know. But she asked for some space. You need to give her that. Let her realize her mistake on her own terms. Don't push her or you'll end up pushing her away. You have a visit with Luis tomorrow, right? It won't kill you to wait one more day to see her."

I tighten my jaw. *It might.*

I hate that I'm using the visit too. I want to see my boy. I have the right to. But I won't lie. I'm one hundred percent leveraging that against her as a way to make her see me. The only communication I've had from Bibiana since last night is a text saying she'll send me the address to Jae's tomorrow an hour before my scheduled time to pick up Luis. That was it. This wasn't even supposed to be our first one-on-one visit. I was going to hang out with her. With them. But I guess she's pissed enough to rush our timeline along. I should be happy about that. I get my boy. But, fuck. I want her too.

She won't even leave her phone on long enough for me to respond. I can't lose her. The thought alone has me feeling paralyzed. Helpless. There's this ache in my chest that won't subside. I don't want to be without her. She's...she's everything. I won't lose her. Not over something like this.

My palms are sweating. I'm picking up my kid from another dude's house. One who I'm sure is enjoying playing house with what is mine.

"Emilio, you need to calm down," Dominique, the voice of reason, says beside me in the passenger seat. Roman and Aaron are sitting in the back, the three of them having collectively decided I couldn't be trusted to handle this on my own. "If Bibiana sees you like this, no way in hell is she letting you leave with Luis."

My lip curls and I scowl at him, flicking on my turn signal as I take a left at the stop sign. "He's my kid," I remind them.

Dom snorts. "Like that fucking matters. Bibi is going to see you and go full on momma bear. Remember what happened the night you found out Luis was yours? She didn't cave to you then and she won't cave to you now. Take a breath. Chill."

I do as he instructs, but the tension riding me keeps me stiff. She's been avoiding my calls. Avoiding me. And now, picking my kid up like this, none of it sits well with me. We pull up to the address she gave me, and I immediately spot Jae's car. I figured he'd be here. It is the fucker's house after all, but she could have at least—I don't know—asked him to leave for a little bit.

I tighten my grip on the steering wheel for a second before I force myself to open the door and step outside. "Breathe," Aaron tells me. "You've got this." The walk to the front porch feels like I'm heading to a funeral, but I have a plan. I just have to keep my eye on the prize. I ramp myself up as if I'm about to step on the field. I've got this.

All I gotta do is explain what actually happened the other night. Make her listen. Once she knows, she'll understand. I get why she's hurt. Angry. Hell, if I thought she stepped out on me I'd be pissed too. But this is nothing. We can get past it. I'm sure of it. I take a deep breath. Stick to the plan.

I knock three times on the door before it swings open and it's Jae's face that greets me.

"Hey," he says in way of greeting and opens the door wider, taking me by surprise. I figured he'd posture or some shit. Try and knock me down a few pegs. He picked her up from the party. He saw what a mess she was. I'm sure she's told him what she thought happened, so I expected anger from him. Or maybe satisfaction. But I get none of that. Just mild resignation.

Despite the greeting, I shake my head. I don't want to go inside. I don't want to be anywhere near this fucker because I am two seconds from going off and slamming my fist into his face. *Breathe,* I remind myself. He can downplay whatever he'd like, but I know he wants my girl and I'm sure he'll use this situation to his advantage. If I were in his shoes, I would.

My worry from last night has morphed into righteous anger. I need someone to take it out on and unfortunately for me, it can't be him.

"Where's Bibiana?"

He sighs and disappears down the hallway leaving the door open for me to follow. I don't. But I can't stop myself from looking around, my eyes taking in the scattered toys and Bibiana's backpack near the door. She's made herself right at home.

A few seconds later she appears, Luis in her arms and a diaper bag hanging over her shoulder. My chest tightens when I see her. Her hair is pulled back into a ponytail and her face is bare, showcasing the dark circles under her eyes. She's beautiful, but those signs of exhaustion worry me.

"Can we talk?" I ask, itching to reach for her, but instead I shove my hands in my pockets and wait.

"Is it about Luis?" she asks, dodging the question with one of her own.

I shake my head. "No. It's about us."

"There isn't an us anymore, Emilio. I think it would be best if we kept our communication centered around our son." Her tone is clipped, without an ounce of emotion in it, but I don't miss the clenching of her jaw.

I bite the inside of my cheek and glance at Jae who is hovering a few steps away. I don't want to have this conversation with him watching, but I can't very well tell him to leave either. And despite what she wants, we're going to talk.

I shift my gaze back to Bibiana, careful to keep my tone calm, soothing even. I don't want to tick her off and I don't want to make a scene in front of Luis. I know he's little. Doesn't understand what we're saying all the time. But I remember my parents fighting in front of me as a kid. That isn't something I ever want to do in front of my son. "It isn't what you think. I didn't—"

"I know." Still holding my gaze, she shakes her head. "I know what happened. I know you didn't cheat on me."

"You do?" Relief crashes over me and my shoulders relax. I take a step forward about to reach for her when she leans away. My arms fall back to my sides. If she knows, then why is she still being like this? My heart squeezes in my chest. What am I missing?

"I talked to Allie. And Kasey. And Aaron." She sighs. "I didn't have much of a choice since they just kept calling and calling, but yeah, I heard about the beer. The shirt. That you pushed Sarah away. I know all of that."

If all that's true then—

"But," she takes a deep breath, "I still can't be with you. Not like that."

Wait. What? "Why the hell not?" I snap my teeth together to bite back the rest of my words, knowing I'll say something I'll regret.

Moisture pools in the corners of her eyes, but she blinks it away before holding her arms out to hand Luis to me, her movements stiff, almost robotic. I take him, careful to support his weight as she hands me his diaper bag. "Because the other night made me realize a few things I hadn't stopped to consider."

I flick my gaze between her and Luis and wait. He smiles, showcasing the two bottom teeth he has, and I take a second to properly greet him. "You ready to spend the day with your old man?" He gurgles and jabbers, swinging his arms and kicking his feet.

Bibiana remains quiet, so I decide to push.

"Like what?"

"I don't trust you."

Ouch. I mean, that much was already clear with how she reacted, but hearing it aloud is still like a knife to the gut.

"But—"

She raises a hand. "Let me finish."

I give her a stiff nod, clinging to my son like a lifeline.

Bibiana's chest rises and falls with her breaths and she turns to Jae for a moment. He gives her a nod of encourage and that alone makes my hackles rise. What is he encouraging her to do here, exactly?

"Luis needs to come first, always."

"He does."

"But he won't if we're fighting. I don't want to risk burning bridges with you. We're both young. A relationship would have never worked out between us. Not long-term."

"You don't know that," I bite out. She's refused to give this a real chance, fighting me every step of the way. She didn't want to get married. Didn't want to fucking date. I don't even know what to call what we've been doing, but even that was half-assed on her part.

But before I can say any of that she continues, "Seeing you with Sarah the other night made me hate you. It made me want to hurt you and the best way to do that is with him." She nods toward Luis. "I don't want to be that person. I don't ever want to use him against you or have him used against me. He isn't some bargaining chip and I hate myself for even considering it."

Air freezes in my lungs as her words hit their mark and my eyes narrow. She folds her arms across her chest and looks away. A single tear slips past her defenses and she hastily wipes it away.

"We can't afford to be at one another's throats. We can't feud and fight. This can't be messy. We have a child together and that's complicated enough. Trying to date, to be whatever it is that you want, it just makes an already complicated situation worse. I think for both our sakes, we need to focus on being co-parents. Not—not anything more."

I stand there, stunned. I expected her anger. Her fury and hatred even. But I was prepared to fight for her. To convince her of my innocence. Now, I don't know what to do. My mind is left reeling. She knows I didn't cheat but she still doesn't want me. I'm not worth the effort, I guess. Not worth her time. And that she even considered keeping Luis from me...

I bite the inside of my cheek harder until blood pools in my mouth, the metallic taste grounding me.

She clears her throat. "Everything you'll need should be in the bag, but if it isn't, call me."

I nod my head.

"He ate about thirty minutes ago so he should be okay for at least another hour."

I nod again.

"Oh, and he's happy and awake now but he usually takes his second nap around two, so you'll notice he'll start to get crabby. His *chupeta*"—pacifier— "is in the right-side pocket and his blanket is in the large compartment. He won't sleep without both of them."

I know all of this already, having picked most of it up during our time together, but I let her run through her list before she tells Luis goodbye.

"Alright. I guess we'll be on our way."

"Okay."

Fuck. Fine. This is not how I planned shit to go. I turn and take two steps towards the SUV when Bibi calls out, "Wait," and I freeze thinking maybe she's changed her mind. Maybe—

She rushes to me and gives Luis a quick kiss on the cheek, running her hand lovingly over his hair. "Okay." She seems to gather herself. "Have a great time together. And if you need—"

"Bibi..."

She pauses. "I know. I'm sorry. I'm not changing my mind. It's your day with him." She visibly swallows. "I know he's safe with you. Just ignore me."

"I'll bring him back at seven."

Another nod. "Okay. Thanks." She gives me a forced smile and this time when I turn to leave, she doesn't stop me.

Fuck. I wish she did.

SEVENTY-THREE

Bibiana

Watching Emilio leave with Luis is torture. Not only because my heart is breaking or because it's hard sharing Luis, but also because any thoughts I had of the three of us being a family, a real family, have been shattered.

Hope—that one word means so much, and I now have none of it.

We're not a couple anymore. I don't know that we ever really were. What we are is co-parents. Two people who need to navigate parenting our child responsibly as a unit.

I watched the videos. Read the books. Listened to the podcasts about effective co-parenting. Anything I could get my hands on this weekend, I binged it. And the biggest take away from them all was how complicated having a romantic relationship with the other parent is. How detrimental it can be to your child's well-being if things don't work out. How it's safest and often best to just shelf any ideas of a romance and focus on your child's needs. So that's what I'm going to do.

Luis has to come first. Always.

I won't lie, I'm relieved Emilio didn't cheat. Relieved he wasn't hooking up with Sarah Draven or anyone else all this time behind my back. Truly, I am. But, this is for the best. Even if it sucks. Even if it feels like my insides are being ripped out of my chest. The pain will go away eventually, right? I mean, it has to. Isn't that how the saying goes? Everything gets better with time? That's all I need. More time.

School is strange the following week. Allie is still my friend. So are Kasey and Aaron, but things are noticeably different. I arrive to school on time as usual and take Luis with me to first period. Like the other days before, Dominique greets me once the bell rings and takes Luis for second since he has a non-schedule.

"Everything good?" he asks. And while innocent enough, it feels like a loaded question.

I force a smile past my lips. "Yeah. Great."

His dark brown eyes drill into me and I can see the word *liar* hanging in the air between us. Thankfully, he keeps it to himself.

"I'll see you at lunch."

I swallow hard and nod, wondering if maybe I should just keep Luis. This is awkward, to say the least. I don't want him to feel obligated to help me especially now that Emilio and I aren't well anything.

"I... umm... you don't have—"

He shakes his head. "Whatever is going on with you and E, that's between you two. It doesn't affect me helping out."

My shoulders sag. "Are you sure?"

He nods and without another word, turns and heads for the library, Luis safe and snug in his arms.

Kasey approaches me on the way to my next class, her expression more subdued than usual. "You doing okay?" she asks, linking her arm with mine. I wish people would stop asking me that.

"As good as can be expected," I tell her, which is the truth.

"You know, you don't have—"

I cut her off. "Yeah, I do. You know I do."

Her lips press into a tight line.

"Kasey, you know how he is with girls. They throw themselves at him every chance they get." And that fear, that doubt, isn't something I can make go away. It will eat at my self-confidence. It will tear at the threads of any relationship we attempt. I'm insecure and I know it. I look at these girls with their perfect looks, perfect bodies, and know I don't compare. Not when my stomach is soft, my skin loose and stretch marks streak across my skin. They're in their prime and I'm, well, not.

Her expression is tight, but she nods. "I know, and I know I've always given him hell for being a player but"—she hesitates—"he was at my house this weekend."

I frown. "What for?" I know he and Aaron are friends, but they don't strike me as close. The relationship between Aaron and the other guys seem to mainly exist because of Allie's influence and maybe Roman's acceptance, though I've never outright asked.

A shrug. "I don't really know to be honest. All the Devils came over and hung out for a bit before going to pick up Luis from you." She bites her bottom lip. "I wasn't supposed to be eavesdropping but...."

When she pauses, my chest tightens, almost like my body is bracing itself for her next words. The urge to shake her and make her tell me everything is whirling through me like a storm, but I force myself to inhale, take a deep breath, exhale. Let it go. It doesn't matter what was said. It doesn't matter if he's upset or relieved or anything. I made my decision. This is for the best.

I squeeze her arm. "It's okay. You don't have to tell me." My smile is forced, but I keep the expression until we reach the door to my next class. "I gotta go, but we'll talk later."

"Oh." Her nose scrunches. "Are you sure?"

"Yup. Don't worry about it."

I wave and go into class, counting my steps as I go. *This is for the best*, I remind myself for what feels like the one hundredth time. It has to be.

Lunch is weird, but what did I expect? Emilio takes Luis as soon as Dominique arrives, and I let him. It's what we agreed to. He isn't coming over every day anymore, so we agreed he could have Luis at lunch and during fourth. He's also picking him up twice a week on Tuesdays and Thursdays. We haven't worked up to overnights yet and I'm thankful for that. I don't know when or if I'll be ready for that step anytime soon, and like we'd agreed before everything unfolded, he's letting me set the pace. I get to make the big decisions and he's not pushing for more than I can give where Luis is concerned.

Dominique, Roman, and Emilio are on one side of the lunch table. Kasey and I on the other. With Aaron and Allie in the middle, acting as a divider between our two groups. The division doesn't go by unnoticed, and already people are starting to look and whisper.

"So, this Thursday," Kasey hedges, "You're sure you want—"

"Yes!" I say, hoping to cut her off before the boys overhear us. I lower my voice to keep our conversation private. "I need the job and I'm really grateful you were willing to talk to your aunt for me."

She smiles and nods her head, blond curls bouncing with the movement.

Kasey's aunt runs the Sun Valley Station, a local diner Allie works at and that Kasey sometimes helps with. Kasey doesn't need a job, nor does she particularly want one, so she was more than happy to put in a good word for me if it meant getting her out of picking up the vacant shifts. It's only two days a week—Thursdays when Luis is with Emilio, and then on Sundays. Monique has offered to watch him anytime I need the help and I gratefully accepted the offer, but I know I need to give Emilio the option first. If roles were reversed, I'd want the option of more time with my son before leaving him with a sitter, even if it was a friend. Co-parenting the right way. Right?

"Okay, then I guess just show up on time and you're all set. Allie works this week so she can show you the ropes."

"Sounds good."

A girl walks up to our table, a determined look on her face. She has a little extra swing in her step and her entire focus is zeroed in on Emilio. She reaches him and says something, but I can't make out the words. She laughs. I look away, but still track their movements in my peripheral. Emilio turns his head to look at me. I can't make out his facial expression but having Kasey close by means I don't have to.

"I think he's gauging your reaction," she whispers low enough for only me to hear.

I sigh hard and shrug. "I don't know why. He can do whatever he wants. He doesn't have to worry about my feelings." I force a smile and climb to my feet. "Thanks again for talking to your aunt."

"Don't thank me yet. I've helped out before and it's no walk in the park. Half the clientele are students and they're mostly assholes so, just try not to let anything get to you. Okay?"

Despite myself, I chance a glance back at Emilio. The girl is gone but he's staring at a small piece of paper in his hands, his expression serious. A phone number. Figures.

"No worries. I'm becoming a master at not letting things get to me."

SEVENTY-FOUR

Emilio

W e've been *co-parenting,* as Bibiana likes to call it, for three weeks now. Torture is a more accurate term if you ask me. Football season is officially over now that we took state, so I don't have anything to occupy my free time with. I considered getting a job, but my brothers shut that idea down real quick. They want me focused on school and Luis. When I argued—because hell, we have bills and I'll be damned if I don't pay my way around here—they informed me Raul had a life insurance policy. Surprise, surprise. Guess the POS was good for something. I guess he and our mom set something up when things were still good between them, and Roberto's made it a point to keep up on the monthly premiums. That right there was thinking ahead.

There was a decent chunk of change there that the four of us decided to split five ways. One portion went to living expenses. It paid off the house and will cover the utilities for at least the next few months. The rest we each put into individual bank accounts for later use. I have no clue what Roberto or Antonio will do with theirs. I still don't really know what Roberto's plans are now that he's back stateside. But Sofia says she's saving for college. Smart girl. And I gave most of mine to Bibiana.

She fought me at first. Didn't want to take it. She said it was too much. But if you ask me, the ten grand I gave her wasn't enough. I had to remind her we agreed I'd pay child support. I wasn't there in the beginning and I didn't have much to give when she came back. This was the least I could do to make sure she and my boy are taken care of. It took some convincing, but when I threatened to have the janitor open her locker and leave it there, she finally took it.

I don't need the money. I have a full ride to Suncrest U. I can live here or in the dorms, it makes no difference to me, and my scholarship will cover my day-to-day expenses once school starts. I was worried about supporting Luis before, but this makes it easier, and if she needs more, I'll give it to her. I'd give that girl anything, even if all it does is make her more comfortable. She's still living with Jae and who the fuck knows how long that will be for, but I don't have a say in the matter. Even if I think I should. With any luck the money will help her get her own place sooner rather than later.

She got a job too. Part time at a local diner. I thought she might quit once I gave her the money, but she didn't, and every chance she gets to pick up a shift, she takes it, not that I can complain. It means more time with my boy, but I can see it wearing on her. She doesn't smile as much, and there are always dark circles under her eyes.

Because of school she works the closing shift and the diner is open till midnight most nights and then classes start at seven thirty. She isn't getting enough sleep. Isn't taking care of herself. And it grates on me that I can't be the one to take care of her.

I miss seeing her and Luis after school every day. And now, I have nothing but time on my hands to sit and dwell on how much I hate this arrangement.

"You wanna grab a bite to eat?" Antonio asks, poking his head in my room. "Roberto and I are taking Sofia to the station."

I shake my head. "Nah, man. I'm good. Not hungry." My stomach decides to call me a liar and rumble.

He frowns. "You sure?"

I nod again. "Yeah, man. I'm good." I'm not great company right now, and I don't need to dampen on my family's good mood. We got the call earlier from social services that they were closing Sofia's case. Roberto is old enough, responsible enough, and has his shit together as a retired vet to be trusted with the welfare of our baby sister. It's good news. I should be with them celebrating but I just—I can't get my mind in the right head space for it.

"Alright. Let us know if you change your mind." With that he leaves, and I do exactly what I've been doing this past week. Think. But no matter how much I analyze my problem, I still can't find a fucking solution. This isn't like a mathematical equation with only one answer. There are too many variables and my brain struggles to figure them all out, but three weeks is three weeks too long. Something needs to give.

My phone pings beside me and I check the screen. A somewhat familiar number flashes and against my better judgement, I answer it. "Hello."

"Hey, E—" A breathy voice says on the other end of the line.

I roll my eyes at the ceiling and throw myself down on my bed. "What do you want?"

There's a pause. "It's me. Kaitlyn."

"And?" I ask. Is her name supposed to mean something to me? I know at least four Kaitlyns. Five if you count Sofia's friend, but I'm pretty sure she isn't the one calling me. There's a different girl hitting me up damn near every day. At first I played along. I wanted to see if it made Bibiana jealous. I wanted to know if she cared. But all it took was the one time I caught hurt on her face for me to put an end to that. Only now, I can't get the girls to back off.

"So, I was thinking, umm, there's this party."

"Pass," I say and hang up the phone, dropping it on the comforter beside me. Rolling to my feet I head for the kitchen, ignoring the buzz of my phone as another call comes in. Leave a voicemail, or don't. Either way, I'm not answering and I'm not calling any of these chicks back.

I'm almost to the refrigerator when there's a knock at the door that stops me. It sounds again. You've got to be kicking me. They're showing up at my house now? This is going too far. I clench my teeth and storm to the door, jerking it open only to be greeted by the one asshole I definitely do not want to see. Not today. Not tomorrow. Not fucking ever.

"What are you doing here?" I bite out, hands fisted at my sides.

Jae stands there like the smug bastard he is. Dressed in black jeans, a white shirt so long it reaches mid-thigh, and a black beanie he glowers at me, almost like he's just as unhappy to see me as I am to see him.

I lean against the doorjamb with zero plans to welcome him inside. "Well?"

His lips tighten and a muscle jumps in his jaw. "I'm here for Bibiana," he says, and I fold my arms over my chest. Right. Because she would totally send this asshole to come find me.

I straighten. Wait. What if she did send him to find me? What if something happened? To her or to Luis. "What happened?" The words barely make it out of my mouth before I'm grabbing my keys off the counter and brushing past him.

He jogs to keep up. "Where are you going?" he asks, irritation in his voice.

"To Bibiana. What happened? Is she hurt? Is Luis—"

"No. They're both fine."

I pull up short. "Then why the fuck are you here?"

He exhales a harsh breath. "I'm here because she isn't and because someone needs to talk some goddamn sense into you."

I bark out a laugh. Oh. This is rich.

"Why the fuck do you care?" I swear it's like I can't catch a fucking break. All week I've had to watch my girl from a distance. I've had to pretend I'm fine with this situation when I'm anything but. I've had to watch her get out of this asshole's car every goddamn morning only to climb back into it at the end of the day. And he's here to what? Rub it in my face that Bibiana doesn't want me anymore? That she was pissed off about something I didn't even do and decided to make decisions that don't only affect her life, they affect mine. *Fuck.* This is bullshit.

"Fuck off. I have nothing to say to you." I turn to storm back to my front door.

His eyes narrow and he takes two steps forward, blocking my way and shoving his finger into my chest. It takes everything in me not to swing for his face. The guy has some fucking nerve showing up while he's moving in on what's mine. And no one can convince me that that isn't exactly what he's doing.

"Fuck me? Really. God, you're such a child. Grow the hell up, man."

My nostrils flare. "Get out of my way."

"Not until you hear me out."

"Why? Nothing you have to say means anything to me. Your opinions are lower than shit as far as I'm concerned, so go crawl back to whatever hole you came out of and leave me the hell alone. You already got the girl. What else could you possibly want from me?"

"God, are you hearing yourself? You're so fucking selfish."

"Excuse me?"

He advances on me. "You heard me. You're selfish. All you're thinking about is how this affects you. Woe is me. Poor Emilio didn't get the girl. How sad." He sneers. "Do you have any idea what Bibiana is dealing with right now?"

"Don't act like you care—"

"I don't. Not about you. But I care about her. I care about Luis."

I snort. "Right. You care so much that—"

"That I went out of my way to talk to the last person I want in their lives. The one person who can take them away from me. Yeah, asshole. That's how much I care, so shut the fuck up and listen."

My jaw snaps shut at his words. I bite the inside of my cheek until I taste blood and wait for him to say whatever it is he came here to say. I'm in no mood to deal with this guy, but he doesn't look like he's going to leave until he says his peace.

"That girl has been through hell, and you don't even know the half of it."

"But you do? Is that it?" I shake my head. If this is some twisted ploy to—

"Shut up! God. You are so goddamn arrogant. Are you too fucking proud to see what you're about to lose?"

My lip curls into a snarl. "I already lost her, or haven't you heard?" I cock my head to the side. What's this guy's end game? Is he here to gloat? Does this little chat earn him brownie points or some shit? So he can go back to tell my girl that he put me in my place. Is that it?

"I can't believe you're this dense. That girl *loves* you."

My heart skips a beat before kicking back into overdrive. I school my expression, refusing to let this fucker see just what hearing those words does to me. I pop my knuckles. Maybe I will punch him after all. If he thinks he can come over here and dangle that shit in my face—lie to me about something so important and get away with it. Nah. Not fucking happening, *cabrón*. Not today.

I'm about to tell him exactly how I feel about what he's doing, but he just keeps on talking, oblivious to the rage brewing inside me.

"You need to man up and fight for her."

"She told me to back off," I remind him, knowing full well he was eavesdropping when she and I spoke.

"*Porca puttana!*" he curses.

"What the hell does that mean?"

He glares at me. His eyes little more than slits. "*For fuck's sake,*" he grinds out. "It's Italian."

"I don't know if anyone told you, but you're Asian."

He stares up at the sky as if answers are going to fall from it.

"젠장, happy?"

Whatever he said sounded like *jenjang.* "Cool, you speak Italian and Chinese. Bravo. Are we showing off now?"

His jaw flexes. "I'm not Chinese, asshole. I'm half Korean, half Italian. Not Asian. Not Chinese." He mutters something under his breath that is probably more swearing, not that I care. "Do you like being called Hispanic?"

My chest puffs up, but then I realize what he's doing. *Fucker.* "Point made."

He grunts.

"Look, I don't have all day and you're not exactly the company I want in my face right now so if you've got something else to say, get on with it."

He scowls and shakes his head. "I don't know why I'm wasting my time."

Cool. Leave then. I don't know why he's wasting his time either. I sure as hell didn't ask for him to come here. He looks like he's about to do exactly that, but then he hesitates.

"You know she had a baby brother?" he asks, and while no, I didn't, what does that have to do with anything?

"He died when he was a kid. She named Luis after him. His middle name."

My brows pull together. *Afonso.* I just figured it was a name she liked or maybe her dad's or something. I don't know. I never thought to ask. But thinking about it now, why didn't I know this?

"After her brother died, her dad left. Couldn't handle the grief, so he bailed."

My jaw locks. Seems we have that in common. Our parents take off when the going gets tough.

"And now, her mom has all but forgotten about her. She's so afraid to be alone again that she's put on rose-colored glasses and can't even see the monster she's throwing her daughter away for."

I suck in a breath. "Why are you telling me all this?" I'm not complaining. I want to know these things about Bibiana's life, but it grates on my nerves that he's known all these things about her and I never even had a clue. I know shit is strained with her mom. It's why she brings Luis to school. But I figured they'd work it out. Bibiana said they were close. Her mom had always been there for her. You'd think she'd snap out of trying to save her rapist boyfriend eventually or at least be a fucking parent.

"So you can get it through your thick head that in her mind, you're already fucking gone. It's always been a forgone conclusion." He tugs off his beanie and runs his hands through his hair, forgetting that it's tied back in a top knot and messing up whatever style he was going for. K-pop wannabe or some shit.

"You're not making any sense."

"Everyone leaves," he tells me. "Her brother died. Her dad left. He mom has all but abandoned her. Everyone leaves that girl eventually, whether by choice or circumstance. She might not admit it, but in the back of her mind, she knew you'd bail. That's why she jumped to the wrong conclusions. Why she pushed you away even after she knew the truth. She's just been waiting for you to leave and right now, you're proving her right."

I bite my lower lip and suck my teeth as a lead weight settles deep in my gut. My own baggage comes back to punch me in the face, and I realize I'm doing to Bibiana what I expected her to do to me all this time—give up.

My nostrils flare. "So you think she *wants* me to fight for her? Despite that being the exact opposite of what she told me she wanted."

"I know she wants you to fight for her. She's miserable. A shell of the girl she used to be."

We're both damaged. Broken beyond repair. Neither of us willing to trust the other enough to make this work but.... I stumble back a few steps and look around, for what, I'm not sure. I just—my brain is moving a mile a minute. Think, Emilio. Think. Everyone leaves. But, what if they didn't have to? What if we could be the missing piece to fill each other's broken spaces?

I've been going at this all wrong. Fuck what everyone else has been telling me. She never needed space. She needed me to push. To not stop pushing. But I did stop. I stopped for three fucking weeks and just left her alone. I did nothing to show her that I was still here, waiting. That I'd always be here.

"Where is she?" I whirl back around to face him, an idea already forming. "Where is she right now?"

Face drawn, he shakes his head. "I don't know but you need to think—"

"I've been thinking." That's all I ever do. I think about how this girl who owns my bleeding fucking heart doesn't want it. How I'm not good enough. How I'll never be good enough. But what if she doesn't see me like that? What if she doesn't think I'm worthless. Even if I am. *Fuck.* I scrub my hands over my face. How could I be so stupid? I've been angry, so goddamn angry that she could just give up on us like that. Throw me away like I meant nothing to her, but that wasn't what she was doing. She was protecting herself.

I need to change that. Convince her I'm not going to leave her. I'm not like everyone else. I'll stand with her if she'll have me. But shit. Will she have me? If I push, can I get her to change her mind? Or is it truly too late now. Three weeks might not sound like much, but it's felt like forever. Did I wait too long?

SEVENTY-FIVE

Emilio

Bibiana doesn't go to work for another few hours. She's working the closing shift, which I only know because earlier this week she asked if I wanted Luis an extra day when she had to go in. I agreed right away. Obviously. But Jae said she wasn't home, and I'm not due to pick Luis up until six. That's still three hours away.

I pace my room as I wait, the minutes ticking by at a snail's pace when the distinct sounds of my brothers and sister returning greet me. They're laughing about something and it's a sound I'm not used to hearing here, in this house. At first, I tense, my body certain that the noise will draw unwanted attention, but then my mind catches up. Raul is gone. We're safe.

I let myself enjoy my baby sister's laughter. Listen to the ease and joy she has and take comfort in knowing she never has to worry about being hit again. Not here in her own home.

I want to hear my son's laughter here too. To have all of the ugly memories I have in this house replaced with new ones. Better ones.

The door to my bedroom opens, my oldest brother leaning in. "What are you doing?" Roberto asks, his tone gruff but not unwelcome. Having him home still feels weird. We were never very close and being overseas the last four years didn't help us get any closer, but I meant what I said when I told him we were good. I can tell he's trying. He goes out of his way to check on all three of us, and he's been great with Luis when I bring him over, really taking on the role of uncle. My hard exterior brother has a soft spot for my boy.

I look down at the football in my hands for a second longer before throwing it in a box. I've been wracking my brain all afternoon on how to show Bibiana that I'm different. That I can change. And this is one of the ways I plan to show her I'm ready to put her, put our family first. I know she's insecure. Has issues with other girls flirting with me and I don't know how to make that shit stop but, I sigh, I need to get the fuck over myself. This is the right move. I had a back-up plan for a reason and an educational scholarship is just a good as a football one and will take some of the attention off of me.

If I have any chance of winning my girl back, I need to put her and Luis first. They have to be my primary focus. Not football. I need to be sensible. Get a real job. Take care of them. And I can't do that and chase my dreams at the same time. I've had nothing but time to think about this. It has to be this way.

"Just packing up some junk," I say, tossing my cleats in next.

He considers me for a moment, and I try and ignore the way his stare makes me feel. Like I'm a problem he can't quite figure out.

My brother is good at that, puzzling things together, assessing a situation and then responding in the manner he thinks is necessary. I'd blame it on the military, but a part of me remembers him always being like this. He sees too much that others don't.

"I never thought I'd hear you say anything football related was junk," he muses.

"We all have to grow up at some point, right? Isn't that why you came back home?" I don't need to look at him to know my words hit their mark.

"Do you love her?"

I take a deep breath and ignore the need to snap at him. Isn't it obvious? If I didn't love her, I wouldn't be this much of a fucking wreck. I wouldn't be packing up all my shit. Closing the door on all the things that matter most to me. And I sure as hell wouldn't be taking Jae's goddamn advice. "Yeah, man. I do."

"Do you love her more than you love being angry with her?"

"What the hell does that mean?" I'm not angry with her. Not anymore. I mean, I was, sure. But I get it now. I understand her damage, or at least I think I do.

"It's a yes or no question," he says.

"I'm not angry," I say with a huff.

He shakes his head. "Yeah, bro, you are. You've been angry for a few weeks now and all I see is you getting angrier by the day."

"Nah, man. You don't know—"

He raises a hand and starts ticking off the reasons he believes I'm angry. "You're mad she isn't giving you a chance. You're mad she's made opinions about you that you don't think are true. You're mad she's got your boy most of the time while you get visitation. You're mad—"

My blood boils over. "I'm not fucking mad." He raises a brow and I exhale a harsh breath. "I don't enjoy being angry with her. I don't want to be pissed off at the girl I care about." But he's right, I am. I'm so fucking angry, even as I'm miserable without her. Even as I convince myself that Jae has the right of it, that she's damaged too and that I have to fight for her because dammit, I want her to fucking fight for me too.

"Do you want to be angry at her for forcing you to sacrifice your dreams, too?"

"It's not that simple."

"Yeah, man, it is. If you give up on football, you're going to resent that girl. You might get her back, but it'll only be temporary. You'll sabotage it. Trust me. I know."

"Then what the hell do you suggest, huh?" How else do I show her that I'm in it for the long haul? I've been sitting here for hours and this is the best I've come up with. If Roberto is saying it isn't good enough, then fuck me, because I don't know what is.

He looks at me like he's trying to explain psychics to a toddler. I wait.

"Let the anger go. It's that simple."

I scowl. "I did. I am. I—"

"The past doesn't matter. The fact you didn't know about Luis for however many months, does not matter." I open my mouth to argue. We've moved past that, but he doesn't give me the chance. "The fact that she got upset and broke things off with you doesn't matter." I bite down on the inside of my cheek until I taste blood.

"All that matters is whether or not you want to be with that girl bad enough to work for it." He watches me for a beat. "Whether or not you want to put in the work to raise your son as a unit and not a broken family."

I clench my jaw and look away. "You already know I do. I'm going to figure this out. I'm going to talk to her. Or try to. I don't want my kid growing up in a broken home like we did."

He nods and waits until I meet his gaze again. "Then you gotta let the anger go. You're hurt. I get it. But your hurt is making you angry and that shit will turn to bitterness in a heartbeat. You can't fix what's broken with you two if you're still broken on your own. Trust me, I would know." I almost ask how but can tell by the look on his face that whatever it is he's angry about, it isn't something he's ready to talk about.

"You want to go storm over there and win back your girl, I see it in your face but that isn't your best move right now."

"Then what is?"

"I cleaned out Dad's room and moved my stuff in there so my old room next to yours is empty now," he says, seemingly out of nowhere.

I frown. "Uh. Okay. Cool." I have no idea why he's telling me this. What does that have anything to do with what we were just talking about? Is he worried I'll give a fuck that he's claiming the bigger room? Not like I plan—my brother smacks me upside the head and scowls at me.

"What the hell, man?"

His scowl only darkens, and the soldier in him is definitely showing. He's standing stiff and straight with menace radiating from his pores. "Do you know *why* I spent all day yesterday clearing my stuff out of that room?" he hisses.

I rub at the back of my head, irritation at the forefront of my mind. "Because you're a selfish prick and wanted the master with a bigger closet and your own bathroom?"

He smirks. "That too. But *hermanito,* I cleaned out the room because Luis needs a bedroom, doesn't he?"

I jerk my gaze to him, scrutinizing his face for any sign that this is some sick joke. His face is dead serious.

I swallow hard. "You think he should have a room here, for when I have him?" I hedge, not entirely sure if I'm hearing him correctly. I mean, I only have him two, sometimes three days a week, and he usually sleeps with me in my room until Bibiana gets off her shift.

"No, stupid." Roberto huffs out a breath and levels me with a look that says *you're a complete moron.* "I think you should go get your girl and my nephew and move them both in here."

Emotion clogs my throat. His plan sounds way better than mine which consisted of some begging and most likely some yelling that she needed to, no, *had to* give me another shot. I mean, I was going to say it a hell of a lot better than that, but that was the gist of it. You're broken. I'm broken. I won't ever leave you. Let's be broken together. Okay. When I repeat it to myself in my head it sounds stupid as hell but this—

I'm not sure what to say, so I state the obvious in case Roberto is late on the pickup. "We, uh. We're not together. Luis's mom and me, I mean. She wants to co-parent. She doesn't want a romantic relationship." With me, at least. So what does moving her in accomplish, aside from getting to see my son every day which I am completely down for but...

He shrugs his shoulders. "She's family now. She shouldn't be living with some other guy who wants to play house with your kid when she can be here. When your son can be raised by both his parents. Together. Whatever your relationship status is, that's between you two. But I for one think my nephew and his mom should be surrounded by family. Don't you?"

I scrub my hand over my face, almost afraid to let the excitement rush in because yeah, they should be here. And put like that, there's no pressure. She doesn't have to be in a relationship with me to move in. We can be roommates. Yeah. She might go for that idea, right? And then maybe with time, she can see that I'm not such a fuck up. That I can be someone she can depend on.

Roberto steps further into the room and pulls the football out of the box, handing it back to me. "You don't have to give up on your dreams because you're a father," he tells me. "If anything, you have to fight harder for them now more than ever. Show Luis what hard work and determination gets you. And if you want to win back your girl"—he pauses—"then let go of all your pent-up anger and show her you at your best. The Emilio who fights for every yard, who smiles through his pain, and who gets up every fucking day and keeps going no matter how hard shit gets. That girl is looking for someone to weather the storm with her, be that person."

I suck on my bottom lip and shake my head. "But—"

"We're family," he says again. "We look out for each other. I know I fucked up when I left you and Antonio. Left Sofia. I should have stayed. Made sure you were all safe." He looks away, shame coloring his features. "I can't change our past. But I can change our futures. I can be here now, the way you need me."

I scrub my hand over my face and blink back the moisture in my eyes. "I don't blame you for escaping this hellhole," I tell him. We all do what we have to do to survive.

He considers me a moment, almost like he's weighing my words before he nods his head. "Appreciate it. But I still fucked up and I'll own that." He sighs. "I know you were going to go to the dorms after graduation, live on campus but this is your home. For however long you want to be here. For you, Bibiana, Luis. Family takes care of family. Alright?"

I nod. "Thanks, man."

"Don't thank me. Get off your ass and go get my nephew."

I look at the clock. It's only an hour before I'm supposed to pick up Luis. Fuck it. I'll take my chances and just hope Bibiana is home. This can't wait a minute longer.

SEVENTY-SIX

Emilio

Knocking on the door and waiting for her to answer has to be one of the most nerve-wracking experiences of my life. I've gone over what to say again and again in my head but when Bibiana opens the door, Luis propped on her hip and fast asleep, all of my carefully planned words escape me. God, she's so fucking beautiful. Her hair is thrown up in a tangle of curls. Dark smudges darken the skin beneath her eyes. She doesn't look to be wearing an ounce of makeup and still, I've never seen her look more beautiful.

"Hey," she says after a full minute passes of me just standing there, drinking her in. "You're here early." She tucks a few flyaway strands of hair behind her ear.

I look down at my sneakers, shoving my hands deep into my pockets to keep from reaching for her. A move I know she would not appreciate right now. "I was hoping we could talk."

Her mouth tightens. "I'm supposed to be getting ready for work."

"I can hold him while you do that. *Please.* I don't want to fight or anything. Just give me five minutes."

She bites her bottom lip but nods, opening the door wider and allowing me to step inside.

I catch sight of Jae in the living room and when he spots me his eyes widen, but he tilts his head in approval, stands up, and heads toward us. "I'm going to grab a coffee," he tells Bibiana. "Want anything?"

"Anything caffeinated," she says, and I know it's meant to be a joke, but hearing her request only confirms she's not getting enough rest. Between school, work, and Luis, she's running herself ragged.

"You've got it." He slips outside, leaving us alone in his house as Bibiana leads me down a hallway that I'm assuming goes to her room. Once inside she hands Luis to me, careful not to wake him before retrieving a makeup bag from her dresser and signaling me to follow her to another room. We make our way to the hallway bathroom where she drops her makeup on the counter and starts pulling out a series of products. I lean against the wall, content to hold Luis and watch as she gets ready. This feels oddly domestic. I like it. The ease and simplicity of it all.

"What did you want to talk about?" The words are casual, but I can see the stiff set of her shoulders like she's bracing herself against a coming storm and I don't want to be that. Something she has to weather.

I meet her bright blue gaze in the mirror and force myself to relax. To set my anger and my feelings aside and say these next words. Take this first step toward the future I want for the three of us.

"I wanted to apologize."

Her brows furrow, a leery expression on her face. "Okay." She doesn't sound convinced.

"I let chicks flirt with me, knowing it would upset you. I contributed to your insecurities and that shit isn't okay."

Her mouth makes a small "o" before she recovers and clears her throat. "Where is this coming from?"

I take a deep breath. "I was also hoping you'd consider something for me. For Luis." I hastily add on, because if there is anything I know about Bibiana, it is that she will always put our son first even before her own wants and needs.

She looks at me, her penetrating stare telling me to go on.

"I have an extra room at my place. I...I was hoping you'd move in. With me. Us. I mean. I live with my brothers—Roberto and Antonio. And my little sister Sofia. You'd like them."

She opens her mouth, but I rush on before she says no without hearing me out completely. I need her to see all the positives before focusing on the negatives.

"You don't want to give a relationship with me another shot. I understand why and I accept it. That isn't why I'm asking you to move in." Lie. It's a part of it, but not the main reason. Not all of it. Baby steps, I remind myself. "I'm not trying to trick you or any bullshit like that. I just..." I stare down at the top of Luis's head. If I look at her face, I'll lose my nerve because the thought of her saying no is soul-crushing. "I want to see my son every day. I want him to have a chance to get to know his uncles and his aunt. I want him surrounded by family where he'll be loved and cherished to the point he'll probably hate it as he gets older because we're going to smother him with so much damn love."

I pause to take a breath. "I know shit with your mom is strained. You have the world on your shoulders. You have school and Luis and now a job. I don't know how you're doing it. But I want to help carry the load. I want to do my part. Watch Luis while you do homework or go out with your friends and help in the mornings when you need to get ready for school because you deserve to graduate. I don't want you giving up on your dreams when you don't have to. My brothers and sister want to help too. If you'll let them. They want to be your family too. Not just Luis's."

The silence stretches between us and I'm almost afraid to look up.

"I don't have any dreams," she whispers.

I raise my eyes to hers, letting her see the sincerity in my own. "Then I want to stand beside you as you make some."

"You want me to move in with you?"

I nod. "No strings. We don't have to be together. You and Luis will have your own space. I just... I want to take care of you. Support you and Luis the way I should have been doing this whole time. That is, if you'll let me." Her lower lip trembles. "Shit. I didn't mean to upset you." *Fuck.* Is the thought of seeing me every day *that* awful?

"You didn't upset me. You..." She sniffs and wipes her tears with the backs of her hands. "That all sounds really great."

"It does." That's hard to believe because instead of looking happy, she looks like an absolute wreck. A beautiful disaster. God, I'm falling hard for this girl. She's strong and smart. Resilient. And braver then anyone I know. No wonder I don't fucking deserve her. But I will spend every fucking day of my life trying to. I won't let this girl down again. And if a relationship isn't in the cards for us, I guess I'll have to accept that. Maybe. Okay, no the fuck I won't, but I don't need to say that out loud.

Bibi's head bobs up and down. "Yeah. Okay. All I ever wanted for Luis was for him to have a family. To be loved, you know? To have people, more than just me or you, that he could rely on to have his back."

"He does. He has Roman and Allie, Dominique, Aaron, Kasey, my brothers and Sofia. We all want to help take care of him. Hell, Roman's mom has even been bugging me to bring him by, so he's got a grandma and grandpa too that are going to love the shit out of him."

Knowing I shouldn't, I reach out and cup her face, stroking my thumb along her cheek. "I will always do right by him. I will always put him first and I will always be there for you. No matter where we stand, no matter what you need, I will show up and I will be there. I promise you I will not abandon either of you, and I think moving in with me is the right move. For all of us."

"Okay." She smiles through her tears and I stomp down the impulse the kiss her. To seal the agreement with our mouths and show her just how great the two of us can be together if only we try. But we're not there yet.

"Yeah?"

She smiles. "Yeah."

"Yes!" I shout, startling Luis, who emits an angry cry. "Shit. Sorry, little man." I bounce him in my arms and manage to calm him down. He yawns once before closing his eyes again and shoving his face between my neck and shoulder.

"Can I help you pack your things?" I ask, eager to get this ball rolling.

She shakes her head, exhaling a strangled laugh. "Let's maybe slow down just a little. I can't move in with you right this minute."

I frown. I thought—

"I have to be at work in less than an hour. How about you come help me tomorrow and we'll go from there."

Oh. Yeah. Tomorrow is good too.

"I can do that." I kiss her cheek. It's quick and chaste, but her cheeks turn a beautiful shade of pink and I have to force myself not to stare. "We'll get out of your way so you can get ready and we'll talk more about this tomorrow."

Her smile widens, a wistful expression taking over her face. "Tomorrow."

SEVENTY-SEVEN

Bibiana

"Bibi!" Antonio—Emilio's brother—calls my name, and I poke my head out of the bathroom door, toothbrush still in my mouth.

"What?" The word is garbled, but he gets the gist.

"You're going to be late. Let's get this show on the road." I groan and duck my head back inside the bathroom, glancing at my phone for the time. Shit. It's almost six. I am going to be late.

I spit the toothpaste in the sink, add a quick layer of gloss over my lips and grab a hair tie, hastily throwing my hair up as I make my way to the front door. Antonio waits for me, keys in hand and a smile on his face. "Ready?"

"Yes. Sorry."

He chuckles. "Don't apologize."

He opens the door for me and ushers me outside where Emilio has Luis in his arms as Roberto runs around the yard, Sofia right behind him as she tries to catch up and tag him, but he's too quick.

Their laughter is infectious, and Luis waves his hands in the air, eager to join the fun.

"I'll be back," Antonio calls out and three heads turn our way. Emilio's eyes meet mine and a smile spreads over his face, nearly taking my breath away. He looks at me like I hang the moon and stars and I still can't understand why. He was right when he said moving in with him and his family was the right move for us. I haven't been living here long, but already it's like a weight has been lifted off my chest.

At first, I was nervous. I thought he was going to push for more than I was willing to give and I kept waiting for the moment when he would demand a relationship, but he never did.

I've been living with the Chavez family for almost a month now and not once has Emilio crossed the line of friendship. We have movie nights as a family and every Sunday we barbecue with our friends. Everyone comes over and we have carne asada and tortillas. Sofia helps me make the rice and beans, and the boys put together the salsa. It's a family affair, and something I look forward to every week.

When I don't work, Emilio and I put Luis to bed together. It's not usually a big deal, just a bedtime story and then we tuck him in my bed. I considered asking Mom for his crib, but I like having my boy snuggled up beside me. And on nights I do work, Emilio puts him to sleep in my room for me and lays with him until I get home, carefully slipping away as I take the spot he vacated.

Only lately, I haven't wanted him to go.

"Let's give Momma a kiss," Emilio says and my heart stutters, but then I realize he's leaning forward to allow Luis to get closer. My boy reaches out to smoosh my face in his tiny hands, giving me an open-mouthed and slobbery kiss on the nose as he tries to all but eat my face. "Thank you, *benzinho,*" I tell him.

"Bibi!" Antonio calls again.

"I'll see you boys later," I tell Emilio. "Gotta run if I don't want to miss my ride."

Emilio snorts. "Antonio wouldn't leave you and you know it."

True, but still... I rush around the car and climb in the passenger seat, making sure to buckle my seat belt. My heart is full as I watch my family continue to play in the front yard, and I wonder not for the first time, if I gave in to my wants, would our lives be even better?

I SLIP IN THE BACK FOR MY TEN-MINUTE BREAK, MY FEET tired and my shoulders stiff. We're deader than dead, which should make my job easier, but it seems to only make the night drag on longer. At least when we're busy time flies by and the next thing I know, we're closing. When it's like this, all I can do is think, and right now I'm not sure thinking is what I should be doing.

"How's it going out there?" Allie asks, setting a stack of plates aside.

"Slow," I tell her, hopping up on the countertop to sit. "I'm taking my ten."

She wipes her hands with a towel and jumps on the counter opposite me. "Cool, I'll take mine too."

She tosses me an apple and I bite into it, swinging my legs back and forth in front of me. "How's living at the Chavez house going?" she asks with a small smirk.

"Fishing?" I ask her, because this question comes up near daily.

She shrugs. "Maybe. Can you blame me? It's been a month and I don't know, it's weird."

My brows furrow. "How is it weird?"

"Haven't you noticed that Emilio's been acting strange?"

I shrug my shoulders, not really sure what she's getting at. He seems like the same old Emilio to me.

"When was the last time a girl gave him her number?" Allie questions.

"I don't know. Probably yesterday." Which sucks but it's probably the truth.

"Nope. It's been at least three weeks."

My eyes narrow. "And you know that how?"

"Because the last time a girl gave him her number, he had Kasey copy it down and give it to every boy in the school. Kasey might have taken things a step further than Emilio intended by telling them all to send a dick pic to that number but—"

I snort and apple flies out of my nose. Ow. Gross. Ow.

"That is disgusting."

"Shut up. You're the one who made me laugh." I clean up my mess and set my apple aside. "Okay, keep going."

She quirks a brow. "Oh, never mind. You're not really interested anyway, right? It's not like you want Emilio or anything."

"Allie," I growl in warning.

She rolls her eyes. "Right. So anyway, its public knowledge now that if you give Emilio your number when he didn't ask for it, every guy at Sun Valley High is going to get it, including the freshman. Penelope Reese had to change her number because the dick pics would not end."

"Why would he—"

"Oh, and prom is next month."

"Really?" Prom wasn't really something I was keeping track of.

"Yep. He's been asked at least eight times that I know of. He's said no each time."

"He's probably just waiting for a better offer," I joke, even as my chest tightens. The thought of him going to prom with anyone else makes me sick to my stomach.

Now it's Allie's turn to snort. "You're kidding, right?"

I shrug. "What?"

"You know how he feels about you, B."

I shake my head. "It's not like that. We agreed—"

She huffs out a breath. "Did you though? Did you both agree, or did you decide?"

"We agreed," I say, but I'm not so sure now. "At least, I thought we agreed."

"You're not dating either," she reminds me.

"I don't have time to date. I have Luis and work and—"

"And Emilio?"

My cheeks heat. "Who is the father of my child and a really great co-parent."

"He is. But now that the dust has settled, are you still sure that's all you want him to be?"

"Yes. No. I don't know."

"Maybe now is the time to be a little daring. Spread your wings and take a chance." Emilio's words echo through my mind. *Spread your wings, mariposa. Fly.*

Things might not have turned out as planned when I first heard those words whispered in my ear, but maybe this is fate's way of telling me I need to do it again, take a chance. I got Luis out of the deal the first time around, and I wouldn't trade him for the world. Maybe...maybe it's time to reach for just a little more.

It's close to midnight when I make it home, having caught a ride with Allie. I creep inside the house, careful to keep my steps silent as I slip off my shoes and coat and leave them near the door. I wash my face and slip into my sleep shorts and tank that I left in the bathroom before making my way to my room.

Luis is curled up in the middle of my bed, Emilio beside him. As I slip inside, the soft glow from Luis's night light shows me that Emilio is fast asleep. I chew on my bottom lip before deciding to leave well enough alone for one night. I slip beneath the covers, curling around my son as my feet accidentally brush up against Emilio's.

His eyes jerk open. Dark brown pools meet my own and a small smile curls his lips before he's forced to stifle a yawn. "How long was I out?" he whispers.

"I just got home, so probably not long."

He nods and turns to sit up, but I reach out and wrap my fingers around his hand before he has the chance to. He frowns, a look of confusion on his face as his eyes flick from my hand to my face. "Stay," I whisper.

His frown deepens and he hesitates.

"Please."

He nods and slips back beneath the covers, facing me with Luis between us. We stare at one another for several minutes, the silence between us heavy, but neither of us brave enough to break it.

I wrap one arm around Luis, Emilio following suit, his arm carefully covering my own. I close my eyes and force myself to relax. To not overthink this moment and for once to just let it be.

SEVENTY-EIGHT

Bibiana

I wake up to a heavy weight in my face and shift my body, attempting to dislodge whatever it is that's trying to smother me. A baby giggle greets me and the next thing I know Luis is sitting up, letting me breathe for a quick second before he decides to body slam my face again.

Ompf.

"Hey, little man," Emilio's sleep heavy voice cuts through my own early morning fog. "We gotta be nice to Momma." Luis giggles again, content to use me as a cushion before shoving his face between my breasts, his way of demanding to be fed.

I groan and roll to my side, tugging my top down to expose my breast without even realizing what I'm doing. Emilio sucks in a breath and my eyes jump to his right as Luis latches on and decides to be extra sweet with a quick scrape of his teeth—the only two he has—to remind me I kept him waiting. I bite down on my bottom lip and glare at him. "Bite Momma again and she might just cut you off," I warn.

He ignores me, of course. Almost a year old now, he's decided to become a boob barnacle every chance he gets. "Sorry," I say sheepishly. "I wasn't thinking when—"

Emilio cuts me off. "You don't have to hide, you know?"

My cheeks heat. "I know." But I have been. Whenever Luis has needed to be fed, I've slipped into my room for privacy. Not because I feel like I need it, but because... Well, I don't know why. But nursing him with Emilio present has always felt intimate in a way I can't quite describe.

"How was work?" he asks, casually changing the subject.

"Long. Slow."

"How'd you sleep?"

I yawn but manage to push through a grin. "Good. But not as long as I'd have liked," I complain. Luis likes to wake up around seven, so without looking at the clock I know it must be around that time.

"Why don't I—"

"Bibi!" Sofia bursts through the door without a care in the world as any middle-schooler would do. "Is he awake."

I chuckle. "Yes, he's awake."

She flicks her gaze to Emilio and raises a single brow. "Why are you in here?"

"Because I'm spending time hanging with my boy," Emilio says smoothly.

Sofia doesn't look convinced. "Did you sleep in here?"

The next thing I know Roberto and Antonio are poking their heads in the door too. "Hey have you seen—*oh.*" Both brothers pause. I turn away, my cheeks heating as I pray they can't all see my tits on display.

"Sorry. We were just looking for—"

Emilio waves. "Right here."

"Right," Antonio says.

'What do you want?" A thread of annoyance filters into Emilio's voice.

"Nothing. Sofia come on. Let's—"

"But I want the baby," she whines.

"Right. Yeah. Grab Luis."

Hearing his name, he rears back, releasing my breast to peer over my shoulder. Seeing his aunt, he lunges for her, crawling over my body and forcing her to make a quick grab for him. "Guess I've been replaced."

"You two, uh... catch up on some sleep. We'll take care of Luis, here," Antonio says.

The three of them leave and the door closes behind them, leaving Emilio and I alone in my bed. I turn to face him, his eyes caught on my breast when I realize I never pulled my shirt back up. "Oh, my god." I rush to cover myself and he snaps out of it.

"Shit. I'm sorry. I didn't mean—"

"No, it's fine. My fault."

We both burst into a fit of laughter as I realize just how stupid this is. It's not like he hasn't seen my boobs before. When I finally get myself under control, my chest is heaving. I wipe the moisture from my eyes and turn to find Emilio staring at me, a wide grin on his face.

"What?" I ask, my heart suddenly loud in my ears.

He shifts closer, closing some of the gap left behind now that Luis is playing with his aunt and uncles. "You still tired?" he asks.

I lick my lips, his eyes tracking the movement.

Spread your wings, Bibi. I tell myself. *Fly.*

To him, I just shake my head. "No. You?"

"No."

The next thing I know, he's closed the distance, his hand cupping my cheek and his eyes boring into mine, giving me every opportunity to pull away. I swallow hard and reach out a tentative hand to trace the line of his jaw. He shudders beneath my touch. "I've missed you." The words slip past my defenses and I freeze, waiting to see what he says, but he says nothing. Instead, his lips press against mine and I melt against him before I realize that I must have the absolute worst morning breath and tear myself away.

"Shit. Did I read that wrong?"

"No. No. Umm..." I jump out of bed. "Wait right there." I rush to the hallway bathroom, brush my teeth faster than I've ever brushed my teeth in my life, and then hurry back to my room, closing the door behind me. My back is pressed against the door, my chest rising and falling as I'm treated to an unobstructed view of Emilio now that he's no longer hidden by the covers. He's sitting against the headboard, the blankets pooled at his waist and his chest bare, showcasing his tattoo.

"You okay?" he asks, worry evident in his voice. "I can go. I mean, I know you said stay but..."

I shake my head and climb back onto the bed, sitting on my knees and facing him. "I don't want you to go."

His shoulders relax. "What do you want?" There is so much unspoken between us, so much left unsaid, but this time instead of letting fear or doubt get in my way, I tell him the truth.

"Everything."

The word barely passes my lips when he's on me. He presses me back against the bed, his body flush with mine and the fact he's only wearing boxer briefs becomes apparent when his hard length presses against my core. I gasp, my back arching off the bed.

"Are you okay? Is this okay?" he asks me, his lips nipping at the column of my neck.

"God, yes," I hiss, clinging to him.

He pulls back and I make a sound of protest in the back of my throat, reaching for him, but he doesn't give. "What is this, *mariposa?*" That single word unravels me.

"I don't know."

He pulls away, sitting back on his knees. I push up on my hands as his dark brown gaze meets mine and he hides none of what he's feeling. All his want, his need, are stamped across his face. But there's something else, a vulnerability I'm not used to seeing.

"I don't want this to be nothing," he says. "If this is just some itch—"

"It's not," I rush to say.

"Then what is it? I need some information here, so I don't go out of my mind." He leans forward, pressing his forehead against mine. "If we go down this road, I don't think I could give you up again. It was damn near impossible the first time. I..." He releases a shaking breath. "No hesitation. No doubts. We do this, we're both all in. One hundred percent."

Is that what I want? Before the question forms completely in my mind, I know it is.

"I'm all in," I whisper, a smile spreading across my face.

"Yeah?"

"Yeah."

"Yes! God, yes!" he shouts. I laugh, falling back to the bed as he towers over me once again. "I am never letting you go again, Bibiana Sousa. Never. "

I bite my bottom lip. "I think I'm okay with that."

He kisses me, his teeth biting at my lips and I open for him, his mouth devouring mine in a hungry kiss before he murmurs, "You brushed your teeth."

I laugh. He moves to pull away again, but I wrap my arms and legs around him, grinding against his length. "You're fine. Keep kissing me."

He groans and does as I ask, his mouth hot against my own.

He takes his time kissing me as his hands roam over my body as though he's trying to commit me to memory. His thumbs hook into the edge of my sleep shorts and panties and I loosen my legs, allowing him to tug them off and toss them to the ground. His fingers trail between my thighs and his thumb finds my clit, stroking me in slow circles that make my pussy clench with need.

God, it feels so good.

He stops just as the pressure begins to build and I cry out in frustration, but he only chuckles.

"Patience," he whispers, his hands sliding up my torso and beneath the hem of my tank. My breathing shudders. He peels the fabric from my skin, baring me to his hungry gaze, and I instinctively wrap my arms around my middle.

"Nah uh. No hiding," he says, tugging my arms free. I wait for his disgust, but the open want in his gaze never changes. He bends at the waist, placing a kiss between my breasts before moving his mouth to kiss one hip bone and then the other.

"Emilio—"

"Shh... relax for me." His gaze is heavy with desire, but it's attentive too, like he wants to make sure I'm okay. And I am. I close my eyes, letting my head fall back as he settles himself between my legs. His hands press my thighs open and I fight the urge to clamp them shut, but I let his eyes drink their fill. "So fucking beautiful, and all mine."

Slowly, he slides a finger inside me, his lips latching on to the sensitive bundle of nerves above my opening at the same time. I gasp and moan his name, unable to hold still as he finger fucks me and sucks on my clit. The pressure builds inside me almost like I'm running a race, and within minutes I'm reaching toward the finish line. What he's doing feels amazing, but I want more. I want him.

I'm already on the edge, my release hovering right there, but I want him buried inside me when I get there. "Emilio, please." Mistaking my words, he increases his pace adding a second finger and I clench around the intrusion. "I need... you... inside me." I gasp and he pulls back to look at me, his fingers still buried in my core.

"I want you to come with me," I tell him, and a savage grin spreads across his face before a flash of irritation has him pulling away entirely.

"One minute."

Still clad in his black boxer briefs he leaves the room only to come back seconds later with a small foil packet in his hands. My shoulders relax and he returns to my side, dropping the boxers and rolling the condom onto his length. I lick my lips.

"You ready for me?"

I nod. So damn ready.

He grabs my hips, pressing me deeper into the mattress as he guides himself to my center, his movements excruciatingly slow. His eyes search mine like he's waiting for some sort of permission, so I nod letting him know I'm not changing my mind.

His body shakes with need as he enters me and I thrust my hips forward, forcing him in deeper. He groans before sinking the rest of the way in and then we just stay like that for several seconds, both of our chests heaving as we savor the feeling of one another.

He kisses my mouth, nibbling at my lips and nipping at my jaw and neck. "I'm going to fuck you, Bibiana. I'm going to show you just how much I've missed you."

"Yes," I moan because God, I want that.

He withdraws his cock only to slam back into me and I cry out. He smiles before his hand comes up to cover my mouth, smothering my cry of pleasure. "Gonna make my brothers think I'm hurting you," he warns.

Oh, my God, I completely forget we are not alone in the house. And they just heard... I groan again, only this time for an entirely different reason.

He chuckles. "Don't be quiet on my account," he says. "I like making you scream."

He keeps his hand pressed over my mouth as his thrusts quicken, his hand muffling my sounds. "That's it, *mariposa*. You like that don't you?" He bites my shoulder and my release slams into me, my pussy convulsing around his cock. He grunts but keeps going, his thrusts coming harder, faster. His kisses grow more aggressive and his hand slips from my mouth to wrap around my throat in a possessive hold.

The fingers of his other hand dig into my hips as he thrusts into me with savage strokes. My sex clenches around him and he grits his teeth, a second orgasm already building inside me. His fingers find my clit, and he rubs quick circles over me, sending me closer to release. Without warning he dips his head, his mouth capturing one taught nipple between his teeth and I sail over the edge, a second orgasm crashing through me like a hurricane.

He doesn't slow his pace, his thrusts erratic as he bites my breasts, my neck, whatever his mouth can find. My hands roam over his back, my nails digging into his skin. It only seems to spur him on. I wrap my legs around his waist, my hands clinging to his shoulders. God, it feels so good.

I can feel the moment he gets close, when his body stiffens, and he thrusts into me one more time before his entire body quakes above me.

He collapses to the bed, shifting his weight at the last second so as not to crush me.

We both lie there, skin slick with sweat, breathing heavily and staring at the ceiling. After a few seconds pass, he rolls to his feet, disposes of the condom, and then climbs back onto the bed beside me and tugs me into his arms.

"I missed you," he says against my hair, and a feeling of contentment sweeps through me.

"I missed you too."

He takes a deep breath, his nose buried in my hair as he says, "You going to marry me this time?"

I choke on a laugh and try to turn to see his face. He's kidding, right?

I catch a smirk and know right away he's just messing with me, so I say, "Nope."

He pretends to be wounded, a mock crestfallen expression on his face. "Fine. Fine. But you'll date me, right? Be my girl?"

I bite my lip. "Yeah. I'll be your girl."

He squeezes me again. "About fucking time. And we're making this Faceplace or Tikgram or whatever the fuck they call it official."

I laugh. "You're not even on social media."

"Don't care. I'll download all the damn apps just to let everyone out there know Bibiana Sousa is *mine*."

BONUS SCENE

My breasts are heavy and god do they hurt. I knew it would be painful once I decided to stop nursing Luis. I just didn't realize how painful. Urgh. I'm dying.

"I'm going to take a shower," I tell Emilio, shoving to my feet. I don't wait for him to respond. I'm about to explode if I don't do something to relieve the pressure.

Stripping as soon as the bathroom door closes behind me, I turn the shower on full blast and groan as I unhook my bra and it hits the floor. It used to feel amazing taking my bra off when I got home from school, but seriously, with this much freaking milk trapped in my tits, I almost miss the damn thing. I feel like I have to hold my chest up, they're so sore.

Holding my breasts in my hands, I slipped past the curtain into the steaming shower. The water hits me and I hiss, the temperature near scalding, but at least it acts as a distraction. I stand under the hot spray, breastmilk leaking down my check and stomach and yeah, fuck it, I'm going to milk myself. This is one of those moments of motherhood no one prepares you for.

I wrack my brain, struggling to remember what the lactation nurse told me to do when I first had Luis. Admittedly, I wasn't paying much attention. I'd just had a baby, and I knew I had a pump. Why on earth would I need to know how to hand express, right?

Except wrong, because here I am. My pump broke a two days ago, and I decided to take it as a sign that now was the time to call it quits. Luis is almost one and barely nursing as it is. Who would have thought I'd miss my breast pump as though it were a body part? Not me.

Okay. Okay. Now what was I supposed to do again?

Hold your breast with your fingers and thumb cupped around your breast in a C shape, near but not touching your areola. The nurse's voice whispers through my mind. *Then, press your fingers and thumb back towards your chest.* Ow! I pause and suck in a breath. *Grin and bear it, Bibi.* It's not like it'll get better on its own.

Compress your breast between your fingers and thumb, moving them slightly towards your nipple without lifting them from your breast.

Dammit. It hurts. My breasts are like two giant swollen bruises. I drop my head back, clench my teeth, and squeeze my eyes closed as my hands work through the motions. After a few attempts, I get the hang of it. Thank God. Opening my eyes, I stare down at my chest and have the pleasure of watching milk shoot out in streams, but not two like you would think. It shoots out in four or five different directions out of each nipple. Why does motherhood come with so many... interesting moments like this?

Ten minutes pass and finally, the ache in my chest begins to subside. I force myself to stop, not wanting to empty my breasts completely despite the inclination to do exactly that. I need to dry up. Not tell my body to make more. Releasing a sigh, I'm about to reach for the shampoo to wash my hair when the curtain is tugged back and a very naked Emilio steps into the shower with me.

"What are you doing?" I hiss, hands flying up to cover myself, like he hasn't seen me naked before, but old habits die hard and the lights are on. Like bright white lights on, which means there is not a single shadow in here doing me any favors right now. Though that means every inch of him is equally exposed and my eyes immediately lock onto his impressive dick. His impressive and growing harder by the second dick. I flick my gaze up to meet his in time to see his eyes darken. He takes a slow pursual of my body, his hands lifting to tug at my own. Reluctantly, I allow him this, knowing he doesn't care about my stretch marks or soft stomach. Emilio has only ever made me feel beautiful.

"Fuck, it was worth it."

I lift a brow. "What was?"

He steps closer to me, his hard body now pressed against mine. "Bribing Sofia to watch Luis so I could jump in here with you."

A smile tugs at the corners of my mouth. "Oh really, bribing your baby sister now? What did she get out of you this time?" Sofia loves to watch her nephew, but she's a smart cookie, that one. I'd swindle my brother too — if I had one. That's what little sisters are for.

"Tacos from the *taqueria* on the other side of town."

"Del Leon's?"

He nods.

"I want some, too!"

Emilio chuckles, a deep husky sound that makes my toes curls. "Hmm, what will I get in return?" The fingers of one hand tangle in my hair as his lips hover over my own. His free hand cups my rear, pressing me tighter against his hard length, and I can smell the hint of sweet oranges and chili that always seem to linger on his tongue.

I pull back, but his grip doesn't allow even the smallest fraction of space between us. "Wait a minute. You bribe her to get naked in the shower with me and now you're trying to black mail me, the naked girl you wanted to be in the shower with in the first place?"

He smirks. "Devils make deals, momma."

I lick my lips. Fuck it, I'll give this man whatever he wants for tacos. Especially tacos from Del Leon's. Trust me, if you had them, you would too.

He must sense my answer because before the words even leave my mouth, he's spun me around and presses my front against the cold tile wall. I hiss. "God, that is cold."

I can feel his smile against my bare shoulder as his lips trail over my wet skin. "Don't worry, I'll help warm you up."

One hand wraps around to cup my breasts, the other slipping between my thighs. I groan and grind my ass against him. "How much time do we have?" I ask, my voice husky. I don't even care that he's squeezing my breast, making more milk come out. The shower does its part to wash it away. Why have we not done the whole show sex thing before?

"Enough." His feet force my stance wider as he positions himself at my entrance. "Do you want my cock?" He asks, his teeth grazing the shell of my ear.

I shiver, dropping my head back against his shoulder as his hand finds my clit, and he works me over with small, quick, circles.

"Mariposa—" there's a warning in his voice, but I ignore it, my body growing tighter and tighter as I strain toward my release. Between Luis and Emilio's siblings, finding time alone has been next to impossible.

His other hand kneads my breast, his touch almost painful, but then he stops and makes a tsking sound in the back of his throat.

What? Why is he stopping?

I move to turn, but he holds me in place.

"I asked you a question," his voice is guttural.

I wrack my brain for what he could have asked, but come up blank.

"Umm... yes?" I say, though it comes out like more of a question than a statement.

"You sound unsure?" Shit. Was that the wrong answer?

The water temperature dips and I know if I want hot shower sex, we better get this ball rolling. And trust me, I do. I really, really do.

"I'm sure. Very sure. Yes!" I say.

He laughs. "Good." Emilio thrusts inside me in one fluid motion, my body clenching around the intrusion, but god does he feel good. He's so big, so thick. My pussy aches as I stretch to accommodate him and my eyes close before his hand lands on my ass with a loud smack that echoes in the room.

I jump, my eyes springing open.

"That's for not listening when I asked you a question," he says, his hand smoothing over my backside and rubbing the sting away.

"Was it the wrong answer?" I ask with a breathy moan.

He bites my shoulder. "No. Which is why you only got one spanking."

Too bad.

His hands move to my hips and I bite my lower lip as he fucks me from behind, a position that has quickly become his favorite. Emilio is possessive in the extreme. It didn't take long to realize he likes having control, especially in the bedroom, and I've learned I am all too happy to give it to him. I love when he gets like this. When he tries to own my body because Devil knows he already owns my soul.

"That's it, Bibiana. You like that?"

"Yes." My release edges closer once again, but then he stills. I smack the wall in front of me with an open hand, a sound of frustration escaping between my lips.

"If you want my cock, fuck it." He tells me.

I glare at him over my shoulder. "And if I don't?"

He steps back, his dick sliding out of me before I thrust my hips back to follow. He grins, his smile both savage and sinful. "I have a feeling you will."

He's so damn sure of himself. I grit my teeth. Too bad he also isn't wrong. Keeping my eyes locked on his, I work my hips back and forth.

Emilio steps back toward me to lessen the gap and groans as I fuck myself on his length, his body locked tight. I know it's killing him right now not to move, to thrust into me like I know he wants to.

I decide to slow down and drag myself along his length. Toying with him the way he's intent on toying with me. "Don't stop," he hisses. "Don't you fucking stop."

Ha! I arch my back, lifting my arms above my head to press against the tile. I tilt my head up to the ceiling, my hair cascading down my spine. His hand fists my hair, tugging me back even further, the sting in my scalp delicious. The way this boy makes me feel...

He uses his grip on my hair to control my thrusts, back and forth. Back and forth, until neither of us can take it anymore, and he thrusts into me, pressing himself impossibly deeper. Fucking me harder. I lose myself to sensation. His hand returns to the apex of my thighs, his skilled fingers finding my bundle of nerves, and I hold on to the wall for dear life. He buries himself inside of me so deep I don't know where I end and he begins. I'm flush with the wall now, my legs shaking as I struggle to remain on my feet. I moan, my release right there, just out of reach.

"Come for me." He says, his fingers working faster. "Now, Bibiana. Come on my cock." His vulgar mouth undoes me. My orgasm tears through me, pleasure cascading over my body. His arm wraps around my stomach, keeping me on my feet as he pounds into me three more times, a near animalistic sound tearing out of him, before he finds his own release.

My chest is heaving, the water now cold, but Emilio stays wrapped around me. "Fuck, I love you." He whispers against my skin.

I swallow hard and crane my head to catch his gaze. Dark brown eyes meet my own, a vulnerability in them I'm not used to seeing. "You love me?" I ask, unsure if I heard him right. Did he mean to say those words out loud? Was it an accident? Heat of the moment sort of thing?

A hesitant smile splits his face. "Yeah. I love you, momma," he says the words again and my heart flip slops in my chest.

I turn in his arms and press my lips against his, needing his kiss. "I love you, too." I whisper against his mouth.

"Yeah?"

"Yeah."

He whistles. "Looks like I need to update the gram or tik or whatever the fuck that thing is again. My girl loves me."

I laugh. "That isn't how social media works."

He shrugs. "Don't care. Still posting it."

God. I love him. I really freaking do.

Cruel Devil

Dominique Price.
Good looking.
Arrogant.
Football-God and my brother's best friend.

He hates me.
He wants me.
He can never have me.

Everything comes so easy for him.

I refuse to be just another game for him to win.

SEVENTY-NINE

Kasey

This year will make me or break me. Personally, I'm hoping for the former. But, as I sit in the back seat of my mother's SUV, I have a feeling it's going to be the latter. There's this sense of foreboding thrumming through me as I look up at the impeccably manicured lawns and twin pillars that decorate where I'll be living this next school year. All one hundred and eighty days of it, plus winter and spring breaks. I'm going to hate every minute.

I'm very much aware that there isn't a seventeen-year-old out there who wouldn't kill to leave the nest a little bit early. And trust me when I say I'm not feeling like my life is about to take a turn for the worse just because I'm moving out at the ripe old age of seventeen. What does have me feeling this way is the fact that I'm joining a sorority. Not by choice, I might add.

Sorority life isn't my scene. And no, I don't have any firsthand experience with sororities, and yes, I'm absolutely judging them based on what I've seen on TV, but let's be real, if you knew anything about me, you'd agree that me and the perfect plastics I see walking in and out of the houses on sorority row aren't a match made in heaven.

When I applied for Sun Valley High's running start program—a program that allows me to attend college courses and earn both college credits and the final credits I'll need for my high school diploma, I thought, *this is exactly what I need.* An escape from the stupid drama that is high school life where I never really fit in. It's hard to relate to the people at school when all they can talk about is how Suzie made out with Jason behind Ruby's back and other stupid nonsense, like who is asking who to senior prom.

Meanwhile, my best friends have all graduated and are planning their weddings and being moms and doing real-life things that matter. It makes it hard to relate to high-school life. Hearing the gossip and then seeing all the back-stabby antics, it's not what I'm interested in. And don't even get me started on the boys.

They're so incredibly stupid in high school. The catcalling and fuck-boy flirting. Urgh. You'd think they'd find a better pickup line than, "You must be an angel, because you look like you just fell from heaven."

Barf.

The guys I go to school with have zero game. Not that I'd be interested in anyone at Sun Valley High anyway. I almost wish I was. It'd make seeing a certain broody asshole on the regular a hell of a lot easier.

Both of us attending Suncrest U isn't going to help, but with any luck I won't see him any more than I have to. Suncrest University is his turf, and here he reigns supreme, not that I'm surprised. Dominique Price and his best friends ran the halls at Sun Valley High as the school's football gods, so of course their reputations would follow them to college as they continue to dominate on and off the field. I used to hate those three for what they put my brother through, but now we're all friends. Hell, more like family. But I don't need people realizing we know each other, especially with the unwanted attention that will bring, so I'd like to keep our association under wraps.

And since I'm in college now, Mom decided it was the perfect time to accept an out-of-state promotion and force me to join Kappa Mu—her alma mater. Guess that makes me a legacy.

Yay.

Not.

The alternative was moving with her—so not happening. The prospect of uprooting my entire life to move halfway across the country holds zero appeal, even if the alternative is, well, this.

"Ready to braid hair and paint your nails bubblegum pink?" my brother—Aaron—asks from the front seat.

I roll my eyes and flip him the bird. "Ha. Ha. You're so funny."

He turns to glance at me, pushing the blond hair from his face to give me a wink. "Don't worry, sis. They'll leave you alone once they realize what a prickly personality you have."

I lunge forward to smack him but he swings open the passenger side door, stepping out, just in time to avoid my swipe.

"Kasey!" my mother admonishes me.

"What? He started it," I tell her as I unbuckle to follow him. Despite the early hour, the house is already buzzing with activity—what looks to be a party in full swing. Girls in all manner of summer wear are flitting about, socializing, drinking whatever is in those red Solo cups—and let's be honest, it's not water—and carrying boxes, doing exactly what I'm here to do. Move in.

I wrinkle my nose and glance at my mom as she slings her oversized purse over her shoulder and moves to join Aaron and me on the sidewalk. "Not too late to change your mind?" Aaron mutters under his breath. "You know you wanna."

I elbow him in the ribs. "Are we telling jokes now?"

When mom concocted this grand idea of me joining her former sorority, Aaron, being the protective big brother he is, was nice enough to offer me the spare room at his place. An offer I was quick to decline.

Under normal circumstances, I'd consider it. We were never very close growing up given the four-year age gap between us, but Aaron has always looked out for me. Most brothers would balk at the idea of living with their baby sister after they moved out, but Aaron genuinely wouldn't mind. He's pretty chill about stuff like that.

The problem isn't living with my brother. It's living with my brother's very hot, very broody, drives-me-insane, asshole of a roommate—Dominique Price. On the best of days, we tolerate one another. On the worst, well, things can be openly hostile.

"I'll pass on living with the devil and take door number two, please," I tell him, and he chuckles.

"Dom isn't that bad."

I snort. "Are we talking about the same person, here?" Dominique Price very much is that bad. He gets under my skin in a way no one else can, and the pull he has over me, urgh. I hate it. Sometimes so much so that I think I hate *him*. When we're in the same room, I want to kiss him and punch him in the same breath. That he makes me question my own sanity is infuriating.

Aaron gives me a light-hearted shove. "Alright, sis, have it your way. But don't come crying to me when you realize the grass isn't greener on the other side."

A gust of wind blows my hair into my face and I hastily push my blond curls out of my eyes. "I won't," I assure him. "The grass on your side is already dead and yellow so the bar is set pretty low."

He smiles, his eyes scanning past me, and I turn to see a familiar black Escalade roll up beside my mother's car. The broody asshole I just mentioned parks his overpriced SUV and three doors open, letting out Dom, Roman, and Emilio. Somebody please shoot me now.

"What are they doing here?" I groan.

Aaron throws his arm over my shoulder and pulls me into a side embrace. "They're being good friends and helping you move into your new place." The fact that he genuinely believes that should be concerning, but I know better.

"Whose idea was this?" I ask.

Already their presence is drawing curious looks from some of the girls. It won't take long for them to realize who they are. God dammit, he is such an asshole. It would have been bad enough if he came on his own, but bringing Roman and Emilio is taking it one step too far.

"Dom's," Aaron confirms what I suspected and my mother being the weirdo she is, gushes.

"Isn't that so sweet of them, Kasey? It makes me so happy to know you'll have such a great support system here. Makes me feel so much better about my baby girl going to college." She sighs, the smile on her face wistful as she turns back to the house. If I grind my teeth any harder I'm liable to break a tooth. She cannot be serious right now.

"Yep. Soooo sweet," I tell her while giving Dominique my most murderous glare. Does he shake in fear like he should? Of course not. Instead he smirks like the cruel bastard he is and heads right for me, Roman and Emilio right on his heels.

I'm going to make him regret this. I cannot believe he'd set me up like this.

The guys do that guy handshake bro hug thing as if they didn't all see each other a few hours ago, then Dom turns his full attention on me and I have to force my expression to remain impassive. Age has only worked to sharpen his features, making him even more striking than the boy I met my freshman year of high school three years ago. With his hair tightly braided away from his face, his sharp jawline and full lips stand out in stark relief, and I can't decide if I want to kiss him or punch him—a frequent struggle of mine, so I do what I'm best at and just antagonize him.

"Are you so desperate for female attention that you have to drop in on the girls of Kappa Mu for a little bit of an ego stroke?" I smile in satisfaction when his dark brown eyes narrow.

Dominique has this edge to him that's difficult to describe. He's both regal and rugged; the juxtaposition between the two is likely what makes women flock to him. He has two thin slashes in his right brow that somehow take him from attractive to dangerous, and after graduation he filled out to a full six-foot-five, stacked with all the muscles you'd expect a division one athlete to have. The effect he has on people is hard to miss.

When he scowls the way he is doing right now, he's damn near terrifying to behold. But when he smiles, a real smile that doesn't hold an ounce of malice—and mind you those are rare—his entire face lights up and for a second it's like standing in the sun after months of nothing but rain. God, I hate him.

"I don't need an ego stroke. Not a single woman here can hold my interest," he says, his eyes boring into mine and waiting for a reaction. One I refuse to deliver. *Asshole.* Of course he'd say something like that. Dominique hasn't dated, like seriously dated, for as long as I've known him. He gets around, I'm sure. What football player doesn't when you have an entire fan club of jersey chasers? But the only girl I've seen him with more than once is Tamara Vinzent. I haven't had the pleasure of meeting her yet, but she's his date to any event or function that requires one. I don't really understand their relationship, and for my own sanity, I try not to think about it too much, but somehow she's outlasted everyone else and has managed to sink some form of a hold into Dominique where no others before her have succeeded.

When Dominique realizes I'm not going to respond, the corner of his mouth curls into his signature cruel smile. "You worried someone will catch my attention?" He scans the growing crowd. "Not really my type, but maybe I can—"

"Yo, Baby Henderson," Emilio says, cutting Dominique off from whatever he was about to say and cutting through the growing tension in the air. "You gonna show us the new digs? Introduce us to your new lady friends?" He winks, and if I didn't know him better, I'd think he was serious. But Emilio is head over heels in love with his girlfriend, one of my best friends, so I know this is for show and he's just helping me out. The softy. Too bad his little act of kindness won't keep him safe if he and the others don't get the hell out of here before anyone realizes the school's star quarterback, wide receiver, and cornerback just showed up.

I shake my head. "Hard no. You three need to leave."

Roman smirks and Emilio clutches his heart as though I just wounded him. "Baby Hen—"

"Stop calling me that and go home or I'm going to tell Bibi about your big surprise," I warn.

He sucks in a sharp breath. "You wouldn't. You love me?" He meant it as a statement but it comes out more as a question.

"Wanna bet?" Because today is day one of campus life for me and I'm not going to let these three muck it up.

Emilio backs away, hands raised in the air. "You win. I'll stay in the car." He turns and jogs back to Dom's Escalade. One down. Two more to go.

I turn to Roman and raise a single brow. "You too, mister."

"You don't have anything you can use against me," he says, his voice filled with confidence he should not be feeling right now. Doesn't he know me? I have something on virtually everyone. It's little sister 101. You always find the dirt and horde it to later get your way.

I prop one hand on my hip. "I don't?" I press a finger to my lips as though thinking before letting a wide smile spread across my face. "Hey, Aaron, did I ever tell you about the time Roman and Allie went to Silverdale?"

Roman's eyes widen briefly before his brows draw together. "How do you—"

I pull my phone from my back pocket. "Allie sent me pictures from that weekend. You two were so cute together. The couples—"

Roman jerks forward, pressing his palm over my mouth. His dark brown eyes fill with a mix of disbelief and fury. "Not. Another. Word," he growls. If he were anybody else, I might be worried by the threat in his voice, but despite his rough exterior, Roman is a big ole softie and his fiancé is one of my other best friends. He wouldn't hurt a hair on my head. She loves me. He loves her. Therefore, I win. So instead of pushing his hand away or trying to say anything, I wait for him to realize what I already know.

It takes only a handful of seconds.

"Fine. Don't say anything else. I'll go chill with E. Deal?"

I nod and he slowly releases me, hesitating for just a second to make sure I'll keep my mouth shut before he turns, slaps Dom on the shoulder with a muttered, "You're on your own, man," and joins Emilio in the car.

"Damn, sis, remind me not to get on your bad side," Aaron says, as if I haven't used this exact same tactic on him before. "Got anything on this one?" He nods toward Dominique, who raises a brow of his own, expression smug because, no, I have nothing I can use against him to make him do anything he doesn't want to do and he knows it.

EIGHTY

Dominique

I smile, watching the gears turn in that pretty little head of hers as she struggles to find a way to get rid of me. Not happening, baby girl. Kasey coming to Suncrest U is a disaster waiting to happen. She's seventeen for chrissakes, and her idiot mother thought it'd be a great idea for her to join the biggest sorority on campus. What a joke.

Football and training for football are what I'm focused on, so it's become a habit of mine to avoid all things Greek, but only a hermit wouldn't know Kappa Mu and their frat counterpart Alpha Ze are the two most notorious party houses here. Problem is, when shit goes down, it gets ugly.

There have been plenty of rumors about girls getting drugged and guys taking turns at some of their parties, and I'll be damned if anyone is going to try shit like that with Kasey.

I can't stand the girl, but that doesn't mean I'll sit back and let anything happen to her, either. I'm not a complete asshole, despite what she might think.

It's why I suggested to Aaron that she move in with us. I'm willing to take one for the team if I have to, not that it'd be some big hardship. I'm barely home during the week. Most of my time is spent in class, on the field, or at the gym, and most Saturdays I have games. Half of them are out of town.

I'm home on Sunday afternoons but usually gone in the evening to see my sister. Sundays are the obligatory Price family dinners. My parents made them mandatory when Monique and I moved out for college, and while I managed to find a way out of them, my sister wasn't so lucky. She goes to school out of state and she still has to fly in for those fucking dinners, so I make it a point to at least catch up with her while she's here and take her to the airport for her return flight whenever I can.

Where Kasey and Aaron's parents are damn near absent, mine take overbearing to an entirely different level.

Aaron liked the idea of Kasey moving in. He's protective of his little sister the same way I am of mine, so it should have been a done deal, except Kasey refused to get on board with the program. The pretty little idiot.

When she shot down the idea, there wasn't shit I could do about it, and Aaron wasn't willing to pressure her. Something about her being independent and responsible and yeah, compared to most females her age, maybe she is. But she's still young. Impressionable. Guys are going to take one look at her small body, perfect tits, and seductive mouth and think she's theirs for the taking.

"Why are you here?" she asks like she doesn't already know.

"I'm helping. That's what *friends* do." I put more emphasis on the word friend than necessary, but sometimes I need to remind myself that's what we're supposed to be. Friends. Not enemies.

Not rivals. She's part of our crew, which means I'm obligated to look out for her same as I would for Allie and Bibiana—Roman and Emilio's girls.

But fuck, the way she gets under my skin, sometimes it's all I can do not to spank her ass to get her to behave. Kasey Henderson is a match just waiting to be lit, and I'm the spark that gets her temper roaring. The way we verbally spar with one another, her tongue like a whip intent on tearing me down, it makes my cock jerk just thinking about how she'd be in the sack. Would she be just as wild and unrestrained? Or would she be shy and submissive?

Get your shit together, D. I fight the urge to adjust myself and force my face to remain impassive. I'm not interested. Not really. I'm just also not blind. Kasey's all grown up. Her waist dips beneath her ribs, giving her an hourglass figure that should be illegal on a seventeen-year-old girl. Her tits are full and round and her ass is more than a handful that I've definitely considered squeezing a time or two. Again, not because I'm interested.

I lock down thoughts like that as soon as they occur. Kasey Henderson is one hundred percent off limits. For one, she is too fucking young. Four years might not seem like a big deal to everyone else, but it sure as shit is when the girl in question is a minor. And for two, I don't do relationships.

Between school and football, I don't have time for one, nor am I particularly fond of having someone all up in my business. Women are needy and temperamental. If the urge arises, I'll find a girl to take home for the night, but that's all I'm interested in. One night.

Besides, I'm pretty sure Aaron would have my balls if I made a play for her. There's an unspoken rule between friends. Thou shall not fuck one another's siblings.

He and I are damn near brothers at this point. No way can I cross that line.

After graduation, the plan was for Roman, Emilio, and I to get a place off campus together. But both fuckers had to go and couple up senior year of high school, so that plan went down the drain real quick and left me with two options. Move into the dorms—not fucking likely—or get my own place off campus. But then money would be tight and I didn't want to ask my parents to cover it. Doing that would lead to trouble. Nothing given was ever given freely, and I didn't want the strings I knew would be attached.

My grandmother set up a trust fund for my sister and I that we got access to the day we turned eighteen. It's not much, but it covers my monthly expenses and would cover rent on a house off campus if I could find a roommate.

The idea of living with a stranger isn't something I could get on board with, so I buried my shit with Aaron and got a place with him since the fucker was the only other one in our crew riding solo like myself.

Since he and the girls are all close, it made sense. We weren't going to be getting rid of him anytime soon. Looking back, it was the right call, even if I didn't love the idea at the time.

Aaron's good people. He fucked up when we were all kids but since then, when any of us need him, he shows up. He's there when it counts, and he's put his ass on the line for me more times than I can count. I won't repay that by banging his sister behind his back, even if there was that one time we kissed, and it still fucking haunts me.

"You good, man?" Roman asks.

I grunt, refusing to take my eyes off the girl in front of me. "Fucking peachy."

Roman snorts and places his hand on my shoulder.

"Right. Well, while you pine over baby Henderson, I'm gonna go get my girl before Emilio tries to steal her."

"I'm not pining," I retort. I don't pine after chicks, least of all a freshman with too much sass and too little sense. What the fuck does she think she's doing right now? And where the hell is her brother. Shouldn't he be watching her or something? At the very least, he should be fending off the assholes who just want to take advantage of her. No way would I let guys be all over my sister like that.

He laughs, shaking his head. "Call it whatever you want but your jealousy is showing, man. Might want to get that in check."

I grind my teeth together, flipping off his retreating back. Rome doesn't know what he's talking about. Baby Henderson isn't anything special. A piece of ass and soon to be jailbait. Not someone I'd be jealous over.

Speaking of Hendersons, Aaron walks up beside me and hands me a Coke. I accept the drink, knowing the fucker is just being nice, and against my better judgement I ask, "You cool with older guys all over your baby sister?" I feign indifference and take a drink of the soda waiting to see how he reacts. It has nothing to do with wondering if the age difference between her and I would matter to him and everything to do with making sure he knows what's going on with Kasey right now.

As expected, Aaron follows my gaze. His eyes narrow and he mutters a curse. "Shit. I'll have to drag her away from a fucking *harem and I'll have to deal with her bitching about it the entire way home today."*

I force a laugh. "She's a handful."

He shakes his head. "That's putting it mildly. I don't know what her deal is, man. Lately, it's like she's looking for trouble." He sighs. "I better go deal with that."

I thrust a hand out to stop him. "Let me." I don't know why I made the suggestion but I don't try to walk it back once it's out there.

His dark blond brows pull together. "You sure, man?"

I nod. "Yeah. Let her be pissed at me. Then on the way home when she's bitching you can pretend to agree with what an asshole I am."

He smiles and slaps me on the back. "Thanks, man. I owe you one." I nod like it's no big deal. Just helping the guy out. I don't have a single selfish reason for making the suggestion.

Allie calls his name and Aaron turns. "Go," I tell him. "I'll get it handled."

He hesitates for a moment. "You sure, man? Kasey can be—"

I cut him off. "Bro, I've got it. Go see what Allie wants." He walks away, heading toward Roman and Allie on the other side of the yard, and without missing a beat, I head straight toward my quarry. She's got herself surrounded by some of Allie's friends from back home. I met the guys earlier, Gabe, Felix, and Julio. They seem nice enough, but that doesn't mean any of them should be talking to her right now.

When I'm within hearing distance I slow my steps, casually walking closer to the group. Gabe, who's on her right, is laying it on thick. He's smiling at her like she's all that he sees. Not happening, asshole.

As soon as I'm behind her, I pull her back into my chest and wrap my arms around her, pinning her in place with her back to my front. I ignore the way she feels pressed up against me and focus on the miscreants in front of me.

Kasey doesn't bother trying to twist to see who's grabbed her. My dark arms banded around her is telling enough. I'm the only black guy here. She doesn't have to see my face to know it's me, and being the smart girl she is, she doesn't bother putting up a fight to get away.

"You know Baby Henderson is jailbait, right?" I direct the question first to Gabe before making eye contact with the other two. Kasey stiffens in my arms and a beautiful shade of pink creeps up her neck.

"For you, maybe," Gabe retorts with a shrug.

The corner of Julio's mouth lifts into a smirk like he's in on some secret, but he doesn't say anything. He takes a drink of his soda and rocks back on his heels, watching things play out. Felix, on the other hand, gives a hard shake of his head. "Ain't no one trying to tap that," he says. "We're all friends. Just having a conversation. No one's crossing any lines."

Gabe snorts. "Speak for yourself," he tells him, and then looks Kasey right in the eyes. "I have no problem saying I am very much interested." He licks his lips and gives her a heated look that makes me want to punch the fucker in the face. "Wanna blow this place? Go have some fun?"

I can't see her expression, but if I had to guess she's probably eating this shit up, if only to irritate me more. "Why not?"

"She's fourteen," I grind out.

"I'm seventeen. Age is just a number, man." He shrugs.

Kasey squirms in my arms in an attempt to get away, but I shift her around, putting her firmly behind me before stepping up and getting in Gabe's face. "She's too young for you, so knock that shit off. No guy here is going to let you put the moves on Henderson's little sister."

Despite having to look up to meet my stare, Gabe doesn't back down. "Did it sound like I was asking for permission?"

Before I do anything that will land me on Allie's shit list, like beating her friend to a pulp, I turn on my heel and grab Kasey by the arm, pulling her with me as I go.

"Dominique, let go of me," she complains, but her steps follow. A glance over my shoulder shows Julio with a hand against Gabe's chest while he mutters something in his ear. Whatever it is, it keeps him in place and that's good enough for me.

I drag Kasey around the side of the house where no one can see us and press her up against the brick exterior, my arms caging her in on either side and offering her zero chance of escape.

Does she look worried? Not one fucking bit. The girl looks pissed and ready to raise hell.

"What is your problem! You had no right—" she snarls, shoving against my chest, but it's like a kitten swatting at a bull. I barely feel it. "You can't manhandle me like that. You are not my keeper. And you do not get to dictate who I hang out with."

"I have every right," I grind out the words and her eyes widen. Shit. I didn't mean for that to come out. The girl gets in my head. Under my skin. She is so goddamn infuriating.

"What is it exactly that gives you the—"

No answer is a good answer, so instead, I close the distance between us and capture her lips with my own to shut her up. At least that's what I tell myself. She jumps, but I don't let that deter me. I step forward into her space, pressing my mouth more firmly against her own and deepening the kiss while grabbing her beneath her thighs and lifting her into my arms. Her legs wrap around my waist instinctively and I press her back against the house. A small moan passes across her lips and I want to hear it again, so I press my hardening cock against her jean-clad center and grind my hips against hers.

She gasps, tearing her mouth away and sucking in a lungful of air. I nip at her full lips and trail kisses down her jawline. Her neck. All while thrusting my hips against her, letting her feel how badly I want her right now.

"What are you doing?" she asks with jagged breath.

I don't answer. Instead, I capture her lips again and drink down her soft sighs and sweet moans. If I were being honest with her, I'd say I had no fucking clue what I was doing, but as soon as I open my mouth to speak, all of this stops and I'm not ready for that to happen just yet.

I shake out the memories from that day and focus back on the here and now.

"We're not friends," Kasey retorts, arms folded across her chest and mouth pressed into a tight line.

I shrug like her words don't affect me.

"We're not even friendly," she adds.

She's not wrong. Since that kiss, shit between us has gone from bad to worse. Kasey and I are like cats and dogs, or oil and water. We don't mix. When we do, things get heated and not in a good way. It's my fault for the way things are between us, and I'm man enough to own that, but when I pressed my mouth against hers and swallowed her soft cries of pleasure I knew right away it was a mistake.

"I'm friends with him." I nod in Aaron's direction. "And I'd be a shit friend if I didn't at least offer to help the guy out. We both know he'll do most of the heavy lifting while you and your mom talk with whoever it is running this show."

Her jaw works and I can tell she's barely keeping herself in check. I love it when she gets like this. All fire and brimstone, ready to raise hell to get what she wants. But before she can say anything else, her mom tugs on her arm. "Kasey, leave the poor boy alone. He's only trying to help. Besides, there are so many things I want to show you before I have to leave." She tugs on her daughter's arm, who reluctantly follows, throwing one last look my way before admitting defeat.

I give her a small wave and her eyes narrow even further. She'll come up with a way to get me back.

I'm looking forward to it.

EIGHTY-ONE

Kasey

I hate him. I hate him. I hate him. I repeat the mantra a dozen times in my head until I convince myself it's the truth. Why does he have to be so infuriating all of the time?

Mom doesn't give me long to dwell on it before she marches me right through the front doors and to the left down a long hallway. We pass a living room, dining room, and kitchen before coming to the open door of an office with a small gold placard that reads, "House Mother."

"Knock, knock," my mother calls before stepping inside, pulling me right along with her.

An attractive brunette looks up and greets us, a wide smile on her face. "You must be Mrs. Henderson?" she says, coming around her desk and shaking mom's hand.

"Ms. Douglas, actually. Kasey's father and I divorced years ago." She throws this out with a laugh like it's no big deal, but I know mom hates it. Dad forced her to change her name after the divorce. Said she didn't deserve it and the perks that came with being a

Henderson. He's an asshole and whatever perks come with my name I'm still waiting on to be delivered, but he's also my dad, so I'm duty bound to love him. Even when he's absent and downright cruel where mom is concerned. "But please, call me Helen."

"Nice to meet you, Helen. I'm Hilary, the Kappa Mu president," she says this with a sugary sweet smile so wide her cheeks are bound to crack. She's not much older than I am. Twenty-one or twenty-two if I had to guess. "And you must be Kasey, our newest legacy. We are so excited to have you."

I'll bet she is. She might be fooling Mom but the fake smile and high-pitched laugh is not fooling me.

"Thanks," I tell her, accepting her offered hand with a fake smile of my own.

"Hills, we're out of—" a girl says behind us but cuts herself off when she sees Hilary isn't alone. "Oh. My bad. I didn't realize you were meeting with parents today," the girl adds almost sheepishly.

I spot the empty liquor bottles in both her hands and know right away what they've recently run out of. I chance a look at my mom and wonder if she'll call the whole thing off with the obvious drinking and partying going on right now despite it only being a little after 10am on a Sunday. But instead of worry or apprehension on her face, her smile is wide, her eyes glazed over, as though she's reliving fond memories before she lets out a little laugh.

"Please, don't worry about me. You girls do what you need to. Are you over twenty-one?" Mom asks her.

"Oh, umm, I ..." She turns to Hilary with wide eyes and a *help me* expression.

Mom laughs again. "Why don't I do you girls a favor and make a quick trip to the store while you guys show my baby girl around. That looks like," she tilts her head for a better look at the bottles the newcomer is clearly trying and failing to hide, "Malibu rum, Sky Vodka, and ... is that Blue Curacao?"

The girl nods but keeps her lips sealed.

"Perfect. I'll be back in a jiff."

Mom brushes a kiss across my temple and then slips past the girl and leaves me standing alone with two very surprised college girls.

"Did your mom just—"

"Offer to go buy you booze after you very obviously failed to confirm that you're legally old enough to drink? Yes. Yes, she did."

"Wicked. Your mom is so cool."

I sigh and force myself to smile. That's Mom. Always one to be your friend rather than your parent. "Yeah. She's pretty chill. I'm Kasey by the way."

"Quinn," the girl says. "Nice to meet you."

"Let's show you around and go over the house rules while we wait for your mom to get back," Hilary interjects. "Quinn, why don't you go make sure the other pledges don't need any assistance."

Quinn nods and leaves to do what Hilary asked, and when I turn to face her, her smile is gone and an annoyed expression rests in its place. "Look," she begins. "I'm going to be honest. I wasn't thrilled when I was told we'd be admitting a new pledge. You skipped our entire application process, didn't show up for a single interview, and didn't have to jump through any of the hoops every other girl who was accepted had to."

I keep my expression blank. Is she wanting me to apologize for something I played zero part in and had no control over? It's not like I asked for this.

She sighs. "But, you're a legacy and our house takes that seriously. It also doesn't hurt that your dad made a donation to Kappa Mu in your name." Huh, look at that. Good ole Dad helping us out. I try not to roll my eyes. He was probably worried I'd ask to live with him full time what with mom leaving. Not that I ever would. I love my dad, but where Mom parents by trying to be my friend, Dad parents with assistants and nannies, forgetting I'm seventeen, not seven.

"So, we're going to make this work." She sounds resigned. Join the club. "We don't want to start getting a flood of running-start applicants. Hanging out with high schoolers isn't really our thing. We also don't want any trouble with the dean's office for exposing you to anything you're not ready for, so for now, keep your age to yourself."

"I can do that," I tell her. It's not like I was planning on letting everyone know how young I was. I'm not an idiot.

"Good. Glad that's out of the way. Like the plaque outside the door says, I'm the housemother, but I'm not going to be your mom while you're here. If you're upset or homesick, phone a friend. I'm not your shoulder to cry on."

"Noted."

"And I'm not your babysitter. The girls here like to have a bit of fun and we're close with some of the campus fraternities. You're responsible for looking after yourself. If you can't handle your liquor, don't drink. And if you do drink, don't be stupid and drive yourself home. Got it?"

I give her two thumbs up. "Anything else?"

"Don't cut classes. Part of eligibility requirements for being a member is maintaining a 3.0 GPA. If you fail any of your classes, you're out. Legacy or not."

"Good to know."

She reaches behind her and grabs an envelope from her desk before handing it to me. "Inside is a map of campus, our events schedule, and your school ID. You're required to attend all Kappa Mu functions so add these dates to your calendar. We don't make exceptions."

I tuck the envelope in the back pocket of my jeans. "Okay." Not like I have a packed social calendar or anything. I hang out with Allie and Bibiana on most weekends but we don't generally plan anything official. It's usually just junk food and movies while the guys lock themselves in the media room to watch videos of past football games. If I have a sorority thing, no one will care if I need to skip a night.

"Your room is on the first floor toward the back of the house. It's just you and Quinn, the girl you just met, on this level. Everyone else is upstairs. There's a back entrance near your room you can use if you need to and additional parking out back if you have a car." I nod. My dad bought me a WRX like Aaron's, only mine is candy apple red, as a 'congrats you're going to college' gift, so that will be convenient. He's supposed to have his driver deliver it sometime this week, so I'll have to let him know they can bring it straight here. It'll save me from needing a campus parking pass since I really only plan on driving when I need to go off campus. I walk everywhere else.

"If you have questions, check with Quinn first. All of our new recruits are assigned a big sister. She's yours."

I nod. "Okay. Cool." Do I leave now? I'm not sure what protocol is here exactly. Should I wait to be excused?

"That's it," Hilary confirms with a huff.

"Great. Thanks." I make a hasty retreat and wander around downstairs, ducking around the other girls in the house until I find a long hallway that leads to the back. I figure I'll get to know everyone later. Right now I just want to track down my room and unpack.

The first door I find is decorated with pictures and drawings. I make a wild guess that it's Quinn's since it's her face in most of the pictures. Further down the hall are two more doors. One at the very end, which I confirm is the door that leads outside. I open it to find a small patch of grass and a concrete slab for parking on my right that leads to the main road.

I close that door and turn to the last one which I'm assuming is mine. I find Aaron lounging on my bed, phone in hand, and take in the rest of the space. It's a decent size. Double closet. I scan the room for Dominique, noting the pile of neatly stacked boxes next to the bed, half expecting him to burst from behind them just to fuck with me. "Where's Dom?" I ask when it's clear my brother isn't going to volunteer the information, too distracted by whoever he's texting with on his phone.

"Coach called. The guys had to leave for some team thing."

Relief sweeps through me and my shoulders sag. I plop down on the bed beside my brother. "I see you found my room?"

He nods, setting his phone aside. "Yeah, one of the girls told us which one was yours so we moved all your stuff in for you."

"Roman and Emilio didn't wait in the car, did they?"

He gives me a crooked grin. "Nope."

"Urgh," I groan, hiding my face with my hands. "Did anyone recognize them?"

Aaron chuckles. "Relax, sis. All they saw were some stacked guys moving boxes. No one asked if they were on the team, though Emilio definitely got his fair share of phone numbers."

I scowl. "He better have thrown them away." Emilio is a notorious flirt, but also absolutely obsessed with Bibi, his girlfriend and the mother of his child. They're doing really good, but I know Bibiana sometimes has a hard time with all the attention Emilio receives. And being a football player doesn't help. I swear all of the guys have their own personal fan clubs.

Aaron leans forward and tugs open the drawer of a nearby nightstand. Five small pieces of paper with girly handwriting in various colors greet me. "Nah, he left them for you so you could make friends. His words, not mine."

I don't bother fighting the smile that spreads over my face. That sounds like Emilio, alright.

Aaron leaves a few minutes later with the promise to help me find my classes on Monday when school starts. "Call me if you need me," he tells me on his way out, giving me a quick hug.

"I will," I promise, and then settle in and unpack my things. The room is a blank canvas. White walls, hardwood floors, and a single window that gives me a glimpse of where my car will soon be parked. There's a queen bed, a single nightstand, and a tall dresser, but nothing else aside from my boxes of belongings. I unpack my clothes first, hanging up what needs to be hung and folding everything else to add to the dresser drawers.

Mom shows up later that afternoon, her arms loaded down with shopping bags and a wide smile on her face.

"What is all that?" I ask, eyeing the pops of pink and gold peeking out the tops of the bags. I'm not a tomboy, but I'm not really a girly girl either. I played basketball throughout high school so I generally go for comfort over style. I haven't decided if I'll play this year. Coach said I could keep my spot, but a part of me would rather move beyond all things high school. I have no intention of playing in college, so stopping now wouldn't really make much difference.

"Pottery Barn was next to the grocery store so I thought I'd pick up a few things you might need. Wait until you see the comforter set I got you," she gushes, pulling out a white down comforter decorated with small pink tassels around the edge.

"Pretty," I deadpan. I'm not sure what the purpose of the tassels is but it could have been worse.

"I know, right? I wanted to make sure you were all set. I can't believe my little girl is all grown up and going to college. I know this is a big step, but I want you to know I am so proud of you."

"Thanks, Mom."

She beams. "Let's get you settled. I only have an hour before I need to get on the road, but that's plenty of time for us to turn this room into your home for the next four years."

I groan. Four years. She really expects me to be a sorority girl for all four years of college?

Her eyes soften. "I know being a Kappa Mu might not seem exciting to you right now, but honey, I made some of my very best friends in this very house when I went to college. Twenty-five years later and I'm still close with them. Sorority sisters look out for each other and you're going to meet some of the best people here. Try to be open-minded."

I sigh. "I'll try."

"Now, let's get this room situated."

EIGHTY-TWO

Dominique

R oman takes off down the field and I step back with my left foot, keeping my feet staggered as I bend slightly at the knees. I raise my left arm over my shoulder, bringing the football behind my head before snapping it forward, focusing on rolling my left shoulder as I do. *Fuck.* It takes all my concentration to get the ball pointed where I need it to go.

The ball whistles through the air, heading straight for Roman, but as soon as he turns to spot the football, I realize my mistake and curse. *Too short.*

"Dammit." I kick the turf and tear off my helmet, frustration coursing through me.

Roman jerks to a stop before lunging forward to salvage the throw. He manages to catch the ball with both hands, tucking it against his chest before rolling to the ground. His momentum throws him into a complete rotation before he springs up to his feet, a bounce in his step over the save. "Fuck, yeah!" he hollers, and jogs back toward me, ball in hand.

"Not bad, man." He throws the football at me and I catch it, fingers gripping the laces.

"That was a shit throw and you know it."

He offers a noncommittal shrug. "Progress at least. And did you see that save? Perfección."

"English asshole. I'm black. Not brown like you."

He smirks. "Perfection."

True enough, and with Roman as my receiver, we have a shot at pulling this off, but it won't matter if I can't get my left arm to go the distance.

Coach called me in for an emergency meeting. I dropped E off on the way but Roman decided to tag along. Nosy bastard. The team doctor took it upon himself to inform our coach of a recent injury. Fucking snitch. If I wanted Coach to know about my shoulder, I would have told him myself.

"You could always sit this next one out," Rome offers, but I shake my head.

"You know I can't." Our second string quarterback—Deacon Hunt—is a freshman without any experience playing at this level. The guy is green. He came from a small school in the middle of nowhere and while he has a great arm, he buckles under pressure. Under normal circumstances, I wouldn't care. The point of bringing him on board is to train with him, get him where he needs to be so that by the time I graduate next year, he's ready and can lead the team. He's got potential and he needs the field time if he's going to grow, but next week we have scouts coming and they're expecting me to play.

If word gets out I'm injured and won't be on the field, there's a chance some of the scouts, maybe all, won't show. I could care less if anyone sees me play, but the other guys on the team, they need as many opportunities as they can get to shine so they have a shot at going pro. I won't be the reason they lose that.

"Let's go again," I tell Roman and he nods, getting into position, but before he starts, a voice from the sidelines draws our attention.

"Price!" Coach yells. "What the hell do you think you're doing?"

I grind my teeth together and wait as he stalks across the field like a bull. Barely six feet and thick around the middle, it's been a hot minute since the man was in his prime, but he still has no problem going toe to toe with any one of us. When he's within earshot without me needing to yell, I tell him, "Practicing, Coach."

"Practicing what, exactly? I gave you explicit orders to rest and—"

"I'm not throwing with my right," I tell him. "I'm using my left. I'll be good in time for next week's game." I have to be.

His brows pull together and I know he wants to fight me on it, but he's aware of the situation we're in just as much as I am.

"Repetitive motion tendonitis is no joke, son. If you don't take care of that arm, you can end your career before it ever starts."

"And if I don't play in next week's game, the guys on my team may find themselves in the same boat."

He takes off his red Suncrest U baseball cap and shakes his head. "They're not your responsibility. There will be more scouts, more opportunities—"

"For Davis and Elliot?" I ask, cutting him off. "They're seniors. They won't have many more chances like this." I know it. He knows it. Hell, even the guys know it, which is why so much is riding on this game. Elliot's a defensive tackle and Davis is a defensive end and they're both good. Better than good. But that won't matter if no one sees them play. They transferred in as seniors from smaller schools hoping to get some face time with scouts, but they're no-name players. Scouts aren't coming to watch them because they've never heard of them. Their best shot is to kill it on the field and have one of the already scheduled scouts recognize their potential and invite them to the NFL Scouting Combine.

Coach mutters under his breath before rubbing his jaw. "How's your right arm feel when you throw with your left?"

It twinges a bit, but I'm not telling him that. "No pain. It's all good."

He considers me for a moment. "What's your range?"

"So far, fifty-two yards," Roman answers for me.

Coach works his jaw. "How long have you been practicing?"

"Since we got out." If I had to guess, that was maybe an hour ago.

He nods to himself. "Alright. We'll try it your way. I want you out of training and practice for the next three days to rest."

I open my mouth to argue. No way can I take three days off if I'm going to get where we need me to be. We're playing Rydeville U. They're a solid team, and while I've always forced myself to throw with both arms, I'm right handed. Throwing consistently with my left isn't a cakewalk for me. I need the practice. "Coach—"

"Three days!" He waves three fingers in my face as if I need a visual. "After that, you throw and you do cardio. That's it. No weights and nothing that can strain your right shoulder. You practice with your left arm and only your left arm. I catch you so much as tossing a towel with your right and I'll bench you. Understood?"

I grit my teeth but nod. I know a losing battle when I see one. Coach is an alright guy. He puts the players' health and well-being first so I have no doubt he'll bench me, even if it means we lose next week's game.

"Good. If this is day one for you and you're already at fifty-two yards, you're ahead of Hunt. We'll make this work. But, if you have a bad performance next week, you might screw your own chances of being drafted early and some of these guys might even decide to look you over next year when the time comes. You prepared to take that risk?"

I nod. Football after college isn't in the cards for me. No matter how bad I may want it. My parents would never stand for it, and despite what some might believe, my parents do in fact have both the money and the means to ensure I go down the path they've carved out for me. This isn't one of those scenarios where I can call their bluff.

Sheridan Peretti Price and Richard Price have enough clout that they've landed themselves on the Business Insiders top ten most influential businesses in the United States six years running. As the founders of Peretti and Price, a multi-billion dollar tech company, they rub elbows with everyone from CEOs to celebrities and grossed over one hundred and eighty-two billion dollars last year alone. Yes, billion. Not million.

The amount of money my parents would need to throw around to ensure no team picked me up is barely a drop in the bucket to them. So no, I'm not worried about fucking up my own chance. I never had a real one to begin with. "It's worth the risk, Coach."

"Have it your way. Now get your asses home and rest. Valdez, keep an eye on him, and if I get wind that you or Chavez are on the field with him these next three days, I'll make you both run so many drills you'll be begging to be benched, do I make myself clear?"

Rome nods. "Crystal."

"Good. Get out of here."

Coach stalks off the field toward the locker room and we head the opposite direction toward the parking lot. "You good, man?" Roman asks once we reach our vehicles.

I nod. "I'm good."

He hesitates, which isn't like him, so I spit out, "What?" only to see him frown.

"What was up this morning?"

"What do you mean?" I open my door and lean against the frame. I have a feeling I know where this is going and I don't like it.

"With Baby Henderson. If she'd asked us to help her move in, we would have. The girl's one of us but ..." he trails off and shakes his head, running a hand through his sweat-drenched hair.

"You're reading too much into it," I tell him, hoping he drops it.

He doesn't. "Nah. I don't think I am. Where's your head at these days? I know you had a thing for her back in high school, but—"

I cut him off before he has a chance to finish. "It's not like that. She's Aaron's little sister."

Roman snorts. "Which meant fuck all when we were in high school and you gawked at her ass every time she walked by."

"Like I said, you're reading too much into it. That was three years ago. Things change."

"Exactly. Have you seen her lately? Kasey's is all grown up and she's filled out in all the right places. Don't pretend you haven't noticed."

I lift a single brow. "Allie know you've been checking Kasey out?"

He chuckles. "No cabrón, because I'm not. But I'm not blind and neither are you. The girl has grown up. A lot. Tension with you two has always been thick, but lately ..." He trails off, giving me a knowing look.

I shake my head. "Nah, man. Things between us are not like that. I can barely stand the girl so, no, I don't fucking like her. Not the way you're suggesting. Whatever you're picking up on is just our usual shit. We get under each other's skin. That's all." I might have the occasional fantasy about fucking her to see if it would make her more tolerable, but I don't let my dick dictate my decisions.

"I was just helping Aaron out. You and E didn't have to come," I add, needing to end this conversation before he gets any ideas.

He gives me an incredulous look. "Really? That's the bullshit you're gonna try and feed me right now?"

"Drop it, man. I'm telling you, I'm not interested. Sue me. I get a kick out of riling the girl up. I saw an opportunity and I took it. That doesn't mean I want her." Though I wouldn't mind her on her knees for me, mouth open and—*Fuck. Drop that line of thinking before you get your ass in trouble.*

Roman levels me with an incredulous look. "I'm one of your best friends, cabrón. I'm not buying what you're selling. I know you better than that."

I let out a tired breath. "Ro, she's just a kid, not even eighteen yet. And you know how I am with females. You really think I'm gonna fuck myself over by trying to get a piece of her?" I shake my head. "I'm not that dumb. Allie, Bibiana, and Monique would all have my ass if I fucked things up with Kasey."

"So don't fuck it up, then. Give shit a real try. bro. You two have been going at it since senior year. You know there's something there. Everyone else can see it. Why can't you?"

"Because there isn't anything to see."

His stare is penetrating as I wait for him to concede the point.

"Is this because of Aaron?" he asks. "You know he'd come around."

"No, fucker. This is because of me. What part of 'I'm not interested' do you not understand?" He opens his mouth to argue but I cut him off. "I don't want hearts and rainbows with any female, let alone Kasey-fucking-Henderson, okay? You're wifed up and I'm happy for you, man. For E too. But I'm only interested in a tight piece of ass and a hot lay and Kasey isn't who I plan on getting that from." I make my words especially crude, hoping he gets the point. "So stop pushing. If shit changes and I decide to fuck her, I'll make sure you're the first to know."

His face hardens, and I can see the second we go from conversation mode to lecture mode. "Don't even think of going there," he warns.

"I'm not," I grind out. "You're the one suggesting—"

The lines around his mouth tighten. "If I have to kick your ass because you—"

I bark out a laugh. "Go home to your woman. Kasey's made it her mission to get under my skin. All I'm doing is returning the favor. Stop reading into nothing. We're good."

He doesn't look entirely convinced, but finally nods. "Fine. You going back to Kappa Mu?"

I should, but if I go back now, it'll give Roman the wrong idea. "Nah. I'm heading home. Gotta ice my shoulder and shit. I'll catch you later."

"Later, cabrón."

I flip off my best friend as I climb into my Escalade, put it in reverse and head for home. I pass by Greek Row and tighten my grip on the wheel until I make it to my street, three short blocks from where Kasey is living now.

Fuck. I need to get my head on straight. I'm not commitment material, and there are too many obstacles in the way, so why is it that the idea of getting past them all makes my dick twitch and brings a smile to my face?

EIGHTY-THREE

Kasey

"**M**om, I have to go."

"Oh, and did I tell you about the time when I was in college and—" She rattles on as though she doesn't hear me.

"Mom," I try again, shifting my bag to my other arm to avoid dropping my phone. "I'm late for class. I'll call you later. Okay?"

"Oh. Just one more thing—"

I grind my teeth together. "Mom!"

"Oh, alright. But before you hang up, can you at least tell me if you're making friends? I worry about you, sweetie." Obviously not enough since you decided to move halfway across the country.

I sigh. She means well and at least she's checking up on me. "Lots of friends. All the friends. Have to go now. Love you. Bye."

"Love yo—"

I hang up and all but run to my last class of the day, my sneakers squeaking as I race down the hallway. My phone buzzes in my hand but I send Mom to voicemail. I've talked to her three times already, and she just left for Florida yesterday. I think she's bored. It's a long drive and she still has probably a day and a half before she'll get there, assuming she doesn't stop to shop along the way.

I chance a look at the clock on my screen. *Shit.* I'm going to be late. I'm almost to the door when another figure turns the corner on my right and crashes into me.

I drop my bag and my books tumble out onto the floor. My body sways with my momentum, but the stranger reaches out, grabbing me with an iron grip before I land face first on the linoleum. "Ow. Crap."

"Watch where you're going," the guy snaps.

Asshole. I jerk my arm free and ignore him, not bothering to look up. This is just my luck. I drop to the floor to grab my things, conscious of the time as I rush to put everything back in my bag. I'm so screwed. It's only the second day of school and I'm going to be late to my english class for the second day in a row.

His feet edge closer. Black Beast Mode sneakers come into my line of vision, making me think of the red ones Dominique wears. *Urgh, and now I'm thinking about Dominique.*

The guy crouches down and retrieves my last book before handing it to me. "Sorry. I didn't mean to snap at you. You just came out of nowhere. I'm late to my English class and my professor is known to be a real hardass. I didn't mean to take you out like that."

I accept the book, rising to my feet and finally look up at the stranger beside me. Honey-colored eyes framed with dark brows meet mine. I suck in a breath, my heart skipping a beat. I'm taken aback by my response to him, but the longer I stare makes me realize I'm not that surprised.

He's gorgeous in a devastating way. Medium brown skin, full lips. I wouldn't say he's light skinned, but he's not as dark as Dominique. He's wearing slim-fitting jeans that are torn in the knees and a long white crew shirt that molds to his body. Add to that the black sneakers and a black ball cap turned backwards and he's stunning. I'm not sure how else to describe him.

Most of the skin I can see on him is covered in ink. Two forearm sleeves disappear beneath the long sleeves of his shirt that he's pushed up to his elbows, and he has a cross tattoo on the left side of his neck. A scroll design filled with script on his right.

But despite looking like Kelly Oubre Jr's doppelganger, there's something about the way he's studying me that sets me on edge.

"It's fine. Sorry for slamming into you," I say.

The corners of his mouth curl into a calculated smirk. He licks his lips and rubs his palms together, almost like a prayer. "Nothing to be sorry about." His eyes roam over me, sliding down from my face, lingering on my chest, and then returning to my face again.

"Alrighty then." I move to step around him but he mirrors my steps, effectively blocking me.

What is he doing?

"You have Fisks for English 101, right? I saw you in the back the other day." His eyes rake me over in appreciation once again. He's not even trying to hide his interest.

Normally, I'd be flattered, but right now I just want to get to class.

"Um. Yeah." I tuck a piece of hair behind my ear and try to ignore the way my stomach clenches. "So you know, gotta run."

I try to go around him again but his hand shoots out, gripping my forearm. "Hold up," his voice pitches low and his eyes lock onto mine.

Mine widen, a flash of trepidation slamming into me before I shove it aside. I don't know who this guy thinks he is, but he can't just grab me. I tug on my arm, but unlike the first time, he doesn't release me. His fingers flex, his grip tightening as his penetrating stare bores into me. Something dark and dangerous seeps into his expression and tension bleeds into the air.

I swallow hard. My gaze darts around us, taking in the empty hallway. Classes started almost over five minutes ago, so it's just the two of us in the halls.

He must pick up on my anxiety because all of a sudden the dark look on his face is gone, replaced with an easy carefree grin. "Safety in numbers, right? Come on." Not giving me a chance to respond he gives me a conspiratorial wink and pulls me the rest of the way to our class, his hand wrapped around me though they've slipped down, his fingers encircling my wrist.

The door to our class is already closed but he quietly inches it open and peers inside.

"How's it look?" I ask, trying to dispel some of the tension still thick between us. I attempt to peer over his shoulder, but he's nearly a foot taller than me so I can't see much.

He turns to look at me, giving me another smile, and I realize he's young. Probably a freshman like me since we're in the same English class. He still has some softness to his face, though that looks like the only place you would find any. His shoulders are broad, his waist narrow and his arms are corded with muscle. Between the body, the arrogance, and the shoes, I'm betting he's an athlete, and since Beast Mode Gear is owned by a former NFL player, I'll assume he's on the football team.

"Come on," he whispers, tugging me through the door with him. He adjusts his hold again, this time capturing my hand with his. I stare at our laced fingers with a frown, but allow him to lead me inside so as not to disturb the class.

Fisks is at the whiteboard, his back to us as he writes today's assignment on the board. We get a few interested looks from other students as we make our way to the empty seats in the back, my hand still locked in his as he raises his finger to his lips, the universal sign to be quiet. A few students nod and grin before turning their attention back to the front of the class.

Once safely in our seats, he releases me and I expel a relieved breath right as our professor turns around to face the class. His gaze lands on me and he frowns but doesn't comment, continuing with his lecture.

"That was a close one," the guy who crashed into me says.

I bite my bottom lip and nod. Pulling out my notebook so I can take notes on today's lecture, I do my best to block out our strange encounter, hoping that's the end of it.

"I'm Deacon," he whispers, eyes straight ahead as though paying attention to Mr. Fisks.

I don't bother to respond. But after a minute passes, he asks, "What's your name?"

I consider refusing to answer, but what would be the point? It wouldn't be hard to figure out if he really wanted to.

"Kasey," I whisper under my breath.

"Nice to—"

"Mr. Hunt."

Deacon tilts his head to our professor, adopting a bored expression. "Yeah?"

"Is there something you'd like to share with the class?" Mr. Fisks asks, and there's a warning in his voice.

"Nah, I'm good," Deacon answers, unconcerned.

"Then I suggest you pay attention to today's lesson. We'll have an exam this Friday." He turns away, droning on about what will be covered on the exam and this week's assigned reading, but I'm not really paying attention. I glance at Deacon through my peripheral, only to catch his eyes on mine.

He reaches into his backpack and retrieves a notebook of his own. His large dark hands make it impossible for me to see what he's writing, but I know it's not anything class related.

He tugs on the page, tearing it out before neatly folding it in half and sliding it onto my desk with an arrogant smirk.

I purse my lips and give him a questioning look. One he returns with a wink. Rolling my eyes, I reach for the note and carefully unfold it so as not to draw Mr. Fisk's attention again.

A laugh bubbles up in my throat and I cover it with a cough when I see what the note says.

He wrote, **Will you go out with me?** on the page in tight neat letters, much neater than I would have expected from a guy, with three check boxes beneath the question labeled, **Yes. No.** And **Maybe.**

My shoulders shake as I struggle to contain a snicker. This guy, is he for real? What are we, five?

I reach for my pen and check the No box before adding a thank you beside it and discreetly passing it back to him.

He opens the note and scowls, his expression a split between genuine surprise and confusion, before he writes something else, his strokes almost aggressive before he folds in the paper in half and passes it back.

Why not?

I chew on my bottom lip. Because you manhandled me. Because there is something about you that screams danger: proceed with caution. And even if none of those things were true, he probably plays football for Suncrest U, which adds two more strikes against him. The first because he's most likely a total player, and the second because that makes him teammates with Roman, Emilio, and Dominique and yeah, that is just a disaster waiting to happen. Aaron's my big brother, but those three can take overprotective to the extreme.

Somehow writing any of that down seems like a bad idea, so instead I write, **I don't know you. What if you're a crazy stalker?**

I pass the note back to him and he makes quick work of his response.

No stalker tendencies present. I'm a nice guy. Promise. I give him a dubious look and he raises his little finger in the universal gesture for a pinkie swear.

"I'm not sure I believe you," I whisper while making sure our teacher isn't looking my way.

His brows pull together. "That I'm a nice guy or that I'm not a stalker?"

I shrug. I mean, really, it could go either way.

He huffs out a breath and snatches the paper off my desk, writing furiously before handing it back, but instead of slipping it on my desk he holds it out between us, his entire attention on me as he waits for me to take it.

A few of our classmates are giving us interested looks, but I ignore them and focus on the boy beside me. He raises his brows and waves the paper in his hand.

Urgh, fine. I hold my hand out and he slowly places it in the palm of my hand, his fingers trailing across my skin before he withdraws. I shiver.

Give me a chance. I can see I made a shitty first impression. Let me fix that.

I fight back an eye roll before scribbling across the paper and handing it back.

What sort of date? I ask.

The corner of his mouth quirks. **Pizza and a movie at my place?** he answers.

Pass. I just met the guy and he expects me to go back to his place with him on the first date? Do I have booty call stamped on my forehead somewhere or something?

Netflix and chill? Not really my thing. I write and toss the note back to him. We're running out of space to write so hopefully this will end soon because his date suggestion only confirms that he is a total player who wants an easy lay. *Sorry, buddy. That isn't* *me*. Then again, what did I expect? He probably has his own personal fan club of jersey chasers who are happy to throw their panties at him.

The note lands on my desk again. **Not what I meant. I figured we could do something low key. Get to know each other.** When he puts it like that, it doesn't sound *so bad*, but it's still bad and I'm not naive enough to fall for it.

Dominique's face flashes through my mind. His lips pressed into a disapproving frown, a silent warning that I better fucking not. My stomach flip flops which only serves to annoy me more. I shake the image of him from my head. *What the hell is wrong with me? I shouldn't care whether or not Dominique would approve. Actually, I don't care. Not one bit.* This is just a side effect of sleep deprivation. I barely slept last night. Whoever is in the room over mine decided to have company over, and let's just say they stayed up into the wee morning hours doing some extracurricular activities, and had zero problem letting the entire house know about it. Yeah, that's all it is. I just need to catch up on sleep.

I give Deacon another look through my peripheral. He gives me a small smile and a tilt of his head as if to say *please*.

I'm not really looking to get into a relationship. I write, and return the paper to him, somewhat frustrated at my unwillingness to give the guy a shot. I know Dominique is factoring into that decision, even if he isn't the only reason, and I hate it. Hate that he has this invisible pull over me when I know nothing will ever happen between us, and that's a good thing. We can hardly stand one another.

Deacon's mouth dips down as he writes out his response.

Not asking for your hand in marriage or to be your boyfriend. Just a chance to get to know you. Maybe be friends?

Friends wouldn't be a horrible idea, but ... I mentally shake myself. I might regret this, but I refuse to let Dominique's imaginary disapproval decide for me. **Okay. Friends.**

His smile grows when he sees my answer. **Any suggestions for our first friend date?**

Not a date. But how about coffee?

Got it. What's your number?

We exchange phone numbers and I discreetly enter his into my phone, praying this isn't a mistake when the teacher draws everyone's attention.

"That'll be all for today. Finish your reading for the week and do not forget about Friday's exam. This will count for twenty percent of your grade, so it would behoove you not to slack off. It will be difficult to catch up should you fail and there will not be retakes so don't think emailing me you're sick the night before will buy you any extra time to study. It won't."

A collective groan rolls through the class as everyone shuffles to their feet. "So," Deacon rubs the back of his neck. "What class do you have next?"

"Health," I tell him as we both walk out the door. His hand brushes against mine and I instinctively bring it to my chest. He doesn't notice my reaction.

"Cool. I'll walk with you. I'm going the same way."

"Sure." I mean, it is a free country. I can't very well tell him, no.

We spend the next ten minutes talking about nothing and everything, and my initial apprehension begins to wane. Deacon is ... charismatic. He's animated when he talks, using his hands, and his face is so expressive. He's one hundred percent as arrogant as I initially pegged him to be but, I don't know, he's not an asshole about it, despite what happened in the hallway, and he doesn't grab me again.

I find myself laughing more than I'm used to after meeting someone new. There's just something about talking to him that is, I don't know, easy. He reminds me a lot of Emilio in that way.

I discover Deacon is in fact on the football team. No surprise there. He's second string seeing as he's an incoming freshman, and he's a QB so he's gunning for Dominique's spot.

He's confident and definitely a little cocky that he'll get it by the end of the year, but I know that won't happen. Not before Dominique graduates at least, so Deacon will have to wait until his junior year to start.

A part of me wonders if the two of them are friends, or friendly at least, since Dominique would be the one responsible for working with him. None of the guys are particularly social unless they have to be, Dominique less so than even Roman, and that's saying something.

In high school, the guys actively avoided everyone not in their close-knit circle, including their fellow teammates, and were called Devils for a reason that had nothing to do with the school mascot and everything to do with the hell they rained down on anyone dumb enough to bother them.

I can't imagine things are any different here. It's unlikely Dominique would bother getting to know a second-string player off the field, but during training and practices, he might be less of an asshole. Maybe. Okay, probably not, but a part of me is tempted to ask Deacon how well he knows Dominique. I try not to dwell on why I want to know that, though.

We reach the school's athletic center and I turn to wave goodbye.

"See you around, Deacon," I tell him, but before I can move for the doors, he clasps my hand with his and tugs just enough to stop me.

"Okay, can you not do that?" I ask.

He drops my hand immediately, lifting his own in a show of surrender. "My bad. I just ..." He adopts a sheepish expression. "I wanted you to know, I'm glad we ran into each other today. Literally and figuratively." He drops his hands and a slow smile spreads across his face."You're not like other girls, Kasey. It's refreshing."

Oh.

"Thanks. I, uh, I'm glad we ran into each other too."

"Yeah?" he asks.

I roll my eyes. "Yeah. You're not that bad, but don't let it go to your head. I've only agreed to coffee," I remind him, and the next thing I know, he closes the distance between us, reclaiming my hand anyway as he brings it to his mouth, gently pressing his lips to my knuckles.

His eyes flick up, holding my gaze, and a small smile plays on his lips before he straightens and takes a step back. "See you around, *friend.*"

"Yep." I turn and make a beeline for the doors, not sure what to think of that, when for the second time today I crash into another warm body, this time hard enough that I stumble back a few steps and fall flat on my butt.

"Seriously!"

A warm chuckle has me looking up to find Dominique's amused stare locked on me. Not who I wanted to run into right now.

EIGHTY-FOUR

Kasey

"Where's the fire?" he asks, peering down at me like the brooding asshole I know him to be.

I open my mouth to snap at him for being a jerk and letting me fall, because I know he did it on purpose. Dominique's reflexes are lightning fast, so there is zero doubt in my mind he could have prevented my fall if he'd wanted to. But before I snap at him, his gaze shifts past me to the doors, a frown marring his face and a flash of anger ignites in his eyes.

I turn, but no one is there. I wonder if he saw me talking to Deacon. If he did, does he care? Probably not. But then why would he be angry?

I shove myself to my feet, dusting my hands on the back of my jeans. "Thanks for the save," I mock.

His attention turns back to me. "Why were you walking with Hunt?" he asks, his gaze probing.

"Who?"

"Hunt?" At my blank look he huffs. "Deacon Hunt. The guy you were talking to on your way over here. Why were you talking to him?"

"Am I not supposed to?" I ask, not bothering to answer his question as I head to my next class. I have ten minutes before it starts, but I'd rather Dominique think I don't have time to talk at the moment. Instead of dropping it, though, he falls into step beside me, his long strides eating through the distance and instinctively making me speed up until I realize what I'm doing and force myself to slow down.

"He's on the team," he says and his frown deepens. He slows down once he sees I'm no longer beside him.

"Why is that a problem? You, Roman, and Emilio are all on the team too."

We walk in silence together for several minutes before he finally says, "It's not the same."

I bark out a laugh. "I'm sorry. How exactly is it different?"

He glowers down at me, but I refuse to be affected.

"You know what jocks are like. They're not better in college than they were in high school. They're worse."

I roll my eyes. "Yes, I'm well aware. I have three guy friends who are damn near football gods with a well-established reputation for being man-whoring assholes. Luckily, two met the girls of their dreams and have since been reformed, the third..." I make a show of thinking it over, tapping my finger against my lower lip. "The third is still up to his asshole man-whoring ways. It's sad, actually. He's a bit of a lost cause."

Dominique's gaze sharpens. "I'm not a man-whore."

I snort. "At least you don't deny you're an asshole."

His teeth grind together. I struck a nerve with that one.

"I don't have to explain myself to you."

"Ding. Ding. Ding. You are one hundred percent right."

His eyes widen the smallest amount, but it's enough to relay his surprise at my words. Oh, he made this too easy and doesn't even realize it yet.

"And I should respect that. So, I will. And since you brought it up, you must also know that I don't need to explain myself to you, either." I grin, my smile widening the darker and more hooded his expression gets.

I know Mom always said you should never poke a bear, but I don't think she realized just how much fun it could be.

A growly sound rumbles deep in his chest.

"He's a player."

I shrug my shoulders. "Cool. I don't really care."

"You don't."

I roll my eyes. "Why would I?" I've already decided I'm not dating the guy, so it's a non-issue.

Dominique goes quiet again before he barks out a mocking laugh. Shaking his head, his mouth curls into a cruel smile, the one he seems to wear more and more whenever I'm around. "I shouldn't be surprised."

I frown. "Surprised by what?" I ask and then kick myself for being so damn predictable. The smart move would have been to ignore his comment. Not to play right into his hands.

His eyes burn with thinly veiled hostility. "That you've become like every other chick on campus. Both stupid and shallow if you're willing to date a known player to gain a little bit of popularity." He shakes his head as though I've somehow disappointed him. "I thought you were better than that." He shrugs. "Guess I was wrong."

I ignore his stab, but then he decides to cut a little deeper. "I give you a month. Maybe two before he cheats." His gaze rakes over me, but there isn't a hint of desire in his eyes as they travel over my body. Instead, they hold mock pity and disgust. "On second thought, just the one. He'll lose interest before you hit the second."

My cheeks heat and I know he can see the blush climbing up my neck.

"Fuck you." My words shake as I clench my hands into tight fists at my side. Why did that hurt so much?

He grunts. "Pass."

Fury spikes my bloodstream, my anger and humiliation at his words filling me like a vicious, violent wave. I don't even realize what's happening until it's done. One second I'm about to storm off and the next, my fist is flying, connecting with his jaw, but only enough to graze it because dammit, he's too fucking tall.

The next thing I know Dominique is shoving me into an empty classroom. The door closes behind us and he locks it before pressing me back into the nearest wall. I suck in a breath and Dominique lifts both arms on either side of me, caging me in with his bulk. "That was an incredibly stupid thing to do." I don't miss the threat in his voice, but I absolutely choose to ignore it.

I fist both hands in the fabric of his shirt and shove him with all of my strength, but it's like trying to move a mountain. "I always knew you were a jerk. But I never knew you were this cruel."

"It can't be considered cruelty if it's the truth."

Tears sting the backs of my eyes before I blink them away. "Never let them see you cry, sweetheart," Mom used to tell me. When Dad left her and filed for divorce, it was the lowest I'd ever seen her, but she never did let him see her cry. She was strong. And she raised me to be strong too. I refuse to break down and cry in front of Dominique all because what? He hurt my feelings? Fuck that. His opinion means nothing to me.

"Well, thanks for clearing that up." My lower lip trembles until I sink my teeth into it, using the pain as an anchor.

Dominique is silent as he stares down his nose at me, eyes devoid of emotion.

"I fucking hate you," I tell him.

Zero reaction.

"You said your piece. Told me I'm stupid and shallow and can't hold a guy's attention. Is there anything else you need to get off your chest? I have a class to get to, and this right here," I wave my arm between us, "is a waste of my time."

His gaze latches onto my arm.

With surprising speed and gentle hands he lifts my arm up, bringing it closer to his face like he's looking for—

I mutter out a curse seeing what caught his attention. Light bruises in the shape of fingers wrap around my forearm. Shit.

Dominique's expression goes from blank to murderous as he grinds out his next words. "Who touched you?" His already dark brown eyes turn even darker, sending a shiver down my spine.

I don't answer him.

"I'm not going to ask again, Kasey. Who. Fucking. Touched. You?"

EIGHTY-FIVE

Dominique

My nostrils flare taking in the yellow and purple bruise on Kasey's fair skin. There's no mistaking that it's from a hand. The shape is too distinct, and the imprint is large. A man's. Someone hurt her.

Whoever he is, he's a dead man.

Kasey's already pale skin has gone two shades paler, making her bright blue eyes damn near glow. Her mouth parts, tongue peeking out to lick her full bottom lip. My dick twitches and I silently curse, willing it to stand the fuck down.

She swallows hard, and I know her mind is racing for a response.

"Don't even think about lying to me," I warn.

In a move I never would have expected from her, Kasey twists her arm out of my grasp and dips beneath the arm I have pressed against the wall caging her in, in a desperate attempt at escape. It takes two seconds for her hand to reach the door, but before she can open it, I catch her by the waist and tug her back against me. "Not so fast, baby girl."

Her anger and hatred for me roll off her in waves as she digs her short nails into my arms and kicks her legs, cursing my name.

I flip her around and press her against the door, using my body to pin her in place. I've tried to keep myself in check, but she is not making this shit easy.

"Get off of me," she shouts, and I cover her mouth with my palm, my hand so large I damn near cover half her face. Fuck she's small. Fragile.

Her eyes blaze and I lean in, ensuring she sees that I am not fucking around right now. Not when it comes to something like this.

"Don't you dare open that pretty little mouth of yours and scream like that again. Do you feel me? Unless you're ready to tell me who the fuck was dumb enough to touch you, or decide to drop down on your knees and wrap your lips around my cock, your mouth is going to stay closed."

Her eyes narrow, nostrils flaring. She's so fucking pissed, and I wish I had more time to enjoy it. I've worked hard this past year getting Kasey to hate me. It makes keeping her out of my bed a hell of a lot easier that way. But damn if seeing her like this doesn't make my dick hard, and the thought of her on her knees for me ... *fuck.* I can't be the only one affected by that image.

Her small fingers wrap around my wrist, pulling to get my hand off of her mouth.

"Are you going to behave?"

If looks could kill I'd be dead right now with the way she's glaring at me.

"It's a yes or no question, baby girl. Blink twice for yes. Once for no."

Her eyes narrow. Seconds pass and the air grows impossibly thick. I'm sure she can feel my hard-on pressed against her stomach, but neither of us is going to acknowledge it.

When a full minute has passed, she blinks twice and concedes. A rush of satisfaction swells inside my chest. I drop my hand, but don't step away. I rationalize that the moment I do she'll bolt. It has nothing to do with how fucking good she feels with her tight little body up against mine. Her lips are pressed into a thin line, her cheeks scarlet. A mix of anger and indignation. She is so fucking beautiful like this.

A few strands of her blond hair fell from her hair tie during our struggle and I slowly reach out, tucking the flyaways behind her ear. Her eyes are guarded as I trail one finger down the side of her face before cupping her jaw. She closes her eyes, a small shudder moving through her.

"What's his name, Kasey?" I ask, and there's a bite of steel in my tone.

Her eyes snap open and she bears her teeth. "You're making a big deal out of nothing. It was an accide—"

"No man leaves a mark on a female by accident." My voice is deceptively calm. I lean down closer to her until our breaths mingle. "Was it Hunt? Did he do that?" The sudden widening of her eyes gives her away, and my vision goes red.

My jaw flexes and I go to step back but she latches onto me, wrapping her arms around my neck. "Whatever it is you're thinking of doing, don't. It was an accident. I don't think he meant to hurt me." I fight the urge to encircle her waist and rise to my full height, taking her with me.

Her arms tighten as her feet lift from the ground. "Dominique—"

"You can't protect your boyfriend," I tell her. "Not from this."

Her feet sway off the floor and her arms tighten around my neck, squeezing to maintain her hold on me since I haven't bothered to help her out.

"He's not my boyfriend. We literally just met because I slammed into him running late to class." My pulse jumps at her words. "I don't even know the guy. We have one class together and this is the first time we've spoken."

I grab the backs of her thighs, hoisting her higher up. Her legs wrap around my waist and my hands move to her ass. I lean her back against the door and wait to see if she'll demand to be put down. She doesn't. Neither does she yell at me for the way I'm cupping her ass right now.

"If you're protecting him—"

She snorts. "I'm not. I have no reason to, so get off your high horse. I'm not some damsel in need of saving."

"Is that so?" I ask, shifting my hips so her center grinds down on my cock.

She gasps. "What are you doing?"

I repeat the movement, and she shakes in my arms. "Are you sure you're not in need of saving?"

EIGHTY-SIX

Kasey

I ignore the way my heart is racing in my chest.

"By the guy who just called me stupid, shallow, and implied I was unattractive and incapable of holding a man's attention?" I shake my head. "I think I'm good."

There's a flash of something in his gaze I can't quite put my finger on. His hold tightens on my ass and his dick strains against his jeans, pressing firmly between my thighs. What was I thinking wrapping my legs around him like this?

As if hearing my thoughts, Dominique smirks. *Asshole.* I decide to give him a taste of his own medicine.

Using his shoulders for leverage I raise myself up a few inches and roll my hips over his length in a long caress. He sucks in a breath, his eyes dark and filled with challenge.

Holding his stare, I do it again, and his entire body trembles with need. I'm not blind. Despite his earlier words, he wants me. He won't after today, but right now at this very moment, Dominique

Price wants to fuck me, and knowing that sends a flood of euphoria surging through me. This means he's no longer in control here. I'm the one with all the power now.

"Don't start something you can't finish."

"Why not? It's not like you could possibly want me, right? So why would me doing this," I grind my pussy against him again, liquid heat soaking my panties, "matter to you? You can't possibly be affected, right?"

He doesn't say a word, but when I give another deliberate roll of my hips, he digs his fingers into my ass and thrusts upward, grinding his dick into me in response.

To my complete horror, a moan escapes me, and he levels me with a knowing smirk.

I dig my short nails into his shoulders as he dry humps me against the classroom door in long languid thrusts and Oh. My. God. That feels good.

One of his hands comes up to knead my breast and I shamelessly arch into his touch. He grunts against the corner of my mouth and the sound snaps something in me, lifting some of the pleasure-induced haze from my eyes.

Why do I let him make me feel like this? I fucking hate him.

Taking a deep breath, I lean forward, licking and biting my way up his neck until my lips graze the shell of his ear. "What would you do if I told you to fuck me?" I whisper and swirl my tongue along his skin.

His sharp intake of breath lets me know I've surprised him and he freezes, pulling back just enough to meet my gaze. His eyes are drowning in need, but there's a hint of confusion too, so I decide to taunt him some more. I make a show of licking my lips and his eyes immediately drop to my mouth.

"You'd like that, wouldn't you?"

He doesn't answer, but his muscles strain against his skin, the veins in his neck protruding.

"I bet you'd like it even more if I begged for it. Got down on my knees and showed you just how bad I—"

His fist tangles in my hair and he yanks my face toward his, tilting my head so his lips can capture my own. His kiss is savage and hungry as he claims my mouth with his tongue in long greedy stokes. I moan into his mouth, and that only seems to spur him on.

His grip holds me in place, leaving me no choice but to accept his punishing kiss. The hand in my hair moves to the side of my neck in a possessive hold while the other continues to hold me up, kneading my ass. He pulls away from the door and carries me further into the room, his mouth never leaving mine until I feel a solid surface beneath me.

Dominique sets me down on a long table, but he doesn't release me. "That what you want?" he asks, and it takes me a few seconds to remember what I said to him before that kiss. "You want me to fuck you while you beg for my cock?"

God, yes. Not that I'll ever admit it out loud. Instead, I lean back, pressing my palms on the table to hold myself up. His hand slips from my neck right as I say, "No thanks. I think I'm good."

I allow a smirk to curl the corners of my mouth as I raise both brows, giving him a disinterested look.

He glares at me in disbelief and then something in him shifts. Tension crackles like lightning between us, and I fight not to squirm under his intense stare.

"You almost had me," he tsks with an amused laugh. "Almost. But if you think for one second I'm going to buy that mouthful of lies, guess again, baby girl." He steps into me, cupping my sex and driving the heel of his palm against me. "You're soaked pussy doesn't lie. I can feel how wet you are through your jeans."

My eyes pop wide and my heart beats frantically against my chest before I can pull myself together enough to bite out, "Screw you."

"You'd like that wouldn't you?" He smirks, palm still pressed firmly against my center. My hips lift off the table of their own volition when he pushes down on my clit. I gasp, biting back a moan, and my cheeks burn with humiliation, but I can't find it in me to tell him to stop. It feels so good.

"I don't like liars," he grunts, his eyes locked on his hand between my legs. *Wait. What?* He drags my hips to the edge of the table until my butt is about to slide off. Then he spreads my legs, creating enough room for him to step between them. He makes no effort to mask his desire as he slams his lips down on mine again and groans into my mouth right before he fists my hair and jerks my head back, tearing his lips from mine and leaving me to stare up at the ceiling. He scrapes his teeth along the column of my throat, nipping and sucking on my sensitive skin.

I gasp, and a fresh wave of pleasure filters through me, igniting every cell in my body.

He runs his nose up the side of my neck, inhaling me as he says, "So, I have to punish you." There's a note of regret in his voice, and the next thing I know, he's spun me around to face the opposite wall. My feet hit the floor, my body bent over the desk and my ass thrust out toward him. One hand presses down on the center of my spine, effectively pinning me in place as the other roams over my hip, trailing down to my ass.

"What am I being punished for?" My heart rate picks up.

"You lied to me."

I shake my head in denial. "I didn't lie." My voice shakes, but whether from desire or fear, I'm not entirely sure.

"There you go again," he tsks.

His hand dips lower, boldly stroking the inside of my thighs as he uses his legs to force me into a wider stance. I grind my teeth together to hold back the moan that threatens to spill past my lips.

"I'm going to give you a second chance to come clean, because despite what you think, I'm not a complete asshole."

I start to laugh, but the sound dies in my throat when I feel the ridge of his cock dig into my ass, hard and demanding. What is he doing to me? We don't get along. We definitely don't like one another. But the level of need I feel right now is like nothing I've felt before, which is both exhilarating and terrifying at the same time because this is bad. So fucking bad.

"Do you want me to fuck you, baby girl?" My mouth goes dry as he thrusts against me, pressing his cock against the crack of my ass as he mimics fucking me. "Do you want to beg for my cock as I thrust deep inside you?"

My pussy clenches and his vulgar words almost undo me. I swallow hard and manage to deliver a shaky denial, "No."

He stops moving and exhales a sigh full of resignation, as if my response somehow pains him. "I did warn you," he says, his voice tinged with regret.

I swallow hard, wondering what he intends to do next. I've never seen him like this. He's always been so restrained. We fight, sure, but with words. This isn't anything like our usual battles. This is like going to war and I am wholly outmatched and unprepared for this kind of fight.

One hand reaches around me and undoes the button on my jeans. "Last chance," he offers, but words die on my tongue. My thighs tighten in anticipation. Is he...are we going to...

His fingers hook into my jeans, dragging them over my hips and exposing my rear. He leaves my underwear in place, but all I'm wearing is a hot pink thong that leaves my entire backside on display. "Fuck," he groans and cups my ass cheeks, spreading them with his fingers while also pushing me forward, father across the table until the tops of my thighs can't go any further.

"Tell me to stop," he growls. "If you're not okay with this, whatever the fuck is about to happen right now, tell me now." He runs his fingers down the crack of my ass until he reaches my pussy and presses his fingers into me through the soaked fabric of my panties. My legs quake.

I should do what he suggests, tell him to stop, but I'm drunk on desire, feeling like I'll explode if he stops touching me, so I keep my lips pressed together and shake my head. I'll regret this come morning.

I won't be able to pretend this didn't happen. I won't be able to forget his hands on me or the sensation of him thrusting between my thighs. This is a mistake and I know it. I just don't fucking care.

Dominique twists his hand in my hair and I instinctively know what comes next. It's no surprise when he yanks on it, forcing my back to arch and my chin to jut forward. He seems to like that, pulling my hair. And I can't say that I'm complaining about it.

I don't have a lot of experience in this arena. I've fooled around before, sure. Given head. Had my pussy eaten out. But I haven't gone all the way with anyone. I'm not saving myself for marriage or anything like that, I just never cared about any of my past boyfriends enough to spread my legs for them.

I've never been with a guy like this. One who my body responds to on a visceral level.

Dom shifts to the side, no longer between my thighs, but he doesn't let go of my hair. He winds it around his fist, tightening his hold as his other hand hooks beneath the fabric of my panties and a lone finger slips between my wet slit.

I moan when he finds my clit, brushing his finger over the sensitive nub.

"Dominique ..." I gasp, and his finger moves faster against me, my hips rearing back of their own accord. The pain in my scalp and the pleasure between my thighs has pure heat zipping down my spine. My toes curl and I'm panting heavy, my release so incredibly close.

"Don't say I didn't warn you," he mutters under his breath right before he withdraws his finger from between my legs and his palm slaps my bare ass cheek. I yelp, jolting forward, but the table makes it impossible to go anywhere.

Holy fuck. "Did you just spank me?"

Instead of answering, he spanks my other cheek and I slap my palm against the table.

"I warned you what would happen if you didn't tell the truth." He massages my burning flesh, lessening the sting a bit, only to slap me again. I cry out, but the sound is cut off when he releases my hair only to wrap his hand over my mouth.

"Shhhh...." he whispers. "Keep making that sound and someone is bound to come and investigate what is going on in here."

I try to shift away from him. When he said he was going to punish me for lying, I didn't expect this.

He chuckles, like my attempt at escape amuses him. "I'm not done with you yet. I think you deserve at least two more." A fourth smack is delivered and I scream, but his palm muffles the sound.

"Your ass turns the prettiest shade of pink," he tells me, and I whimper against his palm.

He squeezes my ass, trailing his fingers over each cheek and between my cleft. He said two more, but he's only delivered one, and the anticipation of what is still to come grips my chest.

Dominique lets go of my mouth and shifts behind me, pressing his erection against me. "Want to try again?" he asks, rocking his hips against me. "Tell me the truth and maybe I'll consider giving you what you want. Beg for my cock the way we both know you want to."

The smug sound of his voice has my eyes narrowing and I lift my head to look over my shoulder. I won't beg for anything. Not from him or anyone else. My gaze collides with his and just as I open my mouth to tell him to fuck off, his palm slaps my ass, harder than all of the times before.

I open my mouth on a silent scream before sucking in a shaky breath as I sag against the table.

Dominique steps back, moving around the table until he's standing in front of me, able to meet my gaze. He casually leans forward, pushing the hair out of my face. I should stand up. At the very least pull my jeans back over my ass, but I can't seem to find the energy to move.

"You know, you're not nearly as insufferable when you're like this."

I raise one hand and flip him off.

He laughs and then, unsurprisingly, walks out of the classroom without so much as a goodbye.

EIGHTY-SEVEN

Dominique

I left Kasey bare-assed in that classroom. Aaron's little sister. Ass cheeks red, courtesy of yours truly, and on display for anyone who walked in to see. This is bad. Already, there is a voice in my head that whispers *you traitor, he's like a brother. He trusts you.*

There's a lead weight in my gut. I shouldn't have touched her. I sure as shit shouldn't still be thinking about touching her.

Thank God I didn't go through with fucking her. Not that what I did do constitutes as much better. A heavy blanket of guilt encompasses me. This can't happen again. Me. Her. I lied when I told Roman I wasn't interested. What I meant was I can't afford to be interested. Not in her. Not like that.

I reach the locker room and make quick work of changing. I'm a few minutes late, but no one will care. I'm not practicing today, still on Coach's mandatory rest period for my shoulder, but that doesn't mean I'm gonna bounce on my obligations. Or miss the chance to give Deacon a piece of my mind.

Kasey might say it was an accident, but I'm not buying it.

Seeing that bruise on her arm ... I shake my head and take a deep breath. It damn near sent me over the edge. The thought of anyone hurting her, anyone who isn't me—and yeah, I realize how fucked up that is—makes my blood boil.

I want to fuck her. Punish her. Soothe her. I want her to ache because of me and I want to be the only one capable of taking that ache away.

Smacking her ass and watching it redden has blood rushing straight to my cock. Seeing her lust-drenched eyes, feeling just how soaking wet her panties are, *shit,* it does something to me.

The door leading to the field opens and Emilio walks in, shouting, "Yeah, yeah. I'll be back. Chill the fuck out," over his shoulder.

"It's about time you showed up. Everything good?" he asks, seeing me on the bench.

I grunt. "Peachy."

He opens his locker, the one right next to mine, and gives me a curious look.

"What'd you do?" he asks.

"What are you talking about?"

He grabs a roll of athletic tape and begins wrapping his wrists. "You look guilty as fuck, man. Where were you before you got here?"

I keep my expression blank. "I think you've been watching too many *telenovelas* with Bibiana, E."

He chuckles. "You got me there, but bro, Señora Acero is savage. That opening scene is *a la Game of Thrones* two-thousand thirteen. A wedding. A massacre. You don't know what you're missing."

"I'll take your word for it."

He finishes with his wrists and tosses the tape back in his locker. "I still can't believe you stopped watching at the ten-minute mark." He shakes his head. "Fifteen more minutes and it would have gotten to the good part."

"I couldn't understand anything."

Emilio scoffs. "Turn on the fucking subtitles. It's fine."

I stretch my back and put myself through a short series of stretches as we bullshit a little longer. I know what I'm planning to do once I walk out on the field, but what I don't know is how to get Emilio and Roman off of it.

"Hunt," I shout, ensuring my voice carries across the field. His head jerks up and he looks around, searching for whoever called his name. As soon as he realizes it was me, he jogs his way over, pulling off his helmet once he's close.

"Yo. What's up?" He tilts his head in greeting, wiping the sweat from his brow with the back of his arm.

"Kasey Henderson." I bite out her name.

He smirks, a glint of excitement in his eyes. "She's fucking *fine*, right?" He rocks back on his heels and gives me a knowing look. Like we're friends or some shit and both in on the same secret.

Until this moment, I had zero issue with Hunt. Thought he was an okay dude with potential, but now... I can't stand the sight of him and I'm two seconds away from punching him in the face, making sure to leave a mark like he left on Kasey.

But I decide to give him a chance and delay punching him right out of the gate by grabbing him by the jersey instead and shoving him against the chain-link fence that surrounds the field.

He brings his arms up in a vain attempt to stop me, but despite the definition he picked up in high school, I have an easy sixty pounds of muscle on him. He's still a kid, and he's not getting away until I'm good and ready to let him go.

"What the fuck, man." His eyes are wide, and I make sure he gets a good look at the fury riding me. "Is she yours or something? Shit, man. She never mentioned having a boyfriend. So if you've got beef, take it up with her." He stops fighting me, both arms raised in surrender. *Idiot.*

"She's seventeen," I snarl, inches from his face.

"What's your point? We're both freshmen. I'm only a year older, probably less than that."

I shake him before slamming him against the fence harder. I can feel the eyes of the team on me, but no one interferes. The only people dumb enough to try are Roman and Emilio, and I made sure both were occupied in the locker room before tracking Deacon down, and that shit took some maneuvering.

"She's a fucking minor," I seethe.

"Bro, lay off. It's not illegal or anything. How do you even know her?"

Shouting comes from the other side of the field. Fuck. I thought I'd have more time, but I guess I'll have to make do with what I have.

"Whatever you think is going on between you two, it ends now. When you see her in class you're going to pretend like you don't even see her."

His jaw tightens, and I know he wants to smart off, but he manages to keep his mouth shut. Only the flaring of his nostrils betrays his emotions. Maybe he isn't that stupid after all.

I drop my hold on him and turn, shouldering past the guys on the team stupid enough to have inched their way closer. Fucking gossips.

"Dom—" Roman calls out, but I shake my head. I'm good. Shit is over. Or at least it should be, but then Deacon goes and opens his fucking mouth.

"I'm not passing on her," he shouts. "If you had your shot and missed it, that's on you. But I'm not gonna look past a fine as fuck piece of ass for your benefit. Not until I've sampled her, at least. When I'm done, I might consider sharing if you still want a taste." He laughs like he's some arrogant frat kid.

My head turns almost as if in slow motion. Everything around me falls away, and all I see is the dipshit in front of me, the three meters between us, and the time it will take me to reach him so I can lay his punk ass out.

"Am I right, boys?" Deacon smirks as he looks around him, meeting the eyes of our teammates. No one responds to him and I watch in satisfaction as his smile slips, and then, I'm on him. I have my left hand on his throat, the right clenched into a tight fist and I draw my arm back.

Right as I move to swing, a hand wraps around my fist, barely managing to stop my momentum. I jerk my gaze to my right only to find Roman holding onto me. Emilio not two steps behind him.

"Your hands," he bites out.

With my left hand still holding Deacon in place, I shake my best friend off. "Fuck my hands." Whatever damage they might sustain will be worth it, only Roman doesn't seem to agree.

"You have a fucked-up shoulder and now you wanna fuck your future just to punch this asshole in the face? Come on, Dom, be smart."

With my eyes locked on his, I ignore Deacon's failed attempts at escape. His hands swing out in a bid to hit me first, save face in front of the team, but my reach is longer than his and all he manages to hit is air. He realizes that he'll never reach me and starts pounding his fist into my left arm.

I grunt, but don't let go.

"Don't be stupid. You're better than this. Don't throw away the season just to punch some punk ass kid."

"Fuck you," Deacon wheezes, not liking Roman's names for him. Personally, I like punk ass more than asshole. It fits him.

My arm is numb. He tagged me on my funny bone and the nerve is spasming, but I'm not about to let up.

Without looking at him, I tighten my grip on his neck.

"My hands will be fine," I snap. "And if they're not, fuck it. It'll be worth it to teach this motherfucker a lesson."

Emilio appears on my other side and both he and Roman work together to shove me back.

I drag Deacon backward with me.

"Dude, let go," Emilio shouts.

"No."

"God dammit," Roman snaps. "For once, will you fucking listen? He isn't worth it."

My nostrils flare. "You have no idea what—"

Emilio curses. "Dammit, Dominique. He's turning blue. Shit. I didn't know black could turn that shade of blue."

I turn to Deacon, eyes narrowing. "Idiot. He's not turning blue. He's turning white. See, around his mouth is muted and almost ashy."

Emilio leans in for a closer look and I use my free hand to smack him upside the head.

"Fucker," he complains, rubbing the back of his head.

"I think you should see a doctor if you think that is blue. Are you color blind?"

Deacon is still struggling, but the strength has been leached out of him and his swings are more like pats on the arm now.

"Not fucking helping," Roman bites out.

"Right." Emilio gives me his best impression of a serious look. "Drop him, man."

I quirk a brow. "That the best you got?"

"What the hell are you all standing around for? Get to moving." Coach shouts, but his voice is far away which means he hasn't caught sight of Deacon yet.

"Fuck." That was Emilio.

"*Hijo de puta.*" And that would be Roman. I've heard *cabrón* out of his mouth enough times to know it basically translates to fucker or smartass, but this one is new.

"What was that?"

"Son of a bitch," Emilio supplies before adding on a groan, "We are so fucked."

I glare at Deacon, seeing the fearful panic in his eyes. I sigh and let go. He slumps to the ground, gasping for breath while clawing at his throat. Coach is about halfway across the field, so we have maybe another minute before this becomes an issue. Enough time for Deacon to get his pussy ass off the ground and fall into line.

I crouch down in front of him, balancing on the balls of my feet, and drop a heavy hand on his shoulder. He's coughing and wheezing, but still manages to look my way, letting me know he's aware of the very real threat I still pose. "You think my issue is that I'm jealous of a punk like you? I'm not. My problem with you is that you left a bruise on Kasey's arm and when I told you to stay the fuck away from her, you mouthed off."

"What the fuck?" Emilio starts, but I block him out.

I'm going to get my point across to this asshole one way or the other. Kasey is off limits, and if he ever lays a hand on her again, I'll fucking kill him.

I grab his chin with a near bruising grip and force him to look up, his back arching from the ground, but he's too weak to fight me. "After today. You're going to pretend you don't know her. You won't look at her. You won't talk to her and you sure as fuck will not touch her. Do you understand?"

He gives a slight nod.

"Good." I release him and stand. "Because the next time I come for you, it won't be anywhere with witnesses."

I stalk toward the field, planning to intercept Coach, when I hear Emilio shout, *"Puta madre, Que te Folle un Pez!"* and turn just in time to see him slam his fist into Deacon's face while he's still on the ground. He knocks him out cold with the single hit.

"What the fuck did that mean?" I ask Roman, a smile curling my lips.

He smirks and tilts his head to the side, thinking. "The literal translation?"

I nod.

"Motherfucker, I hope you get fucked by a fish."

I choke on a laugh. "What? Why a fish?"

He shrugs as Emilio—worked up and chest heaving like he just ran drills—joins us.

"It's harsher in Spanish," Roman adds.

Emilio glares at us both, anger clouding his eyes. "You better start explaining what you meant about him leaving a bruise on Baby Henderson."

Roman's eyes narrow, a vicious glint in his eyes as he takes a step toward Deacon, who is still prone on the ground. I grab his jersey and shake my head. "Not now," I grunt, knowing exactly what he's thinking and agreeing. One hit isn't enough to satisfy any of our need for retribution, which is why he never should have gotten in my way.

His mouth tightens, but he concedes. Then, loud enough for a few of our teammates to hear he says. "Any man weak enough to leave a mark on a woman isn't a man at all. Hunt is going to learn real fucking fast we won't tolerate abusive assholes on this team."

A few of the guys nod their heads, gazes sharpening with that information. Lines are being drawn in the sand as we speak, and I for one can't wait for Deacon to get his next dose of fuck-you medicine.

EIGHTY-EIGHT

Kasey

I ignore the sounds of partying going on in other parts of the house and focus on my textbook. I've done a pretty good job of hiding from my housemates. I probably shouldn't. My mom keeps sending me messages and leaving voicemails asking if I've made any new friends yet. Kind of hard to do when you're actively avoiding everyone.

But there's this strange irrational part of me that thinks if people see me, they'll know.

They'll know that three days ago Dominique Price dry humped me against a wall before baring my ass in an empty classroom and spanking me. And worse, they'll know I liked it.

I groan miserably into my hands. There has to be something wrong with me when that thought alone has me clenching my thighs and aching for something else to be between them.

My bedroom door swings open. "Kasey!" A female voice singsongs, startling me. "Why are you studying right now when you should be hanging out with me!"

Quinn skips into my room wearing a bright orange bikini top and a pair of cut-off denim shorts. She plops down on my bed beside me, an exaggerated pout on her face.

"You're drunk," I tell her.

She rolls her eyes and lets out a huff. "Obviously. And you should be, too." Then with a whine she adds, "I'm sorry."

I frown at her over the edge of my book. "What is there to be sorry for?"

"I'm your big sister. I'm supposed to make your Kappa Mu experience epic, and instead of having fun with us you're holed up in your room doing homework." She throws herself back on my bed dramatically. "I've failed you."

I roll my eyes. Drunk Quinn is an interesting sight to behold. "You have not failed me," I tell her. "You're a great big."

She perks up. "I am?"

I shrug. Why not? It's not like I have anything to compare her to, and I didn't really come here with any expectations. She's answered any questions I've had and she hasn't been a jerk like some of the other girls in the house, so I'd say we were off to a good start.

"Yep. The best." I turn back to my book, hoping that'll be that and she'll see herself to the door.

"Great. Then as your amazing big sister, I demand you party!" She cheers as she jumps from the bed with a fresh wave of energy. "We need drinks!"

"I'm supposed to study," I tell her, resisting her efforts to drag me from my bed.

"You can study later. You need to have fun!"

"I also need to pass my classes," I remind her, but she doesn't seem worried.

"You will. You're smart. So come on. There's no time like the present."

"Fine," I sigh, and let her drag me from my room. After today's nightmare of an English exam that I am eighty percent sure I completely bombed, I guess I can take a short break and hang out for a little bit. Besides, it doesn't look like she's going to take no for an answer.

Quinn pulls me down the hall and through the main part of the house before pausing right as we get to the doors leading into the backyard. "Clothes!"

"Uh, what about them?"

She whirls on me. "You need them!" She makes a show of smacking her own forehead. "Come on. You need to change."

Now I'm being dragged back the way we came, but instead of going into my room where, you know, all my clothes are, she pulls me into hers and starts rifling through her closet.

"What are you doing?"

She pulls pieces out left and right, tossing them behind her on the floor after she rejects them. "You do know you're going to have to clean that up, right?" I remind her.

"The guys from Alpha Ze are here."

Yippee, stupid drunk frat boys. I am so excited. Cue the sarcasm.

"So. Your point?"

She turns and scowls at me, waving what looks like a purple crop top in my face. "So? So, you're wearing that?"

"What's wrong with what I'm wearing?" I ask, looking down at my jean shorts and oversized crew neck t-shirt.

"Are you modest?" she asks, ignoring my question and going back to sifting through her clothes.

"Not particularly. Why?"

"Because you're always covered up. You're in college. This is where you go to see others and be seen."

I open my mouth to tell her I don't have any desire to be seen when she waves a piece of black fabric in the air. "Found it!" She jumps up and down twice. Like she just won a carnival prize. "Okay, here. Get naked and put this on."

She tosses it to me and I catch the black, silky material. "A swimsuit?" I toss it back to her. "I don't want to go swimming."

She throws it at me again. "You don't wear a swimsuit to go swimming, silly. You wear it so you have an excuse to walk around half naked. Now, hurry up and try it on. You can use my bathroom."

I snort, because my room, which is right next door, is so far away.

Quinn gives me her best shot at an *I'm waiting* look, and I decide to humor her. She's basically the closest thing to a friend I have here and pissing her off probably won't do me any favors.

In the bathroom, I strip out of my clothes and hold the swimsuit out in front of me. It's a one piece, so that's good at least. I wasn't lying when I said I wasn't particularly modest, but I'm not a let it all hang out type of girl either. There are what look to be a dozen little ties and crisscross straps, and I'm not exactly sure how to put the damn thing on.

"Are you decent?" Quinn calls, knocking on the door.

"No!" I tell her, one leg in a hole I'm not entirely sure is meant for my leg.

"Too bad, I'm coming in." And she does. When she sees me, naked and jumping on one foot as I try to get my leg out of the weird knot thingy, she covers her mouth and laughs, eyes wide and shoulders shaking.

"I'm still naked!" I say, crossing one arm over my chest and dropping a hand over the apex of my thighs.

"I can see that." She's laughing so hard, her eyes are watering. "Need a little... help?" she waves at me and I huff out a breath.

"Obviously, yes. I don't know how the heck to get into this."

She giggles and moves closer, helping me untangle my foot as I cover up the goods.

"Here, step in through this one." She helps me slip my feet into the right holes. Why are there so many? And then turns her back so I can shimmy into the thing.

The more on it goes, the less it actually covers, if you can believe that. "Okay I'm turning back around," she calls and then helps me find the holes to slip my arms through.

She gives me a critical once over, pulling the fabric here, tightening it there, before stepping back to examine her work. "You look fucking hot!" she says, a gleam in her eye.

I look down for a second before squeezing my eyes closed. "Are you sure you didn't give me lingerie?" I ask, because, wow. And I don't mean that in a good way. Quinn grabs my shoulders and turns me to face the mirror. I open one eye and gasp.

"Holy fu—"

"I know. Right?" She grins. "This one used to be my favorite but since I got these done," she points at her chest, "it doesn't fit anymore. It looks great on you though, so you can keep it."

Keep it? I'm not sure it's even legal to wear. Not in public at least. What I thought was a sleek black one piece is really lingerie pretending to be a swimsuit. The front has a plunging neckline that goes down past my navel, exposing the top of my crotch— thank god I got waxed last week. Holding the two sides in place is a series of crisscross ties that lace up the entire front until they reach my neck where they tie like a halter top in the back. The material over my boobs barely covers my nipples, so I have an insane amount of cleavage, and the back is virtually non-existent. My entire back is on display and half my ass hangs out of the teeny tiny bottoms, giving me a persistent wedgie.

"Stop adjusting everything," Quinn chides, smacking my hand away as she tugs my bottoms up, not down, exposing even more of my ass. "It's supposed to be like this."

I gawk at her. "I'm almost naked. Actually, I think this is more provocative than being naked."

Her smile is wide. "I know, right? Now let's go get wasted! It's Friday night and you've been here a week already. It's time to let loose."

Before I can object, she is literally dragging me out of the bathroom. "Quinn. Stop."

Does she? Of course not. And who would have guessed that my five-foot-four sorority sister was this strong. We're back at the door and not giving me any time to prepare myself, she swings it wide open and shouts, "Time for Jell-O shots, bitches!"

The girls outside laugh and cheer, and then with all the confidence in the world, Quinn heads for the table where said Jell-O shots are lined up in a rainbow of colors. Several of my sorority sisters move to follow her, everyone barely dressed in a multitude of swim attire.

I get a few heated stares from some of the guys and ignore them as I head for an empty chair by the pool where I spot some sunscreen. I'm blond-haired, blue-eyed, and so white that my friend Monique jokes that instead of tanning, I turn translucent.

A joke, obviously, but she isn't far off. I was cursed with zero melanin, so the sun and I have never exactly been friends. Growing up in the summer I would tell Aaron he was born selfish since he stole it all from our mom before I even had a chance. So unfair. A few hours outdoors and he turns a golden color that makes him look like a modern-day Apollo. Meanwhile, I go from white to pink to red in a matter of minutes if I don't slather myself at least in SPF80.

After squirting some sunscreen in my hands, I massage it into my arms and legs when a shadow falls over me, blocking out some of the harsh rays from the sun.

"Want me to get your back?" A masculine voice asks, and I turn to find Deacon behind me, beer in hand and a hesitant smile on his face.

"Oh, hey. What are you doing here?" I ask, and lift a hand over my eyes to see him better. He's wearing black swim shorts and no shirt, and has on mirrored sunglasses so I can't make out his eyes.

"I'm in Alpha Ze," he tells me.

"Ah, it all makes sense now."

He tilts his head to the side.

"What does?"

"That cocky charismatic charm of yours that you're able to flip on and off whenever you like. Nice chatting this week, by the way. Coffee was great," I tell him and he grimaces. After we ran into each other I thought, I don't know, that we'd actually try the whole friend thing, but I guess when he realized he'd be stuck in the friend zone he didn't want to waste his time.

We never talked after that day and in class he wouldn't even look at me. If he wanted me to get the hint, I heard him loud and clear. I just wish he wasn't such an asshole about it. I don't understand why guys can't just be friends with a girl. Why does it always have to be something else?

"About that," he rubs the back of his neck and is silent for a beat before dropping down on the lounge beside me.

EIGHTY-NINE

Kasey

———

Deacon massages his throat and I get the feeling he's working his way up to telling me something I'm not going to like to hear. When the seconds turn into minutes, I shift my focus back to applying my sunscreen. Seriously, if I don't, I will fry.

"I didn't mean to ghost you."

I put a little lotion on two fingers and massage it through the crisscross ties running down the front of the suit. I look ridiculous doing it but a girl has to do what a girl has to do.

"So why did you?" I ask. My feelings aren't hurt by it, to be honest. I have plenty of friends and I'm not actively searching for more. I guess I mostly just find it annoying. I don't get why guys only see value in women if there's a chance of them getting laid. It's bullshit if you ask me.

"Look, I don't want to cause drama and shit."

I wait. I don't know what he's looking for from me, but I'm not going to help him out here. He approached me, so if this is going to be an issue—him talking to me—he's just as welcome to walk away.

"A few of the guys on the team aren't cool with the idea of us hanging out," he tells me and I stiffen. Dammit. Because, of course, Dominique didn't forget about the bruise after he left the classroom. I mean, he had no problem forgetting, but not Deacon. Not when it gave him the opportunity to be an even bigger asshole.

I grind my teeth together and ask, "Was it all three of them?" If it was, then I have three Devils to get back at instead of just the one.

Deacon shakes his head, "I don't think so." He pauses. "Not in the beginning at least. I think only my QB had a problem with it, but those three are tight—"

"Yeah," I sigh. "I know."

We're both quiet for a moment.

"He your ex or something?" Deacon asks.

I snort. "Definitely not. We've never dated and trust me when I say, we never will."

One dark brow raises over the rim of his glasses. "You sure about that? The way Price was acting, it's the way a jealous ex would be if he caught someone sniffing around his girl."

My lip curls. "First, I'm not a dog. No one is sniffing anywhere. And second, yes, I'm sure about that. I've known him since we were kids. We're all sort of in the same friend group and he's roommates with my older brother. He takes the term 'overprotective' to the extreme." They all do. They're the bonus brothers I never asked for. Well, except for Dominique. I mean, I still didn't ask for him. That part is true. But of all the guys, he is the one I most definitely do not see as a brother. Even more so after what happened between us earlier this week.

Asshole.

Deacon nods, and I hate that I still can't see his eyes, so I decide to do something about it. Reaching up, I pluck the shades off his face, folding them down and setting them beside me.

"So, what did those three knuckleheads do, exactly? I'm assuming threats were involved, or did he go on a power trip and threaten to have you removed from the team?"

A flash of fear appears on his face, but it's gone a second later. Shit. Dominique really got to him.

"No. Not that. I'm still on the team." His Adam's apple bobs as he visibly swallows. "He can't get me kicked off, anyway."

I inwardly groan. Why are the pretty ones so dumb? Dominique could absolutely get Deacon removed from the team. All it would take is one phone call to his parents, a sizable donation, and boom. Goodbye, Suncrest U. Hello, community college.

I decide not to tell him that because he seems a little freaked out as it is. If you didn't grow up in Sun Valley, then it's safe to assume you don't know how big of a deal Dominique's family is. Deacon probably knows who the Prices are, the same way everyone in the U.S. knows who Bill Gates is. But, if you saw him walking down the street, you'd probably walk past him none the wiser, and it's not like you'd know who his kids were or what they looked like.

"Yo, D!" someone shouts, pulling Deacon's attention. "Is that her? The chick you got your ass kicked for?" He gives me a heated look, biting his fist. "Damn, man. I get it."

"Reed, fuck off," Deacon snarls right as I give the guy a one-fingered salute.

"Come on, man. No need to be like that. I was just complimenting your girl. I'd tap that for sure." He makes a thrusting motion with his hips and Deacon groans, covering his face with his hand.

"I apologize on behalf of my idiot frat brother. You probably won't believe me, but he's actually a pretty cool guy when he's not wasted like he is now."

Yeah. Not so sure about that but I leave it alone.

"He said you got your ass kicked. That was because of me?"

He sighs. "It's nothing. Can we drop it?"

Uh, no. No, we cannot drop it. I told Dominique it was an accident. Obviously he didn't let it go, but I'd expect him to throw his weight around. Maybe threaten Deacon or try to intimidate him somehow. Physically assaulting him is taking it to another level. Why was he so riled up about this?

"I'm going to need a play by play. I can get that from you or from some of your brothers who, by the sounds of it, are in the know. Up to you."

His jaw flexes, but instead of telling me what happened he asks, "Did you lie and tell him I hurt you?"

"Excuse me?"

He turns narrowed eyes my way. "I've gone over what happened in my head a few times and Dominique said I hurt you. Left a bruise but," he shakes his head. "I never hit you. I don't hit women. I'm trying to figure out why you'd tell him otherwise."

His nostrils flare and damn, he looks pissed. All over again, I get the feeling he isn't someone safe. It's like he hides this dangerous edge about him under layers of confidence and charisma.

"Well?" he snaps.

I lift my arm in answer. When he sees the still purple mark, he grabs my arm and tugs it closer, taking me with it since, well, it's sort of attached. I all but fall into his lap, but he doesn't even notice. His eyes lock on my skin. Flexing his fingers, he wraps them around my arm in the exact same spot before cursing and shoving my arm away.

"I didn't tell him you hit me. I didn't even say this came from you." I sit back and tuck my legs beneath me. "He saw us talking when you walked me to the athletics building. Then he saw the bruise. My poker face is pretty awesome. Sorry about that. He asked if it came from you and well ..." I trail off.

"When we collided?" he asks.

I nod.

He sucks on his teeth. "I grabbed you. Harder than I should have. I get why you got all jumpy after that when I tugged on your hand. I," He pauses. "It wasn't on purpose. I mean, leaving that mark. Hurting you." He hangs his head. "I am not that guy. I'm *trying* not to be that guy."

"Have you ever been that guy before?" I ask, needing to know if he's safe. If he's someone I should be careful around.

He shakes his head, and I exhale a relieved breath. "No. My old man was. But I won't ever allow myself to become a monster the way he was." There is steely determination in his voice. "I'm sorry.

We're getting into deep shit when we barely know each other." He chuckles, but it's forced.

"It's all good. And thanks. For the apology, I mean."

He nods.

"I still want that play by play, though," I remind him.

I wait. He tips back his beer, his throat working as he takes a long pull.

"Stalling will get you nowhere."

He grunts and then shakes his head. "We had some words. It's over now."

"Hey, Reed?" I call out. I stand and scan the backyard, looking for Deacon's frat brother who brought this all up in the first place.

Deacon hisses. "Kasey, drop it."

"Yo!" Reed hollers.

"I have questions." I nod my head and indicate for him to come over. He says a few more words to the guys he was talking to before slapping one on the back and heading our way.

"Kasey—" There's a warning in Deacon's voice. It's cute. I mean if I don't listen when Dominique gets all growly, why would I listen now?

"You're welcome to tell me yourself," I remind him.

He presses his lips into a firm line. Alrighty then.

As soon as Reed is close I say, "What happened with Deacon and Dominique Price?"

Reed whistles. "Aw, man. That was some rough shit." He ignores the death stare Deacon is giving him and dives into his recount of Tuesday's events. Dominique getting in Deacon's face. Choking him. How Deacon nearly passed out.

Deacon is quiet the entire time, chin down and shoulders slumped.

"And then the other guy, what's his name again?" He snaps his fingers before answering his own question. "E! That's what all the jocks call him. So Dominique is walking away, point made, am I right?" He wiggles his brows. "When his buddy, E, starts talking in Spanish and punches Deacon while he's still on the ground. It was fucking savage."

Deacon groans. "Thanks for the recount, man. Appreciate it."

Reeds misses the sarcasm in Deacon's voice.

"Emilio punched you?" I ask. Now, that surprises me the most.

Deacon sighs. "Yeah. I don't think he or Valdez knew why Dominique was in my face. They were trying to haul him off me at first. Talk him down and shit." His mouth tightens. "After Dominique made his point, he warned me off you and mentioned that," he points his beer toward my arm, "Chavez blew a gasket and clocked me. Now that I see it, can't say I really blame him. I'd be pissed too if someone hurt a girl I cared about."

"I'm sorry. The guys can be overprotective."

"It's all good now. Like I said. It's done."

"Fuck no, it's not. D, you haven't told her about practices, man."

"Shut the fuck up, bro," he grinds out, but Reed is drunk, making him oblivious to Deacon's warning.

"What's going on in practice?"

It's Reed who answers. "Deacon is getting his ass handed to him. All day, every day. Left tackles aren't protecting him. He's getting sacked damn near every play he runs. It's fucking brutal."

My eyes widen. "You're kidding?" Why wasn't his team watching his back? The quarterback was the most vulnerable player on the field. One wrong hit and he could be seriously injured.

"Nope. Price's shoulder is fucked up, right?" Wait, it is? What happened to his shoulder? "So all he's doing in practice is throwing. Him and Valdez run drills while Deacon starts on the field. Five plays in on day one and it dawns on Deacon that protection is bad and it's staying bad. He starts to scramble when he gets the ball. Man doesn't want to get hit."

Deacon is rigid, every muscle in his face drawn tight. He doesn't like hearing this.

"This shit goes on for three days," Reed says, waving three fingers in the air. "And then out of nowhere, Price takes to the field, smacks our boy here upside the head, and tells him, 'You're fast. Play faster. Trust your feet.' It was solid advice but Deacon isn't having it. He's pissed."

"Can you blame me?" Deacon snaps.

Reed lifts both hands in the air. "Nope. I'd be an asshole, too. Maybe not to the dude's face like that, but," he shrugs. "Anyway, Hunt is mouthing off. He tells Price he's playing dirty, fucking with his protection, and damn, you should have seen the look on Price's face. He told Deacon if he wanted protection, give them someone worth protecting. And if he doesn't like getting hit, then go play fucking tennis."

I wince. Dominique's never been one to mince words. "That was harsh."

"But, effective," Reed smirks.

I turn to Deacon, who's still glaring, but when he sees me looking he nods. "It did the job," he sighs. "Got my head out of my ass and back in the game."

"And made you a damn better quarterback. Deacon learned in three days what takes most quarterbacks years to figure out, and he's not buckling under the pressure. He's playing smart."

"Has Dom backed off? Is your defensive line helping you out, now?"

Deacon snorts. "No. I'm still on Prices' shit list. But now," he shrugs, "I do my part to not get hit."

"So, he's still getting hit a lot." Reed supplies and Deacon shoots him another glare. "Hey, don't get pissy with me, my friend. You're just mad because that asshole made you a better player and you don't like it."

"Yeah, whatever." Deacon finishes his beer and stands. "I need another drink. You?"

"Uh, sure." He nods and I watch as he heads over to the coolers the girls placed near the pool. Once he's out of earshot, I turn back to Reed and ask, "What's he going to do? Getting sacked in practice is one thing, but he can't be left defenseless in a game. He'll end up seriously hurt."

Reed gives me a sobering look. "I think he's hoping you can help him out with that."

Me? What the hell was I supposed to do?

NINETY

Dominique

Aaron's riding the line again. He isn't sleeping and jumping at loud sounds. I know what's coming and I'm trying to head it off, but the asshole standing in front of me isn't making that easy.

"Bro, we had a deal?"

Aaron throws on his leather jacket and swipes his keys off the table, heading for the front door.

"I'm not going to do anything stupid," he assures me, but we both know that's a lie.

"You heard what the doc—"

His jaw clenches. "I'm going to live my life. Okay? Can you get on board with that, man?"

I grind my teeth together. This is a bad idea and he knows it, but I can see by the look in his eyes I don't have a shot in hell of talking him out of it. I never do. Not when he gets like this.

Henderson is a walking, talking stick of dynamite just waiting to explode. When we were kids, he was always a self-destructive shit, but adult Aaron is on a whole 'nother level. We've all got baggage, but the shit Aaron needs to unpack is traumatic as fuck, and I only know the half of it. But we made a deal. I'm not about to let him weasel out of it.

"When you stop being a lying sack of shit, maybe." I shrug and wait to see how he responds. It can go one of two ways. Brotherhood will get the better of him and he'll back down. Nine and a half times out of ten, he's true to his word and he hates being called a liar. Addicts are liars and Aaron refuses to be one of them.

I see the flicker in his eyes. The moment of hesitation at my words and then... *fuck*. There's that other half. The times when he decides not to give a fuck because he's too far up his own ass to think straight.

"Aaron—"

"You know me," he says, and there's a plea in his voice, so I nod. "You know I've been clean. For two years I've stayed clean. No missteps. I've stayed on the fucking wagon, man."

"I know." Which is why what he's doing now is pissing me off. It's like he forgot what the first year was like. The depression. The withdraws. He was so fucking sick back then he had to take a full semester off. And now he wants to risk it all for a party and a piece of ass. I shake my head. This was a mistake.

"It's a pool party. There will be booze, but we both know booze was never my problem."

No. It wasn't. Aaron's issue started as a little recreational weed until he fucked up. Got behind the wheel while high and wrapped his car around a tree, injuring his passengers—Roman, Emilio, and me. Shit got ugly after the accident and we didn't speak for close to a year after that.

What none of us knew at the time though, was that Aaron almost went to juvie for it. He was a minor driving while under the influence and had over forty grams of weed on him when paramedics picked us up. Once released, he was charged with a class C felony. His lawyer couldn't make it go away. Not entirely. But the DA's office offered him a deal and with approval from a judge and his parent's consent, they signed off on him becoming an informant for the Sun Valley P.D.

Big fucking mistake.

Roman's dad was chief back then and made the arrangements. If Roman ever found out, there'd be hell to pay, which is why even after shit was smoothed out between us all, Aaron never mentioned it.

Shit should have been straightforward. On paper, Aaron was supposed to tip the cops off about corner dealers selling to kids at our school, but what really happened was they forced him into the deep end. They had a sixteen-year-old worming his way into the drug world and shit got messy.

I don't know all the details of everything that went down. I know shit escalated with drugs. Weed turned into molly and that turned into coke. There was a girl he refuses to talk about. And a drug deal went south that Aaron got caught up in. He hasn't shared the full story, but on top of the addiction he got a nice case of PTSD. When he's having an episode things get heavy. The way he reacts, you'd think he'd been to war. I guess in a roundabout way he was.

Aaron worked on getting clean before we moved in together and I helped get him out of the CI program as soon as I learned he was in it. Fuckers didn't want to let him go, but I made sure they realized they didn't have a choice. Sometimes it pays to be a Price. This was one of those times.

But the road to recovery is a long one, and staying clean isn't the only thing Aaron needs to worry about. "Access to drugs isn't what I'm worried about. I know you're good." The first year was rough but the last two, he's been solid.

Aaron lets out an exasperated sigh. "I'll be fine."

"You jumped me when I slammed the back door earlier."

He closes his eyes, hands fisted at his sides. "You caught me off guard."

Yeah. I'd been doing that a lot lately. It's why I've made it a point to be around as much as possible. I go to class, the field, and then straight home. I've met up with Aaron for lunch between classes all week, and when he's felt up for it, he kicks it at the field and catches up on his schoolwork while he waits for me to finish.

It's not ideal. We don't do secrets in our crew. But, this ... this is Aaron's damage. It's not my place to tell my boys. Aaron will do that when he's good and ready, so for now, this is what works.

But part of why it works is because we avoid scenes like what Aaron is about to put himself in. Greek parties are loud. Rowdy. People get into stupid shit and no, I don't think Aaron will slip up when it comes to drugs. He worked to fucking hard for his sobriety. But this week he's been off and I'm waiting for the other shoe to drop.

"There's going to be loud music. Probably shit with a heavy bass. People are going to be shouting. People are going to rub against you when you walk by. How do you think you'll react?" I'm not his dad. I'm not going to order him around, but he needs to see this for what it is. A bad idea.

"I'm going. You wanna babysit, be my guest, but I'm climbing the walls here, Dom." He slams a palm to his chest. "I can't breathe and I know I'm fucked up in the head right now, but this is what I've come up with and I'm seeing it through."

I grab my phone and slide it into my back pocket. "Let's go, then."

Aaron's shoulders relax and we head out. He tells me on the way that the party we're headed to is at Kappa Mu. Kasey's sorority house. *Shit.*

We haven't talked since the classroom. I'm a dick. She knows that already. This isn't some new revelation. But I took shit too far that day. And if Aaron finds out what I did to his baby sister, what I still think about doing to her, I'm fucked.

NINETY-ONE

Kasey

___

"I see you're having fun," Quinn says, a smirk on her face as she moves to stand up beside me. "Any chance your hottie has a brother?"

I follow her eyes and see that she's ogling Deacon. "Not that I know of, but he's not my hottie. We just happen to have English together this semester so, you should go for it."

Her eyes bug out and she whips toward me. "Seriously? You wouldn't mind?"

I laugh. "Nope. He's all yours. Deacon isn't really my type."

She looks at me like I just spoke a foreign language. "Have you seen the guy?" she asks. "That fine specimen of a man right there is everyone's type."

"He's good-looking, I'll give you that. But—"

"But? There are no buts." She places the back of her hand against my forehead. Then my cheeks. "Are you feeling okay? No fever, but I'm worried about you. Maybe you should lie down. All this sun is getting to you."

I smack her hand away. "I'm fine," I tell her with an exasperated breath. "I just don't do players. He's nice, but he's on the football team and he's a Greek. Pass."

"You do realize you're a Greek right?"

I shrug. "So, I'm a hypocrite. Sue me. Are you really going to stand here and continue trying to convince me to go for him, or are you going to take your fine ass over there before one of our sisters shoots their shot?"

"Oh, my God, you're right." Quinn fluffs her hair and adjusts her boobs. Yes, she actually shifted her girls around before glancing at me with an expectant look. "How do I look?"

"Hot! Go get him."

She gives an excited squeal before taking a deep breath and marching toward him. Deacon drifted back to his friend group a little while ago, giving me a much-needed respite after everything he and Reed had unloaded. A part of me wants to help. I feel a little responsible for what he's going through, but a bigger part of me really doesn't want to get involved. I don't want an excuse to seek Dominique out. If I do ... I don't know. But it isn't going to be good. I'm angry and a little hurt, though mostly angry. This is the second time something like this has happened between us and both times he ghosts me.

What the hell is his problem? I'm not asking for a relationship or even a repeat event. All I'm asking for is some human decency. It's really not too much to ask.

But, whatever. This is Dominique I'm talking about here. I turn and grab a water bottle from one of the coolers and head for the pool. There's a pink sprinkle, donut-shaped floaty with my name on it.

One of the Alpha Ze guys helps me maneuver my way onto it without jumping into the pool because not gonna lie, that water is cold.

I'm laying back, enjoying the music and chatter around me when something in the air shifts. I don't know how else to describe it. Sunglasses firmly in place, I turn my head to the side just in time to see my brother and—would you look at that—Dominique, arrive.

For a second, a flash of panic hits me square in the chest and I look down at myself. Fuck. I'm dead. So dead. When Dominique sees what I'm—hold on. I cut that thought off and scoff. What am I even thinking? Fuck what Dominique thinks. Quinn was right. I look hot. No way in hell am I going to let that asshole shame me for wearing this suit. I'm going to own it.

I track their progress through the yard, grateful no one can see my eyes because I'm totally staring. Aaron, being the friendly guy he is, dives right in on the fun and joins a few of the guys at one of the backyard games the girls must have set up. The one where you toss hacky sacks at an angled board and try to get it through the hole.

"Hey, what's that game called?" I ask one of the guys swimming next to me. I'm not sure what his name is. He hooks his arms over the side of my floaty and looks to where I'm pointing. "Corn hole," he tells me, and then instead of swimming away, which was what I'd been hoping for, his eyes do a slow and obvious perusal of my body. "I'm Ignacio, but everyone calls me Iggy."

"Hey. I'm—"

"Kasey!" A familiar voice barks out my name. Well, that took longer than expected. *Not.*

I turn my head to find Dominique, arms folded over his chest and dark eyes ablaze. He's not wearing sunglasses like virtually everyone else here, so I can spot his glare from the edge of the pool and offer him a little wave. His nostrils flare.

Dressed in black jogger pants that taper at the ankle and a white crew t-shirt that hugs his broad shoulders and impressive chest, I have to fight the urge not to lick my lips. Has he always looked this good? Who am I kidding? Yes.

He's wearing his usual red Beast Mode sneakers, but he's changed his hair. For as long as I've known him, Dominique's kept it braided back over his scalp. Sometimes they're thick braids. Other times they're thin. But for the first time, there are no braids. Sometime this week he got his hair cut and damn, it looks good on him.

A line up and fade make his features appear sharper, and he's added a razor part design. Two parallel lines that start at his temple and slant up enough to form a peak before curving down and back. Almost like a lightning bolt.

"I didn't think this was really your scene." I keep my tone casual, my expression carefree. I know people are watching, the girls already trying to figure out how we know one another. This is exactly why I didn't want him and the other guys here when I moved in. They draw too much attention.

"Get out of the pool." His voice is hard.

"Pass. I'm enjoying it here."

I swear steam comes out of his ears.

"Kasey—" There's a warning there. One I should probably listen to, but where is the fun in that?

"Dominique," I retort.

His jaw is tight, a vein bulging in his neck. This is too good. Alpha Ze guy—what was his name again? Oh, right, Iggy—is still clinging to my floaty, but his eyes keep bouncing back and forth from me to Dom and then back again.

"Hey," I draw his attention.

He turns, expression a little nervous. Well, shit. That won't work. I turn my smile up a notch and shift to my side which gives him a better view of my breasts. "Sorry. He's so rude. I'm Kasey." I pick up where we left off, suddenly interested in chatting with the guy.

He swallows hard, eyes locked on my chest.

"So, what year are you?" I ask, and right as I'm about to trail a finger over his arm Dominique snaps, "Rojas. Off limits. Get your ass away from her."

Iggy jumps back as if he's been electrocuted and makes quick work of following Dom's orders. "Yeah, man. Of course. I was just, uh, making conversation. You know?"

Dominique doesn't answer him. He gives Iggy a flat stare before dismissing him with a look and turning his attention back to me. "I won't ask again, Kasey."

I flip him off. There are a few muffled laughs from the yard, and I spot Deacon and Reed barely keeping themselves in check. Dominique sees them too. *Oh, shit.* He stalks in their direction. *Shit. Shit.*

Deacon sees him coming and squares his shoulders, nostrils flaring. Double shit. He's not going to back down. "Dom!" I paddle my arms to reach the pool's edge but wind up spinning myself in circles. Navigation on a giant donut is not as easy as it might seem, but one of the guys is nice enough to give me a push to the shallow end and then I'm off. I jump in the thigh deep water. Gah! Cold. And hop up the steps.

Dominique is in Deacon's face. No clue what he's saying, but it doesn't look like they're discussing the weather. Everyone is watching. Waiting for fists to fly, but yeah, no. Not happening.

I shove myself between the guys and push Dominique in the chest as hard as I can. He moves back a few steps, but only because he was willing to.

"Happy now? I'm out." He's glaring over my shoulder, still not looking at me. I turn and clear my throat to get Deacon's attention. His eyes shift and he looks down, and then all of a sudden I'm shoved back behind Dominique and he's all growly, saying, "Don't fucking look at her."

Then he's tearing his shirt off his head and shoving it down over mine. When my head pops out he helps me get my arms through the sleeves, and then he's back to shoving me behind him again. Whoa. He's seriously losing it right now. I've never seen him like this.

"I thought I made myself clear," he says, voice dipped low and threatening.

"What is your problem, man? She's not your girl. Back the fuck off."

Okay, so true, I am most definitely not his girl, but still, even I know that was the wrong thing to say. *Idiot.* It's like he *wants* to get his ass kicked again. The muscles of Dominique's back tighten, and wow, is it a good-looking back. Why have I never seen his bare back like this before?

More heated words are exchanged, but I'm not really paying attention, too intent on tracing the lines between his shoulders and down his back with my gaze. That accomplished, I reach out and begin physically tracing the lines with my finger.

He stiffens. I don't let that deter me. I follow the path, applying light pressure, and some of the tension falls away. His muscles flex and Dominique takes a deep breath, no longer talking.

When I reach the dip at the base of his spine I lean forward, resting my head against him. A tremor rolls through him. I can feel the twist of his muscles. He peers over his shoulder, but I'm not looking at him so I don't know what he's thinking. I should move away. Stop touching him. *Why am I touching him?*

That thought gets me out of my head and I jerk back, but he's there. He turns, grabs my still raised hand, and pulls me to him. Not in an embrace or anything like that. Dominique doesn't do public affection. Not that he's ever been affectionate with me. No. We fight. I guess we also sometimes angry kiss and dry hump, but whether that was a one off or will be a repeat event is yet to be decided.

So no, no embrace. But I'm right beside him. The heat from his bare skin seeping into me.

"What are you doing?" he asks. I meet his dark-brown stare. He doesn't look mad, at least not right at this moment. He looks ... confused.

"Are you done?"

His brows pull together. "Am I done with what?"

"Being an asshole."

I open my mouth to add that he needs to stop laying into Deacon over nothing, but catch myself. He's calming down. I'd be stupid to say something I know will just piss him off again.

"You wanted me out of the pool. I'm out. Okay? Can we just ... I don't know, go inside? Cool down for a bit?"

He works his jaw, but nods. Relief sweeps through me. Good. "Come on, then." I'm waiting to see if he's going to follow before heading for the door when I catch sight of my brother right as he's turning.

He sees me. Smiles. Waves. When he sees what I'm wearing, a wrinkle forms between his brows.

"What are you—" He eyes the shirt I'm wearing and then spots a shirtless Dominique behind me. "Why are you wearing his shirt?" There's genuine confusion in his voice and my heart starts to race because shit, um ... I go with the first thing that pops in my head.

"Because Dominique is an asshole." Yep. True and relevant. Score one for me.

"Huh?" Why does he sound confused? It's not like this is a new revelation.

I decide to elaborate. "He's a dick and made me put this on because my swimsuit is *indecent*." I make air quotes and glare at Dominique for exaggerated effect. "Did you tell him to cock block me?" I add, turning my glare on my brother. "Because that shit is not cool, Aaron. I know you guys are roommates and all, but I don't need babysitters at my own house."

His eyes widen and he gets this look on his face that screams *abort. Abort.*

I love my brother, but he's never really been one for confrontation. Not with me, at least. I happen to have a bit of a mean streak and a solid record for always getting revenge. What I just said basically implies I'll cock block him the rest of the year if he tries to cock block me. I should feel bad. The panic written all over his face is just too good.

"I wouldn't do that. I—" he sputters, and I fold my arm over my chest, lifting a single brow.

"Bullshit. You absolutely would."

He huffs and then seems to rally himself, which surprises me.

"Was it?"

"Was it what?"

"Indecent. Was the swimsuit indecent?" No. Maybe. Okay, yeah, I mean, have you seen it? It was a lot. But I wasn't going to admit that to my brother.

"It's a swimsuit." I argue. "Top. Bottom. The usual."

"Kasey—" He's glaring. At me. What the hell?

"What is going on right now. This is not how this," I wave at the space between us, "works. Dominique is an asshole. I yell at you and you apologize for him being an asshole. That's how this works."

He just stares for a beat and says, "Fine, let's see it. If he's wrong, I'll apologize for him being an asshole."

My eyes widen. "What? No!"

He gives me an are-you-serious expression. "It's a swimsuit. I've seen you in a swimsuit."

Dominique is shaking beside me fighting not to laugh. I push him. "This is your fault."

He smirks. "Show him the suit, Baby Henderson."

I grind my teeth together. Fine. I'm not embarrassed. I fucking rocked this swimsuit. With my eyes on his, I tug the t-shirt off. Dominique's eyes stay trained on my face, but I don't miss the hitch in his breath.

There's a gasp. "Jesus Christ." That was from Aaron. "Don't look at my little sister like that, you fucking perv." That catches both our attention, but when I look, Aaron isn't talking to Dominique, he's glowering at the guys he's been playing corn hole with. "She's only se—"

"Hey!"

He turns.

"Don't you dare," I warn. If he tells everyone I'm seventeen I will murder him. He must see that in my eyes, because he manages to keep his mouth shut and gives Dominique some weird look. Silent communication passes between them, and then the shirt is being shoved back over my head, only this time when my head pops out it's to see Aaron heading for the door.

I follow him, Dominique right behind me, and as soon as we're all safely inside Aaron whirls on me. "What the fuck were you thinking? Do you know what goes through those guys' heads when they look at you? Shit."

I wait. I'm not really sure what is happening right now. Aaron has always been protective, but he's also always let me do my thing.

This is different. Almost like he's spiraling. I don't think all this anger is really about me. At least I hope it isn't.

"It's a swimsuit. I'm at a party in my own house I might add. I don't care how guys look at me or what goes on in their head. As long as they don't touch me without permission, I'm good. You're overreacting—"

"Overreacting? Overreacting! Jesus Christ." He spears his fingers through his shaggy blond hair.

"You said that already."

"Well, it warranted a repeat."

I smile a little at that. He takes a few deep breaths and then turns to Dominique and gives him a fist bump. "Thanks, man. I appreciate you looking out."

Dominique grunts and meets my stare. There's a warning, as if he's saying *don't you dare say a thing about what happened in the classroom.*

I glare back, my eyes conveying my own response. *I'm not an idiot, asshole.*

"I'm gonna go down to the park. I need to get the image of my baby sister in that," he nods in my direction, "out of my head. I can drop—"

"I'm good. Go ahead. Kasey can give me a lift."

I scowl, but Aaron's not paying attention. "Cool man. I'll see you later back at the house."

He heads for the door, but at the last second Dominique stops him. "Yo!"

He waits until Aaron turns to face him. "If something comes up, you call. You hear me?"

More silent communication passes between them, and damn, is that sort of creepy. I know Aaron and Dominique are friends. Best friends now. But it's like they have their own language, and there is seriously something going on with my brother that definitely has nothing to do with my swimsuit.

NINETY-TWO

Kasey

And then there were two. Aaron leaves to go boarding, leaving me and a very shirtless Dominique behind. Right. Clothes. He needed clothes. Which meant I needed clothes. Gah.

I head for my bedroom, conscious of Dominique's silent steps behind me. Once inside, I head for my dresser and pull out a pair of yoga pants and a sweater. I look down at the shirt. I don't want to give it back. It's soft and comfy and it smells like him. Like cinnamon and sandalwood and yum. *Oh my god.* I cannot believe I thought that. Not keeping the shirt. I am not that girl and no, I am not hung up on him. Just no. He's an asshole. An inconsiderate, domineering jerkface.

I pull it over my head and hold it out to Dominique, who's just standing there. Staring. It's the first time I've gotten a good look at his front and yeah, it's just as good as the back. Better actually, which is completely unfair.

His chest is wide, sculpted. He has abs that should be illegal. And those lines ... you know the ones.

I want to trail my fingers over those lines, lick his hip bone, stroke his abs. Wait. No. Fuck. I do not want to do any of those things. *Come on, Kasey, get it together.*

Alright then. I am not keeping the shirt and he really needs to put it on and leave. I cannot be around him right now. I think the sun addled my brain or something.

"Take it," I say, and give the shirt in question a little shake.

He's not looking at the shirt though. He's looking at me. And the look in his eyes isn't an innocent one. It's the same look he gave me in the classroom. Heated. Hungry. *Fuck.* I drop the shirt.

"Christ." He runs a hand over his head. "That thing is fucking indecent."

I look down at myself and yeah, he's not wrong, but neither was Quinn. I'm glad she offered me the swimsuit. Once I got over the shock of the thing, I decided I liked it. I don't care what anyone else thinks.

I've never had a hard time getting a guy's attention, present company not included, but I'm attractive in a cute sort of way. Not beautiful. Not hot or sexy. Just, cute. I have round cheeks, curly blond hair, bright blue eyes and one of those faces that people look at and think to themselves, *she's cute.*

This swimsuit takes me from cute to sexy and I'm not going to lie, I like it. I like feeling sexy, and as much as I hate to admit it, I like the way Dominique is looking at me while I'm in it. Which, yes, I know that's bad. It's the sun. Totally blaming the sun for my crazy stupid thoughts right now because I shouldn't like the way he's looking at me. In fact, I should be snapping at him for it. But I'm not. I need to steer us back onto safe ground.

"Thanks for the unsolicited opinion," I tell him.

"Put that back on." He nods to the shirt.

"Pass. I don't take orders from assholes."

His eyes narrow. "Put on the shirt."

"No. In case you didn't notice, Kappa Mu is having a party. One I plan on getting back to and enjoying. You should have left with Aaron, but since you didn't, I'll be nice and let you borrow my car. But I'm going to go have fun." I'd breeze past him out the door if he wasn't still blocking it, but because he is, I lean back against my dresser and fold my arms over my chest to wait.

His jaw tics.

"Put on the shirt, Kasey."

"No."

"Dammit. Put on the fucking shirt."

"Make me, asshole."

Okay, that last comment, probably not a great choice of words. Dominique closes the distance between us. Capturing my hips in his hands, he jerks me to him.

"Why do you always have to fight me on shit?"

I give him an incredulous look. "You're kidding, right?"

His nostrils flare.

"You do not get to dictate what I wear or do or anything about my life. You don't own me. Get that through your head." Something in me snaps. All my frustration from before, my anger and hurt at his dismissal comes rushing to the surface. Where does he get off? "You think that, what, since we fooled around in a classroom that you all of a sudden get to make demands? That's not how this works, Dom!" I shove at his chest. "Get the hell out of my way."

He shifts his stance, still blocking me.

"Dominique—"

"Put on the shirt or take off that suit. You're not going out where all those fraternity punks are in that."

I bite the inside of my cheek until I taste blood. "Fine," I snap.

Surprise flashes in his eyes and he takes a step back, giving me some space, but I'm not going to put on his stupid cinnamon smelling shirt. Since he wants me to take off the swimsuit, I'll take it off.

I grab the straps of the swimsuit and tug them down, pulling my arms out.

"What are you doing?"

Ignoring him, I push the swimsuit down past my ribcage, exposing my breasts.

"Jesus Christ!"

A small smile curls my lip and I shove the swimsuit down over my hips, letting it pool at my feet. I swallow hard, but refuse to be embarrassed as I raise my eyes to his. "Happy now?" My voice is surprisingly even, giving none of my nerves away.

Need flashes in Dominique's eyes as he drinks me in. Then, without saying a word, he turns, jerks my bedroom door open, and leaves, slamming it shut behind him.

My phone rings but it takes me a minute to collect myself. I pick up Dominique's shirt from the floor and slip it on. Not because I want to wear anything that belongs to him, but because it's there. And then I dig my phone out of my bag. It's no longer ringing, but I can see it was my mom who called. I'll call her back later. I'm not really in the mood for one of her chats.

I consider going back to the party, but that doesn't sound appealing either, so instead, I drop down on my bed and crack open a textbook, telling myself that my decision to stay inside has nothing to do with Dominique. I just need to catch up on some homework.

Clearly, I am a big fat liar.

NINETY-THREE

Dominique

There are only a few blocks between the Kappa Mu house and my place, so I walk, needing some time to clear my head. If I didn't get out of there when I did, I was going to do something I couldn't take back. I wouldn't regret it. I know that much. Taking Kasey and laying her down on her bed, sliding into her wet heat, yeah, that isn't something I would regret. But it is something that would make shit complicated, and I can't do complicated right now. Almost to my street, I change course and head for the field instead. I could use a run. My body is wound up tight. I need to tire myself out and get Kasey out of my head.

Three miles in and I still can't get the image of her naked body out of my mind. Sweat drips down my back, my calves burning, but I keep up the pace. Two more miles and my chest is heaving, but I still see her perfect tits. Her tiny waist. Her bare pussy. Running isn't going to cut it.

I jog off the track and head for my place. Maybe a cold shower will help.

When I reach my door, I notice Aaron's ride in the driveway, which means he's home. Good.

"Hey, man. You good?" I ask as soon as I see him.

He looks up, eyes bloodshot and unfocused.

I curse. "What happened?"

He shakes his head.

I grab a water bottle from the fridge, uncap it, and bring it back to him. He accepts it but doesn't take a drink. "Bro, you're freaking me out. What happened?"

His hands flex. "I freaked out, alright."

"I'm gonna need you to give me a little more information."

He hangs his head, no longer meeting my eyes. "A car pulled up to me while I was driving. They had music going. I—" He swallows hard. "There were gunshots in the song. I didn't think. Just fucking panicked."

Shit. "But you came home? You're good? Nothing else happened?"

He exhales a harsh breath. "Yeah. I'm good. Just freaked the fuck out."

"Why didn't you call? I would have come back sooner." I rub the back of my neck. He can't keep going like this. He needs help. Like real, professional help. "I think you should see someone—"

"I'm not talking to a fucking shrink."

I open my mouth to argue with him, but a phone buzzing halts my response. Aaron frowns down at his phone, the thing still buzzing.

"Who is it?" I ask.

He shakes his head. "No clue." He lifts the phone to his ear and answers. "Hello?"

"I'm gonna grab a quick shower," I tell him and head down the hall. I make it quick and cold. Enough time to wash the sweat from my body and erase the images of Kasey from my head so my dick calms the fuck down. That finished, I throw on a clean pair of clothes and head back to check on Aaron.

He still has the phone to his ear, but all the blood has drained from his face as he listens to whoever is talking.

"You okay, man?"

It's like he doesn't even hear me. His eyes fill with moisture and my chest seizes. *Fuck.* His hand falls away from his face, the phone still cradled in his palm. Whoever is on the other line is still speaking, but Aaron's no longer listening. I reach for the phone and he relinquishes it without comment.

I bring it to my ear right as he drops his head in his hands, a sob wracking his entire body.

"Who the hell is this?" I snarl.

There's a pause. "Are you related to Mr. Henderson," a calm voice asks almost hesitantly.

"I'm his roommate. What's going on? What did you say to him?" He's not in the right headspace to deal with whatever shit this is right now.

The guy on the other line clears their voice. "I'm sorry to be the bearer of bad news. I was explaining to Mr. Henderson—"

"Aaron," I correct.

"Right. I was explaining to Aaron that there's been an accident." I wait. "His... his mother was in a car accident on the highway earlier today. There was a pileup, and while Ms. Douglas was able to stop before colliding with the vehicle in front of her, the eighteen wheeler behind her wasn't able to do the same."

Fuck.

"Is she okay?"

He's quiet for a beat, and I look down at Aaron. He's hunched over, elbows on his knees and hands on the back of his head. If she was okay, he wouldn't be like that.

"She was rushed to Mercy Hospital but was DOA."

"What the hell does DOA mean?" I bite out, and it's Aaron who answers, his voice dejected.

"Dead on arrival."

"What?" I ask him, eyes wide before repeating into the phone, "What? She's dead?"

Aaron flinches.

"I'm sorry. She's gone. Aaron Henderson is listed as her next of kin. I was contacting him so we can proceed with the next—"

"No. He's not dealing with that today. He just found out his mom is gone. Everything else can wait."

"Sir, if I—"

"No. You can call back in a few days. Give the man some time to grieve." I hang up and toss Aaron's phone on the sofa beside him.

"Hey." He's not looking at me. "What do you need, man? What can I do?"

He hiccups and then gets to his feet.

"Whoa. Slow down. Where are you going?" He grabs his keys and heads for the door, but I block him. "Aaron—"

"I have to tell my sister. *Shit*. How am I supposed to tell her? How do—"

Fuck. I didn't even think about Kasey. Shit. "Okay. It's okay. You don't have to do that right now. We have time."

"Yeah, I do," he shouts, tears tracking down his face. I've never seen him like this before, and fuck if I know how to fix it. "She needs to know. She'd want to know. Now. Not tomorrow or in a few hours. She needs to know now. But how the fuck am I supposed to do that, Dom? She's my baby sister and I have to tell her but—"

I nod my head and grab him in a tight embrace. He clings to me like his life depends on it, hands fisted in the back of my shirt. "I get it, man. But, you're still processing shit right now. You can't drive like this. Just, sit down for a few, okay. We'll sort this out."

His shoulders shake. "She needs to know, man." His voice is hoarse.

"I'll tell her. You stay here and I'll tell her."

He pulls back and runs his hands through his hair, tugging on the strands as he begins to pace.

"You're cool with that? You don't mind?" he asks, not looking at me.

"I got you. I'll tell her. You stay here. I'll have the guys—"

"I don't need a babysitter," he grinds out.

"No, you don't. But you just lost your mom and you don't need to be alone right now either."

He shakes his head, about to argue.

"What about Allie?" I ask. They've always been close, and she lost her mom a few years back. She'll know how to help him get through this while I ... shit. I don't know how I'm going to break this to Kasey.

"Just, Allie?" he croaks.

"Yeah, man. Just Allie."

A nod.

"Okay. I'll call her. Just sit down. Okay?"

Another nod.

I pull out my phone and make the call. An hour later, there's a knock at our door and I let her inside.

"Hey, how's our boy doing?" she asks, voice low.

I peer over my shoulder at the boy in question. "He hasn't moved since I called you. Hasn't talked either."

She nods as I grab my keys. "Where are you going?"

I swallow past the lump in my throat. "He asked me to tell Kasey."

Her eyes soften and she places a hand on my arm. "Dom, that's ... you shouldn't have to—"

"I know. But he can't, and someone needs to."

"I can call Bibiana."

I shake my head. "No. I've got this. You look after him. Don't leave him alone or let him go anywhere by himself. If you need to call Roman to sit on him, do that, okay?"

She nods but..."I'm serious, Allie. He's dealing with some other shit right now too. His mom dying is awful, but the timing couldn't have been worse. Do not leave him alone. I'll handle Kasey, but depending on how she handles things, I don't know what time I'll be back. If you have to leave—"

"I got it. He won't be left alone."

"Good." I leave Allie with Aaron and jump in my Escalade. When I pull up to her place, it hits me that I don't know what I'm going to say to her, so I sit there, my car idling. It's been a few hours since I left and I know she won't be happy to see me but... it doesn't matter. I told Aaron I'd have his back and tell her, so I'm going to do that. He shouldn't be the one to drop this bomb on her. I've got this.

There's a back entrance off the hall that leads to Kasey's room, so I put my ride in drive and head that direction. There's a chance Kappu Mu's pool party is still in full swing. Greek parties are usually an all-day, all-night sort of thing. I don't want to see anyone and deal with their bullshit, so I'll slip into Kasey's room and wait for her there if she isn't inside already.

NINETY-FOUR

Kasey

I'm tired and hungry and decide to fix at least one of those problems by grabbing a bagel from the kitchen. I probably should have put pants on but I doubt anyone is going to come inside, and at least I bothered to slip underwear on before heading to the kitchen.

Dominique's shirt hangs down to the middle of my thighs, which is more than the swimsuit was covering. I should shred the damn thing. All I've had these past few hours is time. Time to think about how twisted up I am about a guy who clearly doesn't give a shit about me. I'm not this person, so why am I letting him get to me?

Decision made, I'm done letting him tell me what to do, or wear. I'm done giving a shit about his feelings or worrying about whether or not he's interested in me. I'm over it.

I'm going to focus on school. I'll date. Yes, I'll definitely date. Maybe Quinn or one of the other girls can fix me up with someone. I need to get over whatever it is that I feel for that asshole.

The toaster dings and I retrieve my bagel, dropping it on a plate before spreading a thin layer of butter on it. Next I add a layer of jelly. I know you're supposed to use cream cheese, but I'm not a huge fan and this tastes a whole lot better. The door leading to the backyard opens and Deacon steps inside.

"Hey," he says upon seeing me right as I bite into my bagel.

I give him a wave and point to my mouth as I chew. He nods and a few seconds later I swallow. "Sorry. Didn't want to talk with my mouth full."

"No problem." He shifts uncomfortably.

"So..." I say.

"Yeah. Sorry. I was just coming in to use the bathroom."

I point down the hall. "First door on your right."

He nods. "Thanks."

"No problem." He goes to take care of business and I put the butter and jelly back in the refrigerator. I take another bite of my bagel and grab a napkin before turning back to the fridge for a bottle of water. Hands full, I head back for my room right as Deacon exits the bathroom. "Have fun," I tell him as I slip past.

"Oh, hey, wait up."

I slow my steps, but I don't stop entirely. "What's up?"

"I was hoping we could talk," he says.

"I thought we already did?" We pause outside my room. I have a bagel in one hand and the water in the other so I'll need to shift things around to free up a hand, but I have a feeling if I open my door, he'll want to come inside, and I'm not sure that's a good idea. Deacon is nice, and hot. But I'm in a weird head space right now, and yes, I definitely want to get over whatever hang-up I have for Dominique at the moment, but I know myself. I'll do something reckless, like throw myself at the guy and just make a bigger mess out of things, which isn't fair to him. I need to find a guy not on the football team. One Dominique can't screw with to get at me.

"We did, it's just—" My door swings open on its own. Correction, the jerkface standing inside my room opens it.

"Leave," he says to Deacon, right as I say, "What the hell are you doing in my room?"

Dominique doesn't look at me, his penetrating stare resting solely on Deacon.

"Look, man..."

Dom shakes his head. "I don't have time to deal with you right now. You need to go. Now."

Deacon's shoulders are stiff as the guys stare off with one another. *Screw this.*

"Hi. I have a better idea. How about you both leave. That'd be great."

Deacon looks down at me, a flicker of hurt in his eyes, and I wince. "Sorry," I tell him. "This one brings the bitch out in me."

That seems to satisfy him, but still, neither guy moves. I turn to Dom. "Why are you even here?" I just decided I'm done with his crap and this is what the universe does? It'd be bad enough if he showed up on my doorstep, but in my room? Really?

Dom looks down at me. "We need to talk."

I scoff. "Pass. I don't have anything to say to you." The universe can shove it for all I care.

He gives me a once over, a smirk curling the corners of his mouth when he sees I'm wearing his shirt. "That looks good on you." He fingers one of the sleeves.

I smack his hand away with my bottle. "Go home, Dom."

"Kasey." There's a warning there.

"She said go home, man. Take the hint and back off."

Surprising me, Dom ignores him. Well, I guess that isn't really surprising, but I expected a verbal jab or maybe even a punch after that comment.

"I just want to talk—"

"No," I snap. Honestly, I don't want to talk to either of them. I want to eat my bagel and then I want to go to bed.

"No?" He rears back incredulously.

"You heard me. No. You were a complete asshole today. You were an asshole last week. You keep fucking with me and for what? I'm tired of this game, Dom. So, no, I don't want to talk to you. Not today. Not tomorrow. Just, go away."

He exhales a harsh breath and his eyes soften the slightest bit. "Kasey, I..." He pauses and turns to Deacon. "Look, I don't like you, but I need to talk to her about personal shit. So, you gotta bounce. Now."

Deacon's jaw tightens, but he nods. "Fine. But only if you get the team to stop fucking me over in practice."

"Done."

A nod. A handshake. And then Deacon leaves, and wasting no time, Dominique pulls me into the room and closes the door behind me.

"Just because you got rid of Deacon doesn't mean I'm going to talk to you. You can go, too," I tell him, setting my water and bagel down on the nightstand.

He sighs, and I know he's going to try again, but I've had time to think and I'm done. I want off his merry-go-round. "What part of go are you not understanding?"

His Adam's apple bobs. "It's about your mom."

A strangled laugh escapes me and I swing my arms wide. "What? What about her is so important that you had to come fuck up my night after already screwing my day?"

He doesn't say anything, just looks at me like I'm a little crazy and so what, maybe I am, but he made me this way. He's the one butting into my life. Interjecting himself where he doesn't belong, and now this.

"Well? What was so damn important that you couldn't just leave me the fuck alone?" He's not leaving. Fine. I'll leave instead. I grab a pair of leggings—I'll throw them on in the car—slip on some sandals, and grab my phone and keys. Jerking my bedroom door open, I head for the side door.

"Kasey!" He calls my name, but I don't stop.

"Go home, Dom," I call over my shoulder as I make it outside.

A few of the girls are outside hanging out on the picnic table. All of them looking my way as I exit the house, Dominique right behind me.

"Kasey, stop."

I flip him off over my shoulder and he growls. Actually growls. I'm almost to my car when he grabs me by the elbow, and I'm about to tear away from him when he bites out, "Your mom was in an accident."

"What?" I shake my head and pull away. "She literally called today while you were in my room earlier."

"Kasey," his voice is soft, eyes somber. A stab of pain hits me in the chest. No. He's wrong. I just talked to her a few days ago and she was fine. And she called earlier today. He doesn't know what he's talking about. I pull out my phone and punch in her number.

"Kasey—"

I hold my finger up, silently telling him to wait.

The call goes straight to voicemail. My stomach sinks, but no, that doesn't mean anything. Mom is forgetful. Her phone is probably dead. Once she charges it, she'll see the missed call and call me right back. It's fine. Everything is fine.

A notification flashes across the screen. I have a voicemail. I smack my forehead. Of course I do. She called earlier and left me a message. I enter my pin and wait for the message to start.

"Hey, sweetheart. I just wanted to check in on my girl. Hope you're having fun. I'll call yo—" her voice cuts off. There's the sound of tires squealing in the background. A shrill scream. The crunch of metal.

Oh my God! "Mom!" No. No. No. She has to be okay. She— Dominique reaches out, but I slap his hand away. I need to find my brother. I need... I drop my phone and shove past him. "Kasey, stop."

I don't. I move for my car, but strong arms band around me, turning me until we're face to face. "I'm sorry. I didn't know how else to tell you."

I shove against his chest, but he doesn't budge. Instead, he holds me tighter against his chest, one hand cupping the back of my head. "I'm sorry, baby girl. I'm so fucking sorry."

I shake my head. "No!" My vision blurs, but I blink back the tears. *"Never let them see you cry, sweetheart."* Mom's words echo in my head.

I sniff and pull away. This time, he lets me go. "She's fine though, right? She's at a hospital or whatever? She's getting treatment?" I rub my eyes with the backs of my hands.

He doesn't say anything. He just stands there looking at me with eyes full of what ...regret?

"Well?" I shout. "You can talk now. That's why you're here, right? Is she going to be okay?" I need to talk to my teachers. If Mom is hurt she'll need someone to look after her. At least until she's back on her feet. I don't know how much time I can miss from school, but I'll figure that out later. Aaron will—*shit.* I need to talk to my brother. Does he know Mom was in an accident?

"Where's Aaron?"

"He's at home."

I frown. "Does he know Mom was hurt? I have to call him."

"He knows," Dominique says. "The hospital called him."

Okay. Good. She's at a hospital. That's good. But, "Why isn't he here? Why are you here telling me about my mom instead of him?" Anger floods my system and I latch onto it.

A tormented look flashes across his face. "He's having a hard time with the news. I don't..." he takes a deep breath, "He didn't know how to tell you."

"Is he packing at least?" I run through my mental to-do list. Pack some clothes. Notify my teachers that I have a family emergency. Book a flight to Florida. *Shit.* I don't even have the new address.

I'll figure that out once I talk to Aaron. I whirl around to go back inside. "Where are you going?"

"I need to pack."

"Kasey!"

"Dominique. I don't have time. If Mom is hurt, I need—"

"She didn't make it."

Something squeezes my chest and all the air whooshes out of my lungs. "W...what?"

My knees shake and everything suddenly sounds far away.

Dominique steps toward me, but it's almost like he's out of focus. My vision is dark along the edges.

"What do you mean, she didn't make it?" My voice is quiet, almost like if I say the words too loud it will make them real. But they can't be real. Mom is fine. She has to be fine.

"I'm so sorry," he tells me. This time, I believe him.

"No." I press the palm of my hand to my chest. "She can't ... no. She has to be okay. My mom," I choke back a sob. "No. She has to be okay!"

Dominique steps closer, his hands reaching out almost like I'm a wild animal he's afraid to spook.

"It's going to be okay."

"No, it's not. It is not going to be okay. This is not okay!"

"Fuck. I know. I'm sorry. That was the wrong thing to say."

I can't breathe. I'm opening and closing my mouth, trying to suck in air, but it's like my lungs have stopped working. I'm like a fish stuck on shore and I can't fucking breath.

"Kasey? Fuck. Kasey!"

A large hand forces my head between my knees. I didn't realize I'd fallen to the ground. "Breath, baby girl. In and out. That's good. Take another breath."

I try to focus on his words, but my chest hurts. It really really hurts.

He rubs circles across my back as I fight to get my emotions under control, but as soon as I manage to suck in a full breath, the tears come pouring out. A distant part of me is screaming to get it together. To push him away and find somewhere private to cry, but I can't move. I want to get up, but it's like the part of my brain that controls my limbs isn't working.

Strong arms scoop me up and the next thing I know I'm nestled in Dominique's arms as he walks me to his Escalade. My entire body shakes like a leaf. *She's gone. She's really gone.* The realization slams into me like a freight train and a new wave of tears falls down my cheeks.

Dominique sets me down on the passenger seat. How he opened the door while holding me, I don't know. He reaches over me and secures my seat belt before cupping my cheeks, his thumbs wiping the tears on my face. "You're going to get through this," he says, his voice somehow both soft and firm.

I hear the words, but I don't believe them. How does anyone get through something like this? How does anyone recover after losing their mom?

The rest of the night is a blur. Dominique takes me to his place, but I don't remember the drive there or even getting out of his Escalade and walking inside.

Aaron is there. Allie too. She hugs me, I think. I'm not really sure.

And then, nothing.

NINETY-FIVE

Kasey

"Kasey?"

I blink sleep from my eyes. Sunlight filters in through the window and it takes me a minute before I'm able to turn my head and find the person who said my name.

"Dom?"

He steps further into the room and I push up on my hands. I'm in bed. But, it's not mine. This bed is a queen but I know mine in my room at the Kappa Mu house is a full. "Whose bed is this?" I ask. My throat is dry and my words come out raspy.

Dominique sits down beside me, placing a hand on my leg. "You're in our guest room. You fell asleep, so I brought you here." He shrugs. "Figured this would be more comfortable than the couch."

That makes sense. "Thanks."

He stares at me intently before asking, "Are you feeling okay? Did you ... did you want to talk?"

I scowl. "Why would I want to—" Last night comes rushing back to me and I suck in a shuddering breath.

"Kasey?"

Oh God.

"Hey. Hey!" He cups both sides of my face and my vision swims. I'm crumbling, and he gets a front row seat to the show. "It's okay."

I shake my head. No. It's not okay. My mom is dead. I'm seventeen and she's fucking dead.

I pull away from his touch and turn to my side, resting my head on the pillow as silent sobs wrack my body. *Don't let him see you cry.* I tell myself. *You fucked that up yesterday. Don't make it worse. Hold it together.*

A rough hand rubs my back, but I pull away from the touch.

"Leave me alone," I whisper.

"Kasey." He sighs, and there's pity in his voice. It makes my tears fall faster. I don't want his pity. I just … I want my mom.

Dominique leaves and I lose track of time after that. Day turns to night only to become day. It happens again and again, day after day. But, I barely move from the bed. I get up to use the bathroom. Sometimes I get up and sit by the window and look outside. The last time I did that I fell asleep, only to wake as Dominique laid me back in bed.

He brings me water. A few times he's tried to get me to eat but I'm never hungry. He's being nice to me and I hate it. This isn't how our relationship works. It's not helping me. It just makes it all worse.

The door to my room opens and I know without rolling over to look that it's Dominique who's come inside. I haven't seen Aaron since I got here. He's dealing with his own grief. Neither one of us is really equipped to help the other right now. I feel like a shitty sister about that, but I'm pretty sure he feels like a shitty brother too, so I figure we're square.

"How are you feeling?" He always asks the same question as if he doesn't already know the answer, so like all the other times, I don't bother to respond.

Dominique sighs and moves around the bed. He crouches down in front of me but I keep my eyes closed, hoping he'll take the hint and go away.

"You're not really asleep."

So? I want to tell him, but I stay quiet.

Another sigh. "The girls are here."

That catches my attention and I snap my eyes open. Dominique is eye level with me, his penetrating stare burning into me.

"They're worried about you. You're not responding to any of their texts."

"I don't want to talk to anyone," I whisper, my mouth so dry the words come out scratchy and raw.

He hands me an uncapped bottle of water. "Drink."

I shake my head. I don't want it.

"Kasey, drink the damn water or I'll hold you down and force it down your throat myself."

I glare at him, feeling mutinous. He waves the bottle in my face, his eyes daring me to push him.

"Fine." I pull myself up into a sitting position and take the bottle. Glaring at him, I swallow a few sips before giving it back. "Happy?" I ask and lay back down.

He grunts out a, "Yes," and places the water on the bedside table. "I told Allie and Bibi you were dealing, but you know how they can be. They want to see for themselves that you're okay. I think they mostly want to make sure I haven't buried you somewhere."

I suck in a breath.

"Fuck. Bad joke. Ignore that." He shakes his head. "I just thought you'd want a heads-up before they came in."

He moves to stand, but I latch onto his wrist, stopping him.

I swallow hard. "Don't let them in."

His eyes soften. "They're worried about you. We all are. It's been four days Kasey—"

I shake my head. "Please. I... I can't."

He looks away, a tic jumping along his jaw. "Allie lost her mom, too. She can help. Aaron's been spending a lot of time with her. Maybe—"

"No!"

He reaches down and tucks a strand of hair behind my ear, his fingers lingering on my cheek. "Okay. I'll tell them you need more time."

NINETY-SIX

Dominique

"**S**he needs more time," I tell Allie, who gives me a worried look.

"It's been days," she says, like I don't already know that.

"I know but she... she asked for more time. I'm not going to push her if she isn't ready."

Allie gives Bibiana a pointed look. "Maybe we can—"

"B, no. She said no. The answer is no." Neither girl looks happy with my answer.

"She has classes. She's—"

"I spoke with the admin. They notified her teachers of the situation."

Allie's eyes widen. "Oh. Wow. That was really thoughtful of you."

I grunt. "She's got enough to worry about." They both do.

Aaron's in the other room, phone held up to his ear. He's been handling funeral arrangements. Trying to get the body transported back to Sun Valley so he can host a funeral, but it's a slow-going process with a lot of paperwork and hoops to jump through.

"How's he doing?" I ask Allie.

She purses her lips. "As good as can be expected. He's talking about it which is good. He's not holding everything in and letting the pressure build but—"

He snaps the phone shut and throws it across the room where it shatters against the wall. Yeah, he's handling shit well alright.

"Aaron?" I call, drawing his attention. "What's up?"

His chest is heaving as he fights to pull himself together. "I have to fly out to Florida. They won't release the body without me physically confirming it's her and signing off on some paperwork."

Fuck.

He runs his hands through his hair, his movements agitated.

"When do you need to go?" I ask.

"As soon as I can get there. I need to check flights and—"

"I got it."

He frowns.

"Peretti and Price has a company jet. I'll set it up. Just tell me when."

He swallows hard and nods. "Thanks, man."

"No worries. You want me to go with you?"

He looks at the door leading to the guest room, and I know what he's thinking. I don't like the idea of leaving Kasey alone any more than he does, but the thought of him dealing with this alone doesn't sit well, either.

"You should talk to her," I suggest, but he shakes his head. "I'm serious, man. She could use her big brother."

"How does that help her? I can't tell her it's going to be okay when I don't believe it myself, man. So what can I do? How can I fix this, because as far as I see it, I can't." He hangs his head and walks out of the room, his shoulders hunched and head hanging low.

"One of us can go with him," Allie says. "You take care of our girl. They'll get through this."

I want to believe her, but it's been four days since I brought Kasey back to our place. Four days and she's barely moved from the guest room. She's not eating. She never talks. It's like the girl has gone catatonic. I don't know what to do and Aaron's been fucking worthless, not that I can blame the guy.

He's either gone to Allie and Roman's or he's locked in his room, and now he's going to fly to Florida. How long will that take? How much longer can Kasey hide before shit gets serious?

"Yeah, okay. I'll make some calls and set up his flight. Just ..." I hesitate, but someone else needs to know. I can't watch them both twenty-four seven. "Can I talk to you for a sec?"

Without needing to be asked, Bibiana excuses herself. "I'm going to head home. Call me if she changes her mind and wants to talk, okay?"

I nod and give her a quick hug goodbye, being careful of her swollen belly. She has a few months left, but already she looks ready to pop. When she's gone, I turn to Allie and consider what to tell her.

"Aaron's been dealing with ... things."

She raises a brow. "Yeah. His mom just died."

I shake my head. "More than that. I can't tell you the how or why. I shouldn't be telling you any of this so don't repeat it, not even to Roman. Okay?"

She nods, worry crossing over her face.

"Aaron has PTSD."

She opens her mouth to ask a question, but I raise my hand to stop her. "Like I said. I can't tell you the why or the how. That's his story to tell when he's ready, but it's been getting worse. He wasn't handling it well before his mom died and now, well, it's not going to get any better. He's just ignoring one problem in place of the other, and eventually the other shoe is going to drop. He doesn't sleep enough. He gets these night terrors where he wakes up panicked and drenched in sweat. And loud noises can set him off. Almost like a panic attack where he feels like the walls are closing in."

"Has he talked to anyone?"

I shake my head. "He won't see a shrink. I've tried but he refuses. I just... you need to know what to look out for because he's getting worse, not better."

She nods. "Okay. What do I need to know."

Fuck. Where did I even begin? "He needs to be in a relaxed environment as much as possible. No parties. No loud, sudden noises. He tries to push it. He thinks if he exposes himself to the shit that sets him off that it'll desensitize him to it, but that doesn't work. Video games with shooters can be a trigger. The smell of smoke. If he doesn't sleep for more than three days he's got pills he's supposed to take to help with that. They knock him out, but he wakes up feeling hungover so he doesn't like taking them, but if he's not sleeping he has to. It gets worse when he doesn't."

She nods. "Okay. I can look out for that."

I take a breath and tell her the last thing. "If you startle him, he can lash out. Physically. He pulls himself back once he recognizes you but he's landed a punch a time or two. For me, that's not a problem. With you or another chick, it will be. Don't surprise him. If you walk in a room and he's spacing out, call his name. Don't touch him until he acknowledges you. Got it?"

"Yeah. I got it."

"Good. I'm gonna make a few calls and get that flight sorted out. Let me know if shit changes with him or if you need me for anything else."

She nods and I go to my room to make the call. My parents will kill me for this. Not because they give a shit if I use the jet, but because we had an agreement I wouldn't use Price assets unless I was willing to be an active member of the family—which I'm not— but it'll take them a while to notice, and what they don't know won't hurt them. It'll just bite me in the ass later.

NINETY-SEVEN

Kasey

H e isn't wearing a shirt. I don't know why I'm hung up on that but there he is, standing in the kitchen barefoot, wearing gray sweatpants without a shirt on.

I somehow manage to step farther into the room. He's at the stove, spatula in hand and he's making ... I peer around him ... pancakes. Dominique is making pancakes. What twilight zone did I just walk out of?

"You're up," he says without turning around.

I clear my throat. "Yeah."

"Have a seat. I'm almost done."

I nod, not that he sees it, and take a seat at the kitchen island, watching the muscles in his back flex as he moves around the kitchen, grabbing syrup and peanut butter before plating the pancakes and setting everything down in front of me.

"You hungry?"

I shake my head.

"When's the last time you ate?"

I think about it, but I don't really remember. "How long has it been since ..." I can't say it, but he knows what I mean and curses.

"You need to eat. I brought food to your room. Why didn't you eat any of it?"

"I'm not hungry."

"I don't care." He tosses two pancakes onto a new plate, spreads peanut butter on both and then drizzles them with syrup before sliding it across the counter to me. "Eat."

I stare down at the food. My stomach twists into a knot and my eyes fill with moisture.

"Dammit." He walks around the counter until he's right beside me. "You're wasting away. You need to eat something. Just a few bites, okay?"

I nod, forcing back the tears. I pick up the fork and knife and cut into the pancakes.

Dominique grabs his own plate and fills it with bacon, eggs, and a single piece of toast. But no pancakes. I frown down at my plate. "Why aren't you having any pancakes?"

"Not on my meal plan."

"Then why did you make pancakes if you knew you weren't going to eat any?"

He grunts. "You order pancakes every time we go to Sun Valley Station. Figured if I was going to get you to eat something, this was my best bet. You mentioned before that pancakes were your favorite food group."

"You remembered that?"

He nods.

I smile at that. Pancakes are my favorite food group. Mom used to make them on Sundays. Always with peanut butter and syrup, how her mom used to make them when she was growing up.

A fresh wave of grief sweeps over me and I blink back the tears, eyes locked on my plate.

Dominique either doesn't notice or chooses not to mention it, which I'm grateful for. "I have practice today. I missed earlier this week, which was fine. Coach wanted me to take it easy because of my shoulder anyway, but we have a game tomorrow and I have to show up. Will you—"

"I'll be fine."

He frowns. "That's not what I was going to ask."

Oh. "What were you going to ask?"

He looks at me, looks at my plate, then waits. I sigh and take a bite.

He grunts. "I was going to ask if you'd come to campus with me. Aaron had to fly out to Florida to take care of a few things and I don't like the idea of leaving you here alone."

"I—"

He cuts me off. "There's a lounge area just off the locker rooms where you can hang out. Maybe catch up on homework or watch some brainless T.V. on the television inside. We usually watch game tapes but I think Coach has it hooked up to cable."

I worry my lower lip. "I'd rather stay here."

His muscles flex and he takes a bite of his food, chewing while he thinks. "Practice is less than two hours. I can leave early if I need to. You won't have to be there long."

I shake my head. "I don't want to go. I never should have gotten up. I'll just go back to the room and—"

"Kasey, I'm not leaving you here alone. Right now isn't the time for you to be difficult. Change your clothes if you want."

I look down at myself. I'm still wearing his shirt. It's been several days. Almost a week and I'm still in the same shirt. The same pair of underwear. Oh god. I probably smell.

"If it's quick, you have time for a shower."

I swallow hard and nod. "Fine."

"Really?"

"Yeah. But I want a shower first."

He exhales a harsh breath. "Okay. Good. Eat some more first. We'll leave in an hour."

I take another bite, barely tasting it, but it seems to make him happy. My stomach growls, so I must be hungry. I just don't *feel* hungry. I'm numb. Empty.

I force myself to eat one whole pancake before pushing my plate aside. "I need to go back to my place. I don't have any clothes or—"

"Your uh, big sister, what's her name?"

"Quinn."

"Right. She packed up some of your things. Clothes. Toiletries. They're in the bag on the bathroom counter. If you're missing anything we can stop by and grab it on the way."

Oh. That was nice. "Okay. I'll go see what I've got." I hesitate. "After practice, are you taking me home?"

Some emotion flashes in his eyes, too fast for me to catch before he shakes his head. "No. You're going to stay here." Something like relief settles in me, but that's strange. Why would I be relieved about staying here? I don't like Dominique. We were literally fighting just a few days ago.

"For how long?"

He shrugs and goes back to his plate. "Until I decide you're okay."

My mouth tightens, and I consider arguing before my shoulders sag and I turn away. "Fine." I head for the bathroom to shower. I'll fight with him another day.

Dominique parks the Escalade near the athletic building, and before I even unbuckle, he has my door open and is helping me out of the car.

Why is he being so nice? Nice and Dominique Price don't go together. I mean, I know my mom just... the word stalls in my brain and I take a moment to breathe through it. Whatever the reason, I don't want him to be nice to me. I need things to be normal. I don't want his or anyone else's pity.

I tug my hand out of his as soon as I'm out of the car. He grabs a gym bag from the back and then we're cutting across the parking lot to the main doors. Inside, I ignore the students in the halls and follow Dominique to the locker room. He opens the door and loud voices can be heard. Blocking my sight, he takes me down a row of lockers before stopping at a closed door. He pushes it open and checks inside before backing up and holding it open for me.

"Yo, Price!" someone calls.

"Give me a minute," he shouts back. To me he says, "You can hang out here. No one will bother you."

We step into a medium-sized room. There are a few sofas scattered around the room and a large flat screen T.V. mounted on one of the walls. "There's a bathroom through that door." He points to the left. "And I'll have Coach hang on to my phone. If you need anything, call me. I'll be done in an hour and a half. Two, tops."

I nod and take a seat on the nearest sofa.

"You're not going to wander off, right?"

"I'll be here."

He stares at me as if gauging my intent. "Good. If any of the guys come in here, tell them to get the fuck out. Got it?"

"Yep."

He closes the door behind him and I take a steadying breath. I find a remote between the cushions and flick on the T.V., stopping on a Disney movie. I don't have it in me to watch anything heavier than that. My phone rings. Aaron's name flashes across the screen. Shit. I haven't even talked to my brother yet. I should have. But I haven't.

I'm not sure what to say to him, and I'm almost certain he hasn't known what to say to me, but he's in Florida handling things I know I'm not in the right headspace to handle, so I need to answer.

I hit accept and bring the phone to my ear. "Hey."

He's quiet on the other end before I hear him release a breath. "Hey."

That one word, hearing his voice, has emotions clogging my throat. "You good?" I ask.

He forces a laugh. "I should be asking you that."

Yeah. Maybe. "I'm okay."

Another heavy breath. "That's good. Dom's not being an asshole is he?"

A small laugh. "No. He's being nice, which is ... weird. I kinda wish he'd be an asshole."

I curl my legs beneath me and sink into the sofa. "Are you calling because..." I swallow hard. "Did you need..." I don't know how to get the words out.

"Yeah. Sorry. I wanted to ask if you were okay with Mom being cremated. It's a lot easier to get her back if we do but if you don't want that—"

"It's fine," I choke on the words.

"Are you sure?"

"MmHmm." My heart squeezes in my chest. We weren't very religious, but I know Mom is—was—Catholic. She'd have wanted a proper burial, but I don't think either Aaron or I can go through with one. This, this is better. "Maybe we can sprinkle her ashes in the ocean or something. Mom might have liked that."

"You think so?" His voice is thick.

I have to blink back my tears before I can answer. "Yeah. I think she would. Remember when we were kids and we went to Myrtle Bay? You got stung by a jellyfish and freaked out trying to pee on your own leg."

He groans, but manages a laugh too. "You promised never to bring it up again."

I snicker. "I know, but we should go there. We used to go every summer growing up. Mom loved that place."

"Yeah, she did, didn't she?"

I sit still, holding the phone tight as we both listen to the other breathe. "I miss her," I tell him, hating how my voice quivers.

"I miss her, too."

This is hard. My eyes fill with tears again, and no matter how hard I fight to hold them in, they still spill down my face. "Will you be home soon?" I ask, needing to say something to fill the silence.

He coughs, clears his throat. "Yeah. I'll be back in a few days. We can figure out what to do after that. There's no rush, okay. We can take however long we want."

I bob my head up and down. "Okay."

"I gotta go, but I'll try and check in later. You'll be okay with Dominique?"

I swallow past a lump. "Yeah. I'll be okay."

"I love you, sis."

"Love you, too." Aaron hangs up and I just sit there, unmoving. I don't know for how long or what time it is when all of a sudden the door opens and Deacon steps in the room.

I look up at him, tears still running down my face and he drops down in front of me. "Hey, are you okay? Are you hurt?" He checks me over as I sit there, frozen in place.

"Kasey." He cups the sides of my face. "What's wrong? Why are you crying."

I look down at my phone. It's still in my hand, fingers gripping it tightly. Deacon sees it and gently pries it from my fingers, setting it beside me. "You're kinda freaking me out here," he says. "I saw you come in with Dominique, figured I'd check in on you. I can't believe he left you in here like this."

I shake my head. "He didn't. I—" *Come on Kasey, pull it together.* "I'm sorry." I blink. "I was just talking to my brother. I..."

His gold-colored eyes stare into me, seeing more than he should. I want to curl into a ball and hide. Turn off the lights and just pretend today isn't here. "Come on." He pulls me to my feet.

"Where are we going?"

"You need chocolate. Or cake. Or both. We're going to get some of that."

I side-eye him as he steers me out of the room. "Why do I need chocolate? And don't you have practice?"

He shrugs, his hand on my lower back as he leads me outside. "I have sisters. When they cry, I give them chocolate. It's the one thing I never get wrong and it works every time, so that's what we're going to do. Come one, there's a vending machine just down the hallway."

I nod but... "What about practice?"

"Dominique is running plays today, so it's fine. No one will miss me."

"Oh. Alright then." We find the vending machine and he shoves a few dollar bills in getting a Reese's, Snickers, Hershey bar, Milky Way, and a Fast Break. Arms full, we find a few lounge chairs to sit in and he drops the candy in my lap.

When I don't move to open any, he grabs one of the bars, a Snickers, and peels the wrapper back before handing it to me. "Try it. I swear it works."

I give him a disbelieving look, but take a bite anyway, letting the chocolate melt on my tongue. I chew and swallow before taking another bite, and the next thing I know, the Snickers is gone and I'm moving onto the Peanut Butter Cups.

Three candy bars in and I feel more like myself. I've wiped the tears from my face, and Deacon catches me up on some of what I've missed in our English class. Twenty minutes goes by, and for the first time in nearly a week I feel like I can breathe. This distraction, it's exactly what I need.

I look down at the last candy bar in my lap and know I'll regret it later, but I peel back the wrapper and take a bite anyway. I moan. Fast Breaks are my favorite, so I saved the best for last.

"You cannot make sounds like that," Deacon says, a small smile on his face.

I roll my eyes. "You'd moan if you had this in your mouth."

He chokes, but covers it with a cough. "You can't say things like that to me either."

I grin. "Want a bite?" I ask him, but a commotion down the hallway catches my attention and I turn. "Shit," I whisper. Dominique is storming toward us, shirt drenched in sweat and a pissed-off expression on his face.

He's already yelling before he's even next to me. "What the hell were you thinking?" he shouts, coming to a stop beside us. "Do you have any idea how worried I was when I opened the door and you weren't there? *Fuck.*" He turns around, hands on his waist and takes a few steps away before turning back to me. "You said you'd stay put. Why did you—" It's then that he notices Deacon. His eyes darken and I jump to my feet.

"Look, I'm sorry. I should have left a note or something."

He scoffs. "Right. A note would have helped."

My anger spikes. I'm not a child. I don't need to be coddled and looked after. "You know what, fine. I'm not sorry." I turn to Deacon. "Thanks for the chocolate and for helping with," I wave to my face, "all of this. It was nice to feel like me for a little bit."

He stands. "Anytime you need a good laugh and some chocolate, give me a call. You don't have to tell me your personal shit, but if you wanna hang, I'm around."

"Thanks. I appreciate that."

He pulls me in for a hug, releasing me just as quickly when Dominique makes a sound in the back of his throat, low and threatening. "I'll catch you later, beautiful," Deacon calls over his shoulder, and then it's just Dom and I.

I sigh and pick up the candy wrappers that fell when I stood up. I shove them in the trash bin and wait for Dominique to yell at me some more, but he doesn't. Instead, he has this pensive look on his face and he refuses to look at me. Somehow, it's worse than the yelling.

When we get outside he opens the door for me, closing it once I'm safe inside the Escalade. I put on my seat belt as he gets inside and I fiddle with the music knob as he pulls out of the parking lot. Five minutes into the drive and he still hasn't said anything.

I hate it.

"Look, I'm sorry. Okay? Can you stop giving me the silent treatment already?"

"I'm not giving you the silent treatment."

I huff. "Then why are you so silent?"

He glares at me. "Do you all of a sudden want to talk? You've barely said a word in five fucking days, but I leave you alone for an hour and suddenly you're chatting with Deacon. My bad. Figured I must be the one guy you refuse to talk to."

I lean my head against the window, the cool glass chilling my skin. "I'm not refusing to talk to you," I tell him.

He grunts. "But you'd rather talk to Deacon?"

"No. I..." I try to put my thoughts into words, but it all sounds so stupid. "Deacon isn't treating me differently."

Dominique scowls. "What the hell does that mean?"

"You're being nice. Like really nice. You check on me all the time. You made me pancakes. You open my door for me."

"So what, I'm supposed to be a dick even though your mom just died?"

My breath hitches and Dominique mutters a curse. "I didn't mean—"

"That," I yell at him. "That, right there. You keep doing things like that. You're apologizing to me when before, you never would have said 'I'm sorry.' That isn't you. That's not us. Not how we communicate."

"You're not making any sense."

"I don't want you to treat me any different. I need things to go back to how they were. The bickering. You being an insensitive jerk."

"I'm not insensitive."

"Yeah, you are. You kissed me when we were in high school and pretended like it never happened. You told me I was shallow. That I couldn't keep a guy's attention. And then gave me the best orgasm of my life, and after, pretended like it never happened. You humiliated me at the Kappa Mu party, made me get out of the pool, basically said I looked like a slut and when I stripped naked in front of you, you left, and big surprise, you pretend it never happened. I'm sorry, how is none of that insensitive? Did you actually consider my feelings even once before doing any of those things?"

He's quiet.

"No. You didn't. And it's fine."

He bangs his head back on the headrest. "It's not fine."

"Yes, it is. It's fine because it's you. It's what I expect. You're a jerk to me. I'm a bitch to you. But this, whatever this version of you is that's nice to me, I can't deal with it right now. I need you to be the same guy you were a week ago. Don't coddle me. I'm not a piece of glass. I won't break."

We pull into his driveway and he turns off the car, neither of us getting out. "You want me to be a jerk."

"Yes."

"Fine. Your mom died almost a week ago, and you're being a baby. You've been hiding in your room for too fucking long and you're wasting away. You've lost weight. You look like shit. And your brother has enough on his plate that he has to deal with, but instead of handling what he needs to, he's calling me five times a day to check on you when he shouldn't have to. Pull yourself together, figure out what you need to do to grieve, and get on with it."

I suck in a shuddering breath and squeeze my hands into fists on my lap.

"Shit. I went too far."

I press my lips together, blinking back the tears and shaking my head. "I'm fine." I tell him, but it's a lie. There's this hole inside of me and his words, hearing about Aaron, it punches the hole wide open. I'm so fucking selfish. My brother shouldn't have to check in on me.

I fight to keep it together. I told Dom to be mean. He did what I asked, so why does it hurt?

He opens his door and the next thing I know he's right beside me, reaching over my lap to unbuckle me. "I'm sorry. I didn't mean any of it. I thought ... I thought this is what you wanted. I thought it would help."

Like a dam breaking, my tears fall down my cheeks.

"Fuck."

I was falling apart. Again. I had an hour where I kept it together and now I was crumbling.

Dom slides his arms beneath me and carries me out of the car. Cradled in his arms, he manages to get us inside and into the living room. My arms are wrapped around his neck, as though holding onto him will somehow hold me together.

He sits on the sofa, still cradling me in his arms. It's intimate and comforting and even knowing I'll hate myself for it tomorrow, I cling to him and cry into his chest.

I feel like pieces of me are breaking one by one, the pain growing more and more with each breath until it's too much. I want to scream, but nothing can get out past the tears. My shoulders shake and I wheeze, unable to catch my breath. Why does it hurt so fucking much.

"Kasey, please." He presses his lips to my temple. "You're killing me here, baby girl. What can I do?"

NINETY-EIGHT

Kasey

"What can I do?" He asks again, and there is something close to panic in his voice. Emotion clogs my throat, threatening to suffocate me, and no matter how hard I try, I can't swallow it down.

I try to speak. To tell him it hurts too much. I don't want to live like this. But I choke on my words, unable to get them out. I scream, choking on my tears as Dominique holds me in place, a wild look in his eyes. One hand grips the back of my neck, the other clutches my hip. "Kasey, I don't know how to fix this. How to fix you. What can I do?" He is almost begging and Dominique never begs but ...

Nothing. There isn't anything he can give me that will make this go away. Nothing that will bring my mom back.

"I don't want to ... feel like... this. It hurts... too much," I finally manage to tell him.

He curses and a nerve jumps in his neck. "One night. I'll go to the store, get a fifth and you can drink yourself into oblivion if you need to, but only for one night. You got me? You get one pass. Will that help?" I nod. Yes. A night of oblivion. A chance to forget.

"Okay, we can do that but, for that to happen, I need to run to the store and I'm not leaving you here, alone like this. You have to come with me. You can wait in the car and I'll be quick, but I'm not leaving you here alone. Will that help? Do you want to forget for one night?"

I do. I really, really do, but it's a temporary fix. I know Dominique well enough to know he's serious when he says one night. That's all I'll get and tomorrow, when the sun rises, all my pain will still be there, only magnified by a hangover.

I pound my fists against his chest. "That's not—" a shuddering breath, "—enough."

"*Fuck*. Kasey, you have to work with me here."

I shake my head. No. "A week," I plead. "Let me forget for a week."

He moves his hands to either side of my face, leaning in until we're only an inch apart, our foreheads almost touching.

"No. You can't go down that path or you might not come back."

"I don't care," I wail.

"I do."

Tears spill from my eyes and hopelessness slams into me. "I hate you," I tell him. "I hate you. I hate you. I hate you."

"I hate you, too," he tells me, but the way he says it doesn't sound like he's telling me he hates me at all. It sounds like he's saying something else entirely.

"I don't want to feel like this anymore." I don't want to feel at all.

"I know, baby. I know. If I could make the pain go away, I would. Fuck, I'd do anything to make it go away right now."

There's that endearment again. I know it means nothing. He's just being nice to me. Using comforting words, but what if it's more than that? Or what if it can be more than that? At least for a little while.

I reach for him, shifting in his lap. "Please."

He holds me tight against his chest. "Anything, Kasey. Help me out here. What will make it bearable right now? This very moment? What else can I do? I can't see you like this and not do something. I have to do something."

I don't let myself think about it. I lean back in his embrace and when he tilts his chin down to look at me, his eyes full of concern, I kiss him.

He responds immediately, his hold shifting until he's grasping the side of my neck and angling me for a deeper kiss. Hot. Desperate. I pour everything I'm feeling into that kiss. My hurt. The pain. The anger over it all.

Our teeth clash. Our tongues duel. He slides his fingers into my hair and devours my mouth. There is no other way to describe it, and the longer he kisses me, the further the pain fades into the background. It's still there, lurking in the shadows of my mind. I'm not naive enough to think kissing Dominique will make it go away forever, but it helps. It gives me something else to think about. Something else to feel.

But, I need more.

I shift until I'm straddling his lap and rock myself against him.

He groans, breaking the kiss. "Kasey..."

I see my own need reflected back in his eyes. He wants this just as much as I do. We may not get along. Hell, we might even hate each other, but this, this he can do. This will help.

"Are you sure?"

My eyes narrow and I shift on his lap, grinding against the hard-on he's sporting beneath me. That should be his answer.

"Fuck."

He captures my mouth again. After that, it's a flurry of frenzied movements as we tear at one another's clothes.

He lifts my shirt off and cups my breast through the thin lace of my bra. I arch closer to his touch, throwing my head back as he squeezes me in his hand.

"We should move," he mumbles against my lips, but I don't let that deter me. I slide my hand into his sweats, wrapping my fingers around him and giving him a firm stroke.

"Jesus Christ," he hisses.

The next thing I know he's on his feet, my legs wrapped around him. He carries me to his room, closes the door behind him, and then tosses me on his bed, my back sinking into the soft mattress. He doesn't miss a beat. In a flash, he's on me. His powerful body pressing firmly against mine.

He kisses me again and I gasp, his tongue seeking out my own and sliding into my mouth. I moan. He tastes so good. Like coffee and spice. His shirt rubs against my skin and I immediately hate it. I don't want anything between us. I need to feel his skin on mine.

I claw at his shirt until he relents and tugs it over his head. Then I reach for the waistband of his sweats.

He smacks my hand away and seizes control. Unhooking my bra, he bares me to him before hooking his fingers into my panties and peeling them off. He doesn't bother with my skirt. What would be the point? With my breasts on full display, he runs his thumb over my nipple before sliding down my body to take one in his mouth.

I whimper.

He peppers kisses across my chest before swirling my other nipple with his tongue.

"Dominique, please."

He glances up at me, his eyes an even darker shade of brown than usual. He watches my face as he kneads my breasts, cataloging every gasp and moan I make. He pinches and pulls on my nipples.

"You're so fucking responsive."

My breathing is heavy as he slips further down the bed until his broad shoulders are nestled between my thighs. He spreads my legs open, and as his face stares down at my sex, his warm breath fans across my skin. I could die and go to heaven with the way he is looking at me right now, his gaze hot and hungry.

He doesn't give me the chance to speak. To get nervous. He locks his hooded gaze with mine and presses a hungry kiss to my core, using his thumbs to spread me open even more.

"Shit," I gasp.

He chuckles, sliding his hands under my thighs and cupping my ass as he tilts my pelvis closer to his mouth. "You like that?"

My teeth sink into my bottom lip, and I nod.

He leans in again and his mouth latches onto my pussy. I cry out, throwing my head back against the bed. He licks my slit before spearing his tongue inside me, and after only a few strokes, the pressure begins to build.

My pussy clenches and my legs quiver as he teases me, licking and sucking, but never putting enough pressure on my clit to throw me over the edge. I thrust my hips up to meet his touch, my body desperate for more friction.

I'm wound so tight I feel like I'm about to snap. "Dominique!"

He grabs my hips and begins to eat my pussy like a man starved. It only takes another minute until I'm crying out and bucking against him, but he doesn't let up. He locks onto my clit, my body hyper aware and overly sensitive as wave after wave of pleasure slams into me.

Limp and sated, my legs shamelessly drop to the bed. I struggle to catch my breath.

I expect Dominique to stop. To climb back beside me, but he stays rooted between my legs. His mouth still between my thighs. When I feel like my heart is no longer at risk of beating out of my chest, he flicks his tongue over my sensitive clit. I moan. Dominique presses his palm over my stomach, holding me down as he devours me all over again, only this time he nudges one thick finger inside me.

My muscles tense, legs quivering. I groan as he strokes me. "Oh, god."

"Fuck, you're tight," he murmurs against me right as a second orgasm hits me out of nowhere and I grind against his hand, riding out my release.

Dominique leans back, his eyes taking me in. "Better?" he asks, rising to his feet.

He still had his pants on. Why is he still wearing clothes?

Despite the fatigue, I push myself up to my elbows. My hair sticks to my neck and forehead and I brush it back away from my face. "Off," I tell him, and tilt my chin toward his pants.

He doesn't move. "Dominique," I growl. "Are you going to stand there or are you going to fuck me?"

His eyes darken, a savage expression passing over his face. "I don't think we—" He hesitates. "We don't need to do that. I can make you feel good in other ways."

Common sense dictates I listen. I haven't slept with anyone before, and a grief-induced fuck fest isn't how I imagined my first time, but I'm past the point of caring. I want this. Need it.

"If you don't want me—"

"I'm not saying that."

I swallow and can feel myself being pulled under again. A mess of emotions swirling inside me. No. No. NO!

I blink quickly as I bite out my words. "Then what are you saying?"

He rubs his jaw, my release still glistening on his lips. "You want me to fuck you?"

"Yes." I thought I made myself clear already. "I'm not going to force myself on you. If you don't want this, want me in this way, I can find someone else—"

"The hell you will," he snarls.

Dominique shoves his pants down and steps out of them, his cock hard and at attention. *Oh my god,* he's huge. A thread of doubt worms its way inside of me. Will it fit?

Without breaking eye contact, he leans to the side and retrieves a condom from the nightstand. He tears the foil packet with his teeth and shamelessly rolls the condom onto his shaft, before stroking himself.

"Say it again," he grinds out as he climbs onto the bed, positioning his cock at my slick entrance. "Tell me what you need."

"I need you to fuck me."

He makes an animalistic sound in his chest, and the head of his cock slides between my folds but without entering me.

"If you regret this in the morning—"

"I won't," I assure him.

Blind desire flashes across his face, but rather than sinking into me as I expect, he sits back on his heels and flips me onto my stomach. My heartbeat kicks into overdrive as he pulls my hips toward him until I'm on hands and knees.

"Dom," my voice quivers with need.

His cock rubs against me from behind.

I shift my hips back and turn my head to look at him. His face is locked in concentration, his expression almost predatory. "Spread your legs for me."

I do what he asks, widening my stance. He presses a hand against the center of my back. "Tilt your ass up," he orders, before sliding that same hand down between my legs. I try to tamp down on my nerves as Dominique presses a finger inside me, rubbing the walls of my pussy before he retreats and lines up his cock. Goosebumps break out across my skin and he leans forward, scraping his teeth over my bare shoulder as his hips thrust against me, his cock buried to the hilt in a single powerful move.

I cry out, a sharp stab of pain spearing into me.

He stills. "What the fuck?"

My legs tremble, but I manage to blindly reach back and grab hold of his wrist. "Don't."

"You're a virgin." He sounds both pissed off and in awe.

Not anymore. I think to myself, but don't say the words aloud.

"Why would you... why didn't... *fuck.*"

My body is tight, my muscles clenching against the intrusion. I force myself to take a deep breath and relax.

Dominique leans over me, his forehead resting between my shoulder blades. "What were you thinking?" he whispers against my skin.

"Dominique?" I say through clenched teeth.

"Yeah?"

"Move." He pulls back and for a second I think he's going to withdraw all the way. "Not stop," I clarify, and he stills. The head of his cock barely inside of me. "I need you to move."

He flexes his hips, an inch sinking back into me.

I moan.

He curses.

"Your first time shouldn't be like this," he growls. "It should be with someone you trust. Someone—"

"Dominique." I give him a second. Looking back, I meet his conflicted gaze. "I trust you."

His nostrils flare. "You do?"

I nod. "Yes. Now please, fuck me already." He sinks in another inch, his eyes carefully watching me for my reaction. He's stretching me to my limits and I can scarcely breathe.

He goes a little deeper.

My body is tight, my muscles clenching against the intrusion.

He pushes into me agonizingly slowly until he's sheathed himself fully. He gives my body a second to adjust and then he moves. In and out as he continues to thrust inside me. I grind my teeth together against the pain. It's not a lot, but enough to be uncomfortable. His body blankets me, his chin resting against my shoulder, breath against my ear. "Relax into it. Let me make you feel good."

I do what he says and force myself to relax, the tension in my body melting away to be replaced with tingling sensations. "That's it."

He leans back, hands gripping my hips as he increases his pace.

I gasp when he hits a particularly sensitive spot. I moan. My mind goes blank and all I can think about, all I can feel, is Dominique moving inside of me.

I push back on my knees, meeting him thrust for thrust, and then I'm coming again, my release spilling out of me on a guttural moan.

He slides out of me and flips me onto my back before sliding right back in, barely missing a beat. He hooks one arm under my knee, lifting my leg up and out to achieve a deeper angle.

I cling to his shoulders as he pounds into me, neither of us saying anything over the sounds of our flesh coming together. One of his hands cups the back of my neck and I stare into his eyes, even as I raise my hips to meet him.

His thrusts come faster, his face tight with tension as he surges inside me. "This what you need?" He forces out the words. I know what he's asking, so I don't hesitate to answer.

"Yes. More. Over and Over." I want to fall asleep from exhaustion. I don't want to lie here and think about my dead mom. About the pain or how helpless I feel. "Fuck me and don't stop. Okay? Not until I pass out. Until neither of us can go anymore."

A tremor moves through him and he nods. Good. We're in agreement.

His mouth crashes down on mine. His tongue licking against my own and his teeth scraping over my bottom lip. At some point the sun sets and the light coming through the windows dims. His forehead rests against my shoulder and my hands cling to his back, nails digging in when he stiffens and groans, pumping out his release.

He slumps against me, our breathing loud in the room. He takes a moment to catch his breath before sliding out of me. I hiss, but don't say anything. Dominique pulls off the condom, leaving to get rid of it before pulling another one out and setting it on the nightstand. I'm not sure how long a guy needs to recover, but he doesn't let me think on it long before he's reaching for me, his fingers sliding between my legs. First, he inserts one finger. Then a second. He works his fingers inside of me, rotating and rubbing every inch inside of me as he thrusts them in and out.

He adds a thirds and I cry out, his mouth crashing over mine and swallowing my cries.

I don't know how long he finger fucks me. Long enough for me to come again and for him to get hard. When he pulls out of me, he licks my juices from his fingers and slides the new condom over his cock.

He positions himself at my entrance again and I nod, letting him know I want this. Want more. He slides into me, a curse slipping past his lips.

"Yes," I tell him. "Don't stop."

We fuck two more times before we're both incapable of moving. After he disposes of the condom, I push up to leave. My legs feel like rubber and my head spins, but I think I can make it back to the guest room, only Dominique stops me.

He slips back into bed beside me and grabs me from behind, pulling my hips against his. My back to his front.

"Sleep," he grunts, tucking my head beneath his chin.

"But—"

"Sleep."

I take a deep breath, close my eyes, and for the first time in a long time, I do what Dominique tells me to do. I sleep.

NINETY-NINE

Dominique

I'm fucked. I am seriously and thoroughly fucked.

Harsh sunlight bleeds into the room. The clock on the wall reads eight AM. Late for me to be waking up, but not late enough that I need to hurry. Kasey is curled up in bed beside me, eyes closed, and blond hair fanning around her pillow. I close my eyes for a beat, breathing in the smell of her apple and vanilla shampoo. I stifle a groan. She smells *good*.

I take in her delicate shoulders, the way she fits perfectly nestled in my arms, her ass pressing against my front. My dick stirs to life.

The thought of rolling her over and sliding my cock inside her wet heat has my dick jumping to attention. I press my hips against her and she lets out a breathy little sigh, pressing deeper into me in her sleep. She feels good in my arms. Right. Like she belongs there. Which is why I can't stay in this bed any longer. If I do, I'm going to wake her up, fuck her, and then we'll both have to face the reality of what happened last night. I doubt she's ready for that. I know I'm not.

I slide my arm out from beneath her and climb out of bed, careful not to wake her. The sheet shifts with me, exposing her creamy skin and her perfect tits. Tits I had my hands on last night. My mouth on. I'm tempted to crawl back into bed, but it's a bad idea. This. Us. I shake my head. Her mom just died and what do I do? *Christ*, I'm a prick. I completely took advantage when she was grieving, when ... my mind wanders and I start to count the days. Shit. Shit. I cover my face with my hand. She's seventeen. *You took the girl's virginity at seventeen.*

Even I know how seriously messed up that is.

Leaving her in my bed, I opt for a cold shower. Five minutes in and my dick is still rock hard, like it knows Kasey is on the other side of the wall, naked and waiting.

I fist my cock in my hand, stroking myself to relieve the pressure, when the shower curtain is pulled back and a very awake and very naked Kasey stands before me. She sees me, sees my fingers wrapped around my cock, and steps inside the shower, dropping to her knees to replace my hand with her own.

My dick jerks at her touch and a smile curls her lips.

"*Shit.*" What is this girl doing to me? "Kasey?" I groan. I'm not sure if it's a warning or a plea.

Her big blue eyes look up at me through her lashes, her fingers barely able to close around my length. My gaze drops to her mouth, and the image of her lips wrapping around the head of my cock has me straining painfully in her grip. It would be so easy to slip between her lips, and I know it'd feel good. A thought trickles into my mind, wondering if she's done this with another guy. Last night, I was the first to take her pussy. Would I be the first to take her mouth, too?

I want that. It's selfish and wrong, but I want all of her firsts. Everything that she'll give me.

Her tongue darts out, licking the drop of pre-cum from my slit and I thrust forward, unable to stop myself. She smiles, and it undoes something inside of me.

"You can't touch me like that, baby girl." My voice is hoarse, the tendons in my neck straining. "If you open that mouth of yours again. I'm going to take it."

I'm clearly insane, or just a glutton for punishment and high on lust, because instead of pulling away from her touch, I press forward, rubbing my dick over her mouth, enjoying the sight of my lingering pre-cum as it paints her lips.

I put one hand against the wall to steady myself, the other fists the back of her head, holding her in place, but I don't push myself inside her mouth. She has to be the one to make that decision. She shows me what she wants. What she's willing to give me.

"Have you sucked a guy's cock before?" Her eyes are dilated, filled with lust and need as she bobs her head.

I grunt. *Fuck.* I hate that answer. My grip in her hair tightens and she hisses, but doesn't try to pull away.

"You want my cock?"

Another nod.

Fuck it. I'm going to hell for this, but I was probably heading that direction anyway.

"Open your mouth, baby. Suck my cock."

She widens her stance, a telling sign that she knows what's coming and she's accepting it. Bracing herself, but not to suck on my dick. She's bracing for me to fuck her mouth.

Her lips part and like the impatient bastard I am, I thrust forward, filling her mouth until I reach the back of her throat. She doesn't gag or pull away like I expect her to. Instead, she relaxes her throat, opening her mouth wider, and takes more of me in. *"Jesus Christ!"*

Her eyes hold mine, tears leaking from the corners, but she doesn't let up. Her cheeks hollow out, sucking me harder while I pump my dick into her mouth.

"Fuck, yeah. Just like that," I throw my head back, groaning.

With both hands now, I hold the back of her head, pumping into her mouth, but it isn't enough.

A growl tears out of my throat, low and rough, my entire body tensing, but I don't want to come in her mouth right now. I want inside her cunt. I want her pussy milking my release from me, so that's what I'm going to have.

I grip her arms and jerk her to her feet. Wide eyes meet mine but I don't answer the unspoken question in them. Turning off the water I don't bother to dry off before I lift her out and set her down in front of the sink. I capture her mouth, my teeth tugging at her bottom lip. "Are you wet for me, baby?"

She moans into the kiss, her body shuddering in my arms. I slip two fingers into her, pushing in deep. She gasps against my mouth, her hands gripping my shoulders for support.

"So fucking wet," I murmur against her lips. I pull out, and instead of licking her juices from my fingers, I bring them to her mouth, pressing them between her lips. I'm transfixed, watching her mouth open, seeing her eyes shudder as she tastes herself. A small moan slips past her lips and my control shatters.

I turn her away from me to face the mirror, her eyes holding mine. Her fingers splay on the counter and I step up behind her, a firm hand on her hip, the other between her legs. Her eyes hold mine captive as I scrape my teeth over her shoulder, and I see the moment she gives herself to me.

I line my cock up with her entrance, her wet pussy coating my head when I realize I'm bare. Shit. I suck in a breath and hold myself immobile. Kasey presses herself back and I grind my teeth together, my hand on her hip the only thing keeping her in place.

"I need to grab a condom," I bite out.

Her eyes widen with understanding, but neither of us move.

"I'm on the pill," she says, voice soft. Hesitant. "I've been on it since I was sixteen. I'm good."

Thank fuck.

I nod. "I'm clean," I tell her.

"Okay."

Okay.

I press into her, watching her face for a reaction as my cock slips between her folds. She gasps, head falling back on her shoulders to expose her neck. Without even thinking, one hand slides up her body, stopping briefly to toy with one nipple, squeeze her full breasts, before wrapping around her throat in a possessive hold.

She moans and I thrust into her harder. Faster. "God, you're tight." I bite out the words as my hips pound furiously into her. I should slow down, ease her into this. She's got to be sore after last night, but I can't muster the control needed to pull back.

She presses her ass into me, meeting me thrust for thrust. My hand flexes on her throat, her cries getting louder. "Oh, god," she moans, the walls of her pussy damn near strangling my cock. Her orgasms rocks through her. She arches her back, legs shaking, and I circle her clit, drawing out her release.

When her legs buckle, I push her forward, pinning her legs between me and the counter. With a hand on her back I push her down until her cheek is pressed against the mirror, her heavy breathing fogging up the glass.

My pelvis slams against her ass, my cock nudging her cervix as I bury myself deep. She isn't even trying to hold in her needy moans, which only serve to spur me on more. Her inner muscles clench around my dick, and I drive into her hard and fast, chasing my own release and grinding against her. My balls draw up tight, muscles clenching, and with one final thrust and an agonizing groan, I'm spilling my cum inside her.

My legs shake and I pull out, Kasey still slumped on the counter. I turn the shower back on, checking the temperature to make sure it's ready before pulling her under the warm spray and washing the signs of sex from both our bodies. Neither of us speaks, but when I move to wash between her thighs, she slaps my hand away.

Right.

We don't do gentle or sweet. We fuck. She doesn't want tenderness from me.

Grabbing us each a towel we dry off and I get dressed in my room. Kasey retreats to the guest room where her clothes are and comes back a few minutes later wearing a pair of white cut-off shorts and a red top. She has a frown on her face and a determined look in her eyes.

"I have a game today," I tell her.

She nods. "You mentioned that yesterday."

"Do you want to come? Allie and Bibi will be there watching the guys. You wouldn't be alone."

She bites her bottom lip, and I have to keep myself from going to her, tugging her abused lip free only to capture it with my own teeth. She doesn't answer.

"What's going on in that head of yours?" I ask, shoving my gear in my gym bag. Between sleeping in, the shower, and the sex, I'm running late and Coach will have my ass if I don't get a move on, but something is going on in that pretty little head of hers. I need to figure it out.

"Aaron will be pissed if he finds out about this."

I grunt. "I'm aware."

"I don't want to be the reason you two have a falling out again. He needs you and the others too much."

I side eye her. "Spell it out for me, Kasey."

"You can't tell him. He can't find out about any of this." She indicates the space between us. I don't like the idea of being her dirty little secret. Not one fucking bit. But, I can't argue with her reasoning. Henderson has a lot on his plate. Me fucking his sister isn't something he needs to worry about right now. Not when me fucking his sister should never have happened in the first place, but after this morning, I can't say it won't happen again.

Dominique

I don't know what came over me this morning. But when I woke up and Dominique was gone, a part of me crumbled, thinking he'd left me there, alone. Then I heard the water running and I just, I needed to know this wasn't going to be like all the times before. That he wasn't going to mess around with me, only to pretend nothing ever happened.

So, I went for broke, and for once in my life, I took my shot. I pulled back the curtain, standing naked and unashamed, and when I saw him standing there with his fingers wrapped around his cock, my need reflected in his eyes, I wanted it to be my hand holding him. I wanted it to be my mouth bringing him his release.

He didn't push me away when I reached for him. He didn't tell me to stop or that he didn't want it. Want me. He moaned when I took him in my mouth. His body shuddered when he spilled his release inside me from behind.

This can't go anywhere, but I don't want to stop. I need whatever this is right now to chase away my grief. To push back the pain.

I'm not stupid. I know who he is. Who I am. I'm not going to pretend that what we have is sunshine and butterflies with a happily ever after at the end of the rainbow. Because the fallout, if things take a bad turn, it isn't just the two of us who will be affected. I'm not sure what is going on with my brother, but I know it has to do with more than Mom. I can't be the reason he loses his best friend, and that's what will happen if he finds out. His protective brother streak won't allow it to be any other way.

"So we're on the same page, then?" I ask, needing the confirmation.

Dominique releases a harsh breath and rubs his hand over the back of his neck. A muscle tics in his jaw, but after a few more seconds pass, he relents. "Fine, we'll be careful. Henderson will never know I'm boning his baby sister."

I bark out a laugh. Way to be presumptuous. "You think this will happen again.?"

He gives me a knowing look, his hooded gaze boring into mine. "You saying it won't?"

I manage a shrug. "Whatever we're doing here, it's casual."

"Agreed."

"This is not a relationship. We're not going to hold hands and go on dates."

He grunts.

"And no catching feelings," I tell him, as much for my own benefit as his.

"I wasn't planning on it."

"Good." I nod. "Aaron can't ever know—" he opens his mouth to interrupt but I rush on to finish, "I know. You said we'll be discreet, but I mean it. My brother can't find out about this. Not even years from now, okay? It never happened."

"Fine. Anything else?"

Nothing else comes to mind, so I shake my head.

"Okay. I have questions. I like shit to be black and white. No gray area." He sucks on his teeth, his expression letting me know he's not playing around.

"Alright. What are they?"

"You and Deacon, what's going on there?"

I shrug. "Nothing. He's nice to me. I told him at the start I was only interested in being friends. He's cool with it." Dominique scoffs, but I don't let it get to me. "Why? Because, just so we're clear, screwing my brains out doesn't mean you own me. You don't get to dictate who I talk to or who I'm friends with."

His jaw clenches and he grunts.

"Anything else you wanna know?"

"I know you think I get around"—I snort at that—"but if I'm fucking a girl more than once, she's the only girl I'm fucking, you feel me?"

I narrow my eyes. "What are you saying, exactly?"

"If you decide being *friends*," he growls, "with Deacon isn't enough for you. If you want his dick or someone else's, do me a solid and let me know before you go testing the waters, alright? I'll be sure to give you the same consideration if I find myself in a similar situation."

Anger flashes through me at the thought of him with anyone else. He sees it, and a slow smile spreads across his face.

"Deal?" he asks.

I want to wipe the smug look off his face, but manage to grit out, "Deal."

"Last question." He waits until I nod. "Do you want a relationship? Is that what you're really looking for here?" His tone is even. His eyes not meeting mine. There is zero inflection in his voice to let me know if he's asking because he wants that, or if he hates the idea and just wants to make sure I don't want one too.

I go with the response I think he's most after because right now, I need him to fuck me when I feel like I'm going to spiral and I need him not to be cagey about it. "With you? Definitely not." His eyes snap to mine, searching. "Look," I tuck my hair behind my ears and lay everything out for him. "You're arrogant, and most of the time, I can barely stand to be in the same room as you."

"The feeling is mutual."

"Right. So, a relationship would never work between us, assuming either of us even wanted one, but fooling around I'm fine with. Does that work for you? I don't need you to beat around the bush, either. I'm not a kid whose feelings you're going to hurt with a rejection." The silence stretches between us. "It's a yes or no question," I tell him, my patience growing thin.

He releases a breath, and without answering, he pulls me into his chest and slams his mouth down on mine. His kiss is all-consuming, leaving my head spinning and my heart racing out of my chest.

A needy moan slips past my lips when he finally pulls away. Dark brown eyes meet my own, and in them I see my own desire reflected back to me. "This works for me," he says. Then he hesitates and asks, "When is your birthday? I know it's coming up, but I don't know the date."

"It was yesterday."

He pulls back, eyes wide. "You turned eighteen yesterday?" I nod. "And no one said shit? No one remembered, not even your brother?"

I shrug. "Shit happened. It's bad timing," I give him a considering look. "Or good, depending on how you look at it."

He smirks. "Yeah, I see what you're saying." He grabs his gym bag and heads for the door, pausing at the threshold to give me a backward glance. "Game's at eleven. I have to get to the field early and warm up." I nod, my lips pressing together. "Show up. I don't want you sitting here alone. You can call one of the girls for a ride if you don't want to drive yourself."

"I'll think about it," I say, and his eyes darken.

"I'll see you there. Eleven. And if you wear my number, I'll think about giving you a belated birthday gift." He gives me a heated look, and before I can respond, he's gone.

What the hell did I just get myself into?

We're just getting started with Dominique and Kasey. Their story continues in Cruel Promise. Be sure to order your copy today!

And if you're curious about some of the other characters mentioned in these books, check out The Savage. Book 1 is Gabriel's story (Allie's friend from Richland in Wicked Devil).

Mischief Managed

Mischief Managed is a short story previously featured in the ***Hallowed Nights Anthology*** (no longer in publication)

Kasey

God, yes. Right there. I'm so freaking close and god do I need an orgasm right now. I'm sure everyone could use the big O bright and early each morning, but I really, really need it. Today more so than most because I am an idiot. I deleted my voicemail inbox. Just wiped the entire stupid thing clean without even registering what I was doing.

Tears prick the backs of my eyes as I think about Mom's last message. Her voice. The fact that I'll never hear it again. It was such a dumb mistake and I hate myself for not paying better attention. For letting my grief and sleep deprivation get the better of me because now I'll never have that message back. I tried. For over an hour, I fought with my stupid phone. I Googled all the ideas. None of it worked.

I blink hard, determined to clear my vision. I'm having sex for chrissakes. Now is not the time to fall apart.

Come on, Kasey. Focus on Dominique. That's why I came over here in the first place. The grief crept in and I needed a dose of dopamine to chase my blues away.

I have a problem. One I am very well aware of and have absolutely zero intention of correcting. At least, not anytime soon. Because it works. It's the only thing that's worked and trust me, I've tried all the things. Drinking away my sorrows—which is more difficult than it should be as an eighteen-year-old college student.

Getting in fights. That one went well. I almost got kicked out of my sorority house, earned myself a black eye, and had not one, but two, hour long lectures, between Dominique and my brother, about how reckless and immature I'd been and how disappointed they were in me. I shouldn't care what they think of me, but pulling the disappointed card fucking hurt.

After that I tried a little weed, but that didn't work out too well, either. I learned, though, that weed is not for me. I think it was mixed with something, or maybe it was a weird strain. I'm not sure. But I hallucinated some shit and wound up even more messed up than I was before.

My bad.

Quinn my Big at Kappa Mu said I kept calling out for my dead mother. So yeah, I won't be trying that again.

But this... sex? It works.

Every time I get in my head, or the grief creeps a little too close, I chase this right here. This feeling of being owned. Claimed. Of his skin on mine and pleasure coursing through my veins. It's the best high out there.

My heart races, my throat already hoarse from moaning and crying out Dominique's name. I showed up on his doorstep fifteen minutes ago having rolled out of bed, looking like hell with messy hair and red-rimmed eyes and Dominique took one look at me, ushered me inside, and the next thing I knew he had me bent me over the dining table and was fucking me from behind, chasing all of my pain away.

Sex is the cure-all for everything but cancer, if you ask me.

And death. It definitely cannot fix death. But anything else — My mind hooks onto that thought. Of dying. Of losing the people you love. Not getting to say goodbye. Suddenly, the sound of tires screeching fills my ears like a roar, and her screams rattle through my skull. Metal crunches.

I close my eyes. *Deep breaths, Kasey.*

This is not where I want my head to be right now.

I swallow the lump in my throat. *Breathe. In and out. Come on. Fucking breathe. You've got this.* I repeat the words in my head. Over and over but... Urgh!

Come. On.

Fuck.

I focus on the feel of Dominique inside me. Of his hands digging into my hips, fingers biting into my flesh. There will be bruises tomorrow, but I don't care. I relish every mark he leaves on my body, and I admire them everytime I need to remind myself of what this feels like. Of how it can make everything else wash away. My breath catches in my throat and I'm overwhelmed by the feeling of his powerful body curling over mine, wrapping me in his heat and his strength. His chest brushes along my back and I shiver beneath him, sucking in another lungful of air.

That's it. Right there. Focus on the good. Another deep breath, in through my nose and out through my mouth.

Don't think about Mom. Think about sex. Think about getting right... there.

I score my finger-tips along the table's edge and my toes curl as I chase my release. So fucking close, if I can just keep my mind in the gutter where it belongs...

I push my hips back and take Dom deeper, clenching my teeth against the sharp spear of pain because he's big, and this angle, it's a lot to take. But as he pounds in and out of me, whatever discomfort I'm feeling is washed away and replaced by a pleasure so intense that spots flicker behind my eyes.

Dominique's hand tangles in my blond curls before he pulls back, forcing my gaze up. I shiver again, swallowing past my emotions. My back arches, the tendons in my neck straining as my body contorts to his will.

I snap my eyes open, but my gaze is unseeing, lost in the haze of lust and want and need.

"You like that?" he growls, his warm breath washing over the shell of my ear.

He's close too and I fucking love it. When he gets like this, rough and dominant and... "Fuck, yes," I hiss.

The sound of flesh against flesh fills the room. This has become a habit the past few months. Him in my room or me in his. We fight. We fuck. Rinse and repeat.

I'm grateful for it. I might despise Dominique ninety percent of the time, but that ten percent when he's buried deep inside me, I actually like the smug bastard.

I crave him. Would give my left tit to have him. Just like this. Every night. And every morning.

Which is why this is so dangerous.

He's Dominique Price for god's sake, and I cannot afford to get hooked on him. Star football player and asshole extraordinaire. He's the starting quarterback for Suncrest U, on the path to NFL stardom, and he's been best friends with my older brother Aaron since they were kids. Now that they're both in college, they live together. Rent this townhouse like two peas in a pod. Proverbial BFFs.

But despite all that, we both know this is one relationship my brother will never approve of, and one I know, without a shadow of a doubt, would never work between us anyway, even if he did. Assuming I actually wanted a relationship with Dominique Price.

Which, for the record, I don't.

And he doesn't want one with me either. We barely get along. If it wasn't for our friends, we wouldn't talk to one another, let alone force ourselves to be civil.

Okay, we're not even that. But I mean, sometimes I try.

It doesn't matter though. None of it does.

I need Dominique Price. I hate to admit it, but it's the truth.

I've gotten more and more reckless as the weeks have passed. And if I don't shape up and start being careful, we're going to get caught. And screwing like this, a whopping twenty feet from the front door, is just plain stupid.

I know this. He knows this.

Did that stop either of us from doing it, anyway?

At the moment, I'm bent over a table with my leggings still hanging off one leg and my ass up in the air, in their kitchen no less, with Dominique pounding into me so... obviously not.

I might be addicted to his dick.

But given that it took him a matter of minutes to get me partially undressed before he was thrusting inside me, I'd say he is equally addicted to my pussy.

Knowing this shouldn't bring a smile to my face. He's an asshole. A Grade A, domineering, arrogant, possessive, asshole.

But God does being bent over by him feel good. It's freaking great, actually.

Which ladies and gentlemen, is why I have a problem. Because I cannot afford to be addicted to Dominique's dick. I mentioned that, right? If I allow this to continue, there is a very good chance I'll get hooked on the person attached to said dick. And that cannot happen.

He'd be easier to quit if the sex was bad. Hell, I could walk away from mediocre, or decent, even. But this— this all-consuming, fucking amazing, screw-me-mindless sex, is impossible to quit. And even though I realize I have nothing to compare it to, given that I slipped Dominique my V-card in a moment of grief induced insanity, there is no way it can get any better than this.

No fucking way.

We've been sneaking around to sleep with each other for weeks now. It's never dull. He's always amazing. I get off every single time. And I swear I always want more. I expected the newness of it all to eventually wear off. For this... craving to go away. But it doesn't. Dominique Price is like tequila to an alcoholic, and a shot of him goes down so damn smooth.

The sex has been an almost every day—or at the very least, every other day—occurrence since we started this up. But football season is well underway, and of course Suncrest U is killing it.

Dominique's time has been limited this week, more so than most. Between training in the mornings, classes in the afternoons, then practice after school and games every weekend, half of which require travel, we barely see each other.

I'm exhausted for him just thinking about his schedule. Not that he'll get any sympathy from me. That's not how this little arrangement works. He scratches my back. I scratch his. And we both satisfy an itch the other has. But lately, something's felt off. Like there's something missing, but I don't know what.

I've tried to ignore the feeling which is easier to do on days like today. When I remember that less than eight weeks ago, my mom died in a tragic car accident. That she was in the middle of leaving me a message when she crashed and that I'd been too busy ignoring her to answer. And now it's gone. Her message is gone. Her voice. The words she spoke, telling me she loved me. It's all fucking gone. And god dammit. Here I go again. What is wrong with me?

I suck in a ragged breath and Dominique's thrusts slow.

This is why I'm here right now. Why I showed up on his doorstep barely after seven AM. Because of that stupid voicemail. It haunts me.

Dominique curses, drawing my attention back to him. He releases his hold on my hair and spins me around to face him. His dick slides out of me with the change in position and a noise not unlike a sob passes over my lips.

"I've got you," he says, and he lifts me onto the edge of the table, spreading my thighs open for him to step between.

Wrapping my legs around his waist, I let out a small sigh of relief as he thrusts back into me. I throw my head back, more than ready for this to continue, and brace myself against the table, expecting Dominique to fuck me hard like he'd been doing only seconds before, except he doesn't. In fact, he does the complete opposite.

Cupping the nape of my neck, he tilts my head forward until he's all that I see. Dark brown eyes framed with heavy brows meet my baby blue gaze and he sinks into me almost painfully slow. I take in the hard lines of his face. The twin slashes that cut thin lines into his brow and his dark brown skin. He's the same arrogant asshole he's always been only now, he looks at me like I'm more than his best friend's little sister. Like I'm more than an easy lay.

His dark brown eyes are soft, gaze heavy lidded. He peppers my face with tender kisses, his lips brushing along my cheeks, my nose, and trailing down along my neck before making their way to my lips and covering my mouth with his. He swallows my sounds of protest and his hand cups the side of my neck, holding me in place but also supporting me with his strength.

Dominique pulls out until only the tip of him is still inside me before sinking into me again. Slow. Methodical. Eyes boring into mine and making the act that much more intense.

It's... intimate.

I don't like it.

His gaze searches mine for something. It's like he's asking me a question, but I can't make out the words to give him a response. His hands roam over my body, skimming over my ribs. He peels my shirt up, exposing my stomach and chest as he tugs down the cup of my bra and palms one of my breasts in his large hands. He rolls my nipple between his thumb and forefinger while I'm struggling to increase our pace.

I dig my heels into his lower back, encouraging him to go faster. To thrust into me harder. But he refuses to budge. With a grimace, he controls himself, thrusting in and out of me at a measured pace, never giving me what I need. Keeping it slow and steady, like he's worried I might break. Or worse. Fucking shatter.

"How's that, baby girl?" His voice rasps over my heated skin as he touches his forehead to mind.

"Fuck me," I snarl and he chuckles, shaking his head.

His thumb grazes my lower lip, and he leans in like he's about to kiss me again, only to whisper a single word against my mouth. "No."

I groan and move to shove him away from me, but pushing Dominique is like trying to move a mountain. "You want me to stop?" he asks, surprise coloring his voice.

"No," I snap. "I want you to fuck me like you hate me. Give me what I need, Dom."

I cringe, hearing the whine in my voice, but thankfully, Dominique doesn't pick up on it. But neither does he do what I ask.

"You can't tell me this doesn't feel good," he demands, continuing to thrust in and out of me. I look down at where our bodies connect, watching his smooth, dark shaft sink into me, and without meaning to, I release another breathy moan.

The sight of his dick does things to me I can't even explain. He has a beautiful dick. Long and thick. He's perfectly symmetrical, the skin smooth and just a few shades lighter at the tip. His hand dips between us, practiced fingers finding my clit.

"I feel that sweet pussy of yours clenching around my cock. You want this. Don't pretend you don't." Keeping with his slow pace, he thrusts into me a little harder, not giving me the friction I want but hitting a deeper point inside of me that has me digging my fingers into his flesh, holding on to his biceps like I need him to anchor me, like I'm worried he'll leave if I don't.

"Fuck." He hits that spot deep inside me, the perfect one that lets me know my release is in sight. His callused fingers strum my clit, increasing the pleasure tenfold. "Harder," I demand.

"No."

"Faster, then."

He nips at my bottom lip.

"No."

"Screw you, Dominique. Fuck me."

His eyes flash with pure lust, and his lips curve into a cruel smile. "What do you think we're doing here, baby girl?"

Sweat drips down my hairline, my chest rising and falling rapidly as I fight to slow my heart rate. Meanwhile, he continues to rub teasing circles around my clit. "Oh God."

"That's it, baby girl. Let go. I've got you," he murmurs, his voice softer than I've ever heard it.

My muscles tense and my eyes flutter closed. A whimper passes over my lips as intense waves build inside me. He's too good at this. No one should be this good at sex.

The hand at my throat tightens, not enough to restrict my airway, but just enough to add a spike of adrenaline to my system, and then I'm flying. My pussy clenches around him as wave after wave of pleasure skates through my entire body. I slump back, my spine meeting the cool wood of the table as Dominique milks out every ounce of my release, leaving me boneless.

Fuck, that was... amazing.

He looms over me, bracing himself on either side of me as he continues to thrust in and out of me, and then his lips are on mine and his hot cum is filling me as he shudders through his own release.

He pulls back enough to meet my eyes. His mouth opens to say what, I'm not sure, because the next thing I know there are familiar voices outside and Dominique is cursing, sliding out of me as I rush to slip my legs back into my leggings and right my top.

Kasey

I jump down from the table, panic rushing through me.

"Kasey..."

"Get dressed," I hiss.

His cum leaks out of my center, but I don't have time to deal with that right now because I'm almost positive Bibiana and Allie are about to walk in right now. I pull the hair tie from my wrist and throw my hair into the fastest messy bun I can manage just as there's a knock at the door, followed by it opening and my two best friends coming inside.

"Hey!" Allie calls.

"Kasey, we went by the Kappa Mu house and Quinn said we'd find you here. Are you kicking it with Aaron today? How's he doing?" Bibiana asks, waddling further into the house. She's close to eight months pregnant now and looks ready to pop. It'd be cute if I didn't know just how miserable she is. The beginning of the pregnancy went well enough, but she's struggling this last trimester. She's tired and sore and from what I've gathered, more than ready for baby Chavez to make his debut.

I hook my thumb behind me and snort. "I was trying to, but all I found was this ray of sunshine." Bibiana gives me a knowing smirk. One I choose to ignore, and claims one of the dining chairs, carefully lowering herself into it, one hand holding her round belly.

"Hey Dom." She exhales a sigh of relief and he gives her a quick kiss on the cheek before moving to grab the giant box in Allie's arms.

"What's all this for?" he asks her.

Allie gives him a mischievous smirk. "We bought forks. It's the day before Halloween and we're going forking."

Dominique drops the box on the table, giving me a heated look while the girls are distracted. One that clearly says he'd like to do some forking, too.

I roll my eyes and a smug look curls the corners of his mouth, so I flip him off and turn my attention to the girls.

"What the hell is forking?"

Allie opens the box and shows us the contents inside. Hundreds of plastic forks greet me. "I'm glad you ask," she says, holding one up. "Forking is when you take a bunch of plastic forks and stab them into the grass. Usually you do this to someone's yard but today we're going to go fork PacNorth's soccer field."

My brows pull together. "Why are we forking their field?" Not that I'm against it. Just curious what brought all of this on.

Her eyes flash. "Because Julio is a butthead."

Bibiana snickers.

Julio is Allie's best friend from her hometown and if she's upset with him, he must have messed up royally because last I checked, in Allie's mind, Julio damn near walks on water.

I grab a fork from the box and hold it out to Allie. "This one is a spork."

She grabs it from me and tosses it back into the box. "I bought all the forks at Pauli's Grocer and sporks were the next best thing. Spoons don't really work."

"What's the point of this?" Dominique asks. "Sticking forks in a university field doesn't seem very effective if you're trying to make a point, here."

Allie huffs out a breath. "Maybe we should fork your field," she mutters.

"Game. Anytime," I tell her, and offer her a high five.

Dominique glowers at us, but we all ignore it. He loves Allie and Bibi as though they're his sisters and they know it, so his scary face doesn't work on them and me. I like seeing his angry face. It means I managed to piss him off, which happens to be my second favorite pastime lately. After the screwing, that is.

"You stick the fork in the field. And when the offending party goes to yank them out. They snap." She breaks one for added effect. "It's annoying as hell and makes unforking the field tedious and annoying. Julio hates stupid shit like this, so it's the perfect kind of revenge."

"Revenge for what, exactly?" I ask. Julio is Allie's bestie from her home town and as far as I knew, the man could do no wrong.

"He got drunk and made out with Adrianna."

I suck in a breath.

"The chick who fucked your ex before he was your ex?"

"Yep. She was Allie's best girl friend at the time, too," Bibiana adds, and I wince. That's a serious girl code violation.

Dominique whistles and steps back from the table. "This sounds like a good time for me to head out. You ladies have fun forking or whatever you want to call it."

"What? No!" Allie whines. "We need a getaway driver. That's you!"

Dominique shakes his head. "Can't. I'm training with the boys today."

She mutters out a curse and smacks her palm over her face. "I knew that. Roman was talking about it last night. I don't know how that slipped my mind." She pauses. "Well crap. Who's going to be our getaway driver now?"

"Why don't you want to drive? You've got the Audi," I remind her.

She gives me the *'please tell you're kidding'* look. "Richland is two hours away." As if that answers the question. "I do not want to have to watch the boring ass road for two hours while you bitches get to relax in your seats." Okay, fair point. I don't want to make that drive either. Being a passenger will be bad enough. There's nothing but farmland between here and Richland, so you can't even take in the view because there just isn't one.

"And I'm pregnant," Bibi adds.

"I think we're all very much aware of that."

She rolls her eyes. "Yeah, yeah. But I'm a shit driver and my stomach bumps into the steering wheel every time I try to go anywhere."

I pull out my phone and go with the phone a friend option. If I don't, then I'm ninety-five percent positive it'll be me stuck as the driver and yeah, no thanks. I turn it on speaker phone, knowing this will get a reaction and feeling entirely okay with that.

Dominique turns to head out of the room, not even bothering to say bye, not that any of us are surprised. He's not much of a talker, that one. But before he's made it far, the call connects and Deacon's voice chimes out of my phone.

"Hey. What's up?"

Dominique's entire body stiffens.

"Hey. The girls and I are heading to Richland to play a prank on some friends. We need a getaway driver. You in?"

He doesn't even hesitate. "I'm down. My schedule's clear since Coach is doing some bullshit training exercise with the starting line players today. When are we heading out?"

Before I can answer, Dominique tears the phone from my hand and ends the call. "No." He barks out.

Silence fills the room.

I glare at him and hold my hand out for my phone.

"Kasey—" there's a warning in his voice. One I choose to ignore.

"I thought you needed to go to training?" I ask.

His nostrils flare. "Deacon is bad news. Find someone else or fuck, don't go at all. But you are not spending the day with that asshole."

He's funny if he thinks that's going to stop me. Hasn't he realized ordering me not to do something just means I'm that much more determined to do it?

Kasey

Twenty minutes and a good fight with Dominique later and we're piling into Deacon's car and heading to Richland to fork the soccer field. Allie is giddy with excitement, but I imagine that'll fade soon. PacNorth is a two-hour drive away, so I settle in for our mini road trip and play with the stereo until I find a station I like. Sueco's *Paralyzed* plays over the speakers and I lean back, letting the music shake loose some of my lingering tension. The argument with Dominique would have gone on longer if it wasn't for the fact he couldn't be late to practice, but when he finally stormed out of the house, I called Deacon back and he was immediately down.

"You owe me," Deacon reminds me.

I roll my eyes and turn to look at him. He keeps his eyes on the road but reaches out and gives me a light shove on the shoulder.

"Pretty sure you owe me for getting Dominique off your ass."

He grunts. "Pretty sure Dominique was only ever on my ass because of you."

He's not wrong. But that's not really my fault either. It's his.

"How much are we betting that this puts me firmly back on his shit list?" he asks, not sounding at all worried. It's stupid really. I mean, I'm glad he agreed to take us. Allie was right. Being stuck in the driver's seat would have sucked. But he knew what he was doing when he agreed. Dominique's gone all big brother over me on his ass before. So have Roman and Emilio, for that matter. And he still agreed to come, so that's on him.

I release an exaggerated sigh. "Ah, the consequences of our actions. Don't you just hate when they strike?"

"What's this about Dominique?" Allie pipes up from the backseat.

"Nothing. Just that he's an asshole," I tell her, a smile in my voice.

"Truth," Deacon mutters and gives me a fist bump in solidarity. Dominique might not be kicking his ass on the field anymore, but those two will never be friends. Dom's inner circle is tight and given the rocky start these two had, it'll be a long day in hell before they ever have anything close to a civilized conversation with each other. A fact which Dominique could give two shits about. He's not looking to make friends. Though Deacon's a nice, personable guy, I wonder if it bothers him how much Dominique dislikes him?

"Dominique is one of the sweetest guys I know," Allie argues. "How you manage to pull the worst out of him always surprises me."

"He really is incredibly sweet. He used to watch Luis for me and Emilio during his non-schedule back at Sun Valley High, remember? That man has a heart of gold," Bibiana adds.

I snort. "He's sweet to you two. To us," I indicate the space between Deacon and I, "he's an asshole. Always has been. I'm his friend's annoying little sister—"

"And I'm the guy gunning for his spot on the field," Deacon finishes.

Allie reaches forward and pats him on the arm. "Hate to break it to you, but until he graduates, you can go after it all you want, but it's not going to happen. Coach will never replace Dominique as the starting QB, and with the way things are looking, he's going to land the Heisman. Again."

Deacon huffs out a breath. "I'm aware. Doesn't mean he doesn't still hate me."

Now it's Bibi's turn to roll her eyes. "Doubt it. He probably doesn't ever think of you." She touches her forefinger to her lower lip. "Though now that I think about it, when Kasey called you to drive us, he did look two seconds away from committing murder. What was that about, anyway?"

"I've always said there's something going on between these two. Maybe he doesn't like the idea of another guy near Kasey." Allie says it flippantly, but in the back of my mind, I'm silently freaking out. If Allie and Bibiana figure out what we're doing, then their significant others—Roman and Emilio—will know too. And if they find out, no way will Aaron not get wind of it. I need to shove them off that trail of thought right away.

"Hardly," I chuckle. "He just likes to play the protective older brother part whenever Aaron isn't around. I've heard him call it some bro code bullshit or something. I wouldn't read too much into it."

Deacon gives me the side eye but thankfully says nothing and after a few comments from the girls about what a bummer that is, and how it would have been so great if we got along and coupled up like they did, I finally get them onto the topic of Bibi's impending birth and get sucked into talks about her birthing plan and the baby shower, and all things baby Chavez.

Thank god for that. They don't really need much input from me, so I relax while they talk about themes and colors, whether Bibiana wants a doula or if she just wants Emilio in the room when the baby comes.

Deacon doesn't join the discussion. Instead, he pulls out his phone, typing a quick, one-handed message before tossing it in the car's cup holder.

My phone vibrates in my pocket and I frown at him as I pull it out, Deacon's name flashing across the screen.

 Deacon: I take it they don't know about you and Dominique?

I scowl at him and type out a response.

 Me: There's nothing to know.

His phone chirps and he reads my message, grunts, and types out a reply.

Deacon: Bullshit. You two fucked in the locker room last week.

I turn wide eyes toward him. Floored. I am fucking floored right now. He saw us? We checked and double checked that no one was in there. How the hell could he—Another message comes in.

 Deacon: Stop freaking out. Your secret is safe with me and I didn't see shit. I heard plenty when I grabbed my gear after practice. Cut back on the 'God, yes. Oh Dominique. Yes.' The man doesn't need the ego stroke. It's plenty big already.

I cover my face with my hand, heat rising in my cheeks. He knows. Shit. No one is supposed to know.

"You okay?" Bibi asks.

I give her a thumbs up, keeping my face turned away from her as my mind scrambles to come up with an excuse. A way to deny this, but I've got nothing. Literally nothing. "Yep. Super peachy."

Deacon, for his part, laughs and I know with that sound alone that, while he might not tell—jury is out on that though because I don't know him that well — he definitely plans to use this against me. *Great.*

Deacon

She's panicking, I can see it in her eyes. The fast flutter of her lashes. Her mouth is stuck in this in-between stage with her lips parted like she wants to speak but has no idea what to say. It's fucking cute as shit. No wonder Price wants her all for himself.

Too bad the fucker can't always have what he wants. He has shit so fucking easy. Life given to him on a silver platter. And if I can't take his spot on the team, then I've got no issue swooping in and claiming his girl as my consolation prize instead.

Don't get me wrong. He's earned his stripes. I won't deny that. Right now, he's the better quarterback. But he's not the better man. Sooner or later, Kasey is going to realize that.

I slide my hand over the center console and give her knee a squeeze. "Relax. I've got you," I tell her. I could fuck Price over with this information if I wanted to. There's a reason he and Kasey are keeping things on the down low. I don't know what they are yet. But I'll find out. And in the meantime, I'll hang on to this knowledge, earn Kasey's trust, and show her why she's wasting her time with a dude who's clearly uninterested in showing her off. *Idiot.* It's like he has no clue what a fucking catch she is. She's younger than him by a few years so it could be that but I can't imagine that's reason enough to avoid laying a public claim on the girl.

She swallows hard, her throat bobbing with the motion, and I leave my hand on her knee for the rest of the drive. I'm not sure if she realizes it's there, likes that I'm touching her, or is just too lost in that pretty head of hers to care.

Either one works for me. I've spent the last few weeks building a relationship with this chick and doing my damnedest to not get stuck in the friend zone, which is a hell of a lot harder than I expected.

I'm an alright looking guy. Getting a girl's attention has never been an issue. But Kasey isn't like other girls. She's feisty and could give two shits what anyone thinks about her, and she never has a problem speaking her mind.

I've managed to make touches like this casual. Normal and to be expected.

She doesn't bat an eye anymore when I toss my arm around her shoulder and walk with her after class, or when I pull her in for a quick hug goodbye. She's comfortable with me. And Price fucking hates it. Knowing that it eats away at him is the only thing keeping me sane these days.

Tuition bills are racking up and if I can't move up to a starting position, my parents aren't going to help with tuition any longer. My pops says if you're not the best then you're wasting your time but I love competing. I was born to play. I'm fast as shit, have quick reflexes, and I'm solid under pressure. No way am I going to let a guy like Dominique Price get in the way of my future. I might not be the best yet, but I can be. He just needs to be knocked off his game.

The drive goes by quickly, the girls talking about babies and all the things I have zero clue about, but it keeps them busy and lets me clear my thoughts before we're pulling up to PacNorth University. Allie directs me to the soccer field and I park at the rear, away from the rest of the cars in the lot. What she's planning seems harmless enough but the girls want to be sneaky and shit, like this is some big covert operation.

We all get out of the car and I keep an eye on the pregnant one. Bibiana. I know she's Emilio's chick and obviously very pregnant. On the drive, I overheard her saying she still has a ways to go but no way can the girl get any bigger. She's small. Over a foot shorter than me and all belly. If I didn't know for a fact she was carrying E's kid, I'd assume she shoved a basketball under her shirt. It's that ridiculous.

With one hand supporting her swollen stomach, she follows Allie and Kasey out of the car and to the field. I take up the rear after claiming the box of forks from Allie's grasp and scan the parking lot for anyone who might snitch on us.

"Thanks," Allie mutters, but I just nod.

My parents and I have a lot of differences, but my momma raised me right. I'm not gonna make a girl shoulder this thing when my arms are free and I'm more than capable.

"No problem. So... what's the plan?"

Allie pulls the hood of her sweatshirt up over her head. "Since it's a Saturday and the day before Halloween, the field should be empty. Everyone is off getting ready for whatever campus parties are happening tonight and tomorrow." Makes sense. "So the plan is to pretend we're supposed to be here."

"Is that why we're doing this in the middle of the day?" Kasey asks.

"Yeah. If we tried to do it at night and someone saw us, they'd immediately assume we didn't belong but since the only people who know what's going on with the field are the players and the coaches, all of whom should be gone already for the day, we should be in the clear. We might get a few curious looks but no one is going to freak out seeing us."

I tug on the back of her hood. "So what's with the cover up, then?"

She rolls her eyes. "Habit. Come on." We rush across the lot and slip through the gate onto the field and I set down the box. Allie immediately starts laying forks out on the grass in some sort of design."

"What are you doing?" Kasey asks, saving me the trouble.

"We don't have enough forks to actually fork the entire field so we're gonna spell out a message."

"What's the message?"

"*Tu madre, traidor.*"

"Which means?"

It's Bibiana who answers. "Your momma, you traitor. It's some weird inside thing between Allie and Julio that none of us understand."

Allie smirks. "You don't need to. Just help me spell out the words. Deacon, you should probably play look out. I don't think we can really get in trouble for a harmless prank but you're an athlete and

PacNorth is technically a rival school. If we get caught, I don't want to be responsible for you getting a suspension."

I nod. "Sounds good. I'll kick it by the locker rooms since that's where coaches or players are bound to head if any show up." I leave the girls to their work, scrolling through social media posts on my phone. There are a few parties going down tonight back on campus I might check out when we get back. I'm not really into Halloween and dressing up. It's never been my thing. But I don't mind when the girls go full on Slutober and display all the goods. It's like Halloween is a free pass to wear the least amount of clothing and not be crucified for it. Something you will never hear me complain about.

Deacon

I t takes the girls over an hour to fork the field and I've blown through all my emails, looked at all the stupid videos on social media, and posted a few images to my Insta feed. Safe to say, I am bored as fuck. But they're having a blast. Bibiana is scooting across the field in a makeshift crab walk so she doesn't have to bend over, and Allie and Kasey are laughing and smiling, talking about who knows what, but it's a good look on them both.

Kasey hasn't smiled much lately. This is good for her. I heard the rumors that her mom passed, and she's had a dark cloud following her these past few weeks, so seeing her be herself again, it's good.

The click of heels on pavement draws my attention and I turn to see who it is only to do a double take. *Holy sh—.* My mouth drops open as I take in the woman walking toward me. She's digging in the oversized bag slung over her shoulder, her gaze directed down and a small furrow between her brows. She hasn't spotted me, but me and every other person—men and women alike—that she walks past, sure as hell spot her.

Wearing white skinny jeans, a low-cut sleeveless silk blouse, and strappy sandals with a small heel, she walks down the pathway like it's a runway made just for her. Her hair is natural, an afro of loose corkscrew curls that billow out around her. Shorter curls hang down in front of her face, almost like bangs. She owns her beauty. Standing out amongst everyone she passes like she doesn't care that she doesn't belong. She's not looking to fit in. She's showing everyone why they wish they were her and could stand out.

She has smooth, dark bronze skin, full plump lips, and dark brown eyes that, even from here, I know I could get fucking lost in.

"Fuck me," I mutter.

She's almost to me and it's obvious she's heading toward the field. Something I can't let happen now that the girls are wrapping up. I'm the look out. No way can I fuck this up when we're so close to the finish line.

I step away from the alcove I've been chilling in and she's forced to come to a halt. She doesn't acknowledge me for the first few seconds. Still digging through her bag until she manages to pull out her phone, which I assume is what she'd been after. She studies me, brushing a coil out of her face.

"Can I help you?" she asks. Her tone is brusque. She gives me a lightning fast once-over, and though I see a flash of interest in her gaze, she masks it and gives me an '*I'm not impressed.*' look.

"Yeah, actually." I let my gaze track over her and let my interest show. "I was hoping you'd be down for grabbing a drink with me later." I shoot my shot, knowing she'll reject it but that's alright. I'm stalling for time here.

"Sorry. I don't date students."

Well, hello there. That means she's faculty or a teacher's aide. Maybe a graduate student who helps after classes. My bet is on teachers's aide. She can't be older than twenty-five, and she doesn't seem the type to sit behind a desk all day in one of the admissions offices.

She moves to step around me, but I sidestep, keeping in her way. She makes an irritated sound and props one hand on her hip. "That's good because I'm not a student."

Her eyes widen before narrowing in doubt. "You don't go to PacNorth?"

I shake my head and step closer to her. Her breath catches, pupils dilating and yeah, she's interested.

"Nah. I just gave a friend a lift. They have a buddy who attends, so we were dropping in to say hello."

She licks her lips and gives me another once over, this one slower. Like the realization that I'm not a student grants her permission to check me out.

"I'm Deacon."

She hesitates before giving me her name. "Jameia."

Jameia. I like it. It's different. Exotic. Like her.

The phone in her hand rings and she tears her gaze from mine to answer it, flicking her eyes up once before she turns her back on me in search of some small measure of privacy.

"Hello?"

I chance a look over my shoulder as she talks to whoever her caller is. Kasey lifts her head at the same time and grimaces, getting the other girls' attention and telling them to hurry the fuck up. Allie rushes the box that'd held the plastic forks to a nearby recycling bin right as Jameia finishes her call and turns back to me.

"It was nice meeting you, Deacon. But I have an appointment to get to."

"Let me walk you," I tell her, falling into step beside her, and we head right for Kasey and the others.

"That's really okay. I'm just going to the soccer field."

I push my hands in my pockets and shrug. "I'm happy to. Besides, I'm heading out soon anyway and I'm parked over there." I indicate the lot and she nods, not having an excuse to send me away. When we get closer to the field, she realizes something is wrong and her footsteps speed up.

"You have got to be kidding me," she curses. I hide my smirk and follow a few steps behind her as she practically runs to the field. "Who did this?"

Before I can answer, not that she was really asking me, more curses fill the air and I turn to spot three Hispanic guys heading our way. "What the fuck happened?" One asks as soon as he's close. He's got tattoos running down his arms. Large roses inked over the top of his hands. His neck is covered in more ink, some colorful card design painting the columns of his throat. The work is solid, the colors vivid and bright.

He gives me a nod in greeting but turns his attention to Jameia, the others closing in around him. "I don't know. I just got here, and it was like this." She waves at the soccer field behind her and I take a few measure steps back. Now is a good time to make my getaway so after I've gone a few steps, I do a quick turn around and head for my car. Kasey's eyes are wide as they look out at me through the windshield and Allie stands beside the back rear door, her eyes bright and her smile wide.

I chuckle. Someone is obviously pleased with themselves.

I'm almost to my car when someone shouts, "Alejandra, get that fine ass of yours over here!"

I turn just as the same three guys who were talking to Jameia run my way. Hell nah.

I'm almost to my car, so I turn to face them and bark out a quick "Get in the car," to Allie. Does she listen? Of course not. Not that I'd expect anything less from one of Kasey's friends. Birds of a feather and all that shit. I hold my hands out in front of me and block their way. "Woah. Woah. Let's relax here for a minute. You three look like you have some business to handle over there," I wave toward the field. "And me and my friends have someplace to be. You'll have to catch your girl later."

Later like when her footballer boyfriend can deal with the hostility coming off him.

"Nah. I'll catch her now. Thanks man."

He shifts to pass me but I shoulder check him and he whirls on me, eyes narrowed and nostrils flaring. "We have a problem, man?" he asks.

His two friends close in and I catch sight of Jameia on the sideline, face pinched in worry, but whether for me or the others, I'm not sure.

"Yeah. We do. Allie's with me and no way am I gonna let some hot head asshole come at her the way you are right now."

He throws his head back and laughs, the other two following suit before he shakes his head and looks over my shoulder at the girl in question. "Alejandra, come out, come out wherever you are. Time to face the music, bebita. Or should I call Rome and tell him you're making friends."

She curses and I hear her storming up the sidewalk behind me. "Don't you dare, Julio. You know how jealous he can get.

Julio smirks. "Yeah. I do." He pulls out his phone and snaps a quick photo of Allie beside me. "Which is why I'mma make sure I've got evidence to back up my claim." She curses and lunges for his phone, but he holds it up in the air with a laugh, playing keep away from her. I frown, not entirely sure what I'm supposed to do here, when the car doors close behind me and Kasey and Bibiana join us.

"Delete the picture and don't be a butt head," Allie tells him. "You're already on my shit list for what you did."

Julio groans. "It was an accident."

"How exactly do you accidentally shove your tongue down my ex-best friend's throat? Hmm?"

One of the other guys steps forward. "It's not what you think, Allie. Adriana took advantage. Kissed him at a party, and when he realized who he was making out with, he pushed her away. Julio would never mess with her. You know that."

She folds her arms over her chest and huffs. "Fine. You're forgiven."

Julio's face breaks into a smile and he whoops before swooping in and throwing Allie over his shoulder. "Julio!" she cries out, and he smacks the back of her thighs. "Appreciate the forgiveness but now it's your turn to repent for your sins."

She squirms in his arms and he chuckles, carrying her like she weighs nothing. "I didn't sin!" she swears, but none of them are buying it.

Julio turns to me, Allie still slung over his shoulder, and holds a hand out. "I'm Julio, by the way. This is Gabe. Felix." He nods to the two boys beside him. "And it looks like you already met Meme."

"Meme?" I ask, looking her way. Her cheeks flush, the skin darkening.

"It's a nickname," she stammers.

I cover my laugh with a cough. "I like it." She bites her bottom lip and I turn back to Julio. "I'm Deacon. Kasey's friend."

"Ah..." He draws out the word. "So that's how these three rebels roped you into their prank."

I shrug. "You have any luck turning them down when they want something?"

He laughs at that. "I do not. Fair point. But we've still got a problem."

I raise a single brow. "How do you figure?"

"You see, I've got a game tomorrow, and a field filled with plastic utensils." He pats the back of Allie's thigh again. "And don't think I missed what you wrote there, Allie girl."

"I have no idea what you're talking about."

Julio huffs out an exasperated breath. "No? If that wasn't you, what brings you to town?" She squirms in his hold and he finally releases her, carefully dropping her to the ground.

She glares at him. Not that it does her any good. Then she turns to me and says, "Deacon wanted to check out the school. See what your football team looks like."

"Really?" Felix asks, not convinced in the slightest, but I back up Allie's lie.

"Yeah, man. I'm not so sure Suncrest U is a good fit. Figured I'd see what PacNorth had to offer."

"For fútbol?" he clarifies putting emphasis on the u.

"Uh, yeah."

Gabe chuckles and shares a look with the other two, some silent communication passing between them. "Alright. How about we make a deal?"

"What are you offering?"

More communication passes between them. "Try to score a goal against me. I'll give you three shots to score, but if you miss, you four have to de-fork our field. Today. Before our game.

"And if I score?"

He shrugs. "You get a free pass and we're stuck here cleaning up the mess."

I glance at Jameia and an idea springs to mind. "Not good enough. I didn't fork your field, your friend there can vouch for me."

She bites her lip, the sight alone making my dick twitch.

"Okay. So if you score, what do you want?" she asks, joining the conversation.

I consider my options and decide I've got nothing to lose. "A kiss," I tell her.

Her mouth parts and everyone around us makes *ooooOOOH* sounds, getting riled up as they wait to see how she answers. She's going to say no. I can see it in her eyes and for whatever reason, I don't want her to. She's hot as hell and while I've got my eyes on Kasey, something tells me Jameia would be a fun interlude.

"But if you're afraid to risk it, I get it. It's not like your boys here stand a chance."

She snorts. "You're that confident you can score against Gabe?"

I look from him to the field. I mean, I've never played soccer before, but how hard can it be? All I've got to do is kick the ball in the giant ass goal. It's not like he can cover the whole thing.

"Yeah. I guess I am."

"Come on, Meme. You know I've got this," Gabe encourages.

She looks at him, her expression pinched before she gives a single nod. "I'm only agreeing because he's not a student. You know my rules."

"Yeah, yeah. No fucking the freshies."

"Oh, so it's fucking we're putting on the table here?"

"Definitely not," she snaps, but I don't miss the heat in her gaze.

I lick my lips. "No worries. I'll settle for the kiss."

The boys lead the way to the field and Gabe grabs a ball and a pair of gloves from the gym bag he abandoned near the gate.

"You need any instructions?" he asks.

"I just have to kick it in the net, right?"

He nods. "It's a little more complicated than that, but yeah. We'll treat it like a penalty kick. You'll start here." He leads me to a line in the field and sets the ball down. "This is twelve yards from the goal line. You have to kick from here. You can't rush me to score, got it."

I nod. "Got it."

He smirks, an arrogant swagger in his step as he positions himself in front of the goal. "Whenever you're ready, man."

I take a deep breath, focus in on that place inside myself where all I see is the ball and the end zone. This isn't football, but the feeling is similar. The goal. The drive to score.

The girls offer encouragement from the sidelines, but for the most part, I tune it out. Taking a deep breath, I take a few steps back, giving myself some room to work with, and line myself up with the goal. I don't want to come at it straight on. He's expecting that. I don't play this sport but I'm sure there's more skill to it than I'm giving it credit. I take in the width of the goal and decide to aim for the top right corner. That will force him to lunge to his left and I have a feeling he's right-handed and is stronger going that direction.

Inhaling deep, I zero in on the ball, bounce on my heels a few times and jog to close the small distance, pushing off and bringing my leg back before I swing forward. I power through the kick, following it all the way through. The ball sails through the air, arrowing right where I intended, in the top right corner at rapid speed. Gabe's eyes widen a second before he lunges for the ball, but that split second of surprise costs him and he misses, his fingers not ever grazing the leather before it collides with the net.

Allie and Kasey are screaming, Bibiana bouncing up and down. A smile breaks out over my face and I meet Jameia's stunned expression. Without hesitating, I head straight for her, my steps confident. She looks to her left and right, as if expecting someone to swoop in and save her. Sorry, pretty girl, not today.

When she's a foot away, I reach out, pull her towards me with one hand on the small of her back, the other cupping the side of her neck, and I press my lips against hers. Hoots and hollers go up around us and she holds herself rigid in my arms.

That's not going to work.

Pressing firmer against her, I nip at her bottom lip and she gasps, giving me the opening I need to sweep my tongue into her mouth. I stroke my tongue over hers and it only takes a few seconds before she's kissing me back, fingers curling into the fabric of my shirt. Sparks of sensation race through my body and I groan against her lips. My dick hardens in my pants and I'm sure she can feel it, but it doesn't look like she minds. Thank fuck for that.

Her tongue darts out and swipes across my lip and I tilt her head, deepening the kiss. Reality must catch up to her though, because the next thing I know, she's biting my lip, hard, and I rear back to glare at her.

"You got your prize," she says, voice breathless.

I lick over my abused lip, tasting blood, and smile at her. "Yeah. I guess I did."

She steps away and the next thing I know I'm being tackled by Allies friends and we tumble to the ground. "Bro! That was sick.

Please tell me Allie was not full of shit when she said you were looking at making a change and yeah, I get it. She meant football, not fútbol but seriously, man. Think about it. We could use someone like you on the team."

I untangle myself from the dog pile and climb up to my feet. "I hate to break it to you but uh, she lied."

Julio shoots her a glare, and she ducks behind Bibiana. "Alight, alright. So that wasn't the plan, but you'll consider it, yeah?"

I shake my head. "I don't know. I mean, I've never played. That was one kick— "

"I know talent when I see it and you've got it. You can score ,and if you already play ball then I'll assume you can work under pressure?"

I nod.

"Great. Next weekend, come back and we'll have you try out in front of Coach. Just tell me you'll think about?"

I press my lips together and shake my head.

"We need a new striker and we've got a full ride scholarship on the table for the right one."

My ears perk up. "Full ride?"

He meets Jameia's gaze. "Wanna give him the deets?"

I frown. Why would he ask her to fill me in? She isn't on the team. She visibly swallows and sweeps the curls out of her face. "Yeah. So if you have what it takes and we invite you to play, you'll have tuition, dorm, and a food credit provided."

Fuck. That's not a bad deal. But I love football. I'm not sure I want to leave the game. Though a full ride means I'm not relying on my parents to help me out with tuition. It's a lot to consider.

"You said we. How do you factor into all this?"

Julio slaps me on the back before hooking his arm over my shoulder. "Meme here is our assistant coach."

My eyes widen at that. So that's why she said she doesn't date students. It all makes perfect sense. My eyes land on her mouth and she touches her lips, thinking about the kiss we just shared. Maybe coming to play at PacNorth isn't a bad idea after all.

Want more?

Check out The Savage to see more from the boys at PacNorth.

Holiday Sext

Holiday Sext is a short story previously featured in the **Scoring over the Holidays** Collection and features Emilio's oldest brother, Roberto.

Twas' the night before Christmas when I sexted my ex ...

Penélope

Coming to Borracho's—a bar close to Suncrest University's campus was my first mistake. Drinking with a bunch of rowdy college kids on Christmas Eve was my second. Did I mention I'm doing all this less than forty-eight hours after a shitty break-up?

Yeah, that's probably mistake number three. The leaving town and drinking part. Not the break-up. The only mistake I made there was sticking around as long as I did and not seeing the glaring red flags from the beginning.

But as with any break up, I'm spiraling. I wasted two years of my life with Patrick. Two years allowing him to whittle away at my self-esteem. To gaslight me and make me feel like I'm the problem. Like everything is always my mistake.

He made me dependent on him and I never even saw it. If it wasn't for walking in on the asshole with his secretary, I'd still be with him. I hate knowing that.

Patrick preyed on my insecurities. He peeled back the layers of who I am and twisted all of my worries and my fears and anytime I disagreed with him or reacted in a way he didn't approve of; I was the crazy one. Irrational. Too stupid to see reason.

A cold prickle of self-loathing trickles down my spine. I won't be that girl. The one he tried so hard to mold me into.

I'm four spiked hot chocolates in—something I never would have been before — when I come up with the grand idea to text my ex. Not Patrick. I'm not so far gone to stoop that low ever again.

But, in my need to rediscover myself, I came back to Sun Valley and I don't know, I'm feeling nostalgic I guess. I haven't talked to my high school flame in years. Not since we graduated, and he enlisted in the army, choosing the military over me. Yeah, it sucked. And yes, I sort of hated him for a while after that.

But being here... it reminds me of him. And it reminds me of the girl I was when I was with him. I liked her. She was confident and filled with life. She was happy. I want to be that girl again.

This is all the peppermint schnapps's fault. At least that's what I'll tell myself if this blows up in my face.

 Me: Are you on Santa's naughty or nice list this year?

NOT MY SMOOTHEST LINE, BUT WE'VE GOT TO START somewhere. We'll see if he responds. I won't hold my breath. Like I said, it's been years. But, I can admit to myself that if he doesn't,

I'll be disappointed. I've thought about him on and off these past years. Always playing the what-if game. What if I gave a long-distance relationship a shot? What if I agreed to wait for him like he'd asked me to? What if I called and told him I changed my mind?

That was the big one but, as the months went by and then the years, it became too late to simply *change my mind*. And then Patrick came along and well, this is where we are now.

Knowing my luck, he's probably married with two point five kids and a picket fence now.

I huff out a breath and visibly shake myself. I refuse to throw a pity party over what-ifs. Forcing myself to make small talk with the small crowd around me, I turn my phone face down on the table. I won't be that girl frantically checking for an incoming message, either. I'm twenty-six for chrissakes, not sixteen.

"Yo, Penn! You're up."

"Coming!" I tell Tyler. He's the one coordinating rounds and taking people's bets for the game. I don't know him. Not beyond initial introductions. But since I'm playing pool with a bunch of frat guys—and kicking their asses, by the way—he's the one guy I've bothered to pay attention to because he's calling the shots and deciding who plays who and when. He also handles pay out and while I don't need the money, I have a competitive streak a mile wide.

If you win your game, you earn fifty bucks. After that, you can keep your money and walk away, or double down and play another round. If you win the next game, that's another fifty. But if you lose, you forfeit all your earnings up to that point.

The first two rounds I win but manage to make things close. I don't want to let on just how good I am. I used to bar tend and on slow nights during the week, the waitresses and I would play a few rounds. Over time, I got good. Then I got better. Stacked against a bunch of intoxicated twenty-one-year-olds and my chances are looking pretty fantastic.

"Whose racking them up?" I ask, scanning the area for my next opponent.

"That'd be Rich, over there." Tyler points to a muscular guy on our left. He's wearing a football jersey with a pair of faded jeans, leading me to believe he's either a player or a really big fan. Given the size of the guy, I'm going to assume player.

"Cool." I chalk up my stick while Rich makes his way over to us and gives me a slow once over, pausing on my chest—rude—before finally meeting my eyes. I force out a smile.

"Hey. I'm Penélope." I hold my hand out. You know, good sportsmanship and all that. But does he shake it? No. He turns to Tyler, an annoyed look on his face.

"Why am I playing some chick?"

I bristle at his words.

"Because she won the last two rounds. Stop being a dick," Tyler says.

"Whatever." Rich heads over to the wall to select his cue stick. I narrow my eyes and make a swift decision. No way am I'm letting this game be close. I'm going to wipe the floor with this guy. It can be the highlight of my holiday weekend.

I'm spending Christmas alone. Which is fine. I really can't complain. I showed up on my parents' doorstep unannounced after my break-up, thinking I'd surprise them for the holidays and have a mini pity party for myself in the process. Only no one was home. Turns out my parents left town a few days ago on some Christmas cruise together.

Great for them. Crummy for me.

Hanging out in my parents' empty house all weekend isn't how I imagined spending my holiday, which is partially why I decided to come here. At least at Borracho's, I have company and entertainment. I almost considered going back to Richland... almost. But that isn't an option. Not yet, at least. Now that Patrick and I have split, I need to figure out living arrangements and I refuse to stay in that apartment while I figure it out. Even if he wants me to. Being around him gives him too much opportunity to mess with my head and change my mind. It's a risk I'm not willing to take.

So, the current plan of action is to have fun tonight, and nurse a well-deserved hangover off tomorrow. Which reminds me... I spot a waitress moving between the tables and flag her down.

"Something I can get for you?" She asks.

"Can I get another spiked peppermint hot chocolate?"

"Sure, love. The drink or the shot?"

I've been going for the drinks, but what the hell, "I'll take a shot." Not like I don't deserve one.

Rich takes his sweet ass time picking out the perfect cue stick, as if they're not all the same. If you need something special, then you're not that great, just pretending to be. Mildly annoyed, I decide to take a quick glance at my phone.

Roberto: Ask nicely and maybe I'll tell you.

HOLY SHIT. HE RESPONDED.

My smile goes wide and I fight the urge to do a little happy dance. I didn't think he would. Or at least, wasn't sure if he could. I have no clue if he's still active military or not. For all I know, he could be out on deployment.

Before I can type out a response, Tyler hollers out that they're ready for me. I set my phone back down. Telling myself I'll message him back after my turn.

Grabbing my pool stick, I do a slow walk around the table while Rich racks them up.

"Here you go." My waitress returns, handing me a shot of dark brown liquor with a dollop of whip cream on top. Here goes nothing. I throw back the shot, wincing at the burn as it slides down my throat. Damn. That was strong. Hand on my chest, I cough to clear my throat.

That might be the one that slips me past the buzz phase and into the drunk phase, but I'm not terribly worried. Pool is my game and even half sober, I can take any one of these fraternity guys on. Certainly Rich over here. He's being such a tool. Sliding the rack around like a hundred times and crouching down to be at eye level with it like there's some magical placement that he needs to pinpoint.

Tyler stops beside me, hands in his pockets, trying way too hard to look casual and I'm not buying it.

"Something I can do for you?" I ask when he continues to stand there.

"Want to make things a little more interesting?" He asks.

I raise a brow, my interest piqued. "What kind of interesting?"

A smirk curls the corners of his mouth and he rubs the back of his neck, almost like he's nervous but I'm not buying this shy guy act. "The drinking kind," he tells me. "For every ball you sink, your opponent takes a shot."

I laugh. "Pretty sure if we go that route, your buddy and I will both wind up in the hospital with alcohol poisoning. You do realize there are fifteen balls, right?"

He shrugs his shoulders, unfazed. "Fair enough. How about you call your shots? If you sink what you say you will, we drink? If you miss, then you drink? Sounds good?"

"The both of you are drinking, or am I just aiming to get Rich drunk?" I ask, because if Tyler's making terms, he should have to suffer through them too.

"Yeah. I can get on board with that but..." he trails off and there's an expectant look on his face now.

"Yes?"

"Well, if Rich wins, he gets the cash. Same goes for you, but there's nothing on the table for me, so I'll be drinking without an incentive."

And that's my problem, why? "What sort of incentive do you need?" I have a feeling this is what he was trying to get at from the beginning.

"A kiss under the mistletoe?" He points to the sprigs hanging just a few feet away from us.

I quirk a brow. "A kiss? Really?" I look over my shoulder at Rich. "You know. I took him for a straight guy, but I can put in a word for you if you'd—"

"You know what I mean?"

I snort. "Okay. So if I win, I get my money, Which I would get anyway," I add.

He nods, expression serious now.

"And if Rich wins, he gets the money and you get a kiss?"

"Your number too, if you're offering it." This guy is not afraid to ask for what he wants. I'll give him that. Too bad he won't be getting that kiss or my number.

I hold my hand out to him. "Deal." He shakes it just as Rich steps up beside him.

"We playing eight or nine?"

"Nine if you can manage it," I tell him. Eight ball pool means you can sink your shots in any order. Nine ball means you have to sink your balls in order. It's a little harder and if I have to call my shots, then I might as well not go easy on the guy.

"Sure you can manage it, sweetheart?"

"OOooo! Damn." Some asshole in crowd calls and yeah, that wasn't condescending at all.

"I'm sure. So why don't re-rack so you can break already? I'd like to wrap this up sometime before midnight." I tell him with a bite in my voice.

He grunts and adjusts the rack since nine ball requires a diamond split, not a triangle. Placing the cue ball on the green top, he leans forward to take his shot.

Crack. We all watch as the balls scatter across the tabletop. At least four hit the sides of the table, so no foul. Too bad. He doesn't manage to sink any balls either, though, so I wait to see if he'll call a *push out.*

"Push out," he mutters. Because of course. He moves the cue ball and lines up his next shot. "One. Left pocket."

He shoots. He misses. Tyler waives over the waitress and orders a round of shots.

I don't bother to smother my laugh when she returns and lays the tray down on a nearby table. "Cheers, boys." I tell them and wait for him and Tyler to down their shots.

Moving to the end of the table, I line up my sights. "One. Right pocket." I lean forward and train my eyes on my mark, letting the sounds of the bar fall away.

Inhaling through my nose, I thrust my cue stick forward on my exhale, hitting the cue ball dead center. *Crack.* It shoots forward, dropping the one ball right where I said.

Rich grunts. "Lucky shot."

Whatever asshole.

I line up my next shot. "Two. Right side pocket," I tell him and take the shot.

"Yo. Penn. Your phone is lighting up." Someone calls.

Shit. My stick barely grazes the cue ball, sending it wide and missing the two ball entirely.

I ignore Rich's smug face and head over to retrieve my phone. I stumble on my way, but manage to maintain my footing. That hot chocolate shot is hitting me now and yep, we're slipping right on past buzzville into drunk town. I snicker to myself.

Missed Call. Mom.

I clear the notification. I'll call her back tomorrow and wish her a Merry Christmas. I'm about to turn back to the game when I remember I never messaged Roberto back. I reread his message.

Ask nicely and maybe I'll tell you.

Hmm. I bite my lip. How do I want to play this? Who am I kidding? I have no freaking clue. But that response was suggestive, right? That means I need to follow it up with something similar. Or I could one up him. One upping him sounds like more fun. Except nothing is coming to me.

God, I suck at this. I never sexted before. Not that I am now. This isn't sexting. I guess I'd call it slut texting. Is that right?

There's a cute blond guy leaning beside my table and an idea pops into my head. I tap him on the arm to grab his attention. "Hey, wanna help me out with something?" I ask.

He turns and gives me a once over, pausing on my rack just like Rich did. Urgh. Boys. "Maybe. What's in it for me?" He asks.

"The satisfaction of knowing you're not a douche."

"Touché." He laughs and I hand him my phone, letting him see the texts. His brows pull together as he reads the messages over before handing it back. His expression is all business now as he drops into the seat beside me.

"This is a hook-up or a—"

"Old flame."

He nods. "You wanting a hook-up from it—"

I shake my head. "He's not around. I just want to rile him up." Maybe remind him what he walked away from all those years ago.

Blond dude nods. "Send a picture," he tells me. "His response means he's interested. If you want to get under the guy's skin, show him what he's missing out on."

My nose wrinkles. "I don't do nudes." I know I called this slut texting, but I meant that in the most figurative way.

"You don't have to," he laughs. "Here, let me show you." He reaches for my phone and I relinquish it to him. "Bite your lip and look straight at my chest."

"Why?"

"You wanted my help, didn't you?"

Fine. I bite my lower lip and keep my eyes level with his chest as he snaps a picture.

"There, send him that and add a *please,* since he wanted you to ask nicely. That'll do the trick and give the guy a major hard-on for you if he doesn't have one already."

"Woah."

The image is cropped, only showing my mouth and the tops of my breasts. My shirt isn't overtly sexual. Just a basic black v-neck t-shirt. But the V dips low enough to give some cleavage and that with the lip biting is surprisingly seductive. Not gonna lie, the red lipstick I decided to wear today helps too.

"I'm trusting you," I tell him.

"You'll thank me later." He gives me a smile before heading to the bar and before I can talk myself out of it, I send it.

 Me: Pretty please. *image attached*

Here goes nothing.

Roberto

My knee bounces as I stare at my phone, waiting to see what she says. I haven't heard from Penélope since we graduated high school and fuck if that text isn't throwing me for a loop. She was my girl until she wasn't. A visceral part of me revolts at the notion that she isn't mine anymore. Fuck that.

What made her decide to reach out?

I can't believe she still has my number. Then again, it's not like I ever deleted hers.

My phone vibrates in my hand and I swipe up on the screen to display the message. "Fuck me," I groan, seeing the picture she sent. Bright red lips and... "fuck." My dick immediately jumps to attention.

My brothers—Antonio and Emilio—sit on either side of me and both turn at my muttered curse. "What's up?" Emilio asks, angling to get a look at my phone. Nosy fucker. I turn the screen away from him. "None of your business." I don't need either of my brothers getting into my business. They're worse than school girls.

"Nice!" Antonio says and I jerk back, realizing in my rush to hide the screen from Emilio, I flashed it right into Antonio's face. "Who's the chick?"

I shake my head and tuck my phone beneath the bar top. "Like I said, none of your business. I thought we were here to watch the game?" I turn my attention back to the oversized TV screen playing the Suncrest U football game and ignore Emilio's obvious smirk, that cocky smile of his spreading wide across his face.

"It's fucking highlights. Besides, I played in that game. No need to rehash it. Come on. Give it up."

Both brothers move to attack, wrestling my arms out from under the counter in a bid for my phone as if we're teenagers again. Just fucking around. I drop my cell on the ground, cursing. These assholes better not break it.

It's Emilio who recovers the phone and after a few swipes on the screen, he lets out a whistle. I grind my teeth together. I knew I should have set up a passcode on the stupid thing.

"Damn, bro. Looks like someone is looking to get lucky for the holidays."

I lunge for the phone, but Antonio pulls me back, jerking my arms behind me. I could easily break out of his hold. I've got a solid thirty pounds on my little brother. But we're at Borracho's and while the three of us know our wrestling around is all fun and games—usually. The bouncers here don't. I'd rather not be banned from this bar the way we were at Fast Eddy's.

"Knock it off, *cabrón*." *Fucker*. "Give it back."

Emilio's eyes scrutinize the image with interest and my jealousy rears its ugly head. "Why the fuck are you looking at her picture so close, bro? You've got Bibiana back home." I remind him. In my bones, I know he loves that girl, but that doesn't mean I'm okay with him looking at *my* girl the way he is right now.

Emilio snorts, not the least bit phased. "Relax. I'm not checking out your woman," he tells me as I jerk away from Antonio. I stalk forward, my fists clenched at my sides and an anger I'm not used to feeling directed at my brothers thrumming through my veins. I don't like the idea of anyone looking at her picture. Not even them.

I rip the phone out of Emilio's hands. "For someone not looking, you sure stared at it long enough."

The asshole laughs. "She's here, fucker. That's why I was looking so close."

My limbs freeze, knees locking into place. *What?*

"What do you mean, she's here?" That isn't possible. Penélope moved out of town shortly after I left. She always wanted to see the world outside Sun Valley and I guess with me out of the equation, it was easier to leave. As far as I knew, she never came back. Had some boyfriend out in Richland she lived with. Not that I'll tell any of that to my brothers because then I'd have to admit I asked around about her. Might have even searched... okay stalked... her socials there for a while when I came back to Sun Valley. But she looked happy. I might have fucking hated it. But I let her be. Not my place to fuck up someone else's situation.

What changed?

Emilio holds his hand out for the phone and I reluctantly relinquish it.

"Look here." He zooms in to the right of the photo just over her shoulder.

"What am I looking at?" I ask. All I see is a red wall with what looks like the outline of... I don't know... maybe a football player.

"No, shit?" Antonio mutters, taking a closer look before I shove his head out of my way. He starts scanning the bar, but I don't pay him any attention. My gaze still trained on figuring out whatever Emilio's trying to show me.

"That wall." He points to it on the screen. "It's a mural for Suncrest U's football team. That mural right over there."

He points at the back of the bar to a dimly lit corner of the room where the pool tables are set up. I look at the wall in question, spotting the mural right away. "It's not the same one," I tell him. It can't be. "She doesn't live in Sun Valley anymore."

"Bro, I'm telling you. It's the same. Maybe she came back to visit family or something."

"There!" Antonio shouts, drawing our attention. He points across the bar. "Left pool table with the Alpha Sig assholes. Same black top. Same red lips."

I follow the direction he's aiming at, my eyes scanning the area, when all of a sudden, I see her. She's leaning against the table, a guy I vaguely recognize leaning toward her, like he's trying to make their conversation intimate or some shit. It's not even that loud here. Why the hell is that asshole so close to her? Before I even know what I'm doing, I'm stalking across the bar toward her, Emilio and Antonio, right behind me.

As we near, I hear her laugh at something the guy says, her smile lighting up the whole fucking room and ice fills my veins. My eyes zero in on her, my body shifting into a stage of alertness that has every one of my senses straining in her direction.

What is she doing here? How long has she been back? A million questions run through my head and only she can give me those answers.

Penélope pushes off from the table, pool stick in hand and moves to the other side. My brows draw together. She plays pool? She bends over, ass aimed in my direction and more than a few heads tilt, giving her ass an appreciative look. My own head does the same until I realize she's on full fucking display.

Anger swells inside me.

"Berto—" There's a warning in my brother's voice, but I'm not hearing it. Antonio grabs me by the back of my arm and holds me in place. "You look like you're about to lose your shit, man. You need to take a beat. Cool your head before you approach her, unless you're aiming to scare the girl away."

I grind my teeth together.

"Is she the chick you dated back in high school?" He asks.

A single nod is my answer.

Emilio whistles. "Wait, that's the girl?"

I turn and glare at my baby brother. "You got a problem?"

He raises both hands in surrender. "Nope. But do me a favor?"

"What," I grind out.

Emilio nods to two guys. The one who'd just been way too fucking close to her and the dude I'm assuming she's playing against, since he's the only other one I see holding a stick. "Those two—Tyler and Rich—they're on the team and we need them for the rose bowl. Don't start shit with them unless you feel like fucking up my season."

"No promises," I mutter. Shaking my brother's grip off, I move up behind her. I don't have a plan. Probably should have thought of that before storming over here. But she was bold, so fuck it. I'll respond in kind.

Penélope hasn't taken her shot yet, still lining up her sights, so I take advantage of her position and press my body against hers. Leaning forward, I brace myself on either side of her and breathe in the floral scent of her shampoo. "Need a hand?" I murmur in her ear.

She stiffens before shoving an elbow into my gut. I grunt. Still feisty, I see. Good.

"No," she snaps. "So back off."

I lean back, giving her some space, but stay pressed against her, my hands settling on her hips.

"Go away," she grinds out.

I smirk, biting back on a chuckle. She's got no idea who's behind her. Will she still want me to back off when she sees it's me?

"I'm good here," I tell her and she bites off a curse before setting her pool stick aside. She pushes off from the pool table, forcing me to take a step back, but before she can turn around, I wrap one arm around her waist and use the other to cup her chin and hold her in place. "You asked so nicely," I whisper in her ear. "But in case it wasn't clear, I'm on the naughty list this year."

Her body goes entirely still at my words. "Roberto?" She whispers, surprise and excitement clear in her voice.

I loosen my hold enough for her to face me.

Her dark brown eyes are wide and glassy. She's been drinking. Did that play a part in her messaging me? Probably. Do I care? Not one fucking bit.

Full red lips part to create a small O and dark brown eyes stare into my own like she can't believe I'm really here. The feeling is mutual. Damn, she looks good. She's still fucking tiny. Five one or two to my six three. I tower over her, which forces her to look up to meet my gaze.

She blinks several times and then rubs her hands over her face. "Fuck. I think I drank too much."

"Probably. But how about you let me buy you one more?"

A pretty blush creeps up her face and it takes everything in me to not cup her jaw and trail my thumb along her skin.

"Hey man. We're in the middle of a game here." A guy calls out.

"Relax, Rich. Don't get your panties in a bunch." Emilio tells him, saving me from yelling at the fucker for interrupting us.

Penélope clears her throat. "I should uh..." she hesitates. "Can you give me five minutes?"

I run my tongue over my teeth. "Yeah. Take your time." I take several steps back to give her some room.

She shakes herself out a bit, loosening her arms and rolling her shoulders before moving back into position over the table. Once again, heads tilt to stare at her ass and I have to bite back the snarl building in my throat.

"Six. Left corner pocket." She takes the shot, sinking the ball in before moving to the side and repeating the motion. "Seven.

Botton right." Her cue stick thrusts forward, shooting at the table's far wall before bouncing forward to hit her target.

The guy she's playing with groans. Shit. She's good.

"Eight. Bottom right again." She takes the shot. Curses go up in the air.

"Fuck, beautiful. You've been holding out on us," a blond guy says. He was one of the ones Emilio pointed out. Tyler. *Fuck Tyler.*

Penélope doesn't respond to his comment, which is the only thing that keeps me from punching the dickhead in the face. I don't like the way he's looking at her. It's clear as day that he wants in her pants.

Not fucking happening.

"Nine for the win," she tells her opponent. "Left side pocket."

Just as she's about to hit, the asshole stumbles forward. It's fake as shit, but does what he intended. He knocks into the table, the noise and movement enough to break her concentration and her shot goes wide, missing the nine ball.

She curses.

"Bottoms up." It's the blond guy again, only this time, he hands her a shot. Nah. I don't like this. She's already swaying on her feet. She doesn't need any more.

"Nah uh," I call out, lowering her arm before she's able to lift the drink to her lips. "How much have you had?"

"Relax, man. We're just playing a game. She's good. Right, babe?"

My eyes narrow. "She's not your *babe*," I grind out.

He doesn't look worried by my tone. Big mistake.

"Whatever, man." He turns his attention back to Penélope. "You can skip the shot and just forfeit the game," he tells her. "Rich will probably land this next one, anyway."

She shakes her head and before I can stop her, tosses the shot back with a grimace. "He'll miss," she coughs.

I pull her up against me and lean down to her ear. "How many have you had, little dove?" I ask her. She shivers in my hold, goosebumps breaking out across her exposed arms.

"Six," she tells me.

I curse. "You're not driving."

"Wasn't planning on it."

She leans back into me, and I take the opportunity to wrap my arms around her. She doesn't push away. Something about this, about having her in my arms again. It feels right. The anxious, always alert part of me stills for the first time in years and a wave of contentment settled in my bones.

Rich misses the shot like she guessed, and I'm forced to release her as she walks around the table to take her own. In my peripheral, I see the other guys throw back their own shots, so I guess this is all just a part of their game. "Nine, corner left." She calls out and this time, before anyone can respond or fuck up her concentration, she strikes.

Crack. The cue ball slams into the nine, sinking it into the corner pocket, and she smirks with her win. "Thanks for the game, boys. I'm cashing out." She holds her hand out and Tyler drops several bills in her hand. She shoves them into her pocket and is about to turn away when he pulls her forward, pressing her close against him. He whispers something in her ear, too quiet for me to hear, and she shakes her head.

I'm two seconds away from storming toward him when Antonio says, "Let it play out. It's been a while for you two. Don't go into possessive asshole mode on day one."

My lip curls. "I'm not a possessive asshole."

Emilio snorts. "Of course you are." He and Antonio both laugh. "Runs in the family."

Penélope

Oh my freaking god, he's here. Tyler is telling me something, but my mind is too muddled to pay attention. Am I hallucinating? I have to be. I blink rapidly. Come on Penn. Snap out of it. Tyler hands me my winnings along with a piece of paper and I shove both into my back pocket. "Thanks," I mutter. Taking a deep breath, I head to where Roberto is waiting.

His arms are folded across his broad chest, arm muscles flexing. He looks good. His dark brown hair is buzzed short on the sides, leaving it a little longer on top.

The style makes him harder. His features more pronounced. There's a tick in his jaw. He's angry. But I haven't done anything to warrant that anger.

Taking in his dark brown eyes and heavy brows, I notice he's not actually looking at me, but rather behind me. Brows furrowed, I glance over my shoulder, following his line of sight.

A slow smile curls around the edges of my mouth. *He's jealous.* Roberto is glaring daggers at Rich and Tyler, both of whom are still watching me. But as soon as I'm in front of him, Roberto snaps his attention back to me, giving me his undivided focus. The intensity of his stare has my body going taut, muscles locking into place. There's heat and want in his eyes and for a moment, I feel strangely naked as his dark gaze bores into me.

My breaths come out faster and my thighs clench in anticipation of something I know isn't going to happen, but god it would be great if it did. That thought has my blood heating and my heart pounding wildly. Is that what I want? It takes no time at all for my mind to give me a resounding yes. We were young. Innocent. Sex wasn't on my radar in high school but now... I've been standing too long without saying anything, so I force out a "Hi."

Urgh. That was lame. You couldn't come up with something better than that, Penélope?

Roberto smirks, that single dimple in his left cheek drawing my attention and doing weird things to my stomach. "Hi."

Okay. So we're both lame. I can work with that.

I swallow hard. "I didn't think you'd be in town. Are you visiting for the holidays?" Where does he live now? Did he move back? I doubt it. When we were younger, he talked about getting out. About leaving Sun Valley and never looking back. That's why he enlisted. It was his way out.

Roberto shakes his head. "No. Family stuff came up. I moved back a few years ago to help out."

Oh. His words sink in. Years ago?

"What about you? Are you visiting or...?" He lets the question hang.

"Visiting." With a shrug, I add, "I think."

"You think?" He raises a brow, but before he can respond, one of the guys beside him slaps him on the shoulder.

"We're gonna bounce. Watch the highlights back at Roman and Allie's, since Bibi is over there with Luis."

"Yeah. Okay. I'll catch you guys back at the house."

The younger of the two winks. "We'll probably crash at Roman's. Don't do anything I wouldn't do." He smiles like a Cheshire Cat. "Actually, please do everything I would do and then do everything else. You need to loosen up, and I think she's just what the doctor ordered."

I smother my smile with a cough.

"Fuck off," Roberto snaps, but the guy seems unfazed.

"Later, bro."

Roberto runs his hand over his face, his exasperation clear, but also there's a bit of... embarrassment. That can't be right. But the tops of his ears have reddened along with the apples of his cheeks. "Sorry about that," he tells me.

"Roommates?" I ask once they're gone.

He shakes his head. "Baby brothers."

My eyes widen. "No way those two guys are your brothers?" at his nod I add, "But they're freaking men."

His eyes narrow. "Yeah." He bites out the single word and I have to fight back my smirk. He doesn't like that I noticed them.

"I guess they do look a lot like you," I tell him. "But damn. I didn't expect them to be so... you know."

He grunts and starts leading me across the room with his hand on the small of my back. Where are we going? Before I can ask, the floor decides to slide out from under me and I stumble forward, but he's right there to catch me.

"Thanks." I cling to his strong shoulders, his face impossibly close. "I might have had a few too many back there."

His jaw is tight and for some strange reason, I get the feeling I'm in trouble. "You did. Do you have any idea how reckless that was?" He pulls me forward and I wobble, but this time manages to keep my feet.

I brush off his rebuke. "It was just a few drinks."

His grip tightens as he spins me around and shoves me back until my shoulders hit a wall. "It wasn't *just* a few drinks. It was reckless." He growls, flinging his arm out back toward the pool tables. "Any one of those guys could take advantage of you and, by the look in most of their eyes, they really fucking wanted to."

I roll my eyes, releasing an exasperated breath, but his expression remains tight.

"You're serious."

"Deadly."

Old arguments rise up to the forefront of my mind and I shove against his shoulders, but rather than stepping back, Roberto steps forward, closing the fraction of space left between us until we're toe to toe. "Fuck you," I tell him. "I'm a grown adult."

"Then act like one."

Heat rushes to my face, but not from embarrassment. This is something else entirely. Memories of Patrick in my face assault me. His words digging into my brain that I'm a whore. That I'm asking for it with the way I dress or behave. That if I'd just get it through my stupid head that he knows what's best for me, everything would be fine. It's my fault he's angry. My fault he hurts me.

Without thinking, my hand flies up and slaps Roberto across the face.

As soon as my palm connects with his cheek, I gasp and jerk it back.

Oh my god. I cover my mouth with my hands, horror washing over me.

Roberto doesn't move, but the red mark of my handprint blooms against his cheek.

His dark gaze sharpens, becoming predatory and my fight or flight instinct slams into me, but I do neither of those things. I freeze like a deer caught in headlights, my heart pounding in my chest.

"I..." I barely get the word out when he closes the scant few inches between us, crushing his lips to mine. I gasp, a jolt of adrenaline drowning out whatever anger I previously felt, and replacing it with a visceral need. His hot tongue takes advantage of my surprise and he kisses me harder. Deeper. A shudder runs through my body and I fist my hands into the fabric of his shirt.

Our kiss grows urgent, hands grabbing at each other as a slick heat builds in my core. I groan into his mouth as Roberto wedges his thigh between my legs, the friction making my toes curl. The fingers of one hand dig into my hip as the other holds the back of my head, keeping me firmly in place.

Using his grip on me, he tilts my head, granting him a better angle to deepen the kiss. I can't get enough air. His tongue strokes my mouth aggressively. His kiss consuming any objections I might have had. I can't think. I can barely breathe. But I don't push him away.

His kiss is raw. Bordering on violence. And with each second that passes, it's like the well of need inside me opens wider. He pushes me more firmly against the wall, his thigh now grinding against my clit.

"You're gonna need to take that somewhere else."

It's like a cold bucket of water has been poured over me. Reluctantly, Roberto releases me, stepping back to glower at the waitress, who interrupted us.

"No sex in the bar," she adds, and he grunts in acknowledgement. Wrapping his strong hand around my wrist, he tugs me forward, leading me outside and through the parking lot.

"Where are we going?" I ask, my feet struggling to keep up with his long strides. Without answering, he leads me over to a black car and pushes me up against the side of it, picking up where we left off. A fire burns inside of me, my hands moving to wrap around his neck.

Roberto presses into me, his erection straining against the rough material of his jeans. I tear my mouth away, sucking in a lungful of air as his mouth trails down my neck and collar bone.

"Fuck," I shiver against him.

He thrusts against me and I moan, clawing at his back and shoulders. "We can't..."

He raises his head, his eyes meeting mine. "We can."

Reaching behind me, he jerks open the passenger door and holds it expectantly. "Get in the car, little dove." His tone is gentle but his expression is hard, warning that he won't take no for an answer. Not that I planned on denying him.

Ducking under his arm, I slide into the car, swallowing hard as the door closes behind me.

A few seconds later, the driver side door opens and Roberto climbs inside. We pull out of Borracho's parking lot and head into the night, anticipation coiling tight inside me.

I turn in my seat and take in the hard line of his jaw and the full pout of his lips. This is crazy and reckless, but the longer I look at him, the less and less I care.

I know where this is going. But when I drove away from Richland, I promised I'd find myself again. That I'd do what I wanted to do, when I wanted to do it. I won't let Patrick's taunting words that I'm easy or a whore ruin this for me. I refuse to deny myself this.

And one look at Roberto confirms that even if I wanted to, I can't.

Roberto

I'm already envisioning what I'm going to do to her. How I'll shove her jeans down, lay her out on my bed, and sink my cock into her pussy. Fuck. I can't wait to be inside her.

The drive from the bar to my place takes ten minutes and as soon as we pull into the driveway, I'm out of the car and pulling her out. Eager anticipation thrums through my veins.

Not wasting any time, I grab her from the back of her thighs and lift her into my arms. Her legs wrap around my waist as her hands hold on to my shoulders. I press her back against the car, grinding my dick into her. The urge to take her spreads inside me like a poison. I need to be inside of her.

Pushing off from the car, I carry her to the front door, my mouth on hers the entire time. She tastes like chocolate and mint and I want to devour her. Shoving the door open, I step inside, kicking it closed behind me as I take her straight to my room, not bothering to turn on any of the lights. Thank fuck my brothers aren't here tonight.

I splay her out on the bed and she tilts her head back, looking up at me through long, thick lashes. "You good, little dove?" I ask, the old nickname rolling off my tongue. Moonlight filters in through the windows, illuminating her figure and casting her in an ethereal glow.

She nods and bites her lip. Fuck. Does she realize how sexy she is?

Climbing over her, I press her back into the mattress. My lips capture hers in a searing kiss, and my hands move to the waistband of her jeans.

I don't have the patience to take this slow. It's been too long, and it's Penélope for chrissakes. Anyone else and I'd be able to hold back, but not with her. I've never had full control of myself when I'm with her.

Tugging the zipper down on her jeans, she lifts her hips, making it easier for me to peel the material off her legs. I leave the thin scrap of lace between her thighs and move up, fingering the hem of her black shirt. I kiss my way up her body as I push up the fabric, letting it bunch beneath her shoulders once I've exposed the tops of her breasts.

"Fuck, I missed these." Her tits are two handfuls of perfection wrapped in black lace. I thumb one pert nipple through the material, watching it pebble beneath my touch. Goosebumps break out over her skin as I lick a path between her valley of her breasts.

"Oh, God." Her breath hitches and I laugh lightly. I graze my teeth over her nipple before sucking her breast into my mouth, and laving at the tender flesh through the lace.

Her back arches. Small noises leaving her throat. I slide one hand down her body, my fingers dipping beneath her panties as I continue to suck and bite at her breasts. Penélope sucks in a breath, but she doesn't tell me to slow down. Instead, she smiles at me and I smile back before I glide two fingers over her aching clit and sink them deep into her pussy.

"Fuck, little dove. You're soaked."

A pretty blush blooms across her face, and I spot the moment she decides she wants to retreat. No way am I about to let that happen. With two fingers still buried inside her, I use my thumb and stroke her clit. She whimpers beneath me, rolling her hips as my fingers fuck her center. "You like that?" I ask.

Her eyes are dilated, but she manages to give me a small nod and I reward her, flicking her clit harder. Faster. She writhes beneath me, legs tightening around my hips as she rushes toward her release.

"Does this belong to anyone else?" I can't shake the thought of the guy she'd been with out of my head. And if she's seeing someone else, I need to know that now. Before I get myself in too deep here.

Luckily, she shakes her head. "No. I'm not seeing anyone," she gasps.

"Good." A smile curls my mouth. "I want to slide my dick in here," I tell her. "Are you going to let me?"

Hands fisted in the sheets, she nods.

Holding her gaze, I sit back on my knees, sliding my fingers out of her to pull my shirt over my head. Her eyes darken and she visibly swallows. Yeah. I look good. Six years in the army will do that to you. Every line of my body is honed. Every muscle tight and on display for her. Rising to my feet, I kick off my shoes and tug down my jeans, taking my boxers with them.

She gasps the moment my dick springs free and I fist my cock, pumping it as I look down at her spread out before me. "Take off the rest of your clothes," I demand.

Pushing up on her elbows, she pulls her shirt the rest of the way off before reaching back to unhook her bra. Flinging it aside, her hands reach for her panties, but I grab her wrist and stop her. "Not those," I tell her. "Not yet."

Climbing back over her, I settle myself between her thighs, letting my dick press against her so she can feel just how hard I am for her. I rub my dick over her pussy, pushing against the thin lace barrier between us.

She moans and I push her thighs further apart. "What do you want?" I ask her, needing to hear the words.

"You."

I continue rubbing my dick against her. "I need the words, Penn. What do you want?"

She swallows hard, her cheeks turning a deeper shade of red. It's fucking adorable. Leaning forward, I nip her ear before laving my tongue along the small sting. "Tell me what you need, little dove. Say the words and I'll give it to you."

"I want..." she hesitates.

"Penn—" I growl.

"I want you inside me."

I meet her flushed expression. "You want me to fuck you?"

A nod. Sliding my fingers beneath her panties, I tug them down her legs, exposing her bare pussy. *Fuck.* She lifts her legs to hide herself, but I'm not having it. Pressing against the inside of her knees, I force her legs wide and bare her weeping center to me. I shift between her thighs, pressing the head of my cock against her. Her breathing hitches and she tilts her hips up, taking the head of my dick inside her wet heat.

"Impatient." I smirk when she doesn't deny it.

I press forward, sinking into her in a single thrust before sucking on my finger and bringing it down to circle her clit. That sets her off, and she moans beneath me. "So fucking responsive," I tell her. She whimpers and I lean forward, capturing the sound with a kiss. It's not a sweet one either. It's wild and crazed and within minutes her legs are shaking, her release hovering close. I put more pressure on her clit and she throws her head back, her entire body growing taut. I fuck her hard through her release, kissing her mouth and scraping my teeth over her jaw and down her neck. I suck on the sensitive skin between her neck and shoulder, wanting to mark her in a way everyone else can see. The need to claim her, to mark her as mine, is visceral and something I can't ignore.

Her fingers grip my hair, tugging on the short strands as my hips buck harder against her. Her pussy squeezes my cock, and I milk every ounce of her release from her before my own slams into me. I brace myself over her, groaning as my cum shoots deep inside her, my orgasm nearly blinding me. "Fuck," I curse, realizing too late that I forgot a condom.

I press into her before rolling off beside her. Pulling her into my arms, I tuck her head beneath my chin and hold her tight against my chest. Our heavy breaths mix together and I run my fingers through the long strands of her hair.

"What was that?" I mutter. I don't expect a response but she answers me, anyway.

"A fresh start."

I smile before kissing the top of her head. A fresh start sounds like exactly what I need.

Penelope

I wake up the next morning with a hangover from hell. Sunlight streams through the open curtains and I blink back against the harsh rays. My eyelids stick together and I rub the sleep from them. A dull ache throbs between my legs, reminding me of what happened last night. Then I feel the warm press of his body behind me. His hard erection wedged against my ass.

"Roberto?" I ask, rolling over to face.

I squirt as his face comes into focus. *God, I am never drinking that much again.* He smiles, his eyes sleepy as his hand reaches up and tucks a strand of hair behind my ear. "Merry Christmas, little dove."

"Oh, shit." I push up into a sitting position, immediately regretting it when my head begins to pound.

"Ow!" I groan and Roberto chuckles, tugging me down beside him and pulling the blank back over me.

The door to his room flies open and a small screen escapes me as a little boy rushes into the room and jumps up on the bed. "Berto!" she squeals, throwing himself into Roberto's arms.

"Hey little man. What are you doing in here? Where's your Mama?"

"Presents!" he cries, but it comes out like *pwesents.*

I lay there frozen as a feeling of horror crashes over me. He has a kid. Roberto is a dad and his kid just walked in on ... Oh my god.

To make matters worse, a beautiful woman walks in through the open doorway, bright blue eyes landing on the man whose bed I'm currently in.

"Shit. Shit. Shit." I mutter, tugging the blanket higher over my naked body.

"Oh. Sorry. I didn't realize you—"

Roberto laughs, unaware of my utter humiliation right now. "Can you give us a few? We'll be out in a bit."

"Oh course. Come on, Luis." She reaches down, picking up her son before turning to leave and closing the door behind her.

As soon as she's gone, I jump from the bed and frantically search for my clothes.

Roberto pushes up on his elbows to watch me. "What are you doing?"

"Getting dressed," I hiss. I find my panties and tug those on. Then I locate my jeans and my shirt but I don't see my bra anywhere.

Fuck it. I throw my shirt over my head and shimmy into my jeans, jumping a few times to get the snug material over my hips.

"Why?" he sounds genuinely confused.

My mouth drops open. "Are you kidding right now?"

Climbing to his feet, he walks toward me, completely uncaring about his nudity or the fact that his very hard cock is pointing right at me. "What just happened?" he asks, closing in on me. He reaches out for me, but I dodge his grasp and hunt for my shoes.

"I need to go."

"Penn?"

I ignore him.

"Penélope!"

"What?" I snap.

He closes the distance between us and I immediately retreat, but my back hits a wall and Roberto cages me in, bracing himself against the wall on either side of me. "Talk to me," he pleads. "What's going on in that head of yours?"

I grit my teeth before the urge to scream at him becomes too much. "You have a kid!" I shout. "A freaking kid you didn't bother mentioning and his mom..." I throw my hands in the air. "She, what, lives here with you?"

His brows furrow in confusion as he takes in my angry expression. "Hold on, you think he's..." he shakes his head. "Luis is my nephew."

Oh.

"He's not yours?"

He shakes his head.

"And the girl?"

"My sister-in-law."

My shoulders relax and I cover my face with my hands. That's — a relief, I suppose.

Roberto pulls my hands away from my face before cupping my jaw. "We good?" he asks.

I nod. "Yeah, but uh..." I trail off. This was great. More than great. I haven't had sex like that in ages, but it's Christmas morning and well, it's time for me to go.

"I'm just going to grab my things, okay?" I duck beneath his arm, but his hand shoots out to stop me.

"Stay," he says.

That has me drawing up short. "What?"

"Stay." He presses. "I know this is new and we need to figure things out but—"

I shake my head. "There isn't anything to figure out," I tell him. "This was fun but—"

His jaw tightens. "Fun?" he bites out.

"That didn't come out, right?"

"So, how was it supposed to come out? Thanks for the fuck. I'm gonna run away now?"

"I'm not running." I tell him.

He barks out a laugh. "Really? You had me fooled, because that's exactly what it looks like you're doing. Again."

I whirl on him so fast I give myself whiplash. "I didn't run back then. You left." I remind him.

"I asked you to wait for me. To give us a chance."

No. It wasn't that simple. "You asked me to put my entire life on hold for you. To give up my dreams and my plans and what, just sit around and pine after you?" My voice rises with every word. "I begged you not to leave. I begged, Roberto."

"You don't understand. The shit I was dealing with back then— "

"The problems at home you never wanted to talk about. That shit?" I ask, my old anger spiking.

"Penn— "

I shake my head and this time manage to shove past him. He stands there, still as a statue as I slip on my socks and shoes and, finding my bra, I tuck the material into my back pocket. A piece of paper falls to the floor from my pocket, and Roberto leans down to retrieve it. Opening it, he curses before shoving it in my face. "Is this really why you're in such a rush? You want to call Tyler? Let him service your needs tonight now that you've gotten your fill from me?"

A sharp stab pieces my chest. "What are you talking about?"

He throws the paper to the ground and storms to the other side of the room. Leaning down, I pick it up and unfold the paper to find a name and a number. This must have been what Tyler gave me when he handed me my earnings.

I gather the nerve to look over at Roberto. This isn't how I wanted to leave things, but... he must feel my gaze on him because his eyes turn to mine and what I see in them breaks a part of me. The part that once loved this boy and thought he'd be my forever. There's pain in his eyes but anger and resentment, too.

"I just got out of a controlling relationship, Roberto. I'm not about to jump into another one." My words are whispered, but he still manages to hear me.

His jaw hardens, eyes flaring with some unnamed emotion. "I'm not trying to control you," he rasps.

My lips press into a thin line. I don't want to argue with him, but I can't seem to drop it either. "You could have had me fooled with the jealous act you're pulling. I didn't even realize he gave me his number."

"You're one to talk. You wanted to storm out of here because you thought Bibi was my woman and that Luis was my son."

Jaw tight, I ignore his accusation.

"And for the record, I'm not jealous." He pushes away from the wall and moves toward me with determination.

Swallowing hard, I hold my ground, watching as he closes the distance between us.

He's so close he's practically on top of me. His breath fans over my cheeks, and I close my eyes as he releases an exasperated huff.

The instinct to retreat hits me, but my legs are locked, my body unwilling to respond to my mind's commands. I open my eyes as he leans closer, his hand coming to cup my face and tilt my head toward his own. His lips feather over mine but never quite touch as he whispers, "A jealous man covets that which does not belong to him." His thumb brushes along my jaw. "But you little dove, have always been mine."

He releases me and steps back, eyes hard as he delivers his next words. "I'm not jealous. I'm possessive and I protect what is mine. Don't confuse the two."

My heart seized at his words, a small gasp parting my lips. My feelings for him are too strong. Too terrifying to acknowledge. "I don't belong to you." Even to my own ears, the argument sounds out weak.

"Look," he starts. "You're freaking out. You said you just got out of a break-up and then you jumped to some pretty serious conclusions this morning and you're spiraling. I get it. This is a lot." I nod, grateful that he seems to understand. "But that doesn't mean this," he indicates the space between us. "Isn't something fucking special, Penn. I lost you once, and I just got you back. Don't make me lose you again. Not on Christmas. You'll ruin this holiday for me forever."

I laugh and some of the tension releases from his shoulders. "Laying it on a little thick there."

He smiles, his dimple drawing my attention. "Just stay. If you have plans later, that's cool. I'll take you wherever you want to go. But for right now, stay. Enjoy the holiday with me for a little while. We don't have to make any promises or anything, just... don't run away. Let's see where this can go."

I lick my bottom lip, considering his words. I liked the girl I was when Roberto and I were together. That girl was carefree. Maybe... maybe he can show me how to be her again.

"No promises?" I confirm.

"No promises."

"Okay. I'll..." I swallow hard. "I'll stay."

His smile spreads before he cups my cheeks and presses his lips to mine in a tender kiss. "Merry Christmas, little dove."

"Merry Christmas."

He bites my bottom lip. "Now that we've got that settled. Let's go introduce you to the family."

WANT MORE? BE SURE TO GRAB CRUEL PROMISE TO FIND OUT what's next in store for the Devils of Sun Valley.

And The Savage for more from the boys at PacNorth.

About the Author

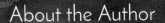

Daniela Romero is a USA Today and Wall Street Journal
bestselling author. She enjoys writing steamy, new-adult and
paranormal romance that delivers an emotional roller coaster sure
to take your breath away.

Her books feature a diverse cast of characters with rich and
vibrant cultures in an effort to effectively portray the world we all
live in. One that is so beautifully colorful.

Daniela is a Bay Area native though she currently lives in
Washington State with her sarcastic husband and their three tiny
terrors.

In her free time, Daniela enjoys frequent naps, binge reading her
favorite romance books, and is known to crochet while watching
television because her ADHD brain can never do just one thing at
a time.

Stop by her website to find all the fun and unique ways you can
stalk her. And while you're there you can check out some free
bonus scenes from your favorite books, learn about her Patreon,
order signed copies of her books, and swoon over her gorgeous
alternative cover editions.

www.daniela-romero.com
You can join my newsletter by visiting
https://hi.switchy.io/VIP